Olivia Goldsmith's be
Wives Club, *Bestseller*,
recently, *Wish Upon a*

Acclaim for Olivia Goldsmith:

'Full of wisecracks and gossip . . . Olivia Goldsmith can keep you reading' *Cosmopolitan*

'A bubbly, fizzy story' *Daily Mail*

'Olivia Goldsmith's forte has always been the writing of revenge novels with great good humor' *Washington Post*

'Goldsmith hands out her characters' rewards and comeuppances like Jane Austen dealing blackjack . . . You keep licking your fingers and reaching for the next page as if it were another potato chip' *Newsweek*

'Fizzing with acerbic dialogue and high-level sexual slapstick' *Good Housekeeping*

Also by Olivia Goldsmith

The First Wives Club
Flavor of the Month
Fashionably Late
Simple Isn't Easy
Bestseller
Marrying Mom
The Switch
Young Wives
Uptown Girl
Wish Upon a Star

OLIVIA GOLDSMITH

INSIDERS

BAD BOY

Grafton

HarperCollins*Publishers*
77–85 Fulham Palace Road,
Hammersmith, London W6 8JB

www.harpercollins.co.uk

This omnibus edition published in 2005
by HarperCollins*Publishers*

ISBN 0 00 773413 1

Printed and bound in Great Britain by
Clays Ltd, St Ives plc

INSIDERS

To Jack Rapke

Because you always knew how good it would be

An imprisoned creature was out of the question – my mother would not have allowed a rat to be restrained of its liberty.

Mark Twain

Book I

1

Jennifer Spencer

What is now proved was once only imagined.

William Blake, *The Marriage of Heaven and Hell*

'All rise.'

Jennifer Anne Spencer watched as Judge Marian Levitt entered the courtroom, her black robes swinging loosely from her shoulders, not concealing her dumpiness, her white hair cut in a simple bob. She climbed the three steps to the bench holding Jennifer's future in her hands.

Jennifer stood beside her lawyer and the rest of the legal team and faced Judge Levitt with what she hoped was a calm and honest gaze. She knew that the photographers would pay a great deal to have a picture of her at the time the verdict was given. But they were barred from the courtroom and for that, if nothing else, she was grateful.

Although she had been assured and reassured that the judge would see things 'their way', it was not an easy thing to stand before the woman as she leafed through her papers.

In fact, although she doubted that she would be judged guilty, she was certain that even if she was, she would be given a suspended sentence or public service or a fine.

Jennifer had to admit that she felt sick to her stomach just standing there. That she had virtually volunteered to be there didn't make it any easier. She felt a fluttering beside her and realized that Tom, her attorney, was reaching for her hand. She entwined her fingers in his and knew that he could feel her trembling. She hoped that the judge could see neither that nor the fact that they were holding hands. But she supposed it wouldn't make any difference to the outcome of the trial.

For what seemed like an interminable time, Judge Levitt paged through the notes in front of her. She had on a pair of half-glasses that were perched at the very end of her long nose. Both Donald and Tom had strongly urged Jennifer to forgo a jury trial. 'This is complicated law,' Tom had said. 'A judge would be more likely to understand the distinctions.' Donald had laughed. 'Let's face it,' he'd said. 'Civilians hate us and would be only too happy to throw the book at you.' Jennifer had nodded. 'We're the fat cats,' Donald had continued. 'We're the Wall Street smart-asses. When they make money during a bull market they resent us for making more. When they lose money they blame us. You can't win when you're on the Street. You'd never get a jury of your peers unless they could get a dozen guys from the Street, and none of them have the time to sit on a jury.' They had all laughed.

But now, looking up at Judge Levitt, Jennifer didn't feel like laughing. She told herself it was all going to be all right. Donald and Tom would see to it. This was the worst of it, and after this she'd be so well rewarded that . . .

'Jennifer Spencer. You have been accused of fraud. I find you guilty. On insider trading I find you guilty on all counts. On . . .'

A loud buzzing began in Jennifer's ears. The word 'guilty' coming from Judge Levitt's lips seemed to move from the bench to her and hit her like a blow. This wasn't what was planned. She felt dizzy and she had to close her eyes for a moment to stop the room from spinning. Tom's hand on her now clammy one did not feel comforting. She wanted to shake him off and wipe the sweat off herself. How could this be happening?

When she could hear again, the judge was intoning something about her sentence. A sentence? If she was found guilty, there wasn't supposed to be a sentence. '. . . three to five years at Jennings Correctional Facility for Women.' The judge paused, took off her glasses, and looked across the bench at Jennifer. 'You are very young,' she said. 'It's better that you learn now that this type of manipulation and illegal profiteering is unacceptable and that it could destroy your entire life.'

Jennifer couldn't respond. Even on that horrible day when the Feds came into her posh office at the prestigious Wall Street firm of Hudson, Van Schaank & Michaels to take her away in cuffs, Jennifer didn't believe that she would spend even one moment in a jail cell. The arrest made her a little nervous, of course, but that was only because she'd never been in trouble before with the law.

'This is just a publicity stunt,' her boss told her. 'They're firing shots over our heads to cool down this overheated market.' That boss was the legendary Donald J. Michaels himself, and Jennifer never questioned his judgment or authority. 'Believe me,' Donald assured her, 'these charges are going to be dropped. And even if you do go to trial, you aren't going to be found guilty of anything. Trust me,' he added with his reassuring smile.

Jennifer did trust him. After all, she *wasn't* guilty of anything. She was just taking the heat for Donald in order to deflect any further investigations into his firm's rather dubious business dealings. If the SEC – the Securities and Exchange Commission – had gone after Donald they would have thrown the book at him. 'And they've got a damn big book,' Donald had joked. 'You know how jealous, how envious, people have been over our success in the last few years.' Jennifer did know. During his Wall Street career Donald Michaels had made not only his own fortune, but had also made dozens, maybe scores – or even hundreds – of other millionaires. Jennifer herself was a millionaire at twenty-eight – but now she was a millionaire who was leaving for prison in less than an hour.

Standing in the courtroom, Jennifer cradled her right elbow in her left hand and her left in her right hand and shivered as she felt both her gooseflesh and nausea rise. How, she wondered, did it come to this? How had Tom, her lawyer, let it happen?

Thomas Philip Branston IV was the sharpest (and most handsome) young counsel on the Street. 'Nothing is really at risk,' he had told Jennifer, echoing Donald's assurances. 'It never is in cases like this. Even if you are convicted – which is virtually impossible – we'll have an appeal before the judge can pound his gavel. Donald has good friends and deep pockets,' Tom said with a knowing smile. Jennifer had no reason to doubt what he said. After all, Tom was not only a Harvard undergrad and Law Review at Yale, he was also much more than her brilliant attorney. He was her beloved fiancé.

'Think of it, Jen,' he had said days ago, 'everyone here will be in your debt. You'll not only have Donald's gratitude, but also the gratitude of the partners and all of the employees, right down to the secretaries and the mail-room staff. They'll all owe their fortunes and their jobs to you.'

'I only regret that I have but one life to give for my firm,' Jennifer had joked on that day when she, Tom, and Donald got together with Bob, the financial officer and Lenny, his assistant, to hatch their plan. There was plenty to drink and lots of laughter at that meeting as they discussed how Tom would prepare her statements, how they'd all sign them, and how Tom would 'turn her in' to the SEC. The Feds would be ripsnorting mad to miss their shot at Donald, but if she confessed they were scotched in their witchhunt, and Jennifer would be back at work within a week.

At the time their plan sounded solid; after all, Jennifer loved the heart-stopping thrill of high-risk deal-making. She loved the power of outleveraging any competitor in a buyout, and she loved the rush of watching one of their IPOs – Initial Public Offerings – burst onto the market to take the lucky or the gullible investor for the ride of his life. She loved it all – but most of all she loved the money and what it bought. She loved the Pratesi sheets on her bed, the silk Kirmans on her floor, and she loved every piece of Armani, Prada, Gucci, and Ferragamo that she kept neatly in her Biedermeier armoire. Even if her Tribeca condo was a little small, it was beautiful and in the best neighborhood in New York. (John Kennedy, Jr. had lived just around the corner.) With the very generous bonus that she was likely to get from pulling off this little charade, Jennifer was sure that she'd be able to move right on up to the penthouse.

'Jennifer, I'm so, so sorry. It's a mistake. Honestly. I thought we had Levitt in line,' Tom said to her now. Jennifer just stared at him, speechless.

The court officer began to move toward her. 'We're going to have to go now,' he said.

'What?' she asked. He must be joking. 'Go where?'

Tom looked away from her, unable to meet her eyes. 'To be transported,' he said. 'To go . . .'

'To go to jail?' she asked, and heard her voice rising. After the indictment she'd been out on bail before the desk sergeant could call the press and tip them off to her presence. 'Ridiculous,' she said, with more bravado than she felt, but the guard came at her relentlessly and when he reached her he pulled out handcuffs. Jennifer almost fainted. 'No,' she said, and it came out almost as a moan.

'Surely handcuffs aren't necessary . . .' Tom began.

'It's procedure,' the marshal said, and it was clear that there was no negotiating. He snapped the cuffs on Jennifer's wrists, then had to stop and adjust them again and again because her wrists were so small. 'Okay,' he said. 'Let's go. We have transport waiting.'

'We're going to have to go out there,' Tom told her. 'There will be a lot of photographers and journalists.' He paused. 'Look, this is only a momentary setback,' he said. 'You'll be there overnight. We'll appeal or we'll get a mistrial. Don't worry about this.'

'Let's go,' the marshal said again and took her, not gently, by the arm.

'Um, could she fix herself for a moment?' Tom asked.

Jennifer, dazed and confused, didn't know what he was

talking about, but Jane, one of the other attorneys, took out a comb and tissue and actually fussed with Jennifer's face as if she were an actor about to go before the cameras. As she was being preened, Tom stood very close to her and she felt something drop into her pocket.

'Call me sometime,' he whispered into her ear. 'Look undaunted,' Tom continued as he stepped back, while she was marshaled out to face the exploding lights and equally unsettling questions. 'Are you sorry now?' a woman's voice yelled.

'What will you do in prison?' she heard someone else shout.

'Jenny, look over here!' a husky voice intoned.

'Jenny!' echoed behind her.

'Jenny! Jenny, here!' was being chanted all around her.

Now she realized why people photographed for the newspapers always looked guilty. She, too, had to hang her head down to protect herself from being blinded by the flashbulbs and strobes. The marshal had been joined by several court officers who were pushing the media out of the way. Jennifer realized that she didn't know if Tom was still with her or not, but when they walked through the double doors and she found herself at a loading dock, Tom was right behind her, though blessedly the wolf pack was stopped in their tracks.

But right now, the idea of prison gave Jennifer another roll of nausea. She tried to quiet her fears with the confidence that she had cut quite a deal with the firm. With Tom in charge of her appeal, and Howard McBane, senior partner of the white shoe firm of Swithmore, McBane pleading it, there was – she reminded herself – essentially no risk. When all the dust was settled, Donald Michaels was going to owe her big time. She may have left the firm in cuffs, but she was certain that she would return as a senior partner.

In the days following her initial arrest, Jennifer focused her energies on practicing her testimony with Tom and deciding what to wear to court. She was charged with investment fraud, so it seemed that she should try to look as *un*fraudulent as possible. She chose Armani over Yamaguchi, because who could appear fraudulent in Armani? And for shoes she opted for Louboutin over Manolo Blahnick. Only a classic Gucci purse would do, and with a new hairstyle and makeup done to perfection, Jennifer was sure that she was dressed not only for success, but for an acquittal.

What she hadn't planned on, however, was the possibility of a female judge. For all of her success, Jennifer had never learned how to deal well with other women – especially the fat, dumpy types who prefer to cloak their femininity in the dark uniformity of robes. When Jennifer saw her judge it was like seeing the ghost of Sister Mary Margaret from St Bartholomew's school. Jennifer had looked to Tom for encouragement.

But as clever and handsome as Tom was in his own impeccably tailored suit, he had no charm over this severe incarnation of Lady Justice. The grand jury hearing was a disaster. Jennifer was indicted and brought to trial amidst a media frenzy that made national headlines. Donald had warned her that the Feds were looking for a high-profile scapegoat. They found one in Jennifer Spencer. Her story kept the tabloids churning out edition after edition, and while the humiliation of the live television coverage was considerable, what really frustrated Jennifer was the judge's inability to see that the charges against her were bogus.

At the van Jennifer cried as Tom held her close. 'This is only a little setback,' he told her. 'It's all going to blow over. We'll get an appeal. You'll get another judge. We'll get Howard McBane for the appeal. McBane is an appellate genius and every judge in the state knows him. Your case will be decided on its merits.' Jennifer tried to remind herself 'No guts – no glory.' The shame of the publicity and the shock of the verdict would be a small price to pay for a senior partnership in the firm – and a lifetime of wealth with her beloved Tom. She'd taken a gamble and if this was the downside of it, the upside was well worth a few days of a little discomfort. 'I'll call ahead,' Tom told her. 'I'll pull a few strings and make sure that you get nothing but white-glove treatment.'

Jennifer nodded as yet another horrible wave of fear, anger, and shame washed over her. She was leaving for prison! She wished Donald Michaels, the author of all this, had come to see her off, but that thought had barely registered when they moved through the doors and, as if out of nowhere, the prison transport van pulled up and two armed officers got out.

The shorter officer carried a clipboard on which various papers were signed and exchanged. Then the taller one opened the doors of the cold parking bay in which they stood. Immediately a second horde of photographers swarmed into the loading area, and in the frenzy and noise Jennifer searched their faces, hoping that Donald might be among them. He wasn't there, but Lenny Benson was. There, in the back of the crowd, Jennifer spotted good old Lenny standing all alone. He gave her a small wave good-bye just as she was told to get into the van.

'I guess I have to go,' Jennifer whispered to Tom. She felt her throat close and her eyes tear up.

'Don't worry. This is nothing,' Tom said, though he looked as pale as she must have. 'It's going to be okay, Jen. Trust me.'

'I do,' she told him, and only later thought about saying those two words in this awful context.

'Come on,' the tall officer urged.

Tom bent to kiss her, but not on the lips – only on the forehead. It made Jennifer feel like the dutiful child she had behaved as. She did trust Tom, but so far he had been wrong when he said that she wouldn't be indicted, wouldn't be tried, and then that she would get off. She looked up and tried to smile into his handsome face. 'Are you sure you're going to want to marry an ex-con?' she asked, heroically trying to joke.

Tom stared at her intently, then took her face in his hands. 'You are so beautiful,' he said in the husky voice he used when they made love. 'You know that?' he asked her. 'Think of this as just an ugly business trip. I'll take care of all the legal aspects. There will be an appeal, we'll win and it'll all be over soon. This will be completely expunged from your record when you're exonerated.'

'I love it when you talk legal,' she told him bravely, but a betraying tear slipped down one of her cheeks.

'Come on! We got a schedule to keep,' the tall officer nearly barked.

Tom looked down at Jennifer's hand. There, on the fourth finger, she wore his ring. 'Maybe you should leave the diamond with me,' he said. 'Just for safekeeping,' he added with an apologetic smile.

Jennifer was stunned. She loved her ring. When he'd put

it on her finger she'd planned to never take it off. But . . . well, of course it was silly, insane really, to wear a three-carat diamond to . . . She tried not to think about what she was doing, but again, like a child, she did as she was told and slipped the gorgeous emerald-cut ring from her finger and gave it back to Tom.

It was almost a relief when the van doors slid shut. As she looked out, hoping for a last glimpse of Tom, she saw nothing but photographers, and then, there in the crowd was Lenny's stricken face. She lifted her ringless hand to wave good-bye through the wire mesh. 'This Jennings place is like a country club,' she reminded herself as the van lurched forward and took her away from her job, her luxurious home, her love. And her life.

2

Gwen Harding

The law is the true embodiment
of everything that's excellent.
It has no kind of fault or flaw,
And I, my Lords, embody the law.

W. S. Gilbert, *Iolanthe*

Whenever Warden Gwendolyn Harding was asked to give the occasional speech to a group of young people or a women's association, she would usually begin by telling those assembled, 'When I was a little girl and people would ask me whether I wanted to be a nurse or a teacher or a mommy when I grew up, I'd answer that question by saying, "No, *I* want to be a prison warden, because then I'll get to be all three of those things at once."' The story always got a laugh, and Gwen Harding liked to think that laughing helped people to relax a bit. If you can make someone laugh, aren't you making his or her life a little better? Isn't it giving him or her a small gift? That was why Gwen was often so disappointed with herself after a long day at Jennings. She couldn't make the lives of the inmates much better, and she most certainly could not make them laugh. She wished that she could.

She also wished that she could make the five representatives from JRU International laugh as well. They were all solemnly seated before her in her sunny but somewhat dusty office at Jennings. This wasn't the first time she'd met with Jerome Lardner, the bald little man with the protruding Adam's apple, but she didn't recognize the rest of his staff. They seemed to be interchangeable in their little suits, their little haircuts, and their little ages. They looked like they ranged between ages twenty-four to twenty-eight. Gwen Harding was used to seeing young prisoners, but her *staff* were mature. Even Jerome Lardner, whom Gwen uncharitably – but only mentally – referred to as 'Baldy', was well under forty.

'What we are hoping to achieve,' Lardner was saying, 'is not just a new level of productivity, but also a new level of profitability within a correctional facility.'

'Well,' Gwen pointed out with a smile, '*any* profitability would be a new level, wouldn't it? Prisons have never made any money.'

'Certainly,' Jerome nodded, 'certainly none of the *public* prisons make money, but the *privatized* ones do.'

That word! Gwen decided yet again that she would not argue statistics with Jerome Lardner. Whenever she called any of his 'facts' into question, he was always ready with statistics. If figures didn't lie, then liars like Jerome certainly didn't figure out anything except how to protect their own position. 'Inmate Output Management Specialists have been very effective in supervising the productivity of privatized facility workers,' Baldy droned on.

Sometimes it took Gwen as long as five minutes to figure

out what the JRU terminology meant. They seemed to avoid using straightforward words like 'prison' or 'forced labor' when they could use their multisyllabic buzz-words instead. It might fool the politicians, but it didn't fool Gwen. 'Whatever you just said, I'm sure you are right,' Gwen responded.

At last! She got a bit of a chuckle and a few laughs from the JRU staff. That would be her little gift to them. Gwen suspected that they were probably laughing *at* her, not with her. She imagined that she was probably the butt of plenty of JRU jokes. But that was nothing new. She knew, for example, that at Jennings many of the women – both the inmates and the staff – referred to her as 'The Prez' – as in 'The President'. This wasn't because of her strong image or authoritative air, but rather because of her somewhat unfortunate name. When Gwen Harding first arrived at Jennings, her nameplate had been erroneously engraved to read: *WARREN G. HARDING* instead of *WARDEN G. HARDING*. She assumed that the error was an innocent one and not a purposeful attempt to make her look silly. She had had the sign redone, but she kept the original one at home and amused friends and relatives with it at dinner parties and family gatherings – back when she gave dinner parties and had a family to gather.

Gwen could laugh about the nameplate now, but it was not the most dignified way to begin her tenure as the new warden. Fortunately, over time, Gwen had noticed that fewer and fewer of the women who were sent to Jennings even knew who Warren G. Harding was. She imagined that 'The Prez' would eventually be replaced with a new name – probably something even more offensive. Maybe it already had. The inmate population grew, changed, and became less educated and more troubled each year. She'd been shocked only last week when Flora, the middle-aged inmate in charge of the laundry detail, apparently didn't know the difference between a city and a country. 'When I get out of here, I'm going to Paris,' Flora had said.

'France?' Gwen had asked her.

'There, too!' was Flora's reply.

It would have been something to laugh about if it wasn't so sad. But Gwen would've preferred that she and Flora had something to laugh about *together*. Jennings was such a sad place, she wished that all of them – the inmates, the officers, the staff – had something to laugh about. But, after all, it was a prison, wasn't it? And she was the Warden – not a clown. And most certainly not a teacher, a nurse, or a mommy. The job wasn't what she had once hoped for. Contrary to what she (and no one else) thought of as her 'amusing public speaking anecdote', being Warden had very little to do with nurturing, medicine, or motherhood. Increasingly, it was a purely administrative position that required an expertise in staff management, food preparation, health services, and custodial care, along with – quite obviously – criminal behavior. If she had to do it all over again, Gwen Harding would've gladly chosen to be a nurse, a teacher, or a mommy. But she didn't and she couldn't.

Gwen looked at the JRU International staff seated before her. She sighed. It was a big waste of time. As she tried to concentrate on the ongoing monotone monologue of the bald one, she realized that she wasn't sure she knew *what* she was any longer; the thrust of her job had changed too much. She had more and more paperwork, less and less contact with the inmates, and virtually no programs in education and rehabilitation. The greatest focus of her work was on cost containment – especially since JRU had begun to explore the privatization of Jennings nearly a year ago.

Baldy finally stopped speaking and a member of his very young crew was now going on about a 'facilities facilitator', who would make the buildings better, stronger, cleaner, bigger, *and* more *beautiful*. It wasn't clear to Gwen how this was going to be achieved without an immense infusion of money. The Jennings infrastructure hadn't been invested in in decades. She couldn't even find money for routine maintenance.

It was very difficult for Gwendolyn Harding to comprehend how an underfunded and crumbling government-controlled institution for the so-called 'rehabilitation' of women could suddenly be transformed into a profitable subsidiary of an international corporate conglomerate. Not only did Gwen have difficulty imagining how it could happen, she was also becoming unnervingly aware that these JRU fools seemed to believe it would be up to her to see that it *did* happen. Ha! Not even *Warren* G. Harding could do the job. The job Baldy had in mind for Gwen to do required an understanding of sales, marketing, and most aspects of the private sector. She had no experience or expertise in any of these areas – nor did she want any.

What if these bozos did succeed in getting a contract from the state? When it came to the state, *anything* was possible. What kind of havoc would ensue then? Gwen envisioned management so cruel and incompetent that an armed insurrection would not be altogether unlikely. She looked at the twentysomethings gathered before her. If each and every one of them were blown away in an Attica scenario she wouldn't be sorry at all. She'd only regret that the inmates would be forced to serve more time. And as far as Gwen was concerned, it would be grossly unfair to serve time when you were just trying to perform a service for humanity.

Gwen was growing weary and angry at these jackals. What if the staff whom she had hired and trained over the years was fired so that some twenty-three-year-old 'executive' could take over? What if she herself was replaced by a 'facilities facilitator' or an 'inmate output management specialist'? Jennings was a correctional facility for women, not one of those 'country club' joints for the white-collar crooks from Wall Street.

That reminded Gwen of the intake meeting that was scheduled for that afternoon. Jennifer Spencer – the Wall Street showboater who the papers said was 'sentenced to three to five at a country club prison' was due to arrive. A country club! Someday Gwen wanted to visit one of those fabled facilities for herself. Maybe they existed somewhere for *male* white-collar criminals, but to her knowledge – which was extensive – there wasn't a correctional facility for women anywhere in the United States that was not miserably overcrowded, pathetically understaffed, and/or dangerously in need of major repairs. There was nothing at Jennings that even remotely resembled the amenities of a country club.

Gwen had all kinds at Jennings. She had women who had violently murdered, and she had a grandmother who had done nothing more criminal than to grow a little marijuana to help her grandson with his MS. And why? Because when the governor declared his war on drugs, and the legislators passed mandatory twenty-year sentences for even the most minor offense, everyone caught in the net – dolphin as well as tuna – eventually wound up on Gwen's doorstep.

And when they did, it was up to her to take care of all of them. She fed them, housed them, put them to bed, and tried to attend to their medical needs. At the same time she did her best to maintain the discipline and decorum that kept the lid on the Jennings pressure cooker of anger, resentment, and – most perilous of all – boredom. In the meantime, there were no full-time medical professionals on staff, the educational and training programs were sub-standard, there were no special facilities for family visits or overnight stays with children, and while there were a few on her staff who were hardworking men and women, Gwen also had more than a few union-protected liars and sadists who she fervently hoped would eventually end up on the other side of the bars. A country club? Gwen hardly thought so. A profit center? That was even more ridiculous. Gwen actually snorted out loud.

Quickly she took the handkerchief that she kept tucked in her sleeve and wiped her nose as if she had sneezed. Well, she thought, as long as Warden Gwendolyn Harding was still at the helm of the Jennings Correctional Facility for Women it would be neither a country club nor a corporate headquarters. It would be a place where sad, damaged, and angry women were locked away from a society that required their removal. And if she had the courage and the stamina to make it happen, when these women were released, they would leave Jennings somewhat healed, more hopeful, and partially rehabilitated and acceptable to society. That was her modest dream.

She shifted in her seat and cleared her voice. As Warden she was used to being watched and obeyed by hundreds of people. Even the slightest narrowing of her eyes usually brought a response. But in *this* meeting she could probably set her hair afire and it wouldn't stop the young woman who was now babbling on and on about telemarketing. Telemarketing?

Gwen glanced at her watch. She'd give them four more minutes and then they were out of there. She had to meet with today's new prisoner, tell her the rules, and assign her to a cell. Jennifer Spencer was going to be a tough call for Gwen. She was coming in as a 'celebrity' inmate. Everyone in America had read all about her long before she had been sent to Jennings. Her story had been in all of the newspapers and magazines, and the photos of her and her handsome young lawyer looked like something right from the society pages. Even when she was led into the courthouse in handcuffs, she held her head high and kept her nose in the air as if she was going to a meeting of the board of directors.

Gwen Harding was afraid that Jennifer Spencer was coming to Jennings to cut herself a deal. In all of the stories that she read about the arrest, the trial, the conviction, and now her imminent incarceration, Jennifer Spencer looked and sounded like a thoroughbred who always came in in first place. Jennifer Spencer was accustomed to being treated like a winner. And that meant that there were probably a lot of losers who were fashioning a knife out of a contraband piece of metal wrenched off a window frame just so they could slash the face of a woman like Jennifer Spencer. Unprovoked violence wasn't epidemic at Jennings, but it did occur and it was a constant worry to Gwen Harding. But she took her mind off it and tried to focus on the snip of a girl in front of her.

'So, in effect,' the young woman was saying, 'the telemarketing personnel could be monitored by only three shifts of management, which would give twenty-four-hour coverage of an operation that could sell nonstop, guaranteeing a –'

That was enough. These people were only visitors. She didn't report to them – yet. Gwen stood up, looked at Jerome and nodded her head. 'Well, thank you,' she said briskly. 'This has been most informative.'

Informative and beyond Gwen's grasp. The JRU people began to shuffle their papers and regroup. They had no idea what they'd be dealing with. Who was going to train the women? And more importantly, *what* was going to *motivate* them? All of Gwen's staffers and all of Gwen's guards couldn't get them to do the laundry with any care, or even to prepare meals that were anything better than slop. Many of the inmates were content to live in squalor, and few took any pride in their appearance or personal hygiene.

Gwen stood, opened the door of her office, and bid the fools from JRU good-bye. They all walked out without so much as a glance toward Gwen's receptionist, Miss Ringling, or Movita Watson, the inmate assigned to Gwen's office from the prisoner population. Movita was the notable exception among the inmates at Jennings. Gwen knew she shouldn't – really *couldn't* – afford to have favorites, but Movita was . . . well, she was one of a kind. She was more competent, more clever, more stylish, with more attitude, intelligence, and tricks up her sleeve than anyone Gwen had even known. Movita ran the tightest crew in the prison, and perhaps ran the prison as well. Her crewmates loved and respected her in a way that Gwen – in her more perversely ironic moods – almost envied.

If the fools from JRU had any sense at all, Gwen thought, they'd be talking to Movita rather than me.

3

Jennifer Spencer

They try to strip you from the very first minute . . .
When they brought me in county jail, the first thing
they did was take my wedding ring and my earrings.
Then they stripped me stark naked and made me jump
up and down on the floor in a squat position – while
they all stood around watching. They have to forget
we're human beings to treat us that way.

A woman prisoner. Kathryn Watterson, *Women in Prison*

As the prison van moved past the crowd at the courthouse and into the city streets, Jennifer put her face up to the smeared, barred window. As the van lumbered through the tunnel and then through poor suburban streets it was as if Jen was traveling back in time. She watched overworked women lugging laundry and groceries through the littered blocks, the kind of low-rent neighborhood in which she had grown up. Tears filled her eyes for a moment. Every one of those women reminded her of her late mother. And every staggering drunk looked like her stepfather.

Jennifer shivered again and rubbed the flesh of her arms vigorously. She hated being in this van, she hated these streets, and she hated the memories she was having of living in streets like them. It had taken motivation, intelligence, and hard work to climb out of the place they were driving through. Ironically, it now seemed as if that same motivation, intelligence, and hard work was bringing her right back, or to a place even worse. Prison! She wouldn't let her tears fall. She reminded herself that this was only a temporary setback. But she was glad that her mother hadn't lived long enough to know about her trial or see her riding in a prison van.

Jennifer turned away from the window. She couldn't worry about the women on the street; she had her own problems. She'd dressed so carefully that morning – as she did every morning – but now the bench that she was sitting on was speckled with God only knew what kind of dirt. The rubber-matted floor smelled as if unspeakable things had been deposited there, and she was afraid to lean against the wall because of the nasty graffiti that was written in – what? Blood? Snot? Magic Marker? Jen thought ruefully of all the taxes that she had paid over the years. She wondered why some of it wasn't spent on keeping prison vans a little cleaner. Well, the horrible interior was probably just a show for the press. As Tom said, they were making an example of her. Things would be a lot better once she actually got to the prison. What had Tom said? It was a country club. Fine. She could handle that for a day or even two. Right now, though, the filth and the stench were permeating her hair and her clothes. Worse, Jennifer felt too tired to sit erect any longer. She gave up and leaned back. What does it matter? she thought. She would take her suit to Chris French Cleaners back on Ninth Street in a couple of days and they would work their magic on it. They would remove the smells and stains, just as Tom was working to make her personal record spotless once again. She thought of pulling out her hidden Nokia and calling him, but the driver might hear and surely he couldn't have accomplished anything this soon. She should just zone out and wait.

Just as Jennifer relaxed into the ride, the driver sped up and recklessly rounded a corner. She was thrown from the steel bench onto the filthy floor. Jen struggled to get back on the bench and, in her surprise, she forgot for a moment just exactly what her situation was. 'Excuse me,' she shouted to the driver through the wire cage, 'but don't you think we're going just a little too fast in a residential neighborhood?'

His head spun around. 'I don't need no driving lessons from a convict,' he sneered. Then he looked straight ahead and drove on even faster.

Jennifer was angry and ashamed of her outburst, but still she insisted, 'It's dangerous. Your driving threw me onto this filthy floor.'

'I don't care if you fall on your ass. You ain't riding in a limo anymore, convict.'

Convict! He kept calling her a convict. She climbed back on the bench and tried to brace herself against the walls of the van. The handcuffs jangled and cut into her wrists. How in the hell had it come to this? Jennifer always followed the rules. She never smoked pot or had unprotected sex. She never took shortcuts; she never had an overdue book from the library. Hell, she never even left dirty dishes in the sink. And he'd called her a convict. Well, Jennifer thought with a shock, she was a convict. For a moment the reality – the smell, the dirt, the ugliness – broke over her in a wave. What was she doing here?

The ride continued endlessly. Jennifer went from nauseated to sleepy to hungry and then back to nauseated again.

Through it all she was frightened. At last the driver made another sharp right turn, and as Jennifer held on as best she could, the brakes screeched and the van came to an abrupt stop. Jennifer peered out the window. The prison gates were opening, and slowly the van pulled into the yard.

This wasn't like any kind of country club that Jennifer had ever seen – and the crazy-looking woman who was squatting in the flower bed was no greenskeeper. Jennifer had no way of knowing her name at the time – nor could she have ever guessed it – but 'Springtime' was the first inmate to greet her with a smile. The old woman's birth name was long lost, as was her youth. Her dark, leathery skin was pulled so tight over her skull that her death-head's grin reminded Jennifer of the cheap skeleton masks all the kids in her old neighborhood used to wear on Halloween. That grin and those loony eyes were Jennifer's first spooky glimpse of prison life. As the van continued forward, the old woman pointed to the flower bed. Jennifer couldn't see what it was that she was pointing to until they were farther away. There, in a withered garden, bright orange marigolds and faded blue argretum spelled out *Welcome to Jennings*.

Beyond the flowers Jennifer saw the terrible glint of razor wire coiled across the top of the chain-link fence. Ten feet behind it was a twin fence, also topped with the same wire. The sight stopped Jennifer's breath for a moment. What was happening to her? It looked as if she were in a Kurt Russell movie. The van approached a high concrete-block wall with garage doors that slowly opened to let them in. The doors closed behind them, the engine was turned off, and they sat in total silence. A burning bile rose in Jennifer's throat and she swallowed hard. She was soaked with sweat. What were they doing? Nobody moved or said a word. Why were they just sitting there in the dark stench of this disgusting van? It was all so unnerving. She needed air – fresh air. 'Excuse me,' she said softly, 'but what happens now?'

'Jesus Christ!' the driver sneered. 'Are you really in such a hurry to get Inside?'

Before Jennifer could answer, an alarm sounded and, as if in response, overhead lights went on. The driver and guard got out of the van, slid open the doors, and reached in to pull her from her seat. Two prison officers had come from somewhere and stood on the tarmac. 'Right this way, Miss Spencer,' the shorter officer said.

'Welcome to Jennings,' the taller one said with a leer.

Jennifer lost her footing as she made the big step down from the prison van and she nearly fell onto the slippery concrete of the Jennings garage. She blinked her eyes against the harsh fluorescent lights and tried her best to regain her balance and maintain her composure. Dizzy, she teetered on her heels.

'Can you walk on your own?' the shorter of the two officers asked Jennifer with what sounded like real concern. Although they were dressed in identical uniforms, the two men couldn't have been more different in their demeanor. While the short one seemed calm and almost caring in his work, it was clear to Jen that the taller officer was wound tight as a spring and seemed ready to explode into violence at any moment. Good cop – bad cop, thought Jennifer. She was studying the faces of her captors when she felt the tall guard's grip tighten firmly on her arm. 'You were asked if you can walk,' he sneered into her face. 'What's your answer?'

Jennifer looked at him. Who was this guy? His nameplate read KARL BYRD, but he was no bird. He was a six foot, six inch, two hundred pound hyena. 'What's your answer?' he repeated. 'Can you walk on your own?' Jennifer only nodded in response, and the officers flanked her on either side and walked her toward the prison door.

Byrd reached up to his shoulder with his free hand and snarled, 'Open One Oh Nine,' into his shoulder-mounted radio. A buzzer sounded and he pushed the door. As Jennifer twisted in an attempt to see the good cop's nameplate, she noticed that he was locking a contraption on the wall that looked like a night depository at a bank.

'It's for our weapons,' he told her, answering her unasked question. 'No guns are allowed inside Jennings.' His name was Roger Camry. Jennifer decided that she liked Roger Camry. He wasn't some vengeful sadist. He was just a short civil servant with a job to do. For the first time since she left home, Jennifer smiled. Well, this was better. The hallway didn't stink and the officers were unarmed, and one of them was even kind of nice. Maybe this was a country club after all.

But then she stepped further inside. What *was* that smell? It wasn't clinical, nor was it sterile. Before Jennifer could take another sniff, the heavy door slammed behind her with a loud and resounding *clank* of metal against metal. It made her jump, and Byrd laughed. It sounded far too final.

Jennifer looked ahead down the long, empty hallway before her. She froze. Even with Byrd's menacing 'Let's go,' she literally could not take a step. The linoleum glinted an anemic lime green. The green mile. She told herself that she wasn't going to the electric chair, but her legs were actually trembling. She needed some air. She needed just a few more minutes. Her legs were shaking so badly she couldn't walk and she didn't want to let them see. 'So, uh,' she stammered, 'I see your names are Roger and Karl.' She tried to sound casual. 'I'm Jennifer Spencer,' she said, and extended her hand.

'We know who *you* are,' Byrd said with a snort that made him sound like a horse. 'Your face has been splashed across every newspaper and TV screen in the country.' But he didn't shake Jennifer's hand as if she were a celebrity. Instead, he grabbed her elbow and jerked her forward.

Jennifer hated it when people did that. It reminded her of being herded along by Sister Imogene John back in parochial school. Byrd's touch made Jennifer flinch, and that was enough to provoke him to tighten his grip even more. Her legs were still weak. She would have paid a thousand – no *ten* thousand – dollars for just a few moments of fresh air. But it wasn't going to happen. She was locked inside. There was no way out. She took a deep breath of what foul air there was, and she knew now what she smelled. It was despair.

The guard pulled her by her upper arm. 'Please don't shove me,' Jennifer said defiantly to Byrd. He said nothing in response, but continued to shove her just the same. 'We're not getting off to a good start here,' Jennifer said, stumbling once again on the highly polished floors.

'You better take off the heels,' the officer named Roger told her, not unkindly. 'Why don't you take them off and carry them? That will help. We don't want you to fall.'

Jennifer looked down at her Louboutins and then at the long hallway before her. She didn't want to go barefoot, but Byrd drew his face right up to Jennifer's, and she could smell the hot, unpleasant combination of tobacco, chewing gum, and . . . With real venom he rephrased Roger's suggestion into an order and barked, 'Get rid of the shoes. Do you understand?' His breath withered Jennifer's anger. She took off the shoes, and then, with one in each hand and a guard on each elbow, she took her first steps into the prison. Maybe it was a defense mechanism, but at that moment, all Jennifer could think about was how much those shoes had cost.

The hall seemed endless. When at last they stopped in front of a closed door, Jennifer suddenly panicked. She actually didn't want the guards to let go of her arms. She was afraid that she might collapse in fear. The sign on the door read INMATE INTAKE. With false bravado she asked Officer Camry, 'Is there another door for *Inmate Exhaust*?'

'In here,' Byrd ordered as he opened the door. Jennifer walked ahead of them and into the room alone.

Inside, a counter cut the small, gray-green space in half. Behind the check-in counter was an open door, and in that doorway lounged a tall, attractive woman. She had the palest skin and the blackest hair that Jennifer had ever seen – a sort of jailhouse Morticia Addams. If she had had a better haircut, she would've been stunning. But even here, in that ugly jumpsuit and in the hideous fluorescent lighting, she was striking. She had the high cheekbones, the long straight nose, and the pale blue eyes of a better-looking Celtic hillbilly. Well, at least now Jennifer could begin the process of getting out of this place. Without hesitation, she strode up to the counter where the desk clerk stood and asked, 'Have I received any messages?'

'Have you *what*!' Morticia asked in amused disbelief.

'Have I received any messages?' Jennifer repeated. 'I'm expecting a call from my lawyer.'

'Oh my Lord,' the woman laughed, 'she's one of *those*.'

And both officers – even the nice one – laughed right along with Morticia. Jennifer cursed herself for her foolish gaffe. Her head was swimming. But she was so accustomed to hotel check-ins, where the faxes and messages were always waiting, that only now did she realize that the jumpsuit the woman was wearing was in fact a prison uniform – she was just another inmate. Jennifer felt her face color.

Officer Camry pulled out a key chain packed more densely than the A train at rush hour and unlocked a door on the wall next to the counter. 'Please step right through here and turn to your left,' Officer Camry said.

Jennifer obliged his courteous request, and found herself in a room with nothing in it but a chair that had a bright orange jumpsuit folded neatly on the seat. She took a step closer to the chair and heard the door slam behind her just as yet another door in the far wall burst open. Jennifer spun around to see that she was alone, then she spun again to see who was about to enter. In her dizzy state she lost her balance, almost fell to the floor, and watched as her expensive shoes slid across the polished surface and into the feet of a tall, severe woman dressed in a long white lab coat.

'You'll need to strip down,' the woman said firmly. 'It's time for your exam.' Her voice was deep – as deep as her waist was wide. She wasn't really fat, but any niceties like a waistline or hips – if she'd ever had them – were long gone. 'Get on your feet, strip, and fold your clothes,' the baritone in white instructed.

'Are you a doctor?' Jennifer asked without standing.

'I'm the intake officer,' came the reply, which Jen noted was not exactly an answer but, it seemed, was all she was going to get. The intake officer pointed to a sign that read, in both English and Spanish: REMOVE ALL CLOTHING,

JEWELRY, AND OTHER PERSONAL EFFECTS, INCLUDING CONTRABAND. HANG YOUR CLOTHES ON THE PEGS OR PLACE THEM IN THE PLASTIC BAG YOU'LL FIND UNDER THE GOWN. WHEN YOUR FINISHED, RING THE BUZZER.

'Can you read?' she asked in her neutral tone.

Jennifer looked at her as if she were crazy. 'Yes, I can read,' she shot back. 'I can read well enough to see the typo.'

'What typo?' the officer asked.

'The second *your*,' Jennifer told her.

'It's not mine,' the officer sighed.

'That's the point. The *your* isn't the personal possessive. It should be the contraction,' Jennifer continued.

'Do you understand what the sign means?'

'Yes,' Jennifer admitted.

'Fine,' the officer said. 'Then forget the spelling and do what you're told.' Then she turned and left Jennifer alone in the room.

Jennifer read the sign again. It might as well have read, 'Abandon all hope, ye who enter here.' God. What could she do? On the other side of the door she could hear the guards laughing. This was no country club and so far she certainly wasn't receiving the special treatment that Donald and Tom had promised she would get. This all had to be some kind of mistake. She must be in the wrong department. That must be it. There was probably some other area, some VIP lounge where decent people were waiting for her. She stood up, gave the buzzer a push, then lifted the jumpsuit and plastic bag off the chair and sat down to wait, mindlessly stroking the nasty synthetic texture of the jumpsuit as if it were a kitten she held on her lap.

The door was suddenly pulled open and Officer Camry walked in. 'Do you have a problem, Miss Spencer?'

Jennifer smiled at him as if she were a debutante who had found herself at the wrong cotillion. 'Well,' she began, 'I don't think it's really a problem. I just realized there's probably been a mistake. I don't think I'm supposed to be here. Is there someone besides the . . . intake officer you could take me to speak with?'

Camry took a deep breath, then shook his head. 'Miss Spencer, you were told to follow the directions on this sign, and while you're here at Jennings, you will not be told anything twice.' God! Even the good cop was turning nasty on her. 'Do you understand that?' he asked. Before Jen could nod she heard Byrd yell.

'She need help pulling off her panties? I'm available for a strip search,' he said and laughed.

Jennifer shuddered, then stood up. She didn't want to lose the only friend she had in the place, but she tried one more time. 'Yes,' she told Camry as calmly as she could, 'I do understand. But do *you* understand what *I'm* saying? I'm not supposed to even *be* here. I'm supposed to be in some other wing, or department, or whatever it is you call it. You've brought me to the wrong place.'

For a moment Camry looked confused. 'And just where do you think you're supposed to be, Miss Spencer?' he asked.

Jennifer used her most intimate and ingratiating smile. 'You can call me Jennifer,' she said as pleasantly as she could. 'May I call you Roger?'

The officer gave her that same look and then said, 'Just follow the rules, Spencer. Put on the smock and let the intake officer get on with her job. You've already wasted too much time. Trust me, you don't want to keep the Warden waiting.'

The Warden! Of course. The Warden. That must be it, Jennifer thought. She just had to get through these formalities and then her white-glove treatment would begin. She smiled again at Officer Camry and said, 'Fine. If I could have some privacy, then.'

Camry nodded and turned to leave, but just as he reached for his keys, the door flew open again and the looming hulk of Officer Byrd strode in. 'What in the hell is going on in here?' he wanted to know. 'What is taking so long?' Jennifer quickly stood and both the jumpsuit and plastic bag fell to the floor.

'Pick that up and put it on,' Byrd shouted at her. 'And leave it unbuttoned.'

'Now wait just a minute!' Jennifer said. 'I think you'll find if you check with the Warden that my lawyer has called ahead, and he has made . . .' Jennifer stopped. She could hear more than a hint of hysteria rising in her voice and she didn't want to lose control.

'Check with the Warden? Ha! I'll let you do that. You think your lawyer called ahead and he made what?' Byrd asked. He was leering at Jennifer. 'Do you think you just checked into a friggin' hotel? Do you think you have special reservations? A room with a view? A table for two?'

'Sarcasm won't get us anywhere,' Jennifer said as calmly as she could.

'That's right,' Byrd agreed. 'You're not getting anywhere until you strip naked. And that is the end of this discussion.' He looked hard at Jennifer. And Jennifer looked right back.

'Fine,' she said. 'I'm not here to make trouble. I won't be here for long, anyway.'

Officer Camry chimed in, clearly trying to make peace.

'Please just follow the directions and ring the buzzer when you are finished.'

Jennifer looked around the room again. 'Do you have any hangers?'

Byrd laughed aloud. 'Use the pegs,' he said as he exited. 'And don't hurt yourself.'

Both Byrd and Camry left the room and Jennifer proceeded with the ridiculous drill. Right, she thought. Roger Camry was right. She was wasting valuable time. Tom would've made the necessary arrangements directly with the Warden. These low-level functionaries knew nothing. The sooner Jennifer got through this Intake stuff the sooner she'd be Exhausted. She took off her Armani suit and the matching silk blouse, wincing as she hung them on the pegs. When she had removed her slacks she hung them with the jacket, only to see both pieces fall onto the floor. She stooped, picked up the clothes, and tried again. And again. The peg gave way and the clothes fell in a heap. With a shiver, Jennifer realized that the pegs were not an April Fool's joke – they were designed to swivel under weight so that no one could hang herself from them.

Not likely, Jennifer thought with a toss of her head. She hung each piece of her outfit on its own peg, then put on the nasty orange jumpsuit. The fabric was harsh against her body – probably Tercel or Herculon or something worse. And it was enormous – probably a 'one size fits all' kind of thing. She didn't want to have to meet the Warden like this. There wasn't a mirror in the room, but Jennifer did the best she could. For years she had managed to make even the drabbest Catholic school uniform look a little stylish. She slipped the alligator belt from her slacks and cinched it around her waist. After just a few tucks and a little flouncing, Jennifer rang the buzzer. She kept the phone in her bra. She was ready to meet the warden.

When Camry returned, Morticia was with him. Jennifer couldn't help but notice that *her* jumpsuit fit as though it had been made to measure. And Morticia was giving Jennifer a good looking-over, too. They both stood there, glaring at each other as only two women who have come to the party wearing the same dress can. When Morticia caught sight of Jennifer's belt, she covered her mouth to stifle a laugh. 'You ready for your close-up, Miss DeMille?' she asked. Jennifer didn't say a word.

'Cut the crap, Cher,' Camry said firmly to the woman. 'Just bag her personal effects. And Miss Spencer,' he turned to Jennifer, 'please take off the belt. It's against regulations.'

'He's afraid you're going to hang yourself,' Morticia smirked, further betraying her hillbilly origins with her accent. 'Also the brassiere and underpants if you have them.'

'What?' Jennifer asked.

'I'll have to pat you down,' Morticia said. 'Then Ms Cranston's goin' to give you an internal.'

Jennifer groaned and did what Roger Camry told her to do, but as she removed the belt she noticed that Morticia had picked up her shoes and was stroking one of them as if it were the Holy Grail. Jennifer guessed that she'd probably never seen a Louboutin before in her poor trash life. Then she turned her back and tried to carefully remove her bra without dropping the cell phone. Just as she was about to secret the phone into the sleeve of her jumpsuit she felt someone standing beside her.

'What is this?' Morticia asked as she grabbed the phone and held it up in the air for the officer to see.

'Where'd you get that?' Camry asked. 'That's what contraband is, Spencer, and it can get you into big trouble here at Jennings. Lucky for you it was found now and not later.' He tilted his head toward the personal effects bag and Morticia went over and slid the phone into the bag.

The white-coated intake officer returned and asked, 'Are we about ready to get on with this?'

'Miss Spencer is ready,' Officer Camry said, and he took hold of Jennifer's elbow. As he steered her toward the door, Jennifer saw that Cher was slipping one of the shoes onto her foot.

'Hey!' Jennifer protested. But Cher quickly pulled the shoe off and put it back on the counter before anyone could catch her.

Camry turned to look at Cher. She met his glare with the blandest look on her face. 'Get busy with that, Cher,' he said. 'Catalogue every piece of clothing and put it all away.'

'Where is she taking my things?' Jennifer asked, but she didn't get an answer from either Camry or the intake officer. Jennifer looked down at the jumpsuit she was wearing. Well, if that Cher person stole her clothes, she'd just have to ask Tom to bring something else for her to wear when he came tomorrow to take her home. She could trust Tom to select something appropriate. He had great taste in clothes and sometimes looked better in his Prada suits than Jennifer did in hers!

'All right then, let's get started,' the intake officer said in the deep voice that gave Jennifer chills.

The rest of the processing was like some kind of surreal out-of-body experience. It was almost as if Jennifer wasn't there. She became just another woman in a prison uniform, and this disassociation actually made it all a little easier to take. She was weighed, measured, and photographed. When the officer fingerprinted her she calmly watched as her fingers were rolled in the ink and then onto the paper. As her prints were being made, Jennifer asked, 'Do you have any suggestions on how to get this ink off your fingers? It's almost impossible to wash it off with just plain soap and water.'

'Well, Spencer,' the officer opined, 'maybe you might try Estée Lauder's Youth Dew.'

The sarcasm wasn't pointed or funny enough for Jennifer to laugh, but she did respond. 'I just thought that, since you worked with the stuff all the time, you might know. I'll make a note to tell our clients at Chesebrough-Ponds to develop some sort of cleansing cream for fingerprint ink.'

The intake officer threw back her head and roared with laughter. 'Yeah,' she chortled, 'you can call it *Out Damn Spot!* Now get up on the table.'

Reluctantly Jennifer climbed onto the stainless steel bench. As soon as this monster was done poking and prodding, she would call Tom. He was probably already well on his way to getting her out of this place. Jennifer knew that everything was going to be all right. And then the officer told her to stand up.

'Bend over and open your jumpsuit,' she said matter-of-factly. She picked up a thin latex rubber glove and began to slowly and deliberately pull it over her hand. When she snapped it against her wrist, the sound sent a shiver down Jennifer's spine. 'Cavity check,' the intake officer said, and Jennifer felt her stomach start to rise.

'Why?' Jennifer whispered. This was too much. She

certainly didn't have a prostate to examine. 'Why do I need a cavity check?' she demanded more loudly. 'I'm not in here for drugs or on a weapons charge.'

'C'mon,' the officer sighed, 'it'll be over before you know it. It's a lot worse when we have to hold you down.'

4

Movita Watson

Rich women have the Betty Ford clinic; poor women have prison.

A prison commentator. Kathryn Watterson, *Women in Prison*

I declared that until I said different, this candy – a name on the Inside for a new inmate – would be known to *my* crew as *Number 71036*. 'She's just another piece of snotty white meat,' I told 'em. 'It's not like we all have to sit up and take notice just because she dragged her sorry ass into this joint. She don't mean nothin' to us.' I'm queen bee at Jennings. And while I know that might not mean much on the Outside, when you're on the Inside it's important to stay on top. Nobody wants to be on the bottom. Not the bottom bunk, not the bottom of the crew, not the bottom of *nothing* in a prison. I've always been on top, and I plan on staying there.

Cher's the funniest, smartest, and baddest in our sisterhood, and she said to me, 'Well let me tell you, that Number 71036's sorry ass was dressed in the best damn silk underwear I've ever seen.'

My crew was sitting at our usual table in the cafeteria eating lunch. Dinner is always at one of our houses but lunch is quick and gotta be in from food service. When you first see us, you might think we're kind of an unlikely group. I'm a proud and beautiful black woman, but all the rest of the women in my crew are white. Unlike men in prison, where black and white rarely mix, women inmates tend to group up based on whether or not they like each other, and what they can do to help each other out. My women make up the most organized, efficient and tight-knit crew in the joint. We're a family.

Like I said, I'm the boss. As the Warden's secretary, I hold a position of power (and opportunity) at Jennings that few, if any, can challenge. Cher McInnery works Intake, and that means that all sorts of nice things flow like a river over the desk in that room where the new inmates strip and leave all their possessions behind. Some of that river of riches, maybe just a small stream, gets diverted in Cher's direction – and some of that gets passed on to my crew.

Right now Cher had an advantage over the others in the crew. She was the only other of us who had actually *seen* Jennifer Spencer. Even though I insisted that she was 'no big fuckin' deal' to me, we had all heard and read plenty about Number 71036 in the news – the fall of 'the Wall Street Princess' – and we were all anxious to talk about her.

You see, inside a prison nothing ever changes. That's probably the worst damn thing about living Inside. Everyone's in the same uniform, Christmas looks just like the Fourth of July, the windows are too high to see out of, and the exercise yard doesn't have a blade of grass that hasn't been examined by four hundred pairs of eyes. There just isn't much to look at except the walls and each other, and women, we like to look at things. I read once in one of the Warden's magazines that the experts call it 'sensory deprivation'. I call it goddamn hard.

'What was she wearing?' Theresa LaBianco wanted to know. She's into 'How was her hair styled? Does she know how to put on makeup?' Theresa used to be at the very top of one of those big makeup sales pyramids. Had a couple of hundred housewives sellin' mascara. I could just imagine what the kites – secreted notes – would say about this new candy.

Theresa worked in the canteen and could always manage to buy us the freshest produce or the best chicken when we got to shop. It wasn't until her husband was caught cooking the books that she found herself on the Inside at Jennings. But Theresa never lost her love for life or blusher. And the bitch could dish. She especially loved to hear Cher talk about all of the new inmates. 'It's kinda like window shopping,' she would say.

'Well,' Cher began, because she knew what was expected of her, 'her shoes were the softest damn leather I ever felt.' Cher shook her head. 'Shoes like that must go for four hundred bucks if they go for a dime.'

'Well, you know what they say about shoes, don't you?' Theresa asked. 'They say, you can't know someone's sorrows until you've walked a mile in her shoes. That's what they say about shoes.' Theresa had a damn saying for everything. She lived by sayings. She said that was how she had motivated her sales force, but they drove me nuts.

'Well, I don't think 71036 has ever had too many problems walking in those shoes,' Cher sneered. 'And I plan to walk more than a mile in 'em,' she told us and laughed.

'Did you take 'em, Cher?' Suki asked, all wide-eyed. Suki Conrad was our crew's innocent – our baby. She worked in the laundry and in Suki's case it wasn't so much what she could do for the rest of us, but what we could do for Suki. I think Suki made us all better women.

'Damn right I took 'em,' Cher said proudly. 'When I saw that those shoes were a size eight, I took that for a sign.' Cher lived by signs and omens like Theresa lived by sayings. 'My parole date is comin' up, and I figure those pointy shoes were pointing directly to my getting outta here.'

'Girl,' I said with a sigh, 'you can't just keep stealin'. You're gonna get caught, lose your chance at parole and damn it, it's wrong.'

'You know what they say about stealing, don't you?' Theresa chimed in. 'They say that God helps those that help themselves. That's what they say about stealing.'

I was never sure with Theresa if she meant to support me or sass me when she said somethin' like that.

'That's not what God meant,' Suki protested. 'God said, "Thou shalt *not* steal."'

'NBD – No Big Deal – I haven't stolen from God since I used to swipe money out of the collection plate at Sunday school,' Cher laughed. 'And I never take nothin' from people who can't spare it. Won't steal from the simple minded, neither,' she added.

Cher was a thief and she didn't mind saying so. She didn't see anything wrong with what she did. What was wrong to Cher was that everyone else had more than she did, and the only way to make up the difference was for her to take what she needed. That's what she'd done to get herself incarcerated and what she did every time a new inmate was processed into Jennings. She just put the things she didn't want into a bag with the new inmate's name and number on it, and she put the good stuff into another bag with a different name and number. No one would ever reclaim the second bag, because the name and number on *that* bag belonged to a dead or released inmate. Cher had perfected the system, and now had plenty of bags hidden right out in plain sight.

'What was she wearing?' Theresa wanted to know.

'Armani!' Cher giggled. 'I've never managed to steal Armani before. It's so damned expensive that the stores usually have it wired to the rack.'

'Well, I don't think 71036 ever had to steal anything,' Suki said. 'It said in the papers that she's really rich.'

'Yeah. And greedy, too. She got busted for stealing that money on Wall Street,' Cher shot back. 'That makes her a thief just like me.'

'But did you see her on the TV news?' Suki asked. 'She looks just like a movie star.'

'Well, you know what they say about pictures, don't you?' Theresa began.

'Yeah, we all know what they say about pictures, Theresa,' I said in exasperation. 'You all act like we never had us a celebrity prisoner before. What about Jackie James, the sick little twist from Montgomery who killed her two babies on a tourist trip to New York, then said they'd been kidnapped by a black brotha'? That was in all the papers.'

'Nobody likes baby killers,' Cher said.

'Or baby rapers,' Theresa added. 'Whatever happened to that teacher, Camille Lazzaro, who decided to teach one of her boy students more than geography? Didn't she just give a whole new meaning to the term "teacher's pet"? She had the baby and the daddy wasn't even thirteen years old yet.'

'Or that Carole Waters over in Unit Three?' Cher added. 'She got her boyfriend to murder both her husband *and* her mother-in-law just for the insurance and the inheritance. She was in all the papers, too.'

'I steer clear of anyone who kills for money.' Theresa shook her head. 'It's one thing if you catch your man screwin' your sister or your daughter. I say shoot 'em. But to kill someone just for money, that's cold.'

'That reminds me,' Cher said, laughing, 'any of you heard that Dixie Chicks song on the radio called "Goodbye Earl"? It reminded me of you, Movita.'

As soon as Cher said that, it got real quiet. 'We ain't gonna talk about Earl,' I said – and I meant it. Cher didn't say another word. She didn't dare to. It's an unspoken but well enforced rule that you don't never talk about anyone's life on the Outside. You specially don't never mention no one's family or her man unless you're invited to.

Most of the women on the Inside are here, one way or another, because of a man. Either she got involved in one of his illegal schemes, or he beat her until one day she fought back and killed him. It's safe to say that most of the women in Jennings wouldn't be here at all if they hadn't been hooked up with low-life no-goods like my Earl. Men are a weakness, like drinking or drugs. I know I was weak willed with my Earl, and fact is I don't like to be reminded of it.

Suki was the first one to speak up again after the silence. 'You think this Jennifer Spencer got in trouble because of her boyfriend, too?' she asked.

'I wouldn't be surprised,' I said. 'I know about book-keeping, and it doesn't matter if it's a dental office in Kew Gardens or investment banking on Wall Street. It all comes down to shifting the books and what you're allowed to get away with. Men still make the rules about that and they probably always will.'

'Well, 71036 seems to be pretty comfortable around men,' Cher said. 'You shoulda seen her flirtin' with dumb ol' Roger Camry. He was all "Miss Spencer" this and "Miss Spencer" that. It was enough to make ya' sick.'

'What about Byrd?' I asked her. 'Was that prick hittin' on her?'

'Not yet,' Cher said with a smirk. 'He'll get her eventually, but right now it looked like he was gonna let Roger have first crack at her.'

As soon as Cher said that, Suki stood up, took her tray from the table, all angry like, and said, 'I'm not gonna sit here and listen to this dirty talk. I gotta get back to the laundry.' She took her tray to the dirty dish window and left.

'Well, what's wrong with that one?' Cher asked, not that she really wanted to know.

'Maybe she's having her time of the month,' I answered, though I was afraid I knew the answer and it wasn't that.

'Well, you know what they say about women living together in prison and their periods, don't you?' asked Theresa.

'Theresa, if we all got our periods at the very same time,' I laughed, 'this ol' building would vibrate so hard from the tension that the cement blocks would all collapse and we'd be able to just walk on outta here.'

Just then old Springtime, who tends the flower gardens, was passing the table and overheard what I said. 'Is someone planning a breakout?' she asked, her voice hushed but all excited.

'Nah, old sista',' I told her gently. She's tried to escape

fifty or sixty times by now. 'We're just waiting for the place to fall down on its own so you can hop your withered old ass right over the pile of rubble and get out.' I smiled at her and she grinned back.

The whole room looked our way as old Springtime's cackle echoed off the steel and cinder blocks.

5

Gwen Harding

Some people think that law enforcement officers are inhumane or uninteresting. Personally, if I became personally involved with every person sitting there crying, I couldn't function in my job. I'm not inhumane – I'm just removed from the emotion.

Georgia Walton, deputy sheriff at Sybil Brand Institute.
Kathryn Watterson, *Women in Prison*

'Good morning, sir,' the new inmate began briskly as she was ushered into the Warden's office by Officers Camry and Byrd.

Gwen Harding didn't get many chances to laugh during an Intake meeting, but the dumbstruck look on Jennifer Spencer's face when she got her first look at 'sir' was almost comical. Like so many other women, Spencer obviously assumed that Warden Harding would be a man with whom she might flirt. The girl was clearly more than just a little rattled by her discovery.

Spencer was thin, taller than average, with big dark eyes and lots of dark hair. Staring at the Warden, those eyes went from registering surprise to embarrassment, and then quickly to something closer to . . . *manipulation*. Oh yes, Gwen Harding thought, this girl was capable of causing trouble. 'Too smart for her own good' was the phrase that Gwen's father would've used to describe Jennifer Spencer. 'Take a seat,' Gwen told her and pointed to the chair that sat directly in front of her desk.

There were two chairs for visitors in the Warden's office. The one beside the desk was rarely offered to inmates or even coworkers. The other chair – which was known as the 'hot seat' – was the chair intended for Jennifer's butt. But Miss Spencer seemed to be past any discomfiture, and, ignoring the 'hot seat', she slipped quite easily into the chair beside Gwen's desk. Officer Camry moved to stop her, but the Warden shook her head. She'd see how this all played out. 'You may go,' she told the officers, and they turned and left, closing the door behind them.

Gwen looked the girl over. There was no doubt that she was going to be a problem. Deciding where to put these high-profile types was always a tough call. She had to get it right the first time, because there was no good way of changing it later. Gwen thought she was a pretty good judge of character, however, and while Spencer might be high profile, Gwen didn't think she'd end up being high maintenance. Number 71036 was too proud for that.

'I trust that your trip here and your processing at Intake was not too difficult,' Gwen began. Gwen realized as she said it that it had been *very* difficult for this young woman. She could tell at a glance that Jennifer Spencer never expected to be stuck in a prison. Jennifer Spencer would've been far more comfortable heading up the JRU meeting than coping with what she was about to experience at Jennings.

'Miss Spencer,' the Warden continued as she opened her desk drawer and took out the inmate manual. 'You'll find this booklet to be indispensable during your stay here.' She handed the bright yellow pamphlet to Jennifer, who took it, set it on her lap, and folded both hands on top of it.

'Thank you,' Jennifer said. 'I –'

'You must read it completely later, but now I'd like you to turn to page three. It's headed *Inmate Responsibilities*.'

As instructed, Inmate 71036 opened the book, but only glanced at the page before she began to speak. 'It's important –'

'It's important that we read this page together,' Gwen interrupted. 'I want to touch on a few items listed here.' The Warden began to read: 'You are responsible for your behavior, actions, and attitude.' Gwen saw the girl shift in her seat.

'Warden Harding,' Jennifer said. 'May I speak frankly?'

'Please do,' Gwen said dryly, waiting for the inevitable. Often Gwen found that if she let a new inmate ramble on long enough, she would catch some pertinent detail, some insight into her personality that would enlighten Gwen on how she might help the woman to help herself. Gwen believed in rehabilitation, not punishment. But she could almost bet that Jennifer Spencer was going to put this belief to the test.

'I guess you've probably already heard from Attorney Howard McBane of Swithmore, McBane, or from Thomas Branston at Hudson, Van Schaank & Michaels,' Jennifer began. 'Or maybe Mr Michaels himself called.' Before Gwen had a chance to respond, Jennifer crossed her legs, leaned in toward Gwen, and continued. 'This situation has gotten a little out of control, I'm afraid. I wasn't meant to come here at all, and I certainly should not have had a rectal or pelvic exam. When I speak with my attorney I'm going to have to mention it and see if legal action should be taken.'

'Legal action?' Gwen asked. She was getting more than just annoyed with this woman.

'Yes,' Jennifer said flatly, 'I am neither a drug offender nor a smuggler. The invasive examination wasn't needed. And your intake officer didn't seem to have any medical education.' She took a deep breath, and Gwen saw that, in spite of her bravado, the girl was trembling. Gwen felt a stab of pity for the girl as she watched her toss her head back and continue. 'Anyway, I'd like to talk about Attorney Branston's arrangements for my special needs while my appeal is being heard.'

'Special needs?' Gwen echoed.

'Did he tell you that I would like a sunny room? And I can't have a roommate because I'll be keeping late hours. If desks and laptops are not standard issue then I'll need to get one of each.'

Gwen merely blinked.

'Also, I'll need access to a copier and hopefully some secretarial help. I don't know if you have a trained staff, but I'd be more than willing to pay for someone to come in.'

Gwendolyn Harding sat in a state of stunned disbelief as 71036 enumerated her expectations of 'white-glove treatment' and 'special considerations'. This wasn't the standard protestation of innocence, but rather a list of demands from the kind of young woman who was used to giving orders – and having them carried out. Not even when women like Margaret Rafferty – someone from a very high social position – were taken in had Gwen run into this lack of reality and misguided arrogance. Did Spencer really think Jennings would revolve around *her*? Who had led her to think such a thing? Her boss? Her success on Wall Street? Spencer's file indicated that she was clearly not from the kind of social background that would justify such an astonishing sense of self-importance.

Gwen took a deep breath. Whatever the reason for it, this was not an attitude that would allow Spencer to survive within the prison population. And it certainly was not endearing her to Gwen, either. The longer Gwen listened, the tighter the muscles cramped in her neck, jaw, and throat. All of her life she had fought a debilitating stammer when confronted with ignorance and pride. Years of speech therapy had taught her to modulate her breathing, focus her thoughts, and to speak in a rhythmic pattern that allowed no time for a stutter. She had managed to control it throughout the horrible JRU meeting, but now she felt that the stammer would return and it angered her. When she was certain that she had mastered her own emotions, Gwen placed her hands on her desk and leaned her face close to 71036. 'Your opinion to the contrary, Miss Spencer, you are not – in charge – here.'

The rhythm of the statement echoed 'On your mark – get set – go.' But the intention was not to start a race, but to stop Jennifer Spencer dead in her tracks. It worked. Spencer shut up and paled. This result pleased Gwen, and consequently she felt the spasm of anger release its grip from her throat. She would not be intimidated by this young woman, nor would she let her forget why they were both here. Jennifer Spencer *needed* Gwendolyn Harding's help.

'*You* are here – to get – help,' Gwen told her, continuing with the steady rhythm of *pa-dum, pa-dum, pa-dum*. '*I* am here – to help – you.' With her anger under control, Gwen took a cleansing breath and continued in a more relaxed tone. 'You will not be given an office or a laptop, nor will you – be assigned – a desk. Or a secretary. You will work on prison work for which you will be paid. Every woman – at Jennings – works. There are no – special favors – here. Have I made – myself – clear?'

The *pa-dum, pa-dum, pa-dum* achieved the desired effect. The new inmate dumbly opened and closed her mouth a few times – kind of like a guppy – uncrossed her legs, and nodded her head with a robotlike rhythm that matched the cadence of Gwen's speech.

Fine, Gwen thought. She looked closely at Spencer's face. She had originally thought of assigning this new inmate to the library, but now she could see that Jennifer Spencer was going to need something very different than the cool and gentle hand of librarian Margaret Rafferty. This girl needed to learn values, cooperation, and probably some humility if she was going to survive incarceration.

The warden relaxed a bit, rose from her chair, sat on the edge of her desk, and continued. Jennifer in turn adjusted her attitude and sat and listened as if she were attending a lesson in the Baltimore catechism.

'First, you have to be passed through Observation for a night,' the Warden told Jennifer. This was SOP – Standard Operating Procedure. It probably wasn't needed in Spencer's case, but it was just possible that under that bravado, she was suicidal or drugged. Gwen knew Spencer wouldn't tolerate Observation well. It was an extremely dehumanizing but necessary evil. However, the real question was, after she was finished with that, where would inmate 71036 fit in?

'Miss Spencer – I assume – that you know that here – at Jennings – we all work. In addition – to the jobs – such as maintenance – there is work – to be done – in the shops.' Gwen stopped and waited to see if any of this was sinking in. She saw the girl nod.

'The pay is next to nothing. You work to help defray your cost to the taxpayer.'

'Yes,' Jennifer said calmly, 'I know. I'm in a very high tax bracket myself.'

Gwendolyn looked to see if there was any attitude or irony in the comment. It was then that she knew exactly where Jennifer Spencer needed to work. 'You will start in the laundry – for now,' the Warden told her. 'I believe that will be for the best. In due time, you may be promoted,' she added with a smile of encouragement. And then, with a deep and meaningful intake of air, Warden Gwendolyn Harding prepared for her big finale. It was a speech she had given often, to each and every new inmate that she welcomed to Jennings.

While she recited the words, she was simultaneously deciding where to put Spencer after Observation. She concluded that she must go right into the middle of Movita Watson's crew. With a good teacher like Movita, Spencer would eventually settle in and learn how to take care of herself. Gwen knew that Movita was fascinated with Jennifer Spencer. She had seen her take the papers and magazines from the library cart that was available to the inmates and read every article that was written about her.

The Warden paused for a moment, then continued both speaking and thinking. There was structure in Movita's crew. She was a good leader with an eye for talent. Of course, no one in that group had ever known the kind of wealth and privilege that Spencer knew, and if that girl looked down her nose at Movita like she had with Gwen –

well, she was likely to have that nose put out of joint. She studied Spencer's face intently. Movita would either take Spencer in – or Movita would take her out. Only time would tell. If she did take her in it would take time.

The Warden's speech was at an end, and she told Jennifer that their meeting was over. She called for Camry and Byrd to take her away to Observation.

Later, all alone in her office, Gwen couldn't help but feel disappointed with the turn of events that day. Jennifer Spencer had actually shaken her self-confidence. Or maybe it was the JRU people who had done that. Why had they all rattled her so? Gwen had seen both Spencer and the women from JRU scrutinizing every inch of her person and her clothing. They all looked like those haughty store clerks at Saks. Except with Jennifer Spencer it was even worse. She walked into Gwen's office like she was coming in for the quarterly earnings report. Gwen didn't know who made her feel the most insignificant, Spencer or Baldy from JRU.

Gwen had kept a daily journal from the first day she began at Jennings. She kept it carefully locked in the bottom left drawer of her desk – where she also kept a bottle of gin, a glass, and a jar of olives.

Most often by the time Gwen finished her journal entry for the day it was deep into the evening. She'd write and sip, sip and read. Night after night she told herself that she found both solace and inspiration in recording her thoughts and observations, but in her heart she knew that it was really the gin that kept her at the office a little later each evening. The gin and the emptiness of her house. So far, she had sternly refused to drink at home. But with her mother dead, her beloved Yorkie gone almost two years, and her husband gone for far longer than that, there was little reason for Gwendolyn Harding to rush home at night.

6

Jennifer Spencer

A cat pent up becomes a lion.

Italian proverb

When Jennifer was escorted out of the Warden's office – sandwiched between the two guards – she was flooded with a feeling of such terror that she had to sink the nails of her fingers deep into her own palms just to keep from screaming or running.

But there was nowhere to run to. Jennifer Spencer couldn't believe that she was actually being incarcerated at the Jennings Correctional Facility for Women. People like Jennifer Spencer didn't go to prison. So she'd been told by Donald and Tom and so she'd believed.

There had been only one person who had warned her not to participate in the deal with Donald Michaels. That was Leonard Benson. He was the financial officer involved, and had always seemed less than enthusiastic about the plan. As the assistant to George Gross, the CFO – Chief Financial

Officer – Lenny was privy to a lot, but not all, of the machinations at Hudson, Van Schaank & Michaels. 'Don't do this, Jennifer,' he had pleaded to her. 'When you play with the SEC, you play for keeps.'

But Jennifer was not only under the influence of too many drinks that particular night; she was also drunk on the praise and the promises that Donald had been lavishing on her. She had turned on Lenny and demanded, 'Hasn't Donald Michaels made *you* rich, too?'

'Yes,' Lenny admitted, 'but . . .'

'He took me straight from school when I had nothing – nothing but loans to pay off, and now – well, you know my net worth.'

Lenny had nodded. He prepared Jennifer's taxes and helped her keep as much of her income as the law would allow. He certainly knew how much she was worth. 'But you earned all of that,' he insisted. 'You worked hard for Don. There's no reason now to take this kind of risk.'

'But it's such a small risk,' Jennifer retorted. 'And it will save Donald. I owe him something.' She grew adamant. 'He's made you rich, Lenny. Aren't *you* grateful?'

'I work my guts out for that guy,' Lenny had protested. 'I'm available twenty-four-seven. And I *am* grateful. But that doesn't mean that I'd take the rap for him.'

'Hey, that's the point,' Jennifer had explained, as if Lenny was stupid, deaf, or not even present. 'There *is* no rap. Donald doesn't do anything that the boys at Salomon Smith Barney or Morgan Stanley or Lazard Frere don't do every day of the week.' She, who had never worked at any of those places, was only parroting back what she'd heard. 'They're envious.'

'You don't know *what* Donald has done,' Lenny had shot

back. 'Nor do I. None of us do. That guy is the most compartmentalized person I've ever met. He doesn't even let his left hand know what the right one is up to.'

Jennifer put her hand on Lenny's narrow shoulder. 'Thanks for trying to look out for me,' she said. 'But you forget that I *like* taking risks. No guts – no glory.'

The grip on Jennifer's left arm grew tighter and she was snapped out of her reverie. Now every step she took away from the Warden's office put Jennifer deeper into the hideous nightmare of the Jennings Correctional Facility. As she was marched off to Observation – whatever the hell that was – she felt that if she didn't get some fresh air to clear her head and her lungs she might actually fall to the floor. The meeting with the Warden had been catastrophic. How had it gone so wrong? Was it her fault? Hadn't Warden Harding been contacted? If not, why not? Donald Michaels was powerful enough to get the governor on the phone in a heartbeat at any time of the day or night. She knew that. Why hadn't he reached the Warden? The answer had to be because he didn't want to. So whom had he reached *instead*? Perhaps, just this once, Donald had made a mistake and aimed too high. If he started with the governor, or even the State Attorney General's Office, how long might it take for the trickle-down effect to take effect?

'This way,' Officer Camry instructed. Jennifer thought she saw a look of pity on his bland, round face. The idea that this thirty-eight-thousand-dollar-a-year civil servant with the thinning brown hair, the flat brown eyes, and the plain brown uniform – the *idea* that this pathetic excuse for a man whose IQ probably wasn't one hundred and one in the shade had reason to pity *her* made her feel both furious and pitiable. She wondered whether Roger's life at home was any better than his life in prison. Who would choose to do a job like this? You had to be nuts, stupid, or very, very limited. She glanced at Roger Camry out of the corner of her eye. He looked like he was probably all three. Officer Byrd, on the other hand, wasn't even *that* qualified. But he obviously received another kind of compensation – women to frighten or even hurt.

Jennifer tried to keep her head as they passed from the administration wing into the prison itself. It all looked oddly familiar, and Jennifer was reminded of how she felt whenever she saw a famous landmark. There's no surprise when you finally see the Eiffel Tower – it looks just like all the pictures. The same was true for Big Ben and the Statue of Liberty. But, despite the familiarity, the same was not true with prison. Sure, it looked just like every jail photo and movie she'd ever seen. But the enormous surprise was the horror that she felt at being here herself. Jen couldn't control the shakes in her hands, so she clenched her fists again. It won't be for long, she reminded herself. What had Tom said? A day. Two at the most. Not long.

The three of them – Jennifer, Roger, and Byrd – walked through one more set of doors, buzzed in this time by an observer in a glass booth, and entered the Observation Wing – at least that's what it said in chipped gray paint over the door.

Jennifer suddenly realized just how tired she was. She would've been grateful to lie down somewhere – anywhere – in the dark and just sleep. If she couldn't have fresh air, then at least give her unconsciousness. But the place she entered almost took her breath away. The room was a kind of office/reception area. It was hard to tell if the stench was more urine than ammonia, but the underscents of vomit and sweat were still strong. For a moment Jennifer thought again of Donald Michaels – this time of his penchant for his costly, custom-blended Floris aftershave and soaps – each bar close to a hundred dollars. She wondered bitterly if one of Donald's scented Floris candles would cover *this* odor.

All right, she told herself. Someday next week, she and Tom and Donald would laugh at this story. She imagined them at Fraunces Tavern or Delmonico's. Donald would laugh and shake his leonine head and wipe the corner of his eyes the way he always did and order another bottle of Veuve Clicquot.

But that would be later. Now she was steeped in this squalor and the noise would not let her mind wander. The sound of another correctional officer's heavy steps, the gruesome static and squawking of his and Camry's and Byrd's walkie-talkies, and the harsh grinding of the gates as they closed behind her chilled her more than she wanted to admit. But the noise and stench weren't the worst things. The light was so harsh it was merciless. Exhausted as she was, if she closed her eyes she could still feel the fluorescence burning through her eyelids. Sleep in this room would be impossible.

There was a lot of paperwork in triplicate and some ribald talk between Byrd and the new officer, a huge black woman. Then she was taken, at last, to Observation.

'Spencer, here,' the huge female officer told the big uniformed woman in a booth at the end of a long catwalk.

'Fourteen,' was all she said in response.

The fat woman nodded. 'How's the other freshman adjusting?' she asked.

'Just about how you'd expect a withdrawing crack whore to adjust,' the woman in the booth snapped. 'But she'll be fine in another thirty hours or so.' The woman officer motioned with her head, took Jennifer by her orange-plastic-coated shoulder, and turned her to the left into one of the cubicles.

'Let's go,' he said.

The space was one of perhaps a dozen concrete cabinets. Jesus, she thought, wasn't Hannibal Lecter confined to something like this? It was achingly bare. A blanket, a mattress, and a commode. Not that she could use the latter, since the entire outside wall of the cell was made of thick Plexiglas and she could be seen, not just from there but also from overhead. There was no ceiling to the cubicle, and as she looked up she could see an officer patrolling along the catwalk that allowed him to look down into each cell.

'Wait!' Jennifer said, and it wasn't a ploy or a power trip; she was truly terrified to be left here. 'Can I please make a phone call?'

The big woman officer laughed out loud, a guttural *haw-haw*. 'Look, this is jail, girl, and you don't have a quarter. You're in prison now,' she said. Then she softened. 'Observation is tough, but it's usually only for a day,' she added almost apologetically to Jennifer. 'After you get out of Observation you can make collect calls from your unit.'

She had barely finished speaking, when someone – or some*thing* – began to screech in a subhuman wail. It was a noise of pure rage and despair. 'I'm sorry about the noise,' the officer said. 'She's going off. But you won't be here long. Maybe twenty-four hours. So try to make the best of it.'

'Oh my God!' Jennifer wailed, then fought and won control of herself. The officer handed her a black booklet to go with the yellow one she still clutched under her arm. 'Maybe this will help,' she said, and Jennifer took it, imagining it must be some religious tract. Only a saint, a sadist, or a cult member would voluntarily work here with this stink and noise. She stepped into the cell. 'You'll get used to it,' the big woman said, and for some reason that was the thing that filled Jennifer's eyes to almost overflowing. She turned her head away. God, she certainly hoped not!

She looked over at the stained mattress and paper sheets. It was only last night – in her own home – that she'd slept in a bed made with Pratesi sheets.

Jen crouched down in the corner of the observation cell and closed her eyes. The light still beat on her eyelids but she tried to transcend to another consciousness. She could stand anything for twenty-four hours, she told herself. She thought of the nights of endless study at college and business school. She'd pulled plenty of all-nighters at Hudson, Van Schaank & Michaels, too, when she was more tired than this. So she'd pull one more now. Maybe her last. All she had to do was concentrate. But on what? Concentrating on her situation was unbearable, and without her cell phone, she couldn't check on deals, her portfolio, or her apartment. Then she thought of it: She'd spend the night concentrating on her closet and every garment in it.

Jennifer didn't have a lot of clothes; when the interior designer had discussed the bedroom Jennifer insisted that she didn't want a built-in closet, just the antique armoire. 'But it's only twenty-seven inches of hanger space,' he'd protested. She'd shrugged.

Now she sat in the corner like a child ordered to take a time out. She remembered what she'd said: 'Twenty-seven inches ought to be more than enough for any woman.' And it was. She'd always longed not for quantity but quality. Now she had it, hanging in her armoire back at home. Aside from the one she had foolishly worn today and doubted she'd ever see again, she had three other Armani suits – one black twill, one black and brown tweed and one dark brown heavy silk. Each one had been well over two thousand dollars, but she'd bought them as an investment, and every time she slipped into one she felt like a million bucks. Next she thought of the two Yamaguchi suits that made the Armanis seem cheap in comparison. She'd considered one for more than a month before she'd bought it, hoping it wouldn't be sold. That was the black one with an asymmetrical jacket; a lapel and a hem were higher on one side than the other. Jennifer couldn't wear it for a meeting that included middle managers or conservative CEOs, but it went over big with high-tech and advertising types. The other, even more costly Yamaguchi was in a neutral gray-beige miracle fiber that she could fold into her purse if she had to and it would unpack as if it had been pressed by Sister Mary Margaret herself.

Jennifer sighed. Thinking was difficult sitting on the cold concrete floor. She began a mental inventory of her drawers. When she was home she wore cashmere sweats that she'd bought at TSE. They'd been very expensive, but nothing was softer against the skin – except perhaps silk. She had a tall lingerie chest, and when she wanted to spend money foolishly she indulged herself in La Perla lace bras and matching underpants or silk wisps from any one of a dozen French and Italian stores on Madison Avenue. She moved her fingers against the tough fabric of her jumpsuit and almost shuddered. Her underwear made her feel special and secretly feminine, and she thought Tom, her fiancé, enjoyed wondering what she was wearing under the sophisticated suit when he saw her at work. Like any good girl,

Jennifer washed her panties out by hand at night – she never threw them in the machine on the delicate cycle because they were too fine for that kind of treatment.

Jen's knees and ankles and butt hurt, but she wouldn't lie on that disgusting mattress, she wouldn't use the cardboard blanket. She wouldn't eat and she wouldn't sleep. Not until she got out of this place. If there was one thing Jennifer Spencer knew about herself it was that she had a strong will. She thought back to the Cooper Corp. deal and the prolonged negotiations at the airport Marriott. Despite the grimness around her now, she almost smiled. Back then – and it seemed like years ago although it was only five months – she remembered how she had complained to Donald about having to stay in a Marriott. 'What a hell hole!' she'd told him. 'This could drag on for days, or even weeks. Couldn't we arrange for a Hyatt at least?'

'Hey, rough it,' Donald had replied. 'It's their corporate culture. Cooper executives travel coach. Even old man Cooper travels coach.' He laughed. 'If it wasn't for me, you'd probably be having this meeting in a Days Inn, so stop bitching and get your ass to sit down at the table. This is all going to be about stamina, Jennifer. I know you can outlast them, but I'm not saying it's going to be easy.' He had paused and laughed again. 'Goddamnit!' he said, 'No one ever makes it easy for you to make five hundred million dollars.'

And, to the credit of her personality and her checkbook, Jennifer and her team had outlasted old man Cooper and his whole lot of Midwestern lawyers. She had sat at that table virtually unmoving, almost unblinking, for hours and hours. Thank God for Cooper's inflamed prostate or she might have never closed the deal. But the fifteen or twenty trips to the men's room he made each day while she sat there, coolly waiting for his return, had certainly contributed to his loss of faith and confidence. Then, when she called Donald in for the kill, it had gone fairly smoothly.

And was this her reward? She opened her eyes.

The shrieking in the next cell or down the hall or wherever it was reached an inhuman crescendo but finally, mercifully stopped. For a moment Jennifer wondered if they'd killed the inmate that had been making the noise. In the blessed peace she didn't care if they had. It wasn't that she didn't feel sorry for the woman – this was a place where misery was not just natural but required and she knew everyone didn't have the self-control that she did – but this wasn't *The Oprah Winfrey Show* and there was no need to share your pain so loudly.

That thought and the relative silence strengthened Jennifer's resolve. She *would* sit here, the lights burning into her eyes. Let them observe that! She wouldn't move. She wouldn't speak. And she wouldn't sleep. It was the only way she could bring some control back to her ravaged sense of self. And then, hopefully very soon, they would take her out of here and she would call Tom and they would send a stretch limo and whatever else it took to get her the fuck out of here.

And when she returned to Hudson, Van Schaank she'd have a hero's welcome. Jennifer closed her eyes again against the unbearable glare and tried to imagine that. Tom, so tall, would be at her side, maybe just lightly holding her elbow as she entered the double-wide glass doors to the floor. She'd buy something new to wear – maybe that suit she'd seen in the window of Walter Steiger, no matter how obscenely expensive it was. Yes, and shoes to match.

And when she walked into the reception area the secretaries and support staff would be there, and they'd all stare and smile. Susan, her top secretary, would give her a big bouquet and say, 'This is from all of us. We admire you so much.' And then she and Tom would walk into the main office area and all the traders, attorneys, partners – all of them, even Dave Jacobs, who hated her – would stand up and they'd begin to clap, and the clapping would rise to a roar and then, the way they did it in European circuses, the clapping would become rhythmic, each pair of hands in perfect unison with the others. And Donald would open his office door and walk toward her and Tom. And Tom, because he was sensitive and wouldn't want to detract from her moment, would give her elbow a little push. 'Go to him,' he'd say, and she would, in front of everybody. And Donald would lift his head and say . . .

She felt wet. Jennifer opened her eyes, back to the gruesome reality of the observation cell, and jumped to her feet. Water was oozing from under the wall behind her! She looked around. In fact, all along the wall where the mattress lay, the water lapped in, much of it already absorbed by the mattress but plenty spreading across her floor. Surely this wasn't part of the punishment, some bizarre test? She ran to the door. There were roaches floating in the water! Worse, they were alive, and trying to find a perch or a nest. 'Hey!' she yelled. 'Hey, someone. What's going on? There's a flood in here.'

The sadistic Officer Byrd was at her door in a moment. He looked in at her, shook his head and yelled, 'Jesus H. Christ! Nine must have wadded the toilet.'

Then, instead of helping her or explaining, he ran off down the hall. Jennifer leaned against the Plexiglas of her door but couldn't see what was going on. She could, however, hear – and in the next moment the howls began again, this time, if anything, even louder and more ferocious than before. Jennifer kept watching, her head pressed against the glass, the water running at her feet, wondering if any of the horror was real. She'd lose her mind if the hideous noise went on for another minute. Then, after one last fiendish screech, the stranger's voice was stilled. Jennifer could still hear curses and grunts. She imagined the officers were making them and, sure enough, in another moment three burly guys were in the corridor, attempting to drag off a big black woman. She was dressed in a shameful orange jumpsuit but now it was partially obscured by the restraint jacket she had on. Though she couldn't move her arms, she was kicking out with both legs, moving her head from side to side, and furiously screaming despite the taped gag that muffled her. Her hair was wild but her face was more so.

The woman was pushed back into a hard black plastic chair that sat as low to the ground as a beach chair. Officer Byrd obstructed Jennifer's view for a few moments but, when he finally moved, Jennifer was horrified to see that the woman had been strapped into the chair at the legs. Then the straitjacket was slowly removed from the woman's body, and the straps were brought over her shoulders in much the same way that an astronaut would be strapped to his seat.

Jennifer, terrified but unable to move, watched as they struggled to wheel the woman past her window. For a moment the startling blue eyes of the African American woman gave Jennifer an intimate look, certainly not one of apology. She winked at Jennifer. Then she was gone.

Jennifer, shocked, didn't know how long she had stood there. There was a drain in the cement floor that gurgled.

She waited for a little while, hoping that the guard would return so she could demand some better conditions. But no one came. Finally she balanced on one leg and peeled off first one drenched sock, then the other. She squeezed them out over the drain. At least half a cup of water ran into the sewage hole, but Jennifer's problem wasn't solved. Now, without socks, her feet were frozen. She couldn't sit on the mattress because it was also disgustingly wet. She didn't know what the correction officer had done with the trouble-some woman. Did they have a firing squad here at Jennings? Could she scream for help or attention? She found she couldn't do it. The woman's blue, blue eye winking at her, as if they were . . . together or . . . bonded somehow had really shaken her. Then she saw, with relief, that Officer Byrd was at the end of the hall about to pass by. Finally she knocked on the glass and he turned to her.

'I'm wet,' she said. 'This whole room has been ruined. You have to help me.' The fear in her voice only made her more frightened.

But Byrd didn't have a clue. He turned his mouth to his squawk box and said something. He stepped into the room and turned around.

'*Tsk, tsk,*' he said. 'You got more than you bargained for.' Jennifer decided not to even respond. Then he looked her over. It was a sexual leer, and she could tell that he wanted her to be uncomfortable. 'I'm alone up here now,' he explained. 'They had to take that one down to the hold. It was her first day in.'

Jennifer actually shivered. 'They'll be back soon,' she said in a flat voice. What kind of man took a job in a women's prison and then tried to . . .

'Well,' said Byrd, 'I could take you down to a cell below

six. That's where the nigger was. She used her towel to stop up the toilet and caused a major flood.' Jennifer recoiled both at the word he'd used and because he'd moved toward her. His voice insinuated that . . . Just then his walkie-talkie spoke.

Roughly Byrd took her under her right arm and moved her out of her little glass box. He was rubbing up against her as they walked past the place where the mad woman had been imprisoned, then moved her to number four, a cell exactly like her previous one.

'Chow will be in a minute,' he said as he slowly released his grip and ran his hand down her arm.

'Food?' Jennifer cried. 'I can't even breathe.' Then she remembered her outfit. 'And I need a new jumpsuit. This one is wet.'

'We'll have supper for you right away,' Byrd said. 'But we can't issue another uniform. Laundry's closed.' Then he moved a little closer. 'Of course,' he almost whispered, 'you could take it off and hang it up. There's nobody here to see you.'

Jennifer looked around at the observation windows, the open ceiling, and the catwalk above. Now she was grateful for them. She wanted someone to keep their eyes on Byrd – or *Vulture*. But she had a creepy feeling that most of those eyes would get a big kick out of her standing around naked. And would they intervene if Vulture touched her?

'Maybe I could get you something else to wear,' he said now, '*if* you wanted to be friendly,' he added.

She couldn't believe what she was hearing. It was a sexual innuendo, wasn't it? 'Forget about that,' she told Byrd.

He shrugged. Had he just offered her something in return for sex? She kept her face calm but swore to herself that she'd have him reported to the governor by tomorrow afternoon. 'Too bad. You'll have to wear the damp one until morning,' he said. He locked the door on the new cubicle and left.

Jennifer was deeply grateful for that. She would have spent some time examining the cell if it hadn't been quite so obviously identical to the previous one. She'd even be willing to swear in a court of law that the stains in this mattress were shaped identically to the one on the other. Hadn't there been that blot that looked like the state of Florida on the upper left corner of the previous mattress? The wetness against her ankles was terribly cold and the rough polyester chafed, but otherwise all was the same. Except that this time, when she sat down in her corner, her stomach rumbled loudly enough for her to hear, and maybe loudly enough for the woman in the next room – if there was a woman in the next room – to hear as well.

But she was still determined that she wouldn't eat anything. And she wouldn't lie down. Even though the day seemed a hundred hours long, she wouldn't allow her hunger or fatigue to get the better of her.

She leaned her back against the wall, pulled her knees up to her chest, wrapped her arms around her cold ankles and tried, once again, to close her eyes and imagine what treats would come her way when she went back to her real life. Donald had better be especially generous with her bonus. In fact, she might not have to wait until the end of the fiscal year. Of course, after December there would be the full partnership and the big office. She took a deeper breath of the fatal air. Concentrate on it, she told herself. Think how beautiful that place will be compared with this one. She knew each partner got a generous budget to furnish and decorate his or her office, but now she thought that she might move her reproduction Beidermeyer desk from home into the office. She'd bill Hudson, Van Schaank and use the money for the dressing table she'd admired in the antique shop on upper Lexington Avenue. She'd . . . she tried once again to get into the reverie but it wasn't working.

She opened her eyes. She couldn't really imagine anything but this room, her freezing feet, the unbearable light and the hunger gnawing at her belly. She tried to remind herself that she was the hero of the Vareen takeover and the heavy lifter in the Cooper Corp. scenario, but she hadn't been cold and wet and humiliated then. Jennifer may have managed not to drink and not to use the ladies' room, but if she had had to pee then, she wouldn't have had to do it in front of a dozen pairs of eyes.

She felt her eyes begin to get wet and forced herself to stand up. Just then a noise outside the cell brought her to the front. Another guard was wheeling a trolley down the corridor. When he reached her, he didn't even look up. He merely bent toward her, his face forward, and slipped a plastic tray through the slot. It almost looked like an airplane meal.

'No,' she told herself firmly one more time. But her cold feet walked, without her permission, over to the tray. She bent and picked it up. Something green. Something brown. And something that looked like it had tomato sauce on it. Whatever it was, she took it to the bed, sat down cross-legged on the filthy mattress, and ravenously wolfed it down.

7

Maggie Rafferty

I was a prisoner long before I was an inmate.

Bonnie Foreshaw, inmate. Andi Rierden, *The Farm*

I know that it will seem a truism, but I must say that shooting your husband, accidentally or otherwise – and even more – having him die from the bullet wound, totally changes your life. The chief benefit is, of course, that he is gone, but there are other benefits, which I'll get to later. The main *drawback*, however, is that in most cases you're deprived of your liberty and might have to live in a place with a library that has only one hundred and sixteen books. That is the exact number of books in the library here at Jennings.

But back to my husband. He could have lived; he died just to spite me. The bullet only grazed his aorta. Serious? Yes – but with his will power, he might have lingered long enough for the paramedics to stabilize him. But no. He always had to get his way in the end. He could turn any situation to his advantage. This was, of course, only one of the many reasons why I hated him so fully and completely, and why the gun I was holding went off while it was pointed in his direction. At the time, I had meant to kill myself. How foolish of me.

My husband was the famous Richard Rafferty, Riff to his friends. At the very minute the bullet was nicking his deceitful heart, his latest book, *The Life of the Heart*, was being talked about on the six o'clock news. A book? On the evening *news*? How can that be? Easy. Richard was sleeping with the woman who produced the show.

And speaking of the evening news, I understand that the new arrival, this Miss Jennifer Spencer, is up in observation hell. She's certainly been news. I've been following her story with some interest, since one needs such pastimes in prison, and because both of my sons are in the same type of business as she is . . . or *was*. From the beginning I could see that she was taking the fall for someone else, probably a man. The only question that remained in my mind was, did she know what was going on? Was she complicitous? I was actually looking forward to seeing her in person, because then I would know.

How would I know? Well, let me explain another result of happening to murder your husband: It turns your brain inside out. Although this is terribly painful at the time and for a long while afterward, in the end it is a good thing. I know this sounds totally insane, but I am a better person for having killed my husband. For instance, I've become nearly as good as a dog at reading people.

Lest anyone think that I am advocating murder as a method of self-improvement, let me correct that impression at once. Yes, I am a better person, but I was a good enough person before. Riff wasn't; he wasn't worth dirtying my hands for. What he deserved from me was the indifference that I only now feel toward him. Trading life and liberty for well-deserved revenge and an enlightened mind is a very hard deal to accept. Jennings, have I said it before, is a kind of hell.

When I arrived here, I fell into despair at once. The trial, Grand Guignol though it had been, was a reason to get up, get dressed, and perform. Here there was nothing. I wanted to die. Imagine. I had been headmistress of one of the most prestigious private girls' schools on the East Coast, and had lived among the very rich and instructed their daughters. On my first day at Jennings, I was told to 'get my fuckin' ass movin'.' I had been in *Who's Who In American Education*. Here I was referred to as 'the old bitch'.

Somehow I got used to the vulgarity. It was the deprivation of every sensory pleasure that was the hardest thing for me to bear. My marriage had not been happy, but I had lived in a beautiful home, traveled to Paris and London nearly every year, spent summers in Tuscany, was a connoisseur of wines and fine foods, collected rare books and Herend, drove an immaculate '62 Mercedes Gullwing, subscribed to the ballet, shopped at Neiman Marcus.

And suddenly I was confined to one of the ugliest places on the face of the earth, twenty-four hours a day, seven days a week. I assure you, no bleaker, duller, more visually offensive place can exist. I'd rather be in Craigmore Prison, dank dark dungeon that it is. It at least has some architecture to boast of. Jennings is the kind of dull, featureless maze they put rats into when they're trying to see if they can stunt their brain development. Even crumbling ceilings or walls would add interest, but here there is no crumbling, just ugly,

1960s efficiency. Jennings was built when there was a soul-sickness plaguing the earth, probably an aftereffect of the war. Buildings were built to last, but beauty in architecture was eschewed. The style could be called 'Plainness with a Vengeance', 'Ugly is Fine', or 'Death in Life'. And I have to stay here for the rest of mine. There are no aesthetic pardons.

So I wondered how Jennifer Spencer was faring in Observation. She had a lower-middle-class youth, upper-middle-class adulthood. A transition to Jennings wasn't going to be easy for her, to say the least. But my interest in the fate and character of Jennifer Spencer was going to be limited compared to the keen interest I have in women like Movita Watson and her 'sidekick', Cher. I had never met women like them before my incarceration and I am fascinated by their unschooled intelligence.

Movita, for example, is someone I pegged as decent the minute I saw her despite her hellfire exterior. She plays tough, and sometimes dumb, but she's generous and clever, too, and has her own eye for 'attitude' in others. She will tell you that when she entered Jennings, I had no 'attitude' at all. This was why we became friends fairly quickly. She was, in her words, 'curious 'bout that weird ol' bitch'. Well, *attitude* is one of the petty attributes that I lost as a result of my husband dying at my hands, or more literally, at my feet. When I came in, I've been told by Movita, I had the look of a 'schoolteacher who'd been wiped out by a nuclear bomb'. Change 'schoolteacher' to 'schoolmistress' and her assessment was pretty much accurate.

But those credentials as a schoolteacher secured my position as the prison librarian. And since that time I have been preoccupied with thinking of ways to acquire more books. Books were always important to me. Well, they are my life's blood really. Before and after my crime.

The Life of the Heart (of which, ironically, we had two copies in the library) was Richard's sixth book. It was supposed to be about the stunning and liberated life that can be ours if we give in to our feelings of love. He'd put me and my two sons through hell while he was trying to write it, just as he had, come to think of it, when he wrote his fourth and fifth. The children were 'distractions'. Somehow I was always doing something 'stupid'. He once accused me of turning pages too loudly. Bryce and Tyler, despite their initial business success, were 'disappointments' to him. But that I could understand. How disappointing it must be for a false, humorless, and arrogant man to have two sons who could see through him and laugh. I, on the other hand – raised to be a right-minded woman – supported the bastard throughout. I fed him, excused him, pampered him, read his drafts, corrected his grammar, gave him ideas, typed his corrections, and hated his editor with him. I did it for thirty-four years. Why stop now, when he needed me more than ever?

It is only now, seven years later, that I can look back at the situation without anger. As I said above, I am a better person now.

I knew that Jennifer Spencer would be given the orientation that included a tour of the facility, a bed assignment, and a work detail. I know what's what here on my own, though I do appreciate the heads up I get when Frances delivers the ice with kites. I had to chuckle at the 'kites on ice'. There *is* no work here in the library. The prison population consists of very few readers and what they *would* read doesn't exist in the library. Needless to say, I would welcome

Miss Spencer to Jennings when she came by later in the day. Lest you think otherwise, this would not be some warm-hearted *Shawshank Redemption* nonsense where I take the girl under my wing. If I had wings, I assure you I'd fly the fuck out of here. Besides, I already have two sons – I don't need a daughter. After a quarter century of girls' schools, I know how much trouble they are.

Jennifer finally came to the library, with that Officer Camry, at about three-thirty, the time I usually fade out, having worked in schools all my life. She had the air of a young woman who was in trouble, there was no mistaking that. Her face was pale and drawn, her eyelids were swollen, and the eyes peering out from between them looked as if they'd glimpsed something horrific, but at the same time she still looked like someone whose car and driver were waiting for her. She had heavy attitude, Movita would say. But I could see right through that. The press, as usual, had gotten it wrong: Thanks to my twenty-seven years of working with schoolgirls, I could see that Jennifer had been a scholarship student. Determination to overcome obstacles was written all over her, so there had to have *been* obstacles. I could see that she had real strength to her, and that when the realization that she was going to be in here for some real time hit her, she would survive the shock.

'Hello,' I said. 'I'm Maggie.' I sounded ridiculous to myself, as if we were in some kind of meeting.

'Hi,' she answered. She was so not present that I was driven to speak to her again. 'This is our library, such as it is.'

She blinked at me, as if she didn't understand why I was talking to her. 'We have the space,' I went on, 'but we have very few books.'

'It doesn't matter to me. Don't worry about it,' she said, a little sharply. Then her expression changed. She was looking at me, wondering who I was, I expect. 'I'm sorry,' she said then. 'I don't mean to be rude. It's just that I'm not going to be *living* here. But this guard has been very nice.' I saw Officer Camry stiffen. It's funny about how prison guards refuse to be called prison guards.

'He's an officer, dear,' I said in a voice drier than the paper of my books. 'Not a guard. You call them officers or COs.'

'Correction officer,' Camry the fool added. He was harmless enough and I nodded at him.

'Oh. Thank you,' the girl said.

Jennifer Spencer surprised me in one way. I, who have met such a wide cross section of women when you consider both my students, my social circle, and my present comrades, could not tell if the girl was essentially good or bad. It's the kind of thing I almost always know at a glance yet I didn't know it then, although I do now. I could see that she was honest.

8

Jennifer Spencer

With keen, discriminating sight,
Black's not so black, – nor white
so very *white.*

George Canning, *New Morality*

After the night in Observation, Jennifer was ready for assignment to a cell. Though it was the relatively benign Officer Camry, rather than the brutal Byrd, who came to take her away, the relentless gloom of the institution put Jennifer into a state bordering on catatonia. If Observation had been hell for her, it was clear that the rest of the place was purgatory. It was all so grim that it was appalling to imagine that women actually lived in this hopeless drabness day after day.

'I need to make a phone call,' she managed to say to Officer Camry. Her head was pounding and she desperately needed some Tylenol – and maybe a Valium – but calling Tom was the most important thing to do right now. 'I have to make a call,' she said again. 'Is there a phone near here?'

Camry stepped back and looked at her intently. 'If there

was, you couldn't use it,' he told her. 'I'm scheduled to give you your house assignment. You can only make calls on your own time.'

Jennifer clenched her jaw and the headache intensified. She wasn't prepared for any of this. She admitted that now. How could Donald and Tom abandon her to this experience? She couldn't imagine the elegant Mr Michaels in a jumpsuit, or Ivy League Tom in the filthy hole. But that didn't matter. She squared her shoulders behind Camry's rounded ones and followed as she was instructed. She would not cry nor would she fuss. This whole ordeal was a punishment; not for the nonsense with the SEC, but for the terrible error in judgment that she had made.

'Right this way,' Camry said, leading her down a long narrow corridor. Then he stopped abruptly and opened a door. 'While we're here, this is the athletic facility,' he said.

Jennifer looked in to see a small room with a couple of flabby volleyballs and a few exercise mats that were so soiled that she had to avert her eyes. So this was the gym. She almost laughed. It was nothing at all like the Vertical Club where she and Tom worked out. Well, she'd be out of there before she needed to go to the gym. But what about the women who had to *use* the place? God almighty.

'You can use the athletic facility in your free time, but not during lockdown or after eight p.m.,' Camry told her.

Jennifer sighed. As if. Once again she turned to Camry and said with great urgency, 'Are you certain I can't use a phone? It is imperative that I get in touch with my lawyer.'

Camry lifted his eyebrows and looked up at the ceiling. He shook his head as if to say, *No, you crazy bitch, no!*

Jennifer knew then that she had made a terrible error. For the first time in her life she had been so confident that she knew everything that she needed to know that she had gone into a test completely unprepared. Prison wasn't like life on the Outside. In here, there was no multiple choice to guess at, and there was no essay that she could bluff her way through. This was all true or false – black and white. This was the test of her life, and she'd willingly come into it unprepared and ignorant.

Tom and Donald had told her that it would be easy. She didn't know why she had believed them – except that they'd never lied to her before. Christ, there was no way this could've been easy. She should've known that. Life had taught her that nothing came easy – it all took work, it all took discipline, and above everything else, it all took a willful determination not to fail. She knew that. She had always been prepared, always one step ahead of the rest.

Jennifer hung her head and looked at the orange jumpsuit that she was wearing. When she was a kid she used to lay out her school clothes before going to bed. She hated uniforms so much that she spent hours figuring out ways to make a plaid jumper and a navy blazer look like something out of *Vogue*. But she did it. She stood out from all the rest.

It was that kind of preparation and thinking ahead that were the big secrets to her success. She got into State on scholarship, and her grades there earned her a free ride into the MBA program at Wharton. When it was time to go out and get a job, Jennifer's research landed her an interview with the already legendary Donald J. Michaels. She walked into his office, clearly a girl from the working class, and she started to talk about his Gulbenkian porcelain. Donald lifted his eyebrows. He knew she was faking it, but he also knew she was *really good* at faking it. Preparation and a poker face were exactly what she needed to succeed in his

Wall Street firm. Donald Michaels not only hired Jennifer on the spot, he put her on his own team. They were known as the smartest and the most aggressive of all the Wall Street shark pool. They specialized in the highest-risk/highest-reward IPOs and some *very* leveraged buyouts. They didn't miss a trick. They were invincible.

'We go down from here,' Camry told her, and Jennifer preceded him down the stairs. She was glad she wasn't with Byrd as they made their way down the dark and damp stairwell.

The trek seemed to take forever, and through it all Jennifer mentally beat herself up. From the first moment she had gotten into the van, things had been out of her control. She tried to control the rising tide of panic that was threatening to overtake her. Why didn't the Warden know who she was? If Tom had called, whom did he talk to? And if she didn't find out, how would she be cushioned and protected from this nightmare? Who was the Warden's boss? Could she go over the stolid Warden Harding's head? She would just have to wait until this ridiculous process was over. Then she would call Tom. Or Don. Or both of them.

At long last, she and Camry entered the cellblock, and Jennifer was taken to her cell. She thought she'd seen the worst of Jennings, but no – they had saved the worst for last.

'This is your house assignment,' Camry told her.

House? This wasn't a house; it wasn't even a dormitory – and it most certainly was not a country club. It was a prison cell, plain and simple. The concrete walls were painted a color that a decorator might claim to be *Dusty Rose*, but to Jennifer's eyes it was a hideous *Battleship Pink*. The beds – four of them – were bunked and bolted against the side walls with only about ten square feet of floor space in between. There was no furniture except a tiny desk that was suspended from the wall, and, beneath it, a single chair. Jennifer wondered if she would have three cellmates, and if the four of them were supposed to share that chair.

The only other place to sit was on a toilet that was quite unlike anything Jennifer had ever seen before in her life. At first glance, the stainless steel creation reminded her of a metal miniature of the Solomon R. Guggenheim Museum. On closer inspection she saw the faucets and realized with horror that it was a monument to prison efficiency. It served as both wash basin and commode, with the seat only inches from the lower bunks. She remembered a snippet of a song parody her mother used to sing: *And my bunk is where the skunk is*. Did someone actually sleep with her head virtually in the *head*? She set her shoulders and tried not to show her dismay. After all, she only had to sit there until Tom came and took her away. She wouldn't be spending the night.

'Home sweet home,' Camry said as he rolled open the door in the fourth wall, which consisted completely of bars. The section slid open, and for a moment it doubled the bars on the left side of the cell. The shadow play they made passing reminded Jennifer of the sun through the windows of New York's elevated trains. But there was no sunshine here. The cells were on a windowless hall, and although each one did have a window, it was so high in the wall that even from the top bunk you couldn't peer through the chicken wire. Camry took Jennifer's elbow and firmly guided her into her new home.

'It's only for a few hours,' she told herself. Maybe now she could finally call Tom. She looked for a moment at Officer Camry, but decided not to ask.

'Get comfortable,' Camry instructed. 'I'll go get your cellmate so you two can get acquainted.'

'Right,' Jennifer said.

'Pardon?' Camry responded.

'I wish,' Jennifer said with a cynical sigh.

Only one of the four bunks was made up, and over it, taped to the walls, were six pictures. One was of a baby – obviously a snapshot – but the other five were clipped from magazines. There was an angel, a toddler on the beach building a sand castle, a fire engine, the Nike logo complete with *Just Do It*, and finally a picture of Jesus, looking a lot like Donny Osmond. Jennifer stood there for a moment, trying to imagine what kind of brain had arranged those particular images in that particular way.

She walked over to the desk. It was bare except for three books: the Bible, a copy of *The Pokey Little Puppy*, and a paperback Baby-Sitters Club book. Jennifer had read the Baby-Sitters Club when she was in fourth grade. Had they put her in a cell with a child or a simpleton?

On the lower bunk on the opposite wall, Jennifer found a rolled up mattress and a set of sheets. Hers, she wondered? She thought about making the bed, but was enraged at the thought of actually making herself 'comfortable' as dopey old Roger had suggested. This was no place to be comfortable. She would never sleep here, and she would most certainly never use the toilet. Anyone – even someone like Byrd – could look right through the bars and see everything that went on.

Jennifer sat on the solitary chair and wondered what time it was. Would Tom still be at home, on his way to the office, or was he already there? She knew his cell phone number by heart, but she wasn't sure if a cell phone could accept a collect call. She stood up suddenly in a rage. Goddamnit! She wasn't a convict. She had her own damn cell phone – and they had taken it. She had a Verizon credit card with no limits. Why couldn't she use it? What harm would there be in that? It had rounded corners, too. She couldn't kill anyone – or herself – with a fucking cell phone. The rage took its toll, and Jennifer wilted onto the made-up bunk. Tom had better get her out of here before the end of the day. This was worse than anything she'd imagined.

'You're sitting on my bed,' Jennifer heard a timid voice say. She jumped up to see Officer Camry standing in the door of the cell with a very small and very pretty young blonde woman.

'I'm sorry,' Jennifer said sincerely.

'It's okay,' the girl said timidly. She looked as if she was terrified of Jennifer, and she seemed to be almost clinging to the smiling Officer Camry.

'Miss Spencer, this is Suki,' Roger said as he gently guided the young girl into the cell. 'You and her will be bunking together.'

Jennifer saw the girl looking at her still damp jumpsuit.

'Were you the one who stuffed the toilet in Observation last night?' Suki asked her. Then she went over to her bunk and looked at the wet spot Jennifer had left when she sat there.

'You can use *this* bedding,' Jennifer said, pointing to the roll on the bunk meant for her. 'I won't be using it.'

'Why not?' Suki asked her.

'I'm not staying,' Jennifer replied.

'Where are you going?'

Jennifer thought she was going to scream. 'Can I just

make a phone call?' she asked, looking past this Suki and talking to Roger.

'Not until after work,' Suki told her.

'But I have to make the call *now*.'

'Miss Spencer – Jennifer – will be working with you in the laundry,' Camry told the young girl. 'Will you see that she gets there this afternoon?' he asked with a smile.

'You bet Rog – uh, sir,' Suki said, blushing.

Roger stood there as awkward as a teenager on a front porch after a first date. Was he going to kiss this girl? Jennifer wondered. But Camry finally turned and walked away. Suki watched him go until he turned for a moment and waved good-bye.

Jennifer didn't know what that was all about, and she didn't need to know. A deafening bell clanged loudly and echoed off the concrete.

'Time to go back to work,' Suki chirped brightly. 'Come on, I'll show you the way.'

Jennifer followed without question. Maybe she could find a phone in the laundromat.

9

Movita Watson

Here I am and here I stay.

Patrice de Mac Mahon

I did alotta work in the office that no inmate should be trusted with, but that was because of Miss Ringling. She was one of those state employees who felt the main function of her job was cashing her paycheck. Most work that required any intelligence was given directly to me by the Warden. The rest of it was given to me by Miss Ringling. But now I was finally shuttin' down the PC and gettin' ready to go to dinner, when Warden Harding strolled outta her office in that casual-like way that says she's got something to tell me.

'Movita?' she asked.

'Mmmm,' I kinda murmured back. You can't really diss the Warden, but by now her and me know each other good enough for me to voice a certain kind of awareness.

'I've assigned Spencer to Conrad. Do you think Suki

will mind having her as a cellmate?' the Warden asked me.

Since when did The Woman worry about what I thought? 'Why do I care what Suki minds?' I answered back. It sounded kinda snotty so I softened it a bit with, 'She'll do fine. NBD. Spencer's no suicide, if that's what you're thinking.'

'I just thought that you might have a better sense of who would be the best to match the new inmate with. You *are* the – uh – main person for the crew. I just don't want to add a problem to an already sensitive situation.'

'Hey, my policy is just like that old president's,' I told her. '"Don't ask, don't tell." That works for me, too.' I knew what she was angling for. The Warden wanted me to take that little white witch to my lovin' black bosom. That's one of the deadly things about prison; you show weakness just once and everyone is ready to prey on ya'. Just 'cause I unreasonably, uncharacteristically, and maybe unfortunately 'adopted' Suki Conrad into my crew doesn't mean I'm gonna do it for every sorrowful new piece of meat that comes to Jennings. It bugged me that The Woman even asked me.

I don't know if the *others* wanted to take Suki in, but I insisted. And when I insist, they don't have much choice. It wasn't like anybody really hated her, and face it, girls, Movita rules. Anyway, the very first day I saw Suki Conrad draggin' her pitiful little butt through Intake, I just took to her. Maybe it was that baby-fine blonde hair or the lost look in her eyes. I got me a pink-skinned baby doll with yellow hair and blue eyes for Christmas once. Didn't I love that dolly! Whatever. Sometimes, though, someone like that just tugs at your heart or some shit like that. I guess I just plain felt sorry for the little thing, and that's the truth. Just 'cause I'm in prison don't mean I got no human feelings. And I felt like we needed a baby in our crew.

Women need family. Don't matter if it's blood or not. In the crew we're like mother and daughters sometimes, and sometimes we're like sisters, and sometimes we're like other family members, too. That don't mean we don't fight and argue and stuff. But when you're in a crew you just try to keep all that to a minimum.

'Please let me know if there's any trouble with the match-up, okay?' the Warden asked me. She was lookin' me right in the eye and I knew she wanted more than a trouble report. She knew how to get at me. 'That's it for today, Movita. You better go to dinner.' She paused for a second. 'What do you and your girls have planned tonight?'

I switched off the monitor and neatened up some stacks of papers on my desk. 'Well, it's Theresa's turn to cook,' I said, 'so it's gonna be a surprise.' Sometimes I get the oddest feeling that the Warden is kinda – well – *envious* of us in the crew. It's like she'd rather come and eat with us instead of goin' to her own house. I don't know much about her life Outside, 'cept that she's divorced and that she works all the time. I doubt she's got much of a life.

When I got back to my house, Theresa was already chopping the carrots that Suki was washin'. 'You want the salad dressing sweet or you want it tart?' Theresa asked.

'I don't care as long as you're making it,' Cher told her. She was loungin' her sassy ass on the bunk, readin' a magazine, and just waitin' to eat.

If prison is the place where society thinks they can make us cons eat shit, they do a damn good job of it. Even though the Warden keeps fightin' with Ben Norton down in Food

Services, the food at Jennings never gets any better. No one – and I mean no one – wants to eat the shit old Ben serves up in the cafeteria. It's nothin' but starch, grease, and real bad meat. People eat it, but only if they have to.

You can eat for free in the cafeteria. So if you're destitute, or spend whatever you got on contraband, or if you can't make even one friend, then you're stuck in the cafeteria eatin' one of Ben's blue plate specials.

But if you got some sense, a little social grace, or any initiative at all, you can buy things from the prison canteen and cook 'em up yourself. You just need to save a little money and get pots and pans and all. There's no real kitchens in our houses, but Harding lets us have a hot plate or an electric skillet. Of course, the canteen doesn't have much variety – maybe only seven or eight kinds of things. You can usually get a chicken, or sometimes beef. They always got a little lettuce or some vegetable. There's potatoes and sometimes rice. And now and then some fruit like apples or bananas or even oranges. Theresa works down in the dispensary, so she always knows what's comin' in. She stashes the best for the crew, and with the money Cher gets from sellin' some of the stuff she steals from Intake we can buy a whole lot of good stuff. Problem is, we don't got refrigeration, and that's why we need plenty of ice. Frances was the lucky one to get to deliver it. Ice is like gold in prison. Without it, lots of our good stuff goes to waste. If we buy a chicken on our own, by the time we eat half of it the other half is no damn good and we're so sick of chicken that we're cluckin'. We don't wanna see no bird *ever* again.

'Hand me that pot of water, Suki,' Theresa said as I sat down to listen to the day's bulletins. I wanted to know if anyone had any more news on Spencer. I thought Suki might speak up, but Cher was the first one to sound off, as usual.

'I hear she's already sashaying round here like she owns the place.' Cher smirked. 'Byrd told old Cranston down in Intake that he's gonna toss Spencer into solitary if she demands to use the phone one more damn time.'

'Well, you know what they say about asking and receiving, don't you?' Theresa said as she opened the Tupperware and measured out some pasta into the boiling water.

'Yeah, well this ain't Sunday school,' Cher shot back. 'And it ain't the movies either. You don't automatically get one call when you get here.'

'It's tough on you white girls when you don't get your way, ain't it?' I said, givin' Cher a look. She was copping some pretty amazing attitude.

'That's not very nice,' Suki said with hurt feelings.

'Movita wasn't referrin' to you, sweetie,' Cher reassured her. She got up and gave Suki a pat on the shoulder.

That was for my benefit. Back when I first took Suki in, Cher made quite a fuss. 'She can't cook, she can't steal, she can't do nothin' but cry,' Cher bitched. 'She's dumb as dirt. That's why she drove the car for her boyfriend.'

I guess Suki actually believed her boyfriend when he said he was goin' into that 7-Eleven for cigarettes. He came out with the contents of the cash register, and little Suki thought she was guilty of nothin' more than keepin' the heater running.

Theresa, on the other hand, was more understanding. 'But she lost her baby,' she said to Cher. 'She's never going to stop crying about that. You know what they say about mothers when someone takes away their babies, don't you?'

Well, nobody answered Theresa's question. It got real

quiet for a moment. You see, I don't like talkin' about children. I never talk about my little girls. Their granny is raisin' them, and that's all I can bear to say about it.

'Just what in heaven's name are you makin' there, Theresa?' I asked to break the tension. 'You trying to kill us all before Cher gets a chance to get outta here?'

'Get out of my way, Movita,' Theresa warned. 'You know what they say about too many cooks, don't you?'

I just laughed and backed off. Havin' a conversation with Theresa was like talkin' to a refrigerator door loaded with sayings. I respected that girl. The goin' never got so tough that Theresa didn't get up and go. 'People say I'm an optimist,' she'd say, lookin' all serious and stuff. 'But I don't think that's necessarily true. And do you wanna know why? I'm gonna tell you why. Because – you know what they say about pessimism and optimism, don't you?'

Theresa never really wanted you to answer her questions, 'cause she had all the answers herself.

'They say the pessimist says the glass is half *empty*, but the optimist says it's half *full*. Well, you know what I say to that? I don't say that glass is half *anything*, I say you're using the wrong damn glass. It's obviously too big. That's what I say.' Then old Theresa always waited a little and let it all sink in before she'd wind up for her big finale. 'And you know what that makes me?' she'd ask. 'That makes me a *pragmatist*! That is someone who has a practical, matter-of-fact way of solving problems. That's a pragmatist and that's what I am – a practical, matter-of-fact problem solver. If you got a problem with how much is in your glass, well then maybe you're just using the wrong glass. You understand what I'm saying here? It just doesn't matter if you think it's half empty or half full, what matters is what you *do* about it.

Get off your ass and get yourself a different glass is what I say. Always remember this: *Answer* is also a verb. You understand what I'm saying here? The door to success is labeled *PUSH!* You can't leave footprints in the sands of time if you're not wearin' work boots.'

I don't know why, but I could listen to Theresa talk for hours. I loved those speeches.

'Get up off your butt, Cher, and grab that plastic strainer for me,' Theresa told Cher, and Cher did it. 'Hold it over the bowl.'

Cher was laughing as Theresa strained her pasta and let the water go down the john. 'You think there's any symbolism here with your cookin' right next to the toilet?' Cher teased.

Theresa's specialty is her pasta. That's somethin' the canteen don't carry, but Theresa's sister sends her a lot of it. That's another thing about who you pick for crew. You want the girls who get lots of packages from the Outside. Theresa gets pasta and salamis and Italian shit like that. And you can't get better packages than Cher gets. Theft runs in her family, so they're always sendin' her stuff. Lots of it is contraband and gets taken out and sent back, but the boxes always have hand creams and shampoos and stuff like that. And now and then she'll get a big ol' canned ham with some spices. The chips and dips and stuff come in on a regular basis. Both girls are real good about sharin' with the crew.

Suki never gets a damned thing. She ain't got a family. Her little girl is in foster care. I don't care, though – we had to take her in. But if we have to take in this Spencer bitch, then that girl better be prepared to do her part.

Dinner was almost ready. Besides the pasta we were

having some lettuce and some bananas for dessert. 'All the ice is gone,' Theresa said, 'and there won't be any more until tomorrow afternoon, so get prepared to eat. I don't want anything to go to waste.'

'Speakin' of waste,' I said. 'I hear Miss Spencer had herself quite a night in Observation.'

'Did Karl Byrd give her any trouble?' Theresa asked, all concerned.

'Karl can do better than get a piece of that sorry ass,' Cher snarled.

'That's not very nice,' Suki piped up. 'I think she seems kind of nice. She's my bunkmate. But she says she's not gonna be here very long.'

Cher was laughing. 'Oh, let me guess,' she said. 'She's just another *innocent* victim, put in the slammer by mistake.'

'That's what she says,' Suki told us, all sincere. Suki doesn't get irony – you might say she has an irony deficiency. 'Jennifer says her boyfriend is coming to get her out.'

'Yeah, just like my knight in shining armor is comin' for me,' Cher snorted.

Havin' Cher as a cellmate helps the time pass. When she first hit Jennings, I couldn't imagine how I'd ever survive being locked up with a wild white woman. But she can be so damned funny. And she's honest – for a thief. She never pretends to be nobody 'ceptin' who she is. For her, everything she sees is just ripe for the pickin'. She always has her eyes wide open and on the lookout for the next chance to take what she wants. And not just for herself, either. Soon as she got here she stole me a Sony Walkman and a feather pillow, and damn it – that hillbilly girl just stole my heart. I never understood how it happened, but I was glad that it did. I love Cher. Now it isn't like we're lesbians. No one in my crew is a lesbian. I know lots of women couple up for a little sex and comfort while they're here, but nothin' like that goes on between me and Cher. But we do love each other. When I think of how I felt for Earl I almost laugh. My feelings for him were pretty shallow and pathetic when I compare 'em with the love I feel for Cher. And even for Theresa and Suki.

About the only action I get from men is from that mother Byrd. He would jump a ladybug or a polliwog as long as they were unwilling. That's what gives 'em the thrill. I keep 'em way off me by never showin' any fear and askin' him if he's got a hard three inches ready for me. Once I made the redneck bastard blush. Made my day, I tell ya'.

I just sat there on my bunk and looked at my crew. Maybe we could take Spencer in. But the thought of it made me feel like I was somehow cheatin' on Cher. Cher was gonna get paroled soon, if she kept her nose clean and didn't get caught stealin' from Intake. Even if she did, Cher had herself a good lawyer on the Outside.

It all made me feel sorta sad and cold. I didn't really resent Cher leavin' Jennings. It's just that it was gonna be a damned lonely and borin' place once she was gone. Maybe we *needed* to take another woman in.

10

Jennifer Spencer

Windows on buildings and vehicles were smashed one day after all the women in the dining room had been 'searched' for tacos as they left the cafeteria. Later the women referred to the incident as 'The Great Taco Shake'.

Kathryn Watterson, *Women in Prison*

'Mealtime,' the officer announced from the control room. 'Stay in single file and follow the brown line.'

Jennifer had absolutely no interest in eating dinner in the cafeteria, but Suki pointed in the direction that she should go and Jennifer had no choice but to follow the others. She had to admit that she was starving, but God only knew what kind of food was being served. She turned to ask Suki if she might know, but Suki seemed to have someplace else to go. Jennifer turned back and followed the woman in front of her.

As the line moved down the corridor it approached a door that was being held open by yet another officer. 'Single file, ladies, single file. Something good today. Officer Summit says it's Reubens since we had ham salad for lunch today.'

'It's about time,' spoke one inmate.

'Now you're talking,' said another.

Off to the side, a woman was having a loud argument with a doorpost. 'You no good, muthafukka,' she yelled, then paused. 'You got no right,' she answered the mute doorway. No one seemed to notice or mind.

As Jennifer finally stepped inside the cafeteria, what she saw was worse than what she had imagined. Yellow-painted concrete blocks, horrible fluorescent lights hung high from metal rafters, cold air blowing from the air-conditioning unit, and a floor that was a solid slab of poured concrete that angled down in the middle with a covered water drain grate at the center. It reminded her of the old meat market her mother used to take her to in her old neighborhood. It was like a slaughterhouse.

Jennifer mechanically imitated the inmate in front of her so that she would be sure not to mess up in mess hall. There were three drink machines: one with grape something or other, one with orange something or other, and then a much less desirable lemonade mixture that was certain to taste more like water than lemon. She took a metal cup from the inverted stack, selected the orange drink, then stepped down the line a little further only to be presented with a plastic tray covered in a clear plastic lid.

'Hey, where's the Reuben?' an inmate asked.

'Yeah, I thought someone said we were having Reubens,' another inmate intoned.

'Well, Officer Summit must have been misinformed,' the officer at the head of the line said.

Oh man, was there going to be a riot over what was served? Jennifer had been through enough already and she couldn't take any more disruption. She'd never felt so out of control in a controlled environment in her life. She took her tray and followed the woman in front of her to the table.

Jennifer stared down at her tray. She watched the other woman at the table dismantle the lid, carefully slide it under the bottom tray, and then unwrap a utensil from a napkin and let it fall in her hand. It was an abbreviated spoon – a shortened bowl with three equally short prongs extending briefly from the center. She stared at the micro landscape of food in front of her. There was a hill of instant potatoes, a wide river of grease, a dying forest of cabbage greens beside a toxic dump of gristle and gray meat. A week ago, Jennifer would have scraped something like this off her shoe in disgust. She was hungry, but eating this would be a challenge, even without the bizarre implement.

A large woman of indeterminate race with light skin, freckles, and kinky red hair pulled back into a knot at the top of her head sat down opposite and gave Jennifer a smile that lacked intelligence and the left bicuspid. 'I'm Big Red,' she said, then lowered her voice. 'You want some brew, you call Big Red.'

'What do you call *this*?' Jennifer asked her dinner companion, holding up her utensil.

'A spork,' Big Red told her, as if Jennifer was the stupid one. 'You never seen no spork before? Used to get them all the time at Kentucky Fried.'

'Are all the forks and spoons gone?' Jennifer asked.

'Get outta here, girl,' Big Red said. 'They don't give us no knives, no forks, no nothing. Don't want us to make weapons out of 'em.'

Jennifer used the spork to scoop up a little potato and gravy, but the gravy ran through the space between the two tines. 'Couldn't they give us just a spoon?' she asked in exasperation. 'You can't hurt someone with a spoon.'

'Oh, say what?' Big Red spoke up. 'Lottie J. took out Sabrina's eye with a spoon.' She was sporking up her food with the kind of relish Jennifer had rarely seen at three star restaurants. 'Lottie J. faked being sick and went to the dispensary and she got herself a spoon there and sharpened it and then when she came back and that Sabrina be botherin' her again, she just scooped out her eye like a melon ball.'

Jennifer put her spork down. The greasy taste of the gravy sat on her tongue like oil on a driveway. Her hunger turned to nausea. The glutinous gray-brown mass that passed as meat couldn't possibly be cut by the spork. 'You finished with that?' Big Red asked, eyeing Jennifer's tray.

Jennifer picked up a plastic cup of pudding and nodded. Before she could get her arm out of the way Big Red grabbed the tray and pulled it over to her, placing it on top of her first tray. She dug in and Jennifer realized that the niceties of cutting the meat were not an issue here; Big Red sporked the entire piece into her mouth and Jennifer watched as she masticated in a bovine manner for a lot longer than it took Jennifer to down the watery tapioca. This was definitely not the Four Seasons and there was no cotton candy cake with sugared violets and a candle on top for dessert.

To help calm her nausea, Jennifer tried to see what the other women were doing to get through their meals. Most of them were talking amongst themselves; some were even laughing. Then, to her absolute horror, Jennifer saw a grown woman trying to make herself a peanut butter and jelly sandwich using a spork. It would've been easier if she'd just used her fingers.

This was humiliation, not rehabilitation! Jennifer couldn't get beyond it no matter how she tried. She wondered if the population was really so dangerous that they couldn't be trusted with real eating utensils. She looked at Big Red, now mopping up the last of the food, and wondered if the story about the spoon was even true. Maybe it was one of those things they told a newcomer to scare her, like the camp story of the parked couple and the bloody hook hanging off the door of their car.

Then, even as she put the thought away, two women began screeching. In less than a second, Big Red jumped up and stood on the table, narrowly missing Jennifer's hand. 'Kill the bitch!' Big Red screamed. Jennifer wasn't sure that even in her exalted position Red could see anything. The imbroglio seemed to be on the floor, on the other side of the table, near the wall. Correction officers were on the two fighting women in an instant, and, although Jennifer didn't want to look, she couldn't help but see one of the officers – she thought it was Byrd – throw a vicious kick at an inmate who was rolling on the floor.

Just then, louder noise and movement broke out to the right. Jennifer looked over, but before she could see what was going on, she noticed a pay phone out in the corridor. This is it, she thought.

As the two women continued to shout, and as several officers rushed their table, Jennifer calmly started to walk backward to the exit. She'd walked against a crowd that way many times in New York's movie theaters when she wanted to get in to a popular show. As she made her way out, she watched the activity in front of her, but also glanced behind her to make sure she didn't disturb anyone by bumping into them. The last thing she needed was to be in a jailhouse brawl. Though she was known as the 'Warrior of Words' at Hudson, Van Schaank, the one thing she didn't know how to do was fight physically. Her path was clear – only another twelve steps before she'd be at the phone! It seemed that no one had noticed her, but her heart was thumping so loudly that she was certain that everyone could hear it, even over the ruckus.

Jennifer looked behind her again; in two more steps she reached the phone. She picked up the receiver and started to dial. She could hear the tones of the numbers in her ears and they drowned out the increasing noise from the room behind her. She dialed collect, and when the automated operator's voice asked for it she gave her name. At the other end of the line, in another world altogether, she heard the phone ring. She imagined Tom's apartment in Battery Park City overlooking New York Harbor and the Statue of Liberty. She'd looked out at the view a hundred times. She heard the phone ring again. Women were screaming and shouting from every corner of the room. It was worse than a snake pit. Jennifer couldn't help it: She instinctively put her hands over her ears, but still the noise penetrated despite her resolution. A tear began to drip from the corner of her right eye along her nose and down to her nostril. But she couldn't take her hands off her ears to wipe it away because the noise was so overwhelming.

Suddenly a squadron of guards surrounding someone was coming her way. Jennifer was bumped into by another woman who was struggling against three officers. 'Lock-down!' she heard an officer shout from the far side of the cafeteria. But Jennifer stayed where she was, listening to the distant ringing. Answer, damnit!

A shuffling line of women approached the exit, and one

woman stood directly in front of Jennifer and smiled. She was almost certain that this was the creature she had seen tending the marigolds on her way into Jennings. The black face split into a skeletal grin. 'Trying to escape this place?' the old woman asked.

At that same moment, a hand reached over and yanked the receiver away from Jennifer. 'You can't use the phone now,' a woman officer said, obviously agitated. 'Damn freshman!' She grabbed Jennifer and pushed her into line. 'Face forward!' the officer snapped. 'You too, Springtime. Step lively! Go to your houses,' the officer shouted.

Jennifer thought that she might just scream, break and run, even though the barred doors visibly truncated the long hallway ahead of her. She had to do something. She *had* to get through to Tom. He and Donald couldn't have known that this place was such a madhouse. Even one more day would be too long for her to keep her sanity. If Observation wasn't enough to make her want to kill herself, another meal like this would be.

11

Gwen Harding

Many laws as certainly make bad men, as bad men make many laws.

Walter Savage Landor

Gwen Harding tightened the sash of her bathrobe, retied the bow, and studied the papers spread before her. In her office at Jennings she was kept busy from moment to moment simply trying to deal with the administrative load, employee problems, staffing, and management. Now for the first time she looked at the JRU International information package and the charts spread out on her dining table. JRU had completed their proposal to the state and Warden Harding, along with half a dozen other state correction professionals, was being asked to write up her opinion of their plan.

She took a preliminary look at the proposal. 'Fact: *The private sector consistently saves government money*. In the past decade, at least fourteen separate independent studies have compared the costs of operating private and public institutions. Twelve of those studies demonstrated that the cost of privately managed prisons is from two to twenty-nine percent less than that of government-managed facilities.' Gwen wondered how they managed to cut costs. Perhaps by firing outdated wardens.

She rose from her chair and passed the counter that was the only demarcation of where the dining room ended and the kitchen began. The kitchen was spotless. She crossed the blue and white tile floor to the stove, where a kettle – the only cooking implement she ever used in this kitchen anymore – sat on the one burner that she ever turned on. She took a mug from the cabinet. It had been a gift from a social-worker friend years ago. It was one of those ready-made but unpainted objects that children and women with time on their hands paint in shops set up expressly for that purpose. On it, Gwen's friend Lisa Anderson had painted BECAUSE I'M THE WARDEN, THAT'S WHY.

When she was given the gift, she and Lisa laughed over the reactions the mug stirred up among the other women at the shop where Lisa had painted it. Now Gwen filled it with hot water and dunked a tea bag into it. She was actually longing for a glass of gin, and the olives in the refrigerator seemed to be calling out to her, but she knew she had to keep a clear head. JRU was waiting and JRU came first. She crossed to the sink holding the steaming mug, opened the under-cabinet and dropped the wet tea bag into the empty trash bag. She didn't even make trash anymore. Gwen sighed. There was a different time and a different place where she used to cook and give dinner parties on a regular basis. And she'd been good – everyone praised her *coq au vin*. 'Jesus,' she thought, walking back to the dining table, 'do people even make *coq au vin* nowadays?' She hadn't seen it on a menu or at a dinner party in years. But then . . . she tried to think of the last dinner party she had attended and couldn't remember one. That couldn't be! She stood still, one hand resting on the back of a dining chair, the other clenched around her mug. There was the dinner at the restaurant at the close of the Eastern States Correction Officers Association. And of course, there was always the rubber chicken at local civic functions. But actual dinner parties – just social time at someone's home, seemed to be a bit thin on the ground.

Gwen took a sip of tea and wondered where her friend Lisa Anderson was now. She smiled. They had had a lot of fun together. Gwen had been divorced and Lisa had been in the process of separating from her husband. The two of them went out at least once a week, but that was . . . Gwen put down the mug and tried to think whether it was six or seven years ago. Could it be that long? She tried to think it out. It had to be. It was just after she got the job at Jennings.

At Jennings Gwen was too busy to see old friends or to make new ones, at least in the beginning. Then, when she had settled in, it seemed as if there were no friends to be made. Certainly she couldn't count any of the Jennings staff as friends. Perhaps her initial conscious distancing had put people off, but she'd only done it because she'd been frightened and overly sensitive about her new position and its required authority. She supposed that by the time she felt secure and was ready to unbend a little, no one else seemed to be so inclined. Well, that was understandable. She took another sip of tea and reminded herself that she'd never been a natural extrovert.

Gwen sat down at the shining waxed dining table, only

sullied by the JRU report. She wouldn't think about anything else right now. Thinking about the emptiness of her life would surely drive her to the olives and she had to begin her response to this proposal. She looked at the inscription once again and smiled ruefully. When she first began working in the Department of Corrections it seemed to her that wardens had enormous power. Perhaps she'd been wrong or had exaggerated what she'd seen, but the position's power had certainly eroded since then. A warden's powers today were so limited, while her accountability was so vast, that Gwen often felt as trussed as a turkey before being shoved into the oven. And now this move to privatize prisons was sure to usurp whatever power she had remaining.

Privatization was a bastard trend that had been born – *mothered* – by Wall Street out of the incredible need for more prisons and taxpayers yelping at the costs of incarceration. If an aging population voted against school-board bond issues and preferred not to spend its tax dollars on educating their own grandchildren, Gwen knew all too well how they felt about spending public funds on strangers in the 'criminal population'. And yet, that population continued to grow. The only solution most agencies saw was building more places to incarcerate offenders. The ineffectual 'war on drugs', mandatory sentences, and a judiciary frightened that they might be perceived as 'soft on crime' had all contributed to a huge increase in prisoners in general, and an even larger increase in female prison statistics.

In fact, Gwen knew that women were the fastest growing sector of the prison population. Since 1980, the female inmate population nationwide had increased by more than five hundred percent. And this was not because women were involved in more violent crimes. It was because, nationwide, people were being imprisoned much more frequently for nonviolent crimes. In 1979, women convicted of nonviolent crimes were sent to prison roughly forty-nine percent of the time. By 1999, they were being sent to prison for nonviolent crimes nearly eighty percent of the time.

So privatization seemed a neat and simple answer to all these problems. Big business claimed it was ready to step in, take the risk, bear the expense, and turn prisons into moneymaking operations. Gwen of course knew that there were two major private prison corporations in the U.S. One of them, Wackenhut Corrections, owned fifty-two prisons 'employing' more than twenty-six thousand prisoners. The other, CCA – Corrections Corporation of America – had control over almost three times as many prisoners in eighty-one prisons. At the last conference for prison wardens that Gwen had attended, there had been a heated discussion over the privatization of prisons. Someone pointed out how large corporations had the incentive and the political clout to encourage the creation of a larger and larger prison population – a larger and larger cheap labor pool. This meant increased sentences and the increasing incarceration of men and women (usually from communities of color). Gwen wondered if this would turn into a new form of slavery.

She shook her head, turned another page of the proposal, and wondered what JRU International stood for. Justice Regulatory Underwriters? Jesus Really Understands? Jails 'R' Us? Jammed Rats Unlimited? Why not be honest and call it PFP: Prisons for Profit? She turned another page of the proposal before her and began to take notes in her small, neat handwriting.

* * *

There was no way this plan was going to work! Gwen looked down at the dozen pages of notations she'd already compiled. Most were written in capital letters and underlined several times. They looked like mad ravings, and weren't far from it. She'd have to somehow turn these blistering observations into cool bureaucratic reportage. She shook her head at the daunting task. What was the state thinking of?

She knew, of course, that her burgeoning budget presented nothing but trouble to them. Gwen knew that while her costs of maintaining one prisoner – including her bed, board, security, and the very limited health and education services that Jennings offered – was increasing to more than fifty-five dollars a day, private prisons claimed they could maintain prisoners at only forty-three dollars a day. She knew she couldn't compete with that.

But how was JRU going to deliver what they were promising? How were they possibly going to reduce medical staff? As it was, she had reluctantly cut the staff dramatically. When she looked at the 'Facilities Management Report' she was actually shocked. They proposed turning the visiting room into a space for a profit-making telemarketing operation. Where would the women visit with their families? They were also proposing to expand the prison itself and enclose the U of the courtyard, to provide additional housing. That meant darkening all the units facing the courtyard. Where would the women exercise? Where would Springtime plant flowers?

She had to be missing something in this ridiculous proposal. After all, though they weren't pleasant, the JRU staff didn't seem to be insane or particularly cruel. Yet the more Gwen studied the details, the more horrifying the plan seemed. It appeared that they expected to house and feed more than two hundred and thirty new inmates, who would be transferred from other facilities, facilities they would later close or would subsume into the JRU empire. Surely there must be a typo, Gwen thought as she looked at the numbers. Then she realized that the current, badly designed cells (which had four bunks but held only two prisoners) were actually going to be used to house four. The additional cells, those built in the courtyard space, would hold the balance.

Gwen did some quick calculations. It was unbelievable! Had those JRU jaspers ever read about Telgrin's experiment with rats? Decent, normal rats from good nests turned vicious – even cannibalistic – when they were overcrowded in their cages. Did they know Amnesty International's position on U.S. prison conditions? Were they so inexperienced that they didn't realize that the four bunk spaces were an error, far too small a space even for two? Clearly, JRU saw the inmates not as human beings or even rats but as a captive labor force. And based on their projection, a *profitable* force at that. How did they hope to transform this angry and sullen population of criminal inmates into chipper and cheerful telemarketers?

Gwen dropped her pen and began pacing around the dining table. This was never going to work. All of her years of experience, not just at Jennings and not just as a warden, but in social work, halfway houses, and other correctional facilities, told Gwen Harding that the plan was bound to fail. And what would happen then? Would there be protests? An uprising? And if there was violence – and with this plan there was bound to be plenty – would the inmates be blamed? Or would it be *her* head on the chopping block? If it all went up in flames – figuratively or literally – could

JRU just abandon the project, leaving the state to clean it up?

She knew very little about businesses and how they operated. She had spent her life working in the public sector. So had her father, who had been a cop, and her mother, who had been a teacher. In fact, aside from an uncle (who had run a dry goods store that failed), she couldn't think of anyone in her extended family who had any real business experience. The corporate world, with its financial realities and its politics, was a complete mystery to her. The one thing that she was sure of was that the executives who had toured her facility had been arrogant and much more prone to talk than to listen. But she'd noticed, of course, how little they wanted to hear from her. It was clear that they already felt she was an advocate of the 'prisoners'. When these people took over – if they did take over – how long would she even get to retain her job?

This situation was awful. Gwen felt the call of the olives in her refrigerator. She had to convince the Department of Corrections that this proposal should – *must* – be turned down. But Gwen had no idea how she was going to convince them that the JRU proposal was not only unrealistic, but also a recipe for failure – or for something much, much worse. She looked at the tea mug, now cold on the table, with its inscription: BECAUSE I'M THE WARDEN, THAT'S WHY. What a joke! No one at the State Department of Corrections listened to what a warden said. Especially a female warden.

She would have to sit down and put together a brilliant counterargument, complete with her own charts and graphs and projections that would not only explain why this plan was flawed but would refute JRU's assumptions. She'd also have to give the state some longer-range alternative strategy for cost-effectively handling an ever-growing prison population. She sighed and picked up the cold cup. How could she possibly do it? Gwen closed her eyes and pinched the bridge of her nose to ease the tension in her brow. In her mind she heard cries of *Attica! Attica! Attica!* Jesus Christ! This was all too much for her. She wasn't young anymore. Who was she kidding? They'd roll right over her. Gwen put the mug down, stood up and walked toward the refrigerator, only stopping on the way to grab a glass and the gin bottle.

12

Jennifer Spencer

Remember that you are always in a better position to ask for a job transfer if you have a good record on the job you already have. Failure to do well on a job may result in demotion or punishment.

'Rules for Inmates' at the Ohio Reformatory for Women in Marysville, Ohio. Kathryn Watterson, *Women in Prison*

Jennifer Spencer survived yet another night in prison, only to awaken to another day of working in the laundry.

Nobody wanted the laundry detail. Undoubtedly that was why Jennifer had been assigned to it. The laundry was a long room in the basement with a low ceiling. Between the steam and the pervasive smell of chlorine bleach and dirty clothes, the place reminded Jennifer of nothing so much as a cheap health club back in what she was beginning to think of as her 'other life'.

There was nothing healthy about this place; the work was heavy and dangerous. All of the prison's dirty laundry – everything from the polyester jumpsuits to regular uniforms to underpants, socks, sheets, and blankets – came through this laundry. So did washrags and blood-soaked pillowcases.

In addition to the stuff that was *supposed* to be washed,

there were two other categories: detritus and contraband. Detritus included bloody gauze pads that had been accidentally wrapped in a towel and thrown into a cart, or the speculum that had been entangled in a dispensary johnny. There were hair clippings from the barbers, stale and rotting food in garment pockets, puzzle pieces, and every possible piece of unbreakable plastic dinnerware (including sporks, pepper shakers, and plastic ketchup squeezers). Jennifer had been issued heavy-gauge rubber gloves and an apron, but it wasn't enough. About the only thing she figured the gloves could protect her from were the roaches she was constantly finding in pockets, socks, or accumulated at the bottom of the bucket.

The laundry at Jennings reminded Jennifer of a blue flannel suit: it attracted everything but men and money. Only two days ago Suki had pulled out a speculum and on another day Jennifer herself had felt a lump inside the tied leg of a pair of slacks. When she untied the bottom the meticulously taped package of cocaine dropped like an iced plum into her hands. 'One day we found a scalpel,' Suki told her.

Laundry came in on industrial rolling carts that, for some reason, Jennifer kept tripping over again and again. The carts were heavy to push, and because the sheets and clothing were often water-soaked, simply untangling the garments and putting her gloved-sheathed hand into the mix seemed almost more than she could bear. The smell of sweating women, the industrial-strength liquid detergent, the cheap perfumes, and the mildew were intolerable to her. I'll call Tom and get him to charter a helicopter, she told herself.

After Jennifer unloaded the dirty linens into the huge

front loader and snapped the lock shut, she would pull the cart back and watch Suki do her magic. It was the only fun that Jennifer managed to get out of the dirty work. When Suki turned on the huge stainless steel industrial washing machines, it was as if the little blonde girl was in control of the space shuttle at Houston. She could barely reach the flip switches on the top of the machine, but she managed to snap some of them all the way up, some in the middle, some all the way down. 'You have to be careful to synchronize the water level push button with the "on" button or otherwise the water runs out over the top. It'll get you wetter than you were when you were in Observation!' Suki yelled over the noise of the tumbling drum.

Once the machine was activated, Suki and Jennifer would stand back and watch the water fill up the front of the glass and watch the bubbles consume the clothes inside.

When all the dirty clothes were sorted and washed it was time to go help out in the clean laundry. There were two black-topped Formica tables butted up against each other where women were folding the clean clothes. None of the women liked folding the jumpsuits, shirts, or undergarments. And forget about doing the socks – that was right up there with the popularity of having to wash silverware. There was always a silent contest, though, when it came to folding the towels and facecloths. It was a competition of speed, neatness, and the crispness of the crease (to insure that the stack of linens would stay vertical). The record for facecloth stacks was held by an older woman named Rory with seventy-five, while Dakota – a black teenager – held the record for twenty-five bath towels.

For Jennifer – who hadn't done laundry since college –

there was a certain fascination in watching the women work briskly, trying to outdo each other. She had to admit that the cleanliness of this part of the work area was nice, the fresh smell of the clean clothes, the heat that radiated from the sheets and towels. It was a homey kind of comfort that she couldn't quite get over.

Later in the day, just after Suki had pushed and emptied a particularly large cart loaded with wet linens, Jennifer saw the girl clutch at her stomach, grow completely pale, and then pass out. Jennifer rushed to Suki's side and caught her just under the arms. In another two seconds, Suki's head would have hit the wet concrete floor. For a moment Jennifer stood there, paralyzed, holding the tiny body upright. She couldn't lay her on the floor, nor could she let go of her grip to get a better hold and attempt to carry Suki to the infirmary. Unconscious, Suki was ninety pounds of dead weight and, unlike the wet laundry, she wasn't on wheels.

Through the din, the vapors of the room, and the jerry-built lighting system, Flora, the supervisor, a middle-aged woman who seemed to really care about her laundry staff, made a motion to another inmate to help Jennifer pick Suki up and lay her across one of the black Formica laundry tables.

A cold cloth was brought for Suki's head and a couple of aspirins were distributed. From her pocket, Flora brought out an ampule and snapped it open right under Suki's nose. Suki's eyes popped open – the bright blue color agitated by all that she could feel going on around her. When her eyelids closed again, Jennifer took a deep breath and almost choked as the supervisor cracked open another capsule of ammonia salt. Once again, Suki's head snapped back and her eyes rolled open. This time, the supervisor cradled her head in her arms and began to ask questions.

'Suki, can you hear me?'

The blonde bounced her head up and down.

'Talk to me. Talk to me, then,' Flora said.

For no discernible reason, Suki began to sing. Her voice was as petite as the supervisor but a good deal more polite 'Don't Cry for Me, Argentina' as she warbled some lines from the flat stage of the linen folding table.

'Are you on your period?' Flora asked.

Suki shook her head.

'We'd better bring her down to the dispensary,' Flora said.

'No, no!' Suki remonstrated. She struggled to sit up, then lost her strength and collapsed again on the table.

'If you take her to medical, they'll do a quick once over and take money from her canteen fund, and she doesn't have that much in it,' Springtime told Flora.

'They make you *pay* for medical treatment?' Jennifer asked in disbelief.

'Yep. A co-pay. Five bucks for a doc, four bucks for a nurse,' Flora explained.

Suki came to again and assured them she was fine. As the group broke up Suki grabbed Jennifer's arm. 'Jennifer, lean over,' she said, and Jen bent her head over the table. 'Can I tell you a secret?' asked Suki, her eyes bright with news.

'Sure,' Jennifer asked, as the supervisor left.

'I'm not on my period,' Suki giggled. 'I can't be.'

'Well, you might be weak anyway,' Jennifer told the young girl, and patted her head. 'Sometimes people are affected differently.'

'No, no, you don't understand,' Suki giggled again. 'I'm going to have a baby.'

For the first moment, Jennifer felt panic. She looked at Suki's flat stomach. Was the girl delusional? Did she think she was going to give birth here? Jennifer had seen her crumple and was sure that Suki hadn't hit her head, but somehow she was out of it. 'Suki,' Jen said gently, 'you're not having a baby. You just passed out.'

'Promise you won't tell nobody?' Suki admonished.

'Oh, I won't tell,' Jennifer told her. But how could she be pregnant? How could she *get* pregnant? Maybe she was just having some kind of seizure. Jennifer looked over at the petite blonde. She seemed to be completely recovered. 'Suki,' Jennifer went on boldly. 'You can't be pregnant, can you?'

Suki just smiled. It was the same smile that Jennifer had seen her give to Roger Camry.

When the workday was over and Jennifer had settled Suki into their cell, she realized that she had a little free time before the bell rang for dinner. One of the phones in her 'pod' wasn't being used. She approached the phone as if it were the magical port that would take her out of this forsaken place. She picked up the receiver and entered Tom's number. But as the phone began to ring on the other end, Officer Byrd came into the rec area of the unit. 'Head count,' he announced. 'Take your places.'

Jennifer kept listening to the ringing. She watched the inmates leisurely move to the entrances of their cells. She, however, was frozen in place. She *had* to get the call through.

Officer Byrd walked up to the first doorway and, with

clipboard in hand, marked off something on his papers. He moved to the next, looked over the women, and marked again. The phone rang again. When he got to Jennifer and Suki's doorway, Jennifer could see Suki leaning against the door for support. Pick up, she thought. Come on. Pick up, Tom.

'Jennifer Spencer,' Officer Byrd growled in a voice loud enough for her to hear all the way down the hall. 'Jennifer Spencer?' he repeated. 'Where is she, the infirmary?'

From her place at the phone Jennifer could see Suki's head shake strenuously and her mouth form the word 'no'. Then she smiled flirtatiously at Officer Byrd and pointed in her direction. He turned around quickly and Jennifer couldn't help but shrink back as he started toward her, though he was a long hallway away. But in what seemed like two steps he was in her face. 'Just what the hell do you think you're doing?' he asked. He grabbed her upper arm roughly. 'It's head count. You're supposed to be in your cell.'

Jen could hear the phone ring. Pick up, pick up, she silently prayed. 'I'm just trying to call . . .' she began.

'I don't care what you're doing!' he snarled. 'You stop everything – even if you're taking a leak – and get to the entrance of your house for head count.'

Then the ringing stopped. 'This is a collect call from . . .' the automated voice intoned.

'Move it,' Byrd was saying at the same time. He jerked her arm. With the receiver still to her ear, Jennifer heard Tom's voice. 'Yes, I'll accept the charges,' he said. And at that moment, Officer Byrd grabbed the phone and jammed it into the receiver.

'Get to your house, *now*, Spencer! You're being written

up for this,' Byrd said, his face flushed almost purple. 'Just two more incidents and you'll be losing visitor's privileges.'

Stricken, Jennifer did as she was told.

13

Jennifer Spencer

Prisoners of hope.
Zech. 9:12

'Back off and wait your ass like everybody else,' the skinny woman hissed at Jennifer.

Jennifer decided not to argue. She wasn't standing any closer to the woman than anybody else was, and like everyone else she'd been waiting in line for more than half an hour to use the phone. But everyone steered clear of the harsh skinny woman. Suki told her that she was from Haiti and knew voodoo. That didn't worry Jennifer, but the crazy look in the woman's eye did. Three women had already used the phone, each for a ten-minute interval, and by rights the receiver should now be handed to Jennifer. But she wasn't going to press the point with this obviously deranged, outraged woman who seemed to be getting some bad news.

Of all the facility problems at this disgusting prison, the phones were the worst. Some bastard in some state architectural office somewhere had to think long and hard in order to make placing a phone call such a humiliating experience. Two antique-looking pay phones hung side by side in the rec room, and *why* they were pay phones no one could say since inmates were only allowed to make collect calls.

Worse, they were placed just high enough on the wall so that you couldn't sit down while using them, but neither could you stand completely upright – if you did, your head was directly in front of the television set mounted on the rec room wall. If the television was on – and it was always on – you had to crouch slightly for your entire call, and then try not to bump into the person who was crouched next to you using the other phone.

Right now the volume on the TV was turned up full blast, and as the women on the phones shouted to be heard, everyone else who was trying to watch the television was shouting at the callers to 'shut the fuck up!' or 'get your goddamn fat head out of the way!' It was chaos.

At last Jennifer was just a moment away from getting to the phone. Barring a lockdown, a head count, or an act of God, she would get to talk to Tom. She stared at the receiver, now being sprayed with spittle as the angry, skinny woman shouted something. Disgusting as it was, that phone was her only lifeline to the Outside.

Jennifer called Tom's office number and heard the phone ringing. Pamela, Tom's secretary, picked it up. The moment she heard Pam's voice, Jennifer began to speak, but the automated operator interrupted her to ask whether or not Pamela would accept the charges. Jennifer felt her stomach contract tightly. My God, what if Pam said no? She held her breath for what seemed a very long moment. When her call was accepted and she heard Pam's voice say hello again, Jennifer felt actual tears of relief in her eyes.

'Pam?' she said. 'This is Jennifer. I need to talk to Tom right away.'

'Jennifer!' Pam said brightly, as if this were a normal situation. 'You're calling from –'

'Yes, yes! I need to talk to Tom right away,' Jennifer repeated.

'Oh, sure. He's in a meeting but –'

'Get him! Get him right now,' Jennifer said.

She held her breath and waited. The thirty seconds of silence seemed as long as her entire previous life. Then, when Tom's voice said hello she felt as if her heart might explode in her chest. 'Jen!' he said. 'Jen, is it you? I've been so worried.'

'Oh, Tom,' she cried, and she was shocked to hear how small and miserable she sounded. 'Oh, Tom!' She looked behind her at the line of women waiting for the phone and lowered her voice. 'Get me out of here. This is unbelievable. You just don't know.'

'What's happened?' he asked.

She realized how wide the chasm from their last goodbye to this hello was. She could never get him to understand. And she certainly didn't have the time now. 'Why hasn't *anything* happened?' she asked. 'You have to get me out of here.'

'Of course,' he said. 'God, I've been so worried. I couldn't reach you and I thought you would call me right away. Why didn't you call?'

'Why didn't I call?' How could she possibly explain to him what this place was like? 'That's all I've been trying to do,' she said. 'But it's not easy here.' Not easy! Ha! This conversation was surreal. She herself wouldn't believe what she'd been through if she herself hadn't been through it. 'Tom, what's going on? When do I get out of here?' She couldn't afford to waste her precious ten minutes on any other topic.

'Soon, real soon.'

His voice, his promise, calmed her. She breathed deeply, the first deep breath of air she'd had since she'd stepped into Jennings. 'Tomorrow?' she asked. She really didn't think she could go back to the filth of the laundry, and more meals in that wretched cafeteria would surely kill her.

Tom said something she couldn't hear. 'What?' she said.

'Tomorrow?' Tom was repeating. 'No, it's not going to be tomorrow.'

Jennifer felt panic rising. 'It has to be,' she told him. 'It *has* to be.'

'Shut the fuck up,' the woman using the phone beside her snarled. Jennifer lowered her voice and crouched even more to keep her head from blocking the television.

'You don't know what it's like here,' she said. 'You just can't imagine.'

'I know it must be rough but . . .'

'You don't know anything!' she said. 'This is no country club. And I'm not getting any special treatment.'

'Where are you?' he asked. 'I can barely hear you.'

How to describe the bedlam of the rec room? 'Never mind that,' she said. 'What's going on? How soon can I get out?'

'Look,' Tom said, his voice soothing. 'You can't expect us to engineer all this right away. You . . .'

Jennifer looked around at the rec room; inmates in grim

uniforms were playing cards, building puzzles, pacing around the room dodging the broken chairs, stopping to stare at the smudges of dirt on the walls. As usual, a clearly psychotic woman was ranting and scratching at herself, but nothing was being done to help her or shut her up. Jen took in the funky smell, the palpable anger and boredom. 'Not right away?' she asked. 'I don't understand. You said it would be just for a day or two. Remember? You said it would be a country club. And that you'd get me right out. House arrest, or a commuted sentence or . . .'

'Look, Jen, I admit it's going a little slower than we'd like,' Tom said calmly. 'You just have to trust me and accept that. We can't just bully our way through the courts on this.'

The courts? They hadn't planned on the courts. 'But what about the governor?' she asked.

'White-collar crime is a big political issue right now. And your case became pretty high profile.' He paused for a moment, and in that second or two Jen thought she'd lost him. 'You know,' he continued, 'the press is still watching us very closely, and if I move too fast they'll be all over it again. And if they are, no judge is going to take the risk of losing his bench over this case. We have to find the right time or we'll be in a worse jam than we are now.'

'We?' Jen asked and heard the bitterness in her voice. 'That must be the royal we that you're using. Because *I* am the one incarcerated, Tom. I am the one who was strip searched. I am the one who slept in a cell with a felon. I'm the one wearing the jumpsuit and eating the crap they call food here.' Then her anger left her all at once and was replaced by a sickening fear mixed with grief. She began to sob. She told herself she had to stop. She couldn't waste her phone time like this, nor let the other inmates see or hear her cry.

'Oh, Jen, I know it's tough,' Tom soothed. 'Look, just try to sit tight. I wish I could do this for you. And I wish I could do it quicker. But you have to believe me when I say that we're doing absolutely everything to get you out of there. It all takes time, Jennifer.'

Time! It already seemed as if everything in Jen's previous life had dissolved, had evaporated, and this dirty room, these miserable and frightening women were all that she knew. 'How long do you think it's going to be?' she managed to whisper.

'Two weeks,' he said. 'Three at the most. And we're already looking into getting you transferred or giving you some special treatment in the meantime.'

Jen couldn't speak. Two weeks! Another fourteen days of this! And maybe more. It was unimaginable. It was literally unbearable. She felt as if her breastbone were cracking, the pressure on her chest was so great.

'Baby?' Jen heard Tom's voice, but she could only answer him with a nod. He, of course, couldn't see her response. 'Baby, are you there?' he asked.

'I don't think I can . . .' her voice trailed off, the pain moving up to her throat and choking her.

'Don't be upset, Jen,' he said. 'You know I love you, don't you?'

'Yes,' she managed.

'Well I promise you that everything's going to be all right.' He paused and his voice became soft, really loving. 'You have to tough it out now, Jen. We're all behind you and we're playing for very big stakes. Just hang on a little while, and think of the reward.'

She clutched the receiver tightly and held it close to her. 'I just didn't know it would be this hard,' Jen whispered.

'Oh, baby. I'm so sorry,' Tom told her. 'You know I would have done it for Donald if it didn't mean I'd be disbarred. You know what *that* would have done to our future.' She nodded again. 'So, can you just hang in there?' he asked. 'Think about the penthouse we'll buy. Think about our wedding. And the cruise we'll go on.' He laughed, then lowered his voice. 'Think about lying on the sand with me on a Caribbean beach.'

'Enough, goddamnit!' Jen heard the words, jumped, and then turned to see the tall dark woman from Intake, the one who had tried on her shoes. She gave Jen a push on her shoulder. 'You've had more than ten minutes. You're not the only one who has a lawyer.'

Jen covered the receiver of the phone with her hand. 'Just another second,' she told the reptile coldly and turned back to the phone.

'Will you come for visiting day on Saturday?' Jennifer asked Tom.

'*This* Saturday?' he asked, sounding hesitant. 'Baby, I've got so much work to do. We're preparing your appeal – just in case, but we're also making a motion for mistrial and going the pardon route.'

'Please,' she begged. 'I only get an hour for a visitor. If I'm going to be here please come.'

'I'll try,' Tom promised.

'Hurry up, debutante,' the woman said, and this time she hit Jen's shoulder harder.

'I've got to go,' Jen said reluctantly, but even after they said good-bye and Tom had hung up, Jen found she couldn't let go of the receiver. She still held it to her ear.

It was Suki who finally pulled Jennifer away from the phone. 'Come on,' she said gently. 'Come away, now.' She brought Jen over to a chair. 'Bad news or good?' she asked, but before Jen had time to answer, a woman CO entered the unit and announced something. Jen didn't catch what she said, but Suki jumped up and got the look of a kid on Christmas morning. 'They're handing out the packages!' she said and grabbed Jennifer's arm, happily leading her across the rec room and into the hall where two of the guards had wheeled in a large cart laden with parcels.

'Are you expecting something?' Jen asked Suki.

'I never get a package,' Suki said, then put her hand on her stomach. 'But I got one here!' she whispered at Jennifer. 'But maybe you got a package today, Jenny,' Suki offered cheerfully. Jen shook her head, but the two of them stood with the other hopeful women.

Jennifer was shocked to see that each and every package was already torn open. Obviously the contents had been rifled through and searched for contraband, but the women all eagerly stood in line and unashamedly shouted for joy when they heard their names called as recipients of these gifts from the Outside. Jennifer watched as each inmate hungrily grabbed her package from the officers and then clutched it to her breast. Most of them scurried to their house or a far corner to examine the bounty of the contents.

Many of the women, the forgotten ones, stood silently off to the side. They knew that they would be receiving no packages today – or perhaps any day. Their looks of envy and of unspeakable sadness nearly brought Jennifer to tears. But when other women – those who were in their crews – got something, the loners gathered around the lucky member of their prison family and shared in the delight of the presents.

Jennifer thought of her mother. Up to now she had been so grateful that the woman who suffered enough in life hadn't lived long enough to witness the shame and humiliation of Jennifer's imprisonment. But right now Jennifer would give anything if she could receive a package from her mother – a package from home. She, too, wanted to open a box filled with cookies and LifeSavers and playing cards.

All around the room there were happy squeals as packages were opened and the contents were discovered. Jennifer found herself smiling as she witnessed the joy a gift of Dr Scholl's footpads could bring. Apparently inmates could buy a few generic healthcare products from the prison canteen, but real happiness was opening a box and finding Caress – Head and Shoulders – Visine – Rolaids – Jergens. The brand names were reverently whispered like the names of the gods of comfort and contentment. And as Jennifer watched she was amazed to see how nothing was taken for granted. Even Tampax and Preparation H were spoken of reverentially. The boxes and bottles were eagerly passed around, and the women, who were starved for any bit of normalcy or sign of life from the Outside examined every word, scent, and color of the products.

'Look! They've changed the Keebler elves,' one woman said with a laugh.

'Let me see.'

'Show me.'

A small chorus of voices responded to each announcement.

'Snickers bars keep getting smaller and smaller all the time,' observed Flora.

'I wish they would just make *plain* potato chips,' said a third. 'I don't think my gut can take Sour Cream and Bar-B-Que Jalapeños.'

Nutritional contents were studied and discussed, and every bit of wrapping paper and packaging was savored and saved. Many of the boxes included writing tablets and pens. One woman received an entire box of greeting cards with all of the envelopes already bearing postage stamps and preaddressed to family members. Women *oohed and ahhed* over the thoughtfulness of that, and they wanted to examine every card.

There were boxes of tissues, tea bags, and Q-tips. In some packages there were sketch pads and colored pencils – even file folders and erasers.

Jennifer's heart ached as she watched the pleasure that such a simple present could evoke. It was too easy to say this was like a birthday or Christmas; it was more important than that. These packages were more than a celebration. They were a reassurance that beyond these pink and green and gray and orange walls there were still shopping malls and pharmacies and grocery stores, all brightly lit. Each package was not only a gift from the Outside, but a momentary trip back into the world of the living. Halls Mentho-Lyptus – Sweet'n Low – Diet Coke – Chun King. Each item proclaimed, 'You're not forgotten,' 'We remember you,' 'We know what you like and what you need.' Jennifer turned away somewhat ashamed; *she* had been having a fit because she'd be here for a week or two.

No one was watching the television now that the packages had arrived, and Jennifer wondered if she should make another phone call to Tom. Maybe if she could stand upright while talking to him it would be easier to discuss all the things that they had to discuss. She wished she hadn't hung up so abruptly. She wondered if he was still in his office. Her mind was miles away from the rec room and from Jennings, so when she heard her name being called it was as if it came to her from far away.

'Jennifer Spencer! Jennifer Spencer!' shouted one of the officers. 'Come on – use it or lose it. We don't have all day for this.'

'Jenny, you have a package!' Suki squealed, and actually jumped up and down.

Jennifer turned to see a small parcel being held out to her by the officer. It was the size of a shoebox, and in her haze Jennifer wondered who would be sending her a pair. She walked across the room and took the package. Suki had come to her side and was eagerly urging her on. 'Open it up!' she kept repeating while Jenny held the box to her chest.

'It's already opened,' Jen pointed out.

'Who do you think it's from?' Suki asked.

Jennifer didn't have a clue. Maybe Tom? But he hadn't said anything about a package while they were on the phone. Who else could it be? Who else was there? Jennifer shivered. There was no one Outside who'd send her anything.

'Let's take it to our house,' Suki half suggested, half begged. 'I never get packages to share with the crew.'

Jen smiled ruefully at the use of the word 'house'. As if that made this all homier. But she looked at Suki's radiant face and couldn't refuse.

Once they settled on the bottom bunk, Jennifer opened the box and peered inside. A tube of Crest – three Oral-B toothbrushes – Tic Tacs. She had to smile at the thought of

Tom taking the time to go to a CVS or Rite Aid to purchase all of this for her. Usually she picked up this kind of stuff for him. And she had to give him credit for remembering the products she liked to use – but Tic Tacs! She'd never used those in her whole life. Well, it's the thought that counts. There were hair care products – a shampoo, a conditioner, talcum, and other things. Tears rose in her eyes. Jennifer took out and fondled first one product then the other: her gifts. It did remind her of going through a Christmas stocking, but no stocking had ever meant so much.

Hoping to find a card, Jennifer lifted the last tissue from the bottom of the box. She saw a trifolded piece of paper. She actually sniffed it in hopes that she would be able to smell the scent of Tom's aftershave on it. With great anticipation she unfolded the Hudson, Van Schaank letterhead.

Dear Jennifer,

I thought you might need some of this. I would like to come and see you on visitor's day if that's okay with you. Because I'm neither a family member nor your attorney I have to get your approval. I've written to the Warden so she should be in touch with you directly. I look forward to seeing you. And try to keep smiling. You have such a beautiful smile.

Leonard Benson

'Who's Leonard Benson?' Suki asked, peering over Jennifer's shoulder. 'Your boyfriend?'

'No,' Jennifer responded, too surprised by the note and Lenny's unexpected kindness to really hear the question.

'Oh – uh, he's a guy at the office. My accountant.' She stared into the box.

Lenny Benson – her accountant – had sent her an entire box of oral hygiene and grooming products?

'Let's go to Movita's house and show the crew what you got.' Suki was so proud and enthusiastic that Jen couldn't really deny her.

Most of the crew was gathered in Movita's cell. Suki good-naturedly teased Jennifer in front of the others. 'Jenny has a new boyfriend! Jenny has a new boyfriend!' she shouted.

Suki gestured all around the tiny room. 'This is Jenny,' she said.

'Jennifer,' Jennifer corrected.

'And this,' Suki continued without taking in the correction, 'is Theresa, the best cook in Jennings.'

'Hi,' Theresa said.

'And Movita,' Suki said. 'She's the boss.'

'She's not *my* boss,' Cher said.

'That's Cher. Did you meet her at Intake?' Suki asked.

Of course Jennifer remembered the Morticia character from Intake. And she remembered her from the telephone line. But she opted to play dumb. 'No, I don't remember,' Jennifer said. Cher sneered lightly in response.

'Jenny got a big load of stuff from her boyfriend. She gave me a new toothbrush,' Suki said. 'Look at it all.'

Cher demanded to 'have a look at what ya' got,' and took the box from Jen. Then she expertly appraised each and every item. 'These Oral-B toothbrushes are top of the line,' she admitted. She looked down at Jen. 'But tell 'em to send ya' something mintier than Crest the next time,' she advised, handing the box back to Jennifer.

'Never look a gift horse in the mouth,' Theresa calmly advised, 'especially this one.'

Movita smiled. 'This boyfriend seems to be a little preoccupied with her mouth already,' she said and smiled at Jennifer.

'He says she has a beautiful smile,' Suki said, as proud as if it were about her.

A little embarrassed, Jennifer shook her head. 'He's just a friend from work.'

'You know what they say about smiles, don't ya'?' Theresa asked. 'Everybody smiles in the same language. Smiles are the same everywhere ya' go in this world. You can smile in English and it means the same damn thing in Thailand. You know what I'm saying?'

'Would my smile mean the same thing in Poland?' Cher asked, smirking.

'If it was *my* smile, yes. But not if it was yours. You don't smile,' Theresa told her. 'You've got a shit-eatin' grin. Uh, pardon my French,' she said to Jennifer.

'Would anyone like the Tic Tacs?' Jennifer asked. She wound up giving them to Theresa. The hair spray went to Cher and a tube of hand cream was given to Movita. Jennifer was happy to be able to share her package with these women. It made her feel like a popular girl in high school.

The crew was waiting for their dinner to heat up. Theresa told Jennifer that she had received real goodies in her package from home: salami, some cheese, a six-pack of Sprite and a bag of Oreos. Tonight they would feast on store-bought, brand-name junk food. 'Well, afterwards you can all brush with Crest,' Jennifer offered.

'So back in New York City what do you usually make for dinner?' Theresa asked Jennifer.

'Reservations!' Jennifer replied.

Suki laughed. 'Get it? Reservations – like making reservations for dinner. Ya' get it?'

Movita looked at Jennifer. 'I have something for you, too,' Movita said, reaching into her pocket. 'It's from the Warden.' She handed Jennifer an envelope.

'Two in one day,' Jennifer said as she opened it and unfolded the note inside. As she silently read what it said, she felt her stomach tighten into a knot. Then she looked up at Movita and asked, 'Is this true? Can we only have one visitor on visitor's day?'

Movita shrugged. 'Not exactly. Ya' get one hour. Ya' decide how ta break it up. Half hour for each or whatever. You'll have to let ol' Gwen know who ya' wanna see,' Movita told her, 'your attorney – who can come any time – or the guy that sent the package. It's up to you.'

'I'd go for the one who makes you smile,' Theresa suggested.

Jennifer wondered which one that would be and decided she'd see both but give more time to Tom.

The bell rang for dinner and Jennifer left the crew to go once again, all alone, to the horrors of the cafeteria.

14

Gwen Harding

Justice should remove the bandages from her eyes long enough to distinguish between the vicious and the unfortunate.

Robert G. Ingersoll

The Warden was drunk, but not so drunk that she didn't know it. More than drunk, she was lonely, and she was afraid that she was going to lose her job. As she locked away her bottle and journal in the bottom drawer of her desk, she considered the irony of her situation. She was probably the only woman in Jennings who didn't want to leave the place; not tonight – not ever. She rose unsteadily and looked out the window at the ugly coils of razor wire and the illuminated double rows of fences. She ran her fingers through her hair, out of place and hanging over her eyes. She had to move.

She stepped through the door of her office, irrationally hoping that Movita would be there, sitting at her desk. She wanted – no *needed* – to talk. But Watson was safely in her cell. And Miss Ringling had her coat on at a quarter to five and wouldn't stay a moment past the hour even if the entire prison staff was being held hostage.

Gwen returned to her desk and wished that she had even one person she could confide in, or laugh with. Gin was not a friend. Gin didn't listen and gin, most certainly, never answered any of her questions or calmed her fears. In fact, Gwen knew that the gin, once a useful painkiller, had become her enemy. JRU, of course, was also her enemy, and Gwen was very much afraid that the State Department of Corrections might also become her enemy. The administration was sick of her and her years of fighting for better conditions and bigger budgets. And the inmates were not, could not, be her friends. Yet all of them – JRU, the Department of Corrections, and the inmates – they all wanted Gwendolyn to be a friend to them.

She looked down at her report to the State Department of Corrections. She prepared it at home and actually went to an outside typing service and Kinko's to do the word processing and graphics. That was because she didn't want anyone within the prison – staff *or* inmates – to read either the proposal or her response to it. It would only breed unrest, fear, and rumors. All her prison experience told Gwen that rumors were one of her biggest foes of all.

She ran her hand across the big report. She'd dropped one copy at the FedEx office herself, and now she had to take this copy and lock it away safely. Along with all of her charts, graphs, and cost projections, which clearly illustrated how and why the proposed prison privatization by JRU International was destined to fail. Gwen had summed up the moral issues with strong harsh words:

In addition to the practical, humane, and financial considerations summarized above, there is a political and ethical issue that must also be addressed. The work of those incarcerated, when exploited for commercial purposes, can easily be interpreted as a form of slave labor. In my opinion, the inmate population of this – or any other – correctional facility cannot and should not be exploited as a homogeneous pool of potential laborers. Their incarceration may void their right to vote, but it does not revoke their humanity.

The new century has brought with it new social and related penal problems. Without doubt, the explosion of the female prison populations has created a daunting difficulty and a major tax burden. But to convert this from a problem to an opportunity for profit-making would, without a doubt, be taking the wrong turn. The myriad and complex problems that these women bring to us must be the focus of our future correctional efforts. To propose the reverse is an invitation for disaster.

Drunk as she was, Gwendolyn was proud of her report and of her work at Jennings. She decided to take a walk through the cellblocks. The lockdown bell had sounded more than an hour earlier, so no one would see her – or get close enough to smell her breath. Just to be safe she turned and entered the bathroom that adjoined her office. Gwendolyn flipped the light switch, grimaced at her reflection, and then rinsed her mouth with Listerine. She splashed some cold water on her face, brushed her hair, put on her suit jacket, and then walked a very straight line out of the door and toward the row upon row of quiet cells.

After the lockdown bell sounds, the inmates have only minutes to return to their 'houses' before the bars slide shut and the guards do the nightly bed check. They are given but a half hour to prepare themselves for bed before being plunged into a sudden darkness that – except for the muffled cries – brings with it an eerie and forbidding silence. Only the click of the Warden's heels sounded against the floor amidst the snores, the sex, the sighs – and the sobs. There was always sobbing.

And the sobbing would get a lot worse if this JRU takeover happened, Gwen thought. The burgeoning population of women's prisons created a bizarre business opportunity. Building prisons, staffing them, and exploiting the situation was something corporate America viewed as a growth industry. And communities, loath in the past to accept prisons, now often welcomed them because of the construction work and longer-term staffing positions they created in towns with failing economies. Who would have ever conceived of prisons as profit centers?

So much was going to be changing all around her that Gwendolyn Harding wondered if it might be wiser to simply resign before she was asked to leave. Every meeting with the men from JRU was more baffling than the last, and as she tried to articulate the folly of many of their proposed changes at Jennings, she herself could hear the defensive and petulant tone that crept into her voice. The men simply smiled and nodded as she voiced her concerns, all of them smirking in that way men smirk just before they accuse you of hysteria.

In the dimness, her feet shuffled along the uneven floors. It took only a split second for her toe to catch a ridge, and she was suddenly pitched forward. She felt herself toppling, but was helpless to stop herself. She managed to twist her shoulder to protect her face before she hit the floor, but the blow was a hard one. She hit the side of her forehead and knocked the wind out of herself. She tried to gasp for help, but couldn't as she blacked out.

The next thing Gwen knew, a pair of capable hands was holding her firmly and helping her up. 'You okay, Warden?' Movita Watson asked.

Gwen was dazed but managed to speak. 'I'm okay, but what are you doing out of your cell?'

'Infirmary visit. That time of the month,' Movita replied.

Gwen raised her hand to her head and felt the bump and the sticky wetness of blood. 'I guess I slipped,' she murmured.

'Just lean on me. It's okay,' Movita said.

Gwen leaned. She saw the young, white face of Roger Camry standing there looking useless. She felt dizzy and there was a sharp pain on the side of her neck.

'I'm all right,' she lied. 'Thank you. I'm all right.' She wasn't sure if that was true, but she hoped so. She found that her legs were steady. The lubrication of the gin had probably cushioned her fall. She tried to stand alone.

'I'll help you to the office,' Movita offered. 'She'll be fine,' she told Camry. 'Just fine. Come on,' Movita told Gwen.

'Warden, can I help you?' Camry asked as he approached them.

'I'm just fine,' Gwen lied, really shaken now. She supposed she was lucky that it was Roger Camry who had seen her fall rather than Doug Slavitz or that bastard Byrd, who would tell the entire prison and state management before morning. Camry was a good sort and would keep his mouth shut. But she was ashamed that she needed to depend on him and his kindness.

Both reluctant and grateful, Gwen went along with Movita. Did she know? Could she smell the gin? It was not far to her office and they walked in silence, Gwen feeling more pain with each step. At the door she fumbled in her pocket for her keys, but as she pulled them out, Movita took them from her hand and unlocked the office door. A total violation, but so was walking alone through the prison under the influence. Movita turned on the light with her left hand while still supporting Gwen with her right. Then the inmate helped the Warden to a chair.

'You sit here,' Movita said. 'I'm gonna get you some ice for that bang you got on the side of your head.'

Gwen again put her hand up to her forehead. It hurt, but was it also visible? Had Officer Camry seen it? How embarrassing! She listened to Movita's retreating steps. She knew how precious ice was for the inmates; it would take Movita some time to get some. Gwen wasn't so naive to what happened in her prison. All she needed was Frances to deliver kites on the rocks tomorrow and the whole population would know of her indiscretion. There was time; she reached into her drawer for the gin bottle, for just a small drink. She needed it.

When Movita came back with the ice, Gwen was slumped over her desk, the injured side of her face resting on a pile of folders. She felt no pain but she couldn't move. The last drink had done her in. 'I'm sorry,' she said to Movita. 'I'm not feeling well.'

Gently Movita lifted the Warden's head, removed the folders, and positioned the ice on the bump. 'I'll make you some coffee,' she said. 'Just a minute.'

Gwen's face was now against the ice. At first it felt good, then it began to burn and hurt. But she couldn't lift her head at all. If Movita was making coffee she must have realized that Gwen wasn't sober. She should know how hard I work, Gwen thought, what stress I'm under. I'm doing it for every inmate – Movita included. When Movita returned, Gwen spoke. 'There's something really terrible happening,' she said to Movita. 'That's one of the reasons I'm not feeling well.'

'I'm sorry,' Movita said casually, busy making a space on the desk and putting down the coffee.

'No, you don't understand,' Gwen continued. 'There's something new, something really terrible that might happen here at Jennings.'

'It's okay, Warden,' Movita said patiently, as if Gwen were a fretful child. 'Ain't nothin' gonna happen while I'm here.'

Gwen tried to raise her head. It was so frustrating. 'I'm not drunk,' she said. 'I'm being serious.'

Movita lifted the coffee cup and set it close to Gwen's head. 'Even the smell will help,' she said. 'Jus' inhale it. Then see if you can drink some.'

'Jennings may be privatized,' Gwen blurted out. 'The state will sell us all.' She heard the melodrama in her voice and she fell silent. She wasn't supposed to tell anyone this. What was she doing?

Movita stopped fussing and looked at her directly for the first time. 'Privatized?' Movita said. 'What d'you mean?'

With a huge effort Gwen managed to lift up her head. It felt good to talk to Movita. 'There's a company called JRU. They're the strangers who have been through here. They want to take over Jennings.' Damn it, she thought. I am drunk. She knew she shouldn't go on, but some lousy devil in her head was intent on blabbering everything. 'And conditions are going to get so much worse . . . It's just a terrible thing.' She felt tears rise and tremble on her lower lids. 'I can't stand it,' she said. She put her head back down, her face against the ice.

'Is this for sure?' Movita asked.

'No, but there's a good chance. They'll run the place like a factory. You and the other inmates will be the machinery and I'll be the oil.'

'Jesus Christ,' Movita muttered, sitting down in the chair next to Gwen. 'Jesus Christ.'

15

Cher McInnery

When Rebecca Cross was sent to prison, it was nine years before her children's first visit with her, because the trip . . . cost more money than she had.

Kathryn Watterson, *Women in Prison*

Cher McInnery shook her head, and her long dark hair flowed. 'Every time it's visitor's day here,' she said, 'you dumb bitches remind me of my daddy's huntin' dog.'

Floyd McInnery liked to kick his dog just to make a point. 'Ya' see that?' he'd ask his beer-drinking cronies. 'Ya' can kick Betty and she jist comes a-crawlin' back and licks your hand like she wants some more.' He'd laugh, take another guzzle and let out a belch; then with a sneer of what looked to Cher like unspeakable sadistic pleasure, he'd land his filthy old boot right in the middle of the poor dog's gut. There'd be a loud yelp, the old honey-brown coon dog would run about ten yards away, and then Floyd would holler, 'Get back here, ya' bitch.' Sure enough, the dog would come crawlin' back, her tail between her legs, her ears erect with hope for somethin' better from the drunken son-of-a-bitch. Most often he'd just kick her again. Sometimes Floyd would even suggest that one of his friends should try the trick. 'Go ahead,' he'd urge, 'kick the bitch. She likes it.'

At first, little Cher pitied the dog. She could barely stand to hear the thud, the yelp, and the laughter, but she couldn't turn away either. She'd stand and watch, and then wait for her father and his friends to leave so that she could go to old Betty and comfort her with a stew bone and some petting.

'Why do you let 'em do that, Betty?' she'd ask, searching the old dog's eyes for an answer. 'Bite 'em the next time,' she'd urge. She tried to retrain Betty to fight. 'Bite me!' she'd snarl at the cowering animal. 'Don't lick my hand, bite it! Fight back, ya' stupid damn dog!' Just once, Cher wanted old Betty to come back snarling with her fangs bared. Just once she wanted that dog to take a bite out of Daddy Floyd's ass.

But the next time would be the same, and so would the time after that, and eventually Cher's pity for the dog turned to anger, then to disgust, and finally to loathing. Cher couldn't help but think of old Betty every time she saw the women at Jennings preparing for visitor's day. She just shook her head when week after week after week they would get their hopes up and be all excited. They'd talk about how their boyfriends or their husbands – or even their daddies – were coming to see them, how the foster mother taking care of their kids swore that *this* time she was going to bring them. And then week after week after week they'd get kicked in the gut when not one of the bastards showed up. But they always went back for more.

'Kick the bitch, she likes it,' Cher would think as she

watched the anxious women rouge their cheeks with dried grape juice and line their eyes with eyeliner made from burnt matchsticks. Week after week after week the women would do their best to look their best for their men – the men who never showed up.

Cher never had a visitor on visitor's day, nor did she fool herself into thinking that she would. Her family was too scattered to come for a visit. But she didn't mind. Hell, with everyone else so damn distracted and actin' crazy it made it easier for her to do a little stealing. For Cher, visitor's day was like a day at the shopping mall. She didn't care if no one ever came to see her; she'd rather lift a few goodies from some dumb bitch who was downstairs getting her heart kicked out while waiting for some shiftless, useless man. As far as Cher could see, they were no smarter than old Betty. At first she had pitied them, too – but then came the disgust and the anger.

When the women came back to the cellblock crying about how disappointed they were, Cher just wanted to kick them and scream, 'Fight back, you stupid damn dog.' But instead, she stole from them, because when Cher was stealing she didn't have to think or feel bad. She remembered her mama and how pretty she used to look back when she and Cher used to go visit Uncle Silas at the Little Rock jail. They never missed one visitor's day all the while he was in there, but even back then Cher couldn't remember ever seeing a male visitor at that prison. No. Cher learned at an early age that the only visitors you can count on are mothers, sisters, and maybe a brave daughter now and then. So it pissed her off when women came back crying because some damn man hadn't showed up. They should be happy that they got to see anyone at all.

The only women Cher did feel sorry for were the ones with kids. Visitor's day was miserable for these inmates whether their kids came to see them or not. If someone did bring them, the babies were usually screaming and crying in fear, and the slightly older ones always asked too many questions like, 'Why are you wearing those clothes, mama?' or 'Why didn't you come to my birfday?' and the worst one: 'When are you coming home?' The older they got, the more ashamed they were to be coming to the prison at all. Since most of them had to grow up without their mothers, as they got older they glared at women they hardly knew, doing nothing to mask their anger, embarrassment, and discomfort. It would've been better if they hadn't come at all.

That's why Cher didn't understand why Movita went through worlds of trouble to arrange for visits with her little girls. Cher couldn't remember for sure the last time they had actually come to Jennings to see their mother. Since Movita hardly ever talked about them, or even showed anyone a picture of them, you sometimes forgot that she had any children. Cher always figured that's what Movita herself was trying to do and respected her for it. But Movita was acting real different lately. Cher could tell that something was bothering her – something was on her mind. When the lights-out alarm rang the night before visitor's day, Cher could tell that Movita was way too nervous to go to sleep. 'Ya' think it's such a good idea for those girls to come here?' Cher whispered to her.

'I'm gonna read 'em a story,' Movita answered. 'Went to the library today and had old Maggie pick me out a book for 'em.'

'That's nice,' Cher said simply. 'My mama used to read me stories.'

'Yeah,' Movita whispered. 'That's what a mama should do. A mama should read stories to her babies.'

Babies? How long since Movita had seen her girls? Cher didn't sleep that night, either. She worried about Movita. She was worried that the kids wouldn't show, or if they did, she worried about what Movita would see when she looked across the visitor's table. Cher sighed and knew there wasn't much she could do. She just hoped Movita would learn her lesson and not turn into a Betty. Then she decided that she'd steal something real nice for Movita. Maybe she could find a new hairbrush or some perfume. Movita loved a nice scent.

The cafeteria was always noisy at breakfast on visitor's day. Theresa in particular seemed to get especially loud when she knew she was having a guest – and Theresa always had a guest. Cher couldn't keep track of how many sisters Theresa had – it might be five, six, or seven – and sometimes there were also women who used to work for Theresa in the cosmetics business who still came for advice and motivation. But it didn't matter who came to see her or who didn't come to see her. As far as Theresa LaBianco was concerned, visitor's day was an occasion for great celebration.

'But don't it make you sad when it's over?' Suki asked her. 'It always makes me so sad when everyone leaves. It makes me lonelier than ever.'

'Well, you know what they say about loneliness, don't you?' Theresa began. 'Loneliness is what we call it when it's *painful* to be alone. But you know, there's another word – and that's *solitude*, and that's the word we use when we *want* to be alone. So when visitor's day is over, I just tell myself that I need a little solitude, that's all.' Theresa struck a dramatic pose and did a very bad imitation of Greta Garbo: 'I *vant* to be alone.'

'You're full of shit,' Cher said with a laugh. 'I love ya' – but you're full of shit.'

'Well, you know what they say about shit, don't you?' Movita asked.

'No,' Theresa said, falling for it like she did every time, 'I don't know. What do they say about shit?'

'Well if *you* don't know, then no one knows,' Movita said good-naturedly, causing the others to laugh.

Theresa laughed with them. Theresa could take a joke. Hell, Theresa *lived* for jokes. 'So is that good-looking lawyer coming to see you today, Cher?' she asked, batting her eyes.

'Yeah. Ain't it a pity that the only guy who comes to see a hottie like me is paid by the hour and doesn't stay long,' Cher chuckled.

'Lawyers are just like whores,' Movita said, picking up a spork full of grits. 'They're both paid by the hour and don't stay long.'

Theresa spoke up again. 'Hey, I *do* know a shit joke. What do you have when you have a lawyer buried up to his neck in shit?' she asked. She looked around the table to see if anyone had the answer. 'You don't have enough shit, that's all!'

The bell rang to signal the end of breakfast, and the crew stood up to return their trays to the conveyor belt. Cher winced when she noticed that Movita was carrying her damn storybook with her along with lollipops from Sally in Unit B. Now as they made their way toward the visitor's room, she stopped Cher. 'You gonna be down there for long today?' she asked.

Cher shook her head. 'Nah,' she answered, 'no reason to. And besides, I got me some errands to run,' she added with a wink.

Movita only nodded, then turned and followed the others out of the cafeteria. After they were out of sight, Cher followed as well. She guessed she wanted to be there to see Movita's face when she saw her little girls.

Cher wrinkled her nose as she entered the visitor's room, which always reeked of body odor and too much perfume as the crowd of nervous women quietly waited, watched, and listened for their names to be called out. Cher stayed at the back, where none of the crew would notice her. She wasn't alone. While most of the women who didn't have visitors stayed as far away as possible from the grim reminder of their loneliness, others – like Cher – stood and watched the more fortunate women with their guests. Cher was nearly on tiptoe, straining to see what was going on, but she could see no sign of Movita.

'Are you expecting someone, Cher?'

The question startled Cher and she spun around to face the debutante. 'Ain't none of your business who's coming,' she snapped at the newcomer. Then Cher caught sight of Movita on the other side of the room. A guard was handing her an envelope, and Cher could see it trembling in Movita's hand. She pushed the rich bitch aside and made her way through the crowd of waiting women.

By the time she got to Movita, the envelope was torn open and was lying on the floor at her feet. Movita was frozen into a statue. With one hand she held a crumpled wad of paper, and with the other she grasped two colorful crayon drawings to her breast, along with the storybook that she had brought with her from the library. Her face was a blank stare. Cher was relieved to see there were no tears; no visible anger. She had simply frozen.

'What happened, Mo?' Cher asked her gently. It wasn't necessary for everyone to see her in her moment of weakness. 'Where are your girls?'

'They ain't comin',' Movita said quietly. 'They ain't comin'.'

Cher took the crumpled letter from Movita's hand and read it. 'Goddamn bastards,' she hissed. 'Fuckin' cruel sons-of-bitches.'

'Watch yer mouth,' Movita shot back at her. 'I'm sick to death of yer filthy talk.'

At that moment Jennifer walked over with her tray of breakfast. Like Mo needed the sympathy of one more friggin' white girl. 'Suki told me you had it all arranged,' Jennifer said to Movita.

'Just who the hell are you to talk to me? Did I say ya' could speak to me? And I don't care what Suki told ya',' Movita snapped. 'Ya' thought I had it all arranged, huh? Well I ain't got nothin' arranged. Ya' got that? I ain't got nothin'.' She moved to push her way past Cher.

'Come on, honey,' Cher tried to comfort her. 'Come on. We'll go get ya' somethin' nice and new. Come on with Cher.'

'Just get your damn hands off me!' Movita suddenly shouted. 'Just keep away from me.' As she tried to push her way past them, the drawings and the storybook fell from her grasp and Movita collapsed onto the floor with them. One of the religion pimps – the churchgoing cranks who were always selling their brand of Jesus to the limp and the lost – started up with 'Sister, it's not too late to see the Lord's work in everything.'

'Shut the fuck up,' Cher told her, and in the moment she turned away the debutante was there kneeling beside Movita trying to help her. But when this Jennifer picked up one of the drawings Movita violently slapped her hand away from it. 'Keep your hands off it,' she snarled. 'That's from my baby. My baby drew that picture for her mama, and you keep yer hands off it. That's from my baby.'

With the paper shaking in her hand, Jennifer gave the drawing back to Movita as Cher helped the now sobbing woman to her feet. For a moment everyone else in the hot and crowded room was deadly silent.

Cher assured everyone that she had everything under control. She looked directly at Jennifer. 'She's my responsibility. I'm takin' her back to the cell,' she said protectively, and the crowd parted to let them pass. At the same time, a guard stepped over to where they were and said firmly, 'Miss Spencer, you have a visitor.'

16

Jennifer Spencer

Everywhere there is one principle of justice, which is the interest of the stronger.

Plato, *The Republic*

Tom hadn't disappointed her! Jennifer was actually going to see him, hold his hand. When she heard the officer say her name, her heart began to thump wildly and she almost ran to the guards to be processed and searched.

But when Jennifer walked into the visiting room, Tom wasn't sitting at any of the empty tables. She looked around, a little panicky; the noise from the inmates, the kids, and the other visitors seemed overwhelming. Then she saw her visitor. Her guest was not Tom Branston, it was Leonard Benson.

He was sitting at a large table, his dark head bent over a copy of *Forbes* magazine. He looked up, smiled, and took off his reading glasses. Jennifer tried to mask her disappointment as she crossed the room to welcome him, but her heart was still racing from excitement at being called. She actually felt the room tilt a little and start to spin. She held on to the corner of the Formica table and tried to take a deep breath. Lenny stood up and gestured to the seat opposite him. 'Lenny, what a surprise!' she managed to say.

'Yes,' he said. 'Thanks for giving me permission to visit. You don't mind that I came?'

'Of course not,' she said, and sank into the chair across from him. 'It's really good of you to come.' The words sounded forced and rather formal for a prison visiting room.

Jennifer's mind began to race. She only had one hour of visiting time. Where was Tom? Was he coming as well? She hadn't heard a confirmation or, for that matter, a decline from Tom, so she knew nothing.

'You look okay,' Lenny said, as if surprised. 'I mean, it's a shock to' – he gestured to her outfit, and to the room – 'you know, to see you here with all this.' He looked toward the officers and bars. 'But you look okay. Healthy, I mean.'

Jennifer looked around without searching for Tom. The room was stuffy and noisy. Most inmates sat across from other women. Children ran back and forth from tables to vending machines, making noise as they argued over soda selections and gobbled down candy bars. Some of the women cried, and so did some of the children. The rare male visitor, dressed in jeans and sneakers, seemed ill at ease.

'I'm all right. But not for long. It's . . . hard.' She didn't want to begin to cry so she forgot to be polite. 'Where's Tom Branston?' she asked Lenny. 'If I'm only allowed one visitor it should be him.'

It was Lenny's turn to mask his disappointment. 'I'm sorry,' he offered and shrugged. 'Tom couldn't make it, I guess. All I know is that I got a call from the Warden's office yesterday. My request for a visit had been approved, so I came.'

'But you've seen Tom at the office?' Jennifer said. 'Did you tell him you were coming? Did he say he was? Or did he give you a message for me?'

Lenny shook his head. 'I haven't told him and I haven't seen him,' Lenny said. 'He hasn't been at the office, or if he was, he kept a real low profile.'

Once again Jennifer searched the room for any signs of her fiancé. 'Well, when I spoke to him he told me he was really busy with my appeal, or even a pardon.' She looked at Lenny directly. His brown eyes seemed to brim with pity for her. Jen hated that so much that she pulled herself together. She couldn't bear to be the object of Lenny Benson's pity.

'Um . . . is there anything you need?' Lenny tried again. There was a long pause. 'Did you get the package I sent?'

Jennifer's eyes, which had been skidding like a rat from table to table, suddenly focused on Lenny's face and his question. 'Yes,' she replied, turning her gaze directly to his. His eyes were kind. 'Yes I did receive it. Thank you,' she said simply. 'Your gifts were wonderful.'

On his side of the table, Lenny blushed. 'I did a little research and read a magazine article about women in pris –' He stopped abruptly, embarrassed. 'About women in . . . places like this. It said that getting packages is very important. It also gave me some ideas about what to send.'

'Where did you read an article like that?' Jen asked, and almost giggled. 'Did they run it in *Forbes*?'

'I looked it up on the Internet,' he said. 'I didn't know if you used toothpaste or gel, so I got both.'

'Listen, it was great to get anything.' She thought of the

day the package came and how touched she'd been. 'It helped me make friends,' she said. 'I certainly didn't expect it or . . .' She was going to say 'deserve it' but she also didn't deserve the punishment she was getting, either. So they were both silent again.

'Did you know that you're not allowed to have dental floss?' he asked nervously.

'No. Why not?'

'I guess you can use floss with an abrasive kitchen cleanser like Comet and actually saw through the metal. I read that online, too,' he admitted. Then he shrugged. 'I'm so sorry for babbling,' he apologized. 'I guess I'm a little nervous.'

Jennifer nodded and another silence hung between them. Jennifer looked around at the gate through which visitors came.

'Do you want me to go?' Lenny asked. 'If you're expecting Tom or anyone else I . . .'

'No. That's fine,' Jennifer assured him. 'I'm sorry I'm so distracted. One of the women here just had a disappointment, a kind of breakdown. It was hard to watch. And I was really hoping Tom would come and, well . . .' She stopped and looked across at him.

'Does everyone miss me at Hudson, Van Schaank?' Jennifer asked lightly.

Once again Lenny colored. Then he shrugged and looked away. Lenny could not tell her anything that was not true. 'You know how people at the firm are,' he said, and Jennifer nodded in resignation. Most of her coworkers were extremely competitive. Selfish. Self-absorbed. Jealous. Vindictive. They hadn't enjoyed watching her huge success.

Still, Jennifer couldn't quite accept or believe what he

seemed to be telling her. Then it hit her. Donald Michaels, of course. He wouldn't just abandon her. He was concerned about her welfare, he wanted to know that she was all right. But he certainly wasn't free to come to the prison, not if he was under the media scrutiny that Tom had described. He must have been the one who had asked Lenny to send the package. And he must have sent Lenny now to try to take care of her until they got this all straightened out. 'Did Donald ask you to come?' she whispered.

'No,' Lenny told her, but perhaps he was being overly cautious.

'It's all right, Lenny. You can tell me.'

Lenny leaned in to the table, put both his elbows on it, and extended one hand across to her. Very gently he touched her forearm, and then held it. His hand was surprisingly big and his fingers wrapped around her wrist like a bracelet. 'Listen, Jennifer,' he said, his voice even more gruff than usual and his eyes – such a deep, deep brown – staring directly into her own. 'Listen,' he repeated, 'I think you're going to be really disappointed if you expect much from Donald. I've been around him longer than you have. I admit that when things go well for him he's a generous guy. But when they don't, or when they get complicated . . . well, let's just say that if he's the general partner and you're the limited partner when the deal gets audited *he's* not going down.'

Jennifer felt her arms go gooseflesh, even where Lenny was holding her. She pulled back from him. 'Don't tell me that Donald has forgotten me,' she said, and realized that her voice had risen. A few of the people at the other tables turned to look. She forced herself to stay calm. 'Tom told me that things are going slower than they expected but that it will be fine. Donald is one hundred percent behind me on this.'

Lenny shook his head. 'Jennifer, I'm afraid Donald is ahead of you. That's my point.' He took his arms off the table.

She felt fury mixed with fear rise in her. She wanted to slap his face right then, throw his glasses onto the floor and stomp on them. 'Donald isn't going to renege. And even if he wanted to, Tom won't let him. He's taking care of everything,' she hissed.

Lenny looked away and nodded. 'I'm sure you're right. I just don't want you to be disappointed,' he said. 'And I want you to know that you can call me anytime, day or night. You have my cell phone number, right?'

Jen shook her head. Why would she need his cell number? She realized that she hated Lenny Benson, with his long nose and his five o'clock shadow and his damned wet eyes. She just wished this negative, boring man would leave. He probably meant well, but he was frightening and upsetting her. She wouldn't tell him to shove off, but she just sat there, silently waiting for him to do it.

'So?' he asked, finally standing up. 'Is there anything else I can get for you or send to you?'

'I'm not going to be here that long,' Jennifer said defiantly. She stared intently at Lenny for some reassurance, but he said nothing. 'I'm *not*. Tom says I'm going to be out of here in just a couple of weeks.'

Lenny nodded, then handed her his card. 'I know the office number,' she said and smiled.

'It has my home and cell on the back. Call me anytime. I mean it,' he said, and he walked away.

17

Maggie Rafferty

Good laws lead to the making of better ones; bad ones bring about worse.

Jean Jacques Rousseau, *The Social Contract*

I looked up from the letter that I was writing to my son to see Movita Watson standing in the doorway. Movita didn't come to the library often. She'd probably read any of the books worth reading before I arrived here. Also, she already had the job in the Warden's office, which gave her something comparatively interesting to do. So when I saw her there, coming to see *me* rather than to get a book, I was pleased.

She glowered. 'You're lookin' glad to see me,' she said. 'Don't make me feel bad. I ain't got no good news.'

I had, of course, heard about the incident in the visitor's room. When you're as high-profile and respected as Movita Watson, something like that doesn't go by unnoticed.

'Brought back some books,' Movita said, and pushed

Make Way for Ducklings and *Sarah, Plain and Tall* across my makeshift desk.

I laughed – something I rarely do anymore. 'I don't expect good news,' I told her. 'I'm imprisoned, not crazy.'

Movita smiled. She had the most beautiful mouth – I'd once seen those lips on the Thanos Venus. 'I got a couple a questions, and you're the only one might have answers. You don't mind, do ya'?'

'Please,' I said. 'Of course not.' I've always respected Movita Watson. When I first came here I was viewed as a thing, a celebrity. She was the only one who looked at me as if I were a person. The other women's eyes glossed over me as if I were invisible. Because I'm old, of course. An older woman brings to prison neither looks nor style, nor anything from the Outside that is of interest to the incarcerated. The one thing that caused unfailing interest among my social peers, the fact that I shot my husband, wasn't an interesting point to anyone at Jennings: It was no big deal as a crime.

Now Movita sat down in the only other chair in the library and frowned at the floor. She didn't usually mince words. When she started to speak, she did so very slowly.

'The first thing I wanna know is, what exactly is "privatization"?'

I almost laughed again. Was Movita thinking about investing in East German railroads? 'It depends,' I said, 'on the circumstances. There's always talk about possibly privatizing the U.S. Post Office, for instance. That means that it would no longer be run by the government but would be purchased by a private company or different companies, and run by them.'

Movita nodded. 'Why do they do it?'

'Well, sometimes it's assumed that the government lacks the skill and ability to run the business efficiently but that private enterprise could.'

'But why would they *wanna*?' Movita asked me, crossing her legs and settling back into the chair.

'For the same reason they do anything. They think that they can make a profit on it.'

'A profit, huh?' Movita frowned at me, then looked back at the floor and was silent for several seconds. I could tell she was torn, something rare in her strong personality. 'Yer sons know all 'bout this stuff, don't they?' she asked.

'As a matter of fact, yes, they do.'

Movita frowned again. I had to admit that I was curious. 'What's this about?' I finally asked.

Movita looked around the empty room, leaned forward and reached into her jumpsuit. For a moment I was afraid that she had contraband, and I was relieved when she took out a sheaf of papers.

'You'd betta take a look at these,' she said, handing the papers to me. They were still warm from her body. 'There's somethin' happenin' here, and from what ya' say, it's a real bad thing.' She looked past me across the room and spoke as if to herself. 'Profit? I didn't understand. Jesus Christ!'

I unfolded the thick pile of papers and saw the business logo at the top of the first sheet. *JRU*. I had never heard of them, but what did that mean? I had a large portfolio, not that it did me any good, but my sons managed it.

I quickly read the first few pages. It was, indeed, a proposal for privatization. I continued to read.

Movita was right. From the beginning it sounded very bad. The way they talked about Jennings, as if it were a poorly run factory or a chicken farm that didn't produce enough eggs, was shocking. In the dozen pages that I quickly read there was no indication at all that there were human beings living in Jennings. I guess JRU didn't consider prisoners people.

'My god,' I said, looking up from the white pages. I'm sure my face was equally white. 'I'm waiting for them to suggest trying out experimental drugs on us as a profit center. Except that there's no mention of us yet.'

'And it gets worse,' Movita told me. She stood up. 'I gotta go back to work,' she said. 'I ain't gonna tell ya' that I never seen that and neither have you.' I nodded my understanding. 'I'm gonna leave it with ya' to read. I'll come back. 'Cause we gotta talk about it.'

I gathered the papers off my desk and put the proposal on my lap. Then I looked up at her. I didn't know what to say.

'It looks bad, don't it?' she asked. I nodded. 'You got it for two hours.'

I took out a legal pad and my fountain pen. I began to read from the beginning, jotting down notes as I went. It seemed as if JRU had done a thorough study of the facility. Every room, including my closet of a library, was measured down to the inch. JRU had found that most of the space was 'underutilized'. The visitor's room was used once a week and sat empty the rest of the time. The cafeteria had a two-hundred-person capacity and only one hundred thirty-five inmates ate there. It also was empty for a good part of the day. The library was 'unnecessary' because books could be listed, the list given out, and then a book cart circulated throughout the cells. Human needs – like the need for air, light, privacy, a place to cry – were all disregarded. I could hardly believe what I was reading, but JRU seemed to be saying that prisoners should spend more time in their cells! When they weren't working, that is.

My chest was tightening up. For some time I've experienced a kind of mild angina-type pain but ignored it as best I could. This, however, was a vise. I waited for it to pass, for the blackness to turn to red and then clear. I took a few breaths and read on.

The plan appeared to be that the inmates must become productive. Jennings was going to become a factory! Now I am the last person to object to work, but this was not work that they were proposing. It was slavery. Pay would be minuscule. Jennings would become a concentration camp. Inmates would be either in the 'production rooms' or in their cells all but one hour of every day. Breakfast and dinner would be 'prefabricated' à la airplane meals and delivered to cells to save time! Lunch would be delivered to 'work stations' and eaten alone.

I was having trouble breathing by this time and should have stopped, but this was my future they were planning. I was sixty-four years old and had had at least my share of hell in my life. I couldn't stand to have any more. I set the proposal down on my lap and looked across the room at the books on the shelf. My eyes teared up. Pathetic of me, I know, but I loved them, even *The Power of Positive Thinking*. A most terrible thought struck me. What if I wouldn't have any time to read?

A person of my age can never experience physical distress without thinking the worst, and I am no exception. I was finding it impossible to get my breath and feared I was having a heart attack. But so what? I thought, perhaps it was better this way. I would rather die than live as a slave to an inhuman system. Every cell of my being rebelled against it. In fact, if I didn't die, I would have to kill myself, I decided, as the proposal slipped off my lap and fell to the floor. Why should I want to live on? Already it was a strain.

I started to weep, which relieved the pressure in my chest. I hadn't wept in years. What a front I kept up, even to myself! Then, to my horror, I heard a noise at the door. If it was that damnable Officer Byrd about to do another malicious shakedown, I thought I might bodily attack him. But it was Jennifer Spencer who walked in. Tears streaked my face, my hair was awry, but worst of all, the proposal was splayed all over the floor. If a CO walked in and found it, it wouldn't just jeopardize me and my position as librarian, it would also hurt Movita and anyone else who'd assisted in getting a hold of the proposal in the first place.

I tried to bend down to pick up the papers, and as I did I felt every year of my age. It isn't easy getting old anywhere, but in prison it's almost impossible. I could only manage to pull myself up to the little table that served as a desk. I must have looked dreadful, for Miss Spencer hurried over to me. 'What is it? Are you ill?' she asked.

'No. No,' I answered weakly. 'I'm just . . . very upset.'

'You're very pale. Should I take you to the nurse? Can I get you something?'

'No. I'm okay.'

Jennifer sat down across from me, where Movita had been sitting.

'Can I help in any way?'

I was touched by her manner. But I couldn't say anything.

Jennifer noticed the papers on the floor and knelt to pick them up. I made a gesture but couldn't stop her. Luckily, in her concern for me she just collected them and set them on the desk without looking at them. Then she looked back at me with a face I'm very familiar with, though I hadn't seen it in a while. It consisted of three parts: recognition and surprise, followed by embarrassment. Jennifer Spencer realized who I was. I suppose it was my ghastly look. I had looked ghastly all through the trial, in all the pictures in the newspapers.

'I see you recognize me now,' I said softly to keep her distracted while I tore the sheets with my notes off the pad and folded them. I was still feeling dreadfully bad, but I could breathe, not that I much wanted to. 'Don't be embarrassed. I'm quite used to people knowing more about me than I do about them.'

'I'm not,' she said. 'It's just a bit of a surprise.' She paused. 'I followed your case.'

'And I yours,' I told her. 'Now, can I help you?'

'Did something just happen, or are you ill? Should I call someone?'

'That's the last thing I want,' I said. 'I'll be okay.'

She nodded, and though she looked a little doubtful, went over to the bookshelves. 'I never thought you were guilty,' she said.

'But I was.'

'How long are you here for? I don't remember the sentence.'

I froze. The question was not a welcome one. It brought back the specter of more years, more and more years. 'My dear,' I said, 'I'm going to give you some advice that you will do well to follow.'

'What?' she asked.

'Never ask anyone here their crime or their time. Not unless you're looking for trouble.'

Her eyes dropped. I must say that at that moment I liked her. I pulled myself up in the chair, took the proposal off the windowsill and secreted it under me along with the notes. 'Did you want a book?'

She looked at me, confused.

'You came in here. Did you want a book?'

'Oh. Yes. I was hoping to look at some law books.' She gave the collection a doubtful look. 'Whatever you have.'

'Torts, I assume.' She nodded, and perhaps she blushed. 'We have one, and it's over there. You can't miss it. It's next to *Grow Your Own Terrarium*.'

Jennifer retrieved the book. She came back to my desk. 'Do I need to sign anything?' she asked.

Wordlessly, I handed her the sign-out sheet.

'You sure you're okay?' she asked again.

I nodded. She signed the sheet, took the book, and with one more look at me left the library.

In prison, like in life, one must learn to trust in very small things for happiness. A shaft of light that falls, just so, across the hall each afternoon. The comfort of soft slippers on the feet. A sugar cookie melting on the tongue. A smile. I sat still, waiting for some kind of clarity to return. When it did, I picked up the report again and read it through, but I didn't have the heart to take notes. As it was, I had to stop frequently to remind myself to breathe.

It seemed hours before Movita returned. When she saw me her face fell. 'So ya' read the thing,' she said.

'Yes.'

'It's bad, huh?'

I nodded.

'It's as bad as it seems?'

'No,' I told her. 'It's much worse.'

18

Jennifer Spencer

> *You better believe that being locked up and at the mercy of these people is hell.*
>
> Delia Robinson, former inmate. Andi Rierden, *The Farm*

Once again, the work in the laundry was unbearably hot and tedious. A seemingly endless train of carts filled with fouled sheets, musty towels, and smelly uniforms was wheeled into the room where the laundry was unloaded, sorted, and stuffed into the huge washing machines. Then the great heavy armfuls of steaming wet laundry were lifted into the dryer, and finally run through the enormous ironing machines. With each new step in the process the temperature in the room rose exponentially as the heat and the humidity transformed the laundry into a tropical inferno.

Jennifer's rage intensified with the heat. Tom had better have some kind of terrific explanation before she would forgive him for this hell she was in. Though she kept telling herself that it would all be over soon, it couldn't be soon enough. Why was it taking so long? What in the hell was he doing? And why hadn't she been able to reach him? Three times in as many days she'd called and gotten only his voicemail.

As Jennifer summoned the physical strength to heft the heavy loads of hot, steaming laundry, she grew emotionally weaker. She thought about the surprise visit from Lenny Benson. Was he just nervous and naturally negative or had he been trying to warn her, prepare her for . . . what? Her tears began to intermingle with the steam and perspiration; her hair hung in a tangled mop of sweat on her brow.

Jennifer stopped to study her hands. They were already red and swollen from the harsh chemicals of the detergents, but at least the ink on her fingertips had finally been washed away. In a way she was sorry to see it go; it was the only enduring reminder of who she had been on the day she entered this place. She continued to stare at her hands and wondered how long it would take to get them back to normal. The chapping might heal and the color would return, but she doubted that the horror of these days and nights would ever fade from her memory.

Try as she might, Jennifer could no longer remember the justification for this gamble she'd taken and the strength of her belief that Tom and Donald were right when they told her that this was all going to be so easy. Why had she been so sure of herself? Jennifer looked over at Suki, who pulled over a canvas cart and emptied it into a dryer. Jennifer felt so sorry for herself and so pathetic that she stood there wringing her hands and mindlessly caressing the naked finger where Tom's engagement ring had once been.

'Hey you! Debutante! Wake up and get to work,' shouted Flora.

Jennifer squared her shoulders, took a deep breath, and

wiped away her tears. The astringent odor of bleach from the wet laundry burned her eyes as she continued with the soul-numbing labor.

That night, back in the cell, Suki took one of her chafed hands, looked into Jennifer's eyes, and asked why she had been crying. 'I think I must be allergic to the soaps and stuff,' Jen told her.

'Yeah? What detergent did you use at home?' Suki asked. Jen was too ashamed to tell her that she hadn't done her own laundry in almost a decade. Instead she merely blamed the red and swollen puffiness on the bleach. She wasn't going to admit to any weakness – not even to Suki. She decided that she was going to close the door on that existential chasm of anxiety threatening to swallow her. She'd trust Tom's love and Donald's respect for her. She had to. She had nothing else in which to trust or believe. There was one good thing about the work in the laundry: She would sleep tonight.

Suki was sitting quietly in the chair next to the table, patting her belly. 'You sure you're okay, Jenny?' she asked.

Jennifer mumbled only a 'Yeah' in reply. Lately, Jennifer had begun to doubt that Suki was pregnant at all. She certainly didn't appear any fatter. It could simply be a pathetic attempt to get more attention from the crew.

'Me and the girls had a pretty greasy supper,' Suki admitted. 'How was yours?' she asked as she stood up and started to get ready for bed.

Jennifer didn't answer. She didn't want to talk about her supper. She didn't want to talk at all. She turned her back to the well-meaning girl and stared at the wall, willing her eyes to pierce the dirty pink concrete and to look beyond to the walls of her own beautiful apartment. What wall is Tom looking at tonight? she wondered.

'I'm sorry,' Suki spoke in a whisper, 'but I have to use the toilet.'

Jennifer merely grunted. A moment later Suki grunted as well. Every tired and aching muscle in Jennifer's body threatened to cramp in the dank, sick chill of nausea that washed over her. She shut her eyes tightly and tried to deny the reality that Suki was suffering from diarrhea just inches from her head. Her own stomach was about to betray her as it churned the prison meal that she had so hungrily devoured.

The lights-out bell rang in concert with Suki's flush, and as Jennifer was plunged into the dark and horrifying reality of where she was, the last thing that she saw was the dirty pink paint on the wall.

'Sorry,' Suki said again as she slipped into her bunk. 'It'll be morning before you know it.'

'I'm fine,' Jennifer assured her. 'I just hate these damn pink walls, that's all.'

'Yeah, I try always to tell myself that it's the color of a sunset,' Suki said.

Jennifer let out a derisive snort of disbelief. 'Uh huh,' she sighed, 'a sunset.' She closed her eyes and tried to envision the sky; she couldn't remember the last time she had really looked at it. Somehow she was always rushing, always looking down at her computer screen or a memo or a proposal.

Jennifer stretched, and in the dark her hand reached out and brushed against something warm. It was another hand and it held hers. Then, all along her left side she felt Tom's long lean body beside her. 'Get closer,' he whispered as he often did when they made love. 'Get closer.'

Beneath her Jennifer felt the sand give and she rolled into position beside him. 'Let's stay like this all night,' he whispered, and she could feel his arms tighten around her. She couldn't speak; there was something in her throat, but she could nod and in her mind she said, 'Let's stay like this forever.'

'Yes, forever,' Tom agreed, and for a moment she wondered how he could hear her thoughts. Then she opened her eyes. 'Look,' he said. 'It's the dawn.' And she could see that they were lying on a beach and that a thin line of light was illuminated along the horizon. The sky was just beginning to color and she remembered that they'd been married and now they were on their honeymoon. How could I have forgotten that? she thought, and she felt Tom laughing beside her. Now that they were married and on this beach, she realized that she would never have to struggle again. It had all been worth it: The studying and the competition for grades and scholarships and the work on the papers she had written and all the time she'd put in on the job had paid off with this. His arms were around her and he loved her and the warm sea was beginning to turn the palest aqua as light continued to fill the sky. It was the most beautiful dawn she had ever seen and Jennifer felt her heart beating in her chest against Tom's own heartbeat. She would never have to be alone or frightened again. She felt a deep peace flow into her as if it had come in on a wave from the Caribbean and washed away all of her anxiety. She was safe. She was loved. She was not alone.

It was the smell more than the noise that woke her. The sour, stomach-rocking scent of vomit was in her nose, down her throat. She opened her eyes and realized with horror that she'd been dreaming. Tom, the sand, the sea and her security were all gone. She was staring, not at the sky but up at the bottom of the bunk on top of her while Suki was making *awe, awe* noises just two feet away from her head.

'I'm sorry I woke you up,' Suki said. Jennifer began to tremble. In the confusion of waking she couldn't tell which was worse, losing that feeling of being bathed in Tom's love or remembering that she was imprisoned here. All she wanted was to close her eyes and go back to that beach and that feeling. She wanted to spend the rest of her life in that dream.

'You okay?' Suki asked. 'You were trying to talk or something in your sleep.' Jennifer knew it was hopeless to try to return to her dream, but giving it up made her feel desperately bereft. She turned her head and looked at the exhausted blonde child who sat on the floor next to the toilet. 'Do you want to talk about it?' Suki asked her.

Jennifer shook her head and turned her back to Suki. No, she still didn't want to talk to Suki about her precious dream. She wanted to live it. She wasn't one of these illiterate, victimized, stupid women. She had a future.

She heard Suki stand up. 'My grandmother said that a dream was God's way of telling the brain something that the heart already knows,' Suki told her as she rinsed the bowl of the toilet.

Jennifer did not – could not – respond. She turned her face to the wall and pulled the blanket over her head and tucked it in. If only when she opened her eyes the next time and took the blanket down she could see something other than the dirty pink paint on the cement walls of her cell. She had a terrible feeling that she would never again feel that tremendous love from Tom.

* * *

Jennifer tried to call Tom the next morning before laundry detail but no one answered his phone at home. His office number and his cell only got voicemail. She thought about the dozens of times he and she had looked at their caller ID and laughed or grimaced and refused to answer. I can't let myself get paranoid, she thought. That night Jennifer tried to remain calm as she attempted, once again, to reach Tom Branston. She got to the phone in the rec room, which was the usual zoo, but she was even more than usually agitated. She was desperate to talk with him. She *had* to. And she had to *see* him. Her heart skipped as the intense feeling from her dream moved through her. She had felt so loved, and so loving. Without the dream she actually felt abandoned. Jennifer shook her head to clear away the ridiculous feeling. Tom wasn't in the Caribbean lying on a beach with her but neither had he abandoned her. He was working to get her released.

She waited in line again and tried his office once more. This time the phone was picked up, but by a secretary whose voice Jen didn't recognize. 'Please put Tom Branston on the line,' Jennifer snapped into the phone. 'This is Jennifer.' She knew several of the women inmates were watching and listening, so she tried to keep her back to them and smile as she waited, but the smile quickly faded when the secretary responded.

'I'm sorry,' the voice said. 'He can't come to the phone.'

'What do you mean he can't come to the phone? You haven't even told him who was calling!'

'He asked not to be disturbed. Perhaps you can call back later.'

Jennifer's voice rose sharply. 'No, I can't call back later.

I'm in prison, goddamn it!' and she slammed down the phone.

Jennifer looked at the clock. She had forty-five minutes before work detail and she absolutely had to hear the sound of Tom's voice. Worse than that, she needed to be reassured that he existed – that anything Outside existed. She was watching the line of women still waiting for the phone when Movita sat down beside her. 'Tryin' to reach your lawyer or your boyfriend?' she asked her, but Jennifer didn't want to bother to explain. She just nodded her head.

'What can a goose do, that a duck can't, and a lawyer should?' Movita asked. Jennifer shrugged. 'Shove its bill up its ass,' Movita said and laughed.

To her surprise, Jennifer laughed, too. She didn't usually like vulgarity, but the joke was so unexpected that it caught her off guard. And, Jennifer thought, it wouldn't hurt to be nice to this woman, considering she could put in a good word for her with the Warden.

'Ya' gonna grind yer wheels right down to the spokes,' Movita volunteered. 'Not that you asked, and not that it's none of my bidness. Speaking of that, what exactly was it that ya' did on Wall Street? You some kinda hot shot, huh?'

'I was in venture capital and IPOs,' Jennifer told her.

'And what would that mean?' the woman asked.

'I help companies raise money to get started or to expand.'

'Any kind of company?' Movita asked.

'Just about.'

'How ya' know 'bout all kinds of companies, all kinds of bidnesses?'

The woman didn't sound hostile, exactly, but she sounded more than idly curious. Jennifer was in no mood to give a lecture on stocks, capitalism, and the American way. 'I don't know everything about every business,' Jennifer told her. 'I just know how to look at the finances of a business, compare it to its past and look at its future to decide if it's a good bet.'

Movita looked intently into Jennifer's eyes. 'Ya' usually right?' she asked.

'Usually,' Jennifer told her.

'Then how come you're here?' Movita asked.

Jennifer shrugged. 'No one seems to understand,' she said. 'I'm not *supposed* to be here.'

Now it was Movita's turn to laugh. 'Honey, ya' don't understand,' she said. 'Ain't none of us *supposed* to be here. What God of mercy would want women penned up in a place like this?'

'Yeah. And kept from your children. I'm really sorry.'

The black woman's eyes flashed. Her whole body stiffened and Jennifer could actually see her elbows, knees, and spine tremble. 'Look, forget about that. You was nice and that was fine, but I don't get visitors and I don't 'spect them. That was just unexpected, that's all. It won't happen again.'

'I'm sorry,' Jennifer said. She hadn't asked this crazy woman to sit down next to her and now she was sorry she had. She looked again at the line and realized that she wouldn't get another shot at the phone before work. Movita followed her eyes.

'Ya' really need to talk to him?' she asked. Jennifer nodded, not that it would do any good. 'Come on,' Movita said and walked to the front of the line.

Jennifer followed her. ''Scuze me, Pearl,' Movita said to the short Latina woman standing there waiting to be the next one at the telephone. 'Do ya' mind if the debutante uses the phone next? Would ya' give up yer place to her as a special favor to me?'

Pearl looked from Movita to Jennifer, then back to Movita. 'Okay,' she said, 'for you, Mo.' She gave Movita a nod and a look passed between them that Jennifer couldn't read. Pearl walked away and Movita motioned for Jennifer to take her place.

'Hey, wait a minute,' said the old crone with a long gray braid who was standing next in line. Movita raised her hand, extending her fingers out.

'Don't you talk at me, Helen,' Movita said. 'We have a situation here. Ya' had one person in front of ya' a minute ago and ya' got one person in front of ya' now. What's your beef?' Helen began to talk but Movita raised her hand again. 'Helen, don't mouth me. Ya' like to take advantage, but ya' know you've been in situations yourself. Hush now.'

And the woman did. Just like that. Jennifer waited a moment to thank Movita, but she didn't get a chance to because the woman on the phone in front of her hung up. Jennifer didn't waste a second and ran to the waiting receiver.

19

Movita Watson

> *I haven't seen my daughters for five years. I know I'm their mother, and I guess they know I'm their mother, but what kind of mother is that? . . . Thinking about it makes me feel dead inside.*
>
> A prisoner at the Federal Reformatory for Women in Alderson, West Virginia. Kathryn Watterson, *Women in Prison*

Even before 'the incident', I'd have to say that the Warden and I have an interesting kinda relationship. Without ever saying a word 'bout it, we help each other. She's a stickler for details and likes to do everything by the book, but she can't be blamed for that. Probably how she got the job. Anyway, she does things for me and I do things for her. It's good for me to have this, not jus' because of the benefits for me and the crew, but also 'cause it keeps me busy and gives me somethin' to think about. The thing I most hate is to have empty time to remember the past and think 'bout the future.

Anyway, the Warden hinted very strongly that she wanted me to take Jennifer Spencer into our crew. 'Movita,' she says, 'you can help that girl.' At first I think, fuck! I should help a rich white girl? What the fuck ever for? But then I'm thinkin' further that maybe she has a point. I'm no hardass mean bitch and Jennifer would probably help the crew as much as we'd help her. She's got a lot of money in the canteen – the fund for prisoners who wanted to buy extra food instead of having cafeteria crap. Of course, even so, I knew I'd have trouble with Cher. Soon as I brought the subject up I did.

It was visitor's day again, and as usual we were all tense as could be, especially Cher.

'Why the hell should we take *her* in?' Cher said, as I knew she would. 'She ain't done nothin' for us 'cept sharin' some toothpaste!' She was rubbin' red pencil on her fingernails, which I thought was ridiculous.

'That's gonna come off soon as you wash,' I said to her. 'Why you doin' it?'

'It's somethin' to do,' Cher said.

'Well, it don't even look good,' I told her, though I didn't blame her. Any stupid thing that passes the time here is worth doin'. Theresa puts together those same jigsaw puzzles and then, when she's finished, she just breaks them down and starts over. Would drive me crazy, but I don't judge her. 'Well, I say we'll benefit from Spencer bein' in crew and that's a good enough reason. It ain't no crime for her to be rich, Cher. You would be if you could.'

'Damn right I would,' Cher answered, holding out her hands. She was trying to admire them, but she couldn't do it. 'Fuck. I gotta wash this shit off.'

'Anyway,' I continued, 'it wouldn't hurt us to have her come over, check her out some more.'

'I checked her in,' Cher said, 'and I'm not interested.'

I looked at Cher, compellin' her to look back. 'Don't matter if you're interested or not,' I said to her, 'Spencer's in. I've asked Suki to bring her on over this morning.' Cher just shrugged, but I knew she was pissed.

You see, the thing is, with the JRU people breathin' down our neck, and with the Warden concerned, havin' someone like Spencer on our side might be a real good thing. Plus, the thought struck me then that once Cher was gone, which wasn't very far away, crew'd just be me and Theresa and Suki. Lord Jesus, it was a good thing the Warden had the idea to bring Spencer in. I was gonna need somebody to talk to.

Cher was still sulkin' when Suki came in with Jennifer. Yeah, I thought as I looked her over, she sure does look like a rich white girl that ain't gonna fit in. But then she says, 'Did you want to talk to me, Movita?' And then she smiled so nice and self-assured that I sorta figured that it might work out after all. Jennifer Spencer has a power attitude. And the Warden needs that right now. Maybe we can, between us, make it so this JRU thing ain't as bad as it could be.

'Sure did,' I said, real casual-like. 'I thought Suki and the rest of us could help get you all ready for visitor's day.'

Cher let out a disgusted little snort, but Suki just squealed she was so happy. 'You can borrow my curlers, Jenny,' she said.

I'm not sure Jennifer Spencer really wanted our help, but she was goin' to get it. Maybe it was kinda like an initiation or somethin'. Anyway, I went over and got Theresa to come and help, and after a lot of laughin' and havin' a good time, our new crewmate was all ready to meet her visitor.

'There. You look great now,' Suki told Spencer.

I damn near laughed out loud when that poor, little rich white girl picked up the mirror and looked at herself. She didn't look great at all. She looked like a cheap whore. After Suki was finished, all that smooth and silky dark hair of hers was a frizzy old mop. But Spencer didn't say a word.

'Great, huh?' Suki asked again.

'Oh yeah,' she told Suki.

'But that's not all,' Theresa said. 'Look what I got for you.' She opened her palm to show her a chapstick, but Spencer just looked at her.

'Open the cap,' Theresa said, but she pulled the cap off herself. Instead of the clear wax the stick was red. 'Adobe Red,' Theresa told her. 'Here,' she reached over and put it on her. 'Want some for your cheeks?' she asked.

'No. No, thanks.' Spencer stood up before Suki could get at her. I could tell that she didn't want to wipe the lipstick off right in front of Theresa, but I also knew she didn't want to wear it anymore either.

'Gosh, I wish someone was coming to see me,' Suki said. 'Even just a lawyer. Cher got some good-looking lawyers.'

'He's not just my lawyer, he's my fiancé,' Jennifer said.

'Oh, wow! Does he know about your boyfriend?' Suki asked her.

'Lenny is not my boyfriend,' Jennifer told her, looking around at the rest of us kinda embarrassed.

'Wait,' Suki said, 'your accountant is not your boyfriend and your lawyer is your fiancé.' Then she shook her head. 'And people say I'm stupid.'

We all laughed – even Cher. And Spencer laughed, too.

'You need some mascara,' Suki said, looking at Jennifer.

'I think Cher's got some,' Theresa said, all cagey-like.

'How do *you* know?' Cher asked.

'Because I saw that Diane from Unit C leaving today.

She was all dressed up, but she didn't have any makeup on. I figure you got to it before she got her effects back.'

Cher laughed in that evil way of hers, and then leaned over to pull a box out from beneath her bunk. 'Stand back girls, it's my turn to help out our little debutante here.' The box was absolutely filled to overflowing with good makeup that Cher had swiped.

I just shook my head at her and said, 'One of these days you're gonna be busted and you'll blow your parole stealing shit like that.'

But nobody paid no mind to what I said. I think everybody was more worried that Cher was gonna put Spencer's eye out with the mascara brush. But pretty soon we were all laughing again. It was already starting to feel like Jennifer was one of us.

20

Jennifer Spencer

I sit here day after day dealing with all of these wounds inside my head. The kinds of wounds that never heal.

Bonnie Foreshaw, inmate. Andi Rierden, *The Farm*

Jennifer raced back to her cell to take a look in the mirror. Tom would be arriving for visitor's day any minute. Did she look all right? What a ridiculous question to even ask. How could she look all right in this shapeless jumpsuit, with her frizzy hair, Adobe Red lipstick, and enough mascara to pass as a raccoon? Tom would take one look at her and think: white trash. But it had been fun to be part of that crew. Even so, she rubbed the cheap lipstick roughly off her lips with the palm of her hand. How could Tom, with his prep school upbringing and his country club expectations, possibly look at her and love what he saw?

But he *did* love her. She took a deep breath and forced herself to think positively. Tom loved her and despite the ridiculous warning she'd gotten from Lenny, Tom and Donald Michaels would do everything in their power to get her out of this dump as soon as possible. He'd make her a lady again, and his wife.

Jennifer got to the visitor's room just as an officer called out, 'Brainard, Jackson, LaBianco, and Spencer. Visitors.' Jennifer raced inside just a step behind Theresa. She craned her neck for a first glimpse of Tom's distinguished widow's peak. Once again she was instantly overwhelmed by the noise, the smells, and the confusion.

'I made you the best chicken potpie!' a woman shrieked, attacking Theresa and enveloping her in a bear hug.

A wave of cheap Wal-Mart perfume washed over Jennifer, almost making her pass out. She pushed by Theresa – and the potpie specialist who must have been her sister, Thelma – and made her way to the center of the room to look for Tom. Everywhere little kids were hanging from their mothers' necks, while grown women tried to shout the latest news over their heads. There were absolutely no men – unless you counted the odious Officer Byrd, standing in one of the corners surveying the crowd. Two female correction officers were on the other side. Where was Tom?

Just then from the corner of her eye, she caught a glimpse of a blue Brooks Brothers suit hanging off broad shoulders. Jennifer rushed across the room and threw her arms around Tom.

'Oh, Tom. Oh . . .' she blurted out. Was it true? Was he finally there with her? This couldn't be another dream, could it? If so, please God, don't let me wake up.

'Jennifer, sweetheart, let me look at you,' Tom said, detaching himself from her and looking her over with concern. Jennifer could feel his eyes on her frizzy mop. She reached up to tame it as best she could.

'It kills me to see you like this, honey,' Tom said. 'But

you look . . . *healthy*, at least. Are they feeding you okay?'

'Oh, who cares about that, Tom? What's going on? When are you getting me out of here!'

'It's all being worked out,' Tom told her.

He reached out and took her hand. It felt so good to have contact with him. Jennifer wished she could kiss him over and over and over again. She wished they could be anywhere except in this miserable room. But most of all she wished they could talk about love and weddings and the future. Jennifer didn't want to talk about the law.

'We know the judge on this one,' Tom said as they sat down at the table, 'and he's not at all keen on holding up the governor's latest fad legislation, so –'

Jennifer cut him off. 'So, no jury trial. A summary judgment and he'll find me innocent, right? And I'll be let out of here?'

'Well . . .' Tom picked up her hand and held it in both of his.

'Well, what?' she asked.

'It's not that simple. The DA's office is being . . . difficult.'

'Difficult?' Jennifer asked. Her heart fluttered in her chest. 'Tom, you don't know what it's like here. I can't . . .' She stopped because she knew that if she went on she'd collapse. She took a deep breath. How could she explain to him how bad it was?

'Look, we feel confident that the judge will go our way this time,' Tom assured her.

Jennifer wasn't convinced.

'Well, what are you going to do to make sure of it, Tom? You've *got* to get me out of here!' Jennifer heard herself beginning to sound a little hysterical.

'Stay calm, sweetie.' He looked at her. 'That's the most important thing right now. Just keep calm and quiet – the model prisoner. Stay ladylike and let us do the dirty work for you.'

She tried to smile. 'Tom, you can't be ladylike here.'

'Oh, babe.' Tom leaned forward across the table and lowered his voice. 'You know Donald's behind you all the way on this one. Do you know the resources he's thrown behind you on this?' She shook her head. 'It's not just Howard McBane. Christ, half of Swithmore, McBane are billing their time to you. You know that Donald won't take no for an answer. So sit tight, and you'll be in the catbird seat when this is all over.'

Jennifer looked at him intently, trying to believe that it would all work out in the end. 'How much longer will it take?' she said finally.

'Oh, under a month.'

'You're sure?'

'Trust me.'

Tom leaned forward and gave her a tender kiss on the forehead. Then he pulled out a pad. 'Now tell me what you need,' he said gently. 'And we'll make sure to get it to you right away.'

'What I need,' Jennifer said, angry with his calm efficiency, 'is some fresh air and for you to get me the hell out of here.'

Tom made a gesture of annoyance with his hand, and then sighed and started speaking slowly, as if talking to a child. 'Okay. I got the point,' he told her. 'You think I enjoy spending my Saturday morning like this? We've gone over this, Jennifer. What more do you need me to tell you?'

As Jennifer looked at him, she realized with a sudden

feeling of horror that Tom had changed. His eyes, his tone of voice, the way he kissed her on the forehead . . . 'Do you still love me, Tom?' she asked abruptly. Something told her that she had to ask, that their emotional landscape had changed, but if the answer wasn't yes, she was certain her heart would stop beating.

Tom's lips tightened and he averted his eyes. 'Yes, of course. But . . .'

Jennifer heard the three-letter word and knew that those three letters shook her world.

'Jennifer, you know I care for you deeply. But, under the circumstances . . .' he stammered and began again. 'You know my family – it would be very bad publicity for them if I was involved with . . . a convict and –'

'Are you insane?' she asked. 'Are you calling me a convict? If I hadn't agreed to do this it would be you and Donald in jail!'

'Jennifer, that isn't even true,' Tom said, stiffening, 'and as your attorney I advise you not to say it again.' He paused and looked down, his eyes narrowed. 'I'm your lawyer. I think it's best if we consider our personal relationship over. When this has all blown over, I'm sure things can go back to normal, but for now it's not a good idea.'

Jennifer stared at him in disbelief. 'What are you saying?'

'I'm returning the engagement ring to the jeweler. I'll make a small statement to the press that we are no longer romantically involved – by mutual choice – but that I am still your close friend and that I will fight your case to the end.'

'Taking back the ring?' she asked. As if the jewelry was at issue.

'It's really for the best. You need to concentrate on your appeal – you don't need emotional complications –'

'But Tom, this is when I need you the most!' Jennifer felt herself on the verge of tears. 'I need your love, I need your support! You *can't* abandon me now!'

'That's not the way I see it – as abandoning. I'm still your lawyer. And really, Jennifer, you need to think of me, too. My position, my reputation.'

'Your reputation? I *made* your reputation. Without my high-powered deals, you would have been nothing. You were a nobody when I met you! And now you have the balls – or lack thereof – to leave me in the lurch? You're a lily-livered coward of a nobody!'

'You're angry, now, so maybe I should just leave. But I'll be in touch soon to talk about your case. I really do care about you, Jennifer. Be that as it may,' he began in what Jennifer had already learned to call his lawyer voice.

'I can't believe this is happening!' she interrupted. 'If you break up with me now, Tom, I swear I –' Jennifer stopped suddenly. She realized she had nothing to threaten him with – she had no leverage at all. No matter what he did, she still needed him to fight her case – he was her only card. Even now, when he was treating her like the worst doormat, she could do nothing to fight back. She felt so helpless, she wanted to attack him, to claw at his face, or at her own, to fall onto the floor and kick and scream. Instead she froze and wished her heart would stop, but it wasn't as easy as that.

'Jennifer, it might be hard to see this now but in the end everything will be okay. Don't worry,' he told her.

If she could have she would have laughed, but all she said was, 'Nothing will ever be okay again.' And then she slapped him. Firmly and soundly, right across his face.

Tom lifted a hand to his cheek. 'I'm sorry,' he said, as if that meant anything. As if saying that helped. He stood up and turned away. She watched him – his tall, graceful figure weaving through the hubbub of the room to the door.

He was gone. Just like that.

Jennifer thought she'd felt the lowest of the low in Observation and during her first meal in the cafeteria, but this was a new lowness of black despair, the kind that she'd never imagined could exist and that she wouldn't even wish on her worst enemy – who was now Tom.

Book II

21

Cher McInnery

A woman always has her revenge ready.

Jean Baptiste Poquelin (Molière)

When Jennifer Spencer finally busted up, she shattered like a bad egg hitting a brick henhouse.

Cher was in the visitor's room, meeting with her lawyer, when Jennifer bent across the table and smacked her visitor across the face with a slap that brought silence to the visitors at tables around her. Cher and her latest lawyer – Jeffery – were just about finished anyway. She bent over and said, 'Enough of this.' Cher wanted to see the fun. She got up quickly and watched Jennifer from a distance. She didn't want to get too close because when someone went ballistic you just didn't know what they might be able to pull out.

But Jennifer didn't go ballistic. She calmly stood up and left the room. Maybe Cher's instincts were wrong. Maybe the poor bitch would just cry herself to sleep. Cher followed Jennifer out of the room and was disappointed when she saw her turn into her cell. It would be hard for Cher to see what would happen next. But Cher stationed herself in the hallway and waited. Sure enough, in a moment Jennifer Spencer, her eyes blank and her face the gray-white of a blue jay's belly, walked out of her house and into the rec room. Cher smiled. Oh yeah. She could see big trouble coming.

Cher watched from the doorway while Jennifer walked to the pay phones and then just stood there and stared at them. Then suddenly she picked up the phone and made a call. Cher moved in closer. 'Collect to Donald J. Michaels,' she heard the deb say. Jesus! Donald J. Michaels was one of the biggest guys on Wall Street. He was bigger than Trump, bigger than Milken ever was. Was *he* the guy the deb had been involved with?

Cher waited, as did Jennifer Spencer. Then Cher heard her say, 'Operator, tell that secretary this is important. He *has* to accept the charges and speak to me. Make it collect and person-to-person from Jennifer Spencer.' Cher watched as nothing happened. Well, nothing happened on the other end of the line, but some huge systems crash was happening behind the deb's eyes. Slowly Jennifer began to shake, then she grasped the telephone for support. She was standing right in front of the TV but didn't hear the women's wails of protest as she blocked their view of the screen, nor did she notice the line of others who were waiting to use the phone. Angry women in the rec room continued to shout at Jennifer to 'move your fucking head, bitch,' while Cher smiled. Some stood and moved toward her to forcibly take her out of the way. It was certain that Jennifer was about to get a real walloping.

But then suddenly Spencer flew into action. She

crammed the receiver into its cradle. She was going off. Cher watched as Jennifer picked up a chair, and with a strength that Cher would not have ever expected, hurled it up and across the room. It smashed against the wall right under the clock. Half of the women were up and out of the way before it bounced to the ground. But Jennifer was moving and didn't wait for the bounce. In three long strides she too crossed the room to a table where Flora and Gloria were sitting. Jennifer slashed her arms across the puzzle they were putting together, flinging the pieces all over. Gloria screamed, and Flora slid from her chair and crouched behind it while the table followed the chair and hit the wall. Cher held back a laugh. She hated those friggin' jigsaw bitches anyway. The way Cher saw it, the debutante was finally coming out.

Meanwhile, the inmates with IQs in the three figures had hit the deck, while a few of the stupid ones were still in the 'Hey, what the fuck . . .' protest stage. Cher realized she'd better make sure she kept her nose clean, because even being a victim now might put her parole at risk. But before she could duck, she was joined at the doorway by a group of other prisoners from the unit. Movita was one of them. 'What's happenin'?' Movita asked.

'Looks like yer new crew member is goin' postal,' Cher told her, lifting an eyebrow but managing to repress a sneer. Behind her the noise in the rec room had increased while Spencer threw chairs, magazines, cards, books, and anything else she could grab hold of. Monopoly money fluttered in the air while half the tiles of a Scrabble game hit the window with hard tiny taps.

'Oh, fuck!' Movita said. Cher had to admit to herself that she was surprised. She didn't think the debutante had it in her. Cher could hear the stampede of COs running down the hall to the unit. Shit, she thought, we'll all be in lockdown in a minute!

Suki came skittering up. 'Byrd, Camry, and Rodriguez are leading a whole squad over here,' she gasped. Then, jumping like a puppy, she tried to get a look over Cher's shoulder. 'Holy shit,' she said. 'It's Jenny.' She started to push past Cher but Movita restrained her.

'Leave her be,' Movita said.

In the rec room Jennifer overturned the last standing table while the rest of the crew watched from the door. Theresa took one look, shook her head, and backed away. 'Do you know what got her goin'?' Movita asked Cher.

Cher shrugged. 'Bad news from her lawyer,' she said.

'Tom?' Suki explained. 'Her fiancé?'

'Oh, shit,' Movita murmured.

'Men. They are no good,' Cher said using a fake Latino accent.

'It's important to release your anger,' Theresa said. 'But it's just as important to do it in a positive, not negative way.'

'Thank you, Doctor Laura,' Movita said, and Cher snickered.

The noise of overturned furniture stopped, and they all froze as a long and painful wail of despair pierced the unit. They witnessed Jennifer Spencer's complete emotional meltdown. Jennifer fell to the floor and began to roll. Her horrifying wails intermingled with the blaring play-by-play broadcast of the television. Cher and the rest of the crew knew better, but one busybody – Carolyn Weltz, the recently born again – knelt beside Jennifer. 'The Lord is my shepherd,' she began, and Cher was pleased to see Jennifer lash out at her like a feral cat cornered in a dark basement.

It was then that the COs, wearing thick yellow rubber gloves, chest protectors, and clear face masks, pushed through the crowd at the doorway. The gear was needed to protect themselves against bites or contact with bodily fluids. Cher had to admit it was a good idea in this case. The debutante probably was a biter, though Cher doubted that her bodily fluids presented a health hazard to Officer Byrd or those other sons-of-bitches. Just to increase the racket, the sirens began. The team surrounded Jennifer as she continued to scream and kick, her arms brutally wrenched behind her back by the bastardly Byrd. Cher saw him knee her before he secured her arms tightly with the plastic cuffs. But the damn deb never stopped caterwauling. She was yanked to her feet but collapsed again to the floor. When she refused to stand, the officers lifted her and carried her from the room, shrieking and sobbing and demanding to see the Warden.

'Lockdown,' Officer Camry cried. 'Let's go. Show's over. Nothin' to see.'

Ha! Cher wouldn't have been surprised to see Spencer foaming at the mouth like old Betty did when she got rabies and daddy finally shot the bitch dog.

'Man, she's in trouble now,' Suki said.

'You will be too if you ain't in your cell in forty seconds,' Movita told her. 'You, too Cher.'

'Lockdown.' The cry went up and was announced over the intercom. All the sheep began moving back to their pens.

Cher wasn't going to admit it to Movita, but she was impressed with the debutante. It took all four of the officers to hold her down and she was giving them plenty of trouble.

And the noise! She could have rented out her lungs to an ambulance. It didn't seem like she ever had to stop to take a breath.

Warden Harding was already waiting at the other side of the bars at the end of the unit. 'Back to your houses, back to your houses,' Officer Camry was still telling them. Cher didn't want a write up – she was too close to parole to take any chances – but she sure did want to see what happened when the debutante passed the Warden. Cher also wondered if Spencer had anything worthwhile to steal in her footlocker. Now would be a good opportunity to go through it, since Spencer would surely get at least forty-eight hours, maybe more, in the SHU for this kind of infraction.

The inmates began moving toward their houses, but Cher tried to move as slowly as she reasonably could. She watched them carry the debutante out past the bars and up to the Warden, who ordered the officers to 'put her on her feet'. They held the panting and nearly spent Jennifer upright as the Warden firmly, but without malice, spoke to her. Cher entered her cell, luckily close to the end of the unit. She wondered if old Gwen would get to stammering but the Warden was completely in control.

'You are an inmate at the Jennings Correctional Facility for Women, Miss Spencer,' the Warden began. 'Can you get control of yourself?'

Spencer made some kind of noise, but Cher couldn't hear it.

'Show's over,' Officer Camry repeated and the bars closed on all the cells. But Cher thought the show wasn't quite over yet. Neither Spencer nor the fat lady had sung. Still, she had to be cautious. A lockdown infraction was serious.

Slowly, Cher inched her way over to the bars. Camry – no boy genius – didn't notice because he was talking with Suki. Cher cupped a hand to her ear, but it wasn't necessary. The Warden's voice carried. 'You are here to be rehabilitated for your crime and we certainly cannot accept this kind of behavior from you or from any inmate in this facility. Do you understand me, Miss Spencer?'

Cher actually heard Spencer say yes and from her tone of voice knew there wouldn't be any more kung fu fighting. She sighed, a little disappointed. But it had been an impressive performance. She had to give Movita credit: There was more to Spencer than she had given her credit for.

The warden was speaking again. 'You are financially responsible for any of the damage to state property that you have done. And you will be spending the next two nights in the Special Holding Unit.'

22

Jennifer Spencer

> *I guess it used to be a whole lot worse in here. Miss Riley, the warden before Miss Wheeler, would shave your head bald for walking on the grass and put you in maximum security for no less than six months.*
>
> Becky Careway, an inmate at the Ohio Reformatory for Women.
> Kathryn Watterson, *Women in Prison*

'Step back, Spencer.'

Jennifer lay sprawled on the concrete floor. 'Back, I said,' the voice barked. 'Or I'll move ya' back.' There was real menace in the voice. Despite her overwhelming lethargy Jennifer forced herself to rise to a crouching position and then managed to stand and move off to the corner of the bare concrete space. 'That's better,' the voice on the other side of the door said. 'Good girl.' She recognized his voice, though she couldn't see him. It was Byrd, the creep. Even in her dazed state, Jen could hear the sexual menace in his voice. As if reading her mind he continued, 'Watch your slot, Spencer. Comin' through.'

The slot at the bottom of the door rattled and a tray was pushed inches beyond the door. Though she felt empty inside, she was anything but hungry. She had either fallen asleep or passed out from exhaustion on the bare cement, and now she had no idea how long she'd been unconscious. The muscles in her lower back and between her shoulder blades ached and one of her legs – the right one – felt sore from the knee to the upper thigh. She reached down to rub it. It was very tender to the touch. Had she been injured in the melee?

She couldn't remember much of what had happened after her attempted phone call to Don. But now, after unknown hours of screaming in rage and sorrow, followed by a deep and disorienting sleep, she just wanted to know what time it was. She took a step toward the tray. Perhaps she could figure out which meal it was by its content. But it was something she couldn't identify, perhaps lunch, perhaps dinner, or even some new brown invention for breakfast. The tray didn't have dishes or implements. It was a single piece of molded plastic with two depressions in it, one filled with the brown substance and the other filled with something that might once have been a green vegetable. But maybe not. She heard the noise of the CO moving away and called out to him. 'What time is it?' she shouted through the door.

'Not time for you to talk, unless you enjoy being in here,' the voice said, laughed, and moved away.

She looked around. No natural light, no clocks, no lights-out, no good morning. In the relentless twenty-four-hour-a-day fluorescent glare of the Special Holding Unit deep in the underground passages of Jennings, Jennifer's hands began to shake uncontrollably. Frightened, she used whatever mind she had left to try to stop them but she couldn't. She left the disgusting meal where it was and walked back to the corner, where she leaned against the wall and slowly, like a deflating pool toy with a leak, slithered down the wall into a squatting position in the corner.

After a time she heard a tiny noise, a kind of scraping. She looked up. Nothing. She heard it again. She looked carefully. And then she saw the roach, big as a waterbug, actually trying to push the plate of slop across the floor. Oh God. From across the cell the bug looked the size of a Chihuahua. She couldn't bear bugs. She felt as if she'd vomit. And then there was a noise in the hall and the bug skittered away.

Her hands kept trembling and she felt as if she couldn't get a breath into her lungs. The air in the cell was incredibly stale. It actually felt as if it were solid, some kind of gel made up in equal parts of body odor, mildew, and the spent exhalations of hundreds of previous inmates.

She still couldn't believe that she had been so unceremoniously dumped by Tom. Their relationship had been so intense, so important to her. Wasn't it true for him? How could he just let it all go? How could he walk away from the love they shared? She had never enjoyed holding, and being held by, any man the way she had enjoyed Tom. Just lying in bed with him, his left arm slid under her pillow, his right arm snaked up between her breasts, cupping one gently in his hand, was an exquisite pleasure. In response she would slide her left hand under the pillow and make a fist, lay it in his palm, and he'd curl his fingers around hers. Jennifer's head would rest just against his chin and he would lift his head a little so that his mouth rested on her ear. His whispers of 'I love you' would make her melt into his body even more.

Even now, after his dismissal of her, as she crouched here in the corner like an abandoned orphan, Jennifer could feel

Tom's body. She could feel her body burn as if his skin were pressed against her own. It was so real it made her whole body tremble. How could he give that up? How would she go on without it? What had happened to Tom since she'd been put in here? Did he fall out of love with her before all of this and just couldn't tell her? No, that couldn't be. Maybe it was pressure from Donald? Maybe it *was* his family and the hounding of the media. After all, she was locked up and had no idea what kind of hell he was going through on the Outside.

Why did he do it? It couldn't have been the publicity and trial because he had been as loving to her as usual throughout all of that. Did his parents only object once the verdict came in? She had met them only three times but they seemed to have liked her. Maybe that was an excuse. Did he see her on visiting day with the Suki hair, the cheap lipstick, and garish eye makeup and get scared away by her transformation? Did she really look like such a monster to him? How could someone who had professed eternal love, who had given her a diamond – her first – which meant 'forever', give her up so quickly and completely?

She thought back to when they first met. It was about two months after she joined Hudson, Van Schaank that she had started working on a huge deal – one that would turn out to be one of the most profitable in the history of the firm – and Tom was the lawyer assigned. They spent many nights working late, ate dinners together, even breakfasts on Saturdays and Sundays as the project neared its close. She tried not to be too attracted to him. Office romances never worked out. But this felt different. He wasn't the usual infatuation, though he was a serious person, and she wasn't a giddy girl. She wondered at first if her growing crush was mutual and began to watch him for signs. First she noticed him looking at her during her presentations to Donald and the other partners. And then there were times when they would finish each other's sentences. 'Great minds think alike,' Tom would tell her.

They were discreet with their affair for several months and were even more careful about not letting Donald know they were an item until they were sure of the seriousness of their feelings. Generally, Donald saw fraternization as a distraction from work. But he didn't have a problem with *them* breaking the rule. When they announced their engagement he was thrilled for them. 'I'll give the bride away,' he said, 'and you can honeymoon in my villa in Umbria.'

How, she wondered again, could Tom just give her up? She felt dizzy. She couldn't bear to think of it anymore. She looked around the cell for distraction. There was nothing to look at, not even graffiti. The light never changed. There was nothing to read, nothing to do, nothing to capture her imagination except her thoughts, which were unbearable. She was, for the first time she could ever remember, completely alone with herself, a self that was soul-sick, frightened, and with hands that would not stop trembling.

She sat and sat and sat. After some time – she'd never know how much – she felt herself undergoing a kind of sea change. The sensory deprivation that left her emotionally numb and staring dumbly at her hands moved her into an altered state. Her fear and anger, all her anguish, seemed to go away, and she saw her hands as if for the first time. Slowly she opened and closed her fists. They were something. They could go from giving the softest caress to the hardest punch. Jennifer opened and closed them again and thought of the marvel of human anatomy that enabled her to perform this simple task. She tried to remember high school biology and the number of bones in the hands but couldn't, though she remembered the names: carpals, metacarpals, and phalanges. She wondered if each of the phalanges had a different name. Perhaps they had numbers.

She was alive; that was all that she felt. Her love for Tom was a physical pain in her chest but all of her emotions were washed away. Maybe this was why they used the SHU. It took away your feelings and left you empty, only partly human. Because, she realized as she sat there staring at her hand, we are not our bodies or our brains. We are our feelings. Without feelings we are not human. She felt as if her humanity had waned. Her anger was spent. Her sorrow was pushed out like an ebbing tide.

Was it possible that Tom had overreacted, that he would regret what he had said and write her an apology? Would he ask to visit again? If he did, what would she do? A man who abandoned a woman in need was not a man who could be trusted. She thought of how her father had run out and what her mother went through. Jennifer had thought that *she* would escape from the bad luck that plagued her family. She had thought she would have money, position, a husband, and, eventually, a family. But she didn't think any of that would be possible now.

Oddly, at that moment, her hands stopped trembling. She had no more hopes, no more delusions of a quick release. She was simply alive in a Special Holding Unit of a prison.

There was no way for Jennifer to know how much time was passing – she could only try to mark the passing of the hours by the delivery of her meals. She counted back the meals that had been delivered. She could remember at least three, though she hadn't eaten any of them. The supper was still there, as was the breakfast and the lunch. She probably had less than twenty-four hours to go. Now, hungry and tired, she crawled over to the trays and was eating what she could when she heard the key in the door. Like a caged animal she quickly retreated to the farthest corner, pulled her knees up to her chest, and stared intently at the heavy iron door.

The door opened very slowly, and Jennifer held her breath. Then, very softly she heard someone whisper her name. 'Jennifa'?'

Jennifer did not answer, but remained frozen in abstract fear. 'Jennifa'?' the voice sounded again.

'Movita?' Jennifer whispered in response. 'Movita, is that you?' Jennifer jumped to her feet and nearly shouted for joy when she saw Movita quickly slip into the cell. 'What are you doing here? How do you get in here?'

Movita held up her hand for Jennifer to be quiet. 'I wasn't sure which of these holes they put ya' in.'

'But you have a key?' Jennifer asked.

'Don't be crazy. Let's just say a guard owes me a favor.' She raised her hand. 'We'll talk about that later. I don't have much time and if I get caught doin' this they'll transfer my tired black ass outta here.'

'What are you doing here, then?' Jen asked.

'I came to see if you're okay,' Movita answered. She looked around the cell. 'No fun, huh?' Jennifer shook her head in agreement. 'This place can break ya' forever. Or it can make ya' stronger. Which ya' think it's gonna do for you, girl?'

'I just want to get back to my cell,' Jennifer said, and realized that it was true. How pathetic. She didn't even say she wanted out of jail. She didn't say she wanted to go home. She said, with absolute sincerity, that she wanted to go back to her cell.

'Ya' certainly acted up enough to warrant bein' here,' Movita said. 'Girl, you were fierce.'

Jen nodded and flushed. 'He dumped me.'

'I guessed,' Movita shrugged. 'Ain't the end of the world. There's lots more lawyers.'

'He was my fiancé.'

Movita shrugged again, then made a noise like a sigh. 'Ain't a woman in the joint who hasn't been dumped by the man Outside.' She looked at Jennifer and, despite the hard words, her face was kind. Her deep brown eyes, virtually the same color as her skin, radiated warmth. 'Ya' still got a day and a half to do nothin' but think in here. I'm goin' to suggest that you think about others as well as yourself.' She handed Jennifer a large manila envelope. 'Since ya' probably figured out by now that you're going to be in here for a while I think ya' should read this.'

Jennifer looked down at the envelope. 'What is it?' she asked.

'It's bidness. Somethin' I don't know enough about, but I think *you* do. There's something goin' down here. It involves a company called JRU. You hear of them?'

Jennifer shook her head. Whatever Movita Watson wanted, Jen didn't care. And she certainly didn't want to be caught breaking a rule and ending up with more time in the SHU. 'I don't care about JRU,' Jennifer told Movita, handing the envelope back. 'Anyway, I may not be engaged to Tom, but he's still my lawyer. I'm not going to be in here that much longer.'

'Goddamnit, woman, face the facts,' Movita spat with a

sudden vehemence, 'you *are* gonna be in here. Ya' still think you're different? Ya' still think you're a special case? You've been fucked over like almost everyone else in this place and you *are* gonna be here.' She shook her head and lowered her voice. 'Ya' have to accept that or this place will destroy ya'.'

Jennifer remained silent in the wake of Movita's passion. The words landed like blows to her gut. 'That's not true,' she said, but for the first time she was afraid maybe it might be. 'I don't mean I'm better than everyone else, I just . . .'

'Oh, yes ya' do. Ya' think someone's gonna pull strings and ya' ain't gonna do time. Ya' think Suki is stupid, and Theresa is a joke, and I'm a gansta. Uh-uh. We're women just like you who fucked up.' She looked Jen up and down. 'Accept it,' she said. 'Live it minute by minute.'

'I can't,' Jen said, trembling. 'I can't take any more of this. I'll die.'

'Then you're gonna have to die,' Movita said simply. Jennifer's head shot up in terror. Was this woman threatening her? Was she trying to force her to do something?

Movita laughed gently at Jen's frightened response. 'Don't worry baby, I ain't here to kill ya'. I'm here to make sure ya' live.'

Jen took a deep breath. 'I don't understand what you're trying to say to me,' she said softly. 'I can't stay here. I can't stay in this place for another day. I can't.' She began sobbing quietly.

'It ain't just 'bout you,' Movita said. 'That's what I'm trying to tell ya'. Ya' ain't the only woman in this place.'

'I know that,' Jennifer responded, hearing how defensive she sounded.

'Do ya'?' Movita asked her. 'There's a difference between knowin' there are others around you and knowin' that *you* are around others. Ya' get what I'm saying, girl? We're all in this together.' She gestured with the envelope. 'It ain't 'bout any one of us, it's 'bout *all* of us. That's the only way we can make it here. Ya' understand that?' Jennifer nodded, and Movita continued. 'And it ain't about forever, either,' she said firmly. 'Ya' got that?'

'I don't know what you mean,' Jennifer told her.

Movita said nothing for a moment. She only stared directly into Jennifer's eyes, and Jennifer didn't like what she saw in them. The pain in those dark eyes was almost more than she could bear, but she sensed that she could not look away – that she *must* not look away. 'I'm gonna die in this place,' Movita finally said. 'Ya' know what that means? I'm never gettin' out of here. Never.'

'But . . .' Jennifer tried to speak.

'Shut up, girl,' Movita said, raising her hand. 'Shut up and listen, 'cause I ain't never talkin' about this again. I killed a man. My man. Earl Watson. He beat me, sure, but I hit him back plenty. One day he went for my daughter. That was it. Still, all of the reasons and justification in the world don't mean shit anymore. I killed him. And I'm gonna live the rest of my days in here. That's *my* reality. It can't be changed.'

'But they can't keep you here forever,' Jennifer protested, horrified. Somehow she hadn't thought about Movita's crime or sentence.

'That's what I'm sayin' to ya', girl. They can, but they can only keep me here one day – one moment – at a time. I just gotta stay in that moment. Ya' hear what I'm sayin' to ya'?' Jen, shocked, barely managed to nod her head. 'I don't think about tomorrow and I don't think about yesterday. I don't even think about ten minutes from now. I just stay in the moment, and honey, if the moment's good, I'm happy. If the moment's bad, like the one I had over this here report, I let it pass. I just take it just one moment at a time, and that's what you have to do, too.'

Jennifer could not begin to accept the reality of a life sentence in prison. What she could sense, however, was the great strength, compassion, and wisdom that were with her in the cold, sterile holding cell. The moment was a good one – good because she was not alone. Movita was there with her. Jennifer looked deeply into Movita's eyes and nodded, and Movita saw that she understood.

'Ya' got more than twenty-four hours in here,' Movita told her, 'so I brought ya' a little readin' material.' Again, Movita referred to the envelope that Jen held in her hand.

'What is it, exactly?' Jennifer asked her, hoping it wasn't some stupid religious tract.

'It's the worst damn thing that's happened to me since the day I picked up the knife and cut Earl's throat,' Movita told her, and motioned to the envelope.

Jennifer, really curious, looked at it. She read the return address: *JRU International*. It meant nothing. 'What is this?'

'It's all in there,' Movita said quietly. 'I want ya to read it.'

'Won't they see me with this? Will I get in trouble?'

'No to both questions. It's been taken care of. I don't have no more time to talk. Shift's gonna change. Once Byrd is off, we both get our asses in a jam over this.' She looked down at the envelope. 'I don't understand all the bidness talk in there, but I do know that if what's in them pages comes true, then I can't go on here. If they do what they say they're gonna do, it *will* be 'bout forever, and I can't . . .'

She stopped and turned away toward the door. Jen wanted to reach out and hold her but knew she shouldn't. 'I gotta get outta here now,' Movita said. 'Read that up and figure out what we can do about it. I got a lollipop for you from Sally to make the readin' more enjoyable.' Jen looked down at the envelope and Movita left as quickly and mysteriously as she had come.

The moment Jennifer heard the key turn to lock her in for another twenty-four hours, she opened the wrapper of the lollipop and popped it into her mouth. The burst of flavor, of sugar, was an incredible comfort. Sugar was the legal drug in Jennings and no inmate could do without it. Tears came into her eyes at the simple pleasure flooding her, and the kindness of Movita. Then, after a few moments, she opened the envelope and began to read.

She read and read. When a meal came in she ate it without tasting it while she was reading. When she finished she didn't even pause – she went back to the first page and began again. She was appalled. JRU International couched their intentions in the politically correct verbiage of 'rehabilitation and job training', but what the privatization plans really described was not unlike a slave owner's plantation in the old South. The report cited 'underutilized' beds and called for an immediate doubling of the inmate population. 'Cost per unit' would thereby be reduced, and with round-the-clock work shifts, the prison would be able to 'more fully realize existing and proposed profit centers'.

She finally looked up from the world she was in to find herself back in her cell. The proposal was an unbelievably callous and cruel assessment and Jennifer grew angrier with each and every word that she read. JRU International was going to turn the place into a factory. In the name of rehabilitation, the women – the 'units' – would be worked twenty-four hours a day. And double the population? Jennifer scanned the rest of the report. Where were the plans for increased health care and better nutrition to keep this slave labor force working? Where were the cost estimates for the repairs and modifications that would transform this hell hole into something better than a kennel? Where was the reality, the humanity in this report?

Jennifer knew she wouldn't be at Jennings for long, but Suki and Theresa and poor Springtime and Flora – all of them would. Who and what was this JRU? She would have to get in touch with Lenny and ask him to do some research. But not over the phone. Nor could she write to him – letters were read. Maybe he'd visit. They could talk about it more then. Just as these thoughts were going through her head, her eyes focused by chance on the page before her and landed on the word 'visitation'. She read the paragraph closely.

> *Research shows that inmate visitation frequently leads to unrest and deviant behavior. In addition, far too much space is dedicated to this purpose. While we cannot eliminate visitation entirely, we can reduce the magnitude of the problem by a general dispersal of the inmate population to other JRU-controlled facilities across the nation, and in turn, transfer new units into this facility. Research shows that relatives and friends will rarely travel more than three hours for a prison visit.*

People were 'units'. Visitation caused 'deviant behavior'. Jennifer could not read one more word of the report. She thought back to what Movita had told her: *'It's not about you and it's not about forever.'*

'Mealtime, Spencer,' a woman CO's voice said. Jennifer scrambled over to push her old tray out the slot in the bottom of the door. Then another meal was silently shoved into the room, without a mention of the contraband report in front of her. She was so upset, so angry, that her first impulse was to kick the damn tray. Instead, she picked it up, sat back down on the floor, picked up her spork, and started to eat. She needed to think, but not too far ahead. She had to stay in this moment.

Tom might not love her, he might not want to marry her, but he wasn't going to abandon her without counsel. But it looked as if, without possibility of an immediate action from the governor or a judge, she would be here for some time at least. Perhaps she could use the time to do some good. She looked at one of the charts in front of her. This was what she knew how to do and it would keep her busy, as well as make a difference to her quality of life. She could focus on this for distraction, and help a woman as powerful and tragic as Movita Watson.

23

Gwen Harding

A leader is a dealer in hope.

Napoleon I

Warden Harding sat in her car in the parking lot of Jennings. She looked at her watch. Her self-regulated lunch break was over and she hadn't done what she wanted to do. Nor had she eaten lunch. She had driven around town for forty-five minutes, parked outside a church for fifteen minutes, and then drove back to Jennings, stupidly passing a McDonald's and a Taco Bell without picking up anything to eat. And she was hungry. Ravenous, actually.

Angry at herself, she got out of the car, slammed the door behind her, and went inside, stopping at the employee lounge and going straight for the snack machine. She put in change and got two candy bars. The hell with it. She'd eat them and make coffee in her office.

Movita was at her desk while Miss Ringling was working at the copier. Movita looked up at Warden Harding and smiled. 'Nice lunch?' she asked. It was unusual for the Warden to go out during the day and she knew Movita well enough to know she noticed every little thing.

Gwen again felt a rush of gratitude, embarrassment, and shame. For several nights in a row she'd dreamed of her drunken tour of Jennings, and although each dream differed slightly, in all of them she was caught by COs and fired. It had been a narrow escape. How fortunate she was that Movita and Roger Camry had found her and not anyone else! But how had Movita managed to get out of her cell? Did she remember the inmate saying 'infirmary'? Well, these women were clever and resourceful. That Gwen knew for sure. She wouldn't ask and Movita wouldn't tell. At least the story wouldn't get all over the prison. She self-consciously reached up and touched the bruise on her jaw. 'Fine,' she said. 'Just a sandwich with a friend.' Movita smiled and went back to her work. Movita Watson was a fine person, Gwen thought, a very fine person. What a pity . . .

'You got one message, Warden,' Movita said. 'Somebody called from that JRU. They wanna make an appointment for a tour.'

Gwen felt her face flush. It made the bruise more tender and she hoped Movita didn't see. She turned away and tried to compose her features, but found herself instead thinking of the gin in her desk drawer. How she would've loved a drink at that moment! Don't think of it, she told herself firmly. 'Fine,' she told Movita, and turned to her office, where she'd at least have the comfort of privacy, caffeine, and chocolate.

But Movita continued. 'And there's somethin' else I expect you'd like to know 'bout.'

'What's that?' she asked, though her feet kept moving her to her office. Movita followed her and stood just inside the doorway while Gwen sat down at her desk. She could feel the gin, behind the drawer front next to her left leg.

'Well, I know what caused Spencer to go berserk. I heard all about it.'

The Warden looked at her. 'I'm interested,' she said, and meant it. It had been a disappointment to see the new, highly visible inmate so out of control. Perhaps she'd been taunted, or worse. 'What was it about?'

Movita crossed her arms and leaned back against the door. 'She had provocation.'

Warden Harding gave her a skeptical look. 'Movita . . .'

'Warden, I ain't excusin' it. You know I ain't. But she's just a kid and it was a terrible thing for her.'

'Okay Movita, I believe you,' the Warden said, folding her hands on her desk and putting the thought of a drink firmly out of her mind. 'Tell me.'

'She met with her lawyer and apparently one of the other women heard mostly everything,' Movita began. 'She said the man was very good-lookin', wearing a suit and a shirt that was starched and ironed so stiff it looked like it could cut his neck and wrists. But he was also stiff and mean lookin' too. Well, it seems he wasn't just her attorney. He and Spencer was engaged, and he comes here and breaks the engagement. He tells her he can't be involved with no convict 'cause a his family and his position so he's breakin' it off.'

Gwen Harding shook her head. 'Bad timing, I'd say. They love to kick you when you're down.'

'But there's more,' Movita added.

'Go on.'

'Well, Jennifer's sayin' to him, "but you know I didn't do nothin' except what you said I should do." Or somethin' like that. I didn't hear the whole rap, but it sounded like she took the fall for him, or someone else.'

The Warden sat very still, biting her lower lip. Her eyes were staring across the room. She was thinking. How many, what percentage of women were imprisoned because of their involvement with men? Far more women's lives were destroyed by men than the opposite, she thought. Maybe that was painfully obvious. But why? The women were often smart, clever women, women with jobs and children, educated women, women who should know better. Even in her own life she'd . . .

'Anyway, he left and she got twisted.'

'Did she love him, you think, Movita?' Gwen asked.

'How can we know that? But if I had to guess, I'd say she did. She don't seem the kinda girl to get hooked up with someone she don't love.' Movita opened the door. 'She didn't have no fight over the TV show they was watching or nothin' like that. She just went crazy.'

Gwen nodded and Movita left her alone.

She fully intended to write up a report for the file on Jennifer Spencer. That was what she always did when an inmate went into the SHU. It would, of course, affect Spencer's time and parole. After Movita's news she thought that maybe she should forgo the report. This was all disturbing, and the JRU call, and her drunken incident were all on her mind at once. Hadn't she been granted another chance? She'd never been tempted to hush up an incident before. Was she being a more responsible person or was she disintegrating? She wasn't sure.

The Warden had to call the people at JRU. No hurry on

that one. She'd eat her junk food and take a look at Spencer's file, then she'd make the phone call. There would be plenty of time, once JRU took over, for her to jump at their command.

One of the tragedies of prison was that prisoners with relatively light sentences, a year or two, increased their time through breaking rules and bad behavior. She knew that sometimes the women were provoked by others, sometimes they acted out of self-defense and, shamefully, they were occasionally egged on by COs. She'd known a woman who'd started with a twelve-to-eighteen-month sentence and ended up serving nine years because of her troubled reactions to authority. She'd tried to help that poor soul, but couldn't get through to her. She certainly didn't want the same thing to happen to Jennifer Spencer. The trouble was, it became a vicious cycle: Every punishment increased the anger and the anger led to worse behavior.

Gwen wolfed down the Butterfinger bar and felt better. With her sugar high she might be up to calling JRU and setting up an appointment. But after she'd done that her mood soured again. She looked at her watch. It was only three-thirty. She looked down at her drawer, the one with the gin. This was impossible. She took out the bottle, secreted it in her purse, and stood up. 'I have to leave early today, Miss Ringling,' she said, ignoring the surprise in Movita's face. Did the fact that she hadn't left early more than once in almost a decade mean she had to explain why? No, it didn't, she told herself.

She walked out of the office, a false front over an unquiet interior. It was okay, she told herself, for while Movita saw all, Movita didn't judge.

Back in her car she felt the same terror that she'd felt

earlier in the day. She was amazed at the deep and simple quality of the terror. She hadn't been this frightened since childhood. Then her misbehaviors had always been minor. Now, her misbehavior was not. Being drunk at work was terrible. It was shocking. And she had done it. She was so distracted by her thoughts that she nearly went through a red light. She stopped just in time. What was next? A DUI?

She rolled down her window, took the bottle from her purse, and poured it out the window. There.

She was spurred on by that act of courage to drive directly back to the church. It was important that she go. That she do something.

This time, afraid she might not go in if she didn't do it immediately, she got out of her car as soon as she had parked. Putting one foot in front of the other, she walked up the narrow path between two patches of well-kept lawn, and entered the side door of the stone building. There was a sign on the wall directing her to the basement. Not so easy. She held the rail firmly as she descended, because her trembling had increased.

She heard people talking and went toward the doorway the voices were coming from. Then she entered the smoky room and stood in the back. She was just in time to see a woman rise and hear her say, 'Hello, my name is Pat, and I am an alcoholic.' Gwen heaved a big sigh. She was where she ought to be.

24

Jennifer Spencer

Self is the only prison that can ever bind the soul.

Henry Van Dyke, *The Prison and the Angel*

Jennifer Spencer came out of the SHU a different person from when she went in. It wasn't just the rage, the disappointment, and the pain that swept through her, leaving her empty as a broom-swept New York apartment. And the change wasn't all internal either. As she was led back to her cell Jen caught sight of herself in a smudged stainless steel door: The white face, the gray around the eyes, the dark marionette lines between nose and mouth, all looked like they belonged to someone else; none of it looked like her. The face she saw looked ugly to her, but what the hell did she care? It didn't matter anymore without Tom.

When she got back to her cell, just before head count and lights-out, all she longed for was darkness. She wanted to climb into her bunk and collapse.

But Suki had other plans. She was lying on her narrow

lower bunk clutching her belly. 'Wow! You're out! We were worried about you.'

'Really,' Jennifer managed. She couldn't imagine who the 'we' was.

'Time in the SHU is tough. Are you okay?'

Jennifer shrugged, too tired to talk. 'NBD,' was all she could manage. She heaved herself into her bunk, and pulled the pillow over her face. Then she remembered Suki's condition. 'Are *you* okay?' she asked. 'How are you feeling?'

'I'm better. I haven't passed out since that once. And I'm not nauseous all the time anymore,' she explained. 'Only when I eat something my stomach don't like.'

'That could never happen at Jennings,' Jennifer said with as much sarcasm as she could muster. She replaced the pillow.

Through it she could hear Suki laugh, but Jennifer kept her face covered. Nothingness was all she wanted. The nothingness of sleep to match the nothingness inside her.

'You know something funny?' Suki asked. Apparently it was a rhetorical question because she continued. 'I keep having this appetite for German potato salad. The kind with vinegar and bacon bits. Isn't that weird?'

Reluctantly Jennifer took the pillow off. 'No,' she told Suki. 'Pregnant women crave all kinds of things. It's normal.'

'Is it? Oh, good.'

Silence reigned, for which Jennifer was grateful. But lying there she couldn't help but wonder how much Suki knew about pregnancy, childbirth, and child rearing. She assumed that the baby picture on the wall was hers. But she had never asked. Jennifer turned on her side so that she could speak quietly but Suki would be able to hear her.

'With the food here, how can you be sure you're getting enough nutrition for your baby?'

'Oh, I got some vitamins,' Suki said proudly.

'From the dispensary?' Had they finally figured out Suki's condition?

'No. I don't dare go there till it's too late for them to take the baby. Cher's sister sent 'em.'

'They're not enough,' Jennifer told her. She pulled her knees up to her chest and her blanket up to her nose and retreated back to her pillow. 'Goddamn place,' she muttered. 'I have to sleep now,' she said, and merciful darkness closed in over her.

Jen wasn't able to retreat from reality for long. It seemed only minutes before the morning bell rang. It was her time to shower, and even if it was with a group that was being watched over by an officer, she didn't care; the SHU had to be the most disgusting place she'd been in, and she had to wash all of it off. She could hardly believe that she was supposed to get up and shuffle along with everyone else as if everything were fine. As if being locked in an SHU was just one more life activity you learned to deal with. As if giving up your future and your entire former life and accepting this present one was no big deal. But she just had to stay in the moment.

The next task was breakfast. As she set her plate of reddish beige glop on the table and sat down at her place, a surge of anger made her exclaim, to no one in particular. 'Fuck!'

Theresa looked at her from across the table. 'Keep your chin up,' she said. 'Better times are coming.'

Jennifer rolled her eyes. 'How do you know that,

Theresa? Maybe *worse* times are coming.' She thought of the JRU proposal and how that would make this ghastly place so much worse.

'Can't be a pessimist, you know,' Theresa said cheerfully. 'It gives you wrinkles and makes bad things happen.'

Jennifer, expressionless, looked across the table. 'Optimism makes bad things happen, too.'

Theresa smiled nervously. 'I don't think so,' she said softly.

'Fuck! *Anything* can make bad things happen,' Cher said, joining them. She sat down across from Theresa, Movita right behind her. 'They're just out there, like accidents, only more so, waiting to happen.'

Theresa looked down at her plate.

'Shut the fuck up,' Movita barked at Cher. 'Theresa's just tryin' to make Jennifer feel better.' She looked at Jennifer. 'You might try to be grateful when someone's nice to you,' she said.

Jen made a face and took a few more stabs at the Cream of Wheat on her plate. 'What the hell is this stuff? Boiled packing peanuts?' She looked over at Suki. 'Can *you* eat this?' she asked her.

Suki shrugged. 'Sure, as long as you pour fourteen teaspoons of sugar over it.' She loaded her bowl with the sugar and so much margarine that the yellow grease made a puddle across the top of her bowl. 'It's okay,' she said with a shrug. 'I like it better than most of the stuff they serve.'

Jennifer dropped her spork on the table with disgust. The others pretended not to notice. She sat perfectly still, ate no more and said no more. Why bother?

When Suki reminded her that they were supposed to be in the laundry soon, Jen rose and followed her like a robot.

As they walked to the laundry, down one after another of the bleak institutional corridors, the vision of her life as empty and frightening came back to Jennifer, as it had when she had been down in that dreadful hole. Even if she could actually stay here at Jennings and serve her time, remain in this horrible place for years without going crazy – which she strongly doubted – there would be nothing, not a goddamn thing, waiting for her when she got out. The thought of the endless emptiness ahead made her exhale a puff of air, leaving her lungs as empty as her life. The horror of it all suddenly made her want to scream in terror, to clutch at Suki for comfort, for help. But Suki, so little as she walked in front of her, pregnant in this women's prison, couldn't help her. Suki was helpless herself.

'Are you okay, Suki?' she asked her.

'Fine. How about you?'

'Fine.'

Jennifer wouldn't have a job when she got out, no money coming in at all, and that terrified her. She wouldn't be able to go into stores and buy what she wanted. She wouldn't be able to travel. She would be poor. And she would have a criminal record.

A feeling of panic was coming over her. Poverty was like prison, she knew that. Poverty kept you from living, just like prison did. It kept ahold of you, it kept a grip on you, it said no to this and no to that, no to everything. Just like Jennings. It made you eat crap, made you sleep on an uncomfortable bed, made you wear shit, made you do without good medical care. Just like Jennings.

They'd reached the laundry room. Jen followed Suki mechanically but she was so out of it she was almost in a trance. Suki was already lifting the piles of dirty laundry into bins to sort it out while Jen just stood there, a broken machine. Then she remembered Suki's condition. Wasn't there something easier for her to work on?

'Don't!' Jen said to her, snapping out of her fog. 'Don't lift that.' Suki looked up at her. 'Come on, I mean it,' she said when Suki didn't stop immediately. 'I'll do that. You just do the sorting.'

'It's okay,' Suki assured her.

'No it's not.' Some of Jen's emptiness got filled with anger. 'Jesus! They don't give you any medical care, or tell you how to take care of yourself! Or your baby.' Then the anger was gone. 'At least let me do the lifting here, okay?' Jen asked. 'I can't stand it otherwise.'

Suki looked at her with a touch of confusion. 'Okay,' she agreed.

So Jen did the hard work, while Suki did the smaller but tedious tasks: the emptying of pockets, the sorting of colors. Still, it was hot in the laundry room and after less than an hour, when Jen looked across at her, Suki looked pale.

'Sit down,' Jen commanded. 'You're white as one of these sheets is supposed to be. I'll get Flora.'

'You are, too,' Suki said and laughed. 'But don't call Flora. I'll be okay,' Suki reassured her.

Jennifer looked down at Suki's stomach. Suki had never told her how she'd gotten pregnant, only how much she wanted the baby. She spoke about it nearly every night before she went to sleep. She was just starting to show, but the uniforms were roomy enough to camouflage her for quite a while longer. Her plan, she said, was to keep the pregnancy going until abortion wasn't possible. Jennifer sighed. Suki would never win any awards for intelligence, but she was optimistic, generous, and good hearted. She'd be a good mother. Jennifer was afraid to ask at what point they separate mothers and babies.

As they folded sheets she thought about the JRU threat. Whatever punishment Suki might get because of her pregnancy now, it would be mild compared to what JRU would probably have in store for her. Since she'd first read the proposal, Jennifer had backed off a little bit. After all, getting involved too deeply could get her into a world of trouble. But poor Suki. Jen didn't know what her sentence was, but armed robbery had to be years and years.

The shift was endless. Breaks were short, lunch inedible, and when the day finally finished Jen could barely stand. She realized it was time to go back to their 'houses' and cook something for dinner. Now that she was in the crew, it was her turn to cook. While she could manage a hostile takeover or an IPO, she didn't know how to cook very many things. This was no time to try anything new; that would only open herself up to Cher's contempt. The idea of being in the crew – something that she'd kind of liked at first – now felt like a burden. She didn't want to talk to these people today or any day. She wanted privacy. But when she thought of the cafeteria, she knew that she *had* to stay in the crew to survive. She'd just cook, eat, and not try to get involved with them beyond that. She'd have to order something decent from next week's canteen that would fit the bill for an acceptable meal.

Everybody was gathered when Jen and Suki walked in. So what? She didn't greet any of them because she wasn't thinking of anything but how the hell she was going to make dinner. Groceries were spread out on the makeshift counter. Her eyes rested on the chunks of beef and unidentifiable pale green vegetables that sat with it. It looked like she was supposed to cook Chinese, which she had never done in her life, thank you.

'What am I supposed to make out of this?' she asked bluntly.

No one answered.

'Well, if you don't know –'

'Will ya' please cut the brat attitude?' Movita suddenly shouted at her. 'We know you were in the fuckin' hole, but you're not supposed to bring it back up here to us. Do I have to tell ya' that we got it bad enough already? And that many of us been down there ourselves and don't need no revisit? Go back to ya' cell till ya' get over it.'

'I'll shut up and cook,' Jennifer said, as coldly as she could.

'Awright,' Movita said. 'Then go ahead and make somethin' good.'

Not knowing what to do, Jen started heating up the oil in the pan over the electric coil. 'Where's my knife?' she asked. She got only chuckles in reply. She tossed the meat into the smoking oil, and as soon as it started to spatter, tears started streaming down her cheeks.

'It'll be okay,' Theresa said, putting her hand on Jen's arm.

Jen didn't reply. She felt sullen and wanted to be left alone. But Movita wouldn't do it. She came up to the stove. 'You're gonna burn this meat, girl. And if you do, you're outta crew.'

Being yelled at was the last straw. Jennifer began to sob uncontrollably, but she continued to cook. She turned the meat quickly and lowered the flame, sobbing all the while.

'Just a minute,' Movita said. 'We don't need no tears in our food. Theresa, take over here. Jen, come with me.'

Jen set the spatula down and followed Movita, still sobbing. She tore a scrap of the crude brown paper towel off the roll and held it to her face.

'Siddown,' Movita ordered.

Jennifer sat.

'You got a choice, Missy. And you gotta make it right now.'

'I don't have any choices,' Jen wailed.

'Shut up. That's just what I'm talkin' about. "*I don't got no choices*,"' Movita mocked. 'You got as many as the rest of us. No. You got more. But what you got that's a problem is feeling sorry for yourself, thinkin' you're some kinda special. Well, let me tell ya' somethin', ya' not. You let those lousy cracker dudes leave ya' with the rap. I think that's a dumber move than anybody else here did. Ya' think ya' educated – hate to tell ya' babe, Maggie in the library is more educated than you. Your education is nothin' compared to the life experiences of these women. So what ya' got left that makes ya' better'n us? Nothin'.'

Jennifer felt the words come down on her like weights. She had nothing left and now she was supposed to be nothing. All she'd lived on all her life was being special. Being special was what got her scholarships and good jobs and rich. So now she was supposed to be nobody special.

It made her feel sick.

25

Maggie Rafferty

The jury, passing on the prisoners life, may in the sworn twelve have a thief or two guiltier than him they try.

Shakespeare

A tragic heroine. That's what I thought of when Jennifer Spencer walked into the library about a week after she'd been released from the Special Holding Unit. She looked ravaged, an Antigone, with perhaps a pinch of Medea underneath. In other words, the rage was there too, but buried under the grief.

I know my literary allusions make me seem both a bluestocking and a heartless observer. Rest assured, I never share them with anyone. Not that there's anyone to tell. The point is, it's important in this place to keep one's thoughts to oneself and one's feelings small. Waste none of them on pity. But there are times when I am sympathetic, and this was one of those times.

Jennifer Spencer looked pounds thinner, years older, and hollow eyed, as if she'd glimpsed something horrific. And of course, she had. She'd been in 'the hole'. I remembered the last time she had come in here, when I'd been reading the JRU information and felt as if I were having a heart attack. She had tried to help me. Now our roles were reversed.

She approached my little table. 'Movita asked me to come and talk to you,' she told me. 'Is this a good time?'

I smiled. She may have faced the horror of prison, but she hadn't yet fathomed the meaninglessness of the word 'time' here. Of all things, boredom is the greatest torture in prison. There is nothing to do for hours on end. Except for the endless daily head counts, lineups, and occasional lockdowns, all excruciating in their tediousness. Not to mention the hours and hours in your 'house' – a cruel joke of a term – and finally the monotony of prison labor. Time is meaningless. 'It's fine,' was all I said.

She lowered her voice. 'She's told me about this JRU thing.'

'I know.' Ever since I had read the report I had not been sleeping well. Or eating well. Or doing anything well, even breathing. I repeatedly called my sons, but I was afraid to speak about it openly (our pay phones are computer recorded and randomly monitored). At any rate, Bryce was in Hong Kong while Tyler was in London for business. They had both promised to visit as soon as they returned.

Jennifer stood there, clearly not comfortable. 'She wants me to help.'

'I know,' I said again.

She was displaying reluctance even to talk about it. 'I'm not sure I should,' she said finally.

'I see,' I said, making it clear by my tone that I didn't see at all. If anyone can spot denial and a resistance to being involved, it's me. After all, I lived denial through thirty years of my marriage. And here at Jennings I'd been totally uninvolved for years. Oh, when I first came to the prison I tried to teach reading and set up child-care, GED, and other classes, but I gave up long ago. Now I could see that Jennifer Spencer had reluctantly accepted being stuck here at Jennings – at least for now – but she wasn't ready to get involved. She certainly wasn't going to start hatching plots with fellow inmates. I totally understood. But unfortunately we needed her. I knew what my role was, and I began to do it. 'You might give it some thought,' I said blandly. 'After all, what else have you to do?'

'It's not that,' Jennifer said, lowering her eyes, 'It's . . . well, you know where I was last week.'

'Yes, I know.' I could see her shame. 'I'm afraid you have the wrong impression of me,' I told her. 'Maybe because I was a school headmistress and I've now become the staid librarian of Jennings.' I paused. 'Sounds like an epic poem, doesn't it? *The Staid Librarian of Jennings*.' She looked at me and smiled, at least a bit. 'Anyway, when I first arrived here, I was down in the hole so often that I was called "The Old Woman Who Lived in the SHU."'

Jennifer looked at me in amazement. 'No! What did you do? And how did you stand it?'

'Oh, I don't know. I was adjusting, I guess. And for me the hole wasn't any worse than above ground. I had a lot of thinking I needed to do.' I looked at her. I believed Jennifer Spencer needed to do some thinking as well. I smiled. 'Not to mention the fact that I was in such a rage at that time it was almost better for me to be alone.'

'God,' Jennifer said. 'I could never stand to go down there again.' Her lip trembled. 'It was horrible. Horrible.' Then she paused. 'Look, I don't expect to be here long. And

I'd like to help, but I never want to be put through that again. And I don't want to spend one more day here than I have to. Not one more day.'

I asked her to sit down. And I smiled at her before I began my lecture. 'They won't put you down there for trying to do a little business deal. Warden Harding is humane. They can't. It's for contraband and violent offenders only.'

'A little business?' Jennifer said. 'What an understatement! And even if it's not violent, working in any way on this JRU thing is a SHU violation. Even the report is contraband.' She paused again. I could see she was a woman used to being in control of herself as well as others – or at least having that illusion. Losing that control had been decimating. 'Look, I'm planning on being good. I want time off for good behavior.'

'That's good behavior in the most passive sense,' I replied. 'The kind of good behavior you're talking about is actually, according to ethicists, the opposite. The worst sin is for good people to stand by and do nothing when they see evil being done.'

I was surprised to see her face redden. Ah, guilt. The working class is rife with it, but I didn't think she would respond so readily. No doubt nuns had educated her. Worse than Jesuits. Of course, she was also still raw from the SHU.

'Even if I help, there's not much I can do,' she protested. 'I mean, I worked in the private sector. I have no government contacts and I'm not sure my lawyer . . .' She paused yet again. 'Well, Hudson, Van Schaank has close contacts with the governor but . . .'

'We don't know how or what we're trying to do yet,' I told her. 'And it isn't all your responsibility. I've already spoken to my sons and once they get back to the U.S. and hear about this they'll be willing to help. You know that they have . . . connections, and power. They may even add an air of respectability to the endeavor.'

'That depends,' Jennifer said.

I was offended. There were those who accused my boys of playing fast and loose but Jennifer Spencer was in no position to throw stones at glass houses. 'Why not? Aren't you being very negative?' I asked, trying not to get upset.

'No. It's just that there's very little we or they can do. Look, I'll ask my contacts to find out all they can about JRU and I'll see if there's anything . . . shady or questionable about them. If we're lucky the CEO, Tarrington, is a declared Satan worshipper and the public will rise up and make it a political hot potato. But that's a long shot.' She turned to the door, as if to leave.

I sighed, the way I used to sigh at my students when I wanted more from them. I can be so manipulative, I thought as she turned around. But it was as much for her good as mine.

'Jennifer – may I call you Jennifer?' She nodded. 'Aren't you being incredibly selfish? Didn't Movita tell you what kind of changes JRU will impose? Doesn't the idea of what they're going to do scare you?'

Before the girl could respond I heard the heavy footsteps of Officer Byrd coming down the hall. 'Shhh,' I whispered, and put my index finger up to my lips. 'He's trouble.' Then I quickly sandwiched the papers in between two boxes of books that had to be reshelved.

'How's the book business today, ladies?' Byrd asked as he stepped into the little room. Neither of us responded to him. 'I think it's time for a little spring cleaning in here don't you?' he asked as he started reaching for a book and then dropped it on the floor. 'Oops,' he said and continued down the wall pulling out books and dropping them on the floor. He often liked to come in and toss part of the library, just for fun. I was used to it by now, but Jennifer froze in horror.

I gave Jennifer the look that meant 'stay in your position'. Karl Byrd had an attitude and arrogance about him to the point of being repulsive. He went around the room disrupting everything from books to magazines to chairs. I eyed Jennifer when he got close to the boxes that hid the JRU papers. He took both hands and caressed the top of the box and looked right at the scared girl but she didn't look away from him. Then he moved his hands away from the box and went to the edges of a table and felt the underside of the wood. Jennifer tried not to show anxiety because, like a dog, Byrd could always smell fear. He ran his hands down two legs of the table and knocked it and its contents onto the floor. 'I guess you ladies have some cleaning up to do in here,' he said with a sneer.

Once he was gone, we both sighed in relief. 'That was a little too close for comfort,' I said.

'He's such a jerk,' Jennifer said. 'And if one thing is going to happen with this transition with JRU it had better be that he's removed from this facility. But none of this can be done single-handedly. It's obvious that the public wants prisons to cost nothing and warehouse monsters. I'm just one person. I can't change that.'

'Look, you won't be doing this all on your own. Responsibility will be divided. And I think the main thing you have to remember is that if JRU gets a hold on this place, gets a hold on *us* . . . well, we'll all wish we were down in the SHU. It's going to be much worse being up here.'

'Listen, I'll ask my sources on the Street about JRU. I'll try to think of anything I can but I . . .' she trailed off, but I thought she was weakening and I pressed on.

'That's all I ask. We can get you reassigned to be my assistant here in the library. And you can use the time to do research. I'll give you whatever help I can,' I volunteered.

'All right,' she sighed, but I felt like dancing. Well, dancing as much as my arthritis would allow. Still, I managed to conceal my elation.

'So, first – if you can stand it – reread that proposal and give me your notes,' Jennifer told me. 'Anything about the prison that is incorrect, unlikely, or unlawful.'

'Already done,' I smiled at her and pulled my notes from inside my copy of *Waiting* – a rather slow-moving but excellent novel by Ha Jin.

'Fine,' she said, and took them, folded them as carefully as a kite and put them in her uniform. 'I'll look for irregularities in the financing or management of JRU, and for unrealistic projections in their business plans.'

'Good,' I said, and watched her leave. I sat there after she was gone, stunned for a moment. I was experiencing a kind of pleasure I hadn't felt in years. It was excitement. And even the tiniest bit of hope. I didn't know what, exactly, I was hoping for, but it felt good.

26

Cher McInnery

I don't want the cheese, I just want to get out of the trap.

Latin American proverb

'Okay. My chicken is served,' Theresa told the crew. For a Yankee the girl knew how to make her chicken. Cher felt her mouth water, but she sat down to dinner with resentment. She knew something was up but wasn't sure what it was. That bothered her. Movita had been busy, and Frances had been delivering a lot of kites along with ice. Cher had heard that the debutante wasn't going to work in the laundry no more. Cher knew Movita was a private person, but when something was on, she let Cher in. Not this time, though.

Cher didn't like to be dependent on no one. In fact, she felt it was best not to get too close to no one. But she had never had a friend like Movita. She had never had no black friend at all, and she had never known a woman who was as on top of things, smart, and resourceful as Movita was. The thing about her was that she was like Cher, but she wasn't like Cher. She was like Cher because Movita was smart, tricky, realistic, and funny as hell. But she wasn't like Cher because she didn't just use her smarts for herself – she was always figuring out a scam or a way to involve or help other people. Of course, the crew came first. Movita tried to keep peace among everyone. Unlike Cher, she was willing to make an extra effort to make things better for someone else. At first Cher had thought she did it to get power over people, or to get something else back. But time and observation had taught her that Movita was also a natural leader. She couldn't help straightening things out for other people. It was her way. Sometimes Cher admired it, and sometimes it was big goddamn pain in her ass.

Like her, Movita was secretive – she was one of the two or three women in the whole damn prison that could keep something to herself. But though Cher had trusted Movita to keep a few secrets of her own, she didn't like it when something was afoot and she was left out. She also didn't like it that it seemed Movita was trusting the debutante with some kind of secret that she was keeping Cher out of.

What do I care, Cher tried to tell herself as she helped herself to the largest piece of the fried chicken. I'm out of here. But she looked over at the debutante and then over at Movita. It irked her. Before the plate was passed on she took another piece of the chicken. What the fuck. Theresa raised her eyebrows but Cher paid no attention.

'Have some coleslaw,' Suki said, passing her the bowl. 'We have plenty of *that*.'

Back in Arkansas, Cher's mama used to say, 'Girlchild, we shoulda spelt your name S-H-A-R-E, 'cuz you are absolutely *obsessed* with that word.' And Mama had been right. As one of nine hungry children in a poor white trash family, Cher learned very early that survival depended on *learning* to share, *doing* your share, and *getting* your share.

Now Cher ignored Suki's hidden admonition. Like Suki knew jack shit about anything. 'The only thing we had plenty of when I was growin' up was work,' Cher told the crew. 'And if you didn't do your share of the work, you didn't get your share of the food. It was just that damn simple.' Everyone had filled their plates and had begun eating. Nobody spoke, so Cher continued. ' 'Ceptin for my baby brother Ellis.' Cher shook her head and took another bite of the chicken. 'Mama spoilt him somethin' awful. She was too damn old by then to have another kid, and little Ellis was so pathetic and weak that she made sure he never had to lift a finger his whole life. And, 'cuz I was the oldest, I was supposed to do his share of the work *and* share my share of the food.' She laughed, but she hadn't laughed then. And nobody laughed now. It pissed her off. She looked over at Jennifer Spencer, so sweet, so damn demure. 'Jesus Christ, I used to think I had two names,' Cher said. 'Alls the time my mama would be shoutin' at me: *Share, Cher! Share, Cher! Share, Cher*! I got damn sick of it then, and I'm damn sick of it now!'

Movita put down her cup hard. 'What'n the hell you jabberin' about?' she wanted to know.

Cher indicated the whole table with her chin. 'They think I didn't share the chicken,' Cher said sulkily.

'Did anybody say that?' Movita asked. 'I didn't hear it. And if you knew what people were thinking, you'd be worried about more serious stuff than that.'

'You know what I always say?' Theresa, the peacemaker, asked. 'Enough is as good as a feast.'

'This *is* a feast,' the debutante said, like she hadn't been eating in four star restaurants her whole damn life.

'Yeah? What did you ever make for dinner but reservations?' Cher asked.

Jennifer stood up. She looked through Cher as if she were invisible, which only pissed Cher off more than ever. 'Thanks, Theresa,' she said. 'Great chicken. Sorry about the coleslaw. It wasn't very good.' She moved toward the cell doors and Cher wished they'd rack the gate and scrunch the skinny bitch. 'I have to make a phone call,' the deb said. 'I'd better go now before the line gets too long.'

'Oh, is that where our little Miss Armani is going?' Cher countered. 'Every time we get done eatin' she's outta here without doin' one damn bit of the cleanup.'

'She helped me make the supper,' Theresa said. 'She made the coleslaw. It's a lot of messy work. And you know the rule: Whoever cooks don't clean up.'

'You call that sharin'?' Cher snarled. 'Nobody ate any of that crap she served up. Coleslaw! Just makes the cleanup all that messier. Can't even get it to flush down the john.' She looked at the bowl, still almost full. It was so vinegary it had made Cher wince. 'Should make her eat it all.'

'She said she's got a phone call to make,' Suki said as she stood to help Cher with the dishes. 'I'm on with you for the cleanup, Cher. I don't mind a little work.'

'I don't mind work either!' Cher snapped back. 'I know how to work and I don't mind doin' my share of the work if everyone else is doin' *her* share of the work. That's all I'm sayin'. You can bet your ass that she's gonna stick around and do cleanup tomorrow night after *I* cook. And I'm gonna make one hell of a mess, too. You can count on that.'

Movita shook her head. 'Girlfriend, you have been

sputterin' and spoutin' about this now for the last fifteen minutes! Don't you got nothin' better to do? Like maybe practice talking about how well you've learned to live with others for your parole speech?'

Cher sat down again. Was that what this was all about? She was shut out because she was leavin'? Was that it? And Mo had picked the debutante to take her place. Cher got a real empty feeling under her breastbone and a pulling at the bottom of her stomach. She didn't like those feelings.

'Fine,' she said. 'I will.' She got up and angrily slammed a kettle down onto the hot plate. Despite her ire, the fact was she liked these women. In all her travels – and Cher had crisscrossed the country more times than the lines on her palm – she'd never met anyone like Movita, and Theresa – for all her wacky optimism and stupid aphorisms – and Spencer – with her smarts – were women Cher would like to keep on knowing. But once paroled she was forbidden to see or speak to any prison inmates. She couldn't even write to the crew without permission from her parole officer. That was cold.

And it was just as cold for the crew to replace her . . . and with Jennifer. Cher felt something unfamiliar, an unpleasant emotion. She was so self-assured, she generally felt so superior to the skanks and hos and marks around her that it was rare that she felt this annoying emotional tic, but she realized with a start that part of her dislike for the debutante was based on jealousy. From the day that girl had arrived in her Armani panties she had seemed an affront to Cher, and if she didn't come right out and say, 'I'm better than any poor white trash like you could ever hope to be,' there was something in her posture and attitude that said it just as plain as speech. And there was no denying that

Movita favored her. Cher was jealous of Jennifer. It wasn't a nice feeling to have, but she supposed there was very little she could do about it. It was a pity that Movita felt that Jennifer was crew material, and it was clear she was planning to replace Cher with the debutante.

It wasn't that Cher blamed Movita – hey, it would be as much as her parole was worth to even jot her a postcard once Cher was out, and she knew she wouldn't think of Jennings or the other women. She could walk right by Theresa on the street and not notice her. But somehow Movita's friendship really mattered. Movita had to take care of herself because she was doin' a long stretch and Cher knew it but somehow seein' herself replaced with the little debutante caused her a pang.

She turned to face Movita. 'And just why are *you* kissin' her uppity white ass?' she spat.

'You ain't go no idea about *what* she's doin'!' Movita spat back. Cher could see that Movita was about to say more, but she stopped abruptly, shut her mouth, and remained silent – avoiding Cher's glare.

Something *was* up; Cher could always tell when a scam or a grift was going down – after all, she'd been grifting for twenty years – and something was definitely going down now. She narrowed her eyes and stared intently at her old friend Movita. The kettle water wasn't heated enough to really clean but she didn't care. She poured the lukewarm water into the plastic dishpan. 'What's going on here, Mo? What ain't you tellin' Cher? Huh?'

'I'm just sayin' we should cut Spencer some slack, that's all,' Movita said quietly, scraping the remains of the chicken bones and most of the coleslaw into the trash. 'That's alls I'm sayin'.'

Cher snorted. No one had ever cut any slack for Cher in her entire life. If there was one thing she had *never* gotten her share of, it was slack. And now she would be damned if some snotty little rich white girl from New York City was going to get all of that, too – especially from Movita, known by all to be tough as hell. It had taken Cher months to get hooked up with Movita. And now the deb was her new best friend?

Cher would never admit to fear anything, and she wasn't *afraid* to get out but . . . Cher let the empty kettle fall to the floor with a clang and headed for the door. 'I'll cut that little bitch somethin', and it won't be any slack,' she hissed. She shoved Suki out of her way. Cher heard Movita say something and follow her out of the cell, but she didn't look back.

The pay telephone was at the far end of the rec room, and Jennifer stood hunched there with her back to the line of women waiting for the phone. She held the telephone receiver to her right ear with her shoulder, and with her left hand she was covering her other ear to cut out some of the noise from the blaring television set. With her right hand she was frantically making notes, stopping now and then to put up her palm to the impatient inmates.

That's all Cher had to see. She crossed the room in less than four strides and without hesitation yanked the receiver from the startled Jennifer and slammed it back into its cradle on the phone. 'What the hell do you think you're doing?' Jennifer asked.

'You need to learn how to share, Missy,' Cher said to Jennifer.

'I wasn't finished and that was a *very* important call,' the deb told her, then reached to pick up the receiver again. But

Cher was having none of that and put her larger and stronger hand hard on top of Jennifer's.

'I wasn't finished and that was a very important call,' mocked Cher. She had mastered her impersonation of Jennifer, and her performance earned great guffaws of appreciative laughter from the rest of the women in the rec room. That is, from everyone except Movita, who had witnessed the whole confrontation and now came to the front of the group.

'That's enough, you two,' Movita ordered. 'Spencer's got to finish her call.'

'The hell she does,' Cher shouted. 'What's so damned important that this little bitch gets to hog the phone?'

There were murmurs of assent from the other inmates.

'I have *business* to take care of,' Jennifer shouted in response.

'Business?' Cher spat incredulously, 'What business do *you* have? Anyway,' she taunted, 'I thought *you* weren't going to be here long.'

The rec room was dead silent and all eyes were on the three of them. Cher knew she'd broken the first rule of any crew – no fighting or dissing in front of outsiders, but she felt wild with loneliness, disappointment, and futility. 'Both of you, shut your mouths,' Movita said. She looked hard at Cher. 'Gettin' outta prison isn't always somethin' that's good for a person, you know?' Cher felt herself color. Lord Jesus, she hadn't blushed since she was twelve years old. Movita motioned to the hall. 'Come on over here with me,' she told Cher. Then she turned to the deb and said, 'Get on the end of the line and finish your call.' She looked at the inmates gawking and waiting. 'That all right, girls?' she asked. The women in the line nodded. Jennifer walked to the end and Movita didn't say anything more, except to turn to Linda, the first woman waiting to use the phone, and indicate with a nod of her head that it was her turn at the phone.

Cher followed Movita out into the hallway. 'What in the hell is goin' on here?' Cher demanded the minute they got out of earshot. 'Somethin's up. I can always tell when somethin's up.'

'There ain't nothin' up that concerns you,' Movita said quietly.

'Then why are you dissin' me like that?' Cher asked almost petulantly.

'*You* were dissin' *Spencer* in there,' Movita explained. 'I don't want my crew fightin' with each other. Especially in front of that Jesus-freak group in the rec room. Spencer is *crew* now, Cher. She's one of us, and she was makin' a call I asked her to make, not that it was your bidness. And for a woman who has managed to get her hands on plenty of cash, I'd remind ya' that to diss someone for their financial success might be hypocrisy. It ain't no crime for her to be rich. You just jealous that her scams are bigger than yours.'

Cher went to bed determined to find out just what was going on with Jennifer Spencer. She wanted to know what Jennifer was up to, and she wanted to know what Movita knew about it and why she wouldn't tell her.

The next morning on the way to breakfast Cher managed to mutter a half-assed 'I'm sorry' to the debutante, though that cost her. Cher got her breakfast and parked herself in the seat next to the deb. Theresa was babbling about some new computer program she was learning, and Suki told them about how Gloria finally gave up and started 'dating' Georgette, a stone butch who had been courting her for months. When there was a pause, Cher took the opening. 'So, where do you live in New York?' she asked.

'Tribeca,' Jennifer told her.

'Umm. That's near Wall Street, right?' Cher asked, like some dumb-ass cracker. 'Isn't that where JFK, Jr. lived?'

'Yes.'

'You live on the same street?'

'No, he was on North Moore Street. I'm on Washington.'

'No kiddin'?' Cher said. 'What number? I know someone who lives on Washington Street.'

'I'm two-oh-one.'

'Nah,' Cher said. 'He must have been further uptown.'

Movita joined them then with her usual breakfast – three cups of coffee and a half bowl of sugar. Suki got up and returned with her plate heaped high with something that passed for home fries.

'You know,' Cher said as she picked at her plate, 'I'm really sorry about that boyfriend thing. I've had my own run of bastards. Movita will attest to that.'

Movita, silent as she was most mornings, just raised her head and grunted. 'They ain't worth dog shit but they can make you feel *real* bad.'

Cher looked over at Movita, who seemed oblivious. 'What was your guy's name? Tom Branson?'

'Tom *Branston*,' Jennifer corrected.

'He's a fancy-ass Wall Street dude, right? Loaded and everythin'?' Cher asked, trying not to be too obvious.

'He's an ass, a lawyer, and loaded with shit,' Jennifer answered, and Theresa and Suki giggled.

'You two lived together? He got your crib?'

'No. We were going to get married, though.'

'So who's watchin' your place now? Who's takin' care of your cat and waterin' your plants?' Cher took the opportunity to get on the better side of the deb. 'That call you were on last night, was it to him?'

'No,' Jennifer sniffed in reply. 'But I do need to finish that phone call,' she said.

'You won't be makin' any phone calls till after work,' Cher told her. 'But I won't interrupt you again. Like I said, I'm sorry about that. But what'n the hell's so important about them phone calls anyway?' she asked. Cher wanted Jennifer and Movita to take her into their confidence, but Jennifer made a point of turning her head away.

'What's the guy's name and number?' Movita asked Jennifer. 'Gwen has a meeting and she won't be in till noon. I'll get 'im on the phone and then I'll call down to the laundry and tell 'em that the Warden wants to see ya' in her office, okay?'

When Cher heard that, her forced good humor left her and she couldn't help snorting in disgust. 'You're gonna get your ass in some kind of real jam, Movita honey. And for what? So that this one can talk to her lawyer or something? She won't even tell us what's goin' on.'

Movita dismissed Cher with a wave of her hand, then wrote down the name and telephone number that Jennifer told her. Cher memorized it. When the bell that signaled the end of breakfast rang, there was the usual groan and the women slowly rose to begin their day of work.

Cher began her walk down to Intake but shook her head. What was wrong with Movita? It would be against every regulation in the book for Movita to let Jennifer Spencer use the telephone in the Warden's office.

But Movita shook her head and said, 'I just wanna hear

what she has to say to her lawyer, honey. That's all that this is about.'

Cher worried all day about Movita and the phone call. If she got caught it wouldn't just be time in the SHU, she'd lose her job with the Prez for sure. And Cher couldn't imagine Movita peeling vegetables or delivering ice for the rest of her life. Damnit! Why would she take such a chance for the debutante? Was she in love with her?

None of the women in their crew were lesbians. Neither were a lot of the women who hooked up. Many just did it out of loneliness, or because they were wooed by dykes. Once they left prison they never thought about it again. But there were the stone bulldaggers who were career lesbians. Cher didn't care if people fucked philodendrons, but she couldn't imagine that Movita had gone so nuts that she wanted the deb in that way. So why all of this risk and special treatment? Why even bring her into the crew in the first place? As she processed the candy that came into Intake that day she worried herself over it.

Cher was relieved to see Movita at dinner. Better than in the hole. She waited patiently with the surprise she had figured out, until she had a chance to get the two of them alone in her crib. Cher looked at Movita and then at Jennifer. 'You finally gonna tell me what's goin' on round here?' she asked, but neither woman would answer her question.

'Things might be changing around here real soon,' Movita said as she sat on her bunk. 'I'm not just talking about your parole.'

'Fine,' Cher said, 'don't tell me. I'll find out soon enough.' She walked over to her own bed and sat down.

'But it seems to me that whatever is going on, Miss Armani here needs to use a telephone real bad to make sure it happens. Am I at least right about that much?'

'Yeah,' Jennifer admitted with a nod. 'You're right about that.'

'Did ya' get your call out?' Cher asked Movita.

'Nah. The Warden was in her office all day. There wasn't any time to get away with it,' Movita admitted with disappointment.

'Well, then,' Cher said as she lifted the corner of her mattress, 'I always like to do my share to help.' From beneath the mattress she pulled a cell phone and handed it to Jennifer. 'Here ya' go. Lifted it from a new inmate earlier in this week.'

'What is it?' Movita asked.

'It's a cell phone,' the deb said. 'My God, it's a cell phone!'

'Let me see,' Movita asked. Cher handed it to her. Sometimes she forgot that Movita hadn't been Outside for a long time. 'Where's its base?' Movita asked.

'It don't have a base,' Cher said. 'Whaddaya think, it's a blues band?'

'It just works like this?' Movita asked. 'No base, no electric line, no nothing?'

'It needs a battery and a charger. They get plugged into an outlet,' Spencer said, and looked over at Cher.

'I got 'em,' Cher told her. 'You got 'em now. But you get caught with this, either one of you, and they ship your ass to Iceland.'

'Does it work?' Jennifer said, staring at the cell phone as if it were the Holy Grail.

'Hell yes, it works,' Cher said proudly. 'I called my own

lawyer from it to confirm my parole hearing.' She extended it to Jennifer. 'Consider it a gift – a peace offering from me to you.'

Jennifer turned to Movita and exclaimed, 'Do you know what this means?' Then she turned back to Cher and stammered, 'I don't know what to say. This is – this is just wonderful.'

'Man, if they toss the cell and find it, it won't be wonderful,' Movita said. 'But it's great, Cher.' She looked at her straight in the face for the first time in days. 'Thank you.'

Movita reached out and took Cher's hand. 'Look,' she said. 'I didn't want to trouble ya' with this. You got enough on your mind with your parole and gettin' out. But something real bad is goin' down here and Jennifer has been tryin' to help.'

Cher shrugged. 'What are you talkin' about? The Spanish Inquisition?'

'Maybe worse. The priests left you alone if you were Catholic,' the deb said. 'This will affect everyone.'

Then Movita told Cher about the report she'd copped off the warden, and the plans to privatize, and what that meant. It took them a little while, and Cher listened closely, then shook her head. 'Man,' she said, 'when it comes to scams ya' can't beat rich white men for comin' up with the best. And legal, too. I hope there is reincarnation,' she said, ' 'cause I wanna be a rich, fat-assed white man in my next life.'

27

Jennifer Spencer

Freedom suppressed and again regained bites with keener fangs than freedom never endangered.

Cicero, *De Officiis*

'Spencer,' Officer Mowbry called out in her little girl voice. 'Visitor. Stevenson, Vassallo. Visitors. McInnery, lawyer.' Jen stood up, glad of any distraction. She knew it was Lenny so there was no reason to be excited, but it would be interesting to hear what he had learned about JRU.

As Jen walked to the visitor's room along with a cluster of her fellow inmates, she had a thought that made her hate herself. For a moment as she looked around it seemed to her as if she were one of them – she looked like them, she smelled like them, and the longer she was at Jennings the more she felt herself slipping lower and lower into their degradation. She almost felt she was a part of the prison now.

When she'd agreed to try to help Movita with JRU she'd immediately been transferred from the laundry job to the library – leaving poor Suki to fend for herself. She felt guilty but relieved. The thing was, she actually *liked* several of her fellow inmates: Suki, of course, and Movita, and even the laundry supervisor, Flora. She'd even stopped being afraid of Springtime – now she identified with her for trying too hard to get out of this place.

She walked through the security check and into the visitor's room. She didn't bother fluffing her hair – or anything else for that matter – she wasn't worried about her appearance. Instead of her gorgeous Tom, it would only be Lenny. There was the usual noise and chaos in the visitor's room. She looked around for Lenny and saw him waiting. He was average height, a trifle thin and narrow in the shoulders. His suit was gray – she hated gray suits – and wrinkled. Stop it, she said to herself. Sick, sick, sick. It was great of Lenny to show up at all. Remember, Tom is a bastard, not fit to serve food to some of the people here. She smiled to herself at the thought. Flora, walking next to her, saw the smile and smiled back. 'He your man?' she asked, and without waiting for an answer continued. 'Isn't it wonderful?' she asked. 'I *love* visitor's day.'

Jennifer felt thoroughly ashamed of herself for her earlier thoughts. Flora was such a damn sweet woman. She tried hard to be fair with all the women who worked under her in the laundry. And she was a better, cooler manager than some of the men at Hudson, Van Schaank. She certainly had to deal with more troubled employees – although, neurosis for neurosis, the day traders at Hudson, Van Schaank & Michaels could stack up against any inmate here. But as she made her way toward Lenny Benson she admitted to herself that she was a snob. There were, as usual, some children in the crowd, and one voice overpowering the rest sounded like it belonged to one of Theresa's relatives. Her entire extended family seemed to be overly gregarious, and they all cursed more than a commodity trader.

Lenny moved toward her and took a seat at a table between Maria's sister Blanche and Theresa's Aunt Helen. Lenny's modesty was as conspicuous as Tom's pride. He had a large box in front of him wrapped in camouflage-patterned paper. Jennifer had to smile. That was funny. Had he meant it as a joke? she wondered.

'Hi,' she said to him as she took the seat opposite. 'I can't thank you enough for coming.'

'Hey, yes you can,' he answered. 'In fact, you already have. I'm happy to be here.'

She looked around the room at the chaos, tears, and noise, then looked back at him and laughed. What was his private life like if a visit to Jennings Correctional Institution made him happy? But he looked as if he meant it.

'Did you have much luck with the research I asked about?'

'I found out a lot of interesting stuff,' he said. Then he patted at the box in front of him. 'And I brought a lot of interesting stuff. What do you want first?'

'You shouldn't get me gifts. Really,' she told him. 'I have money and I insist on paying you back.'

He waved his hand as if insects flew before his face. 'Forget it,' he said. 'But who is managing your money now? And what about your condo? Who's dealing with the carrying costs and the real estate taxes?'

'I gave Tom power of attorney,' Jennifer admitted. Maybe that hadn't been such a good idea, she thought now. 'I thought he was trustworthy,' she said. 'And he'll keep my canteen fund filled,' she laughed, albeit a bit bitterly. 'I'm only allowed to spend ninety dollars there every two weeks. So it's not a lot of money.'

Lenny just looked at her and was silent.

'I'm anxious to hear about you-know-what. Did you find out much?' Jennifer continued to break the silence.

'Yeah. As much as there was to find.' He picked up his briefcase, a very nerdy one she noticed, not Gucci like Tom's. She looked away, around the room, while he fumbled through the bag.

What she saw amazed her. Flora and Maria, as well as other women she'd seen around – workers from the laundry, inmates from her unit – they all looked so different here! Their faces were transformed by some kind of . . . life, she guessed it was. And even the ones crying, obviously getting bad news about family members or being disappointed, even they looked – well – alive. Jen looked over at Theresa. Even *she* looked happier, if such a thing was possible for a woman on a constant high.

And JRU was planning to curtail visitation? Jennifer felt a surge of anger. She turned back to Lenny. 'So let's cover the situation first. What did you find out?' she asked him. 'Keep your voice down.' She leaned in to him across the table.

'Well,' Lenny began, 'for one thing, JRU is privately held, and pretty closely. It's not easy to get anything on them but . . . well, let's just say I have my sources.' He smiled, and she noticed for the first time that he had a dimple on his left cheek. She wondered why she'd never noticed it, but it could have been because she'd never seen Lenny smile before.

'How big is it?' she asked. 'JRU.'

'Small. It only does about thirty million annually. It's a

start-up. And it's doing nothing in profits. They've gotten these couple of prison contracts all in the last three years.'

Jennifer's eyes brightened. 'That's good, for a start. At least they're not Philip Morris with a fleet of fucking lawyers.'

'Yeah, but news from the other prisons, the couple that they are managing, isn't good. It looks like they're trying to avoid any capital expenditure and milking the facility for profits by cutting costs to the bone.'

'Shit! How much worse can the food get?' she asked. A start-up that wasn't profitable but still going for more of the same. 'So how does this make sense?'

'I did a lot of digging and I think they might be setting themselves up to be acquired by Wackenhut, or something. They, of course, are the "prison as gross industry" superstars.'

Jennifer's face darkened. 'It *is* a gross industry,' she muttered. 'Who's the CEO? Is it Steve Ross, starting out with parking lots or what?'

'John Tarrington. A senior VP from Wackenhut. Other than him, they're just a bunch of financial guys with *gotz* for industry experience. They're obviously using his contacts to get the contracts, and he's using their expertise to put together the proposals. I got their previous ones, by the way.'

She smiled at him. 'Cool,' she said. 'So what's up?'

'They're not setting it up to go public, and it isn't going to make them risk. I figure they gotta be setting themselves up for acquisition. Their only real assets are those contracts.'

Jen thought about it and nodded. Maybe so. Or the CEO, this Tarrington guy, had a hard-on for someone he'd worked for and wanted to make a point. You never knew with men.

'Whatever it is, they're underfinanced,' Lenny added, then took out some spreadsheets and explained the basics of their financials. They paused. 'Okay,' he said. 'I did as you asked and I haven't bothered you with a single question. But why all this interest?'

'They're going to take over this place.'

'So I heard.'

'How did they get the contract if they're so . . .'

'Hey, since when does the government make sound business decisions? I don't know their political connections. Or their board. But I'll have that information in a couple of days,' he told her. Jen had to admit she was impressed with Mr Benson. 'Jennifer, what are you thinking about?'

'I don't know,' she told him honestly.

'Maybe some . . . interaction with JRU?' he offered.

Jen nodded, then turned her face away and looked again at Flora, Maria, and all the other women. 'This place is awful, but it could be even worse,' she told him. 'I'd like to help stop that.' She leaned even closer to him and lowered her voice further. 'I'm in a bind, though,' she said quickly. 'I don't want to do anything that would be considered "bad behavior" here. I've got to make my stay as short a time as possible.'

'Of course you do,' Lenny said.

They were both silent for a moment.

'I'm sorry,' he told her.

'You were right about Tom,' she said. 'And maybe about everything else.' All at once Jennifer had to struggle to keep from crying.

Lenny reached out and took her arm. 'Don't waste tears on him. He's a yellow rat bastard.'

Jennifer laughed in spite of herself, and felt a little better.

'A yellow rat bastard?' she asked. 'I thought that was a shop in Soho.' At least she could speak. 'I had to go into the SHU last week,' she began, and told him all about what had happened when Tom visited. Lenny listened, his eyes warm with sympathy. After she got to the part about her hands she stopped and looked at him. 'I shouldn't burden you with this. It's all so weird. I'm sorry. I just need to tell somebody.'

'Please,' Lenny said, holding both of his hands out and open. 'Tell me. I'm interested.'

So Jen kept telling him: about the crew, and the trouble with Cher, and especially about Movita and what she'd revealed. As she spoke she looked down and unconsciously wrapped her arms around herself. It wasn't until she was finished that she realized that she was not only hugging herself but also rocking in her chair. She stopped, embarrassed, and looked at Lenny Benson, expecting to see disgust or disapproval. But he was looking at her with such sympathy that she was taken aback.

'Amnesty International officially condemns the U.S. prison system,' he said. 'Did you know that? They list it as the worst in the world. And since 1980 the female inmate population has increased by more than five hundred percent.'

'God!' Jennifer said. 'That is so . . . so . . . terrible. You see, these women' – she moved her eyes to include the other inmates in the room – 'a lot of them never did anything really wrong. They acted in self-defense, or they were in the wrong place at the wrong time. Can you imagine?'

'Hey,' he said. 'I've read up on the subject. How about Rebecca Cross, who was sentenced to twenty years without parole for a first offense? *Possession* of fifty-five dollars' worth of dope.'

'Yeah,' she replied. 'Unbelievable. But only some of them are totally innocent.'

'Like you,' Lenny said.

She shook her head. 'Uh-uh. I'm afraid I wasn't *totally* –'

'Close enough,' Lenny interrupted. 'It's not *you* who should be in prison.' He paused.

'You warned me,' Jennifer admitted. 'I was greedy. And stupid. I was looking for a shortcut.'

'Forget it,' he said, and his expression changed from pensive to efficient. 'Let's get back to JRU. Let me tell you what I think. If you want to influence what they do, we could try to get someone on the board. Or influence people already on it. Do you remember the first Bush administration?'

'It's not something I like to focus on,' Jennifer admitted.

'Well, he followed Reagan, and the Republicans had already had a field day with deregulation. They set all the savings banks free and hotshots bought them up left and right. Then they started giving out loans to their hotshot pals so all the little moms' and pops' and widows' and orphans' savings were lent out to golf-playing Republican scammers like Keating.'

'Oh,' Jennifer said. 'I remember *him*.'

'Yeah. Another yellow rat bastard. Anyway his pals defaulted on the loans, but he'd already been paid off for lending them money and the friggin' bank failed. And then, because of the FDIC, the taxpayers had to bail out the banks.'

'I do remember that now,' she said. 'Wasn't one of the Bush boys involved?'

'Yeah. Silverado. Another big bank that went bust. He'd been put on the board. Not that he knew dick about banking. Anyway, the point is, I think that there's a parallel here. Back then they deregulated savings banks and there was a big opportunity to drain them. Now they privatize prisons and another opportunity exists to collect the fees from the state, pay almost nothing to keep up the infrastructure and take care of the prisoners. They make a few bucks from their labor before selling off quick for a profit or declaring bankruptcy.'

'That's a cheerful scenario,' Jennifer said. 'Hey Lenny, what do you know about the Rafferty boys, Bryce and Tyler?'

'They've dipped their wicks into things no one else would touch,' he said, then blushed. 'Sorry. I didn't mean to be vulgar.'

Jennifer bent her head down so he wouldn't see her smile at that. Everyone on Wall Street swore like sailors – it was a prerequisite. 'The question I want answered about them is if they fuck over their partners as well as investors.'

'I don't know,' he said. 'But it's easy enough to find out. Call me Tuesday. I'll have some info by then. Anyway, why do you ask? You think they might have some influence at JRU?'

'I'm not sure why I'm asking,' Jennifer admitted. 'I don't really have a plan yet. I just want to have . . . options.'

'Well, I wish your option was to forget all of this and get out of here,' Lenny said.

'Tom promised me he's going to really push Howard McBane.'

'I wouldn't trust anything Tom said,' Lenny told her glumly. 'And I'd reconsider that power of attorney. If he goes near your portfolio, I'm going to stop him. I'm telling you that right now.'

'Look. He might not want to marry me, but he's not a thief and he doesn't want me ratting him out, either. And Donald is good for his word.' Lenny looked away. 'I won't be here much longer,' Jennifer told him. 'But it would be terrible to let this happen to the other women. Most of the ones I've met aren't criminals, they're victims.'

Visiting time was almost over, but Lenny wasn't prepared to leave. 'Wait,' he said. 'You have to open the box of stuff I brought. Don't you want to?'

'Are you kidding?' Jen said and smiled. 'I'm the original material girl. I liked stuff before but you can't imagine how we *love* stuff in here.'

'It was all really nicely wrapped,' he said, and sighed, 'but they opened everything. Kinda ruined it.' He held up a bright red bow and a piece of newspaper. It was a page of the *Wall Street Journal*. 'It was black and white and red all over,' he said. 'I figured you'd have fun reading it.'

'Hey. Waste not, want not,' she told him. 'I'll take it. Unusual reading matter here.' She looked into the first opened box. 'Oh God! Floris soaps! How did you know I love them?'

Lenny shrugged, then colored.

Jennifer looked at the other items in the parcel. There was more toothpaste, deodorant, and breath mints. There were Pringles, and onion dip, and Balsen cookies and there was even a box of high fashion chocolates – Richart – that had also been torn apart. 'I'm sorry,' Lenny said. 'They opened it all up.'

'Looking for contraband,' Jen told him and shrugged. She looked down at the tiny, delicate chocolates, each one decorated exquisitely. 'God, they're beautiful! At least they didn't eat any. My crew will go nuts over these.'

'I'll bring you one every week if you like them that much,' Lenny said.

Jen looked at him. Could a man be this nice? Yeah, but only if he was boring, she thought, scanning his face. But the thing was, Lenny – at least the Lenny visiting her and working on this JRU thing – really wasn't boring. He wasn't like the close-mouthed, shut-down, unenthusiastic guy he was at Hudson, Van Schaank & Michaels. How interesting life is, she thought. You never could judge by appearances and maybe all men weren't . . .

'What did you call Tom?' she asked him.

'Tom? I said he's a yellow rat bastard. And he is.'

'Right,' Jen said. Maybe all men weren't yellow rat bastards, she thought, looking at Lenny.

'What's the matter?' he asked. 'You're so quiet.'

'Nothing,' she said. 'I'm fine.' And she went back to opening her box of goodies.

28

Gwen Harding

Illegal for many years, private companies employing prisoners directly was again made legal in the mid '70s.

Prison Activist Resource Center

The intercom buzz brought Gwen out of her reverie. 'The parole board is waiting for you, Warden,' Miss Ringling's voice sang through the speaker.

"Thank you, I'll be out in a minute.'

Today was judgment day for Cher McInnery. And Gwen had nothing but good things to report on the woman. It was a blessing that someone was going to get out before Jennings took a dive. Gwen just hoped that Cher didn't cop an attitude like she had the last time she was up and screw herself out of the opportunity of being released. Sometimes it happened, though. The fear of the Outside and the unknown combined with the smugness of the parole board members was sometimes too much for the inmates and they would do whatever was necessary – even get into trouble – to get to stay in Jennings. But Cher McInnery was not a career convict. She'd been watching her step for a long time and Gwen thought that she had seen a positive change in her attitude since Movita had taken Spencer in to her crew.

There were a lot of rules in the penal system designed by men for men that didn't work for women. One of the ones that caused Gwen the most profound pain was the enforced parole statute that prohibited ex-inmates from fraternizing with other convicted offenders. Among the male population this made a lot of sense because many young men had come to prison on a first offense, then learned illegal crafts and scams from more experienced prisoners, and then were pulled back into criminal behavior by their prison buddies once they were released. But women – particularly those incarcerated for long periods of time – often made deep and meaningful friendships with other inmates. Prohibiting them from making contact with their prison 'families' Outside always struck Gwen not only as harsh but as counterproductive. For a woman to be cut off from all of her social contacts at a time when she was reentering society and needed all the support she could get seemed ridiculous. It was cruel and unusual punishment to pull someone like Cher out of her crew of 'sisters' and legislate that she could never again communicate with Movita or Theresa or Suki, that she could never see them again or know how they were progressing not only in prison but afterwards when they were out.

So, Gwen pulled the McInnery file from the folder stacks on her desk, walked out of her office, and actually smiled at Movita. 'Change is good for everyone, Movita, it really is,' she said, and went to be Mom, Teacher, and Caring Nurse perhaps for the last time.

After the board meeting Gwen tried not to disclose by her expression the outcome to Movita. She knew that she and Cher were tight, but the word for something so important as parole should come from the board, not through gossip or guesswork. Gwen Harding was so deep in thought that she actually jumped as the intercom buzzer sounded. 'Yes?'

'The JRU people are here to see you,' Movita's voice crackled through the tinny speaker. Was the disturbance static in the system or was it actually Movita's reaction to the group that was on their way to her office?

Gwen knew that Movita Watson wasn't a stupid woman and may well have figured out change was in the air here at Jennings. And on Gwen's night of drunkenness she may have revealed more than she should have, though she couldn't remember. Neither one of the women had ever referred to it.

Gwen pushed the red button on the intercom. 'Send them right in when they get here please, Movita.'

'Yes, ma'am,' the woman's voice responded.

She would miss Movita Watson more than anyone, Gwen thought as she placed her hands on the edge of her desk, pushed her chair backwards, and slowly stood up. She walked over to a small mirror that hung discreetly on the back of her door and looked at the small patch of discoloration that remained on her forehead. At least the visible signs of that incident had all but vanished. Gwen pulled out her makeup and covered the bit of bruise, then freshened her lipstick. She began to pace around her office, waiting for the group to arrive. She couldn't help but wonder how long it would be until she was fired. Perhaps it would be today. She stopped to look out one of the three windows of her office, all of them overlooking the yard. Maybe there would be a transport van in the sally port waiting to take her away once the tour was over and the new JRU representative took her place.

Since the state's response, the JRU staff had been busy as ants at a picnic. There wasn't a corner of the prison they hadn't combed. If anything, Gwen felt more and more apprehensive about the changes coming. Today, she supposed, she was going to hear about them.

As always, it took a while for outsiders to clear security and be brought to her. Gwen's suit was nearly soaked with perspiration by the time there was a knock on the door. She took her seat as Movita popped her head in to announce the arrival of her 'guests'. But there was a strange look on her dark face and she mouthed, 'Only one,' while she raised her index finger into the air. What was going on? Gwen thought. Had JRU canceled the tour and only sent her replacement?

As Movita opened the door wider, Gwen tried to smile as she greeted a tall, thin woman with as hardy a 'good morning' as she could muster. But she shouldn't have bothered. The woman was all business and cut right to the chase after the customary exchange of professional and personal niceties.

'I'm Marlys Johnston and I've come to let you know what we – JRU – expect from you, Warden Harding, during this transition period,' she said even as she slipped into the chair across from her. The woman had a powerful aura. She was even more arrogant and self-confident than Jennifer Spencer had been the first time she stepped into her office, Gwen thought. Perhaps it was because she was older – thirty-six or thirty-eight by the look of her.

Marlys Johnston leaned forward and placed her leather briefcase in the middle of Gwen's desk. It was obvious the woman was well paid because never in all her working years had Gwen been able to afford such a beautiful accessory. The woman's fingertips gleamed in the overhead light as they wrapped around the edges of the case – professional manicure, where the tips of the nails were white and the rest was natural color. If Gwen could have afforded it she would have known what it was called. There was a loud click as the latches of the briefcase flew open and Ms Johnston pulled papers from the suede-lined interior.

'You'll find everything you need in this report,' the Marlys woman said as she handed Gwen a neatly bound report. *Thinking Outside the Box* was printed in bold letters on the cover, along with the JRU logo. Gwen smiled. Somehow the phrase reminded her of Springtime, who was about due for another escape attempt. 'I think reading this will help you to see the potential here at Jennings,' Marlys said with an emotionless smile. 'I think you'll find that the observations that you made in your report to the state will look a little different if seen from another perspective.'

Gwen slowly lowered herself into the chair beside her desk. She looked down at the booklet. She hadn't had much doubt that she had lost the battle. But this news told her she was going to have to surrender. That her complete report submitted to the state, which was supposed to be confidential, had been passed on to JRU was the final nail. It made things very clear that the state was not – had never been – on Gwen's side. And Marlys Johnston was definitely not on Gwen's side, either.

But as the meeting continued it became equally clear that Marlys Johnston had been sent to Jennings neither to ignore Gwen nor to fire her. She had been sent to wear her down or scare her away. 'There is so much underutilized space here,' the consultant kept saying over and over and over again. 'You have both indoor *and* outdoor recreational areas, as well as a visitation center, and both a library *and* an events and programs facility.'

Gwen would've itemized the same spaces as a locker room, a parking lot, a hallway, a virtual closet with some old books, and another closet with a folding table. *An events and programs facility?* Who in the hell was she trying to kid? And a *visitation center?* It was little more than a hallway divided by bulletproof glass. But her objections slid off Ms Johnston. 'Perhaps' – Gwen tried to calm herself so she wouldn't stammer – 'if you saw these spaces. Let me show them to you and you see what you think.'

'I'm quite capable of reading a blueprint, Gwen. May I call you Gwen?'

'We prefer a more formal approach here. I call the inmates "Ms" or "Mrs" and they refer to me as Warden. We expect the same of the COs.'

Marlys Johnston simply raised her brows and said nothing.

'We're concerned that you're at about fifty percent capacity at this time,' Marlys observed as they passed through the cellblock. 'These are four-man cells,' she said, while noting the fact again on her legal pad.

'Yes,' Gwen agreed. 'As I've explained to JRU staff time and time again, they were designed in the dark ages to be four-man cells, but now they are *two-woman* cells.'

Marlys didn't seem to catch the intent of Gwen's reply. She went on to see only what she wanted to see. 'So, Gwen, I'm assuming that all other facilities here at Jennings are equally underutilized.' She continued with her list. 'The kitchen, therefore, was designed to serve twice the number of inmates,' she began, 'and the laundry was designed to do the same. I'm assuming that the health care department would also be more than sufficient for the number of inmates currently housed here. Am I right, Gwen?'

Gwen gritted her teeth. She didn't want this woman to call her 'Gwen'. But she took small, shallow breaths to try to keep her composure and to avoid the possibility of speaking in a stammer. 'Perhaps if the equipment was all updated and we had a medical staff,' Gwen told her. 'Then it might be sufficient.'

'Oh, don't be so negative, Gwen.'

'Miss Johnston,' Gwen said sternly, causing her guest to look up promptly and stop taking notes. 'You and I both know that what you are saying only makes sense on paper. This facility was built over thirty years ago. No doubt with asbestos and then painted with lead paint. All penologists agree that there are and must be differences between prisons for men and those for women. If you read my report, you can't possibly suggest that Jennings could operate with twice the number of inmates.'

'Warden,' Marlys said as kindly as Gwen was stern. 'I'm here to help. I'm here to work with you to make this transition as smooth as possible. I want to work *with* you, Gwen – not against you. We just have to get you to think outside the box, that's all. Okay?'

Gwen wondered what the penalty would be if she slapped Marlys Johnston, but she nodded and tried her best to muster a cooperative-looking smile. She feared that Marlys Johnston was her last chance – small as it was – to get herself heard before more changes were made that would forever destroy everything she had worked all these hard years to build. 'I believe that any transition must be done at a slow pace,' Gwen told the woman. 'A prison population can be volatile.'

'I agree! That's why we'll make the first change small. We'll start with visitation day.' Gwen held her tongue. 'To best structure the work week, the midweek visitation day will be eliminated. As it stands now the inmates have to earn merits to get that day applied to them anyway, so we'll just have them work that day instead.'

Gwen actually gasped. 'But the visits are very important to inmate morale here at Jennings. And some family members work weekends, particularly in lower-level jobs. You can't just . . .'

Marlys Johnston smiled again. 'Yes, we can, Warden. You just have to begin thinking outside the box. And I want you to make the announcement at dinnertime tonight about next Wednesday's visitation. Let the ladies sleep on it.'

'I don't think they're going to sleep after hearing that. And don't you think it's best to give more notice? Some people plan a month or more ahead for visiting.'

'Warden Harding, we need to move forward as quickly as we can so that the facility starts to earn a profit by the second fiscal quarter,' the beastly woman said. 'That will mean cutting costs, cutting staff, and gearing up for productive work – work that industry will pay for.'

'And how will that improve the lives of the inmates? I can't believe . . .'

'If you want to succeed with JRU, Gwen, you're going to have to start thinking more positively.' The woman gathered her papers, closed her fancy briefcase with those fancy painted fingers, and nodded a good-bye to Gwen, who only had the strength to nod back.

Gwen sat at her desk and thought about how badly she needed a drink. She *had* to have a drink. With the JRU International stage set and geared up for 'transitions' she needed a drink. Gwen reached over to her drawer and pulled it open. She looked down at nip bottles she had lined up in rows. She pulled one out and twisted the cap open. She poured the liquid down her throat, replaced the cap back on the glass bottle, and inverted the bottle in the row in the drawer.

It was all psychological. She had to have routine in her life. She couldn't give up everything completely. No cold turkey for her at this time in her life. She had heard that people trying to quit smoking would often have a cigarette handy, hold it, pretend to flick the ashes and place it in the ashtray, even put it in their mouth and try to inhale. But the trick was to *never* light the cigarette. So she improvised with her gin. She bought little glass bottles, filled them with water, and kept them in her drawer. It was a false sense of comfort for her, but she needed comfort now with all the changes going on around her.

Well, she hadn't been fired but she might as well quit. It was going to be a nightmare – hell it was going to be an uproar, a riot – when the inmates found out about visitor's day. Even with all the disappointment that sometimes happened with visitors not showing up or not staying for the full hour, the prisoners worked very hard to earn those days. She didn't want to be the one to have to disappoint these women with the change. They were so sensitive to these sorts of things – not because they were women – but because they were used to a schedule. Jesus, she could remember what a disturbance there had been when the food service took off scrambled eggs and added pancakes. They expected everything to stay as it was. Change was not favored here at all.

Gwen couldn't help but think that she didn't like the changes that were going to have to take place in her life because of JRU. If she left now, she'd have a reduction in her pension or perhaps lose it altogether. And where would she get another job? She chuckled at the thought of seeing herself as a door greeter at Wal-Mart on a part-time basis. Collecting hardly any pay, no insurance coverage, but boy, oh boy, she'd get an employee discount and even more of a break on Tuesdays when it was Seniors Day.

She picked up her cup of coffee and thought of the biblical reference, 'Let this cup pass from my lips.' How true this was. She felt like she was being crucified.

29

Jennifer Spencer

From jail, it is difficult to prepare an adequate defense – while on the other hand, a person who can make bail usually is able to search for a lawyer, round up witnesses, secure a job, and make a good case for herself in court.

Kathryn Watterson, *Women in Prison*

The only mail that came into Jennings that wasn't ransacked and examined was the privileged communications from attorneys. When Jennifer received the thick envelope from Howard McBane, she immediately went to her bunk and tore it open. There were pages and pages. She picked up the cover letter and read it.

Dear Miss Spencer,

After careful analysis of your case and a reading of the trial transcripts, we believe that there are no significant grounds for an appeal. Discussions with your counsel, Thomas Branston, indicate that he is in agreement.

We could, of course, proceed with the appeal on some minor grounds, but that is a time-consuming and costly undertaking. If, in the face of this advice, you determine to continue, we will represent you, but we first wanted to apprise you of the likely outcome. The firm will also require a sizeable retainer.

As you can see, I have enclosed a detailed estimate, as well as the opinions rendered on your case by several of our senior partners, along with annotated trial transcripts where relevant.

Jennifer looked at the letter with horror. She tried to take a deep breath but the air wouldn't go into her lungs. She read it again to be sure she hadn't made some mistake.

Of course she'd made a mistake, but it hadn't been in reading the damn letter. She'd made a huge mistake in choosing where to place her trust. First, she had been promised by Donald and Tom that she wouldn't be found guilty. Then, when she was, they had guaranteed her a suspended sentence. When she'd been sentenced to prison, they had told her that most likely she would get an immediate pardon, and when that fell through Tom had told her the appeal would take only a matter of weeks. Then Tom had broken up with her, but assured her that Howard would see that the appeal went smoothly. And now she was being informed by Howard that 'there are no significant grounds for an appeal.' How about the fact that it was Donald Michaels, not she, who was guilty?

She turned a page. And the next one made the first seem like good news! It literally took what little breath she had away. It was a request for a $280,000 retainer. Jennifer must have made a noise, because Suki, who had just entered the cell, asked, 'Are you all right?'

Jennifer couldn't answer. She had no air in her lungs and she was sick to her stomach. She moaned a little. God, here she was, thinking she was smarter and better than all the other women in prison, and she was probably the most sophisticated dupe in the joint. She wondered for the first time if perhaps she had been set up from the very beginning to take this fall. Maybe the whole romance with Tom, the engagement, everything, had just been a way to find someone willing to be the victim. She actually felt dizzy and leaned back onto the flat pillow of her bunk. Suki stepped over to her and took her hand. Jen moaned again.

'Are you all right, Jenny?' Suki asked again. 'Should I get Movita?'

Jennifer just shook her head. She wasn't all right, but how could Movita or anyone help? Donald Michaels had been doing questionable IPOs since before the dot-com boom. He and all the rest of Wall Street. But he'd played just a little faster, a little looser, and a lot more visibly than others. He'd always been aware that the SEC and the market self-regulatory agency were tracking him. It occurred to her that it was just possible he had hired her with the idea that a good girl like her, from a Catholic school, might be the perfect one to catch the flak if it ever flew. And she'd thought it had been her rap about Gulbenkian porcelain.

'Jenny? Jenny, you're scaring me,' Suki said.

'I'll be all right,' Jennifer managed to tell her. Then she concentrated on trying to breathe. The brain needed oxygen to think. 'Sit down, Suki,' she told the girl, though she was barely conscious of whether her cellmate was sitting or standing. She had no energy to talk to Suki now. She had to think. 'Leave me be,' she said.

Well, though Howard may have given up on her, Donald

had promised her that they would be responsible for her legal expenses, and she was going to find another firm that felt she had a better shot at an appeal than these puppets at Swithmore, McBane. And they would pay for it, because if they didn't, she would call the SEC on the phone in the rec room and begin to rattle off every secret she knew. And she would hope that the call was monitored, because she would want not only the prison authorities, but the FBI and the IRS to hear about this shit.

She sat up, jumped off the bunk, and turned to Suki.

'Help me,' Jennifer said, and they lifted the bed so she could get to the cell phone secreted in the pipe of the leg.

'Watch out,' she told Suki. 'I have to make a really important phone call.'

Suki just nodded, but her eyes opened wide. Jennifer punched in Tom's cell phone. Despite his caller ID the son-of-a-bitch didn't know this number, so she wouldn't get voicemail. Sure enough, the bastard answered on the first ring.

'Tom Branston,' he said.

'I know who *you* are,' she said. 'You better not hang up when you know who *I* am.'

'Jennifer?' he asked, and she could hear the surprise and dismay in his voice.

She didn't bother with preliminaries. 'Did you see the letter from that creep, Howard McBane?' she asked.

'It's privileged information Jennifer. I haven't seen the letter, but he did communicate with me that . . .'

'Cut the crap, Tom. The first question I have to ask is, was I railroaded from the very beginning? Or was I merely the most convenient dispensable player?'

'Jennifer, I can't really talk to you now . . .'

'Wait a minute! Don't you dare hang up!' Her tone of voice was enough to ensure that he didn't. 'The second question I have to ask is whether you have the phone number of Charles Hainey at the SEC handy, because I'm about to call him and drop a dime on the two of you, as we convicts say.'

'Jennifer, I . . .'

'Listen to me, you liar. If you and Donald don't *immediately* find, and pay, some lawyers who can get me out of here, you're both going to be really, really sorry.'

There was a dead pause, and for a moment she was afraid that they had been disconnected. But then his voice came through as clearly as if he were standing in the cell with her. And his voice wasn't pleasant, but there was an undercurrent of . . . was it fear? she wondered.

'Jennifer, don't do anything crazy. I haven't seen this letter from Howard, but I'll call him right away and I'll get ahold of Donald,' he told her. 'You know we're behind you. But if you're guilty . . .'

'If I'm guilty!' Jennifer screeched. Suki turned around and gestured to her and she lowered her voice. 'Listen,' she said with more intensity than she had ever used in her life. 'I did what you told me to. *Because* you told me to. We all agreed. And if I'm the least little bit guilty, then you and Donald are very, very guilty and in trouble big-time. Maybe you've forgotten I know all about the Fischer offering, and that was before my time. And Sam Sutton told me all the details on the Omnigroup IPO. Not to mention the way Donald bragged about it when he had a few martinis in him.' That ought to put the fear of God into him.

But his voice went cold. 'Jennifer, you're on a cell phone.

This call can be overheard, and it sounds like you're threatening blackmail.' He paused. 'Just because I broke off our engagement is no reason to seek revenge.'

'Revenge? Are you insane?' she asked. 'Don't try to make this some woman-scorned bullshit. Trust me, Tom, this is strictly business.'

His voice was formal. She'd heard it like that when he was about to walk out of a negotiation. 'On behalf of Donald Michaels and Hudson, Van Schaank, I have to tell you that we won't be party to this kind of shakedown,' he told her.

Jennifer actually stared at the mouthpiece of the phone. How crazy was this son-of-a-bitch? And how had she confused him with a decent man?

'You can try and pretend for the record that what went down didn't go down,' she told him now. 'But I need to hear an assurance from you and Donald Michaels, within the next three hours, that Alan Dershowitz or somebody even better has been retained and paid for on my behalf. And if I don't . . .'

'Jennifer, this is a nonproductive conversation at this point. In fact, based on your guilt it may represent a conflict of interest. But I'll try to speak with Howard and Donald. Call me tonight around ten o'clock.'

'I can't call you at ten o'clock,' she virtually spat at him. 'I'm in prison, remember? I'll call you at eight. And you better have some answers by then.'

She hit the end button of the phone, Suki came over, and the two of them got the phone back into its hiding place.

Jennifer could not breathe. She could not speak or move or even swallow the bile that was threatening to choke her. It burned the back of her throat.

'I don't know how much longer I can keep this secret,' Suki said, totally out of the blue, as she rolled over in her bunk.

Jennifer sat up. It felt good to be able to sit upright. Suki had asked to switch bunks since she kept getting up during the night to pee. And the girl never stopped talking about the baby when she was awake. 'You have to be careful about any of this,' Jennifer warned Suki. 'You'll get us all in trouble.'

'How can *you* all get in trouble? It doesn't involve any of *you*,' Suki whined.

Sometimes it was hard to tell if Suki was dumb or just played dumb. 'Like hell it doesn't,' Jen told her. 'We'll all get put in the SHU.'

'Me being pregnant won't do all that,' Suki said.

Jennifer actually laughed out loud. She'd thought, of course, that Suki was referring to the hidden cell phone and all the unusual activity.

'It's not a laughing matter!' Suki said with much more than the usual vehemence. 'The whole thing was a terrible experience. It brought everything back. You know, from when I was twelve and my cousin Travis forced me to do it with him and his friends.'

Jennifer was shocked at hearing this confession. 'I can't imagine Camry being capable of such an aggressive act.'

Suki swung her head out from under the bunk. 'It wasn't Roger. He's the nicest CO in here,' Suki said with anger.

'I just assumed that . . .'

Suki moved her head back into her pillow and talked into the bottom of Jennifer's bunk. 'God! You're crazy. It was Karl Byrd. I hate him.'

Jennifer was stunned – and nauseated. She remembered

the overtures and smirks from Byrd, and wondered how close she had come to being raped. But Suki had never seemed resentful about her pregnancy. She didn't seem to connect the man she hated with the baby she was carrying. For some reason Jennifer remembered a tribe she had read of in her college anthropology course. They had never connected the sexual act with pregnancy. Didn't it bother Suki that the baby she seemed to already love was Karl Byrd's baby as well? Jennifer realized Suki was talking and bent to listen.

'I had just been reassigned to working in the laundry. Byrd worked days then.' Suki stopped for a moment as if to build up the courage to continue. 'We were in the dirty laundry area with Flora when a buzzer went off on one of the washers. He sent Flora to take care of it and he escorted me to the back to get more dirty laundry. There he told me to get a bag.'

Suki stopped again. She must have been starting to cry because Jen could hear her sniffle and see the shadow cast on the floor of her arm going to her face. She was wiping away tears. 'We wore one-piece green dresses before you came here, and when I bent over . . .' She took a deep breath. 'He came at me from behind. He cupped his hand over my mouth and pushed me into the pile of dirty clothes. I didn't know what was happening at first. My face was pushed into the stinking laundry and his hand covered me so I could hardly breathe. He pushed himself on me. He was so heavy, and then I felt his thing – his dick.'

Jennifer jumped off her bunk and bent down to Suki. She felt sick. 'Why didn't you report it? He can't get away with that. You can't just rape someone.'

'Ha. He did. Right then, and he got off twice, Jen. Twice!

The second time I fought him hard. I turned over so we were face-to-face. But he got me by the throat.'

Jennifer felt tears run down her face. 'Oh, Suki. I'm so sorry! The first day I came here, I knew he was no good. But why didn't you say something to Movita or Cher?'

'He told me that he'd hurt me if I told anyone. He said it would be his word against mine and that no one would believe a frightened, lying little whore inmate.' She paused. 'He also told me I was lucky he wasn't a nigger. That's what he said.'

'We've got to do something,' Jennifer insisted. 'It's not right.'

Suki grabbed Jen's arm and squeezed it hard. '*We* will do nothing,' Suki said looking directly into Jennifer's eyes. 'At least I've managed to get far enough along so nobody will try to get me to abort. And even though I got pregnant in a bad experience, I *want* to have this baby. I lost my other to foster care and I'll never get her back. I want to have someone to love, someone that will love me back.' She patted her belly. 'A baby is a new chance, Jenny. And Roger says he'll take care of me – when I'm on the Outside – and he'll be a good daddy to the baby.'

Jennifer sat on the cold concrete floor. She couldn't believe how naïve, and brave, and stupid this woman was. She had been violated in ways that Jennifer had a hard time comprehending, but Suki found the positive in all of it. 'I get it,' she said gently, and added her hand to the girl's belly. 'Mum's the word. No pun intended.'

Jennifer barely ate dinner that night, though Movita's cooking was good. She moved the food around on her plate until Cher asked her, 'You gonna eat that or hang it on your wall?'

She didn't even respond while the chatter went on around her. She was a human stopwatch, counting down the minutes until eight o'clock. She needed to be sure she was first on the line for the phone and she rushed through the washup as quickly as she could. She couldn't take a chance on using the cell phone again, partly because she might be seen by a CO and partly because she was afraid Tom might have caller ID and investigate. Anyway, the cell phone was only for JRU business, not for her personal convenience. Movita asked her a question, but she didn't hear it, and the woman just shook her head, leaving Jennifer to stow the plates in the footlocker. When she was finally done, she rushed down the hall to the rec room.

The noise was already deafening. The television was blaring loudly, and two groups of tough-looking women had taken on sides to cheer on some event. As always, one of the psychotics was ranting, this time at an empty chair. Jennifer moved directly to one of the phones, stooped to make sure she wouldn't block the view of the set, and urgently placed her collect call to Tom's apartment. Her knees were shaking as she waited and rehearsed in her mind the outrage she would unleash upon the betraying Tom. Jennifer could barely hear the operator when she asked, 'We have a collect call from Jennifer Spencer, will you accept the charges?' and she turned and glared at the noisy sports fans, but then she heard Tom's voice. 'Jennifer,' was all that he said. His tone stopped her cold.

'This is the last call I'm going to accept from you,' he said flatly. 'Should you call my home again I will contact the Warden and tell her that you are harassing me. Is that understood?' Jennifer could not speak. 'Is that understood?' Tom repeated.

'Is this Tom Branston?' Jennifer asked weakly. 'Tom, it's Jennifer.' There was silence on the line. 'Tom?'

'I'm sorry, Jennifer,' Tom spoke more quietly. 'But nothing more can be done. We've looked into it and it's clear to everyone involved that you were actively complicit in what was going on at the firm and you got caught. You were a little too ambitious, a little too willing to take shortcuts. There's nothing more I can do about it.'

Jennifer didn't sleep that night but she didn't spend one minute of it crying. She did curse herself for being stupid, for thinking she was smarter than she was, and most of all for trusting men who had made their careers and all their money by taking advantage of the trust of idiots like herself.

But she knew that to continue looking backward would kill her. She told herself that, compared to the other women sleeping in 'houses' all around her, she had been lucky. She had to tell herself that, repeating it like a mantra, or else she might begin to shake so badly she would split down the middle like a log hit by an ax for kindling. She wouldn't split, she wouldn't come apart, she told herself. She thought of Movita's dark eyes and her words of advice when she had come to her in the SHU. 'This place can break you forever. Or it can make you stronger.'

Jennifer had a three-to-five-year sentence. For the first time she tried to imagine what that meant. With good behavior she'd be out in a year and a half. She felt as if she'd already served a lifetime. It was too easy to lose track of time. How would she get through it?

She had always been an optimistic person. She thought it was probably genetic. And she knew how to work hard.

She thought of her condo, the silk rugs, the antique furniture, and the soft, soft Pratesi sheets. The blanket on her bunk, pulled up to her shoulder, was a parody of comfort, but it would have to do. She was lucky, she reminded herself, one of the lucky ones. Unlike Maggie Rafferty, or Movita Watson, she'd be going home, and though she wouldn't mind killing either Tom or Donald, she certainly wouldn't want to pay the price they had. Nor, she realized, did she want to go back to her old job or even that industry – not that she'd be allowed to. Movita and Maggie had been right: She'd been selfish. There had to be more than simply working sixteen hours a day, buying lots of gifts for yourself and taking some splendid vacations sometimes. During that long, long night it became clear to her that dealing with JRU and the situation before her was a responsibility that, for some reason, had been placed in her hands.

She hadn't prayed in a long time. She wasn't sure that she believed in the God the nuns had taught her about, but she still believed in destiny, in fate, or perhaps some higher power that placed people in situations for a reason. As the night wore on she was certain that her fate was connected to these women and their future at Jennings. In this month she already felt closer and more connected to them than she ever had to either her partners or adversaries at HVS – Hudson, Van Schaank.

She tried to find a more comfortable position on the lumpy mattress. It was virtually impossible. She heard a CO go by on patrol. By now she could already distinguish the sound of their steps. It was probably Mowbry, a heavyset, African American woman, who seemed to show a lot of compassion to the prisoners. What this place needed, first and foremost, was a lot more compassion. After that, of course, it needed about a million other things, from more library books to inmate classes to a maternal visitation wing to . . . well, the list was endless.

Jen tossed again and again. She now had no doubt that she would have to serve her sentence and, for the first time, she admitted to herself that it was fair that she do so. She *had* participated in manipulating and insider trading. Of course, it was de rigueur. And she, Tom, Donald, virtually all the men she had worked with at Hudson, Van Schaank, and the other Wall Street experts at other firms did the same thing on a daily basis. But that didn't make it right that she had. More unforgivable was that she'd been so proud of it.

Yes, that had been her big sin. Being proud that she, Jennifer Anne Spencer, had been smarter than the other girls, had figured out a way to get herself out of the life she'd been assigned and into what looked – on the outside at least – like a much better one. But her brain was something she didn't deserve any credit for. It had been an inherited gift, no different from the pretty blue eyes she had, or the money that so many of her classmates at Wharton had inherited and that she had so resented. She had taken her gift and her energy and she'd squandered it on Beidermeyer armoires.

Jennifer lay on the thin mattress, the worn and ugly blanket pulled over her, and decided not to look back. She had always had a strong will and she would use it now, not only to help herself but to help others if she could.

Tomorrow she would talk with Maggie and see if she could reach the Rafferty boys. They were thought of as outlaws, Wall Street gunslingers who played the very edge of the line, but she no longer had to worry about her reputation. There, in the dark, she smiled, if a bit grimly, and began to do what she did so well: try to find the solution to a business problem in front of her. Comforted with the familiarity of it, she fell asleep just as the small strips of sky visible through the high windows were beginning to lighten.

30

Movita Watson

We're not allowed to communicate with the girls after they get out. They can call or write us here, but we can't answer unless they get special permission from their parole officer.

Ms Bonnie Brown, a registered nurse at a state prison.
Kathryn Watterson, *Women in Prison*

The first time I laid eyes on Cher McInnery I thought she was nothin' better than a piece of wild hillbilly white trash. But Cher didn't mind; she never pretended to be anything nor anybody other than who she was. And if I tell you she was smart as a whip, ya' better believe it. Cher was a thief – everythin' she saw was ripe for the pickin'. But she wasn't just a booster; she'd been involved in some complicated scams. She lived without pretense and with both eyes wide open. She was always on the lookout for the next opportunity to take what she needed, and when she got to Jennings, she knew that what she needed was a friend.

So, on the day Cher met me, the thief decided that she would just have to steal my black girl's heart. I wasn't sure I understood how it happened, but until now I was damn glad that it did. She made me laugh, and I could set her off, too. Neither one of us was much of a crier, but if I did have to shed a few tears I would have rather done it in front of Cher than anyone. I knew that Jennings was goin' to be a damn lonely place for me after she was gone.

Those last days before Cher's release were hard on me. I admit it. Cher knew it and she tried not to talk too much about her meetin' before the parole board, her future plans, or any of it in front of me. But it was almost impossible for an inmate not to be excited (and a little nervous) when she was getting out of prison after almost four years. And the others – especially Theresa – couldn't seem to talk about anythin' else.

The evenin' after Cher's parole hearing wasn't easy for me. I wished her well. I'm not a godful type so I didn't pray or nothin' but if I was I would have.

'Well, take a look at Miss McInnery over there,' Theresa crowed when Cher got back to our crib. 'Doesn't she just look like the cat who stole the canary?' Her parole hearin' must have gone well. Cher was not only a great mimic but a really gifted actress – the girl could make a man believe she was a virgin while she was givin' head.

Anyway, real unlike her, Cher said nothin' back to Theresa – except to mumble a halfhearted, 'No way.'

'No way?' Theresa pressed on. 'Cher, you're positively glowing with excitement. I could make a fortune if I could bottle your skin color right now! You look like you're ready to take on the world.' She shot a glance over at me. And again, Cher muttered the same, 'No way.' I could see she didn't want to make no federal case out of it. But Theresa – a woman happiest when beating a dead damn horse – refused to let the subject drop, and after a few more words of enthusiastic encouragement – always followed by Cher's 'no way' – I finally snapped.

'What in the hell is this "no way" shit you keep sayin'?' I demanded.

'Oh, everybody on the Outside says it,' Suki chimed in. 'My sister says that my niece is *always* saying it. You know, "no way" this and "no way" that.'

'Well, it sounds dumb as hell,' I snarled. Sometimes, when I've missed some slang or didn't know they made bite-size Oreos I feel bad. Like the world is passin' me by. Cher just stood up and walked away.

She was tryin' to be kind, but I knew things would never be the same anymore between me and Cher. They couldn't be. Cher was leavin' this place – but I was never gettin' out, and when one of the crew left I always went through a low time. But it would be really hard to lose Cher.

She got her parole and we celebrated, but it was still a bittersweet supper that we all shared on Cher's last night. Theresa tried to make jokes about it bein' the Last Supper, but the laughs were forced and the smiles were pretty sad. Cher would be gone in the mornin'. Her time was up. No one could think of anythin' more to say that would make sense of the situation. How could Cher be anythin' 'cept happy at the thought of gettin' out of prison? But how could any of us be anythin' 'cept envious or real damn sad at the thought of losing a friend? Our conflict of emotions couldn't be put into words.

Over dinner I studied Cher's face. How did she feel knowin' it was her last night on a lumpy mattress, her last night of starin' up at bedsprings? How would it feel to me? I couldn't imagine it. Her face, angular and no longer young but not yet middle-aged, showed nothin'.

I hoped she had changed, but I doubted it. She might have been punished in Jennings but she sure hadn't been rehabilitated. If anythin', it seemed like Cher was only tougher and hungrier for more thievery. No one said it, but in their hearts I think all the crew suspected – maybe even hoped – that Cher would be back before long.

'So, what exactly are your plans, Cher?' Jennifer asked. The two of them had become much more friendly since the cell phone incident. Cher had spent hours in their house, rubbin' Suki's swollen feet and talkin' to Jenny about her business, Wall Street, and all kinds of shit. Now Jen asked, 'Will you be staying with your family?'

Cher shook her head. 'Do you have any kind of job lined up or anything like that? It seems like after this it might be kind of hard to adjust again.'

'Don't worry about me, Jenny,' Cher said with her smile. 'I have plans.'

'Such as?' Jennifer asked.

'Well, I thought maybe I might become a stock broker like you,' Cher replied. 'Seems to me that you and your kind have figured out a legal way to steal. You just dress better while you're doing it, that's all.'

Jennifer's laughter was uneasy. Then she shrugged. 'I don't think felons can become registered brokers. But if you need a recommendation, just let me know.'

I watched Cher look directly into Jennifer's eyes. I knew she was sensitive about havin' been busted – it hurt her pride. In all her years of stealin' she'd been busted but never convicted before. With a cold calm she said, 'Thank you Jennifer, but you've already helped me more than you can know.'

I should have put two and two together and seen what

was comin' then, but I didn't. The uneasy silence that followed Cher's remark was of course, broken by Theresa. 'Maybe we should have a toast,' she suggested as she refilled their glasses with grape juice. When everyone was ready all eyes turned to me, like I was some kind of toastmaster.

'You know,' I began after some thought, 'I haven't seen my babies now in quite a while. And it breaks my heart to think about how much they must've grown since I last saw 'em.' I stopped and closed my eyes tightly for a moment before continuin' with the toast. 'A mama is supposed to want her babies to grow *up*, but there's not a mama I know that wants her babies to grow *away* from her. But babies gotta go out on their own. And so does Cher, I guess.'

'You calling me a baby, Movita?' Cher asked in mock protest.

I got over my mood. 'You know what I'm callin' you honey,' I shot back. 'I got this crew together so we could take care of each other in this place. And we have one of us is leavin' and it ain't so easy to see her go. I'll worry about ya', girl. Who'll cover your back?'

Just then Suki screeched. 'Oooh! The baby's moving!'

It was a mood changer for sure whenever Suki shared the baby's activity. I went over to her and put my hand on her belly. The baby kicked again. 'He's gonna be a football player with a kick like that,' I told her.

'It's gonna be a girl,' Suki said matter-of-factly.

'Now, just how do you know that?' Theresa asked.

'My sister Louisa says that when you carry in the front it's a girl, when you carry in the back it's a boy,' Suki said.

Jennifer came over to Suki. 'Can I?' she asked, indicating her belly.

'Sure, everybody else does. Heck, I should start charging

for the feel. What do you think it's worth? A bag of Fritos from the canteen?' Suki asked.

I went back to my seat and watched Jennifer with Suki. She seemed a little bit scared of the whole thing and, when the baby kicked, Jennifer actually jumped back, startled. I had to chuckle to myself. I had to admit it was kinda weird to know there was a baby in Suki's still relatively flat stomach. I wished I had been able to conceal my belly durin' my pregnancies. But I gained fifty pounds. I started to get lonely for my girls so I had to start talkin' again. 'So what kind of names do you have picked out?' I asked Suki.

'I like Allison,' Suki said.

'How about Juanita?' I suggested.

'Oh Jesus,' Cher said in mock panic, 'don't listen to a black woman when it comes to naming a baby!'

'What in the hell is that supposed to mean?' I asked her.

'Oh, please!' Cher said, 'if she listens to you that baby will end up with some kind of name like Metamucil or Mylanta.'

'Is Stephanie, Bethany, Tiffany, or Brittany any better?' I asked, and made her laugh. 'You're gonna need Mylanta if you don't shut your dumb honky mouth,' I threatened good-naturedly.

They were all laughin' so hard that no one noticed as the Warden stepped into the cell and gently put a hand on Cher's shoulder. 'Sounds as if you're enjoying yourselves,' she said.

Cher pulled her shoulder away and said, 'We're just trying to make the most of my last night.'

'I just came by to wish you well, Cher,' the Warden said. 'And to see how you ladies were doing. I guess it's going to be rather different not having Cher around, isn't it?' She looked around the room but made eye contact with me.

No one said anything. So I stood up. 'Thanks for comin' by, Warden,' I said.

The warden nodded at me. 'Well, I'll leave you to enjoy each other's company,' she said, and she turned and walked down the hallway.

Once she was gone, all the women fell back in their seats and bunks and let out a simultaneous sigh. 'Whoooeee!' Cher exclaimed. 'That was a close one. You girls better be careful with her; ya' never know when she's gonna pop in. As for me, I'm gonna be gone.'

I turned and looked first at Cher, then at each of the others. The pain in my eyes was almost more than they could bear, but not one of them looked away. 'I'm gonna die in this place,' I said simply. 'I'm never gettin' out of here. Never.'

'But . . .' Cher tried to speak.

'Shut up, girl,' I said, raising my hand. 'Shut up and listen, and make sure you don't make the same mistake I made. You hear me? Don't you trust no man when ya' get outta here. They set ya' up and then they let ya' down. I was dumb enough to trust my Earl. I let him keep his drugs at my place 'cause he told me it was just petty dealin'. But when the cops showed up and arrested me right in front of my babies, Earl was nowhere to be found.' I shrugged. 'When the police released me for turnin' Earl in, he hurt me. He hurt me real bad. But all of the reasons and all that shit don't mean a damn thing anymore. I killed him. And now I'm gonna live the rest of my days in here.' I walked over to Cher and took her hands. 'Much as I love ya', girl, I don't want ya' comin' back here, ya' understand? When ya' leave here tomorrow, I don't want to ever see your face again. I just love ya' too much.'

Cher only nodded. She understood all too well.

'We're gonna miss you, Cher,' Theresa said with uncharacteristic brevity and no Hallmark bullshit.

'I'm gonna miss all the stuff you steal,' Suki added. We laughed.

'Don't worry,' she told Suki. 'The very first thing I'm gonna boost is a layette for the baby.' We all laughed again. 'And I might just miss all of you, too,' Cher admitted. 'But I'll come back on visitor's day. Wait'll you see me then. I'm gonna get me a face-lift and a nip and a tuck . . .'

'How are ya' gonna steal a face-lift?' I asked. Of course she couldn't come to visit. But Jennifer raised her glass and the others followed. She said, 'Here's to our new and improved, soon-to-be-free Miss Cher McInnery.'

'Hear! Hear!' the others chimed in.

I couldn't really tell what Jennifer was thinkin'. It wasn't like her and Cher ever got along real well, though since the phone thing they'd been chummy. I'm sayin' they respected each other – but they weren't tight. Oh, she was jokin' and laughin' with the rest of us – but I couldn't tell whether she was happy for Cher – or happy to see Cher go. And then that girl did the nicest damned thing. 'I've brought something very special to the party,' she said with a smile, and she pulled out the fanciest box of candy I had ever seen. 'It's Richart Chocolat,' she said – in French! 'Lenny brought them for me.'

The crew couldn't get over these things – each one no bigger than the size of a sugar cube but all decorated up like a work of art. Some had dots – some had squiggles – some were striped. Each one a tiny little masterpiece. Who takes the time to paint on a piece of candy? And what does it cost? 'Cher goes first,' Jennifer said.

I think Cher liked that. She reached into the box, fished out a deep dark cube. 'It's almost too pretty to eat.'

She was about to put it in her mouth when Theresa, who was looking at the card or such that came with the chocolate, let out a screech. 'Stop!' she shouted. 'You're not eating it right.'

'I'm not what?' Cher asked.

'There's this little book here with the candy,' Theresa explained. 'And right here there's a whole page on "tasting technique".'

'You mean I can't just eat it?'

'Girl, I been eatin' chocolate all my life and it seems just fine. Never got arrested for it,' I said.

'No. If something's worth doing, let's do it right,' Theresa said. 'Everybody get a chocolate.'

We did. She began to read. 'Now, "To really taste the base and primary flavor notes, wait a few seconds after you place a piece of chocolate into your mouth. To release the secondary flavors, expand the chocolate's surface area by chewing five to ten times. Let the chocolate melt slowly by pushing it gently against the roof of your mouth. Make note of the flavor, the texture and the way the chocolate lingers on the tongue."' Theresa read.

We tried to do it just like the book said, but I was laughin' so damn hard I nearly choked. Suki drooled some chocolate down her chin. Jennifer shook her head and just walked out.

Cher took another piece.

'Wait,' Theresa commanded. 'Is that a plain chocolate or a filled chocolate?' she asked.

'It's a good chocolate,' Cher said.

'It's a filled one and there's a different way to eat them,' Theresa said.

'Get the fuck outta here,' Cher said and grabbed the little booklet. She looked it over. 'Holy shit,' she said. 'It's true. Look at this. They tell you to chew the filled chocolate only three to five times!' She then read aloud from the book. '"New flavors continue to appear as the two melt in your mouth. Finally, make note of how long the flavor lingers on the tongue."'

'Are they talkin' about eatin' candy or givin' a blow job?' I asked.

'Screw it,' Theresa finally gave in. 'Let's just eat the damn things. Besides, what kinda world is this?' Theresa asked. 'They got pages and pages on what wines and what teas you can mix with this stuff. Who had the time to think this shit up?'

Everyone laughed but Cher. 'That's the world I'd like to live in,' Cher said.

You ain't allowed to see an inmate off. I don't know why they would think there's a security risk. Cher wasn't gonna try and make a break for it – she was free as a bird. No one else would, because even Springtime with all of her botched escapes wasn't dumb or crazy enough to try to escape out the front entrance of Jennings while the officers and the guns were right there. I didn't expect to see Cher again but The Woman, tryin' to be nice, I think, invited me to join the escort party to take Cher out.

Fact was, I didn't want to. Night before I had had a few bad readings after the good-bye party and in the mornin' I didn't even look in Cher's direction before I went up to the office. What's gone is gone, and another ten minutes with Cher didn't seem like no favor, since both she and I knew that we would never see each other again. Livin' Inside ya' gotta learn to cut your losses and let go. I had been in the process of lettin' go for weeks and this wasn't gonna be nothin' but painful. Still, I knew I couldn't explain it to the Warden, so I got up and went with her.

I know it was sorta an honor to be invited. They don't let no convicts into the group and I suppose – since I was never gonna see it any other way – it was interestin' to check out the release procedures. But the fact is, I could hardly look at Cher and she could hardly look at me. The two women officers were quiet in front of the Warden, and although Gwen was present it couldn't make up for the awkwardness between me and Cher. I watched as she traded her uniform for the clothes she had worn in. She looked real good in them, too. She got a bagful of possessions, the cash from her canteen fund and the money the state gives you to start a new life – a pathetic amount that wouldn't pay for a bus ticket past Pennsylvania. There was a lot of paperwork – the stuff I saw afterwards and often had to file and put away, and Cher was busy signin' her name on a lot of sheets and copies.

I kept my head down and my eyes on the floor durin' most of it. Fact was, I was jealous that she was goin'. I was sad to see her leave. I was happy for her, and I was generally miserable. Finally we got to the exit and The Woman gave her some little talk about somethin' and Cher, bein' Cher, cracked wise. I don't remember what she said but I remember what happened next. 'Well,' Gwen Harding said, 'I guess you two will want to say good-bye.' I guess she expected a warm prison scene, somethin' where the two of us hugged and cried on each other's shoulders or somethin' like that. But I had already been in enough pain and Cher was too eager to go to be bothered with that.

Cher and I stood there. I looked up from the floor. Somethin' was expected so I put my hand out. 'Good-bye,' I said, and Cher took my cold hand in her cool one.

'Good-bye,' she answered. She turned around and I looked at her back, dressed in some real nice jacket. I figured that would be the last time I'd ever see her again, and I turned around and headed back into Jennings.

31

Maggie Rafferty

Murderers – the people we fear the most – make up a minority of the prison population, and most of them have killed a mate, not a stranger. They represent no danger to society.

Kathryn Watterson, *Women in Prison*

For a murderess serving a life sentence, I'm lucky. I'm also well aware of the humor of that statement, but it doesn't make it any less true. I have a room to myself, a constant flow of books from the Outside, two loving sons who try to make my days as interesting as possible and visit me often. I'm also lucky in having an understanding warden who doesn't go out of her way to 'bust my chops' – as they quaintly put it here at Jennings. So when I poured boiling water into my tea cup and bowl of McCann's oatmeal as I did each morning rather than eating in the mess hall, I also opened the pages of the *New York Times*. One of the small pleasures of imprisonment has been having enough time not only to read the *New York Times* daily from cover to cover, but also to read the *New Yorker* each week before the next one comes.

When my oatmeal was ready and the tea steeped, I had a spoonful of one and a sip of the other and then continued to thumb through the *Times*. When I reached the business section I paused and nearly spilled my tea. I looked down at a picture of Tom Branston and Donald Michaels. They were standing next to – and *smiling* with – the investigator who had charged and arrested Jennifer Spencer for investment fraud. The headline over the photo read: FURTHER INVESTIGATIONS INTO HUDSON VAN SCHAANK & MICHAELS CALLED OFF. The caption below the photo quoted Branston: 'Hudson Van Schaank gave full cooperation throughout the investigation, and the weight of evidence now convinces me that Jennifer Spencer – and she alone – was the "bad seed" at our firm.'

Bad seed, indeed! Was there no end to the perfidy of men? It was then that Frances came to the cell door to deliver ice, and this time it wasn't just the frozen H_2O I received but also a kite. Frances, as always, was careful to fill the cooler to the very top. I thanked her and waited until she was gone to open the note. *Meet me and the deb during recreation at 2:30.* It wasn't signed – kites are contraband and it would be stupid to sign one – but I knew Movita's handwriting and who 'the deb' was.

Recreation always struck me as a particularly sad word for the ninety minutes that we were allowed outside the walls of Jennings every day. In effect, though we were outside we were still within the walls because the three wings of the prison created a U-shape and the open part of the 'U' was blocked by double fencing. Still, it was a chance to see the sky. I have never understood how many of the women could bear to go on without any view of the sky at all or why the prison architects consciously decided to create prison cells – and I'm not talking about the ones in the SHU – that had no windows at all. Oddly, at least to me, because they were in a newer part of the building they were considered very desirable by many women, but I would never give up my window, small and too highly placed as it was. Recreation for me was the time I tried to do what the Buddhists and contemplative nuns call walking meditation. I usually started by keeping my feet moving around the perimeter of the yard and slowly closing in. I took a breath with every other step and if I was lucky – which I admit has been rare in my life – I could complete a constantly shrinking square until I ended my ninety minutes in the very center of the recreation yard. But more often than not, arguments, interruptions, distractions, or athletics prevented me from my pilgrimage. Still, I looked forward to the time and the challenge. I wasn't really pleased to think of spending it talking, but I knew this was, of course, important.

The weather was what I used to call gray and drizzly but now I thought of as 'soft'. Somehow the light and the dampness were kinder than the sunshine against the brick and I, like all the other inmates, needed as much kindness as I could get. But I took it as a good sign and although I saw Movita from the moment I got out to the recreation area I made sure that I began my walk as usual.

Movita hadn't been herself lately. Of course it was particularly difficult on us lifers when an inmate 'graduated', since we never would. And it was particularly cruel that they were not allowed to communicate with us or us with them. But as a lifer I had learned to let changes like this flow over and through me. It was unusual that Movita had gotten close enough to Cher that her leaving upset her. This is one of the lessons prison teaches: not to care too much about anyone.

At any rate, Movita was moping and I did not join her. It wasn't my way. Inmates, particularly female ones, are attuned to *any* change in the pattern of the day, and this was not a meeting we needed to have attention drawn to. Still, it wasn't unusual for me to be interrupted a dozen or more times when I was doing my walk.

Jennifer Spencer joined us shortly after Movita and I met and we decided to keep walking, although not in the deliberate way I usually did. I liked Jennifer Spencer. I admired her spirit and I was amused by the personal naïveté that I occasionally glimpsed behind the mask of a sophisticated and shrewd businesswoman. I felt that I understood Jennifer Spencer – her dreams, her determination, her now bitter disillusionment with a man she thought she loved. I certainly respected her business acumen. 'Okay,' she said to both of us now, and she spoke with complete authority. 'Based on what I know, I think we have a situation here.'

'Well, we all know it's a situation,' Movita said darkly.

'I misspoke,' Jennifer said. 'I meant to say we have an opportunity.' She began to explain the financial status of JRU. How the company was underfinanced and looked like a candidate for takeover. 'I've been thinking,' she said, 'better than trying to influence the board, or take one of those paths with an uncertain outcome, like trying to buy an influential minority of private stock, I think we should buy the company.'

Movita shook her head. 'This is not the time for jokes.'

But I knew Spencer wasn't joking. 'How much would it take?' I asked, with the first feeling of hope I'd had since the day I read the report.

'That's hard to say. But they're very underfinanced. The other two prison contracts they have haven't yet turned the corner and become profitable. I'm not sure whether either a CCA or a Wackenhut would step in at this point. And my information leads me to believe that they're not going to have much more capital.'

'What would it take?' I asked her again.

'I don't know, but I think it's time to meet with your sons.'

Movita looked at the two of us. 'You bitches are crazy,' she said. 'Or else you're richer than I ever thought, and bigger thieves than Cher McInnery on her best day. How you goin' to buy a big company like that?'

'I don't know,' Jennifer told her. 'I don't know if we can do it, but sometimes a leveraged buyout works. That's what it's called. You just need to offer some of the private owners more money for their share of the company than they think they'll get any other way. And if they're greedy or they've lost confidence in the business, they say yes and there we are.'

'What do you mean, "we", white girl?' Movita asked. And I actually laughed out loud. 'Then can you open all the doors and let us all out?'

'Look, you know perfectly well that JRU can't do that. You know they can't change our sentences, affect our parole, or give us extra prison time. They are only going to administer the facility for the state. But if we were doing the administration . . .'

'The changes we could make! We could institute classes again. We could create a wing for the really deranged inmates. We could have more exercise time, better work details, a better library,' I said.

'Hold on, hold on,' Jennifer Spencer said. 'We can't lose money or throw it away. We would have to come up with a way to make reform pay. But maybe we could do that. Still, we're getting ahead of ourselves.' Jennifer turned to me. 'Could you ask your sons to come up here for a meeting?'

'Of course,' I told her. 'And let the games begin.'

Both of my boys are good-looking. Bryce is thirty-five and divorced. Tyler is thirty-nine and he's never been married. They have all of my brains, their father's charm, and more than a little of his larceny, but they have managed to direct it into an enterprise where brains, charm, and larceny – with the latter kept within limits – create a healthy profit. Both of them are rich in their own right, aside from the trusts they inherited from my parents and the not inconsiderable sum I will leave them.

Yet, I have always felt nothing but sorrow for the women they have become involved with, beauties with brains whom they seduce and inevitably abandon. I have, however, stopped blaming myself and have to believe it's either genetic or learned behavior from their father. That was only one of the reasons why I felt most uncomfortable when Bryce and Tyler came to Jennings for the visit and, though they sat across from me, kept their eyes on Jennifer Spencer. She, too, had a visitor, a nonentity named Leonard Benson whom I had to admit, after a little while, did impress me with his understanding of the situation. But when it came to first impressions Jennifer was making a large one on both of my boys. And it seemed to me she was quite taken with Bryce. As usual, that only served to incite Tyler's greater interest.

Needless to say, from the Jennings Correctional Officers'

point of view the meeting was not supposed to be a meeting but coincidental simultaneous visits. In the mayhem of the visitor's room – and with the invisible help of Movita – we were assigned to adjoining tables. It wasn't difficult for the five of us to talk without attracting too much attention.

I had already gotten the JRU proposal and its acceptance to my boys. They were appropriately outraged and worried for me but eager to listen to Jennifer and – somewhat less so – Lenny Benson. When they had finished Bryce began. 'It's inspired,' he said. 'It gives a whole new meaning to the prison term hostile takeover.'

'Yeah. Now it doesn't mean Attica,' Tyler laughed.

'You know, if what you've told us is reliable,' Bryce said to Lenny, 'I don't think it would take much to leverage a buyout.' He turned to his brother. 'Don't you know that schmuck Tarrington, CEO?'

'Yeah. Went to Yale with him. Dumber than Dubya and a lot more greedy,' Tyler said. 'We could make him an offer. And I think our firm could throw seven or eight million behind this.' He turned to me. 'Things went well in Hong Kong despite that sucker Murdoch.' The boys don't curse in my presence, even though everyone else here cusses at the drop of a hatpin, much less a hat.

Jennifer opened her eyes wide. 'You'd invest that much?' she asked. She turned to Lenny. 'Would that be enough?' she asked.

'Marginal,' Lenny told her. 'We'd get a large minority position but not necessarily control.'

Bryce looked a little crestfallen.

'Sell my damn house and put my money into this,' I directed them.

'Sell your house?' Tyler asked, as shocked as if I'd just yelled 'motherfucker' at the top of my lungs.

'But you've always wanted to hold on to the house,' Bryce said. 'Always.'

'Until now,' I told him.

'Do you know how much that "damn house" is worth?' Tyler asked me. I replied to this question with a smile and a shrug.

'In for a penny – in for a pound,' I told them. It was the most liberating moment I had known in many years. I had clung to the idea of the house – my adult home and garden – for many years. In my head I redid the perennial beds, thought about painting the hallway a light yellow instead of its current blue, and sometimes looked at catalogues, thinking of what I could buy to make the house more comfortable, more attractive, more homey. The problem was it wasn't my home and it never would be again. I realized I could play the same mental games without owning the place. And my life was here and its quality was far more important.

'That may be as much as ten million dollars,' Bryce said. 'Real estate in Greenwich had skyrocketed,' he reminded me. 'And they're not making any more waterfront land there.'

'Yes, I know,' I said with a faraway look in my eye. 'I can't imagine why anyone would pay ten million dollars to live in such a monstrously huge house in such a miserably petty place as Greenwich.' I laughed. 'I don't think it was the infidelity that made me shoot your father, I think it was that place.' I stopped and thought about what I had just said. 'We should've sold it years ago,' I told the boys. 'It's not where you boys grew up. I have no good memories of the place.' I was lost in the past when I suddenly brightened and turned to Jennifer. 'What do you think you could get for your apartment, if you sold it?' I asked.

Jennifer thought about it for a minute. 'I imagine it'll bring a little over four.'

'Four thousand! Is that all?' I asked.

She laughed. 'No, Maggie – I meant four *hundred* thousand. Maybe even five.'

'But I thought it was a loft.'

'It's a very big one bedroom,' she smiled, 'but I wasn't up to the million-dollar level. But now the market is such that you get four million for real lofts – whole floors – in old factory buildings.'

I shook my head and had to laugh. 'Well, I guess if someone is willing to pay ten to live in Greenwich they'd be willing to pay four to live in a factory.' I stopped laughing, turned quite serious, and looked around. 'You know, if we actually do end up owning this place,' I said, 'perhaps we should turn it into condominiums.' I stopped again and waited until they all realized I was joking and laughed.

'Hey, if we're going to put out that much, let's really do something with JRU once we own it,' Tyler said.

'Well, of course we will,' I told them. 'Isn't that the point? We'll make this a far better facility. We'll actually train and rehabilitate those who are willing and capable.'

'That wasn't exactly what I was talking about, Mom,' Tyler said. 'I meant make some money with it.'

'Are you certain you should risk everything you own on this scheme?' I asked Jennifer.

'You are,' Jennifer countered. 'Anyway, I might not have to sell it, yet.'

That was true. 'But I'll never leave here, Jennifer. You,

on the other hand, will need a place to go to. I'm never going back to that house anyway,' I said. 'And if selling it can make life in here a little bit better – not only for myself but for everyone else – well, I really have nothing to lose, except the money.'

'We'll call it the Jennings Estate for the Criminally Rich,' Tyler said.

'Yeah. Milken, Boesky, Trump, maybe Leona Helmsley,' Bryce said.

'Great. The campaign can be, "You don't have to be a felon to live like one."' Jennifer smiled.

'It would definitely be a gated community,' Lenny contributed, totally straight-faced.

'One of the biggest concerns I have is how I am supposed to communicate with you. I mean, it's not as if you're my lawyers and can show up every day,' Jennifer inquired. 'And they monitor the telephone calls from the pay phones.'

'We can set you up with a Palm Pilot with a communications option. Get you the newest and smallest laptop or perhaps a cell phone that can be linked to the Internet. But then our problem is getting them to you,' Bryce said.

'None of this is without risk,' Jennifer told them. 'But it can be done, can't it, Maggie?'

'Sure, if we're careful. We'll ask Movita. She'll figure out a way and we'll let you know what to do,' I told my boys.

I was worried not for my sons' investment firm, but for Jennifer Spencer. I saw the look in Bryce's eyes as Jennifer and that accountant shared their plot of prison takeover and reform. Bryce was a dreamer – a trait that he had inherited from his father. But Bryce was a ruthless and manipulative dreamer – traits that had gotten his father a bullet between the eyes. I hoped that I wasn't watching anything starting here, and that Jennifer Spencer would not someday want to murder my son, but it seemed to me that the chemistry between them as they concocted this scheme in the hour of a prison visitation could lead to nothing but trouble.

During my time in the prison library, I had listened to some pretty bizarre plans as inmates desperately tried to research new ways to beat the system. For myself, I harbored no hopes of beating the system. I had stopped the boys from their constant attempts at appeals, throwing good money after bad. I was in prison for life, and, as the old adage put it, 'If you can't beat 'em – join 'em.' Experience had taught me that 'joining 'em' was a whole lot better than 'killing 'em'.

As Jennifer Spencer and 'Son Number Two' enthusiastically spun their web of intrigue and revenge, I couldn't help but wonder how different my life might have been had I been born into this new generation. Up until now, it had never occurred to me that instead of 'join 'em' or 'kill 'em', 'buy 'em' might actually be a delightful way to beat your enemies at their own game. Seeing the glint in Jennifer Spencer's eyes made me feel young again.

32

Jennifer Spencer

The narrower the cage, the sweeter the liberty.

German proverb

On the nights when Byrd wasn't on duty after lights-out Movita would work her charms on the officer filling in so that Jen and Movita could meet Theresa and hunker down in her house to go online with the slim, sexy laptop. Jen would hand over the memos, letters, and emails she had drafted during the day in the library, and Movita, who could type over a hundred words a minute, would get online and knock them out.

Bryce and Tyler did most of the negotiating with Tarrington for his share of the JRU stock and its options. In the meantime, Lenny Benson set up not one, but two significant loans for the financially strapped firm, but made sure that the small print gave the lenders not just veto power over financial decisions but also the ability to vote for board members. Bryce and Tyler became board members the moment the loans were delivered.

Both processes were fast and fairly simple; after all, Jen explained to Movita, it didn't take much to get people to accept an offer of free money. The next bit would be trickier. Normally they would not have needed a majority of shares to own a controlling interest in the company, but in this case more than forty percent of the issued stock belonged to Tarrington, who would take any questioning of his power badly. 'We don't want to have to buy all sixty-two percent of the remaining friggin' stock. And by the way, you've got great eyes.' Bryce emailed her. Movita read the message too and just gave her a look. 'We've named ourselves to the board, and with what Benson and you can manage to dig up we can probably unseat Tarrington, but that doesn't mean we want to spend more money than we have to control this fucker. Any thoughts?'

'What the hell are they talking about?' Movita asked.

'It's simple,' Jen told her. 'You can sometimes control a very big company with a fairly small percentage of their stock if you can get other large stockholders to vote with you. If you know the holdings are really widely dispersed among a lot of small stockholders, then unless Tarrington can get 'em all to vote with him, you can also get control.'

'Okay. I got that,' Movita nodded. They were crouched in the corner beside the commode, over which Theresa had placed a cloth and a puzzle box so they could use it as a workstation. Tonight they were lucky because Officer Mowbry was patrolling the unit until midnight and she was too big and lazy to walk much. But even so, once in a while she walked past the cell and then Theresa signaled them. They had to be prepared to get into her bunk while Jen plastered herself under Theresa's bunk as close up against the wall as possible. They crawled back together and Movita asked what else could be done.

'Well,' Jen explained, 'the only other option I know of is buying more of the privately held shares. Or setting the place on fire.'

'What would that do?' Theresa asked. 'Get insurance money?'

'I was only joking,' Jen whispered. 'I was trying to dramatize how important it was to get controlling interest of the stock. I could still sell my condo,' she murmured. 'Lenny tells me it would raise about half a million dollars after I paid off the broker and the mortgage.'

'Girl, ya' got a half a million dollar crib?'

Jen tried not to smile. In Tribeca a half a million dollars bought a one-bedroom apartment, but there was a limit to the economic lessons she was going to teach tonight.

'You gotta keep your home,' Theresa said firmly. 'You're young and you're not going to be here forever.'

'There has to be some other way,' Movita said.

'There sure does,' Jen sighed. 'Because half a million dollars wouldn't do much to get us controlling interest.'

Movita shook her head. 'Those JRU men aren't just mean bastards,' she said. 'They're rich mean bastards.'

'Honey,' Jen told her. 'Now you're startin' to understand Wall Street.' She answered Bryce's email, resisted flirting with him electronically, and sent another message to Lenny. By then it was almost midnight and Officer Mowbry was going off shift. Jennifer slipped off to her own cell.

It was the next morning that Jennifer came up with the plan. She was so excited that she had to tell Maggie. That wasn't enough, though. She took the chance and punched in Warden Harding's phone number into the cell phone. She was lucky that Movita and not Miss Ringling answered the phone. 'I got it, girl,' Jen told Movita.

'I knew ya' would,' Mo said calmly, but Jen knew her well enough now to read the pleasure in her voice. 'The Warden is in a meeting right now. Can I take a message?'

'We're going to take them public.'

'And that would mean . . .' Movita said.

'We offer Tarrington and the rest of his crew a minority position in a company that gets publicly traded.'

'And that would mean?' Movita said again.

'We tempt them with the idea of getting paid out when we raise a lot of money for them to take them public. They'll have a smaller percentage of the total stock but the stock will be traded on Wall Street and because their holdings are publicly traded they can cash out whenever they want to,' Jennifer explained.

'And that would benefit the situation because . . .' Movita inquired.

'Because then we'd control them!' Jen said, and she actually giggled.

'You white girls got a strange sense of humor,' Movita said, her voice lowered, and then she chuckled. 'I'll tell the Warden, as soon as she's out of her meetin'.'

Jen hung up and went over the whole plan again with Maggie, then phoned Lenny and presented it to him. 'Do you think you can you put together halfway decent financials for an IPO?' she asked him.

'Sure,' he told her. 'As long as you save a bunk for me in your cell.'

Jen smiled. 'I think for that you go to Allenwood,' she told him.

'Yeah, I hear it's a real country club,' he cracked. That made her laugh out loud and Maggie raised her eyebrows and looked over at her. They had to be as circumspect as possible because the door to the library had to be kept open and an officer was always merely steps away.

Jen had to make all of her calls from the corner of the library by the window to keep the static down. The cell phone got the best signal there but it meant that she could be seen from the doorway and Maggie had to spend her time watching out for the authorities. Worse yet, now Jen was working on the laptop – running spreadsheets and projections based on a set of givens that were so far from given that they were more like fairy tales. But she had to start somewhere. Working on the laptop was even more dangerous than using the cell phone and when she used it Maggie actually had to stand in the doorway, her arms crossed, pretending to be doing something while she kept an eye out for an officer. 'It's my punishment,' she had said. 'For being the authority in so many classrooms for so many years. Now I'm chickie. Do they still call the lookout that?'

'I don't think so,' Jen admitted.

Maggie sighed. 'I think it would have been more fun to spend my life misbehaving.'

Keeping her back to the door and being far enough back from the library window so she couldn't be seen from the yard, Jen worked on convincing Lenny. 'Look,' she said, 'we don't have to promise them anything financially in the IPO. We break it out, separate from the other JRU holdings. Prisons right now are a glamor stock. It's a growth industry in an uncertain economy.'

'Well, *there's* a stunning indictment of the American Way if I ever heard one,' Lenny told her.

She looked down at the spreadsheet she was running. 'The point is, we'll get buyers. Then Tarrington and his boys will get some money to further dilute their holdings, and for our services we retain the lion's share.'

'The lion's share, Jennifer, means everything,' Lenny told her. 'Most people get that wrong and they think it means the majority. But the lion takes all.'

'Well, there wouldn't be anything wrong with that, either,' Jen said. She paused. 'Please, Lenny. Do you think that you can do it?'

'Maybe,' he admitted.

'Can you get an accounting firm to rubber-stamp it?'

'You know the answer to that.'

Simultaneously they said, 'For the right price.'

'Do you want me to try to get HVS to underwrite it?' Lenny asked.

Jennifer thought about how poorly he was regarded at HVS as a rainmaker. She doubted they'd pick up any deal Lenny Benson brought in. Plus, she didn't want any of those sons-of-bitches to have any idea what she was doing. 'Nah,' she told him. 'I think we can do better. You think the Rafferty boys would place it?'

'Those pirates? They'd mutiny if you brought in anyone else. Anyway, if we actually do take JRU public we'll want to use every greedy bastard there when the IPO's floated to buy the thing and hype it.'

'The point is, Lenny, could you use Hudson, Van Schaank cards, stationery, and letterhead now to make them think that HVS is interested? Then we can switch later once they've taken the bait.'

'Ah, the old bait and switch,' Lenny said.

You have lovely eyes. The phrase from Bryce's email – for

no reason she could think of – came into her head again. She put it out. 'Well, we've got the HVS bait,' she said.

'It won't just be bait, Jennifer, it'll be money.'

'Yeah, but it won't have to be so much. Not if they think there's a shot of a public offering. They'll dilute themselves. Then, once we are in an ownership position . . .'

'Look, I don't want to rain on your parade but I'm just pointing out they may not want to dilute their stock if they think there's going to be a public offering. It depends on how greedy they are.'

She paused. He was smart and he was right. 'Okay,' she said. 'Then we make it a two-step waltz. First we give them some money infusion for some stock. Not just the loans. Then we tempt them with a possible offering or an acquisition and dilute them further.'

Before she could hear his response, Maggie hissed at her. 'Byrd,' she said, and Jennifer hung up, just like that, stashed the phone behind the books on the self-help shelf (after all, they were helping themselves), closed the iBook and crossed the room to the pile of books waiting to be put back alphabetically. It was a good thing, Jennifer thought, that in all her years in prison Maggie had never been caught with contraband.

Movita handed the kite to Jen at dinner. She opened it and read it. 'Could you join me this evening in my cell. Maggie.' Jen looked over at Movita, who nodded and Jen nodded back.

It was an odd thing, but everybody knew not to visit Maggie, at least not in her house. Unlike everyone else in Jennings she neither ate in the cafeteria nor with a group. She could always be approached in the library on any prison business, somehow the unwritten rule 'not in my cell' totally applied.

Jennifer and Movita were walking down the hallway with an escort to get from one unit to another, but with Movita's connections, the officer only went as far as the metal door that closed her wing off from Maggie's. Once the door closed behind her, Jennifer proceeded down the corridor. She felt as if she were on her way to see the headmistress of her school. Then she chuckled. Actually, she was going to see the headmistress. When she approached Maggie's house door, she knocked softly on the metal door frame.

'Hello,' Maggie said, and Jennifer followed Movita in.

As far as Jennifer knew, Maggie was the only inmate at Jennings who had a private cell. Sometimes others, for a time, didn't have to share when inmates were released or reassigned, but nobody ever seemed to be assigned to Maggie's cell. Looking around, Jennifer was amazed. She had never seen such order or cleanliness. The woman must scrub the place with a toothbrush, she thought. She noticed that the blanket on her bunk was pulled very tight – military style. Her magazines were stacked neatly by date on the floor near the head of her bed. All of her hygiene products were lined up along the ledge of her high windowsill. But the one thing that wasn't visible for inspection was the fact that Margaret Rafferty had privacy, and that was what Jennifer craved most of the time.

Maggie sat down on the chair and gestured toward the bunk. 'Have a seat,' she said. And then took out a plate – a real plate with a line of gold around the edge and twining leaves and flowers on it. Jennifer realized she hadn't seen china or a real cup or bowl in months.

She took the plate from Maggie's hand. On it were small

wedges of cheese, each one centered on a Ritz cracker and topped with a pimento-stuffed olive. There were also a few thin stalks of celery, with a white strip of what looked like cream cheese on it. Was it possible? It made Jennifer think of Sunday afternoons at her grandmother's.

Movita took an hors d'oeuvre, as if having canapés at six o'clock was the norm at Jennings. Following her lead, Jennifer picked up a celery stalk. Meanwhile Maggie took out three perfect martini glasses. Just the sight of them gave Jennifer a stab. Of course, they were totally contraband, but they made Jennifer long for the days that she hung out in bars and drank Cosmopolitans until she was pie-eyed. She knew better than to ask how Maggie managed to keep them hidden from random cell searches.

Maggie cleared her throat. 'Movita,' she said, and inclined her head toward Mo. 'Jennifer.' Jen felt the woman's eyes on her. 'I know that you are both very bright and very motivated. I certainly don't think I underestimated you, yet working together I feel as if in the past I didn't know the full breadth of your abilities.' She paused for a moment and, to Jen's astonishment, she took out a martini shaker. 'Blocking the dreadful JRU takeover is going to take a lot of work, could fail, and may very well cause us enormous problems.' She looked from Jen to Movita. 'This afternoon I realized just how much was involved and how much is at stake. The question I want to put to you is whether or not you want to pursue this, balls to the wall, no matter what?'

Movita reached for another cracker and then crossed one long leg over the other. 'I don't see that we have much choice,' Movita said. 'If we don't do nothin' life here will be unbearable. If we try and fail or if we try and succeed at least we know we tried.' Movita smiled. 'Am I startin' to sound like Theresa?' she asked.

Jen shook her head. 'I know what you mean. I guess I am the one among us with the most to lose since I don't have to do as much time as you do,' she told them. 'But the truth is that I have a lot at stake as well. Because I may die or go crazy if I continue this way.' She looked down. Everyone was silent for a moment.

'Well then,' Maggie said, and her voice was so cheerful that Jen managed to look at her and see that she was pouring the martini glasses full. 'Onion or olive?' she asked. And to Jen's complete amazement she had both.

'Onion,' Jen breathed and was rewarded with a perfect martini, two pearls lying side by side in the V at the top of the stem. Jen was smart enough in prison ways not to ask how, why, or how often Maggie managed to put together a treat like this. She just grinned and nodded to Movita, who grinned back at her.

'So,' Maggie said. 'We're going to do this thing.'

'Absolutely,' said Movita.

'Absolutely,' Jennifer echoed. And the three of them drained their glasses.

33

Gwen Harding

Better starve free than be a fat slave.

Aesop, 'The Dog and the Wolf,' *Fables*

When Movita Watson asked Gwen Harding to see Jennifer Spencer, the Warden just shrugged. She had been living with nothing but complaints, problems, and pressure for weeks and weeks now. Not to mention her own fear and despair. She felt what she imagined a nun who had served in a convent for years and lost her vocation must feel – empty, futile, and afraid.

But despite that she hadn't had a drink. And she supposed part of her emptiness came from the lack of gin that had filled her bloodstream and her life for so long.

Seeing Jennifer Spencer was no worse or better than the other tasks she had to do, though she wondered at it. It seemed to her that Jennifer Spencer had settled down and settled in. While she wouldn't look forward to a meeting with her, she nodded. Her days at Jennings were numbered and she didn't know if she would then be transferred by the state to some prison elsewhere, whether she'd be offered early retirement, or whether she'd quit. She felt as if leaving would be a betrayal of the women she had tried, so ineffectively, to protect and assist. But it was clear to her that all of this was out of her hands now and far too difficult and complex for the likes of her to grapple with.

She had already brought a couple of cardboard cartons into her office. There would also be a lot of things to be fed into the shredder, but she could wait on that until just before the ax fell. Bit by bit she was packing the personal mementos and the relics from her years at the prison. There were the gratifying thank-you letters from inmates who had moved on and were succeeding in a life Outside. There were the sadder but just as meaningful notes from women who had gone on to other prisons and wrote for advice or help. She had the meaningless awards that she had won both from the community and the state. They were empty of any feeling of achievement now but she supposed she'd take them. She was trying to do the packing discreetly, but she knew that Miss Ringling, Movita – and probably every inmate in Jennings – knew what was up, though she was almost certain Movita hadn't said a word. Still, when there was the knock on the door Gwen put the box, along with two others, under her desk.

'Come in,' Gwen said, and Jennifer Spencer entered the office. This time she stood and waited to be asked to sit down. Gwen thought of Marlys Johnston of JRU and her arrogant behavior and grimaced. When Gwen made a move indicating that Spencer could take a seat, Spencer – appropriately – sat across from the desk rather than next to it. Yes, Gwen thought, the girl had changed and perhaps for the better although Gwen no longer knew what 'better' and 'worse' meant.

'Warden Harding,' Spencer said. 'I have some news for you.'

Gwen felt her eyebrows raising. Perhaps she'd been premature in thinking that this girl had gained some humility. Gwen, as she often did, sat silent and waited.

'Maybe I should begin by saying I've known about the JRU takeover for some time,' Spencer said.

Gwen wasn't surprised. Between the visits the JRU staff had made, the communications with the state, and the contacts this girl had in business, it was inevitable that people, inmates included, would know about the change. 'Yes,' she said.

'Well,' Spencer continued, 'there's been a recent change in management at JRU and I think that will affect what goes on here.'

'Really?' Gwen asked. 'In what way?' She wasn't sure if she should tell the girl to shut up and get back to the library, or listen. She had to admit she was curious, but she wondered if Spencer thought she could trade information for favors. Wasn't that kind of insider stuff the very act that had landed her here in the first place? Perhaps the library wasn't enough of an upgrade and she was hoping for a job in the office here. For all Gwen knew, the girl wanted Movita's job; maybe she felt she could help JRU. Gwen stopped herself. Perhaps of everything having to do with the inmates, Gwen Harding felt worst about having to leave Movita in the hands of these profit mongers. No doubt she'd be useful to them initially, but Gwen didn't want to think about where she might end up longer-term. Well, Gwen shrugged and figured she had nothing to lose in talking with Spencer, though she wasn't making any deals. Somehow she still didn't seem the kind of girl who would step on others, although her crime indicated that her values might be less than correct. 'What kind of changes?' she asked. 'Although JRU doesn't inform me of everything, I'm sure that I'll be told anything important.'

'Well, JRU doesn't actually know this yet,' Spencer told her.

Was this some gossip from Wall Street? 'Yes, Spencer. What is it?' Gwen snapped, her voice showing her impatience. 'I have a lot of work this morning.'

'The fact is, JRU has been acquired.'

'Acquired?' Gwen repeated. 'Acquired by another firm?' God, Wackenhut or CCA had eaten up JRU.

'Not exactly,' Spencer said. 'They've been bought out by another management group.'

'I see,' Harding said. 'And when did this happen?'

'Just in the last two days. Some of the staff there might not even know about it.'

Gwen thought of Marlys Johnston and a small smile came to her lips. Did she know? Perhaps Gwen herself could call Ms Johnston and give her the tips. She couldn't help think how lovely it would be if this change affected that woman in a negative way. Live by the sword, die by the sword, she thought. But, life being what it was, no doubt this would only benefit the Marlys Johnstons of the world. She'd probably wind up as president. 'How do you know this information?' Gwen asked Spencer. The girl looked down at her lap for a moment.

'Well,' she said, 'I acquired it.'

Had Inmate 71036 gone mad? She had come into this office months ago with a chip on her shoulder and an air of arrogance to boot and here she was saying she'd 'acquired' Jennings? Gwen knew Spencer was smart in business but just how in the hell did she expect her to believe that she had done a quiet takeover of her facility? That would mean that *she* now worked for *her*. Unbelievable! 'What?' Gwen asked, reduced to single syllables to avoid stammering more than ever.

'Not me personally,' Spencer told her calmly. 'A group of investors. But I have been, well, the point man, I guess.'

Gwen stared at her. It still wasn't safe for her to speak. She thought that one of the two of them had gone mad, probably her. Was Spencer delusional? It was possible, but it was equally possible that Gwen herself was hallucinating. And if she wasn't, she'd not only completely underestimated this girl, but also totally failed to supervise her. 'Run this by me again,' she demanded, not knowing what to hope for.

'A group of investors have bought JRU. And I kind of led the acquisition.'

'From here?' Gwen asked. 'You managed a Wall Street acquisition from within Jennings?'

Jennifer nodded. 'And I know it doesn't change our relationship as inmate and warden,' she added. 'But for the time being, until we can find the proper management, I will serve as de facto chief of operations.'

Gwen began to laugh. Once she started it was very hard for her to stop. In fact, it wasn't until she saw the alarm on Spencer's face that she came back to herself. 'Surely, if this is true,' she said, 'you see the bizarre implications of this.' This couldn't be happening, Gwen thought. This woman might be good, but she wasn't that good. And how had she done it alone? Gwen herself had set up the connection between Movita and Jennifer, and she also knew that Spencer had been getting chummy with Maggie. That was understandable; eventually most of the girls ended up going to her for comfort, advice, or just to be around someone who was more cultured and mature than most of the other inmates. But surely those two women, and little Suki Conrad or big-mouthed Theresa LaBianco were a poor and puny team for a caper like this. Gwen took a deep breath to manage her speech. 'I hope you don't think for a minute that you're going to be acting in a warden capacity. That just isn't going to happen. You may be able to fire me but the state charter makes it clear that the prison will continue to be run by penologists.'

Jennifer nodded again. 'I can promise you I didn't choose this,' she said. 'It kind of chose me.'

Gwen bent down, took out one of the boxes from under her feet and put it on top of the desk. 'Well, regardless of the truth of this, in the words of the late Richard Nixon: "You won't have me to push around anymore." I'll be resigning. I was going to do it anyway.'

Jennifer Spencer opened her eyes very, very wide. 'Oh, no,' she said. 'You can't do that. No, you can't do that at all. You can't leave, I'm going to need your help. Together we can make a change.'

'I can leave and I will,' Gwen assured her. 'You may already be my "de facto chief of operations", but even if you are, you can't stop an employee from resigning.'

'No,' Spencer said, 'not unless she's a prisoner, working for JRU. Then no matter what job she's been assigned to, she can't quit, she doesn't get vacations, and she'll barely be paid.'

Gwen stopped putting things into the box. 'I gave

you credit for being smart,' Gwen said. 'But maybe not enough credit. Is what you're saying true?'

'Oh, yes,' Jennifer assured her. 'In fact, I thought we might start simply by going over the list of JRU personnel you'd like to see fired.'

Gwen actually laughed again. 'You're serious,' she said.

'Oh, yes,' Jennifer told her again. 'I'm not sure I want this job but now that I have it, I'm going to do it.'

Gwen sat there for what seemed like a very long moment. 'Let this cup pass from my lips,' she murmured.

Jennifer heard her. 'Yes,' she said. 'That's sort of it.'

The girl didn't know that Gwen had been talking to herself. Gwen thought about all of the nonsense she'd been hearing in meetings about 'higher power' and the like. This was not going to make her a believer but it certainly looked like a Hand was involved. Then she narrowed her eyes. 'Is this some kind of Wall Street scam to get you out of here sooner?' she asked. 'Because it will not work. I don't care if you are the chairman of the company, it won't get you one day less for your sentence.'

'I know that,' Jennifer said. 'There's no reason for you to believe me, but I actually *am* thinking of others.'

And, for the first time in a long while, Gwen believed in the possibility of the redemptive power of Jennings. She looked at Jennifer Spencer as if for the first time. This woman might believe she, as warden, would be resentful or punitive, but all Gwen Harding felt was gratitude. Jennifer Spencer had taken her talent, intelligence, and experience and used them all, along with her financial contacts and God knows what else, to do good. The very end of the morning sunlight flickered in through the window and Gwen, who was not a fanciful woman, could almost swear that the light reflecting on the corner walls behind Spencer looked like the dancing of angels' wings.

Gwen extended her hand and, after a moment's pause, Jennifer took it. 'Congratulations,' Gwen said. 'I'm very pleased and proud of you.' She thought she saw another flicker, this time one of pleasure, in Jennifer Spencer's eyes. Gwen smiled. She thought of the changes they could begin to institute and began to get truly excited, but then felt that, after the surprise she'd been handed, Jennifer should be punished. She gave her best stern look to Spencer.

'I realize, of course, that you must have broken a great many rules to manage to do this from inside our institution,' she said. 'Your position of ownership doesn't change that fact.' Then she raised her hand and shook a finger at Jennifer. Using her best schoolmarm voice she told her, 'This is going on your permanent record, Missy.'

After a moment they both began to laugh. When their hilarity calmed, Gwen thanked Jennifer Spencer with all sincerity. 'You've saved a lot of women a lot of pain,' Gwen told her.

'Well, I'd like to save a lot more women a lot more pain and there's one way we can do that immediately,' Jennifer said.

'Good afternoon, Officer Byrd,' Gwen Harding said as the CO walked into her office. He looked around and Gwen glimpsed the panic that he quickly covered when he saw Jennifer, Suki Conrad, and Theresa LaBianco sitting in her office.

'Yes, Warden?' he asked, his voice deep and fairly strong. It didn't sound like the voice of a rapist, but then whose did?

'Officer Byrd, I'd like to introduce you to the new owner of Jennings, Miss Jennifer Spencer. Minority shareholders include Suki Conrad and Theresa LaBianco.' Byrd just nodded silently. It was obvious that he was trying to think fast, but was simultaneously confused by the lay of the land.

'New owners?' he asked. And Warden Gwen Harding hoped she heard a tremble in his voice.

'Yes,' she told him. 'The prison is no longer a state agency. It's been sold. The point is, you are no longer working for the state, nor are you union protected. And Miss Spencer, the new chairman of JRU International, has something to share with you.'

'Yes?' he asked, turning his head.

'Miss Spencer would like to read you something from the *New York Times*.'

'That's right,' Jennifer said, and took out a piece that she held before her.

> *Amnesty International documented custodial sexual misconduct toward female prisoners in forty-eight states. This may not be surprising given that the number of women in prisons and jails has tripled in the last fifteen years and that at least forty percent of those guarding women are men. But until two years ago, sexual abuse of prisoners by correctional officials was not even a criminal offense in fourteen states. Today, thanks to the efforts of Amnesty and other groups, only five states remain without such laws. What remains is to enforce them.*
>
> *Curt Goering, Deputy Executive Director of Amnesty International* USA 4/15/01

Gwen could see Byrd lose all his color. Good, Goddamnit. She had to stop feeling sorry for everyone. 'Unfortunately,' Jennifer said, 'we are in one of the states where you can't be tried for the rape of Suki Conrad or the other victims that were documented, or for sexual harassment of myself, Theresa LaBianco, Flora Cravets, Pearl Mendoza, Sally Waterman, and probably a minimum of two dozen more.'

'What?' the lunkhead began. 'What do you mean?'

'Please don't insult us,' Jennifer said. 'You know perfectly well what we mean.'

The warden stood up. 'What I'd like to see is you carried off in handcuffs, ready to spend some time being raped by men in a different facility.' She sighed. 'Since that's not possible, we have only two words for you.'

For a moment the women looked at each other, as if an obscenity might be said. But real power was so much better than words, no matter how obscene.

'You're fired,' Jennifer Spencer told him.

Book III

34

Jennifer Spencer

It is the nature of desire not to be satisfied, and most men live only for the gratification of it. The beginning of reform is not so much to equalize property as to train the noble sort of natures not to desire more, and to prevent the lower from getting more.

Aristotle

As Jennifer stared at the pages of notes spread before her on the library table she felt as if she were back in Catholic school and some nun had just handed her an impossible word problem: If it takes ten men nine hours to dig a fifty foot long ditch four foot deep by two and a half feet wide, how long would it take one female with the help of several friends to turn around the attitude, facility, and costs in a women's prison? Actually, it was more of an essay test: You own a correctional facility for women. In one thousand words, explain how you would a. make it humane, b. make it effective, and c. make it profitable. (Neatness counts.)

Jennifer didn't know where to begin.

Back in school Jennifer had always known what the nuns wanted to hear; she knew how to give a snow job to a nun. But this was different. This assignment hadn't come from a nun or Donald Michaels. This wasn't a snow job or a blow job. For the first time in her life she wasn't doing intellectual exercises or selling an idea and running. She had never in her life been responsible for the daily management of anything – not even an apartment. It was a challenge that Jennifer had willingly taken on herself, but it was going to take a lot more than one thousand words to make Jennings a. humane, b. effective, and c. profitable. It was going to take thought, planning, training, and money – lots and lots of money. So where should she begin?

She had been sitting and stewing over the paper before her for two days. Then, all at once Jennifer smiled. The lyrics to 'Do-Re-Mi' suddenly popped into her head. *The Sound of Music* had been her favorite movie when she was a kid, and she remembered Sister Maria's suggestion that the beginning was a very good place to start. 'Nuns!' Jennifer thought, shaking her head. 'They always have all the answers.' She chuckled as it occurred to her that she might have to become a nun herself after all this was over. Convents were one of the few employers she could think of that welcomed ex-cons.

Jennifer knew how she'd begin, but turned to her computer and clicked on her email account for new messages. One of the perks of being the new official assistant librarian was having an official phone line installed for her use in the library, plus a DSL line for fast Internet access. Gwen Harding had suggested the change in Jennifer's position, acknowledging that Jennifer needed a private place to work from and communicate with the people at JRU, but that a private office could look dangerously like favoritism and bring down a lot of anger and jealousy from other inmates. Jennifer knew she could trust Maggie, Movita, Theresa, and

Suki to keep quiet about the recent turn of events at Jennings, but beyond the crew it could be dicey. Now Jennifer opened her email account, and a new email message from Bryce popped up marked 'URGENT – OPEN IMMEDIATELY!!' Her stomach sank. Something must be wrong. Feeling sick, she clicked on the message.

> *Yo, Jen! Just joking! I just wanted to get your blood pumping a little, I know you don't get enough stimulation in there. Actually, everything's fine. Everything's going really smoothly on my end. Don't worry about a thing.*

Easy enough for him to say, Jennifer thought. But she breathed a sigh of relief that he was just joking around.

Then she read the rest of the message and felt a blush bloom on her face.

> *But seriously, urgently, I do wish I could see you face-to-face again soon. Visitor's day just seems way too far off when you really get along with a person, you know? I was very impressed with all your ideas last Tuesday, not to mention your other . . . assets.*
>
> *Anyway back to business . . . Listen, we're going to make this thing work. Trust me, and have a productive day!*
>
> *Bryce*

She read the message again with mixed feelings. She hated when guys said 'trust me'. It almost invariably meant the opposite. But she thought he was sincere, at least about the business end of the deal. Regarding the other stuff, she wasn't sure. He's just a typical financial prankster, Jennifer thought. They littered Wall Street. Deep down, though, she was flattered by his attention. He was good-looking and smart and self-assured and it was nice to have a little flirtation with a man, even if it was only over the Internet. She was pretty starved for male attention here in an all-women's prison. You couldn't really count the male officers as men – most of them were no better than dirt under your shoe. She laughed to herself as she read over Bryce's email again. But she promised herself to try to keep all her communications with him strictly business.

She shot him off a note saying that things were going well on her end, and mentioning the fact that she was currently working on plans for a Proposed Profit Center at Jennings, and organizational and management tactics.

'Have you come across something humorous?' asked Maggie when she heard Jennifer laugh.

Jennifer laughed again as she looked up at Maggie, reflecting that it was odd that she was here in prison with Bryce's mother. Wanting to cover the real cause of her laughter, she said, 'It just seems so surreal.'

Maggie nodded. 'I imagine so. It probably also seems impossible.'

'Let's just say extremely, very, extraordinarily, unimaginably, overwhelmingly difficult.'

'Well, as long as you have a positive attitude,' Maggie said. 'Let's see what you've come up with so far.' She walked over to Jennifer's table and looked at the plethora of lists, charts, and proposed reorganizational plans that Jennifer had made. 'What's your main objective?'

'To make this place a little better for the women who live here,' Jennifer said matter-of-factly.

'And what do we need to make it better?' Maggie pressed on.

Jennifer shuffled the papers until she found the one on which she had already itemized a response to Maggie's question. 'First,' she began, 'better living conditions – especially better meals, increased privacy, improved relations with the staff, and different uniforms.' She looked to Maggie for a confirming nod and smiled when she got it. 'Secondly, improved health care – I was going to itemize here, but basically we need health care of all kinds.'

'I agree,' Maggie said.

'And finally, better educational programs for basic skills like reading and math, GEDs, life skills, mothering. And more substance abuse and twelve-step programs. Then job training,' Jennifer lowered the page and looked at Maggie.

'But there's something they need first. Self-respect and discipline.'

'Hey, I went to a psychiatrist all through college and graduate school and I'm not sure I go there,' Jennifer joked.

'Well, I realize that we can't change people from the cellular level on up. But we can improve their clothes, address them by name, insist on timeliness and courtesy, increase their privileges if they deliver and learn the rules and the problems they incur from breaking them.'

'Spoken like a true headmistress,' Jennifer said.

'We also have to create a wing for the women who disturb the peace. The ones who are mentally ill and habitually scream all night and disturb everyone's sleep, the ones who go off at the slightest provocation, the ones who harangue guards endlessly. Nights of sleep uninterrupted by screaming would do a world of good for everyone, and it wouldn't cost anything.'

'We also need a better orientation for the candy when they first get here,' Jennifer said.

'Yes. And we need better training for the COs so they are more consistent. And we have to weed out the corrupt ones and the abusers.'

'That would do a lot for morale,' Jennifer agreed.

'So would some physical changes: a real gym for wet days.'

'Now you're starting to talk money,' Jennifer commented.

'And where is the money going to come from?' Maggie asked.

'We have to earn it,' Jennifer said with a sigh, and in anticipation of Maggie's next question, she shuffled the papers once again and produced the chart entitled *Proposed Profit Center for Jennings*.

Maggie studied the chart for a moment. Then she said, 'This is a wonderful start, Jennifer. Income-producing businesses.'

'I'm not sure I can make it work,' Jennifer admitted.

'It *has* to work,' Maggie told her.

Jennifer nodded. 'Without money, nothing can happen here.'

'But if this plan is going to work, you're going to need as much of the full and – I might add – *enthusiastic* cooperation of the women here as possible.' Maggie sat down next to Jennifer at the paper-strewn table. 'Do you have a plan for that?' she asked.

'Not really,' Jennifer admitted. 'We have to improve the general attitude around here, but the only ways I can think of to do that are the things that cost the most money, and since we don't have the money we can't improve the attitude, and if we can't improve the attitude we can't raise any money, and – well . . .' She stopped with a helpless shrug of her shoulders.

'It's a bit of a chicken-and-egg kind of problem, isn't it?' Maggie observed.

Jennifer nodded as she shuffled the papers yet again until she found the *Inmate Handbook* that she had been given on the day of her incarceration. 'I've been looking through this,' she said. 'I thought maybe we could change some of the rules and that would improve morale.' She opened the manual and went on. 'Like this one,' she said, pointing to a page. She read, '"Each inmate is allowed only six photographs on the cell wall." Why can't we have eight, or ten, or as many as we want?' She closed the manual and questioned Maggie: 'Don't you think if we changed some of those stupid rules it might make everyone feel a little better?'

'For a while, perhaps,' Maggie said sadly. 'But women without any pictures will be jealous. And because some of these women need to push authority, eventually, Jennifer, some women would have hundreds of pictures and cover other inmates' walls and then there would be trouble.'

'Oh,' Jennifer said dismissively, 'what trouble can there be in pictures?'

Maggie reached across the table and picked up the manual. 'I've been here a long time, Jennifer,' she began. 'And I have come to understand that there is not one rule in this manual that is either arbitrary or nonessential. Each and every rule has been made in response to a problem – *the* problem. We can each have only six pictures, because that way no one has more pictures than anyone else does. We must all wear uniforms, because that way no one will be better dressed than anyone else. Do you understand what I am saying – do you know what the problem is?'

Jennifer shook her head.

'Inequality,' Maggie said simply. 'Some *have* and some *have not*. It's the root of every conflict and crime in the world's history. And in here, every effort is made to eliminate inequality. We're all in the same mess, eating the same slop, and wearing the same hideous uniform. It's what keeps us from killing each other.'

Jennifer considered what Maggie had said and then observed, 'It sounds like communism, and communism isn't exactly the plan I had in mind for making money. Look what happened to Russia.'

Maggie laughed. 'You're getting way too far ahead of yourself, dear,' she said. 'Start with the basics: food, shelter, and clothing. Make the meals a little tastier, make the place a bit more hospitable, and maybe make the uniforms slightly less hideous. Give more, but not unlimited choices. Start with those things and then see what happens next.'

'Do – Re – Mi,' Jennifer sang in response.

'That's right.' Maggie smiled. 'Food – Shelter – Clothing. But we've got to really think about how we're going to change these women's attitudes. Most of them have been so used to being ordered around and having so few choices to make – even before they ended up in prison – that they probably don't really know how to make responsible decisions for themselves. And that's going to be a big problem when you're trying to change the atmosphere around here and turn these women into productive, self-motivated people,' Maggie continued.

Jennifer nodded. 'It's true. I always thought I got to where I am because of my own hard work, but I forget how many advantages I had. Even the nuns, who I hated, gave me a better education than I would have gotten elsewhere. But until I got to Jennings I didn't know I was privileged.'

Maggie nodded. 'Some of these women have never had anything and they're just too cynical to believe that they'll ever get anything. They were never taught anything so they think they can't learn anything. When they do get a shot at a meal, or clothes, or money, or love, they grab. And grab. They cram it in. So we must move with moderation. It's like giving food to somebody who's starving: You have to be careful not to give them too much or they'll vomit. We have to make these changes very gradually, so that nobody gets sick.'

'Point taken,' Jennifer said. She really admired Maggie as a woman and an educator. She wondered what kind of a mother she'd been to Bryce. 'Ideally,' Maggie continued, 'if we can inspire inmates to be a productive part of the changing process instead of just empty vessels taking handouts, then there's a chance we might make them "good citizens" of Jennings. And if they learn how to be "good citizens" here, then they might be able to become "good citizens" of their communities Outside when they're released.'

'Hear, hear! You're really on a roll today, Maggie,' Jennifer teased her, but she was impressed.

'Oh, stop it.' Maggie looked away. 'I guess I'd gotten cynical myself, but now, since this miracle, I'm getting rather enthusiastic at the possibility of improvements. But I'm going to get back to work now, as should you, or none of this is going to become a reality.' Maggie smiled, and wandered back to her shelves to reorganize a newly arrived carton of books.

Jennifer turned back to her computer. She was surprised

to find another new email from Bryce. Already? She clicked it open.

It's the sunniest day here. I walked to work and it almost broke my heart when I thought of how you and my mother probably aren't getting any sun in that dungeon of yours. I wish I could email you some. Because every email from you is like a beam of sunlight in my day.

Bryce

He's really laying it on thick, Jennifer thought. She didn't know how to respond to this email or if she even should. Instead, she decided to send Lenny an email, and thought it would be funny to use Bryce's little 'URGENT' trick on him. She started typing up the message.

URGENT – PRISON RIOT!

The positive changes here have already become too much for the inmates and now they're holding me hostage in the library . . . Just kidding! Lenny, I wanted to get your attention right away. I feel like we haven't talked for ages. I'm trying to put together plans on how to make this place profitable, and I just wanted to write and tell you how much I appreciate all that you've done for me. And your visits . . .

Jennifer stopped typing, trying to think of what to say. Then it came to her.

. . . are like sunshine. Thanks.

35

Gwen Harding

Of a good beginning cometh a good end.

John Heywood

'Let go and let God,' Gwen said to the reflection in the small mirror that hung in her office. It was one of the slogans they repeated endlessly at the AA meetings she continued to attend. She was still afraid that, despite the rule of anonymity, she'd be seen by a CO or a correctional staff's relative or even an ex-inmate who had stayed in the area. It shouldn't, of course, matter to her, with anonymity being such a rule, but she couldn't imagine bumping into Miss Ringling and not having word get out all over the prison. On the other hand, she could always raise her eyebrows, look Miss Ringling – or whomever – in the eye and ask, 'And what are *you* doing here?' She wasn't sure she'd have the balls, but that idea gave her the confidence to walk into the church basement door each time she attended.

She needed a different kind of confidence this morning.

Today was the dawning of a new beginning at Jennings. She had gotten over her surprise – no, shock – at Jennifer Spencer's disclosure and she'd even come to appreciate what the girl had done. They had agreed to work together to save Jennings and its inmates. And they had also decided it was best to keep Jennifer's unusual situation quiet. She could keep working in the library and the changes they planned could be implemented by Gwen and her staff.

She hoped that the announcement she had to make at breakfast would go well. If it didn't, she'd have egg on her face – literally. Most people didn't like change. Oddly enough, it was the people with the least to lose who were most often resistant to something in which they might, in the long term, gain. Between Jennifer Spencer, Movita Watson, Maggie Rafferty, and the new consultant they had brought in, they had a formidable team and had already begun to make significant changes. But, she reminded herself again that people did not like changes, even for the better.

Gwen tugged on the front of her pant legs to help reduce the creases from where she had been sitting in her chair. They had all decided to make the wake-up time more pleasant. Instead of the heart-stopping, dream-shattering clang of the wake-up bell, today the pleasant sound of the Cat Stevens song 'Morning Has Broken' was softly wafting throughout the halls and cellblocks. Of course, it was possible that some people might not like the old hymn, but since the man had converted to Islam they couldn't be accused of being insensitive and Theresa LaBianco had put together a multicultural morning mix for the future including the Beatles' 'Good Day, Sunshine,' the show tune 'Oh, What a Beautiful Morning,' and some hip-hop boy singing about how good it felt to wake up. Gwen suspected it meant waking up after almost overdosing but she listened to the lyrics and approved the song.

Gwen cleared her throat. She had worked with Spencer and Maggie Rafferty on the announcement about JRU. She had practiced it until she had it memorized, but she was still afraid she might begin to stammer. She took another deep breath. 'Good morning, ladies,' the Warden announced over the speaker system. 'Today is Thursday. Please be advised that breakfast will be served in the cafeteria in just fifteen minutes. And an announcement will be made. Please attend. Thank you.' Then, without the usual blast from the bullhorn, the cell doors slid open and the music continued. Gwen took fifteen minutes and spent it walking up and down the halls. Women were actually smiling. People seemed to be moving to the cafeteria in a more quiet and orderly way. Gwen herself smiled. Why hadn't she thought of this? What an improvement. It hadn't cost a dime to do, but the effect was priceless!

Gwen, no longer reporting to the state, had fired Ben Norton and they had replaced the head of food services. For the last few mornings she had eaten her own breakfast there and had made certain that all of the breakfast foods were hot and looked recognizable. No more would her girls be seeing blobs of gray oatmeal, no more rubbery squares of Jell-O. There was more fresh fruit, and they had added healthy cereals with skim milk. Breakfast was actually a more pleasant meal now and it was cheaper per person because there was less spoilage.

Today the Warden stood at the front of the breakfast line and handed out trays with plastic utensils wrapped in paper napkins. She greeted each woman with a hardy good morning. She could see from the expressions on their faces that they couldn't decide if they should go along with her or fear the calm before the storm.

The line did not move quickly. The inmates weren't used to having so many choices, and breakfast had always been such a horrendous meal that many of them stood frozen, without making a choice. 'Scrambled or boiled?' – 'Hash-browns or home fries?' – 'Bacon or sausage?' – 'Orange or cranberry juice?' – 'Coffee or tea?'

The inmates were nearly speechless as they were confronted with each new choice. And unlike Ben's staff, the new food-service personnel seemed positively delighted to be able to offer the choices. There were smiles and pleasantries exchanged, and the warden was pleased to notice that the food was served with greater pride and accepted with less belligerence.

It took longer than usual for people to get their meals and take their seats. Then Gwen gave them some time to luxuriate in the unexpected quality of the food in front of them. When she could put it off no longer, the Warden stepped to the front of the room and asked them all for their attention. She greeted them with the same tone that she had used on the public address system. 'You have probably noted some changes,' Gwen began. Some inmates laughed, a few clapped and cheered. 'We hope you approve,' Gwen said. 'There has been a change here at Jennings. It is called "privatization". This means that the state has asked a company, in our case one called JRU, to manage the prison. It doesn't mean I stop being warden but it does mean that there will be other changes. We hope all of them will improve our lives here.' She could smell the suspicion in the air, and throughout the room rumblings were heard as

Gwen continued to explain the 'changes in management and changes in attitude'. Nobody liked change and to these women any change in their blighted lives had meant a change for the worse. She needed a way to tell them that change could be a positive thing or else she, Movita, and Jennifer might be saddled with a mutiny. Every warden lived in fear of a hostage situation, and if the new owners of the prison were actually a part of the prison population it would not make things easy.

But luck and a deeper problem that she had known about now served her well. 'I would like to announce,' she said, 'that as one of the first changes Officer Byrd has been fired.'

There was a moment of silence, maybe two. And then the population broke out into such cheering and table banging and whooping and clapping as Gwen had never heard. Applause was a powerful thing. Gwen met it and felt it hit her face and belly and move past her. But the wave of approval kept coming. Every woman was on her feet, stamping them and, as people said today, 'putting their hands together'. Gwen was shocked by their reaction and by how clearly Byrd had been universally despised. She put aside her shame at not having known it herself and instead focused on her delight at seeing all of the women united in a single feeling. She tried several times to speak but the applause and hooting continued. At last, she got them to sit down. 'I hope *all* of the changes will meet with that kind of approval,' she said.

She was pleased that she wasn't stammering and she got through the rest of the announcement. She did not ask if there were any questions, because there were so many that she couldn't answer that she herself was reeling.

'I don't like this,' Springtime said to Movita. 'I don't like this at all.' But as Rodgers and Hammerstein was followed with the Fifth Dimension's 'Age of Aquarius' on the PA system, many of the women started to smile and laugh and even to dance a little in their seats as they ate their breakfast.

'What in the hell is going on here?' Theresa nervously wanted to know.

'I think it's kind of nice,' Jennifer said encouragingly.

'I think it's damn weird,' Springtime countered. Springtime suddenly leapt up from her table and ran toward the Warden. Quickly the officers tried to intervene, but Springtime managed to elude their grasp. Gwen was nearly paralyzed with fear as she watched helplessly with the other silent inmates. But Springtime did not attack her; she only whispered in her ear. Then, the Warden nodded and indicated that two officers should take Springtime from the room. 'Please continue with your breakfast, ladies,' the Warden instructed.

As the women ate, the Warden explained how new programs were going to be implemented, that health care staff would be on duty three days a week, that visitation would be expanded to include Mondays and Sundays. That church services would be able to be attended with visitors and that a play area was going to be added for the inmates to interact with their children in.

Someone started to tap her tray with the plastic utensils and was soon joined in by the rest of the population. Gwen couldn't suppress her happiness. She smiled and nodded to the group. Here she was mother, teacher, nurse, and bearer of good news.

Gwen Harding put her hands up in the air gesturing for

quiet. 'We have one more little surprise,' she explained. And as she spoke, a beaming Springtime entered the cafeteria carrying a tray. On it were plastic cups filled with the marigolds taken from the sign that Springtime tended in front of the prison. The musical tape was playing 'Good Morning, Starshine,' as Springtime placed her small floral offerings in the center of each table.

36

Movita Watson

You get privileges, you get to wear one of them print blouses instead of the T-shirt uniform. We mostly all want 'em. When someone new is down, one of us say 'Don't worry. Some day your prints will come.'

Kristen S., interviewed by Olivia Goldsmith
(anonymity requested)

Ain't nobody don't got a secret wish, 'bout what they mighta been, or woulda really liked to do. Mine, and I'm sure nobody in the world knows it, 'cept maybe my baby Jamorah, was always to be a fashion designer. Funny, I can hear people actually laughin' at me in my head every time I even think it. But anyway, even though it's harder to believe than a good time at Jennings, I'm actually doin' it! Designin' fashions! For some reason, doin' new uniforms was the job that got given to me. I didn't ask for it, 'cause I got this superstition that whatever I really want, and especially what I ask for, I ain't gonna get. I know I got the job I wanted in the Warden's office, but that's all the more reason to know I couldn't have another good thing happen to me. The chance of *two* good things happenin' to a black woman inmate like me is slimmer than Jada Pinkett's thighs. But somehow it happened anyway. The Lord moves in mysterious ways, I guess.

Warden Harding and Jennifer asked me if I wanted to do it. I said, 'Are you kiddin' me?' And there I am sittin' with paper and crayons. (They still didn't let us use pencils on account a their weapon possibilities.) It took me all of two minutes to start drawin'. Man, I know every woman in the joint is gonna have a preference, a problem, a beef. I don't expect no gratitude. It's the doin' of the job itself. I got a million ideas.

The first thing I'm thinkin' to change is the material these jumpsuits we gotta wear are made out of. It's some kinda polyester junk that chafes like crazy. By the time it gets soft it pills and there are these ugly little gray balls all over. The seams feel like rope and if you got a active job the seams hurt at the knees and elbows and under the arms and the crotch. I've decided to make the new uniforms out of some kinda cotton that ain't so stiff and weird. Jennifer gave me a budget per piece, and Miss Ringling, believe it or not, was assigned to help me bid on some fabrics from our previous suppliers. But when I showed Jen the prices she laughed. 'That's the seven-hundred-dollar toilet seat,' she said. 'You remember they sold a toilet seat to the government for seven hundred dollars. I think hammers were four hundred.' She shook her head. 'I can get this in New York from an Indian fabric dealer on West Thirty-eighth Street for three dollars a yard. Why don't I have him send some samples? He'd be thrilled for the business.'

Boy, when those samples came it felt like Christmas. It wasn't just the cotton. Ravi had also enclosed some Thai silks and they came in ten thousand colors, one more beautiful than the other. And, girl, they were cheap. So I got the idea that we would make curtains for the cafeteria out of the sky-blue fabric and do the same thing in the visitor's room with a bright pink. And then I thought that if the stuff washed good – and we tried it and it did – we could sell some of the other colors in the canteen and that women could make bedspreads and curtains out of it. Just havin' somethin' pretty to spend their money on would be a real lift. Plus, the raw silk came in about thirty colors, so even if every cell was the same, it could be different because the colors were so different. Of course, I had to discuss it with the Warden, Jennifer, and Maggie, but they were all for it. Then I got me an even better idea: Why not make up T-shirts and sashes and neckerchiefs out of some of the colored silk? It would mean that women could do all kinds of shit – be in uniform but also be individual.

Then I started thinkin', why a jumpsuit at all? What are we, Oompa Loompas? Why not pants and shirts like everybody else in the world wears? I didn't think separate pieces got weapon possibilities. I checked with the warden and she said it was okay.

So I'm really cookin', drawin' away, and Theresa comes into the Warden's office. Just what I needed. I'm sure she thinks she'd be better than me at this. I don't think so. 'What are you doing?' she asked, in a tone which said she knew damn well what I was doin'.

'I'm designin' new uniforms for us. New clothes, Theresa,' I said. 'And ya' gotta try and not hold it against me.'

'I don't hold it against you,' she said. 'You don't mind hearing my opinion, though, do you?'

'I guess not, but I just started, you know. I'm thinkin' about what they should be made out of.'

'Clothes make the woman. They have to be neat and

flattering. And not wrinkle. So they have to be permanent press.'

'Hell, no!' I said, beginning to draw again. 'I'm so sick of this synthetic garbage. I say cotton all the way. It looks natural wrinkled. And puttin' it on fresh in the mornin' feels good. If I ever get outta here my kids are gonna wear nothin' but cotton.'

She looked down at my drawin'. 'Not bad,' she said. 'But slim down the pant leg. You've got the legs too wide. It's not flattering. Not everyone's as tall as you are. And put some darts in the top so that they have some shape. If a woman looks good, she feels good.'

'No fuckin' darts,' I answered. 'How's somebody like Renee or Mavis from Unit B gonna wear somethin' with darts?' Renee and Mavis are both at least two hundred fifty pounds. They bulk up so their bellies blend with their breasts and they wind up with no shape whatsoever.

Theresa shrugged and made a disapproving noise.

'Hey,' I said. 'We ain't gonna be goin' for job interviews, you know, Theresa. We're just gonna be hangin' out here as usual, and we want to be comfortable.'

'Maybe we could have different outfits for visitor's day.'

'I doubt it,' I said. 'There's a budget issue, ya' know.'

Theresa made a face of givin' up and walked out of the office. That made me feel good.

Anyway, it took me three days to design a bunch of pieces. I did long pants, Bermuda shorts for the summer, two different styles of shirts – one sleeveless and one sleeved – a skirt for visitor's day or Christmas or that kinda thing, some T-shirts and a couple of jacket styles for when it's cold out and we need some warmth. The only thing still to decide was the colors. I thought I'd get the opinions of some of the others about that. It proved very interestin', besides bein' a big pain in the ass. The crew talked about it over dinner.

'Can they be light blue?' Suki asked. 'Please?'

'They're already light blue, girl,' I said to her. 'Whaddaya mean?'

'They're not light blue, they're gray.'

We laughed, even though it wasn't funny. They had started out some kinda gray-blue, but now they were gray. Suki was right.

'Light blue's too light,' Theresa said. 'We need a color that won't show the dirt.'

'Or be so boring,' Theresa said. 'How about prints? Animal prints. Leopard or tiger or something like that. Safari.'

I nearly spat out my food laughin', picturin' Jennings crawlin' with animal prints. 'That's wild, Theresa,' I said. 'But I don't know if we could stand lookin' at it.'

'Well, then, how about black? Black is always cool,' Jennifer chimed in as she entered the cell.

'Black is a depressing color. We need to find out what colors of the spectrum are psychologically uplifting. Like red or orange, or coral maybe. Maybe the library has some books on color,' Suki said.

I shook my head picturin' a sea of coral-colored inmates. God. Some people ain't got no vision.

Jennifer came up with the practical suggestion of khaki, which I thought was too dreary. Then someone, namely me, suggested dark blue denim. Everybody was shocked that they hadn't thought of it. 'It's 'cause I'm a fashion designer,' I said, teasin' 'em. 'It ain't by accident I get ideas.'

Jennifer Spencer sweet-talked the Paragon Uniform

company in Yonkers to do up some samples for us, tellin' 'em they'd get a big order if they did. In the interest of a little variety I decided to have 'em do some pieces up in black denim and some of the shirts in a lightweight khaki. I often realize later that an idea is good and then I'm not afraid to do it, even though someone else thought of it. But we didn't order no animal prints.

Then we had a most amazin' event at Jennings, no doubt at all the first time anything like it happened. We had an honest-to-goodness fashion show!

At first everyone wanted to be a model and Warden Harding thought we were gonna have fights or at least a very bad scene. But funny thing was, as the day and the actual doin' it got closer, most all of 'em that wanted to turned chicken and backed out and we didn't have enough. Suki's belly was slightly rounded now, but she wanted to be in and we let her. Why the hell not?

The occasion itself had to be the most fun we ever had at Jennings. We moved the tables in the cafeteria together lengthwise to make a catwalk – this was Theresa's idea. Then we set up the chairs in rows on each side and put fashion pictures from magazines on the walls. I had the new curtains for the windows and they were beautiful – yards and yards of the most gorgeous sky-blue silk. The day before we hung 'em Warden Harding authorized repaintin' the cafeteria and instead of that dirty old color we got it a clean pearly white and my curtains made it look like a kinda heaven. I mean, you were still in the joint but it looked like the nicest joint ya' ever saw. Cher woulda been shocked, and then she'd probably try to cut off a piece of the curtain to turn into a skirt. I had to laugh. Maybe it was just as well she wasn't here.

I stood at one end of the catwalk and I gotta say I was real nervous as all the inmates filed in and took their seats. There was a little printed brochure on each chair and they all started reading it right away. It had an allowance for each inmate and little drawings of the different tops, pants, jackets, and accessories. I'm not a shy person, but that was a tough crowd and I was a little worried about the dykes. I'm not afraid of speakin' my mind but that's different from speakin' in public. So the models were ready – we used Flora and Frances and Theresa. Cher woulda been great to go down the catwalk but we got a tall, thin new girl named Lorrie instead. Jennifer wouldn't do it, even though I begged her. And Maggie just laughed, even though I told her we needed someone to represent senior convicts. In the end I had seven women. And I made sure that their outfits fit and that they were scheduled so they had time to make changes in between each appearance. Maggie and Suki were in charge backstage.

So, once the cafeteria was full and the COs were leanin' against the wall with their arms crossed, the warden introduced me. I started talkin', well, readin' from my cards 'cause I was too damn nervous to even look up. Old Gwen had explained that this was the new choice of uniforms and that everybody would get seven pieces – after that they could buy 'em. No one could have more than twelve. But the first seven came to you as a gift. So then out steps Frances and I say, 'Ladies and bulldaggers, presentin' Prison Blues.' And the music comes up loud and those girls began to strut just like they were real models and for a couple of minutes, well seconds really, nobody in the audience does nothing 'cause it was all so different from what we was used to. And then the place went crazy – but in a good way.

Theresa and Flora and Lorrie and all those model girls came out in my clothes and the women started to whoop and cheer. The dykes were whistlin' and the music kept playin' and for a minute I thought we was going to have a riot – not the good kind – but it was just everybody's enthusiasm and they were clappin' for my things. Then they started arguin' with each other about which would be better to have and I could hardly believe it. But I kept on talkin' and I explained that we were settin' up a production sewin' unit and that anybody who was workin' for a higher-level pay scale could apply. And we'd be makin' these uniforms and other stuff as well. And by the time the whole show was over I looked up from my cards and it wasn't just everybody in the audience clappin' but it was also Jennifer and the Warden and Maggie and every single one of the COs.

I never felt so proud of myself in my whole life.

37

Jennifer Spencer

Through all the drama –
whether damned or not –
Love gilds the scene,
and women guide the plot.
Richard Brinsley Sheridan

There weren't enough hours in the day. Jen felt pumped, the way she used to feel during high-stakes negotiations at Hudson, Van Schaank. But now it wasn't indirect. She would receive benefits from what she was doing that would daily influence her quality of life and that of others. When the music came on for wake-up, the lassitude and depression she had faced each morning since her arrival had gone. She hopped out of bed, full of new plans and new tasks.

It seemed as if the IPO package she and Lenny had worked so long and hard on might be acceptable, but it presented Jen with another financial issue. She needed, of course, for the IPO to go smoothly and for people to buy up the stock. She also needed some money with which to buy as much stock as she could and to help in making the offering look as good as possible.

That day at the library she got on the phone and called Peter Grant, one of the dumbest brokers she knew, and the one with the biggest mouth. Donald had used Peter when he wanted word circulated out on the Street. 'Peter?' she asked when he picked up the phone. 'It's Jennifer. Jennifer Spencer.'

'Hey! Great to hear from you!' He lowered his voice a decibel or two. 'Sorry about that trouble you were in. Glad it's over.'

'Yeah,' she said. She shook her head. He probably assumed she was out of prison. It was hard to remember that you were not the center of everybody else's life and interest. 'I took the fall for Donald but I'm getting repaid big time now.'

'I figured it was something like that,' Peter said, voice booming. 'Good for you!'

'Yeah,' she agreed. 'It's not like a grand larceny conviction stops you from getting invited out.'

He laughed, a real *har-har-har*. 'Actually, it's more of a social asset,' he told her. 'You know what they say: The unindicted are uninvited.'

What a jerk! 'Well,' she said, 'my social life *has* been looking up since I got out.' Why not let him continue with his assumption. She lowered her voice conspiratorially. 'Listen, Peter, I'd like an account. I'm going to do a lot of . . . well, just between you and me, a lot of things Donald's told me to, but I know I can count on you for absolute discretion.'

'Absolutely.'

Absolutely the opposite, she thought. That's why I'm calling you, you schmuck. Then his stupidity and greed gave her another idea. 'Could we put it in his name?' she asked. 'I'll get it in writing or put him on the phone if you like.' She held her breath.

'Hey, I'd be honored,' Peter said. He paused and she thought that perhaps she'd gone too far and the jig was up. Then he continued. 'You know, he opened one before. Remember? It's been inactive for a long time. I've been very disappointed about that.'

It had been inactive because Donald had only used Peter Grant's account when he wanted every dumb bastard to jump on something. You couldn't keep an account like that going for long because the SEC monitored big gains and would be on his back. But it was a great bit of luck that he had never closed the account. Jennifer thought as quickly as she could and smiled.

Peter was the kind of guy who would watch every trade Donald made and would jump on any wagon, no matter how rickety. 'Great,' she said. 'Let's just use that one. Send all the info to my new email address and you'll be hearing from me. We'll make a small initial deposit, and then probably work on profits from then on.'

Peter laughed again, his stupid *har-har-har*. 'Hey, Donald's credit is always good with me.'

Yeah, she thought, you and every other greedy bastard on the Street. 'Trades may come from other email addresses, phones, or faxes,' she told him. 'You know how it is.'

'Yeah,' he said. But he didn't know anything.

'But let's for security's sake use a code word to insure authenticity.' She thought for a moment. Then she said, 'Could you hold? I just want to ask Donald,' she said.

'Sure,' Peter said. 'Tell Don hello for me.'

A, Donald didn't know Peter Grant from a Chinese wok and B, anyone who knew him knew he *hated* to be called

Don. Jennifer put Peter on hold and tried to think of a code word that only Donald and his closest associates might use. SOB? YELLOW RAT BASTARD? She thought of Lenny and smiled. Then it came to her. Oh, it was so great! Yes! She got back on the line. 'Peter, I've got it. It's Grendel,' she told him and spelled it for the ignoramus. She doubted that he knew Grendel was the monster in *Beowulf*. Or that it was the name of Donald's female bull mastiff. 'Oh, and he says hi,' she lied.

'Great!' Peter said. 'Tell him we ought to get together sometime for a round of golf.'

'I'll tell him,' she said. The guy must have been named Peter because his mother knew he was going to grow up to be a dickhead. Donald hated golf, and an invitation like that from a guy like Peter would be enough for him to sic lawyers on the dumb bastard. Lucky for Peter Grant this interaction with Donald Michaels was all imaginary or he might wind up in trouble. Well, with any luck, he'd wind up in trouble anyway.

'Great!' Peter told her.

'He says he'll call you. Well, gotta go. Thanks for your help.' She paused, just for a moment. 'Oh, and Peter?'

'Yes?'

'I may ask that some of the . . . profits,' she giggled, sounding as close to a foolish, guilty girl as she could. 'Well, some of the profits – not much, but some – we might want distributed in cash.'

'Hey,' he said, 'under ten thousand dollars and we'll give you a cashier's check. If you want I'll run down to the bank and cash it for you. In pennies, nickels and dimes if you want.'

'What a guy,' she said. And at least that line was true.

'Gotta go,' she told him again. She took the concealed laptop from under the table top, opened it up, and went online. She picked several dozen penny stocks, did a Google search and selected the handful that looked like there was some way to sex them up. She put in a buy order and then she began the ancient process known in the trade as 'pump-and-dump'. She visited chat rooms and Web sites, and sent out emails to brokers and mutual fund managers, all touting the stock. Needless to say, she used different screen names, different writing styles, and gave Movita several dozen similar messages to post from her work-station. When Miss Ringling was out to lunch they signed on and sent another few dozen messages from there. Then she called Bryce.

'Hey, gorgeous,' he said when he picked up the phone. 'Can I send my car for you?'

'If only,' she said. 'No, right now I'm in a little money-raising compulsion. No time for a ride.'

'Hey,' Bryce said. 'Those rides are the best of all.' And Jennifer was sure he believed that to be true. 'What can I do for you?' he asked.

'I'm buying ten thousand shares of a company called Rivdek.'

'What is it?' he asked.

'What do you care?' she answered. 'It's a vehicle right now. Since I can't use your car. Anyway, I need you to buy some too.'

'Sure,' he told her. 'How many ya' want?'

'Well, right now it's priced at a dollar nine,' she said. 'I'd like you to buy up to thirty thousand shares, but not if the price goes higher than a dollar twenty.'

She heard the smile in his voice. 'I see,' he said. 'And

you will let me know when I'm supposed to unload these suckers.'

'I certainly will,' she promised him.

'And you will also let me know whether you think I'm a manly man,' he added.

He was a ridiculous flirt. He could dish it out but she wondered if he could take it. 'I thought I already told you that,' she said.

'Did you?' he asked.

'Uh huh,' she said, 'but only in body language. Perhaps you don't read body language.'

'I not only read it, I speak it fluently.'

Set and match, she thought. 'Well, I look forward to a more complete conversation at some other time,' she said. 'Gotta go.' Bryce was fun to flirt with, but between the two brothers she thought Tyler had a little more depth. Not that that mattered. She had missed flirting, being looked at like she was attractive. God, it must be hard for women who spent the best decades of their life in prison. She had forgotten how nice it was to communicate with attractive men. She didn't wonder that some of the women inmates would do almost anything to get a male CO's attention.

She dialed a number on the cell phone. 'Lenny Benson, please.'

'Accounting.' His voice sounded stern.

'It's me, Jennifer. I need your help transferring money so I can buy some Rivdek stock,' she told him.

'Hi, there.' She could hear his voice soften. 'Before I do that, have you gotten the power of attorney back from Tom?'

'He should have all the papers by now and everything should be transferred.'

'Well, just in case they're not in place, I'll bring the papers up for you to sign,' Lenny said, and she thought she heard a bit of excitement in his voice. 'And since it's of a business nature I shouldn't have to wait for visitor's day.'

'But I've already signed them.'

'Well, it's just an excuse to come see you,' Lenny said quickly as if she wasn't supposed to hear it.

What was going on? First Bryce, now Lenny. Was there a certain thrill to hitting on a woman who's incarcerated? She had to get him back to business. 'Look, I want you to do whatever you need to do to get the stock purchased and I want you to hype the hell out of Rivdek.'

'Okay, and if I have to I'll float you a loan,' he assured her.

'Thanks, Lenny. Well, I gotta go.' She pushed the red button on the cell phone and went back to the laptop.

She bought a little over ten thousand shares of Rivdek and watched the quotations. Her purchase at a dollar ten was fine but when you added all of her touting and then Bryce's purchase the stock rose to a dollar eighteen. Then a dollar twenty-seven. She'd already made twenty-five percent additional but it wasn't enough, so she sent out more messages of congratulations to many of the Web sites and chat rooms until, by closing, the stock was up to two ten. She put a call in to Bryce. 'Sell,' she said. And she did, too.

She doubled *her* money that day, and then did it again the following day. She'd always had nothing but contempt for day traders but she could see the compulsive pleasure one could take in the game. If everyone in the prison were given an account with Peter Grant, she thought, there would be no more acting out. They'd all be busy buying and selling stocks. Of course, like all outsiders, they'd eventually get burned. But even that would give them something to think about.

That night, over a dinner of tortellini and 'gravy', Jennifer didn't have the energy to talk much, but she felt as if she'd had a really good day.

38

Cher McInnery

The hardest thing to face getting out is the decisions. For months, for years, you haven't been able to decide anything for yourself. Then all of a sudden, you're supposed to be able to decide everything, make every kind of decision. It's just too much.

Emma Green, parolee from the state prison for women in Lansing, Kansas. Kathryn Watterson, *Women in Prison*

Cher wriggled her toes with pleasure in the thick pile of the silk Kirman. She loved watching her flat-screen TV in her new Tribeca loft.

On the day she was released from Jennings, Cher regretted that she had to be somewhat selective in what she actually took with her. It broke her heart to leave so much of her hard-earned bounty behind, but she had no intention of leaving those items that belonged to Jennifer Spencer. She took them all, and when her processing was finished, Cher McInnery walked out of the Jennings Correctional Facility a free and well-dressed woman. She had served close to four years for grand larceny, and she couldn't wait to get started again. Except this time there would be no petty coins, no boosting from stores, no grifting. After all, Jennifer Spencer's Armani suit was a perfect fit, and there was no reason to think that everything else in her closet wasn't going to fit Cher as well. She was grateful to Jennifer for opening her eyes to a larger world, one where stealing and manipulation was a respectable way of life.

It had always seemed dead wrong to Cher that everyone else had more than she had, and stealing was the only way she knew to settle the score. She only had one rule when it came to thievery: Never steal from no one that's poorer than you. And besides, it was a lot easier to steal from people who had more than they needed.

They got sloppy and did stupid things. They took their house keys to prison. It didn't take a rocket scientist to find the doors that those keys unlocked. When she first got to Jennifer's address, Cher was somewhat surprised to see that Jennifer's place was in an old meatpacking plant or something, but once she got inside she knew that she had struck gold. The views out the window from the huge living room looked south all the way down the Hudson River. Cher could even glimpse the Statue of Liberty in the distance – a good omen for her for the beginning of her new freedom.

She left prison with over thirty-eight hundred dollars that she had managed, bit by bit, to accumulate by acquiring and selling things on the black market. She was shocked to see how quickly money went here. She couldn't get into a taxi or eat a slice of pizza without breaking a ten dollar bill. And Cher didn't like to live tight and have to watch her pennies. She preferred to make lots of Benjamin Franklins rather than watching every George Washington. But Cher had plans. She had learned something in prison and it wasn't any crap about reforming. She had learned that she'd been thinking on too small a scale – that what she had considered success was penny ante. Prison had opened her vistas. Just like this view down to the New York Harbor did. And both were courtesy of Jennifer Spencer. She had to be grateful to the girl, and she was, in her own way.

Cher went to her purse – well, it had once been Jennifer Spencer's purse but it was her purse now – and took out the phone numbers she had hidden there beneath the tiny slit she had made in the lining. She was finished with the short con or even the big con. Blowing off the mark had become more and more difficult and they were more and more likely to bleat – go to the police. In the old days, marks were too embarrassed after getting conned to do anything about it. That was the whole point. Cher didn't plan to spend any more time Inside ever again.

She looked down at the phone number in her hand. JoJo ran a boiler room and a bucket shop here in New York. Cher had no interest in sitting all day, trying to make scores over the telephone, talking old ladies in Des Moines out of their savings, but the bucket shop might work. That was, if JoJo gave her a chance. His brother was a pickpocket with a whiz mob that sometimes worked New York, but JoJo looked down on him. She didn't want to try to talk herself into a job with him over the phone – she doubted if that would work, even with her refined tone of voice. But if she could find out where he was, go in for a meeting, or get him to take a walk, she was certain, dead certain, that she could move up.

But enough daydreaming. Cher had luxuriated in the pleasures of her new digs long enough. It was time to get to work. There was a whole lot she needed to get done before sunset. She clicked off the TV with the remote control and headed for the kitchen. It was a damned nice layout, but it didn't look as if the debutante had ever prepared a meal here in her life. Cher thought back to the crap Jennifer had served up at Jennings. Hadn't her mama taught her how to cook? The only useful thing Cher found in that kitchen was the drawer stuffed full of menus from places that delivered. She remembered Theresa's favorite joke: 'What does a debutante make for dinner? – Reservations!' Hell, this girl didn't even do that, she made phone calls. Well, if that's the way they did things in Tribeca, that's the way Cher would do it, too.

She decided she'd get a delivery from Balthazar. She was crazy for sticky buns, and she wanted to see what a sticky bun that cost five bucks tasted like. It was an extravagance that she couldn't really afford, but she'd worry about that later. As soon as she was working with JoJo she'd eat three five-dollar sticky buns a day if she wanted to. She dialed the number on the menu and was surprised when the voice on the other end answered with, 'Good morning, Miss Spencer. How may I help you?'

A lot had changed in the five years Cher had been at Jennings. Every damn place in America had new telephone systems that let them know who was calling before they even asked and a computer record right there with everything they needed to know about you. But Cher didn't miss a beat. 'I'd like to order breakfast,' she said casually.

'Would that be your usual order?' was the next question.

Cher thought, why not? 'Sure,' she said. 'Send over the usual.' Her stomach knotted at the thought of how much she was spending, but she was curious to know just what 'the usual' was for someone like Jennifer Spencer.

'And we'll just put that on your American Express as usual, right?' asked the order taker.

When Cher heard that, the knot in her stomach instantly untied and she was suddenly hungrier than she had ever been before in her life. 'You bet,' she said. 'Just put it on the American Express.'

'Very good, Miss Spencer. Your breakfast will be there in ten minutes.'

It was better than very good, thought Cher, this was damn good. With breakfast on its way, Cher picked up the phone to make another very necessary call. She flipped through Jennifer's address file until she found 'Branston, Tom,' and she dialed the number. She felt a deep sexual itch that just needed to be scratched. Tom Branston was a very handsome man – maybe a bit of a slimebag, but one in very nice packaging. Cher had always been attracted to those Wall Street types in their fancy suits. Now she had one of her own.

'Good morning, Tommy,' she cooed when she heard him answer. 'I'm all settled in.'

The first thing Cher had done after she got to New York City was to look up Jennifer's old beau. From what she had heard from the debutante, this guy was a bit of a dim bulb who thought primarily with his crotch. Cher had known plenty of guys like him. You had only to stroke the ego – and nothing else – to get what you wanted. Branston was no exception, and Cher played him like a cheap piano. When he heard that Cher was just released from Jennings, he was more than anxious to meet with her. Of course, Cher intimated that the deb had told her more than old Tom wanted anyone to know, and fearing blackmail, he willingly agreed to meet for a drink. That's when Cher surprised him with an easy way out. She had faked a letter from Jennifer asking for Tom's help in securing a 'sublet' on the apartment for Cher. 'She wants me to look after her belongings,' Cher assured the initially dubious attorney. When she showed him that she had Jennifer's keys, he believed her. Tom cleared Cher's way with the co-op board, and she moved in.

'I just wanted to say thank you,' Cher told Tom over the phone. 'Maybe I can do that personally sometime, huh?' she teased. She imagined that Mr Branston, like every other healthy young stud in the world, woke up ready for action. She would've been happy to help out with a little phone sex, but breakfast had arrived and Tom would have to finish up on his own. She bid him 'bye bye' and hung up. Always leave 'em asking for more, Cher thought. She smiled as she thought about how she might eventually pluck that chicken naked.

It seemed Jennifer Spencer shared Cher's taste for sticky buns. The 'usual' suited Cher just fine – as did everything she found in the closet. It was like dying and going to fashion boutique heaven to pick out an outfit from the debutante's closet. Cher tried on every damn suit in the wardrobe, but finally settled on the Prada. The others would have to wait. There'd be plenty of time to play dress-up just as soon as she got set up in the bucket shop. Cher was ready for business – looking good, feeling good, and ready to bite into the Big Apple – right down to the core.

It was good to walk the streets of New York City again. It always inspired Cher to feel the pace and the pressures of the pavement. But damn, the shops were distracting. With Jennifer's Gucci purse slung over her shoulder, Cher could just hear those credit cards calling out to her: *Use me – charge it – buy it – have it.* What the hell, Cher thought, and she succumbed to temptation and strolled into Agnes B. for a new outfit of her own. One thing that hadn't changed while Cher was gone was just how snotty the sales clerks could be at these fancy clothing stores. But now Cher was wearing Prada and that seemed to make all the difference in the world. She just started tossing stuff on the counter like she knew what she was doing. And little Isabelle the store clerk couldn't ring it up fast enough.

'You do deliver, don't you?' Cher asked, haughty as hell.

'Oh, yes,' Isabelle assured her.

Cher flipped out Jennifer's American Express and tried to act casual as she waited for the reassuring 'bleep' of approval from the credit card terminal. It sounded, and Cher started breathing again. She gave the address for the delivery and was about to be on her way, when she heard a voice behind her exclaim, 'Miss Spencer? Miss Spencer?' Cher froze, then turned very slowly. An older woman had appeared from the back office and was staring at her intently.

'Yes?' Cher asked.

'Is that you, Miss Spencer?' the woman asked. 'Have you done something different with your hair?'

'Dyed it,' Cher said quickly.

The woman squinted slightly and tilted her head as she considered Cher's answer. 'I like it,' she said finally. 'It changes your whole look.'

'Thank you,' Cher said with a smile.

'Anyway, I'll let you go now,' the woman said. 'I just wanted to say hello and to welcome you back. I'm glad you didn't forget us. We look forward to seeing you again soon, I hope?'

'Oh, yes,' Cher said as she turned and left the shop. Her heart was racing. She'd have to be more careful in the future. Tribeca was a small pond where Jennifer Spencer had been a very big-spending fish. From now on, Cher would do her shopping uptown.

39

Jennifer Spencer

Opportunity makes the thief.
English proverb

'I can't believe this shit,' Jennifer snarled to anyone who might be listening in the rec room. She waved around the letter that she was holding in her hand. 'I got this notice from my co-op board saying that I'm in violation of my contract with them because,' and she started reading directly from the letter:

> *In your absence, you have illegally subleased the unit to a third party which is in direct violation of building by-laws. When sublets are approved – which is done on a case by case basis – the lettor must be present.*

'I don't know what in the hell they're talking about,' Jennifer said aloud. 'I haven't sublet my apartment. I don't know what in the hell is going on, but I'm afraid Tom Branston has screwed me over once again!'

'Rich girls' problems,' Movita said.

Jennifer stalked over to the pay phone. She dialed Lenny's number. He helped fix everything. What would she do without him? 'Do you know what's going on with my loft?' she asked when Lenny picked up.

'Not a clue. Are you behind in maintenance? I've been sending it on the first of the month.'

'No. Nothing that simple. The co-op board is threatening to take me to court because of my illegal sublet. What sublet?'

'It must be a mistake.'

'I hope so. I don't need to be convicted again for crimes I didn't commit. What in the hell is happening out there, Lenny?'

She waited for him to castigate her for ever giving Tom Branston power of attorney. As Jennifer's accountant, Lenny had never been comfortable with the arrangement. As her . . . friend, she knew he resented Tom every moment of every day.

'I'll look into it, Jennifer,' he assured her. 'I'll talk to Tom and I'll talk to the people on your building's board. I'm sure that it's just a misunderstanding, or a paperwork screwup, okay?'

'But they say someone's living there!' Jennifer insisted.

'It's probably me they're talking about.' Lenny reminded her that during the secretive days of the holding company's formation and the subsequent buyout of JRU he had occasionally used her loft as his headquarters for the clandestine operation. 'Someone probably saw me coming and going and just thought I was living there, that's all. I'll straighten it all out. Stop worrying.'

Jennifer wanted to stop worrying about her place, just

like she wanted to stop worrying about her prison, but she couldn't shake the fear that whatever was happening on the Outside was somehow a direct threat to what she was trying to achieve at Jennings.

Those fears were realized when Lenny arrived at Jennings just two days later to report to Jennifer on what he had discovered. They sat together at a table in the visiting room and he started to explain.

'Look, you're sure Tom's name isn't on your co-op? He doesn't own shares, does he?'

'Absolutely not!' she told him.

'Well, he's living there. Or he's using it, a lot.'

'What? How do you know?'

'I followed him two nights ago. He didn't see me,' Lenny assured her. 'I snuck over to the newsstand and watched him from behind a magazine.' The mild-mannered accountant was almost panting with the intrigue of his adventure. Actually, Jennifer thought, he would have made a good John le Carré spy. 'At first, I just figured that maybe Tom was using your loft,' he said. 'After all, you two were engaged and he obviously still has a key. But then I thought, "Why would Tom start living here now? He has his own place."'

'Lenny, please,' Jennifer begged, 'just tell me what you found.'

Lenny was a little crestfallen that Jennifer did not find his tale of sleuthing as intriguing as he did, but he picked up the pace and continued. He told Jennifer how he had waited until he was certain Tom was gone, then he took his key and set off on his own expedition to uncover the truth. Before the elevator had even reached Jennifer's floor, Lenny could hear the blare of music that emanated from the loft. 'The thought of actually finding someone living there was pretty scary,' he told Jennifer. 'So I stayed in the elevator for some time, peering at your door through the wooden slats. And just when I mustered the courage to go in, the door to the apartment flew open and some woman came out with a bag of garbage!'

'Who was it?' Jennifer demanded to know.

'I don't know,' Lenny said, 'but she was obviously living there.'

'So what happened?' Jennifer asked.

Lenny took a deep breath, stared intently into Jennifer's eyes, and continued. 'I'm not sure you want to know,' he said sadly. But Jennifer *did* want to know, and from what Lenny told her, it soon became clear that Tom Branston was using Jennifer's loft to keep another woman.

'I can't believe it!' Jennifer said. She didn't want Lenny to think she still had feelings for Tom – she did, but they were all angry ones – but jealousy did flare up. She was holed up in this . . . this *convent* while he . . .

'How does a guy like Tom Branston sleep at night?' Lenny asked. 'Do you know how lucky you are to be rid of that guy?'

'Was she wearing my diamond?' Jennifer asked him.

Lenny stared at Jennifer for a moment. 'After everything I just told you, is that all you can think about?'

'Was she wearing my diamond or not, Lenny?' Jennifer insisted.

'I don't know,' Lenny answered in exasperation. 'I doubt it. I think she's just a . . .' Lenny hesitated.

'A what?' Jennifer wanted to know, but Lenny said nothing. Neither spoke for a moment, then Jennifer asked hesitantly, 'Is she pretty?'

Lenny couldn't take it anymore. 'She's a whore,

Jennifer!' he almost shouted. 'Whores are not pretty, and they don't get diamond rings.'

Jennifer couldn't sleep that night. She didn't want to disturb Suki, so she got up from her bunk and walked out into the dayroom. It had been one of her life's sweetest victories when the battle was finally won that allowed the inmates to leave their cells at night and spend their sleepless hours in the rec room if they chose, playing cards or doing jigsaw puzzles. You could always find someone to talk with, no matter what hour of the night it was. Most people had troubles worse than hers. Jennifer was glad of that tonight when she walked in and saw Movita there.

'You can't sleep either?' Movita asked when she saw her.

Jennifer shook her head and sat down across from her at the table.

'What's the problem?' Movita wondered.

Jennifer shrugged. How could she explain to Movita that she feared her eventual release from prison? How could she tell a woman who was serving a life sentence in prison that she was worried about a luxurious loft, her ex-engagement ring and her ex-fiancé. She didn't want to tell Movita that that was the reason she couldn't sleep, because she was ashamed. She was ashamed of the art, and the rugs, and the antiques. She was ashamed of the Biedermeier armoire filled with designer clothes. She was ashamed that her life had added up to nothing but a lot of stuff, and now that the stuff might be gone, she was ashamed that she might not know what to do without it. 'I'm just not sleepy,' Jennifer finally said in answer to Movita's question.

Movita nodded, as if to say that she too would rather not talk about the real causes of her insomnia. But Jen knew her daughters' names, and that Mo's pain was too deep to probe. So, after an hour or two of small talk and prison gossip, they were both tired and relaxed enough for sleep. Jennifer crept quietly back into her cell, careful not to wake the snoring Suki.

To keep peace among the inmates who were complaining about Jennifer working in the library, the Warden had her start to divide her time between there and the laundry. So her work detail for today was in the sweat pit of the Jennings laundry. She staggered quickly across the laundry room floor under a bundle of sheets almost as big as she was, because if she didn't get everything into the machines fast, Suki would be picking up laundry and Jennifer got sympathy pains in her own abdomen just thinking about it. Suki was nearly nine months pregnant, and Jennifer had nightmares worrying about the silly girl. Suki would bend over and pick up laundry as if it were perfectly okay to do.

'Just sit down!' Jennifer said to Suki now as Suki wandered dangerously near to the piles of whites. 'Don't you understand that it's easier for me to do it than to watch you do it? Please! They've still got lousy health care here and if you're premature it'll be a terrible thing!'

'I'm fine,' Suki answered. 'My sister was working on the day her first baby was born. And she was a telephone lineman.'

'A lineman had a baby? Was she up a pole?'

Suki shook her head, as if Jen were serious. 'Uh-uh. But she had it in the truck. And fast.'

'Really?' Jennifer asked.

Suki nodded, bent down, and picked up some towels.

'Towels are too heavy! Leave those!' Jennifer said, walking up to her and taking them out of her hands. 'Sit.'

'I can't just sit,' Suki said, looking down at her belly as she pulled the material of her jumpsuit tight across her abdomen to reveal her bulge. When she held her baggy suit against it you could see. It was stupendous.

Jennifer increased her pace, sorting and carrying laundry faster than she ever thought she could. But then, a couple of minutes later, out of the corner of her eye, she saw that Suki had, in fact, sat down.

'Are you okay, Suki?' she asked, turning to her. Suki didn't answer at once, and it seemed to Jennifer that she had a strange look on her face. 'Suki?' she repeated. 'Are you in pain? Are you having contractions?'

'No,' Suki answered. 'I'm just getting . . . feelings.'

'Feelings?'

'Yeah.' Suki was sweating, tiny beads coating her upper lip and nose.

Jennifer stared down at her for a minute, made sure she was all right and then went back to work, but now she looked over at Suki every minute or so. 'Are you okay?' she asked again. 'You don't look so good.'

'I think I might be sick,' Suki said. 'I feel a little sick.'

Jennifer dropped the sheets she'd just folded on a table and went over to help Suki up. 'C'mon, Suki,' she said. 'We better go to the infirmary. You can't be too careful about these things.'

'No, actually I feel much better now,' Suki said. 'I think it was just gas.'

'Are you sure you're not getting contractions?' Jennifer asked her.

Suki seemed to think about it. 'No,' she said, 'this is not

what I read about in the book. And it's over already.' She looked up at Jennifer and shrugged. 'False alarm,' she said.

Jennifer looked at her. She couldn't very well force the girl to go to the infirmary, so she just went back to work, sorting, hefting laundry in and out of the machines, folding, and all the while watching Suki. An hour later, work duty was over and it was nearly time for dinner. Suki slowly walked back to the cells with Jennifer. She would stop every now and then to remark on something. Jen thought it was to rest as well, but Suki said she felt absolutely fine. Jennifer guessed that it had been false labor. The fact that Suki ate very little dinner didn't mean anything either. Suki hadn't had a consistent appetite since early on in her pregnancy.

So it came as a total surprise when, just after lights-out, Suki sat bolt upright in her bunk and announced that the baby would be coming soon.

'Oh my God! What do you mean, Suki?' Jennifer cried. She was very alarmed, and frightened for the girl. 'I thought you weren't even having contractions!'

'I guess they must have been what I was having all day. But now they're getting closer together and worse. They're getting really bad, Jen. I think you're gonna have to help me.'

Jennifer jumped out of her bed and sat down next to Suki. She took her hand and told her to just keep on breathing calmly and deeply.

'I'll call a CO,' she said. 'They'll get an ambulance.'

'No. No, please,' Suki begged in a whisper. 'Don't tell. And don't be mad at me.'

'I'm not mad at you, Suki,' she said, 'but will you please tell me why you kept this a secret? What were you thinking of?'

'Oh God, Jenny,' Suki said, beginning to cry. 'I just

couldn't stand to be in handcuffs and . . . and . . . have my legs shackled to the table. I just couldn't stand it.' She gripped Jennifer's hand tightly. 'I'm not afraid to have the baby, but I'm afraid to let them take me away. I could have the baby here, Jen, before anybody comes. Please help me. I don't want to have my baby in cuffs. Please.'

'God, Suki!' Jennifer said. The strength and weakness of each woman overwhelmed her. 'You pretended all day?'

Jennifer felt Suki nod in the darkness. 'Ohhh,' she groaned. 'I want Roger.'

Jen called for an officer. It was Officer Ryan, thank God. She thought the white-haired older man would at least try to help them. 'We have a situation,' Jen said to him. 'Suki's going to have her baby.'

'Oh my God!' Ryan whispered. 'Infirmary's closed. Locked up. What do ya' wanna do?'

'I think you should call the Warden and tell her,' Jennifer said. 'She'll know what to do.'

Suki was making groaning noises now and Jennifer went back and sat with her. Ryan called the Warden and then brought the phone to Jennifer.

'I'm breakin' the rules and lettin' you talk on my phone,' he said. 'Don't you ever tell anybody I did it.'

Jennifer almost laughed aloud. She could lend him *her* cell, but instead she just took the phone.

'Suki Conrad is in labor?' the Warden asked.

'What should I do?' Jen asked back.

'I think you should take her down to the infirmary,' the Warden said. 'I'll tell Ryan to get Movita and Theresa to help you, and I'll pick up my friend Lucille and come right over.'

'Who's Lucille?'

'She's a doctor. Not an OB-GYN but a good internist.'

'Good. Thank God.' Jennifer handed the phone back to Ryan and went back to Suki. 'C'mon, girl,' she said, 'we're going to go for a walk.'

Officer Ryan turned on the auxiliary lights and unlocked their door. He spoke to another officer on his walkie-talkie and told him to bring Movita and Theresa to the infirmary. Then the three began to walk. Suki was fine between contractions, but they were coming every minute or so and she'd have to stop and bend over with each one.

'I wish we could ride,' Jennifer said. 'This is such a long walk for her.'

Officer Ryan shrugged. 'It ain't a bad thing to walk at this time,' he said. 'Gets things movin'. Did it with my wife for all three of our kids.'

Jennifer didn't say it, but she thought things were moving plenty fast enough already, and she was right. They didn't make it to the infirmary. Suki started to scream that the baby was coming right then. Jen nearly passed out, but Suki was wrong. Before she could drop to the floor and lie down on her side, her water broke and gushed all over the floor. Fortunately, Movita and Theresa came down the corridor just then and neither one seemed rattled. Officer Ryan went with Theresa and Jennifer to get the things that Movita, who was already down on the floor with Suki, said they would need.

'Pillows and blankets,' she said, picking Suki's upper body off the floor and cradling her in her arms. 'A good pair of scissors and antiseptic, and one a them aspirators to clear the baby's nose out. You know what I mean? And then we're gonna need some warm water and little blankets. I don't know where we're gonna get those.'

Jen assured her that they'd get everything Mo wanted, but she was praying all the while that the Warden would come with the doctor, because she was sure that there wouldn't be any of what Movita needed in the closet. Suki was moaning and making another noise that didn't sound good.

'Breathe, girl, breathe,' Movita said. She looked up at Jen. 'Go with that CO and look in the infirmary for the necessary supplies.'

There was a blanket and there was a pillow, but nothing else. They went into the infirmary itself next and found another pillow. They saw a pair of scissors and antiseptic in a glass-doored cabinet, but Officer Ryan didn't have the key to it. Jennifer was about to beg him to break the glass when she heard talk coming from the corridor.

'Listen! Maybe the doctor's here!' Jennifer cried, but it was Roger Camry, with Officer Mowbry dogtrotting along.

'Where is she?' Camry asked, and Jen pointed. They all ran together.

By the time they got back to the birth scene, Suki had Movita and another woman – the doctor, Jen realized – caring for her, and the Warden was sitting next to her on the floor holding her hand. After that it was just a matter of time. 'Roger! Roger!' Suki cried, and he took her hand. Officer Ryan left and a kind of peace descended. Lucille was calm and efficient and had everything under control. She and Movita were working like partners, both telling Suki when to push and when to let up. Suki looked up at Roger Camry and Jen saw the Warden look at them both. Suki was grunting loudly with each push and collapsing with fatigue in between. But with each push Jennifer could see the patch of baby's head get a little bigger, and she was mesmerized. So was Theresa, who stood next to Jen. When the little head finally popped out, accompanied by a yelp from the mother, Jennifer let out a cry herself. It was a sight she would never forget, the birth on the floor of the prison unit of Suki's innocent, seven-pound-six-ounce baby girl.

40

Jennifer Spencer

> *When one has been threatened with a great injustice, one accepts a smaller as a favour.*
>
> Jane Welsh Carlyle

Jennifer felt as nervous as if she were giving birth. It wasn't as if she hadn't done an Initial Public Offering before, but somehow, even when it had been at the beginning of her career and it mattered a lot, it hadn't felt as important as this. If they could raise money, improve the prison's infrastructure, and generate a little profitability, it would be what Martha Stewart called a 'good thing'. Jennifer wasn't sure that she wanted to grow JRU until it was a behemoth like Wackenhut, running a couple scores of prisons, but the choice in America was grow or perish and she supposed this was the lesser of the two evils.

The Rafferty boys had put together a syndicate but against her better judgment she had allowed them, rather than the investment group of Tucker Anthony, to be the lead managers. She hoped that they hadn't been too aggressive in setting the price per share at somewhere between five and eight dollars. She thought about the classic job that had been done when Yahoo! went public and had been so undervalued because older analysts hadn't seen the technical revolution that was about to bite them in the ass. The lead manager had low-balled it and when Yahoo! came to market the price was so low and demand was so great that it had risen four hundred percent and gained tremendous publicity. She didn't need that, but last night Bryce and Tyler had set the price at eight dollars a share and this morning they were calling the sales people in the syndicate, allocating the shares among them before the market opened and hoping that the demand would be greater than the allocations. Since the tech market had cooled, pharmaceuticals were at an all-time high, and prisons were – unfortunately – a growth industry. Jennifer was hoping there would be a demand that exceeded the available stock.

Bryce had promised to allocate plenty of shares to Lenny, but Jennifer wanted to be sure that the risk was limited and that no other salesmen at Hudson, Van Schaank would get access. She took a deep breath. It was 9:25. The allocations were being made in New York right now, and when the offering took place this morning she would see how they fared.

Because she couldn't bear to sit still, she got up from her desk and paced around the newly expanded library. It was great to see the orderly rows of books, the reading tables, the encyclopedia, and the law books in the reference section, as well as the two computer workstations that gave the library users access to library databases. In the alcove there were five women, their heads bowed over books as if they were in prayer, learning to read. Maggie, strict but patient, was quietly teaching them, while other women sat at tables, reading for pleasure or taking notes. This is worthwhile, Jennifer thought. I've made a change, and it's worthwhile.

The problem with the success was that she had less privacy. Although as assistant librarian she was granted the privilege of a desk in the corner with her back to the rest of the library, she couldn't make phone calls easily and she certainly couldn't receive them on the cell phone. Inmates were nothing if not observant, and any infraction, any special treatment was immediately spotted, commented on, reported, or envied – sometimes all of the above. Jennifer did not want to improve the prison at the cost of her own safety.

She decided it was best to go up to the Warden's office. There she had Miss Ringling to contend with, but she could talk with Movita and go online. What she wanted to do was go into the rec room and put the television on to watch CNBC and follow the quotations, but she didn't think that the women addicted to *Live with Regis and Kelly* or *Ricki Lake* would allow it, never mind trying to get the use of the TV during the soaps. She smiled at the very thought. There were two factions – the CBS addicts, who watched *The Bold and the Beautiful, The Young and the Restless,* and *As the World Turns,* seemed to be winning the war against the ABC addicts who watched *All My Children, One Life to Live,* and *General Hospital.* At least that's what she thought. She didn't even know what was on NBC because Jennifer hadn't been home to watch television in the afternoon since grammar school, when she had flirted briefly with Luke and Laura on *General Hospital* but could never stay sincerely interested.

Now she had to ask Maggie to telephone the Warden's

office and send her on some kind of trumped-up mission. She hated to interrupt Maggie during a class but motioned her aside. 'Restless, huh?' Maggie asked her.

'Shouldn't you be?' she asked. 'Your whole fortune is riding on this. If the offering is successful you can sell off your holdings in JRU and recoup some of your investment.'

Maggie looked around the room. 'I've already recouped my investment,' she said, smiling at the books, the library, and the women busy at the tables. She gave Jennifer a copy of *Corrections Officer Monthly* and said, with a voice slightly raised, 'Would you take this up to the Warden's office? They requested it.'

Jennifer walked down the hall toward the center of the prison. She passed the section of the old kitchen facility that now housed the sewing room. They had only been able to buy fourteen professional sewing machines, but they already had two teachers and the new uniforms were being cut and sewn. Beyond the kitchen and the cafeteria was the canteen, which was already stocking a wider and healthier selection of foods, including protein bars, more fresh fruits and a selection of half a dozen frozen vegetables. Outside the canteen, on a wall at least twenty feet long, photographs from the fashion show and the actual garments were pinned up along with a box where order forms could be placed. Jennifer sighed. It was very little but already the prison felt like a different place. Not all but perhaps half of the women were clambering for job assignments so they could earn more and buy more.

Movita and Warden Harding had already begun to put together a list of the deranged or extremely difficult inmates. They would be reassigned, all together, to a new wing where, Jennifer knew, bedlam would reign, but everyone else would get a sounder sleep and have an easier day, including the COs. Warden Harding was looking for COs with psychiatric hospital backgrounds to staff the new disturbed wing.

Jennifer got to the Warden's office, passed Miss Ringling's desk, and walked straight to Movita. 'Have you seen yet?' Movita asked.

'Seen what?' Jennifer had no idea what Movita was talking about.

'The offering,' Movita told her. 'It opened at eight and a quarter. And it's already up to ten and a half,' Movita said, sounding as if she'd been selling in a boiler room for the last ten years.

'You've got to be kidding,' Jennifer said, really stunned. My God, she thought. How much money would that raise for the prison?

She pushed Movita on the shoulder and tried to share her seat. 'I don't have it online,' Movita said. 'I got a call from one of my friends.'

Jennifer stared at her. 'You have friends at the market?' she asked.

'Hey, girlfriend, you don't know everything about me.'

Just then Warden Harding put her head out the door. 'Miss Watson, Miss Spencer, would you join me in the office for a moment?' she asked.

Jen and Movita followed her in and she closed the door behind them. She had a small television sitting on her windowsill tuned to CNBC. Without even thinking about it, Jennifer sat down on the floor. She was mesmerized by the numbers flashing across the bottom of the screen. She was looking for JUI, the initials that had been assigned to the company (apparently there was something else that was

JRU). It took a while, but eventually it showed up and it was at fourteen and an eighth. Jennifer actually half rose from her lotus position and screamed. This was a good sign, a really good sign. 'What's up?' Movita asked, Warden Harding right behind her.

'We're in the action,' Jennifer said. 'It looks good. We're up to fourteen.' She looked at the time. 'And it's only ten ten. Of course, anything could happen, it could have been a burst of enthusiasm early in the day that'll be followed by a crash. It could be a plateau, but even then . . .'

'You mean we've doubled our money?' Gwen Harding asked.

Jennifer smiled at her as if she were a simpleton. 'Well, you would have doubled it if you had had it in the market on this stock in the first place.'

'But I do,' Gwen Harding said.

'Oh, no!' Jennifer moaned. 'I can't take any more pressure. Don't tell me you invested personal money. This is a business. We always do it with other people's money.'

'Well, I'm another person,' Gwen said. 'And I don't believe I'm alone. As far as I know there are quite a few people here who have invested.'

'Who?' Jennifer asked, but then was distracted by hearing something mentioned on CNBC.

'One IPO that seems to be on the move today is JRU. And here to discuss it is Chris Olsen, of the investment firm of Tucker Anthony.'

An attractive woman with short platinum hair nodded at the camera. 'This is an interesting public offering, Bob,' she said. 'We were hoping for an allocation of five thousand shares but while we feel good about it and we have additional demand, we didn't get any allocation at all at the seven-dollar opening price. I think the investment bankers may have been a little too conservative on this one. JRU is a new firm but it has three lucrative prison management contracts and when you look at their major competitors, the giants Wackenhut and CCA, JRU looks like a David to their Goliath. It's a feisty young company, they have some good staff and I'm expecting demand to continue. I think our clients might be willing to buy it at as much as twenty dollars a share.'

'Oh, my good Lord!' Movita cried. 'They talking about the stock tripling?'

Jennifer's heart was thumping in her chest but she tried to keep calm for the sake of the others. 'Hey, it's only ten thirty. It could drop to three bucks by nightfall.' She looked at the television. 'Although this certainly didn't hurt,' she said. She looked at the two women. 'May I remind you that I am here in part because of dealing in so-called "insider information". I hope you haven't made me guilty of that again.'

'Hey, I'm not goin' to drop a dime on you,' Movita said. 'How 'bout you, Warden?'

Warden Harding just laughed and Jen couldn't tell if it was over the mild joke or the fact that the woman had just made a few thousand dollars.

It was time for a head count just before lunch and they made their way back to their hallway. After the cafeteria, Jennifer and Movita went back to the library to tell Maggie the news, but Maggie was already in the know. 'Bryce and Tyler called the Warden and she relayed the information to me. Isn't it just grand, girls? You know, it's up to twenty-four and a quarter,' Maggie told them.

Jennifer opened her eyes wide. 'Your sons have been . . .'

Maggie smiled a full, slow grin. 'Are you trying to tell me I'm not the only criminal in my family?' she asked.

Jennifer couldn't help it – she went back to the Warden's office and spent the rest of the afternoon alternating between the telephone, the television, and Movita's online service while she watched the stock climb and climb. By the end of business that day it was at thirty-seven and she made sure that she called everyone she knew to tell them to get out.

'Hey,' Bryce said when she spoke with him. 'We've only just begun.'

'Please, Bryce,' Jennifer told him. 'Just get out. Let it cool off.'

'Not on your life,' Bryce told her.

41

Maggie Rafferty

Time discovers truth.

Lucius Annaeus Seneca

America's insatiable hunger for novelty is a constant source of bewilderment to me. I, who have never hula hooped, visited any Disney Kingdom, eaten buffet in Branson, Missouri, or petted a rock (domesticated or wild), find it inconceivable that there are those who have not only done these things, but who have willingly parted with generous sums of their cash in order to do so. As Mr Barnum would say, well, we all know his theory on the frequency of patsy births.

That great showman's maxim was never so gloriously affirmed as it was at the Jennings Correctional Facility for Women. With suckers proliferating nationwide at a rate of one per minute, it only stood to reason that whoever came up with the next 'new thing' to satisfy their infantile oral cravings would become very rich indeed. And what better way to satisfy a sucker than with a lollipop? That is how 'Prison Pops' came to take America by storm – and for an even 'buck a pop'. It was a glorious thing to behold.

Ice was long the rarest of commodities here at Jennings. In the pre-privatization days, residents here were forced to rely on primitive methods of refrigeration to keep any precious food provisions from spoiling in the prison cells. One's weekly allocation of ice was used for this purpose, and rarely did it last long enough to do the job adequately.

A greedy but ingenious woman in Unit B by the name of Sally Waterman had come up years ago with a marvelous confection that came to be known as 'Prison Pops'.

It was a really rather simple recipe that required only coloring, gelatin, enough caramelized sugar to rot the teeth of an entire kindergarten class, and a secret flavoring that Sally wouldn't disclose. Richer than a Tootsie Pop and a Sugar Daddy put together. Prison Pops were the new taste treat that the suckers in America longed for. Initially we produced only small batches of the pops during the new professional cooking classes that had been instituted as part of the training courses. Lacking proper sticks, the sweet and icy delight was served in bowls and eaten with a spork. It was actually Suki Conrad who suggested that the pop be frozen right onto the spork, and old Springtime who observed, 'These are good enough to sell in a store Outside.'

Well, that's all Theresa LaBianco had to hear. Given the new technologies of the computer and the Internet, it wasn't long before that business-mad mind had developed a telephone sales plan, an outline for a mail-order catalogue, and a Web site. Jennifer Spencer got behind it and made a presentation (including a taste test) to my boys. Well, Bryce had always had a real sweet tooth. Soon we were, as they say, in business. I don't really want to speculate as to why Internet users might be searching for Web sites with the name 'Prison Chic Candies', but it seemed to be an immediately popular site. We had thousands of 'hits' within just hours, and hundreds of orders within days. Theresa trained a staff of nearly twenty women to handle the orders. Jennifer bought the equipment to mix and make and wrap the stuff in big batches. It was nothing short of amazing. Dear old Gwendolyn Harding was delighted to see that this burgeoning new enterprise was equipped with everything it needed for success. It was a rare occasion that you didn't see the Warden with a pop in her mouth.

At first the demand was nearly overwhelming, but Theresa managed to turn our inability to meet the orders into a brilliant marketing ploy. 'PPs' became as rare as those homely stuffed dolls once were at Christmas, and shops like Neiman Marcus, Gump's, and the like clambered for them. They weren't to be found in supermarkets or candy stores but only via the exclusive shops, our catalogue, or the Prison Chic Web site. As I say, it is our nation's insatiable hunger for novelty. You just can't underestimate gullibility.

Anyway, when Prison Pops were unexpectedly 'picked' by *People* magazine in their 'Picks and Pans' column, the visionary Miss LaBianco was ready to take Prison Chic Candies to a whole new level of operation. Sally was testing recipes for new flavors while the Web site was constantly updated with 'Sweet Thoughts from the Prison Chics'. It was originally thought that I might be of some help with this project, but it soon became apparent that this particular old prison 'chic' did not possess the verbal skills that Web-browsers were surfing for. You might say that I laid an egg. However, as the new products emerged from Sally's lab, my tongue was loosened by their sweetness, and it was I who dubbed her pistachio fudge nut brownies 'Prison Bars'. They were an immediate success. It was also I who named the hard confectionary division 'Jailhouse Rock Candies'. They became big holiday sellers. I even tried my hand at advertising copy, but it seems that I'm far too verbose for the succinct and 'punchy' requirements of that particular medium. Well, we all do what we can.

This unexpected revenue stream provided not only cash flow, jobs, and training but also secured for JRU the kind of publicity on Wall Street that you simply cannot buy. The stock skyrocketed as everyone wanted to cash in on the phenomenon that was called 'the next Ben & Jerry's' in *Barron's* and 'a sweet deal' in *Forbes*. Meanwhile every inmate in the joint came up with some family recipe or secret ingredient that could be the next big thing. Several of them are actually in development, and two look promising. As if all of this wasn't enough success for Jennifer Spencer, it wasn't long before our cottage industry captured the attention of several food-manufacturing giants across the nation, and Miss Spencer and my sons are currently in negotiations for a buyout. Tyler and Bryce were both instrumental in securing billions for a similar operation that was begun by two hippies in Vermont. They are working on this as I write. In the meantime, I understand Frances, the ice queen, is concocting her own version of a marshmallow-based puff that will be ready for Halloween. I've been conducting focus groups to determine a name, but thus far we have not decided between 'Gallows Ghosts' or 'Dungeon Devils'. The girls in copy are anxious for us to make up our minds in order that they can develop the verbiage for the

Web site. Then, of course, the packaging must be designed.

As they once said back in the seventies, 'We've come a long way, baby.'

I do wish I could write a punchy line like that.

42

Jennifer Spencer

A business with an income at its heels furnishes always oil for its own wheels.

William Cowper

Jennifer thought that Movita was a hoot. She had never seen anybody become as totally obsessed with anything as Movita had become with fashion. She begged Maggie to use library funds to subscribe to every fashion magazine and though Maggie refused her most of them, Movita did prevail with *W* and *Women's Wear Daily*. She spent her own money on *Vogue*, *Bazaar* and even more arcane ones. She pored over them night and day and was always sketching improvements and additions to her line of prison wear. Only Theresa had the patience to look and listen to her constant stream of fashion talk, and even she eventually grew tired of it. But no matter how long Mo worked on a shift in the sewing room she always came back excited and filled with new ideas. Jennifer felt just a little bit as if she'd unleashed a monster.

She was also worried about the financial realities of

running the prison. Although the IPO had raised money that could be used for capital improvements or the actual budget, there didn't seem to be a lot of income re-creation possibilities. Prison Pops and Bars were selling strong and the new catalogue they were producing would probably increase sales, although right now it was just cost. But Jennifer knew she couldn't count on the candy to support all of them. It wasn't as if they were a tiny convent and baking bread would do the job. In its original proposal that won the bid, it was clear that JRU had planned to take a loss simply to build a presence. Unless she wanted to be taken over by one of the larger prison management firms – which she definitively did not – Jennifer couldn't see a way to make their projection and she knew what that would do to the company's financial rating. Wall Street analysts went nuts when there was any surprise. They weren't even thrilled with surprise profits. Well, okay, they were thrilled with surprise profits but they went nuts buying stock as if it was the first offering of Bell Telephone.

Movita was trying to talk Jennifer into doing a mail-order catalogue of casual clothes, but Jennifer felt it was far too risky and that the catalogue business was probably saturated. After dinner that evening she actually missed Cher, who, if she had still been there, could have probably come up with some thieving scheme that might actually work. Just then Theresa, who was thumbing through one of Mo's magazines, interrupted her thoughts with an expletive that she rarely used.

'Holy shit!' Theresa said. 'I don't believe this and I'm seeing it with my own eyes. Did you see this, Movita?' she asked.

'Oh, yeah,' Movita said. 'Isn't that a scam and a half.'

'What's that?' Jen wanted to know.

'It's this company, a French one called Imitation of Christ,' Theresa said, the outrage in her voice apparent.

'A charity?' Jennifer asked.

'No, a fashion company,' Theresa said.

'Well, it does make a statement,' Movita said.

'Like what?' Theresa said. 'That French people are fuckin' nuts? It says here that they buy old clothes from the Salvation Army and other shelters and thrift shops and then they tear them up or draw on them or add different buttons and sell it as high fashion.'

'Well, it is high fashion,' Movita said. 'First of all they're French and they have good taste and secondly they don't pick just anythin' from the thrift shop. And it's what they do with it that makes all the difference.'

'Let me see,' Suki said, shifting the weight of baby Christina from one hip to the other, then bending down to take a look at the magazine. 'God, that stuff is ridiculous. And the prices. Holy . . .'

'Let me see that,' Jennifer demanded. She took the magazine from Suki. It all seemed to be true, hard as it was to believe. Well, two years ago she might have been convinced that homeless chic was a look. She speed-read the article looking for the names of the American distributors and retailers who sold the garbage. She shook her head and wrote the names down.

'You gonna buy some?' Suki asked and moved the baby to a cradle position in her arms.

Jennifer didn't even deign to answer her.

The next day Jennifer got on the phone as quickly as she could. Her French was lousy – she hadn't used it since college – but she managed to get in touch with Imitation of

Christ, and through them with another firm that was larger and less avant-garde. She spoke to a Pierre Duchamps who, luckily for her, spoke English and was a big fan of *Con Air*. 'I love zee cinema of Jerry Bruckheimer,' he said. 'We can get zese real prison clothes? But for women? *C'est fantastique. Merveilleux.* Can you fax me zee choices? You have many sizes, many styles?'

Jennifer looked up into the air at the library ceiling over her head and wasn't sure if she was thanking God or giving up. The world Outside was sometimes so very, very weird. 'Sure,' she said. 'I'll fax them to you.'

'But with prices you must also tell me if it is exclusive for Duchamps Couture. We will pay more but it must be exclusive to us. *Comprenez-vous?*'

'Oui, je comprends.'

Jennifer made almost four hundred and sixty thousand dollars from the uniforms and realized that after it caught on in Paris there was a good chance it would move to London and New York. And, she thought, she had an endless supply of used ugly prison gear because the candy were still being issued jumpsuits until they settled in. When she and Warden Harding discussed it, neither one of them could keep back their laughter. But conservative projections indicated that they could expect to make close to a million dollars in pure profits as long as the trend lasted.

In the meantime, virtually every prisoner was bringing in recipes from their grandmothers, their great aunts, their mothers' sisters' cousins who had candy recipes that couldn't be beat. After dinner in the cafeteria on Thursdays and Sundays they had tastings as a kind of rough market research. Though Jennifer noticed there was definitely a tendency to go for milk chocolate instead of the more expensive – and delicious – dark chocolate that she preferred. She figured it was a class thing. Two winners that they added to the collection were hard candies that were beautiful to look at and stored well. That was important, because while they valued freshness, it was impossible to guarantee at what temperature and for how long things would be stored while they were being shipped.

At Jen's insistence, Maggie had begun joining them at dinner and once Maggie had even cooked, making coq au vin. 'I don't think anybody makes this anymore,' she admitted to all of them. 'But in my day it was the classy dish, sort of like my mother's chicken à la king.' Everybody ate the chicken happily, simply because it was something different. 'I had to cheat, of course, with the wine,' she said. 'I suppose you can't call it coq au vin when you're using flat grape soda.' She lowered her voice. 'But I did add a little alcohol. Bryce smuggled it in to me. He injected some vodka into oranges that he brought me.'

'Man,' Movita told her. 'You lucky with your sons but you stupid with your cookin'. I would have rather just sucked that orange instead of eatin' this chicken.'

Maggie smiled. 'Believe me, Miss Watson, I had already sucked several of them.'

'You bad,' Movita said. 'And smart. Tell your boys to bring me a few dozen oranges next time.'

Maggie laughed. Jen smiled as everyone else at the table began clambering for the liquor-laced fruit. 'Bryce is coming up on visiting day,' she admitted. 'But it's to talk business with Jennifer.' She looked across the makeshift table at Jen. 'Apparently, our little JRU is doing very well,' she said. 'It looks as if my ship has come in.'

'What does that mean?' Suki asked, holding little Christina to her breast.

'It means we all made money,' Theresa explained.

Jen smiled at her naïveté. 'No, it means that JRU made money for its stockholders. You only make money if you own stock and get a dividend or if you own stock, its value rises, and you sell it.'

Theresa smiled a big smile and said, 'I do own stock and the value has increased and I may sell it.'

'You own stock in JRU?' Jennifer asked.

But before Theresa could answer Movita began bobbing her head. 'I own stock,' she said. 'You think I'm gonna let the two smartest financial women I ever met get into a new venture without me takin' some of the ride?'

'Are you serious?' Jen asked.

'Um-hum,' Movita told her.

'Where did you get the money?' Jennifer asked. 'You've been in here for quite a while. How did you . . .'

'I've got some money on the Outside. I got my ways,' Movita said. 'There are quite a few of us that got on board.'

'But you weren't supposed to say or do anything with this, Mo, it was too much of a risk. You could have lost everything.'

'Yeah, well, considerin' we're in here it doesn't really much matter if we win or lose, now, does it? Besides, we didn't lose – we came out rich as we ever been.'

Jennifer sat herself down on the bunk in total shock.

43

Movita Watson

A deer with a chain of gold, if she escape, will run to the forest to eat grass.

Malay proverb

A couple of weeks before my kids were gonna be comin' to see me, I sent off to a toy store catalogue and got 'em all presents. I got a dall for Kiama, a chapstick for Talitha, and an art set for Jamorah.

Of all the things that Jennifer Spencer has done since she got started improvin' conditions at Jennings, helpin' kids come to see their mothers on visitin' day is the best of all. By far, I think, and I'm not alone in this. I hadn't seen my kids in four years and you can bet I could hardly stand the wait once I knew I was gonna see them. We had been writin' to each other all the time and I talked with 'em on the phone but of course none of that's the same as bein' actually with them. I couldn't sleep for the excitement and got myself so worn down that I was cryin' about the slightest thing.

'Can you please stop?' the candy who had been assigned

as my new cellmate said to me, puttin' her face over the side of the bunk. 'I can't sleep.'

'I would if I could,' I answered her. 'I just can't.'

She put her pillow over her head and I buried my face in mine. I don't know why I was cryin' so much, but I guess it was just because it was such a terrible thing, me bein' separated from them for so long.

The day finally came. I got dressed in a pair of denim pants and a white shirt and a jacket. I had stopped cryin' and now I couldn't stop smilin'. The presents were wrapped up and sittin' on my bunk.

I went to the cafeteria but I couldn't eat lunch. I was so nervous. Then, finally, it was almost one o'clock. I took the toys and the wrappin' and went to the visitor's room. People were already comin' in, but I had time to quickly put the paper back on, lookin' up at the door constantly. Then I saw 'em.

I don't suppose there's any better sight than your kids after you haven't seen 'em in a long time. I was so amazed at the looks of 'em that I couldn't even speak. I just stared, smilin' and even laughin'. They were smilin' too, except for Kiama who's six and hardly knows me. She came walkin' over, real serious.

'My babies,' I cried, holdin' my arms open big enough for all three.

'Mama!' Jamorah said, and then Talitha after her. 'Mama! Mama!'

I scooped 'em all together in my arms and we was kissin' and huggin' and cryin' and laughin'. I couldn't get over how beautiful they were. It made me sad that they weren't dressed nice enough, but they were so beautiful! They were pictures of health to me.

'I got somethin' for each a you,' I said, after we'd calmed down.

'What, Mama?' the two older girls asked together. Kiama looked at me, still wonderin' who the heck I was.

'First Kiama's,' I said, ' 'cause she's the youngest.' I handed her the dall and helped her open the package. Her fingers were still so small and soft! When she saw the dall she took it and hugged it and finally smiled at me. I was gonna cry again if I didn't turn my attention to the others.

They opened their gifts then and were so pleased with 'em. I never felt better in my life, havin' 'em there with me and happy. I took Kiama up on my lap and put my arm around Jamorah.

'How are you all, my sweet little girls? Tell Mama all about everything.'

Well things just started spoutin' outta them, things about school and their friends and their rooms at home.

Kiama sat pattin' her lil' dally and then she started to talk, too. 'Will you come home with us, Mama?' she asked.

Jamorah got a sad look on her face and Talitha started appylin' the chapstick to her lips.

'Mama can't go with you now,' I said to her. 'Mama's got to stay here for a while more.'

'But you know somethin'?' I continued. 'There's cookies and juice over there that we ain't even had. Let's go and get some.'

So we walked over to the refreshment table where Jen was pourin' juice for everybody. 'What beautiful children you have, Movita,' she said, smilin' at them.

'Thank you,' I said, and introduced them. I was so immensely proud of them at that moment. They were fine, well-behaved children. I could see Jen was impressed and I felt like I had done at least somethin' good in my life.

The end of our visit came way too soon. When the ten minute warning came, I felt so bad all of a sudden I didn't think I'd be able to stand it when they left. I was afraid I'd scream and sob and had to think of some way not to. Maybe Jen would help me, I thought, and took my kids back that way to say good-bye – under the pretext of gettin' some more cookies.

Then I told 'em all that I loved 'em and that I had each one's picture up in my room and that I prayed for 'em every day. I said they could come again to see me soon. When I actually had to watch their little backs walkin' out, leavin' me, I took hold of Jennifer's hand. She seemed to understand and put her arm around my back. I started cryin' the minute I couldn't see 'em no more, and I cried nearly the whole rest of the day, except for when I was feelin' good, thinkin' of 'em playin' with their presents.

44

Maggie Rafferty

> *'Association' is one of the most noxious of restrictions placed on people released on parole. 'Association' means that the parolee is not allowed to communicate with any person who also has a prison record . . . [T]hey are not able to associate with any of their old friends and buddies.*
>
> Kathryn Watterson, *Women in Prison*

Working with Jennifer Spencer was a great pleasure. And she brought other pleasures into my life. I must admit that I had cut myself off from people and my feelings, and that for me it was a more comfortable way to live. But Jennifer, with her intelligence, her enthusiasm, her optimism, and her can-do attitude, revitalized me. Perhaps she reminded me, just a little bit, of myself at her age. As problems were hurled at her daily she responded with solutions. Once she had a mission she was busy, optimistic, and good company.

And Jennifer Spencer did a lot more than improve my quality of life. She improved the quality of life for everybody at Jennings and she brought people together. After years of keeping to myself, she forced me to deal with Warden Harding and I found that I had been a snob and that I had not given her enough credit for her intelligence and imagination. She had been hog-tied by the system but she had never lost her compassion. Jennifer also forced me to interact with her crew. Movita Watson, Theresa LaBianco, Suki Conrad and her adorable baby. We had so many meetings that it was easiest to meet over dinner. I found myself enjoying their company, even that of the platitude-spouting Miss LaBianco. And the baby! Neither one of my boys has made me a grandmother but little Christina brought out all my grandmotherly feelings. Despite my arthritis I even began crocheting again.

As I sat in the library crocheting, I would sometimes be overwhelmed with sadness. The problem of feeling pleasure again is the fact that it also brings pain along with it. It is impossible to catalogue the myriad soul-numbing cruelties that are visited upon us as we serve our time in prison. It is impossible, and it is of no value to try. We need not be reminded of these degradations, for we submit to them daily.

There is, however, a particularly cruel regulation that tears at our hearts only on occasion. And even under new management this rule couldn't be changed. That is when a beloved friend – or as they say 'crewmate' – is released from incarceration. From the moment she passes beyond these bars, the law prohibits any further communication between that woman and the friends that she leaves behind. After five, ten, or perhaps twenty years of friendship – of living together, laughing and crying together, comforting and nursing one another, and growing together as sisters and friends – it is all brought to an abrupt end. No letters, no phone calls, no visits – nothing. We dare not even mourn, for we know our friend has not passed away. As I say, it is a particular cruelty that can still tear at hearts that have long been hardened to such sorrow.

I am speaking, of course, of Miss McInnery's – Cher's – absence. It was keenly felt by all of the women in her crew, but most painfully, I believe, by Miss Movita Watson. I myself never permitted my heart the luxury of an intense friendship such as the one these two women shared. What one does not have, one cannot lose. And yet, given the new circumstances of life at Jennings, I found my resolve to protect my heart was weakening, and quite before I knew what was happening, it seemed as if I was now a member of Miss Watson's crew. I shared meals with these women, shared dreams with these women, and after many years of willful solitary exile, I felt at home with these women. It was so very good – and so very hard to witness their loss of their dear Cher. They did not speak of her – as many primitive cultures refuse to speak of the dead – but the sorrow of her absence was keenly felt by all.

Imagine then, the delight, when the cagey Miss Cher somehow managed to slip a communication past the prison postal officials and into the hands of a nearly ecstatic Movita Watson. It came as a simple tourist postcard from New York City – fittingly with a picture of the Statue of Liberty – and bearing this message:

Girls –

Having a wonderful time – wish you were here! I'm looking good, feeling good, and taking my own personal bite out of the Big Apple and enjoying every minute of it.

Love from Lady Liberty

Miss Watson put on a brave and defensive show of snorting disregard and ridicule of the message, and yet I could not help but note that she held tight to that postcard throughout the dinner we shared that evening. Everyone was talking about Cher – speculating about Cher – and in doing so, bringing Cher back into their presence, if only for that moment.

It was Miss LaBianço who first suggested that we collectively return correspondence to Cher. She strongly opined that given the new leadership and conditions at Jennings, we, too, were looking good, feeling good, and – while not taking a bite out of the *Big* Apple – enjoying more fresh fruit in our diet than ever before. All agreed that we should share with Cher just how nice it had become to be imprisoned. I'll admit that I was intrigued. However, as no one knew of Cher's whereabouts, it was impossible to send our greetings (and, may I say, our gloatings?) to her.

It was Miss Watson who then informed us that she, having access to the Warden's files, could easily find a mailing address for her friend. I recognized the address at once as being that of an infamous mailing service that enables the pretentious to lay claim to an Upper East Side address. So exactly where Miss Cher was actually residing could not be determined, but I can assure you that it was not on East Seventy-third. However, that was the address we had, and so it was decided that we should – in flagrant violation of the regulations – post a letter to Cher.

It fell to me to pen this epistle, as I was the only resident at Jennings to possess both personally engraved stationery and (if I may be so immodest) a most beautiful calligraphic mastery of penmanship. Although my Mont Blanc had long ago run dry, I managed with an inexpensive disposable ballpoint to compose a lengthy letter to Miss McInnery in which I shared each of the 'crew's' personal taste of this heretofore rotten – but now considerably rosier – apple we know of as Jennings. I share it with you now.

My Dearest Lady Liberty,

Greetings from 'The Crew'. We were so delighted to receive your most welcome communication. We too, wish we were there. However, as you are no doubt aware, the privatization of Jennings has led to numerous improvements in our living conditions, and so while we cannot be there, being here is not nearly so bleak an experience as it once was. Each of the crew has asked that I share some specifics with you.

I shall begin with Miss LaBianco, as it was at her suggestion that this letter was written. Theresa has brought her considerable business acumen to bear in the development of an entire curriculum of instructional courses covering all aspects of occupational training. From composing curriculum vitae and practicing employment interview techniques, then on to instruction in modern business practices and telecommunications skills and computer use, the course of study fully prepares each participant to reenter the competitive employment market. It is a pity that you could not have availed yourself of this fine program prior to your release. I am certain it would have been of great value in your efforts to find gainful employment in New York City. Be that as it may, Miss LaBianco is both a brilliant teacher and an inspiring motivational speaker. Whenever a student voices a doubt as to the efficacy of the class work – often citing the problems inherent in applying for employment as an 'ex-con', Miss L. launches into one of her familiar lectures. 'Problems?' she'll ask. 'You know what they say about problems, don't you? Problems are just opportunities to find solutions! That's what they say about problems.' She is absolutely right, you know. It is much better to believe that we have opportunities for solutions than to wallow in our problems.

Which brings me to Miss Conrad. She is the proud mother of a healthy baby girl she named Christina. Suki, too, is benefiting from the changes wrought here at Jennings. In addition to the aforementioned classes in professional training, there are numerous instructional opportunities for expectant mothers, both in pre- and post-natal care. These courses are part and parcel of an entire program of improved medical services. Full-time medical personnel are readily available twenty-four-seven, as they say, and, in addition to improved health care, we have instituted a fine program in preventative medicine as well: nutritional classes, exercise regimens, and effective treatments for substance abuse are available to all.

You do know, of course, that Miss Spencer is largely responsible for the improvements here at Jennings. While I recall that you and she did not always see eye to eye, I trust that you will agree that she has been a tireless champion of the women here. She continues to conceive, develop, and implement innovative programs and services that seek to rehabilitate rather than to punish. Her legacy is worthy of any philanthropist. She is quite a remarkable young woman.

As is, as you know, your dear friend Miss Watson. Now while I would not choose to write such sentiments myself, Movita has insisted that I quote her exactly: 'You tell that honky bitch that she'd better keep her snotty nose clean or else she'll be draggin' her sorry white ass right back in here!' I trust you can read beyond the harsh bravado of those words and see the underlying truth of her love and devotion for you. In addition to her continued service to the Warden, Movita has been instrumental in the development of improved visitation services, and, with the overnight facilities for families nearing completion, it won't be long before she will enjoy lengthy visits with her daughters. Miss Watson misses you dearly, and while I'm sure she does not wish it for you, be assured that should you ever drag your 'sorry white ass' back to Jennings, she would welcome you and it most warmly.

Which brings me at last to my own distinctive – if somewhat diminutive – contribution to the betterment of Jennings. I have drafted and introduced to both the staff and the residents a most thorough and rigid 'Code of Courtesy'. It is my hope that I shall live to see the day when we no longer refer to one another as B——s, c——s, and w——s. Instead, I have insisted that we treat one another with the respect that we deserve. The code calls for everyone – residents and staff alike – to use 'Miss' or 'Mrs' while addressing residents, and to use 'Officer' or whatever title is appropriate while speaking to staff members. While many have mocked and ridiculed this code, others have grown to appreciate the new civility and can now see the benefits of good manners and proper decorum. Miss LaBianco has suggested that I teach courses in deportment, and I believe I shall agree to do so.

And so, Miss Liberty, we remain your less-tired, less-poor, and not-so-huddled masses yearning to be free.

Sincerely,

Margaret Rafferty

I was especially satisfied with the closing. However, upon sharing the letter with Miss Watson, prior to its posting via my son's hand, she opined that Miss McInnery would well require the use of a dictionary to assist in her reading of the missive. In fact, what she said exactly was, 'We asked you to write to the bitch in English. She can't read no foreign language.' I thanked her for that pithy observation. But as a woman involved in education most of my life, I always champion any effort to broaden one's vocabulary. As one can probably infer, it is, in fact, difficult for me to articulate the renewed vigor that the changes at Jennings have brought to my life. I wake up without lethargy or depression. It is of no mean import to know that a life's sentence need not terminate one's life's work.

As for Miss Watson, I doubt I shall ever be as great a friend to her as Miss McInnery was. However, despite the difference in our skin color, our backgrounds, our vocabulary, *et al.*, given the shared nature of our incarceration, we shall never have to say good-bye to one another. In total fairness, I should say that I – being many years her senior – will likely never have to say good-bye to her. I trust when the day comes that she bids me farewell, she will understand and forgive my selfish devotion to her. She is my new friend.

45

Jennifer Spencer

Making it out there ain't no easy thing, honey. We're as good as lepers out there.

An older woman parolee. Kathryn Watterson, *Women in Prison*

'You know what they say about advice, don't you?' Theresa asked Jennifer. 'They say, if you can tell the difference between good advice and bad advice, then you probably don't need any advice. That's what they say about advice.' Theresa leaned back and let her words of wisdom sink in.

'What kind of advice is that?' Jennifer wanted to know. 'If I didn't need any advice, I wouldn't have asked for any advice.'

'That's what I'm trying to tell you,' Theresa explained. 'You've been asking for advice about this parole hearing from every woman in the joint, and has everyone advised you to do the same thing?'

'No,' Jennifer answered. 'In fact, it seems like everyone that I talk to has a different idea of how to act at a parole hearing. Some say I should be all passive and regretful, and others say I should be confident and strong and really show them that I'm rehabilitated. And Flora said I should just stay quiet and only answer the questions.' Jennifer paused. She really was nervous about this. She could be out in weeks if the board passed her. But lots of inmates had told her that the board was reluctant to parole anyone on their first request. Jennifer was confused. 'I keep thinking, if they all know so damn much about it, why aren't *they* out on parole? So the point is, I don't know what to think. That's why I'm asking *you*. What's *your* advice?' She looked at Theresa, who wasn't an idiot, though she sounded like one sometimes.

'I just gave it to you.' Theresa smiled. 'You have to figure out whose advice is good advice and whose advice is bad advice, and then you won't need any advice at all.'

'I can't believe you actually made millions talking like this,' Jennifer said in exasperation. 'You just talk in circles.'

'Okay, fine,' sniffed Theresa. 'Let *that* be my advice. My advice is "What goes round, comes round." It all goes in circles.'

'That doesn't tell me a thing either,' Jennifer sighed.

'Then try this,' Theresa continued as she fit another damn piece in the puzzle. '"It is in pardoning that we are pardoned." That's right from the mouth of St Francis, and you don't get much better advice than his.'

Jennifer didn't say anything in response – not right away. She was giving serious thought to what Theresa had just said. 'That's great advice, Theresa,' she finally said, 'but who is it that I'm supposed to pardon?'

'Who are you pissed at?'

Jennifer's brow furrowed as she considered Theresa's question. Who was she pissed at? Tom? Not anymore – not really. She hated his guts, she despised everything he stood for, and she was sorry as hell that she had ever met the guy. But she wasn't really pissed at him anymore. She didn't have the time to be pissed at Tom. Donald? Same story. That sorry son-of-a-bitch would get his eventually. She just hoped that she would be there to watch it happen. Donald Michaels had played her for the fool that she was, and if she was pissed at anyone, it was herself. She was pissed at herself for idolizing a monster, loving a weakling, and letting them both bring out the absolute worst in her. And she was pissed for being stupid, greedy, and gullible. 'Me,' she finally said in answer to Theresa's question. 'I'm pissed at me.'

Theresa just smiled. 'Well, my advice still applies. It is in pardoning that we are pardoned. Go in there and tell that parole board everything that you're sorry about, and then tell them that you've worked damned hard to forgive yourself, and then tell them you would appreciate it if they would forgive you, too.' Theresa paused for a moment, then asked, '*Are* you ready to pardon yourself, honey?'

'Yeah,' Jennifer answered. 'Yeah,' she said again, 'I think I am.'

'Then you shall be pardoned,' Theresa concluded – and then, like the Pope, she actually blessed Jennifer with the sign of the cross. 'Now go, my child, and sin no more.'

'*That's* why you got paid the big bucks,' Jennifer laughed. 'You really are good at this shit. You know that, don't you?'

'Well,' Theresa demurred, 'you know what they say about modesty, don't you? They say modesty is the art of letting other people find out for themselves just how wonderful you are. That's what they say about modesty.'

'I'll remember that, Theresa,' Jennifer said. 'You are pretty wonderful.'

'You are, too, honey,' Theresa replied. 'You are, too.'

That afternoon, when the time finally came for Jennifer's parole hearing to begin, she was not surprised to discover that everything that Theresa had told her was absolutely true. It all had to start with Jennifer forgiving herself.

As she walked down the hall, she smiled. She couldn't believe that she was about to go to a major meeting without first spending several hours deciding what to wear. Never in her life had she ever gone before any kind of board meeting without her hair styled and her makeup done. But she couldn't do any 'homework' for this meeting, and she hadn't prepared one single thing to say. Two years ago she would've never forgiven herself for being so badly prepared, but today she knew that she had to forgive herself for having been so *mistakenly* prepared in the past. The Jennifer Spencer that stepped into that parole board hearing had forgiven herself for being herself. She could only hope that Theresa was right, and that others would be willing to forgive her, too.

'I've never given a more heartfelt and forceful recommendation for parole in my life,' Gwen Harding said. She was waiting outside the meeting room to take Jennifer in. 'And it wasn't easy for me, Jennifer,' she said, wiping away a tear. 'If I could have my way, you'd never leave here. I don't know how I'll do it all without you.'

There wasn't time for Jennifer to reply to Gwen's words. The bailiff opened the door and instructed her to 'appear before the Westchester County Board of Parole'. Gwen reached out and took Jennifer's hand between hers and gave it a squeeze. 'Good luck, Jenny,' she sniffed. 'Good luck.'

There were five of them. Three men and two women. They all looked so severe as they sat perched behind the long wooden table. They were all dressed in various pastels and plaids, and before each of them was a high stack of papers. The older of the two women gave Jennifer an encouraging smile, but the other remained quite grim and said, 'Have a seat, Ms Spencer.' The three men all cleared their throats in unison, then one of them asked, 'Are you ready to begin?'

'I am,' Jennifer said quietly as she sat in the chair in the middle of the room.

The proceeding began just as everyone said that it would. There was a painful retelling of her crime, her arrest, her trial, and her conviction, and when it was over Jennifer was asked if what she had just heard was complete and accurate. She nodded and said that it was. Her record of incarceration came next: her work record, her time in the SHU, the various reports that Byrd had written up – it was all there. And again, she was asked if the record was complete and accurate, and again Jennifer nodded and said that it was. Jennifer's mouth was so dry that her tongue was sticking to the roof of her mouth and all she could think about were the five pitchers of ice water that were on the table where the board members sat. 'May I have something to drink?' she asked them.

The youngest of the men stood and brought her a glass. Jennifer thanked him for it, drank deeply, and then held the glass in her lap, waiting for the hearing to continue.

'Warden Harding just presented a glowing review of you, Ms Spencer,' the older woman said. 'She assures us that you have been a most cooperative visitor here, and that in her mind, you are both remorseful for your crimes and fully rehabilitated. Would you agree with that assessment?'

'Yes, ma'am,' Jennifer replied. 'I would agree.'

'Do you have anything to add to that?' the other woman asked.

Jennifer was unsure as to what she should say. She hadn't heard Gwen's review, so she didn't know whether something had to be added or not. 'I – uh,' she hesitated. 'I'm not sure what Gwen – I mean, I'm not sure what Warden Harding told you,' Jennifer said, 'so I'm not sure what to say.'

'What would you like to say?' the older woman asked.

Jennifer thought for a moment. What would she like to say? She didn't really know. All she knew was that she just wanted to be released on parole. So that is what she said. 'I'd like to be granted parole, ma'am,' was her answer. 'That's all I really have to say.'

The older woman and the handsome young water-bearer chuckled softly. He was the next one to ask her a question. 'And why do you believe you should be granted that parole?' he asked with a smile.

'Because there's nothing left for me to do here,' Jennifer answered without thinking.

The members of the board seemed to be dumbstruck with her answer. The older man poured himself a glass of water, while the other one shuffled his papers. The kind old woman smiled and leaned back in her chair, but the younger one leaned forward in hers and studied Jennifer's face. This time, it was the very severe middle-aged man who spoke up.

'Do you believe that you were sent to this facility to do mission work, Ms Spencer?' he snapped at her.

'Excuse me?' Jennifer asked, looking at him. He might've

been Donald Michaels's brother. There was that same smug, self-satisfied and all-knowing smirk on his face.

'Do you *know* why you were sent here?' he wanted to know.

'Yes sir, I do know,' Jennifer answered. 'You have read my records, we have agreed that they are accurate. There is no question of why I was sent here. It was my understanding that today was going to be about why it was time for me to leave.'

'Please, Ms Spencer,' the older woman counseled. 'Do not jeopardize your freedom by responding so harshly.'

'That's right, young lady,' the older man echoed. 'It is our responsibility to determine whether or not your behavior warrants parole. It is not in your best interest to behave badly, don't you agree?'

'Yes,' Jennifer replied, 'I do agree.'

'Then would you like to reconsider your answer to my question?' the young man asked her.

Jennifer blushed. 'I'm sorry. I can't remember what your question was.'

The Donald Michaels clone and the snippy younger woman both let a snort of disgust, while the older woman just shook her head in despair. But now the old guy was almost chuckling, and the young man smiled broadly as he repeated his question. 'Why do you believe you should be granted parole, Ms Spencer?' he asked. 'Why do you think you should be released from this prison?'

'It's not a prison,' the young woman snapped. 'It's a correctional facility.'

Jennifer let out an involuntary chuckle.

'Did you find something amusing, Ms Spencer?' the woman asked.

'I'm sorry,' Jennifer answered. 'But you see, it doesn't matter what you call this place. We used to call it a prison, or the pen, or the clink. Now we call it a correctional facility. I guess it's the difference between believing in punishment and believing in rehabilitation. I don't know.' Jennifer stopped. She fully expected to be silenced at any moment, but it appeared as if she had their undivided attention. She continued. 'I do know that when you're on the Inside, the difference is between feeling like you've been *thrown away* like a useless piece of trash, or feeling like you're being *recycled* into something that resembles a "law abiding and productive member of society". But whatever you on the Outside call it, when you're locked up on the Inside, it all feels pretty hopeless – and not just for us inmates, but for the warden and the staff as well.'

'Why hopeless, Ms Spencer?' the old gent asked.

'Because rehabilitation is damned hard work when you don't have the tools you need to do it. You can't rehabilitate in a place that's set up to punish. You're going to have to decide if you want to punish us or rehabilitate us – or even both. But just be honest about it.'

The snorting man snorted again. 'Thank you for that advice, Ms Spencer.' He smirked. 'I'm sure everyone here will value your wise words on honesty.' The bastard was almost dripping with irony.

'Well, you know what they say about honesty, don't you?' Jennifer asked. 'They say that honesty is the best policy. That's what they say about honesty. And honesty is the new policy here at Jennings. I can tell you quite honestly that I was guilty as charged. And I can tell you quite honestly that I have been severely punished. And I can also tell you that I am quite honestly rehabilitated. This "pinstripe mama" will never wear Armani again.' Jennifer was standing by now.

'Did you know that we can pay a nurse a full month's salary with what it cost to buy just one Armani suit?' she continued. The man only glared in response.

'That's why I think I should be granted parole,' Jennifer said. 'Because I came in here wearing Armani and I thought that made me invincible. I was wrong. I'd trade all the Armanis in the world for a full-time medical staff. I'd sell every silk Kirman I could find if I could have the money for educational programs. My shoe budget alone could keep all of Unit C well fed and healthy. That's why I think I should be granted parole. Because now I know the difference between right and wrong – and between Armani mamas who can read a balance sheet and the real mamas who just want to be able to read to their children. No, sir, I wasn't sent here on a mission. I was sent here to be punished. But I lucked out. The missionaries were waiting for me when I got here.'

Jennifer collapsed into her chair. She couldn't believe that she had lost control. She'd never get out of Jennings now. Never. She lifted her hands to her face and began to sob uncontrollably. Theresa would be so disappointed in her.

And then – she heard clapping. Just the slow, rhythmic sound of one hand slapping against another. And then she heard some more. And soon it became applause. She braved a look between her fingers. Her handsome young water-bearer was on his feet applauding! The old woman rose to her feet as well – and then, so did the old gent. They were applauding her and smiling. And even the snippy one was smiling, too. But Donald's look-alike wasn't pleased. No, not at all. As the others stood and smiled, he angrily swept up the pile of papers before him, threw them into his briefcase and slammed it shut in disgust. Grim-faced, he glared at Jennifer. But she didn't mind. She couldn't please them all – and you know what they say about pleasing all of the people all of the time?

Theresa was going to be so proud.

46

Gwen Harding

Times change, and we change with them too.

Anonymous Latin translated by John Owen in *Epigram*

Gwendolyn Harding sat in her office, looking out the window at the blue sky and smiling at her own thoughts. She'd just heard that Officer Roger Camry had given Suki Conrad an engagement ring.

It was crazy, she knew, but she felt maternal pride. She had no children of her own and, as prison warden, she had always felt that she was running a home. Suki was as close to a daughter as she'd ever have. This was a good thing. She had no regrets.

The fact that Suki had been incarcerated because she'd let some man get her into trouble made the situation even more poignant. The girl deserved a break and hopefully she was getting one.

'I think Camry's okay,' Gwen said to Movita, who sat at a desk working a little distance from her.

'Unfortunate that the baby is that bastard Byrd's,' Movita replied.

'Look, Movita, I know how difficult the whole situation was, but Byrd's gone and Suki really loves this baby!'

'I know, but it still doesn't make the whole thing right.'

The Warden looked at Movita with concern. 'I'm hoping he loves her. I don't want her to marry him if he doesn't!'

Movita grinned. 'I'm sure you don't have to worry about that, Warden. He's a good man.'

Warden Harding reached for Suki's file and began to browse through it. The girl was actually twenty-four. And of course she was a mother twice over. Camry seemed caring – no – besotted with her. The warden had done little about their 'misdemeanor'. If she'd been so blind as to not know about Conrad's rape or pregnancy, she could close her eyes to their innocent love. Let there be one happy story to come out of Jennings. Love is such a powerful force that even the head of a prison can't control it.

What the Warden was interested in now was the wedding and the happily ever after. Deep down, she knew that Movita was of the same mind as she was. Between the two of them and with the help of the 'crew', they could give Suki a nice wedding, even if it had to take place within prison walls, and keep it low-key. But the Warden thought she'd first have another talk with Roger Camry. Gwen had him come to see her in the office. The young man looked a little shamefaced when he arrived. 'I think it's time to stop looking guilty, Roger,' Gwen said to him. 'You're soon going to be a married man with a daughter.'

He turned a shade pinker and Warden Harding decided he would probably make Suki a decent husband. He was no cavalier but he was no rogue either.

'So let's get down to business,' she continued. For a moment she wondered if he was as clueless as Suki. 'You're going to need a best man.'

Roger beamed. 'My best friend, Barry White.'

'Good,' she said.

Then Suki came in to talk about what she would like, which gave Gwen a chance to hold little Christina. 'We want to give your mommy a nice wedding,' she said to the infant, who stared at her, puzzled, and then started to cry.

'I'd like to invite my family,' Suki said, taking back the infant. 'Would that be possible? How many can come?'

'Make a list of them and bring it to me. We'll invite as many as we can. Of course your mother will come.' Suki nodded.

'Sure my mom'll come. She wants to come the night before.'

'I was wondering what you're going to do about a dress.'

Christina began to cry again and Suki opened her shirt to feed the little girl. 'I have two cousins who got married this year and both of 'em have dresses. They're gonna send me pictures so I can decide.'

'Real wedding dresses?' the Warden asked.

Suki looked surprised. 'Of course,' she answered. 'You can't get married in no other kind of dress.'

'Of course,' the Warden answered, amazed for a moment at how the world outside functioned.

'We'll get a justice of the peace to do the ceremony. Is that fine with you?'

'As long as he dresses proper and isn't fat.'

The Warden was puzzled. 'What do you mean "isn't fat"?'

'When my sister Doreen got married three years ago, the guy who did the wedding was so fat that everybody laughed. It practically spoiled the whole thing.' She looked up at Gwen as little Christina nursed on, her tiny mouth moving confidently. 'Doreen had a *gor*geous gown. It was satin. But it turned yellow in a year so nobody else could wear it.'

The Warden looked down at the file on her desk. She knew Suki's father was dead and that there was a brother a few years older than she was. But something told her not to mention him. He'd never visited her. 'Have you thought about who you would like to give you away?'

Suki looked unhappy for the first time. 'No,' she said. 'I don't know who should.' She paused. 'I'd ask Bobby but there's no way he'd ever do it.'

'Why not?'

'He doesn't like me.'

It was the first time the Warden had heard her say a negative thing about her family. Rather than probe, she lookcd down at Christina.

'Why don't you take her back to your room and sit on your rocker,' she said instead. 'You'll both be more comfortable.'

Suki smiled. 'Okay.' She took her breast out of the baby's mouth gently, but the little girl frowned and whimpered.

'Okay, quit fussin',' Suki said gently, kissing a chubby cheek. 'I love you.'

What a sweet girl, Gwen thought. At that moment Warden Harding decided that she wanted to give Suki away at the wedding. She wouldn't exactly offer, but she'd tell Movita the idea and maybe she could suggest it to Suki. Maybe Suki had someone else, maybe there was some uncle or other who she would want to walk her down the aisle, but she sincerely hoped it could be her to do it.

Once Warden Harding had granted permission for the wedding of Roger Camry and Suki Conrad, the crew decided to have a little 'springtime' party for Jennifer and have the ceremony at the same time. Low-key all the way. When the Warden gave her blessing to the affair, preparations began in earnest. Everyone who was going to attend had to have something to wear. And everyone wanted to give Suki something special. These are difficult tasks Outside, very difficult Inside a prison.

But the crew outdid themselves preparing for the event, and Movita and Jen came to the Warden with their plans.

'We want to have it in the visitor's room,' they said.

'Why not the cafeteria? Like the fashion show?' the Warden suggested.

'Since we can't have any visitors here we don't need that much space,' Jen said. 'I know how much Suki wanted her family here for this but maybe sometime later they can renew their vows.' But in the end, there really was no place else.

So with the help of Theresa, Flora, Springtime, Maggie, and Mo the cafeteria was decorated again. Gwen smiled when she walked in, remembering the fashion show and how much the inmates had enjoyed it. But this little soiree was going to be a very mixed bag of emotions. Gwen was going to play mother to Christina while the ceremony took place. She would be teacher when it came time to organize the inmates for the gathering and then nurse when it came time to comfort the women when they said their good-byes to Jennifer Spencer.

Springtime had taken some flowers from the new greenhouses and decorated the small altar they had made out of the stainless steel table at the far side of the wall. Movita had a few extra yards of fabric to lay out on the floor as a 'red carpet' for Suki to walk down.

As for the guests, Gwen thought it best to make the attendees only the immediate crew, and it was understood by Suki that it had to be done this way. But in her innocence and happiness she was pleased to be allowed even to have the marriage take place.

After the justice of the peace concluded the vows, Roger gave Suki a quick peck on the lips – most certainly he wanted to be more passionate, but due to the stipulations Gwen had put in place, he was more than understanding about it.

Everyone went around the cafeteria and hugged and kissed Suki, and Gwen handed little Christina off to Roger to hold. 'Here's your daddy, little girl.' The baby cooed at him as if she knew who he was.

Then it came time for everyone to approach Jennifer Spencer, the newly paroled inmate at Jennings. All the women had such great admiration for her, the work she had done to get Jennings to be a more humane place to have to stay in.

Movita, Maggie, Theresa, and Suki were sitting at the table waiting for Jennifer to finish talking with Roger and playing with Christina. As she came to join them, they greeted her with strangely subdued enthusiasm. They had mixed feelings about Jennifer leaving. They were jealous, they were envious, they would miss her terribly, and they were unselfishly happy for her. All of them had all the feelings.

'Oh God, girlfriend,' Movita said, giving her a hug. 'I'm gonna miss you!'

'Let's not say good-bye yet,' Suki cried, tears filling her eyes. 'Not until we have to.'

'Okay,' Movita said, 'let's eat. You won't believe what we made for the bride and groom and the parolee!'

'Come and sit down,' Maggie said. 'Theresa and I will bring it out.'

The table was set with paper place mats decorated with crayon drawings.

'Movita, these are adorable,' Jennifer said. 'I see another business here.'

'If you're not careful,' Warden Harding warned, 'Movita's going to buy this prison out from under you.'

Movita laughed. 'Then I'll throw myself out!'

They all laughed; Jen slapped the table in her hilarity. Gwen could see the happiness bubbling up inside her eyes like an eruption beginning deep in a volcano. The woman was intoxicated with the thought of freedom so close.

Maggie and Theresa came out of the kitchen carrying trays of covered dishes, which they set down with a flourish. 'Macaroni and gravy!' Maggie cried. 'What do you think of that!'

'It's our favorite,' Suki and Jennifer said simultaneously.

Their raptures were interrupted by the noise of the cafeteria door opening. For a second they all feared an unpleasant interruption. Then they saw that it was Warden Harding carrying out a tray full of flavored crushed-ice drinks. 'To help the cake go easier,' Frances said as she popped her head out from behind the Warden. 'I figured you'd want one last ice delivery.'

The small group laughed and Warden Harding set the

tray down in the middle of the table. 'Drink up!' she said.

Everyone grabbed at the drinks. There was no argument over who got what color, since they were all green. There was silence for a moment as they sporked up the ice pellets. 'It's really too bad you can't find Cher when you leave and let her know how we all are doing,' Movita said.

There wasn't a dry eye at the table after that, and Theresa was the only one who could speak. 'The food's getting cold,' she said softly.

'Wait, I have something else,' Movita said, and disappeared into the kitchen. She returned with a two-tiered cake. It was signed by the entire crew in colored frosting.

'It's got a bride and groom on it,' Suki said.

'And look at this, they put "Good Luck Jen" on the back side of it.'

Gwen cleared her throat and lifted up what was left of her ice drink. 'To the future!' she declared, and everyone raised their cups in unison.

47

Jennifer Spencer

> *He hath sent me to bind up the brokenhearted, to proclaim liberty to the captives, and the opening of the prison to them that are bound.*
>
> Isa. 61:1

After serving almost a year of a three-to-five-year sentence for investment fraud, Jennifer Spencer was finally leaving the Jennings Correctional Facility for Women. In many ways she was as terrified to leave the place as she had once been to come to it.

As she waited nervously for her release to be officially processed, she remembered so clearly the day of her incarceration. She was so sure of herself back then – so arrogant, so certain that she had everything under control. She knew – or thought that she knew – exactly who Jennifer Spencer was. But what she didn't know was what *prison* was, and she didn't know what prison could do to her. Now, ironically, she knew prison life all too well, but she wasn't so sure that she knew herself. Who was Jennifer Spencer now? And what would life outside prison hold for her? The only thing she knew for certain was that neither she nor Jennings was the same. Jennings was a far better place – and Jennifer wanted to believe that she was a far better woman. A better woman with the permanent record that the nuns always said she would have.

Jennifer smiled as she remembered how they had meted out detentions and demerits for each and every minor infraction of their Byzantine rules. Then, even after you served your time and suffered your punishment the nuns always threatened, *This is going on your permanent record!* Jennifer had never once believed that such a record actually existed – until now. Now, the complete account of her arrest, trial, conviction, and prison sentence – along with her fingerprints and mugshots – were part of a nationwide law enforcement database. Jennifer Spencer was an official ex-con. She left Jennings with a permanent record – but little else.

It came as no real surprise that the bag bearing Jennifer's name held no trace of the clothing or personal belongings that Cher had bagged and tagged on the infamous day of Jennifer's incarceration. Jennifer was neither surprised nor outraged; she didn't really want to leave Jennings in an Armani suit anyway. Probably whoever took over Cher's job in Intake managed to confiscate her clothing. What the hell, Jennifer thought, they wouldn't fit me right anyway – she'd lost weight during her stay in Jennings. Jennifer was going to be on the Outside – and she didn't have a damn thing to wear.

'Oh, Jennifer,' Gwen sighed when they discovered the thievery, 'there's nothing in your bag except someone's old torn blue jeans and a T-shirt.'

Jennifer just laughed. 'Give 'em to me,' she said. 'If they fit, I'll wear 'em. It doesn't matter.'

'But you can't wear these,' Gwen protested. 'Do we have time to call Lenny and ask him to bring you something from your apartment?'

'It's fine,' Jennifer said as she changed into the clothes. 'And besides, these match my record, don't you think?' The sneakers in the bag were far too large for Jennifer, and it was decided that she could wear the shoes issued from the prison. 'I'll return them,' Jennifer assured the Warden, 'I promise.'

Gwen just shook her head ruefully, then offered her hand for a handshake. The handshake turned into a clumsy embrace, but Gwen insisted that Jennifer should not get all maudlin and sentimental. 'I would like to believe that we both learned a great deal from each other,' she said warmly.

Jennifer nodded, wiped her eyes, and watched as Gwen Harding hit the final 'enter' button that sent Jennifer's record to every computer in every prison, police station, and precinct house in America. The theme song from *Cheers* popped into Jennifer's head, and even though she didn't have anything she'd come in with – or a purse to put it in – she walked out of Jennings with a smile. She hummed the theme song. Perhaps everyone would know her name, but she would be free, and that was all that mattered. She didn't want the things she had thought she wanted. Clothes and furniture and Sub-Zero refrigerators were not important. What was important was her freedom and though most people took it for granted, she would never forget that.

Roger Camry was there to unlock the gate for her, and Lenny was waiting next to his car. 'What are you singing?' he asked Jennifer as she approached him.

'It's too warped to explain,' Jennifer told him. 'C'mon, let's get out of here.'

'Are you wearing that?' Lenny asked in surprise.

'It's all I have,' Jennifer said with a shrug. 'Are you embarrassed to be seen with me?'

Lenny blushed. 'No,' he said softly. 'It's just that I brought you a gift.'

Jennifer shyly accepted the gift and eagerly opened it right on the spot. Inside was a beautiful silk scarf that she lovingly lifted out of the distinctive gift box from Gucci. 'Oh Lenny,' she cried, 'it's lovely.' And she brought the scarf to her face and caressed her cheek with the luxurious silk. 'It's lovely, Lenny,' she said again, 'really so lovely.' Then, with a flourish, she expertly tied the scarf about her neck and said very haughtily, 'Jennifer Spencer has always been a trendsetter. I predict that in less than a month every woman on Wall Street will be wearing silk with denim.'

'Every woman on Wall Street will probably be *here*,' Lenny joked.

'Oh,' Jennifer sighed sadly, 'haven't the people here suffered enough already?' As she opened the door to step into Lenny's car, she saw Springtime in her flower bed. 'It's looking real good, Springtime,' she shouted and waved. Springtime's smile was no different than it had been the day it first sent shivers down Jennifer's spine, but now Jennifer knew her; now the smile had a name, and that made all the difference in the world.

'What's a little old lady like that doing in prison?' Lenny asked.

'She had fields and fields of pot growing north of Albany,' Jennifer laughed. 'She sold it to her friends with glaucoma.' Jennifer took a final long look at Springtime, her flower bed, and the prison walls, then she turned to Lenny and said, 'Take me home now. I'm ready to go home.'

Jennifer and Lenny's eyes met for just a moment, and as always, Lenny nervously looked away. But he didn't move from where he stood next to her. 'It's going to be okay, Jennifer,' he said, looking at his feet. 'Everything will be back to normal before you know it.'

'I don't even remember what normal is,' Jennifer told him.

Lenny lifted his head and stared into her eyes. This time, neither of them looked away – nor did they say anything. Jennifer smiled at Lenny. 'Let's go,' she said, and she opened the door and sank into the front seat of his car. It was the softest thing that she had sat on in almost a year. She closed her eyes, heard Lenny start the engine, and never looked back as they turned out of the prison drive.

As they neared the city, Jennifer kept her nose almost pressed to the window to take in every sight along the way. It was almost too much. After a year of dusty rose, dirty green, and battleship gray, the rich and wonderful hues of New York were almost dizzying. It wasn't long before she felt right back at home. All the stores, all the people, all the traffic. It was all wonderful. 'Hey,' Jennifer shouted, craning her neck as they drove through the street, 'I think that woman back there used to be at Jennings.'

'Lock your doors,' Lenny said reflexively. 'This is a rather rough neighborhood.'

'Bigot,' Jennifer reprimanded him. 'I bet a person isn't any more likely to be robbed on this street than she is on Wall Street.'

'Touché!' Lenny conceded.

It wasn't long before Jennifer realized that they were headed for her loft in Tribeca. She felt her stomach knot in nervous anticipation of her return. How many times had she dreamed of being home? How many times had she returned to this place in her imagination? Now again, she closed her eyes and envisioned her loft. She could see the living room, the kitchen, the bedroom. Nothing was changed – everything was there. But now, in the living room she saw Movita, in the kitchen stood Theresa, and in the bedroom she saw another bed, and on it lay Suki. She opened her eyes and smiled sadly. She was going home – and yet, she feared that she was still going to be homesick.

'You're home,' Lenny said as they rounded a corner and pulled up in front of Jennifer's building. He cut the engine, jumped out of the car, and came around to open her door. 'What's wrong?' he asked when Jennifer made no move to get out.

'I'm afraid,' she replied with a whisper.

Lenny held out his hand. 'Come on,' he said softly, 'there's nothing to be afraid of.' Then he added shyly but with genuine valor, 'I'm right here with you.' He helped her from the car, then took her arm and walked her to the door. 'I don't have my keys,' Jennifer said suddenly as they neared the building. 'When they went looking for the clothes and things I checked in with, all of my stuff was gone,' she said.

'Don't worry,' Lenny assured her. 'I have keys and I made another pair, just in case.'

They let themselves into the building and rode the rather cumbersome, but atmospheric, freight elevator up to Jennifer's loft. Had she ever really lived in this place? Jennifer thought, as the ride brought back memories of a life she thought was gone forever. She tried to remember being here, living here. She tried to recall the nights of making love with Tom. Had he ever really loved her? Did she love him? She didn't know. She supposed the answer was no – and yet, she had enjoyed his company and she did care deeply for his well-being. She could've probably made a marriage to Tom Branston work. Their kids would've been terrific, she thought ruefully. The elevator clanged to a halt and Lenny lifted the wooden gate and escorted her to the familiar door.

Lenny took his key, and without hesitation opened the door and gestured for Jennifer to walk in. The sight of all her beautiful furniture before her caused her to want to cry out in happiness. She reached for Lenny's hand to help her calm herself and to keep from collapsing. She walked around the living room caressing the tabletops and the upholstery fabric. She picked up a throw pillow or two and hugged them to her chest. She walked into the kitchen and ran her fingers over the stove top. A real cooktop. No more hot plates. Then she went into the television room. When she opened the door she was taken aback. 'What are you doing here?' Jennifer asked more calmly than she expected. 'Why are you in my apartment?'

Lenny came over and stood behind Jennifer.

'A friend of yours said I could stay here until you got back,' Cher said, mustering her familiar bravado.

'You're lying,' Jennifer spat back at her.

'No, I'm not,' Cher answered calmly. 'And besides, this isn't what it looks like. I've been looking after your place for you until you got out.'

'And by the looks of you you're taking care of my clothes, too,' Jennifer snapped. 'You took my things from Intake didn't you?'

'Hey, you weren't going to need them anytime soon,' Cher said.

Then there was noise from the bedroom and a man's voice – a familiar one – called out. 'When are you coming back in here?'

'Oh, and you decided to have houseguests too? How convenient,' Jennifer said.

'Well, it's not like he's unfamiliar with the . . .'

Just then the bedroom door swung open and Tom walked into the room wearing nothing but his expensive blue silk boxers. 'Are you going to join me?' he asked and then looked up.

Jennifer stared at him in dumbstruck amazement. She was almost glad that he was giving her yet another reason to despise him. She just looked at him.

'Jennifer?' Tom said in horror, 'Jenny – is that you?'

'Yeah, Tom,' she said sadly, 'it's me.'

'I'm uh – I'm sorry, I uh – didn't think you'd –' he fumbled.

'What's the matter? Aren't you glad to see me?' she said angrily.

'You uh – you, well – you . . .'

Jennifer didn't speak. She felt herself slipping into a rage, and she didn't want to relinquish control of this moment just because she was angry. After taking a deep breath she said quietly, 'I cannot believe that you have done this, Tom. Haven't you hurt me enough already?' There was no more rage left in her, no more hurt – only a deep and powerful sense of indifference. It was, perhaps, the most terrifying emotion she had ever known. She felt Lenny take hold of her hand, and once again she was grateful for this man who had seen her through the darkest days of her life.

'This must be very uncomfortable for you, Jenny,' Tom finally said, breaking the silence.

'And are you comfortable, Tom?' she asked.

He sighed heavily and hung his head. 'No, Jenny, of course I'm not comfortable,' he answered her.

'Please don't call me Jenny,' she said coldly.

Tom only nodded in consent.

'I want to explain what's happening here,' Cher said calmly from where she sat. 'I know you ain't gonna believe this,' she continued, 'but I really am very sorry for what I've done.'

Jennifer snorted in disbelief. 'You've apparently stolen everything that I had,' she said angrily, 'and what you didn't steal you ruined. What gave you the right to do that?'

'What gave you the right to have it?' Cher shot back, standing up to face Jennifer.

'I earned it,' Jennifer snarled at her. 'I earned everything that I had and you took it.' She willed herself not to give in to the sobs that were threatening to erupt from her clenched and aching throat.

'I said I was sorry, Jennifer, and I meant it. I was just watching over everything for you. Trying to help you out.'

'Help me out?' Jennifer repeated, and in spite of her every effort, she burst into tears. 'You've taken over my home, you even took my old boyfriend.' She hated how ridiculous those words sounded. She felt as if she were back in junior high. Her old boyfriend!

'I did not take your boyfriend,' Cher said. 'You gotta let me explain.'

'Explain?' Jennifer snapped. 'There's nothing to explain. I'm not blind. I can see what the two of you have been doing.'

'It's not what it looks like,' Cher insisted.

Lenny had remained silent through this all, but now he

let go of Jennifer's hand and stepped between her and Cher. 'Stop it,' he said with uncharacteristic disgust. 'You two are spitting at each other like a couple of alley cats over a guy who isn't worth the time it would take to run over him with a car.'

Jennifer couldn't believe that Lenny had spoken the words that she heard.

Cher, on the other hand, was laughing. 'You're damned right about that,' she said, and she sat back down on the couch.

Jennifer stared at Cher and considered what she said. Cher had used Tom – just like Cher used everyone. But Jennifer wasn't worried about Tom. 'How have you been managing to live here, Cher? Did you rack up my credit cards? Did you take money from my bank accounts?'

'I did what I had to,' Cher answered.

Jennifer sighed and said nothing more.

'I'm sorry I did it,' Cher offered again.

Jennifer looked at her, then she looked at Tom, then she looked back to Cher. 'I'm sorry you did, too, Cher,' she finally said.

Jennifer looked around at the place she called home. Somehow it didn't seem to matter to her anymore. 'Let's go,' she said to Lenny, then grabbed his hand and led him to the door.

48

Jennifer Spencer

Few rich men own their own property. The property owns them.

Robert Green Ingersoll, address to the McKinley League, New York

Her fury, Jen decided, was actually a good thing. She left her apartment with Lenny and she was shaking with rage, but that gave her the motor she would use. In the meantime, Lenny took her shaking hand. 'I'm so sorry,' he said. 'It's my fault. I should have gotten into the apartment. I should have . . .'

She looked at him. He was a truly good man and his sense of responsibility was, unlike most men's – deeply overdeveloped. 'No permanent harm done,' Jennifer said. 'I'll take care of it tomorrow.'

'We'll take care of it,' he said. She looked at him and nodded. 'So what do you need right now?' he asked.

'Something clean to wear. Some new shoes. A bath in a big tub with good bath salts, a haircut and a room in a hotel.' She looked around Greenwich Avenue. 'Let's go to Soho,' she said. It was only a few blocks away, and though Lenny asked if she wanted a cab nothing felt better to Jennifer than walking outdoors in a straight line for as long as she wanted. She thought of poor Maggie making her endless spiraling from the outer corners of the yard to the center and then back again. 'You know what I'd like to do?' she said. 'Maybe the day after tomorrow?' He waited for her to go on. 'I'd like to walk from Broadway down here all the way up to the Cloisters!'

Lenny laughed. 'That's over two hundred blocks,' he said. 'You'd have to walk through Soho and the Village, the Flatiron District, Midtown, the Upper West Side, Morningside Heights, Harlem, Washington Heights –'

'Yeah,' she said. 'Wouldn't it be great? I'd end up at the Cloisters.'

'You'd end up a cripple,' Lenny said.

'Nah, I'm no softie. I'd grease my feet and I'd get a new pair of Nikes and I'd just go.' She looked around West Broadway. 'And there would be shops and cafés and restaurants and businesses and apartment buildings. There would be doormen and people at bus stops and window boxes and garbage and Korean fruit stands and shoe stores and probably nine Gaps and about fifty Starbuckses and I swear I'd have a good cup of coffee in every single one along the way. Boy,' she said, 'you really come to appreciate the little things.' Then a dress in the window of a shop caught her eye. It was a pinkish red, and out of a silk that seemed to shine with a subtle iridescence. 'Oh,' she said, 'that's what I want.' She'd never had a dress like that in her life. It was girly and sexy and absolutely inappropriate for business. But it wasn't cheap. It had a subtle fluid motion to it; the fabric had been cut so that, simple as the dress was, the slight iridescence of the material seemed to make the shadows on it move. 'I want that,' she said.

'Then you shall have it,' Lenny said, took her arm and led her into the shop.

They bought her shoes at Otto Tootsie Plohound, makeup at Sephora, silk underwear and a beautiful nightgown at Joovay and a bagful of fun jewelry at Girlprops. Then they sat down, both of them exhausted, at Penang, a restaurant where the shrimp was fabulous and the décor transported you to Southeast Asia. They had their own little booth, a sort of opium den made of bamboo, so small there was hardly room for the two of them and all their bags.

Lenny had insisted on paying for everything. And once she had realized that her credit cards were useless – since Cher had had access to everything – she allowed him to. 'I'm exhausted,' she said. 'But in a good way.' She looked down at their leftovers. 'I wish Movita and Theresa and Suki could taste this shrimp,' she said. 'They wouldn't believe it.' She closed her eyes for a moment and while they were closed Lenny must have reached out to her, because she felt his hands enclose hers. She opened her eyes, and he kept his hands wrapped around hers. It felt really good. 'I want to thank you,' she said. 'For being such a good friend. For really being there for me.'

'Oh,' he said, 'come on. You know what really happened.'

'Did I miss something?' she asked. 'I thought that was what really happened.'

He shook his head. 'I've wanted to be closer to you for years. Almost since you came to the firm. Your misfortune was just an opportunity for me to get to know you better. It seemed in a way like taking unfair advantage.'

She laughed. 'Oh, yeah. Those visits in that stinking room were really unfair to me.'

'You know what I mean,' he said.

'Let me tell you what I mean,' she said. 'You saved my life. I don't know how I would have gotten along without your help. I don't think I would have. Thank you, Lenny. Thank you for everything.'

He smiled. 'You're welcome. You know,' he said. 'I'm a little bit frightened that I won't get to see you much now that you're out and free. I'm ashamed to admit that, but it's true.'

'Oh, don't worry,' she said. 'You're going to get to see a lot of me. After all, we have a business to run.' She took a deep breath. 'God, I'm tired,' she said.

He shook his head. 'I'm so sorry about the apartment, I –'

'Don't be ridiculous. I don't think I'd want to go there right now anyway.'

'Well, you're welcome to come to my apartment.'

'Where is your apartment, Lenny?'

'On the Upper East Side,' he admitted. 'Kind of in a boring neighborhood.'

'Does it have a really big bathtub?' she asked.

'I don't think so,' he admitted. 'I shower.'

She nodded her head. 'Yeah, guys shower,' she agreed. 'But I have to have a really good long soak. You know, we only got showers once every three days. And we were watched the whole time.'

Lenny shook his head. 'I'm so sorry.'

'Don't be,' she told him. 'You know it was good for me. It's made me a different person.'

'Well, I like the person you were before,' he said. 'But I think I love the person you are now.'

She grinned at him. He was awfully shy. She figured he didn't have much experience with women, and if she slept with him and it was bad it would be so upsetting, so mortifying to both of them. She wondered for a few minutes about men and women and what was important, and then realized that a few lifetimes wouldn't be enough to figure that one out. It was probably safest for them to just go on with the friendship, working together and enjoying each other, because if she slept with him and then rejected him, it would be too hard for him to take. No man could put up with that. She thought back to her nights with Tom. He was so tall and his shoulders were so broad. She had felt like a little doll when he wrapped his arms around her. Lenny was perhaps five foot eight or nine. His shoulders and hips were narrow and she doubted that he weighed twenty pounds more than she did. But she liked his long, narrow nose and the compassion and feeling in his dark eyes. 'I think I'd like to check into a hotel,' she said. 'Maybe the Mercer has rooms.'

The Mercer Hotel in the very center of Soho has a kind of Zen elegance. The rooms are not large and the décor is a soothing one with dark woods and white walls and luxe but discreet upholstery that doesn't call attention to itself but makes you feel immediately relaxed. The attraction for Jennifer, however, was the bathroom: double doors swung open to reveal an enormous white ceramic tub in the very center of the room. The tiny white mosaic tiled floor seemed to go on for an acre around it and the white marble double sinks, the closets, the Egyptian terry cloth towels as large as bedsheets along with a whole range of FACE shampoos, conditioners, shower gels, bubble baths in big, simple containers instead of those tiny little annoying froufrou sample packs.

'Oh, yes!' she cried as she ran to the tap and started to fill the tub. My God, you could swim half a lap in it or, alternatively, have half the swim team bathe with you.

'My God,' Lenny said as he set the bags down on the bed. 'Is that a bathtub or a sarcophagus?'

'Either will do for me,' Jennifer told him. 'I want to soak for hours and if I die, well, it would make a great last resting place.' She poured all of the bath salts into the swirling water of the tub and looked over at him. He was shifting from one foot to the other. He looked suddenly very uncomfortable. Poor Lenny. He was a nice looking man, his face long, his jaw square and shadowed now with the beginning of the need for a second shave of the day. Maybe that's why his skin was so nice. She had read somewhere that men's skin benefited from being exfoliated by shaving. She walked toward him.

'I guess I'll have to go now,' he said, obviously regretful.

She made a serious face. 'But Lenny,' she said. 'You hate wasting money. I'm paying for a double room. There's a double bed.' She swung open the closet door. 'And there are two robes. I can't wear both of them.'

He looked at her for a moment, not comprehending. Then the implications of her words sank in.

'You can stay over,' she said. 'And you can make love to me. And we can sleep together all night and we can have a room-service breakfast together and read the paper together. But you have to make me two promises.' He nodded. 'The first one is, if we never do it again you'll still be my good friend.'

'Of course I will,' he said.

'Oh, don't speak so quick. Men's egos, you know.' Meanwhile she thought, what the hell? He might not be a very experienced or good lover but he was an experienced and good man. She could at least try it. After all, she'd been in prison for the last eleven months. It had to be better than that.

'What's the second promise?' he asked.

'That I get to take my bath for as long as I want all by myself.'

Lenny smiled. 'Can I at least watch?'

'You have to watch,' she said. 'And maybe you have to wash my back.' He was just her height and he took her face gently in both his hands and brought her mouth to his. His lips were soft, gentle. He tugged at her lower lip with his own, then bit lightly. They both smiled, looking at each other. From that close, he was blurry. She closed her eyes again, letting herself be pulled into those soft lips. She tasted his breath, fresh, like sweet corn. It was so long since she'd kissed a man! Now they kissed harder. The pressure against her lips felt so good. This *was* good, she thought as she reached up to touch his neck. She brushed his cheek, feeling the bristle, caressing it for a moment, scruffy, manly. Then she held on to the back of his neck, his head, caressing his hair. She found it was softer, finer, than she'd expected.

He was caressing her back now, massaging her, pulling her close to him. She felt as if she'd come alive all over. She could go on like this for a long time. This was *very* good.

What a surprise! The man really knew how to kiss. Maybe he knew more . . .

Then, as Lenny pulled away for a moment to touch her cheek, she opened her eyes and saw the tub behind him about to overflow. 'Oh, my God!' she said. 'Oh, my God!' The two of them got there in time to turn off the taps and to throw towels down to take up the water that had overflowed. They laughed hysterically, half from nerves and half from the fun of it.

The bath she took was warm, luxurious, exciting, and relaxing. And she liked having Lenny watch her and soap her back, prolonging the anticipation. Then, when she was fully dried off – the fluffy white towels of the Mercer Hotel were so luxurious after the skin-scraping rags she'd become accustomed to – she let herself be enfolded in Lenny's arms and pampered some more. At first, everything was soft and gentle and all about caressing her and soothing her aching body, but then things suddenly turned. He touched her nipples, gently, then harder and harder until she moaned. When she opened her eyes he smiled at her. It was a wicked, teasing smile. 'You like teasing?' she asked, and she moved her hand down to him, touching him until he was so hard she could feel his pulse. Then she withdrew. Her teasing made him vigorous and energetic, and she found herself tangling with him on the bed, almost sparring. He held her shoulders down, at last, and rolled on top of her. She was surprised and delighted to find such voraciousness beneath Lenny's calm exterior. And her own full-body participation, as well as his passion and teasing skill, brought her a welcome release after so many months of unfulfilled longings.

49

Jennifer Spencer

As long as possible live free and uncommitted. It makes but little difference whether you are committed to a farm or the county jail.

Henry David Thoreau

Jennifer woke up in the big bed of the Mercer Hotel, Lenny lying beside her, and for a moment – a long moment – she didn't know where she was. She wasn't home and she wasn't in prison. Had it all been a dream? Or was this a dream? Then she remembered not only their day together, but their night, and smiled. In that mysterious way that lovers have Lenny must have sensed she was awake because his eyes opened slowly. She'd never noticed before what long lashes he had. 'Hello, gorgeous,' he said.

'Hello, sexy,' she told him.

Before they had a chance to compliment one another any further the phone rang. She looked at him. He shrugged. 'Does anyone know you're here?' she asked.

He shook his head. 'Are you kidding? It must be the desk,' he said. 'They'll call to see if we're checking out.'

'At this time of morning?' she asked.

'What time is it?' he asked.

'I don't know,' she said.

They both laughed and he reached over for the phone. He listened for a moment and his eyes opened wider. 'Oh,' he said. 'Hello.' And looked over at her. 'It's Cher,' he mouthed.

Jennifer grabbed the phone. 'You have nerve,' she said. 'How did you know we were here?'

'Oh, please,' Cher said. 'You think I don't know Lenny's credit card numbers? You think I can't find out where anyone is if they've charged something?' Jennifer threw Lenny a look of disbelief and shook her head. 'What do you want?' she asked Cher.

Cher's voice was insistent. 'I'd like to meet with you and explain a few things . . .'

'You're a thief and a bitch. No explanation needed,' Jennifer cut her off. She heard Cher sigh on the other end of the line.

'Well,' Cher said. 'Both of those things are true, but it's my motivation that you have to examine.' She paused. 'I did it for you,' she said.

Jennifer laughed out loud. Lenny looked over at her as if he were ready to get on the line and end any problems she was having. Jennifer waved him away; she could handle this herself. 'Thanks, Cher. That might work on morons but not on me.'

'Listen, I've gotten into Tom's portfolio and files, as well as his pants and your apartment,' Cher insisted. 'I've bankrupted him. He doesn't know it yet, but he's penniless.'

Jennifer reconsidered. Still, it was probably just Cher's selfish motivations that made her steal the money. 'Well, thank you for that. It was very selfless of you,' Jennifer said sarcastically.

'Hey, don't go off on me,' Cher told her. 'Your boyfriend is a bad guy as well as a bad fuck. I think you ought to meet with me.'

Jennifer sighed. She wished this was all over with and she could just have her home back. But there was nothing she could do. 'Okay,' Jennifer agreed.

An hour later, Jennifer found herself sitting across from Cher at a stylish, minimalist table at the Mercer Kitchen, the restaurant in the hotel. She couldn't get over how different this was from camping out over a simple home-made dinner in Movita's cell. The silverware, the napkins, the service, and the delicacy of the Euro-Thai cuisine were a continual shock to Jennifer. Unfortunately, Cher was distracting her with a play-by-play of her bad love life with Tom.

'Didn't you ever take the time to teach him how to go down on you?' Cher asked in disbelief. 'Okay, at his age he should know how, but you were engaged to the dumb fuck. You were going to live with that boring tongue action for the rest of your life? Is he a man or a Labrador retriever?'

Cher looked great. All of Jennifer's clothes seemed to suit her, and Jennifer didn't know whether Cher had started going to Angelo or not but her hair looked fantastic as well. It had been cut two different lengths but was now straight and shiny. She had something that had seemed missing before. Not that Cher was ever stupid, but now she seemed, well, classy. Jennifer had never believed that clothes made the man but in this case they seemed to have made the woman into a lady. No wonder she could fool everyone, Jennifer thought. She was a chameleon. If I didn't know where she came from, if I didn't know for sure about prison, I would never believe it.

'Look,' Cher said. 'I know I haven't treated you well and I know you probably don't like me or trust me and I don't blame you. But you can't blame me for the way I used to treat you because you used to be a bitch.'

Jennifer stiffened. 'What's your point, Cher? Did you drag me out to insult me?'

'No, I mean you changed.' Cher calmed her down. 'When you first got to prison you walked in it like you were God's only child and we were dirt. And I'm willing to admit that I took attitude against you but I think you can understand why.'

Jennifer interrupted. 'Well, you were a real bitch to me when I first came in.'

Cher nodded. 'I know I was, and for that I'm sorry. Once I saw you being so good to Suki and to Movita, and then when I saw what you did when you found out about what those bastards were up to at JRU, I was really impressed. And I don't impress easy. You jumped right the fuck in.'

Jennifer couldn't stop herself from smiling. She'd never heard Cher praise her before.

Cher continued. 'I know you took a risk doin' that. It was good of you. And what ya' done since, well I don't think no one but you coulda done it. Oh, the Prez, she woulda wanted to, but she didn't know how.'

'Cher, if you were so impressed with me,' Jennifer had to say, 'then why'd you get out and take over my life?'

'Let me finish,' Cher insisted. 'I gotta tell my story my way. That's just the way I am.'

Jennifer signaled the waiter for another glass of wine. She was going to need it.

'You took the best each person had to give and you found a way to make it work for the good of everyone,' Cher continued. 'And there wasn't nothin' in that for you. I thought you were a selfish bitch, and suddenly, to tell you the truth, I had to admit you'd changed. By the time I stole you that cell phone and got it set up for you, I was startin' to kinda like ya'.'

Jennifer was getting a little tipsy from the wine. 'I liked you too, Cher. You know I couldn't have done it without that cell phone.'

'Oh, you woulda found a way,' Cher insisted. 'Anyway, you don't have to believe me or nothing. I can disappear long before you can stop me. But the point is I didn't do this to hurt you or steal from you.'

'How can you say that when you're sitting there in my suit?' Jennifer protested. Suddenly, she looked around the restaurant, wondering if anyone was overhearing this crazy conversation. She bet that the Mercer Kitchen had never been witness to a conversation between two ex-convicts before.

'Okay, okay,' Cher admitted. 'At first I needed a place to crash and I thought maybe I'd wear your clothes for a little while, but then, well, I heard what you were doing and I just thought someone should do something for you.'

Jennifer almost spat up her wine. 'What? How is living in my place for free and stealing my clothes and my boyfriend your idea of a reward?'

'Shit, girl, I wouldn't fuck him for money.' Cher took a swig of water. 'I established myself. It didn't take me long to get a new social security number and a new name and I got a job. I'm working on the Street.' She lifted her eyebrows. 'Not as a prostitute, on Wall Street. I found a boiler room a friend of mine had set up and from that I moved up to a discount brokerage firm, but I was sellin' so much goddamn stock that the sons-of-bitches kept moving me up and now I'm managing portfolios.'

'Cher!' she said. 'What do you know about portfolio management?' She couldn't believe her. But it was an even crazier story to make up.

Cher grinned. 'I know enough to get your boyfriend to put his money in my hands.' Jennifer raised her brows. Tom was greedy, but he was very cautious. 'I doubt that,' she said.

'Hey, look. We got an expression: No one easier to con than a con.' She paused. 'Okay, I admit I had to have him put a few other things in my hands, but it was a small price to pay.'

'A small price to pay for what?' Jennifer asked, completely out of patience.

'For watching him go broke,' Cher said with a deeply satisfied smile. 'He doesn't know it yet but I've put him into every bad deal I could find. I've given him positions even a contortionist couldn't survive.' She laughed. 'But that isn't all,' she said.

Jennifer laughed, too. She couldn't take all this in. 'What do you mean? There's more?'

The lunch crowd had begun to thin out and Jennifer was on her third glass of wine. It was going to her head more than in the old days, before the eleven-month abstinence of prison.

Cher nodded. 'I also got copies of all of Tom's files and I have the goods on him and Donald Michaels on your deal and a few previous ones. In writing: contracts and memos signed by them.'

Jennifer shook her head. 'But how did you gain Tom's trust? Didn't he find you in my apartment?'

'I just told him I was a friend of yours, and once I got set up at my new job, he believed me. It's amazing how gullible these smart guys can be,' Cher shrugged. 'Hey, Jen – were you ever raped in prison?'

Jennifer turned white. She'd heard too many stories. 'No, thank God.'

'Well, Tommy boy is a little too pretty for his own good. I'm tellin' you once we get his lily ass in prison, that bitch is gonna be cleanin' somebody else's house.' Cher smirked. Then she reached into her pocket. She took out a big wad of cash. 'Look, I owe ya' this from when I first moved in. I had to use some of your charge cards and shit and here's all the rent I woulda paid ya'. I'm not even askin' for a discount.' She handed Jennifer a wad of bills. All hundreds.

Jennifer looked down at the roll and wouldn't count it right then, but there had to be ten, maybe fifteen thousand dollars, maybe more. She stuffed it into her new purse. And to think she had been worried about money when she shopped yesterday afternoon.

'Thanks, Cher,' Jennifer said finally. 'I didn't expect this.'

'I know ya' didn't,' Cher said. 'But listen, if you still want to turn me in you can call the police, or Tom, or my parole officer, who – by the way – I'm fuckin' too, and he knows how to do it.'

'No, Cher, I would never –' Jennifer started.

Cher cut her off. 'Good, 'cause what I'd like, what I'd really like is for you to just get back at these guys who railroaded you and then maybe leave me in my job without blowin' the whistle. I never thought I'd say it, but I kinda like being legit. Not that it's all that different from what I used to do.'

The waiter came by to see if Jennifer wanted more wine. 'Actually, I'll have a Cosmopolitan,' Jennifer said. This sounded like a celebration.

Cher made eyes up to the ceiling. 'Oh, Christ, Deb. Nobody drinks those anymore.' Cher ordered a top-shelf, single-malt scotch on the rocks.

Jennifer just had to sit there for a few minutes to take it all in. 'So, I still don't get something.'

'You need me to tell you the whole friggin' story again?' Cher asked.

'No,' Jennifer said. 'Just tell me again, how did you get Tom to trust you?'

Cher laughed. 'Oh, come on. These kinda guys never think women have enough brains to screw them. We're the screwees. All I had to do was offer it up and hang around for the ride. If ya' keep your mouth shut most of the time except when you're praising them or they've got their dick in it, they'll believe anything. Don't pretend you don't know that.'

Jennifer stared at Cher and then she began to laugh. 'You,' she said, 'are a real piece of work.'

Luckily, their drinks arrived just then, and they were able to toast to that.

'Duh,' Cher teased her. 'And you just noticed, huh? No wonder they could railroad you so easy.'

Jennifer didn't take offense. It was true, so she began to laugh and laugh and then for a few minutes she actually couldn't stop. It was a little frightening, but all of the adjustments that she had had to make in the last twenty-four hours, from leaving Jennings to her shock at the apartment to her spending spree and her incredibly wonderful night with Lenny upstairs at the hotel were, she had to admit, a bit much for any girl.

Cher pushed her hand from across the table. 'Don't you go off on me,' she said. But then she started to laugh, too. 'Friends?' she asked.

'Oh, yeah,' Jen said. 'Friends. But let me tell you about the little plan that I've worked out that you might want to help me with.' She leaned forward. 'Do you really think Movita and Suki and Theresa should still be in prison?' she asked.

'Holy shit,' Cher said. 'I am not getting involved in a fuckin' jail break.'

Jennifer laughed again. 'Oh, come on, Cher. I appreciate the compliment but I'm not that bold, or that stupid. Still, I do have a plan.' She leaned forward again and quietly began explaining.

50

Jennifer Spencer

You're so sure you're not going back to the same crowd. But pretty soon you be hanging out with the same ol' crowd again, just to feel like you belong somewhere.

Theresa Derry, an inmate at SCI Muncy, Pennsylvania.
Kathryn Watterson, *Women in Prison*

Jennifer went over every detail with Lenny to make sure that she hadn't left anything out. He had to admit two things: that the plan could work, and that he wouldn't mind staying on at the Mercer for a little while. 'It's just for the towels,' he said.

Jennifer laughed, grabbed him around the neck with the crook of her arm and pulled him down onto the bed. 'Miss Spencer,' he said. 'What are you thinking of? The chambermaids just made this bed.'

'Dumb move,' she said, and then she showed him a few of her own.

Later, stretched out in the bathtub, she thought she'd never take a bath again without appreciating it. Now, when she looked back, she realized that she had thought she knew

Lenny, but she hadn't appreciated him. She shook her head, wetting her hair. Well, she'd have a professional cut today to prepare her for this evening's showdown. She thought for a few moments about what other preparations she might need. Cher promised to have the written records and the computerized ones of the questionable Hudson, Van Schaank transactions ready. Lenny, she was sure, could serve as a witness with a lot of clout since, unlike herself and Cher, he was not a convicted felon. She allowed her feet to float in the deep tub and stared up at the ceiling. She wondered why these rooms, so simple as to almost be stark, were beautifully pleasant while the rooms at Jennings were so hideously ugly. She stared up at the white ceiling and let her entire body float on the warm pillow of bath water.

Lenny lay asleep in their bed. He was an amazing lover, and she wondered if he always had been or if this was a special effort inspired by her. If it was the former she'd just been stupid and blind; if it was the latter she was touched and grateful. Speaking of touched, she felt her fingers pruning up. Underwater they looked like white raisins. Perhaps she'd been in the bath long enough. She looked over at the white freesia that Lenny had bought for her. She could smell them from the tub, though they weren't splashy or even particularly rare. They were just beautiful, the green of their stems so perfect, long and thin as dancers, the white of their blossoms creamy, and the graceful way the blossom moved horizontally across an extension perpendicular to the stem, with each flower or bud getting smaller and smaller. Oh, it broke her heart that she had gone without a single blossom for almost a year. She stopped and counted. Well, there had been the chrysanthemums at Christmas and Springtime's marigolds, but she didn't think she could ever like those flowers again.

Prison had wasted more than eleven months of her life, but wouldn't they have been equally wasted at Hudson, Van Schaank? All she'd been doing, her apartment, her antiques, her Kirmans, and her portfolios . . . When she'd been sent to Jennings she had been a selfish, narrow young woman. She had lost touch with her old friends and didn't have any new ones – except for her so-called fiancé and her boss, both of whom turned out to be . . . she searched for Lenny's term. Oh yes, yellow rat bastards. Her judgment, her values, her goals, and her viewpoints had all been questionable. Prison had set her free. She knew the most important thing wasn't how much money she made, or how successful her next deal was, or how many people envied and respected her, or how powerful her friends were. She shivered, though the tub water was still warm. She had taken for granted all of life's most important pleasures and she had been a pouting child when they'd been taken away from her. She had never admitted her guilt, nor taken responsibility for losing her way as she had. Jennings had been dreadful, but through imprisonment she'd found freedom. She was no longer afraid. She didn't need to keep a big apartment, or a large paycheck, or a big wardrobe. She needed to keep her friends, and her freedom. She wanted to be free of fear.

Though she had changed, one thing in New York certainly hadn't. Balthazar was still the hottest restaurant in the city and dinner there on a Friday night wasn't easy to plan. The room was massive and the crowd was loud. The décor was such a perfect re-creation of a French bistro that she had heard the O'Malley brothers had actually imported French dust that they had ground into the tile floors. The red banquettes with chairs opposite were desirable, but not as desirable as the semicircular seating on the east and south wall. Above them hung squares of old mirrors pieced together to form large mirrors, ornately framed. The ceiling, a dark beige pressed-tin, still had a few playing cards stuck to it where previous parties had taken place. Jen remembered a Christmas party where Donald Michaels had reserved the whole restaurant for a soiree. A magician had been hired and one of the tricks was to have a participant sign his name to a random card in a deck. When all the cards were thrown into the air the only one that stuck to the ceiling was the one that had been signed. Jen looked down at her own feet as she and Lenny entered. Her foot was beautifully covered in the new Otto Tootsie Plohound shoes. The floors were beautifully covered in tiny mosaic tiles. They walked through the crowd to the deep mahogany bar, but it was so crowded that Lenny took her to the back where all the luscious seafood was laid out on beds of crushed ice.

It was a good place from which to observe the crowd, a combination of downtown hipsters, Wall Streeters, beautiful women, and the occasional rich family or older couple celebrating some anniversary or event. Despite the crowd it was easy to spot Tom and Cher when they came in. Cher, who seemed to have given up her flamboyant style, still managed to glow. While she had adopted a patina of pampered grooming there was still something raw and vibrant about her that shined through. For a moment Jennifer could hardly bear to look at Tom – not because she still loved him but because she was ashamed that she had ever thought she did. He looked so untouchable and self-satisfied that for a moment she really wondered if she could pull this off. His harsh judgment of Lenny and his off-loading of her weren't justified by his smooth good looks, his perfectly tailored suit, and his aura of impeccable breeding. Then she pulled herself together and got ready.

They were seated at table fifty-three – one of the best circular banquettes – by Zuair, the maitre d'. 'Let's go,' she told Lenny, and took his hand for a moment. He gave her hand a squeeze, as if he knew she'd been shaken. She led the way through the crowd.

'Well, hello,' she said, looking down at the two of them. Tom looked up and for a moment his face froze. Then he managed a smile.

'Oh, surely we're not going to have another scene, Jennifer.' He looked over at Lenny and registered surprise, or was it . . . contempt? Whatever it was, it enraged her.

'A scene?' she asked. 'Certainly not.' And she slid into the banquette next to him while Lenny slid beside Cher. There was no way he could get out, short of ducking under the table and scrabbling away. She knew Tom well enough to know that he'd rather die than make a public spectacle.

'I don't remember asking you to join us,' Tom said. 'Lenny, why don't you take Jennifer out of here.'

'Why don't you listen to what Jennifer has to say,' Lenny told him.

Tom turned to Cher. 'I'm sorry about this,' he said. 'It's almost like having a stalker.'

'Shut up, you motherfucker,' Cher told him.

Tom blinked. 'What?' he managed to ask, as if his ears couldn't take the obscenity in.

'Shut the fuck up, you douche, and listen to Jennifer before I get your knees broken.'

Tom blinked again. 'I don't understand,' he said.

'Well, it's necessary that you do,' Jennifer said. 'Now listen, I'll cut to the chase: I have all the documentation I need to put you in prison for the next ten years at least. And believe me, it won't be a country club.'

'Don't be ridiculous,' he said.

'I'm talking about the Anderson deal, the Thompson acquisition. I'm talking about your insider position on the Bayler-Crups merger. I'm talking about the secret purchases you've made for Donald. That's leaving out how you perjured yourself and misrepresented my case. It's also leaving out Donald, and how he'd throw you to the wolves in a heartbeat – if he had a heart. If it would protect his ass from the FCC.'

'I have more,' Lenny added. 'And some of it I witnessed. I can testify under oath.'

'Do you think you're scaring me?' Tom asked.

'I don't really care how you feel,' Jennifer told him. 'I'm just telling you the drill: You go to Donald. You get me the money he owes me – the money he promised me – as well as a pardon from the governor.' She handed him a piece of paper. 'And you get a pardon for these women as well.'

'I will not even discuss this,' Tom said. 'I am an attorney. You're talking about privileged information . . .'

'Well, I'm a thief,' Cher interrupted him to say. 'And I've stolen quite a bit of privileged information myself. All of your portfolio statements, your files, your correspondence on the Thompson and Bayler-Crup deals. I even have a few tapes of you and Donald talking about your latest scheme, that Canadian petrochemical company.'

'What are you talking about?' Tom asked. 'What do you mean you stole this information?'

Cher yawned. 'I mean that I went through your mail and your desk and your briefcase. I have copies of your phone bills, I duped your laptop files.'

'How, how could . . .'

'It was my pleasure,' Cher said. She reached over and took Jennifer's hand. 'Anything for a pal,' she said, and smiled real wide at Tom.

He got very pale. Jennifer could see the perspiration forming in tiny pinhead drops on his upper lip and just over his brows.

'The only reason why a woman – other than dumb Jenny here – would fuck you, pencil dick, is because she needed access to your wallet, your contacts, or your data bank. Make sure you remember that the next time you climb up on top of some little heifer, 'cause you've climbed up on me for the last time. Thank God.' Cher looked over at Jennifer. 'Please, promise me I don't have to fuck him again. It's so damn boring I'm afraid my heart will just stop beating. Even as a favor to you it's been tough to swallow, you should pardon the expression.' She smiled brightly at Tom. 'My friend here wants you to be the intermediary with your boss. I suggest you do it. I tell you, I know a lot of men in prison and I think you'd dislike getting fucked by them even more than I disliked getting fucked by you.'

Just then the Balthazar waiter approached the table. 'Would you like to hear the specials?' he asked.

'No, thank you,' Jennifer said. 'I've just gotten out of prison and I have an enormous craving for seafood. Could we get the triple crown and a vintage bottle of Veuve Clicquot? I didn't have any champagne in prison either.'

The waiter laughed. 'Any other drinks?' he asked.

Cher shook her head and indicated Tom with her chin.

'He doesn't get any choices,' she said. 'And the funny thing is, he pays the bill. But I'd like a bottle of champagne, too.' She turned to Tom and smiled. He seemed to be in a state of shock, speechless, or maybe beyond speech. 'He'll just watch,' Cher said.

51

Jennifer Spencer

Injustice is relatively easy to bear; what stings is justice.

H. L. Mencken, *Prejudices: Third Series*

'But I wanna come.'

'And I want to be an astronaut. But it's not going to happen in this lifetime,' Jen told Cher.

'But why? I did so good with Tom.'

Jennifer put down the blow-dryer and checked out her makeup in her bathroom mirror. She and Cher were both there, though Cher had found her own apartment in Chelsea and was moving in on the first of the month. 'You know, Cher, I don't want to hear the details of what you did with Tom,' Jen said.

'Oh, come on. I did it for you. Please, please can't I come to the meeting with Donald Michaels?'

'No, you can't.'

'Just give me one good reason.'

'Because you tried to set him up as a future mark.'

'Okay. Point taken. But give me another good reason.'

Jennifer hated to admit it, but she actually liked having Cher at her place. And though she did have a real concern that at any moment the bunko squad might knock on the door and take her off in cuffs, she was proud of Cher for going so far toward legitimacy. (The fact that Cher, with all of her predatory traits, was thriving on Wall Street was only another indication to Jennifer that perhaps it wasn't tragic that she would no longer be permitted to be in that line of work.)

In fact, she had almost definitely decided that she wanted to continue working with women in prison. She wasn't sure how yet, but she knew she didn't want to go back to a life where her comforts and her plans were the only important things in it. Jennifer looked at herself in the full-length mirror. She wasn't wearing one of her business suits – that was over. She instead had on a pair of black slacks and a simple white shirt.

'You look great,' Cher told her. 'Like you just got outta prison. So give me one more reason.'

'I am not giving you another reason. It's something I have to do on my own.'

'Don't bullshit me,' Cher said. 'And put on a little more lipstick. You don't have to look like a dyke.'

Jennifer picked up a tube of Nars and remembered the Adobe Red Cher had handed out at Jennings.

'Lenny's coming with you,' Cher said, and sounded exactly like a four-year-old.

'No, he isn't,' Jennifer told her. 'This is something I have to do myself. But if I need reinforcements you and Lenny will be the first two people I'll call.'

'You suck,' Cher said.

'This, from a woman who had sex with my ex-fiancé,' Jennifer responded, then picked up her purse and went out the door.

Nothing in Donald's office had changed, least of all Donald himself. He sat, well buffed, well coiffed, well dressed, and well fed, his feet – well shod as ever – up on the desk and crossed at the ankles as usual. The only time his feet came down from the desk was when he had to walk to his limo or kick someone's ass, Jennifer thought. Somehow, staring at his shoe sole – certainly the only soul he possessed – bothered her more than coming into the Hudson, Van Schaank & Michaels building, going past the receptionists and ex-coworkers, waiting in Donald's private reception area or even seeing Tom, slightly pale, enter the room. She had once read that, during his presidency, Lyndon Johnson used to go to the toilet and defecate during meetings, expecting his cabinet members to follow him while he continued the conversation. Somehow staring at the bottom of Donald's shoe was like that.

'I want it very clear that it is only as a courtesy that I am seeing you,' Donald began. 'Tom came to me with your demands, and I want you to hear this very clearly, Jennifer: You have no grounds for these allegations and I am not intimidated. Now, if you have something else to say, say it, because I have a meeting – an important one – in ten minutes.'

So it was going to be like that. Jen just shrugged. 'I don't have a wire on,' she told Donald. 'You don't have to bother with your broadcast to the troops.' Jennifer stood up and in less than three seconds opened her shirt, unzipped her pants and dropped both to the ground. She turned around briefly. 'There,' she said. 'See?' One thing prison had done for her was buff her up. She wanted to show these two jerkoffs something perfect they'd never have. She didn't look at the two men's reactions. She merely bent down, pulled up the slacks, buttoned the waist and slipped back into her top. After the group showers and everything else she'd been through at Jennings, this was no big deal, but it made a hell of an impression on the two of them.

'Are you offering yourself to me?' Donald asked.

Jennifer actually laughed aloud. 'Yes, and I've converted to Islam,' she said, then sat down and crossed her legs. She shook her head. 'Don,' she said, consciously using the nickname he hated. 'Don, I wouldn't fuck you with Tom's dick. Now, let's get serious. I don't know if you are recording this, but that nonsense about blackmail can be disregarded. Let me make this short and sweet. We made an agreement. I took the fall for you and you were going to pay me.'

'Jennifer, there was no wrongdoing on my part,' Donald began. 'You know perfectly well.'

'Don, say that one more time and I'm going to have to make you strip. I'll take off my clothes and start to scream rape. So just cut the crap and let's get down to cases. You owe me eleven months' salary, bonuses from two Christmases, and the down payment on a larger apartment. You never promised me that last one, but since prices appreciated while I was in prison, I'm adding it instead of interest. Consider it the vig.'

Donald was silent for a minute. 'What else?' he asked.

'I want him out of here,' she said.

'You mean, fired?' Donald asked, looking at Tom.

'Hey,' Tom said. But neither of them was paying much attention to him.

'No,' she said. 'Although it's an interesting idea. I just want him out of here now.'

'Is that really necessary?' Donald asked calmly.

'Donald, as your counsel, I . . .'

'Shut up,' Jennifer told him. She looked directly at Donald. 'This is not negotiable,' she said.

'Thomas, would you excuse us?' Donald said, as smooth as marble and just as hard.

Tom tried to object but Donald made the movement of his hand that meant no discussion was possible. Slowly, reluctantly, Tom stood and looked at Jennifer, the expression in his eyes the one she had waited for for almost a year: fear. It took all of her willpower not to smile. He stood up and walked hesitantly to the door. She didn't allow herself to turn around, but she watched Donald's hand and knew that Tom had tried to speak before he closed the door.

She sat for a moment and let the silence build. Before prison she never could have tolerated the pressure but now talking to Donald – Don – was NBD. She waited and then waited. He spoke at last. 'All right, Jennifer. What's it going to be? I'm not saying that I'm committing to anything but at least let me hear your demands.'

'I don't look at them as demands, Don,' she said calmly. And she felt calm. 'I look at them as choices. Choices for you to make.' She reached into her purse and took out several dozen pages. She put them at the edge of his desk so he had to put his feet down to get at them. He rifled through them and, though he was famous for his poker face, she thought she saw a flicker of concern. He put the papers down and his feet back up.

'Is that your whole hand?' he asked.

'Oh, no,' she said. And she told him all of the information

that Cher had gathered, along with the corroborating evidence that Lenny Benson and others would give. 'We've been through all the files,' she said. 'And accessed your computer. And you've been very negligent in the trades you've been making in the last year and a half with Peter Grant.' She handed him the file on those. 'The SEC will be calling you on that,' she said. 'Sooner or later.'

Donald looked down at the statements. 'I didn't do these trades,' he said.

'And I didn't do your crime,' she told him. 'But I did do your time. Hey, it's your name, social security number, and your code word. By the way, how is Grendel?'

'My dog?' he asked. And she saw the light dawn in his eyes. 'How much more of this stuff is there?' he asked.

'Plenty,' she told him. Though in truth her quiver was just about empty. Still, it would serve.

'Jennifer, you know the money isn't an issue. So what is it you want?'

She handed her last sheet of paper to him. 'Gubernatorial pardons for those three inmates. You have their numbers and the pertinent information.'

'Jennifer, one of these women is a murderer. I couldn't even get *you* a pardon.'

'You didn't even try,' she told him. And when he began to argue she made the hand motion he always used. 'We've had an election since then, and I know that your contributions got him reelected.'

He stopped. 'Is that it?' he asked.

'There's one more thing,' she told him, and allowed herself a smile. He waited. 'About Tom,' she said.

52

Movita Watson

All that we know who lie in gaol is that the wall is strong.

Oscar Wilde, *The Ballad of Reading Gaol*

'I don't like this, Theresa. I don't like this one bit,' I said, looking at the paper in my hand. 'I think this has got to be baaad news!'

Theresa had the same kinda paper as me and was readin' it like I was. It was a summons to go to the Warden's office. I don't mean an official summons, like to go to court. I mean that the Warden was tellin' us that we had to come in there. Now I see her nearly every day and if she's got any news for me of a decent sort, even if it ain't great, she just tells it to my face or sends someone to bring me up there. But this was a note – handwritten by her, and signed.

'Don't assume,' Theresa said. 'It makes an ass of you and me.' I swear I almost tole her to take her happy little readin' away with this worried expression.

'What do you think it could be, Movita?' Suki asked, holding her baby and an envelope just like ours.

It was just what I was afraid of. I threw my summons down onto my bunk. 'You got one, too. I'm almost sure that it has to do with Suki and Christina. That child's gonna be twelve months old and that's about the limit for keepin' her in here. She's gonna have to let her go.'

'Oh, no!' Suki moaned.

'Are you sure?' Theresa asked.

It was all I could do not to cry, seein' 'em there happy and so much a part of each other. I told Suki my idea as quickly as I could. She went through all kinda expressions on her face as she listened and then broke into tears and hugged Christina to her.

'I know that's what it's about,' she said. 'I been sick about it.'

'Well you bein' sick ain't gonna do no good at all,' I whispered loudly.

'Then why does she want to see *us*?' Theresa asked.

'Obviously 'cause she don't want Suki to be by herself,' I said. It irritated me when Theresa didn't just listen when I knew somethin' for sure. 'It's like havin' the family in. She wants us there helpin' the girl. Me because I went through it with my kids, and you because you're so damn fulla wisdom.'

'How terrible! Suki's going to be heartbroken.' Theresa looked at me with that look she's got like a helpless animal. For someone who's always tellin' others not to give up, she gives up awful fast herself.

'Not if it don't happen,' I said. 'We got to think of some way for her to keep her longer. She's up for parole in a little over a year.'

I went over to the sink to wash my hands, and got one of those pangs that I always get over my own kids. Damn it all to hell, I thought, it never changes. I'm always wantin' so bad what I can never have.

'I think we should tell the Warden that Christina is sick,' I said, turning around to Suki and Theresa, 'and that for the time bein' she needs to stay with her mother.'

Theresa looked at me and then the baby, real doubtful. 'That child is the picture of health,' she said.

'Sick children don't always look bad,' I answered. 'Besides, the way I see it, the Warden favors Christina and Suki both and if she could think of an excuse to help keep the baby in here, she would do it. We just got to give her one.'

'But a doctor is going to have to see the baby. And you can't fool a doctor,' Suki cried.

I snorted. As if. 'Yes, you can,' I said, tucking my shirt in. 'The child can't speak, so you'll just say that she has some kinda symptoms during the night, like cramps or something.'

Theresa shook her head. 'I don't know . . .' she said.

'Theresa,' I warned, 'we gotta try. That child is still just a baby and needs to be with her mother. It's barbaric to separate 'em and you know it. The Warden knows it. Now c'mon!'

We called Officer Mowbry over and told her we were ready to go. She unlocked the door and we all walked to Warden Harding's office, but we walked real slow, like it was the last mile. During the time we did, I tried to think of more possible symptoms we could say that Christina had. I was rememberin' my own kids' problems, like with teethin' and colds and stuff, but none a that was serious.

Suki started to cry and that started Christina fussin'. Which was no bad thing, if Suki would shut up.

'Now stop that,' I tole her. 'Act like it's all a surprise. And you gotta think a some way that Christina's sick.'

Suki just kept on cryin'. By this time not only her and Christina but Theresa had tears in her eyes, too. We were a miserable-lookin' group when Warden Harding opened her door and asked us to come in. We walked in like goin' to the gallows. And then the confusin' thing was that the Warden herself looked happier than the day we got the prison back from them JRU bastards. She just started cooin' at Christina, which I thought was a damn cold thing to do, considering she was about to see her handed off to foster care.

'How's my favorite little girl?' she asked, lookin' at the baby and positively radiatin' happiness. I was about to scream, thinkin' that maybe the Warden liked the idea of Christina leavin' the prison.

The Warden gave Christina back to Suki and sat down. She looked at all of us, still smilin' like crazy.

'I have news for all of you,' she said. 'Very important and very good news.'

None of us said a word or moved a muscle. I swear, even that baby was still. What could it be? 'Our friend Jennifer Spencer has done it again,' the Warden said. 'She has secured unconditional pardons from the governor for all three of you.'

I musta been crazy right at that moment. I know it's a sin to admit, but I got a feelin' of terrible, terrible sadness, thinkin' that the three was Theresa and Suki and Christina, and that only I was goin' to stay there forever. But the Warden was smilin' at me most of all, and there were tears in *her* eyes, but not of sadness.

'You too, Movita,' she said, as if she read my mind. 'You're free to go home.'

I have never in my life felt anything like I did that moment in that office, not even when I was sentenced to life without parole by the judge. It was as if what the Warden said had to go through my whole body, like a physical thing, before I could even hear it. It started at my shoulders and moved down my arms like some kinda pain. Then my legs were weak and I couldn't a stood if I had to, and then it went to my stomach and I bent over in the chair and felt as if I was goin' to be sick. Then finally it went to my head and I heard the words. But I didn't believe them. I got the horrible thought that she was just lyin' to me.

'Oh, please, Warden,' I groaned, still bent over in my chair. 'Don't say that if it ain't true.'

'It's true, Movita. I'm sorry.'

I knew that was kinda funny, her apologizin', but I couldn't laugh. I was starting to feel a tiny kinda happiness creepin' on me, but then I was afraid, real afraid like this was just another dream and I'd wake up and see the pink wall again. I still couldn't straighten up. My mind was somethin' like paralyzed. I heard Theresa talkin' and Suki cryin'. I was far, farther away. They were huggin' each other and someone touched me, but I could hardly feel it.

'Oh my God!' I heard Theresa say. 'How did she do that? Oh my God, that girl is a saint. I would've been here two more years before I maxed out. I'm going to faint.'

Suki was cryin' away, rockin' Christina, sayin' 'We're gonna go home, baby. We're gonna go home, baby.'

I still couldn't believe I was goin' home. I just sat there and listened to the Warden goin' on about what Jennifer had done.

'She got you all unconditional pardons, which means you are *out of here*,' she explained. 'You don't have to go before any board. This is *not* parole. You may not know this, but it also means you can be in touch with each other on the Outside. It means you won't have to check in, or be checked on.'

I straightened up and looked around the room. Theresa was sittin' on the edge of her chair as if she was already on her way out, and Suki also had a different look about her already. Like she was a more important person.

The Warden stood up and told us to go and pack up our things, whatever we wanted to take, and to come back to her office. And then I got really afraid.

'Do you mean now?' Suki cried. 'We can leave now?'

The Warden laughed. 'To tell you the truth,' she said, 'after twenty-four hours I'm going to have to throw you out. You are no longer inmates here.'

I'd never fainted in my whole life, but after Warden Harding said that and everyone laughed I got woozy in my knees, like I wasn't sure they'd hold me up no more, even though I was sittin' in a chair. And my face and hands got all hot, like I was burnin' up. I could feel beads of sweat breakin' out on my forehead and under my arms, and when I looked at the light over the Warden's desk – that light I've seen maybe a million times – it suddenly got real bright and started to drown out the whole room. I looked over at Theresa and Suki, maybe for some help, but they was gettin' whiter and whiter, and seemin' further and further away. They was lookin' at me like they was worried, but before I could say anythin' they faded into the light and I felt myself slide sideways off the chair. Then everythin' just seemed to stop.

I woke up on the floor with the Warden and Theresa fussin' over me. The Warden was holdin' somethin' strong-smellin' under my nose. Theresa had some ice. I pulled myself up but I didn't say nothin'. I couldn't say nothin'.

'Come on, Movita,' Theresa said to me. 'Pull yourself together. Let's go to our cell. I'll help you.' Her voice was real serious. Somehow she musta known what I was goin' through.

The Warden put her arms around me. 'It's gonna be okay, Movita,' she said real quietly. 'In fact, it's gonna be more than okay. Go get your things and come back here. That's all you have to do.'

I got up and told Gwen I was all right. Theresa hugged me, and so did Suki, and Gwen Harding – she was just beamin'.

'Go on back and take it in,' she told me. 'Then pack yourselves up.'

I thanked her and nodded and we left the office. Once we got to the long corridor I started to cry but kept walkin' along with Theresa next to me, Suki in front. I sobbed on and on like I would never stop. I was sadder durin' that walk than I ever been in my life, which sure was strange. It was as if I was suddenly thawed out or somethin' and thinkin' that maybe I was not some kinda rat that is supposed to be kept in a cellar. I didn't think those words then, I couldn't think any words, but that's what I remember the feelin' bein' like. I think I let myself cry for all the times I didn't all the years before.

Back in our cell, Theresa started sortin' through her stuff. I had stopped cryin' but I couldn't move. She told me to just take what I wanted, and leave the rest. I think it was one of her stupid slogans, but for once it was useful. I took the pictures of my children and the pack a letters they sent me, and I don't know what else.

'Now where are we goin'?' I asked Theresa. I stopped cryin' and was just kinda numb by this time.

Theresa stopped what she was doin' and looked at me. 'That's actually a good question. I don't know,' she said. 'And how will we get wherever we go?'

Then she smiled. 'Look, I'm sure the Warden will help us. We get our money – everything in the canteen fund plus what we earned working plus a hundred dollars. And then, if we sell our stock, we're rich. Don't forget that.'

'But it all takes time.' Crazy as it sounds, I think I was scared.

'She knows we can't just walk out of here.' Theresa made like she was lost in the universe, wavin' her arms and lookin' at the ceilin'. She was jokin' but it was how I really felt, and I bet she knew it. She had sisters and all kinda family to go to. I had the girls but . . .

She came over and looked at my little pile of stuff.

'Don't you want to take anything else?' she asked me. 'What about a few clothes? You'll need something to wear.'

So I started puttin' together a bundle but the pants and shirts that I'd designed now just looked useless to me. Toothpaste and washcloth. I was finished in a minute and went and stood by the door, like I always used to, but this time when I leaned against it, it moved.

'Theresa!' I said. 'Ryan didn't lock the door!'

She came up behind me and pushed it open. 'We are no longer inmates of this prison, Movita. We're outta here.'

I followed her out into the corridor holdin' my stuff, and then turned around and looked back. I looked at my bunk and the sink and the wall without my kids' pictures on it. It was the most horrible lookin' place I ever saw, but I stared at it for a minute, 'cause it was where I lived for all those years.

In a kind of a daze we went to Suki's cell, 'cause she had a lot more stuff to carry than we did, all the baby paraphernalia and the baby – who was sleepin' quietly in her bassinet. I realized I didn't want to say good-bye to nobody who wasn't gettin' out right then with us because it would be too damn cruel. Then Ryan escorted us back to the Warden's office. I was afraid maybe she'd say 'April fool' or something, but she didn't.

'Come with me,' she said, puttin' her arms out like she wanted to hug all of us at once. 'I'm going to walk you Outside.'

We followed her out, walkin' along as if we were just visitors at Jennings, like the JRU groups and the tours that sometimes came through. Everybody we passed was lookin' at us different than they had the day before. You can't never keep a secret in a woman's prison.

'But where will we go, Warden?' Suki asked. 'I can go to Roger's but . . . well . . .'

I knew she was feeling sorry for me. I hate that. 'I'm not sure I got a place to go,' I admitted.

'Oh, I don't think you have to worry about that,' she said. 'There's someone picking you up Outside and we're all going out for lunch. After that we'll take care of where you're all settling down.'

Well, I may be crazy but I ain't no dummy. I knew it'd be Jennifer Spencer waitin' out there for us. Still, it was the greatest feelin' in the world to come out into the actual Outside and see her standin' there. It was then that I knew it was for real.

And of all the amazin', outrageous things, she had come with a huge stretch limousine! Must have been six windows on each side. And when the driver opened the door, about fifty helium balloons poured out and up into the air.

'Freedom!' Jennifer said.

This just started me cryin' all over again. I was so grateful that I couldn't even speak, so I just hugged Jennifer. Then that bitch Cher stepped out of the car! 'You like her better than you like me?' she asked. I swear, I was bewildered, but I hugged that girl and let everyone else do the talkin'. Cher told me later that this was the only time she ever saw me bein' quiet.

Everybody climbed in the big car, even the Warden, and we drove away from Jennings. For a moment everybody was quiet as we pulled through the gate. I was waitin' for the Warden to say somethin' about Cher and Jennifer bein' in violation of their parole – they weren't supposed to be together. But ol' Gwen said nothin'. Me and Theresa looked out the tinted window, but Suki didn't 'cause she was busy with Christina. After that I just looked at Jennifer. To me she was the best and most beautiful person in the world and I knew I'd never live a day without thinkin' of her and bein' more grateful than I could ever say. Didn't matter she was white. She was my sister. I don't think anyone can understand how it feels to be released. Even I don't understand it and it happened to me.

Jennifer couldn't get over how Christina had grown. She had to wake the child up to admire her. 'She's gotten so big! Honestly, Suki, she's the cutest baby I've ever seen!' she said. 'She's a big chubby doll!' She took out a box, all wrapped nice. 'Here, I have something for her. Why don't you put it on her now?' I just loved that the box was wrapped up beautiful and *not* rewrapped. I noticed right away.

Suki opened the box and inside was a little flowered dress with a sweater to match. She took off Christina's rompers and put on the new outfit. We were all just overcome by the beauty of the child. We began laughin' with pleasure, 'cause smilin' and words were just not enough.

Then Jennifer told us what we were goin' to do. First we would have lunch, after which the Warden would have to go back to Jennings, and we would go into New York City. She said we could all stay at her apartment for the night and then the next day we would go home. She'd arranged for drivers. It was like a dream, I was thinkin', and I bent my head down so that I wouldn't faint again.

We went to lunch at some fancy restaurant, which I thought was the most beautiful place I'd ever been in, and I said so. I was also the only African American sittin' down, though there were several waiters and service people. I forgot how white the world Outside was. But I was so happy, nothin' could spoil it. But when I got the menu I kinda froze up. Too many choices. I felt my fingers tighten on the card. How to choose? What to eat, what to drink? It was way too much.

Jen saw my problem. 'Let's all have the Cobb salad,' she suggested. I had no damn idea what the Cobb salad was, but I said sure, and to this day that blue crumbly cheese is the taste of freedom to me.

'Missy, I'm gonna take you places that make this look like nothin'!' Cher said to me. But I shook my head. I don't think any place is ever gonna look so beautiful to me. Still Cher was full of fun, and she looked the bomb, and a lot younger than when she was in with us.

But the best came last. When we came out of the restaurant, there in the parkin' lot was another limo and out of it poured three of Theresa's sisters, Roger Camry, his mother, and then, one by one, my girls: Jamorah, Talitha, and Kiama, all dressed real nice.

'Mama!' Jamorah cried, and ran across the tarmac, her arms open wide to give me the best hug of my life.

53

Maggie Rafferty

I suppose society is wonderfully delightful. To be in it is merely a bore. But to be out of it is simply a tragedy.

Oscar Wilde, *A Woman of No Importance*

One by one they had become dear to my heart and one by one they left me. First Jennifer Spencer was paroled, then Miss Watson, Miss LaBianco and Suki Conrad along with dear little Christina – all were pardoned. I didn't resent their new freedom, but I did miss them. Of course, I was very busy in my new, expanded role as inmate coordinator. Dozens and dozens of women needed counseling, direction, a chance to share their grievances, and an intercessor. I filled the bill. And I wasn't abandoned by my friends because they were pardoned, so all of them were free to write and visit me, and they already had – and frequently.

I had begun to take my meals alone again, but the food was now so much better in the cafeteria that I frequently picked it up there and then brought it to my cell. It was a peaceful respite for me after dealing with people all day long. But when I heard the rumor that Warden Harding was leaving, and then heard it confirmed by a CO, I felt a pain that pierced my heart. Two, or sometimes three, times a week we had been having tea and sharing gossip and inmate problems in her office. Now that would be denied me, too, and I felt deeply bereft. It wasn't that my days were empty – to the contrary, they were filled with interesting and useful activity. There were many young women I had already come to like, and with the clearly psychotic housed in their own wing, I was no longer troubled by the screaming, cursing, and bizarre behavior that could so often disrupt a meal, sleep, a class, or even a conversation. I had also come to have deep affection for Springtime, whom I worked with each morning in one of the new gardens. She rarely spoke, but her presence was soothing and I believe that somewhere in her troubled consciousness she felt the same about mine. Springtime had finally stopped trying to escape, and would have been outdoors, nursing her plants and flowers or in the new greenhouse with her seedlings twenty-four-seven, as they say here, had it been allowed.

Since the yard had been grassed and the young birch trees planted, recreation had been extended to an area all around the perimeter of the building. I no longer had to walk in circles, figuratively and literally. A whole team was working on landscaping what we called the 'woods walk', a winding path all around the prison that would be visible from the guard towers (so no mischief could take place there) but would give the illusion of something approaching Arcadia to the walker. Already about a third of it was completed, and the azaleas, rhododendrons and plantings of annuals and perennials looked both natural and inviting.

Many of the inmates had become really interested in landscaping and nursery work as a career and I had made sure that Flora, who had inherited my job at the library, was collecting a significant selection of horticultural books and books on careers in the nursery and gardening fields. The perimeter walk was one of the new privileges at Jennings and it was so coveted that good behavior had certainly increased among the inmates to ensure their outdoor time.

The news, though, of Warden Harding's departure shocked and upset me in a way I simply wasn't prepared for. Of course, it was only a rumor, but I called her office and asked if I might come up to speak with her. The dull Miss Ringling had at last been replaced by a pleasant older woman named Ethel Schutz. No one, of course, could take Movita's place. But a new young woman named Tulip had been, at my suggestion, given a chance. Tulip put me on hold and came back on to tell me that I could come right up. That was a comfort, but when I got there I had to wait almost twenty minutes, and the phone calls and the faxes seemed to indicate that the rumor might be true. I could, of course, ask Tulip, because she did owe me a favor, but I didn't like to use that kind of ploy. I merely sat, my hands in my lap, and looked down at them.

They were the hands of an old woman. It was clear that they had done a lot of labor and the speckles on them showed that I was well past menopause. They were hands that had raised two boys, diapered and burped them, hands that had touched a man with passion, hands that had gestured and demonstrated and remonstrated to countless students, and they were hands that had killed a man. I stared and stared at them, going into an almost trancelike state. Well, I thought, they were hands that would have to do without the warmth of a cup of tea with Warden Gwendolyn Harding.

When the intercom buzzed Mrs Schutz looked up and politely told me I could join the Warden. I walked into her office expecting the worst and prepared for it. 'So,' I said, 'is it true, Gwendolyn?' After years and years of calling one another by title, we had only recently gotten onto a first-name basis (although I was always careful not to use her first name in any setting but her office).

'Yes, Margaret,' Gwendolyn said, smiling broadly. She seemed not to have the slightest regret that she was moving on. Well, I couldn't blame her.

I tried not to show my disappointment. 'Congratulations,' I said, and smiled back at her.

'You seem troubled, Margaret. Are you okay?' Gwendolyn asked, concerned.

'I'll be all right. Really,' I tried to reassure both of us. 'Do you know who'll be coming in to take over for you?'

'Take over for me?' Gwendolyn asked. 'What makes you think I need to be taken over? Haven't we been through that already?'

'Well, if you're going to be Director of Corrections, I merely assumed that . . .'

'That I was leaving? No. I made the agreement to take on the job only if I could use this office as my base.' Gwendolyn paused. 'Oh, dear. If you think I'm leaving so does everybody else,' Gwendolyn shook her head, then leaned back in her chair. 'I'm sorry if you've been worried about all of this, Margaret. But I'm not going anywhere. Yes, I've been given more responsibilities and a new title but I'm still going to be based here at Jennings. They'll have to lease an administrative building nearby, but I thought that you might be very involved in that work.'

I instinctively hugged myself. Tears rose in my eyes. 'Oh, thank heavens! You don't know how much that means. I . . . just don't think I could take any more change around here.'

'Well, there will be changes, but they'll be good ones. Speaking of changes, did you get one of these?' Gwendolyn handed a white envelope to me.

I took it, struggled to pull out the enclosure, and glanced at it. It was an invitation to Jennifer Spencer's wedding. 'No, I haven't gotten one, yet. I can't say I'm surprised, though. Lenny is a lovely man.'

'But won't it be fun?' Gwendolyn asked.

Perhaps I was muddled over the reversals of the morning. All I know is I said, 'She deserves every happiness. Still, it doesn't much matter since I can't go to it anyway.'

'Actually, you will be able to go,' Gwendolyn said.

'Gwendolyn, you can't let me leave the grounds to go to a wedding. She's not even a relative. I know things are different, but they're not *that* different.'

'Have wedding, will travel,' Gwendolyn said, and chuckled. 'Look at the invitation, Margaret. Former Inmate 71036 is coming here to be married!'

'Here?' I asked. 'Where? Where will it be?'

'Margaret, you'll have to go out to the shed.'

They hold a lot of weddings at men's prisons. I don't pretend to understand the phenomenon, but it's surprisingly common that a woman will correspond with a prisoner, become involved, and marry the criminal, even if he's guilty of a heinous crime. Perhaps, as my friend Gwendolyn opined, it's because when your husband is in prison at least you always know where he is. I think the situation feeds into a woman's need for fantasy and 'romance' – if he's not around underfoot, if you can see him only briefly, if the sex is rare or actually impossible and only imagined, a woman is capable of turning any frog into a mental prince. But weddings in women's prisons are virtually unheard of. And women love weddings. So, you can imagine the stir that the event made at Jennings.

The garden shed had been converted into a bower of flowers. White lilacs, roses, lisianthus, lilies, and ivy covered it. Seats had been put outside, with white ribbons streaming from them. Inmates had volunteered to work on a long white runner, hand hooked, that ran from the shed to the entrance of the yard. The wedding was truly beautiful. Jennifer looked radiant. Her dress was simple; a white swath of silk designed by Movita, covered with tulle that created a ghostlike effect as it shadowed the dress beneath. Jen also had what seemed like miles of tulle flowing from her simple headdress, and a wreath of flowers prepared by Springtime. Leonard – I was the only person who refused to call him that undignified name he was known by – looked very elegant in a simple black suit. I regretted, a bit, that it wasn't Bryce or Tyler Jennifer was marrying, so that she could actually become a member of my family – until I realized that neither of my boys was good husband material, and she was a member of my family anyway. I will never lose track of her or she of me.

Before the ceremony I had helped prepare the bride along with the other 'girls', Movita, Suki, Theresa, and Cher. Jen had asked that I give her away and, as she had neither mother nor father, I was pleased to do it. I had spent years serving *in loco parentis*, and I probably was more loco than parental at this point.

I was a little worried about misbehavior on the part of any of the inmates but I had two weeks to prepare them and I was delighted that their deportment was excellent. I have no idea what Leonard Benson's mother and aged father thought about the venue, but I could see that they were delighted with their new daughter-in-law.

I hadn't been to a wedding since my Tyler was married and that had been some fifteen years ago. And I couldn't attend any ceremonies for either of my boys anymore so this was definitely going to be an extra exciting time for me. The wedding march had started to play – the warden had brought in a CD player – and all the girls and I got in line and waited nervously for the right time to enter the yard. Theresa and Cher walked out first as the bridesmaids, then Movita as the maid of honor. The flower girl was Christina, who was accompanied by Suki for assistance. They were all stunning, dressed up in their lavender dresses, wearing real makeup, with their hair done beautifully. Once the girls had gotten twenty steps out – I had to try to keep count as they walked away – I gave Jennifer's arm a little squeeze and she smiled down at me through her veil. 'Let's get outta here,' she said, and gently took my hand.

When we stepped out of the doorway and into the sunshine and fresh air I felt like it was the first time I had ever been outside. A sound, something between a sigh and a gasp, came from the many inmates and guests assembled. I felt rejuvenated. The colors of the maid of honor's and bridesmaids' dresses against the green of the lawn and trees was breathtaking. As we approached the pastor I squeezed Jennifer's arm again. I didn't want to let go of her at the end of the white runner but I did. As I let go, Gwendolyn came up behind me and helped me to my seat. 'Isn't she ravishing?' I asked.

'Without a doubt,' Gwendolyn whispered.

The ceremony was emotional for everyone. Even the bulldaggers cried.

When the pastor pronounced the two of them man and wife, Leonard leaned forward and took Jennifer's face in his hands. I was right next to them and I had never noticed what lovely, long, strong fingers he had. He tilted her face toward him and the kiss that he gave her was as deep and long and passionate as I hoped their marriage would be. Jennifer colored, and the blush was one I remembered from the days when Riff was exciting in a good way. She was a wise and good girl, Jennifer Spencer Benson. She had picked her mate, a decision always fraught with the potential for catastrophe for a woman. She had picked her mate wisely. Leonard clearly cherished her and I had the strongest sense that he would continue to do so.

And when it came time for Jennifer to throw her bouquet, I must say it was the hungriest, most eager group that I had ever seen. Jennifer, with Lenny's help, stood up on a chair, closed her eyes, and threw her flowers. As the bouquet was released, arms shot up into the air as if the women were waiting for the delivery of packages from home. Several of them used basketball blocking moves. The bouquet suddenly disappeared from the air and the women were scrambling. I couldn't see who caught it and no one was holding it up in victory. Were they ripping it into pieces so they each got some? What were they doing?

Then I saw the bouquet come out of the crowd. Behind the flowers I saw a dark leathery face and loony bright eyes.

I was distracted for a moment by Jennifer, who was still standing up on the chair, and who had started to laugh and point. When I looked back to the group of inmates still collected, I spotted what Jennifer was laughing at. Behind the colorful flowers I saw Springtime with the biggest grin on her face, the recipient of the bridal bouquet.

Epilogue

If I had been present at the creation, I would have given some useful hints for the better arrangement of the Universe.

Alfonso the Wise, King of Castile

I didn't feel sorry for myself despite all that I had gone through. And I didn't feel sorry for Tom Branston when he was disbarred, or when he found out that he was virtually penniless due to Cher's shenanigans. I never spoke to Donald again, and I never asked for a pardon from the governor, because I was guilty. Not as guilty as Donald, who has never been punished, but if I had learned anything at Jennings, it was that there may be plenty of laws but there's very little justice.

I have been luckier than most. I was born with a good brain, I was raised by my own mother, I managed to get into university and even graduate school. That it was the wrong one, and that I wasted some years on Wall Street, doesn't seem like a major mistake compared to the mistakes that other people make with their lives. And I did learn how the system works as I combated the system. Certainly, my time at Jennings wasn't wasted. I learned the value of liberty, something I had always taken for granted. I learned about injustice, and how prevalent it is. I had the chance to reevaluate the importance of money versus human needs. In this country, in this century, financial considerations will virtually always win out over human ones, but Jennings put me on another path. My work now is focused on helping other women, women not so lucky as I.

Mostly, I raise funds. Movita Watson is now the director of the outreach program that we've created. My husband has worked hard to get us the not-for-profit status that we need. He's started his own practice, which makes his time as flexible as mine is. Sometimes, on very busy days, he'll watch the twins. Otherwise I take them to the office or drop them with Suki, who is running a day-care center. Roger's quit his job as a correctional officer and is now a guard for Brinks Security.

Cher is still on Wall Street. So far she hasn't been arrested for stock fraud, insider trading, or alienation of affection. At last count she'd had three affairs with moguls, and she's a big contributor to our outreach program. 'Nobody ever gave me nothin',' she says, tough as ever, 'but since it's tax deductible, I may as well.'

Theresa has opened a restaurant with one of her innumerable sisters, or maybe it's her cousin, or her sister-in-law. It's in Brooklyn, and we all get together there at least once a month and eat 'macaroni and gravy' and drink too much red wine.

Gwen Harding now heads the State Corrections Authority and is engaged to be married! And to a judge! We could hardly believe the news when we heard it but Gwen says she can hardly believe it either. Movita was the first one to meet him and she says he's a pretty good guy for a judge. We all expect to meet him at a party they're throwing in Albany next month.

And finally, there's Maggie Rafferty. I visit her regularly, and she seems happy and busy in her many roles at Jennings. She runs our outreach program from Inside and feeds inmates into our programs as they become ready for them. If I have any regret at all, it's that I couldn't get Margaret Rafferty out of prison. But her case was simply too high profile and other members of the Rafferty family (not her sons) were too politically connected to allow it. While men murder their spouses at an alarming rate, women who kill the men in their lives are rarely forgiven. It's dreadful to imagine that Maggie will end her life in Jennings, but she does seem adjusted to that fact, and to be, to some extent, at peace.

The sale of JRU back to the state made Maggie a tidy sum of money, but she donates virtually all of it to various programs protecting women caught in the legal system. And, in the last two years or so, a change has come over her. She seems, in a way, to have transcended her physical boundaries. I don't know if it's my imagination or if it's true, but she seems to have found some kind of peace that makes me think of the saints I read about back in parochial school. She seems not just satisfied but actually fully realized, and, although incarceration is a cruel punishment, after all these years it seems as if Maggie Rafferty has found a mission and a raison d'être. She's godmother to both of my twins as well as Christina, and I know Suki plans to ask her to be godmother to the new baby as soon as it's born.

Movita's eldest, Jamorah, has just aced her SATs – with

a little help from her friends – and plans to become an attorney instead of a fashion designer as she had once planned when she was younger. Talitha has also been doing well. The youngest, Kiama, has been diagnosed with a learning disability. Now she's being tutored three times a week.

As I said, I have no regrets. I'm not as optimistic as Theresa, who believes that everything is part of God's plan, but I do know that serving time in Jennings has brought me my life's mission, my husband, my best friends, and my little boys, Tyler and Bryce. Needless to say, Maggie dotes on them and is their honorary grandma, since my mom is dead.

I think now that my mother would be proud of who I am, and though I know I can never do enough, at least I'm doing something. I'm busy all the time. Of course, there are times when I'm overwhelmed, depressed, particularly exhausted, or upset. But those are the times that Lenny reminds me of what Thomas Jefferson wrote: 'Eternal vigilance is the price of liberty.'

Acknowledgments

Of all of the novels that I have written in my career, I must admit that *Insiders* has been the most difficult. *You* try to write a charming, uplifting, funny, and empowering story about a woman who wrongly goes to jail! I wrote this book to expose some of the evils and inequities that exist in the prison system, but I felt certain I could find the fun and dark humor of strong women being taken advantage of by a bad system (as I have previously done in *First Wives Club*, *Flavor of the Month*, *Fashionably Late*, and *Young Wives*). But in doing my research for *Insiders* I found there was very, very little that was charming, uplifting, or empowering in prison. What I learned within prisons, from prisoner advocates, prison superintendents, inmates, and correction officers has helped in the creation of this novel, but a great deal of pain and misery had to be jettisoned. The characters are, I hope, lifelike, funny, and inspiring; but their situations (except for the most desperate parts) are far better than what real inmates experience. It is important for readers (and all women) to be aware of our incarcerated sisters and to know that:

- Women are the fastest growing sector of the entire prison population. Since 1980, the female inmate population nationwide has increased more than 500 percent.
- Health care for female prisoners is incredibly insufficient. (Pap smears, mammograms, annual gynecological checkups, are almost nonexistent.) It is common practice for prisoners to be denied medical examinations and treatments.
- Every time a woman is incarcerated her innocent children are also punished. They are sent to family members or – tragically – sent out to foster care.
- Women prisoners spend, on average, seventeen hours a day in their cells with only one hour outside for exercise (far less than for male prisoners).
- Despite the minimal services, it annually costs more to send a woman to prison than to Harvard University.
- Privatization of prisons is creating a female slave labor force. (Prisoners are forbidden by law to unionize or strike.) Unprotected by minimum wage laws or the Fair Labor Standards Act, they cannot voice complaints or even refuse to work without receiving *severe* retaliation.

It takes a special kind of person to do good work in a prison, jail, correctional facility, or whatever you choose to call the walls that incarcerate women. To choose to be locked inside a building full of misery, addiction, illness, and pain, where there is virtually no privacy, and where you – as an employee or volunteer – experience the heartbreaks of so many women, takes tremendous courage. To witness the pain of the return of a previously released inmate, when family or friends don't arrive for visitor's day, when early release is jeopardized by a single mindless act, or when bad news from the Outside is received, is more difficult than most people can imagine, much less bear. Without the assistance of those listed below, I wouldn't have been able to interview inmates, tour facilities, obtain necessary statistics or the 'insider' information that I needed to write this book. So, special thanks to:

Randy Credico of the William Moses Kunstler Fund for Racial Justice, a hero who has worked at freeing more unjustly imprisoned women than anyone else I know.

Kathyrn Watterson, author of *Women in Prison,* for the definitive book on the subject, as well as her generous permission to quote from it.

Andi Rierden, author of *The Farm,* a human and humane look at female prisoners.

Robert Gangi, executive director of the Correctional Association of New York, for his insights, as well as his entrée to prisons and halfway houses in New York and elsewhere.

Jennifer Wynn, director of the Prison Visiting Project, for her help in doing the difficult work necessary to get clearance for me to visit women prisoners.

Mishi Faruquee, director of Women in Prison Project. Keep up the good work.

Margaret Owens, executive director of the National Center for Women in Prison. Thanks for being there, and for the tremendous job you do.

New York State Senator Velmanette Montgomery of the 18th Senate District in Albany. Thanks also to Sandy Stewart, her able administrator.

Superintendent Eleine Lord of Bedford Hills. Her savvy, compassion, and wisdom impressed me enormously (and I'm not so easily impressed).

Superintendent Wayne Strack of Fishkill Correctional Facility for allowing us to tour the Beacon, New York, women's prison.

Superintendent Susan Schultz of the Beacon Correctional Facility for Women, who not only gave us a tour but also gave us lunch and free access to talk with inmates.

The Prison Activist Resource Center of Berkeley, California. Their tremendous work on behalf of prisoners all over the U.S. and the statistics that they have gathered were absolutely invaluable.

Nan Robinson, my able and loving (as well as much beloved) editorial assistant, who toured many facilities with me (and the Cheshire County Department of Corrections in Westmoreland, New Hampshire, without me).

Superintendent Richard N. Van Wickler of the Cheshire County Department of Corrections for giving Nan Robinson a personal tour of his facility and for taking the time to explain procedures, observation areas, Special Holding Units (which I am glad to report have been turned into storage closets), and for answering so many of our questions. Thanks too, to the staff: Kerry, Penny, Julie, and the many COs, and the medical staff Nan met during the tour.

Nan would like to extend a special thank-you to the group of women who were housed in the Cheshire County

Department of Corrections at the time of her visit for allowing her to walk through their wing, watch a little television, and – most important – to be interviewed during their lunch time.

The book is, unfortunately, unworthy of the subject. So, most important of all, I would like to thank the women inmates who took the time and made the effort to talk with me despite cynicism, depression, or fear. Ironically, I cannot give copies of this novel to any facilities until it comes out in the paperback edition because hardcover books are considered contraband (items can be hidden in the book binding). But in the meantime, women on the Inside need to be visited by women from the Outside. And while I took small gifts to many of the women I visited, I received so much more than I gave.

Special thanks to the inmates in the Beacon Horticultural Program who gave me the terrific houseplants. They are still going strong, despite my black thumb. I have one on my kitchen windowsill and I like to think of the plants as expressions of the strength of the women who helped to start and nurture the seedlings.

A final thanks to Tracy Fonville, an inmate sentenced to an unjust twenty-three-year sentence, and who was released early. Our joy at meeting in front of Rockefeller Center had to be experienced before I could write about newfound freedom with any truth.

On the last page I list a few books that I recommend to readers who want to be more aware of the prison problem in America. And I remind us all that:

He that judges without informing himself to the utmost that he is capable, cannot acquit himself of judging amiss.

John Locke, *An Essay Concerning Human Understanding*

Recommended Reading

Books:

The Farm: Life Inside a Women's Prison. Andi Rierden. University of Massachusetts Press.

Women in Prison: Inside the Concrete Womb. Kathryn Watterson, Meda Chesney-Lind. Northeastern University Press.

The Celling of America: An Inside Look at the U.S. Prison Industry. Daniel Burton-Rose, Dan Pens, Paul Wright, eds. Common Courage Press.

Criminal Injustice: Confronting the Prison Crisis. Elihu Rosenblatt, ed. South End Press.

Live from Death Row. Mumia Abu-Jamal. Avon.

Lockdown America: Police and Prisons in the Age of Crisis. Christian Parenti. Verso.

Race to Incarcerate. Mark Maurer. New Press.

States of Confinement: Policing, Detention, and Prisons. Joy James, ed. Palgrave.

Articles/pamphlets:

'The Prison Industrial Complex.' Eric Schlosser. *Atlantic Monthly*, December 1998.

BAD BOY

To Nunzio Nappi

As long as I can sit in the front seat

Acknowledgments

A special nod to all the natural-born bad boys who helped with their contributions: Nick Ellison, Ivan Reitman, Tom "My-Sister-Bought-Your-Apartment" Pollack, Michael Chinich, Dan Goldberg, Joe Medjik, Jeff "Ice" Berg, Cliff Gilbert-Lurie, Skip "Bait-and-Switch" Brittenham, Paul "No Coast" Mahon, Bert Fields, Lenny Gartner, Dwight "The-Mean-One" Currie, Jim "Lincoln-Logs" Ragliamo, Tom LaPoint, Jerry "Rat-on-Acid" Balargeon, Carl "CJ" Benenati, Philip "Frisky" Kain, Justin Levy, Andy Fisher, Paul "Hang-'Em-High" Toner, not to mention Miracle Relocators—Nissim, Keith, and Patrick.

And thanks as well to all the bad boy wannabe men: Bob "You-Keep-the-Money" Levinson, Ross "She-Called-Me-a-Dick" Cantor, Alan "The Sweetie" Ladd, Jr., Lewis Allen, Jerry "Let's-Do-It" Offsay, John Moser, Harold "Just-One-More" Sokol, Tony the Line Dog, Jeff Kreutziger, Paul "The Dozer" Rothmel, Ed Harte, Michael "Hatrick" Elovitz, Peter "Overshoes" Davis, Ben Dower, Lenny Bigelow, Michael "The-Nice-One" Kohlmann, Charlie "You Write-'Em-I-Buy-'Em" Crowley, Mohammed Rahman, Eric Breitbart, Howard "Just-One-More-Bill" Schwartz, David "Oh-That-Ginkgo!" Gandler, Louis "Editors! I-Hate-Editors!" Aronne, all the guys from James Lee Construction, Kami Ashrafi, Efrain Butron, and Herb Gruberger, my drivers from Mirage, Rob "Temple Bar" Hundley, and Anthony "Just-a-Little-Longer" Susino at Louis Licari.

An extra special nod to all the women in my life that have put up with or do put up with bad boys. Sherry Lansing, Barbara "Returning-My-Call" Dreyfus, Nancy Josephson, Ann Foley, Jacki Judd, Barbara Howard, Laurie Sheldon, Jay Presson Allen, Rachel Dower, Ali Elovitz, Susan "Slugmeister" Jedren, Lorraine "Marysue" Kreahling, Sara "The Equalizer" Pearson, Lynn "Have-I-Got-a-Guy-for-You" Phillips, Linda Grady, Jane Sheridan, Deborah Levitt, Kathy Isoldi, Lisa

Welti, The Bitch of Perkinsville, Rosie Sisto, Carol Sylvia, Robinette Bell, Debbie, Katie, and Nina LaPoint, Nancy Lee Kingsbury-Robinson-Delano, Rita Benenati, Pat Rhule, Judy Aqui-Rahim, Freeway, Mary Ann Chiapperino, Gladys, Rebekah, and Sarah Ashrafi, Lynn Goddel at Louis Licari, Edith Cohen at Marc Tash, and Mary Ellen "Bring-It-on-Home" Cashman. Special thanks to Martine Rothblatt who can put herself into any of the above categories that she chooses to. Last but not least, Louise and both Margarets.

Thanks also to the Canine Americans in my life: Mish "The Fish" Dubinofsky-Romanoff, Spice "The Rack" Escobar, New Baby "Jelly Roll" Levinson, Lexie Elovitz, and Max "Sergeant Ryan" Delano.

A very special acknowledgment must go to Pat Handly for introducing Nan to Rose Marie Jones, an endless resource for native Seattle lingo and sights. Thanks to the Seattle-King County Convention and Visitors Bureau for the tourist maps, to Jason Stamaris a special hello and thanks for identifying the location for exchange 807. Thanks to Jeff Cravens at REI for helping me with my rock climbing terminology and for the layout of the REI store in Seattle. Another big thanks to Margaret Santa Maria of Eastern Mountain Sports in Manhattan. I'm still not going to use a fefe hook, but that's a good thing.

Finally, kudos to my new friends at Dutton: Laurie Chittenden, Carolyn Nichols, Brian Tart, Louise Burke, Lisa Johnson, Michael McKenzie, and Carole Baron. Here's to all of you!

Bad Boy

Chapter 1

The sky was the same gray-white as the skim milk Tracie poured into her coffee. But that was what she loved about Seattle. It definitely wasn't Encino, where the sky was always a glorious blue, as empty of clouds as her house had been empty of people. As an only child with parents in "The Industry," Tracie had spent too many hours staring at that sky. No more empty blue for her. It made her feel as if she should be happy when she wasn't. Here in Seattle, any happiness against the overcast arc above seemed a reward.

Before Tracie had come here to college, she'd considered East Coast schools, but she wasn't brave enough for them. She'd read about Dorothy Parker, Sylvia Plath, and the Seven Sisters. Uh-uh. She knew, though, that she wanted out of California and far enough away from home that weekend visits wouldn't be possible. Unlike the heroine in a fairy tale, she couldn't say that her stepmother was wicked. Just passive-aggressive. So she'd picked the University of Washington, and the bonus had been that, aside from a pretty good journalism school, she'd made good friends, gotten a decent job, and fallen in love with Seattle. Not to mention that when the music scene got hot, she'd found a string of drop-dead-sexy guys. Of course, Tracie admitted to herself as she took her first sip of morning caffeine, Seattle was famous for its bad boys, good coffee, and Micro Millionaires. And, staring up at the cloud-filled sky, Tracie Leigh Higgins considered herself an aficionado on all three.

Sometimes, though, she thought she had them in the wrong positions: Maybe she ought to quit the bad boys completely, cut back on the coffee, and start dating the Micro Millionaires. Instead, she got serious with bad boys, guzzled lattes, and only interviewed and wrote about Micro Millionaires.

Tracie looked up at the sky once more. Her boyfriend, Phil, was giving her problems again. Maybe I should quit coffee, date the Micro and Gotonet guys, and write novels about the bad boys, she thought, and considered the idea as she stirred a little skim milk into her brew. She considered one of the chocolate and yellow-cake muffins, but then she scolded herself because they were addictive and she was off them for good. Somewhere in the back of her mind, Tracie realized it was either the thought of giving up Phil or writing a book that made her so upset she craved comfort. Did she have the courage to quit her day job to write books? And what did she have to write about? Too embarrassing to write about her ex-boyfriends, she decided. Tracie loved the quiet time she spent each morning reading out-of-town papers and staring out the coffeehouse window, but she'd be late if she didn't get moving. She had another Nettie profile to write. Boring.

She took another sip from the cup and glanced at her watch. Wait. Maybe I should quit bad boys and write about coffee. . . . It was all too confusing this early in the morning. She was a night person. She couldn't sort out life issues this early in the day. She'd wait until next New Year's to make some resolutions. Today, she had a deadline. She had to finish the article about one more Seattle TechnoWunderkind.

Then she'd see Phil.

Tracie tingled at the last part of her thought and picked up the coffee, which was now an almost-undrinkable temperature. She took a last gulp anyway and wondered if she could leave work early to get her hair done before seeing Phil.

She pulled out a Post-it notepad and wrote, "Call Stefan for a c,w & bd," then gathered her purse and backpack and walked to the door.

But as Tracie walked down the *Times* hallway, she was stopped by Beth Conte, eye-roller extraordinaire. "Marcus has been looking for you," Beth hissed. Even though Tracie knew Beth was a drama queen, her stomach took a little dive, and the coffee in it didn't like the plunge. The two of them kept walking toward Tracie's cubicle. "He's on the warpath," Beth added unnecessarily.

"Is that term politically correct?" Tracie asked Beth. "Or would it be considered a slur on Native Americans?"

"Putting Marcus in any ethnic group would be a slur on them. What is he, anyway?" Beth asked her as the two of them hurried along the corridor. "He's not Italian-American. I know that," she added, putting up her hands as if to defend her own ethnic background.

"He sprang from Zeus's forehead," Tracie conjectured as they turned the last corner and entered her cubicle at last.

" 'Zeus's forehead'?" Beth echoed. "Is Marcus Greek? What are you talking about?"

Tracie took off her raincoat, hung it on the hook, and stowed her purse under the desk. "You know, like Diana. Or was it Athena?"

"Princess Diana?" Beth asked, wrong and one beat behind, as usual.

This was what happened if you talked Greek mythology with Beth before 10:00 A.M. (or after 10:00 A.M.). Tracie took her sneakers off, threw them under her desk, and rooted around for her office shoes. She was about to explain her joke when the doorway to her cubicle was darkened by Marcus Stromberg's bulky form. Tracie pulled her head out from under her desk and hoped he hadn't had more than a few seconds look at her butt. She pushed her feet into her pumps. Facing Marcus barefoot was more than she could bear.

"Well, thanks for the lead," Beth squeaked, and slipped out of the cubicle.

Tracie gave Marcus her best I-graduated-cum-laude smile and sat down as coolly as she could. She refused to be cowed by Marcus. He wasn't so tough. He was a much smaller bully than all the men that her dad worked with back in L.A. He wasn't even as big a bully as her father. Just because Marcus had hoped one day to be Woodward or Bernstein and had wound up only being Stromberg was no fault of hers.

"How kind of you to drop in," Marcus said, looking down at his wristwatch. "I hope it didn't interfere with your social schedule."

Marcus had a habit of acting as if she considered herself some kind of debutante. "You'll have the profile by four," Tracie told him calmly. "I told you that yesterday."

"So I recall. But as it happens, I also need you to do a feature today."

Shit! As if she didn't have enough work to do. "On what?" Tracie asked, trying to appear unconcerned.

"Mother's Day. I need it good and I need it by tomorrow."

Tracie's beat included interviewing high-tech moguls and moguls-to-be, but, like everyone else, she was occasionally given other assignments. To make matters worse, Marcus had an uncanny knack of assigning the very story that would ruin your day. To Lily, an overweight but talented writer, he'd always assign stories about gymnasiums, anorexia, beauty pageants, and the like. To Tim, who tended to be a hypochondriac, he'd assign stories on new hospital wings, treatments. Somehow, he always found their weakness, even when it wasn't as obvious as Tim's and Lily's. Since Tracie rarely saw her family and didn't particularly like holidays, she was usually stuck covering the special occasions. And Mother's Day!

Her mother had died when Tracie was four and a half. Her father had long ago remarried, divorced, and remarried. Tracie could barely remember her mother and tried to forget her current stepmom. She considered Marcus's square jaw and the beard, which, to be accurate, should be called "10:00 A.M. shadow." "What's the angle?" Tracie queried. "Or can it be a sensitive essay on how I plan to spend Mother's Day?"

Marcus ignored her. "How Seattle celebrates its mothers. Mention a lot of restaurants, florists, and any other advertiser you can stuff into it. Nine hundred words by tomorrow morning. It'll run on Sunday."

God! Nine hundred words by tomorrow would kill any chances of fun with Phil tonight. Tracie looked at Marcus again, his curly dark hair, his ruddy skin, his small blue eyes, and wished, not for the first time, that he wasn't good-looking as well as totally obnoxious. Looks aside, Tracie made it a policy that she'd never give Marcus the satisfaction of knowing he'd upset her. So in keeping with her policy, she merely smiled. She knew that would bug him, so she tried to make it a debutante smile.

" 'As you wish,' said Wesley to the princess," she added.

"You're the only princess around here," Marcus grumbled as he turned and took himself off to darken the cubicle of some other poor journalist. Over his shoulder, he added, "And would you please try to get that Gene Banks profile fluff-free? I don't want to hear about his schnauzer."

"He doesn't have a schnauzer," Tracie called after him. Then, in a lower voice, she added, "He's got a black Lab." It was true she mentioned the Micronerds' pets and hobbies in her pieces, but that was a humanizing touch. Anyway, she liked dogs.

The phone rang, and it reminded her she'd have to call Phil about tonight, but at five after ten, it couldn't be him. He never got up before noon. She lifted the receiver. "Tracie Higgins," she said in as brisk and upbeat a voice as she could manage.

"And for that I am eternally grateful," Jonathan Delano teased. "What's wrong?"

"Oh, Marcus just had an aneurysm," Tracie told him.

"Isn't that a good thing?" Jon asked.

Tracie laughed. Jonathan always made her smile, no matter what. He had been her best friend for years. They'd met in a French class at the university. Jonathan had the biggest vocabulary and the worst accent that Tracie had ever heard. Her accent was pure Paris, but she couldn't conjugate a verb. She'd helped Jon with pronunciation and he'd helped her with grammar. They'd both gotten A's, and the partnership had thrived ever since. Only Jon or her girlfriend Laura could tell from four syllables that she was upset.

"I have a huge new assignment and I wanted to go out tonight. Plus, Laura is threatening to visit, so I gotta clean up my place."

"Famous Laura, your friend from Sausalito?"

"Sacramento, actually, but what's the dif? Yeah. She broke up with her freak boyfriend and needs some recovery time."

"Don't we all? What kind of freak was he?"

"Oh, just the usual 'I'm-sorry-I-didn't-call-you-can-I-borrow-three-hundred-dollars?-and-I-didn't-mean-to-sleep-with-your-best-friend' kind of freak."

"Oh. A freak kind of like Phil."

Tracie felt her stomach drop as if she were in the Needle elevator. "Phil's not like that. He's just having a hard time working on his writing and his music. Sometimes he needs help getting by, that's all."

Actually, Tracie more often felt Phil didn't need her help at all. While she always asked him to read her pieces, he rarely shared what he wrote. She still couldn't tell if it was because he was too sensitive to criticism, or if he didn't respect her opinion. Either way, Tracie felt attracted to that in him. His self-containment was so unlike her too-eager hunger for acknowledgment. He was cool. She was not.

Jon snorted. "Phil's a distraction from things that matter."

"Like what?"

"Um. Like the story of your mother's early death. Your complicated relationship with your father. Your *real* writing."

"What writing?" Tracie asked, playing dumb, though she'd been thinking the very same thing over coffee that morning. Jon meant well. He believed in her, but sometimes he . . . well, he went too far. "I don't do any *real* writing."

"Sometimes it creeps into the middle of a puff piece," Jon said. "Your real stuff is good. If they give you a column—"

"Ha! It will be forever before Marcus lets me have a column." Tracie sighed. "If he'd just stop cutting them and I got a few features published the way I wrote them . . ."

"You'd be a great columnist. Better than Anna Quindlen."

"Come on. Quindlen won a Pulitzer."

"So will you. Tracie, your stuff is so fresh that you'd blow everyone away. Nobody is speaking for our generation. You could be that voice."

Tracie stared at the receiver of the phone as if hypnotized. Neither one of them said anything for a moment and Tracie put the phone back to her ear. Then the spell broke. "Come on. Marcus doesn't even let my punch lines stay in my features. I'll be writing holiday features until I'm old and gray."

Jon cleared his throat. "Well, maybe if you focused more on your job . . ."

Tracie's other line rang. "Hold a minute, would you?" she asked Jon.

"I'll hold for Marcus but not for Phil," Jon said. "I have my pride."

Tracie punched the button, glad to hear Laura's soprano. "Hey ho, Tracerino. I phoned because I'm actually getting on the plane now."

"Get out. Right now?" Tracie asked. "I thought you were coming on Sunday."

"Face it. You thought maybe I wasn't coming at all. But I am. I really am. I'm just calling to say I packed up all my stuff and left my pots and pans with Susan."

"So that's it? You've told Peter?"

"I don't think I had to tell him. He saw the look on my face when I caught him going down on our next-door neighbor in our bedroom. Plus, he told me Quincy was an asshole."

Back in high school, Laura'd had a tremendous crush on Jack

Klugman. Tracie could never understand why, but sometimes the two of them drove through Benedict Canyon and staked out the house where somebody had told Laura he lived. They'd never seen him, but there wasn't an episode of *Quincy* that Laura didn't know by heart.

Tracie's eyes widened. "He didn't like Quincy?" she asked in mock horror. "And he went down on your neighbor?" she continued. "Was your neighbor a man or a woman?"

At least Laura laughed at that; it was better than tears. By Tracie's count, Laura had cried fifteen gallons' worth over Peter already. "So what's your flight number and what time should I meet you?" While Laura fumbled for the info, Tracie thought of her deadline and her date, but Laura had been her best friend for years. "I'll meet you at the airport," Tracie said, trying to assuage her guilt.

"You don't have to do that. I'm a big girl," Laura said, and laughed. Laura was six feet tall, and not skinny. "I'll just take the bus to your place," she offered.

"Are you sure?" Tracie asked.

"Yeah. I'll be fine. Besides, you've got work to do. You still get *Quincy* reruns in Seattle, don't you?" Laura added.

Tracie smiled. "Yup."

"Great. So hang up. I don't want to hold you up," Laura said.

That reminded her. "Oh no! I've got Jon on hold!" Tracie exclaimed.

"Don't worry, he's still there waiting for you. Hey, I'll get to meet the nerd at last." Laura laughed. "See you later," she said, and then hung up.

Tracie pushed the button for line one and, sure enough, Jon was still on the other end. "What's up?" he asked.

Chapter 2

"You're sure this isn't going to be inconvenient?" Laura asked, her sizable butt in the air, her head in the bottom drawer of the bureau Tracie had cleared out for her. She was putting away her T-shirts. Tracie had always marveled at how neatly Laura folded her shirts. Of course, once she put one on, it became as messy as her wild dark hair.

As she watched Laura, Tracie realized that she'd been really lonely for a girlfriend. She was pals with Beth and a few of the other women at work, but they were just work friends. Jon was her close pal, and though she adored him, it was nice to have Laura back again.

"I'm sure this *is* going to be inconvenient. Living in a one bedroom with a friend, not to mention a boyfriend as a frequent guest, is going to be very inconvenient, but it doesn't mean it's not going to be *fun*. I'm thrilled that you're here." Tracie squealed the way she had back in high school and opened her arms.

Laura gave great hugs. Sometimes, Tracie thought it was Laura's patient, listening ear and her great hugs that got her through. They had met in the seventh grade and for the next six years had spent less time apart than most married couples. In all that time, they'd never had one fight or disagreement—unless you counted the time Laura wanted to buy a dress with a fake fur bolero jacket for the junior prom. Tracie had absolutely forbidden it because (although she couldn't say so) it made Laura look almost exactly like a gorilla.

Tracie thought that they'd grown so close because they both were so needy at the time and yet so different. Laura was as tall as Tracie was short. Laura was big (God alone knew her weight) and Tracie was thin (104, but no more bulimia since she'd promised Laura not to throw up). Tracie was boyish, had almost no chest, and wore her hair short and streaked with blond. Laura was a brunette earth mother, had huge breasts and an unruly mane. Laura had always loved to cook; Tracie wasn't sure there'd been a kitchen in her Encino house.

"You can stay here as long as you want. As long as you don't bake farm cakes," Tracie told her girlfriend as they ended their hug. "I think you should move to Seattle permanently. But you do whatever you want as long as you don't go back to Peter."

"Peter, Peter Woman-eater. Hadda neighbor, hadda eat her," Laura sang.

"Was that really what he was doing when you walked in on them?" Tracie gasped.

"Sure was. Somehow, it was a lot worse than if they'd been fucking," Laura said. She stopped unpacking and sat down on the edge of Tracie's bed. "A guy can fuck a girl he doesn't even like, but he doesn't . . ." She paused and then shook her head. "Jesus, he hardly ever went down on *me*." She sighed, diving back into her bag to take out yet another perfectly folded T-shirt.

"Well, it doesn't matter," Tracie told her. "You're just never going to see him again. He's going to miss you."

"I don't know about me, but I do know he's going to miss my short ribs with braised cabbage and mango-apple-cranberry coulis." Laura laughed. "But enough about Peter. I can't wait to meet the famous Phil."

Tracie waggled her eyebrows in a poor imitation of Groucho Marx. "Well, you're not going to have to wait long. You finish unpacking while I work on this stupid feature. Then we'll get something to eat. After that, I'll take you to meet Phil at Cosmo."

"What's Cosmo?"

"It's easier to take you there than to explain it," Tracie told her friend. "You'll see tonight."

Cosmo was jammed by the time Tracie and Laura walked through its black glass double doors. It was enormous—three separate dance floors—with neon lights running along the black-painted walls and strobes and black lights picking up the slack, as if there was any. Laura eyed the scene. "An epileptic's nightmare," she quipped as they made their way to the crowded bar.

"Wait till you see the computerized light show," Tracie yelled above the din.

"They make it snow in here?" Laura yelled back.

"Light show—SHOW!" Tracie yelled, then saw by Laura's grin that she'd gotten her. "Yeah, yeah." Tracie grinned back.

Cosmo was bustling with habitués, all under thirty, thinking they were terminally hep. Personally, Tracie always thought there was something weird about the jeunesse dorée of Seattle. They had a lot more money and a lot less style than people in L.A. or other places Tracie had been, but she liked them for it. They either looked like they had forgotten to dress up before they went out or as if they'd put themselves together for some convention. In fact, the majority of Seattle young people seemed like Trekkies who had recently transferred their manic interest to some other sphere. Now a swing band was playing and couples danced, many of them in forties zoot suits and period dresses. Tracie thought the dresses were kind of cool actually, but otherwise, she just didn't get it.

"Me, neither," Laura said, as if Tracie had spoken her thoughts aloud.

Tracie picked up her drink, tossed it back, and tried to order another. Phil was late, as usual.

"Hey, how many of those did you have? And it's not even midnight yet," Laura commented.

"I'm just . . . uptight. You know, Mother's Day weekend always bothers me," Tracie admitted. And the story. And Marcus. And Phil being late. And . . .

"Look, take it from me: Having a mother can suck, too," Laura told her, and put her arm around Tracie's shoulder.

Tracie stood on a rung of the bar stool to look over the crowd. Her hair fell in her eyes and that, along with the lights, made it impossible to see. No Phil. Instead, Tracie motioned for another drink, and this time the bartender saw her. "I'd just like to know that I'm going to go home with Phil tonight and cocoon tomorrow in bed."

"While I quietly weep on my cot," Laura said, then added, "Hey, you deserve it, working so hard on that Mother's Day story. Marcus shouldn't have assigned it to you. It's totally harshed your buzz."

"Newspaper editors are rarely noted for their sensitivity. And my roommates always have big mouths."

"I'm not a roommate," Laura interjected. "I'm only visiting till I get over Peter."

"God! That'll take years."

"No. It took years to get over *Ben*." Laura stopped, considered, and continued. "It'll just be months to get over Peter. Unless he calls and begs."

"Tell him to drop dead."

"What?"

"Tell him to forget it."

"Regret it?" Laura yelled.

Tracie pulled out a Post-it notepad—she was never without one—and scribbled on it. She slapped it on the bar. It read "*Just Say No.*" In a corner, a group of die-hard punk rock musicians sat in a booth. They were sucking down beers. "The Swollen Glands," Tracie said, and indicated to Laura. "Phil's band."

"Well, they don't look like my type, but it's better than sitting here. Let's join 'em," Laura suggested. "Maybe they'll buy us a drink."

"Yeah, maybe they'll win a Congressional Medal of Honor, too." The two girls made their way through the crowd and over to the group in the corner.

"Hi, guys," Tracie said. "Glands, this is Laura. Laura, the Glands." Tracie sat down next to Jeff.

"This music sucks," Jeff, the regular Glands bass player, said.

"Yo, Tracie. Doesn't this suck?" Frank, the drummer, asked as Laura took the seat beside him. There was a silence until a beautiful blonde walked by.

"Yum, yum. Come to papa. I've got something for ya," Jeff said.

"Forget her. She works with me at the *Times*. She's a barracuda."

"Well, I've got something I'd like to hook her with," Jeff said.

"Now I know which Gland you are," Laura said. She turned to Frank. "And you? Lymph, perhaps?"

There was a commotion at the door. Tracie brightened as Phil entered. She gave Laura a look, and Laura turned her head. "God. He *is* tall. And good-looking." Tracie nodded. Her guy had a lot of grace and charm—when he wanted to use it. In his hand was a bass guitar, but she was disturbed to see that beside him was an extremely thin, pretty woman. The two made their way through the crowd and approached the corner table. "He doesn't walk," Laura said. "He swaggers. And who's the skank? Heavenly Host, he's worse than Peter."

"You haven't even met him yet," Tracie protested, though she was already nervous about the so-called skank herself. "Give me a break."

"Hey, girl. I got out late from rehearsal." Phil put his arm around Tracie.

"Phil, this is Laura," Tracie said, introducing them. Uh-oh, one look at Laura's face and Tracie recognized her mood. It was overly protective. She was staring at Phil as if instead of being late and accompanied by this nobody he had thrown acid on her face. Laura tended to overreact in situations like this. On the other hand, Tracie had the same tendency when Laura was being mistreated.

"Hi, Phil. Nice to meet you, too. Oh! And what have you brought us? Your tuning fork?" Laura asked. Tracie gave Laura a discreet kick in the ankle. When Laura had gone too far with Tracie's wicked stepmother (known to them always as W.S.M. and never Thelma), Tracie had used the same editing system. No one had hated her stepmother as much as Laura—not even Tracie herself.

As if dealing with Laura, Phil, and the skank wasn't enough, Allison drifted over, too. Just because she had to work with Allison at the *Times* didn't mean she had to introduce her to anyone.

"Hi, Tracie," Allison said.

It was the first time Tracie could remember Allison saying hello to her or anyone. She wasn't even nice to Marcus, and he never gave *her* deadlines.

In a way, Tracie knew she should feel complimented and she did. Phil was so attractive and had so much presence. His height, his clothes, his hair, and his attitude all worked. Hey, they had worked on her, and she had snagged him, and she was thrilled every time she looked at him. But, other women were constantly being snagged as well and she had to be ever vigilant regarding her potential rivals and Phil's attitude toward them. Luckily, he was so used to female attention that he usually ignored it. Tracie sighed. She would have to introduce them. "Laura, Frank, Jeff, Phil, this is Allison." And even though she knew she shouldn't, Tracie looked at Phil and said, "And this would be . . ."

"This is Melody," Phil said. "She needed a ride over here."

"From where? Your apartment?" Tracie asked, and then wanted to bite her tongue.

Laura shifted slightly in her seat, so there was no room for anyone else at the banquette. Tracie had to hand it to her friend. Phil still ignored Laura as he tightened his embrace around Tracie's shoulder. "You look like a warm stove on a cold night," he whispered into her ear. "See you later, babe," he said to Melody, who was then forced, albeit reluctantly, to melt into the crowd.

Tracie eyed the girl's back as she left.

"Unchained Melody," Laura muttered with satisfaction.

"Righteous Brothers. 1965. Phillies label," Jeff said.

Best to just ignore her and what might have gone on, put it away, like a sweater at the back of the closet in summer. Not that she wouldn't hear all about it from Laura later. "So, are you playing tonight?" she asked Phil.

"Yeah. Bob is letting me do the second show."

Bob led the Glands, but not for long, if Phil had his way. "Great!" Tracie said, distracted. She looked back into the crowd to see if Melody was hanging around. She didn't seem to be, which was a relief. Tracie trusted Phil, but only within certain parameters. She'd better stay the whole night, then. When you mixed music, alcohol, and Melody, you were outside the parameters. "When is Bob arriving?"

"Well, there's the question," Phil said with a frown.

"Which Gland is he?" Laura asked. "The adrenal? The pituitary?"

"The asshole," Phil said.

"Oh. Then that would more properly be called 'the anal gland,' " Laura said smoothly.

Though Phil was the newest member, he was already jockeying to be leader. But why he would want it, Tracie could not fathom. It seemed like a lot of work: begging for unpaid jobs with club owners, making endless phone calls about rehearsals, begging vans from friends to schlep equipment—all just to pick the lineup of songs. Big deal. She supposed picking the lineup would be fun, but she couldn't imagine Phil organizing everything else. She thought, There must be a responsible side to him after all.

"You know," Jeff said for what had to be the three hundredth time, "I'm not so sure about our name." Tracie looked up to the ceiling and sighed. When the guys weren't fighting with one another or rehearsing or drinking, they spent their time arguing over the band's name. Tracie had managed to do a feature about them—overcoming a lot of resistance from Marcus—and she'd used the latest name that they had agreed upon: Swollen Glands. But now, once again, Jeff voiced an objection. "I saw this sign, and it was really cool," he continued. "Up in the mountains. They had them everywhere. It just said FROST HEAVES. Great name, huh? And, like, free advertising. Cool, huh?"

"How about Watch for Curves?" Laura joked.

"Nah," Jeff said, serious. "Too limp."

"Well, there's always Yield to Pedestrians," she suggested.

"There's nothing wrong with Swollen Glands," Phil said. "I thought of it, and anyway, the name's in the paper. We don't want to stop the swell of publicity that's building. Right, Tracie?"

Tracie didn't have the heart to mention that one article was more a pimple than a swell and that tomorrow there'd be another band in the paper. "Right," she said, and caught Laura rolling her eyes. She hoped Phil hadn't seen it.

Luckily, Phil was trying to get the bartender to fix him a drink. He then nuzzled closer and whispered into Tracie's ear, "I'm happy to see you."

Sometimes, Phil was a jerk. And Tracie knew he probably wasn't ready to make a commitment, but there was something about his wild good looks, the way his hair brushed across his cheek, the way his fingers hardly tapered, but instead came to an end in flat, smooth nails. Phil was heat to her coolness and passion to her planning, and sometimes he made her forget all of the bad. Tracie responded to his whisper with a blush.

Laura picked up on Tracie's blush and shook her head. "I think I'll try to buck the trend and do something socially responsible, like picking up a merchant seaman. Later," she said as she boogied off into the crowd.

"What's up her ass?" Phil asked Tracie.

She just shrugged and sighed. It was too much to expect her friend to like her boyfriend and vice versa. She turned to her laptop. She'd completed her profile at work and begun the Mother's Day feature, but she still had some polishing to do on it.

One of the things Tracie really liked about Phil was that he was also a writer. But, unlike her, he didn't write commercially. He was an artist. Phil wrote very, very short stories. Some less than a page. Often Tracie didn't get them, but she didn't admit that to him. There was something about his work that was so personal, so completely contemptuous of an audience, that she respected him.

Although Phil had roommates, and had always had a girlfriend, Tracie knew he was essentially a loner. He could probably spend five years on a desert island and when a ship landed to rescue him he'd look up from his writing or his guitar and say, "This is not a good time for me to be interrupted." He'd certainly said that enough to her, and she respected his integrity.

Sometimes she thought that journalism school and her job had spoiled her talent. After years of being told, "Always consider who might be reading your work," she found Phil's commitment refreshing, even if he looked down on writers like herself who took on commercial subjects.

Now she knew exactly who would be reading her feature: suburbanites over morning coffee; Seattle hipsters munching bagels at brunch; old ladies at the library. Tracie sighed and bent her head to get closer to the screen.

After just a minute or two Phil nudged her. "Can't you put that down and enjoy the scene?"

"Phil, I told you I have to finish this feature. If I don't get it in on time, Marcus will pull me off features altogether. He'd love the excuse. Or I could lose my job," she snapped.

"That's what you say about every story," Phil snapped back. "Stop living in fear."

"I mean it. Look, this feature is really important to me. I'm trying to do something unusual about Mother's Day."

"Hey, you don't even have a mother," Jeff announced.

Tracie turned to Jeff as if he was a child. "Yes, Jeff, it's true that my mother died when I was very young. But, you see, journalists don't always write about themselves. Remember, I wrote an article about you guys? Yet I'm not a Swollen Gland. Not even a mammary.

Sometimes, journalists write about current events. Or they report on other people's lives. That's why they call us 'reporters.' "

"Wow. The irony is so heavy in here, it's breaking my drumsticks," Frank said.

"Man, what time do we go on?" Jeff asked.

"Not till two, man," Frank told them.

Tracie kept herself from groaning. Two! They wouldn't be out of here until dawn.

"God. Was that the best Bob could do?"

"I hope these jerks clear out by then and we get a decent crowd," Phil said.

"I'm sure you will. The Glands are really building a following," Tracie assured him. She herself felt no such thing. In fact, the crowd could turn ugly if you cut off their supply of big-band standards.

Laura emerged from the dance floor, a short guy dressed like a forties bookie close behind her. Tracie noticed that a lot of small men went for Laura. The attraction was definitely not mutual. "Mind if we join you all? Or do you turn into rats and pumpkins at midnight?"

"Rats and Pumpkins. That would be a good name," Frank commented.

Tracie looked at her watch. "Oh God. I've got to get this in." She turned back to the laptop.

The band members were still giving one another glum looks. More dead soldiers littered the tabletop. Tracie snapped her laptop shut.

"This music sucks, man," Frank repeated to the uninterested table.

"Yeah, it sucks," Jeff echoed.

"Thank you for this introduction to Seattle. The conversation here really is a lot more sophisticated than in Sacramento," Laura quipped.

Tracie looked up. "It all gets better when my work is done and the guys play," she promised. She started to stand up.

"Where ya going?" Phil asked.

"I have to fax this to Marcus at home," Tracie explained.

"Hey, don't leave the table," Phil said, catching her hand. "You're making the band look bad. Don't you realize other girls would die to sit here with us?"

Tracie shrugged and laughed. It wasn't easy to find modem service in a bar. It would be hard enough to find a Yellow Pages, listing a twenty-four-hour copy center. Phil was being cute but difficult, and she couldn't afford to get Marcus in an uproar. She'd have to do what was necessary to get her piece in and hope Phil would relax. If she could leave, she'd get back before the band's performance. There'd be hell to pay with a pouting Phil for the rest of the night if she didn't get back in time.

When she finally returned twenty minutes later, a swing-dance girl was in her seat. "I made it in just under the wire," Tracie said, standing beside the table.

"Congratulations," Jeff said, handing her a beer.

"So what's new since I left?" Tracie said directly to Phil.

"Well, I hear the music still sucks, and I think there's a new mascot," Laura told her.

Tracie tapped the girl on her shoulder to get her seat back, shooting Phil a dirty look because he should have told the girl to move. "Hey, it's not my fault," Phil protested as the young woman walked away.

"I don't know why these bitches want to dress up like Betty Crawford anyway," Frank said.

"What assholes," Phil agreed.

Laura leaned across the table to Frank. "It isn't Betty Crawford."

"What?" he asked.

"There's no 'Betty Crawford,' " Laura informed him. "You must be the drummer, right?"

"Huh?" Frank grunted.

"There was Betty Grable and there was Bette Davis. There was also Joan Crawford. But I don't think Joan Crawford ever danced to swing," Tracie explained.

"Whatever," Jeff said.

"Yeah. Who cares? Whatever, man," Phil said to Laura.

The band began to play "Last Kiss." "Pearl Jam," Jeff said. "Epic Records. 1999."

"That was just a cover," Laura said. "It's an old fifties song."

"It is not. Pearl Jam writes all their own material," Jeff said.

"Wanna bet?" Laura asked, raising her brows in a dare.

"Why don't we bet each other a dance?" Jeff said. "Then I'll win either way." Tracie looked back at Laura, whose eyes had widened to match her brows. Wordlessly she extended her hand, and Jeff, who had to be less than half her size, took it and pulled her out onto the dance floor. God knows, Tracie thought, I'd rather give my jewelry to Allison than dance with Jeff.

"Where's Bob?" Phil asked.

"Yeah. Where is he?" Frank echoed, obviously disgusted by Jeff's departure. He and Laura were really getting into the music. Tracie had forgotten how well Laura danced. "I ask myself what would Guns N' Roses do if they were here?" Frank continued.

"Pull out an automatic weapon," Phil told him. Tracie had to laugh.

"Man, Axl Rose would turn over in his grave if he saw this," Frank added.

"Is Axl Rose dead?" Tracie asked.

The band members turned to look at her as if she was crazy. "What are you talking about?" Frank asked.

"You said he'd turn over in his grave. I just . . ."

Phil put his arm around her. "She's not smart, but she sure is beautiful," he told Frank by way of excuse, then gave Tracie a long, wet kiss.

Chapter 3

Jonathan Charles Delano rode his bicycle through the morning fog on Puget Sound. The road wound along the misty shore. He wore his Micro/Connection jacket—only given to founding staff with more than twenty thousand shares—and a baseball cap. The wind caught him broadside as he made a turn and then, as he swung into it, the wind inflated his open jacket as if it were a Mylar balloon. Riding was good therapy. Once he hit a rhythm, he could think—or not think, as he required. This morning, he desperately wanted not to think of last night—a night he'd spent standing in the rain getting stood up—or of the exhausting day ahead. He was actually reluctant to get to his destination, but he pedaled his heart out as if participating in the Tour de France. Mother's Day was always tough for him. For years now, he had been following this tradition, one he had invented out of unnecessary guilt and compassion. He figured that as Chuck Delano's son, he owed something. And anyhow, as an only child, these visits were the closest he got to extended family. Anyway, that's how he rationalized the visits.

As he pulled around the next curve of the coast road, the fog cleared all at once and a breathtaking view across the Sound opened.

Seattle appeared as green-fringed and magical as the Emerald City—and he noticed that Rainier was out, the towering mountain that reigned majestically over the city when visibility was good.

As one of the four actual natives of Seattle—it seemed everyone else had moved to the city from somewhere "back east"—he'd seen the sight a thousand times, but it never failed to thrill him. Now, though, he could only take a moment to enjoy it before he continued pedaling across Bainbridge Island and finally up to a shingled house. Jon jumped off his bike, pulled a bouquet out of the basket, and ran his fingers through his hair. He looked at his watch, cringed, and bolted up the path to the front door. The name plate on it read MRS. B. DELANO.

He knocked on the door. A heavyset middle-aged blonde in a zippered sweat suit opened the door. Jon couldn't help noticing Barbara was even bigger than last year. She had an apron on over her sweats. That made Jon smile. It was so . . . Barbara.

"Jon! Oh, Jon. I didn't expect you," she lied in the sweetest way as she hugged him. Barbara was his father's first wife, only slightly older than Jon's own mother, but somehow from a different generation.

Jon tried to be all the things he should be: in touch with his feelings, a good son, an understanding boss, a loyal employee, a good friend, a . . . Well, the list went on and on and made him tired. Being a dutiful stepson was the part that made him depressed, as well.

Something about the first Mrs. Delano really saddened him. It was her relentless cheerfulness. She seemed happy in her little cottage in Winslow, but Jon imagined that the moment he left, she'd begin to pine. Not for him—Jon knew no one pined for him—but for Chuck, Jon's father, the man she had loved and lost.

There was no reason for Jon to feel responsible, but he did, and he guessed he would always feel it, so he'd prepared in advance for this day. He brought the flowers from behind his back. "Not expect me?" he asked, as cheerful as she was. "How could you not? Happy Mother's Day, Barbara." Jonathan presented the bouquet with a flourish.

"For heaven's sake. Roses *and* gladiolus. My favorites! How did you remember?"

Jon figured this wasn't the time to tell her about his automated calendar, tickler file, or his Palm Pilot.

Barbara hugged him again. He could feel her soft bulk. She obviously didn't use the track suit on the track. "You're such a good boy, Jon." She stepped to the side to let him have access to the foyer. "Come on in. I'm making biscuits for breakfast."

"I didn't know you could bake," he lied, reluctantly. He didn't want breakfast and . . . well, once she got started, Barbara could really talk. And there were two questions he dreaded: the overly casual "Heard from your father lately?" and the even worse "Are you seeing someone special?" Though Chuck rarely communicated with Jon and though Jon almost as rarely had a date, Barbara never tired of asking. But that was probably because she was lonely. She and his father had no kids and she'd never remarried. She seemed isolated, not just on the island but in her life.

"You have to have coffee," Barbara said.

"Maybe just coffee. I don't have a lot of time. I really ought to . . ."

Barbara extended her hand and drew him into the house. "So, are you seeing anyone special?" she asked.

Jon tried hard not to flinch. If he didn't already know that the little time he spent on his personal life was a fiasco, last night would have been proof enough. He and Tracie, his best friend, had spent years trying to determine whose romantic life was less romantic. This week, he'd finally be the definitive winner. Or maybe that would make him the definitive loser. As he followed Barbara into the kitchen, he knew that whichever one it was, it wasn't good.

An hour later, Jon pushed his bicycle, careful not to skin the heels of anyone as he followed a crowd of people disembarking the Puget Sound ferry on the city side. Everyone but him seemed coupled up. Sunday morning and arm in arm with their sweeties. Except him. He sighed. He worked all the time—relentlessly as all the whiz kids. Seattle loomed over the waterfront, with its silly Space Needle and the newer towers gleaming. He mounted the bike, quickly passed the crowd, and pedaled wildly onto Fifteenth Avenue Northwest.

In less than ten minutes, Jon stopped abruptly outside a luxury apartment tower. He checked his watch, took another bouquet out of his basket—this one all tulips—and locked his bike against a parking meter. He entered the lobby of the building, an overdone mirrored space he used to visit when his dad took him for weekends. He pressed the elevator button, the door slid open, and he entered, pressing the number 12. Though it was only seconds, it seemed like a long ride.

The elevator stopped and the bell beeped as the door slid open. Jon sighed again, walked out of the elevator, and paused to gather himself. Then he knocked on an apartment door where the name below the brass knocker read MR. & MRS. J. DELANO, with the MR. & crossed out. A woman—almost middle-aged but younger and far better preserved than Barbara—opened the door. She was dressed (or even overdressed) in what Jon guessed was considered "a smart suit."

"Jonathan," the woman cooed as she took the tulips from his hand as if they were expected. "How nice."

"Happy Mother's Day, Mother," Jon said to Janet as he kissed her the way she'd taught him to: carefully on each cheek, being sure not to smudge her beautifully applied makeup.

"You don't have to call me 'Mother.' I'm hardly old enough for that," Janet replied with a little laugh. There was something about Janet's voice that had always made him feel uncomfortable. When he was younger, he'd felt that she was gently mocking him. More recently, he'd realized that she was actually flirting. "Let me just put these in water," she said. She opened the door wider to let him inside. He'd never felt comfortable with Janet.

The apartment was as overdecorated as Janet was herself. She wore way too much gold jewelry and had way too many gold buttons. The apartment had too many gold frames and too much cut glass.

When he was twelve years old and had visited his father here, she'd spent most of her time cautioning him not to touch anything.

Nothing had changed since last year except his flowers. It was frozen in time, like Janet's face or the palace in *Sleeping Beauty*. But no prince was making it up here for Janet's wake-up call. Jon liked Barbara, but he couldn't actually feel anything but pity for Janet. Now she played with the flowers in the little sink of the tiny kitchen. "Have you heard from your dad?" she asked, trying to sound casual.

"No," Jon said quietly. It was the question he most hated hearing. It made his father's exes seem vulnerable. Now he felt even more sorry for Janet and he'd have to stay longer.

"No? No surprise," she said, and her flirty voice changed and became hard. She pushed the last tulip into the vase too hard and broke the stem, though she didn't notice. "And how's *your* social life?" she asked, and Jon felt she might already know the answer wasn't good. She eyed him up and down, taking in his baggy khakis, his old sneakers, his T-shirt. Then she sighed. "Well, where shall we go for brunch?"

Jon's heart sank. "You know," he said uncomfortably, "I thought maybe we'd just have coffee here. I mean, I could afford to lose a few pounds. . . ."

"You mean *I* could," Janet said, smiling and using that flirtatious voice again. "I'm always on a diet. But since it's Mother's Day, any brunch calories I eat are exempt. Even for a stepmom."

Jon gave up and gave in. Until he left her, Jon's dad had always given in to Janet, too.

In less than ten minutes, Jon found himself standing in front of a chic Seattle café. Thank God there was no line yet, but by the time they'd finished and he'd waved good-bye to his second stepmother, more than two dozen people were waiting. Jon consulted his watch, panicked, and hopped on his bike. He pedaled like a madman, out of downtown, past the park, through the wealthier part of Seattle, and into his old neighborhood.

At Corcoran Street, Jon pulled his bike into the driveway of a brick bungalow. The house was covered in creeper and surrounded by flower beds. He ran past a well-tended bed, which reminded him to double back to the bike for yet another bouquet, the largest one.

He grabbed it and ran up to the door. There under the buzzer, the brass name plate read J. DELANO. Before he could knock, the door was thrown open by an attractive dark-haired woman who actually looked a lot like Jon.

"Jonathan!" his mother exclaimed.

"Happy Mother's Day, Mom!" Jon embraced her warmly, crushing the flowers between them.

"Right on time!" his mother said. She took the flowers and patted his cheek with obvious deep affection. "Oh, honey. Peonies! God, they're way before season. They must have cost you a fortune."

"It's okay, Mom. My allowance is bigger than it used to be."

She laughed. "But how's your appendix?" she asked.

"It's still missing—but I'm good," he said. He'd had an emergency appendectomy three years ago and it had frightened the hell out of her. She still asked about it, but it had come to mean his health in general.

"Did you see Rainier today?" she asked.

"Yes. And Mount Baker," he told her.

They went through the living room and into the kitchen. "You came alone?" she asked.

"Yes. Why?" Jon asked.

"I thought maybe you'd bring Tracie."

Jon smiled. Though he and Tracie had been close friends from the time they met, his mother still hinted or hoped they were more. Or that he'd bring some other girl—a real girlfriend—home. While all of Chuck's ex-wives focused on who Chuck's new girlfriend was, his mom focused on who Jon's girlfriend was. He knew she wanted him to be happy, and that she wanted grandchildren for herself and for him. It wasn't that Jon wouldn't love to meet a woman and settle down, it was just that women he met seemed to want to settle down with someone other than him. In his social life he was a disappointment to himself and others. He sighed. He'd have liked to oblige, but . . .

". . . This holiday's always hard on her," his mother was saying as she put the flowers in a vase.

Jon didn't bother to tell his mom that he'd thought of Tracie—sometimes he thought he thought of Tracie too much—but that she was booked up with the latest loser and her old friend from San Bernadino or somewhere.

"She was busy. But I'll see her tonight. You know, our midnight brunch."

"Well, give her my love," she told him.

"Sure," he agreed as he reached into the pocket of his jacket and pulled out a small wrapped box. He put it on the counter between them.

"Oh. A present? Jon. It's not necessary."

"I know that traditionally on Mother's Day you're supposed to steal your mom's bank card and go on a spree. I just thought this once we'd be untraditional."

Jon made a lot of money. Well, it was not a lot of money compared to what the four initial founders of his firm made, but it was a lot of money for a guy his age. And he didn't spend it on much, since he was usually too busy working to have time to shop. Plus, he didn't want anything. He had all the toys—stereos and laptops and video equipment—he could possibly want and very little time to listen, play with, or watch them. When he wasn't working, he was thinking about work or sleeping. So, for him to spend some bucks on his mother was no big deal. It was deciding what she might like that was difficult. In the end, he had let Tracie pick something out. She was great at shopping.

"You're so thoughtful. You sure didn't get that from your father." There was an uncomfortable pause, just for the tiniest moment. His father was the one subject Jon had asked that they not speak about. His mother laughed and unwrapped the gift. She held up the jade earrings. "Oh, Jonathan! I love them!" And it was clear she really *did*.

Tracie always knew stuff like that. His mother went to the hall mirror and held them up, then preened for a moment. It made Jon happy. "So, are we going to Babbette's for lunch?" she asked as she at last put the earrings on.

"Don't we always?" Jonathan responded without hesitation, despite the protests that Barbara's breakfast and Janet's brunch were making in his stomach.

"Let's capture the moment," his mother said as she grabbed her Polaroid and led Jon outside to the wisteria bush. "All I have to do is figure out the automatic timer and we're all set." She took about half an hour doing it, while he waited as patiently as he could. Then she scurried from the camera to him before the timer went off.

And, with a flash, the moment was over.

Jon was exhausted. He was only twenty-eight, but he wondered how many more Mother's Days he could survive before they killed him. He had three more stepmothers to get through, despite the three meals distending his gut. But tea, an early dinner, and a late supper were all on the agenda before he could meet Tracie at midnight. Grimly, Jon climbed on his bike and pedaled off into the Seattle rain.

Chapter 4

Tracie raised her head, trying to see the clock. She could, but that didn't help, as it clearly had been unplugged so that Phil could use the one overburdened outlet to plug in his guitar. No wonder he was always late.

Phil's apartment was a typical poet/musician's hellhole. He shared the space with two other guys, and it seemed that none of the three of them had heard of power strips, extension cords, vacuums, or the advent of dish-washing liquid. Tracie closed her eyes, turned away from the squalor, and cuddled up against Phil's warm side. She knew she had to get up, get dressed, and go meet Jon—as she did every Sunday night—but this felt so good. And today was Mother's Day. A quick wave of self-pity washed over her. She told herself she only wanted a few more moments in the gray zone between sexual exhaustion and sleep. She dozed there for a while, then slept again, and when she next awoke, the streetlights had gone on and she knew it was getting late.

She began to untangle herself from the wrinkled sheets, trying not to wake Phil. But as she stood up, Phil, only half-awake, grabbed at her with his long, long legs and pulled her back to the bed. "Come here, you," he said, and kissed her. He smelled so good—like sleep and sex and bread dough—and she responded; then her mouth guiltily pulled away. "I'll be right back," she promised, and Phil mumbled and turned over.

Tracie crept out of bed, slipped into her clothes, and snuck out to get the Sunday paper. It was already quarter past nine! God! No wonder she was ravenous. She'd better pick up some coffee, eggs, and bread for toast. Then she thought of the state of Phil's kitchen and gave up that idea. Maybe just a couple of cheese Danishes. She'd leave the cooking to Laura. Tracie felt in her jacket pocket for money. She'd only need a few dollars. Most importantly, she wanted to get the Sunday paper and see what the Mother's Day article looked like in print.

It was funny: She'd been working at the *Times* now for four years, but she still got a thrill seeing her byline. Maybe that's what kept her a journalist. She knew she could probably earn a lot more money hiring on as a technical writer at Micro/Con or any of the other high-tech companies in Seattle. But she didn't have an interest in writing manuals or ad copy. There was something magical to her about the immediacy of newspaper work. The gratification of working on an article and seeing it—with her name at the top—just a day or two later kept her hooked.

She walked to the deli closest to Phil's place. It wasn't clean, and the food wasn't good, but, as they said about Everest, it was there. Across the door was a hand-lettered sign that said HAPPY MOTHER'S DAY. She ordered a couple of coffees, bought a pint of Tropicana juice, but couldn't manage to sink to the level of the stale-looking pastries in the smudged case in front of her. She just went for a paper and called it a day. Then, even before she could leave the store, she had to look at the feature. She opened to her section. It wasn't on the front page. She began to look through it. And kept looking. Not on page two or three. Not even on the following two. Then she found it. On the bottom of six. Truncated. Overedited. Sliced and diced. Trepanned. The thing had been cut up and then stitched back together as badly as Frankenstein's monster. She actually felt sick to her stomach. Goddamn it! Tracie scanned it again. It couldn't be as bad as she thought, but it was. It really was.

She threw the rest of the paper on the counter, turned, and walked out with the Sunday section still in her hands. She almost stuffed it into the first garbage pail she saw and did go as far as crumpling it up, but her outrage was so strong, she needed to hold on to it, just to share it with Phil and look at it again. She walked through the spring night, back toward the apartment. Why did Marcus do this to her? Why did he even bother giving her an assignment if he was going to rewrite it? She could swear he did it out of spite. What was the point? She could never use this as a clip. Potential employers would think she was a moron. What was wrong with Marcus? What was wrong with *her* for putting up with Marcus? Or why did she even bother to struggle over her work? Why not just hand in bad stuff and let him revise it as much as he wanted?

She was to Phil's door when she realized she'd forgotten both the coffee and the juice, but now she didn't care. She just wanted to crawl into bed and blot out everything. It was too bad that she had to see Jon later. Usually, she looked forward to their midnight meetings. But now she felt like being alone, crawling into a hole somewhere. She couldn't go home to her apartment because Laura was there and would be cheery and busy. Of course, when she showed her the paper, Laura would get even more upset then she was, and then she'd have to spend her time calming Laura down. Laura would tell her to quit, to get a new job, one where they appreciated her. But it wasn't so easy to get a job as a journalist writing features for what the *Superman* show used to call "a large metropolitan daily." Without a nice portfolio of well-written articles, her value had actually gone down since she had left school with her masters in journalism.

Tracie sighed as she walked up the dirty stairway to Phil's apartment. She wanted to be held like an infant. She walked in the door, then through the living room, trying to ignore the month's worth of accumulated dirty dishes, the piles of clothes, CD cases, and the assorted sordid detritus of three pathetically dirty man-boys. She walked into Phil's bedroom.

"Hey, where you been?" he asked. "You took so long that my feet are getting cold. And where's my coffee?"

She sighed. Sometimes, Phil was incredibly self-involved. " 'Hello, Tracie. How did you sleep? What's wrong? Mother's Day a little tough on you?' " she began, imitating his voice. " 'Oh! Marcus, your bully editor, cut your Mother's Day feature to shit? I'm so sorry. And you worked so hard on that story.' "

He didn't show any remorse, but he sat up in bed and opened his arms. "Hey, come over here, baby."

Tracie hesitated, but the newspaper crumpled under her arm made her feel so bad that she needed comfort more than pride just at that moment. When Phil gave her *that* look, everything seemed better. He needed her, and Tracie felt so desired that work seemed instantly unimportant. She crawled in beside him. He gave her a deep, hot kiss. Tracie melted into his arms.

"Life is always hard for the artist, baby," he said, holding her tighter and starting to rub her back. "You know, I just finished another story."

"Really?" Tracie knew Phil could write only if he was inspired. He didn't believe in deadlines. "They kill your creativity," he'd said. "That's why they call them deadlines." "What's the story about?" Tracie asked shyly. Secretly, she'd always hoped he'd write something about her. But so far, he hadn't.

"I'll show it to you sometime," he said, and pressed both of his hands on either side of her spine. It was soothing. He was so much bigger than she was. It felt great to be held against his wide chest, encircled by his arms. This was what she wanted. Not sex, not words, just dumb comfort. She nuzzled against him. Then he turned her to him. "Nobody kisses like you do. You love me?"

Tracie nodded and hugged him back. "And my ironing isn't bad, either," she said. "But I have to go. I'm meeting Jon."

"Fuck Jon," he said, then lowered his voice. "No, fuck me." He nuzzled her ear. "I want you," he whispered.

"Phil, I have to go or I'm going to be late. I have to meet—"

"The computer weenie." Phil shifted his weight so that his whole length was against her. "Why don't you stay here with my weenie instead?" he asked.

"Phil, I mean it. I *have* to—"

He grabbed her again and pulled her to him. "You look so sexy right now. . . ."

"You only say that when you're horny."

"I'm horny all the time, so you always look sexy to me."

They struggled with each other until Phil was on top of her. She gave him a deep kiss. Oh, she liked him to touch her so much. When he began to unbutton her shirt, she stopped struggling. He wasn't always hot for her. Tracie was smart enough to notice that Phil withheld sex sometimes. She thought it was one of his power plays: make her want it and then pretend to be bored.

The sick part was, when he teased her it made her hotter for him. Most of the men Tracie's age were only too happy to grab her and stuff their thing inside her. Phil was the first man she'd known who knew how to hold off until she was almost ready to beg for it. She shivered just a little, but he was close enough to feel it. "I know you like me," he whispered. "You can't help it, can you?"

"No," she murmured, and he lifted her at the hips and pulled off her jeans as if she were no heavier than an infant. He ran his tongue from her knees all the way up to her breasts.

"So pink and so pretty," he said, and she felt a little thrill run from the back of her neck directly to her groin. He hooked his thumb under the elastic. "These always remind me of those frilly paper things that cupcakes come in." He kissed her again. "Come to me, my little cupcake." For an insane moment, Tracie thought about the farm cakes she craved, but when Phil moved his thumb elsewhere, she was right back to business.

And business was good.

Tracie's eyelids fluttered open. She hadn't meant to fall asleep again, but the sex had been so good, and being held by Phil and slipping off to sleep after a really satisfying orgasm had been too hard to resist. Not a bad way to spend Mother's Day, or any day, for that matter.

She remembered Jon again. She sat up and began to gather her clothes. Phil groaned, rolled over, and grabbed her back. He put the side of his face in the crook of her neck so that his mouth was just at her ear. "If you didn't have to leave," he whispered in her ear as he caressed her arm, "I'd be tempted to start kissing you right here." He was quiet while he kissed the nape of her neck, then her shoulder. His breathing was getting heavier. "I'd move my way down to your nipples and then I'd . . ."

Tracie felt Phil's erection against her leg. "Still playing hard to get?" Tracie asked.

"Hard, anyway. And you know why? Because of you, baby."

Tracie reached down to the inside of Phil's leg. "Oh, yes," she cooed. She took one hand and began to kiss his fingers. But then she stopped. "What is this?" She held up his hand. They both looked at it. A phone number was scrawled in blue pen across his palm.

"Uh." There was a tiny pause, the shortness of which only an experienced girlfriend could interpret. Was it the pause to remember or the pause to make up a plausible lie? "One of the guys' new phone numbers. From the band," Phil said.

"An 807 exchange? You're telling me this is a Gland's phone number?" she asked. "Frank's? Jeff's? I don't think so. Since when did they move to Centralia?" She looked at Phil, hoping to see truth in his eyes.

"Jeff moved awhile ago," he said, pulling away from her. He swung his long legs over the side of the mattress, sat up, and reached over to the night table for a cigarette. "I have to call him about rehearsal tomorrow," he told her.

"Whose number is it, Phil?" Tracie asked. She picked up the phone, prepared to dial.

"Jeff's," he said, his back still to her. He lit a match, sucked in a deep lungful of smoke.

She hated him right then. She wasn't stupid, after all. It was probably the phone number of that skinny little girl from Friday night. She should have known! She began to dial. "Phil, if I dial this number and I don't get Jeff, I'm going to cut off your hand, so your penis never has a friend again."

"Go ahead, baby," Phil said calmly as he did a French inhale. "Of course, you'll look like a psycho bitch and I'll look like an asshole, but hey, I don't mind."

Tracie paused. Was he being casual or just acting as if he was? She couldn't tell. And did she really want to know? Phil took a deep puff, then exhaled. "I mean, I can't help it if Jeff's old lady answers the phone and gets mad. She hates him to get calls there. Especially from women. And so late."

"Late? It's only ten-thirty." God! She'd be late for Jon!

"Why don't you stop fussing and come here and get what you really want?" Phil asked her. Sometimes she hated him. He put his cigarette down and opened his arms again to her.

"I miss you already and you're not even gone," he said, and rolled on top of her and kissed her again. His long body wasn't heavy enough to really pin her against the bed, but she liked the sensation of almost being pinned. His mouth tasted sharply of tobacco, but his tongue was so warm and alive. It searched hers like a friendly little vole looking for a home. Tracie dropped the phone and reached for the water bottle she kept on her bedside table.

"I'd like some of that, too," Phil said, and started to get up on his elbows.

"It's all yours," Tracie replied, and doused him with it. Just in case he was a liar. He yelped, but she paid no attention. She had no time to find out—and maybe she didn't want to know. She'd be hellishly late for Jon. She pulled on her clothes, slipped into her shoes, and crossed the floor. "I'm outta here," she called from the door, laughing. Her last look at Phil was of him untangling the wet gray sheet from his lanky body.

Chapter 5

Jon's office was impressive in size and location, occupying the corner of a building on the low-rise Micro/Con campus, with a view of the topiary garden. But instead of the usual corporate chairs and sofa he had been offered, Jon had used his decorating budget to buy vintage beanbag chairs upholstered in leatherlike Naugahyde. A lot of Naugas must have died, 'cause there were at least half a dozen shapeless mounds of chairs spread around the room. In the center of them, there was a coffee table actually made of coffee beans suspended in a clear acrylic. Jon particularly liked the coffee table. Narrow shelves lined one wall—not for books, or even software CDs, but for the vast collection of action figures he had acquired for work (he had a huge annual budget for them). They shared space with his numerous Pez dispensers (his own private collection). Jon had more than four hundred, including the rare Betsy Ross, the only Pez dispenser ever created based on a real person.

He more than liked the nonsense of his office. There was a method to his madness. It put people at ease, and encouraged playfulness, hence creativity. But there was no nonsense on his desk. Only three photographs were set at the corner of the shining (renewable) teak surface: a picture of his mother, a picture of Tracie and him at college graduation, and a picture of a much younger Jon standing with his mom next to his father, just after they'd planted the wisteria around the doorway of their house and just before Chuck had split.

Now he pulled out the Polaroid his mother had taken earlier in the day and inserted it into the corner of that frame. He stared at the picture: Jon Delano, twenty-eight years old, embracing his mother, and for a moment, it changed before his eyes. It turned black and white and suddenly there was no mature blooming wisteria nor a mature Jon. Instead, a very young Jon and his young mom were embracing while Mr. Delano walked past them, struggling with two suitcases. Jon blinked and the actual Polaroid returned. Spooked, he got up and walked away from the desk.

Well, he was really tired. Not to mention stuffed. Thank God Toni, his last stepmom but one, had canceled at the last minute, or his stomach would probably have burst. He looked out the window to the lit garden and the darkness beyond. It was almost 10:00 P.M., but that didn't stop people from working on Sunday at Micro/Con. All the staff prided themselves on the incredibly long hours they put in. Sunday was just another workday, and even now the parking lot was almost half-full. Jon patted his belly and sank into a beanbag, wiggling his butt until it assumed the position. There was something about Mother's Day that depressed him, and it wasn't merely surveying the trail of human wreckage his father had left behind.

Jon had grown up listening to the women's complaints. It wasn't only his father's various wives, though; it was also the women who gathered for coffee at his mother's house. Other women had even worse stories about their exes, stories that he'd listened to, hiding behind the couch, when he was seven, nine, and fourteen. His mother's friends seemed incapable of ditching their husbands or finding ones who treated them well. Why'd they stay? he still wondered. He thought of Barbara and her baking. After the biscuits had come the inevitable question: "Hear from your father?" He thought of Janet's skinny shoulders when she turned her back on him, pretending to arrange the flowers, and asked, "Have you heard from your father?"

It wasn't Mother's Day, Jon decided. Not for him. For him, it had been Heard from Your Father Day and Have You Got Anyone Special Day. He shook his head, closed his eyes, and, with his right hand, removed his glasses so that he could massage the reddened flesh under the nosepiece. Jon had almost two hours before his customary midnight date with Tracie and, although he had piles and piles of work to do, if he just kept his eyes closed and napped for just a minute, ten minutes at the most . . .

Jon was eleven and sitting in a leatherette booth across from his father. A plate of untouched eggs, their whites runny, the yolk congealing, sat undisturbed in front of him, while his father was busy tearing pieces of the running egg albumen with a side of his fork, then pushing the nasty stuff onto a burned corner of toast and popping it into his mouth. Jon was aware that he was asleep, yet the man in front of him was so real, so perfectly reconstructed in his dream, that it was impossible to believe the guy was not there. Jon could have counted each bristle of his father's five o'clock shadow. Chuck finished the last bit of egg, wiped the plate with some of Jon's toast, and began to chew it up. He leaned forward. "Just remember this, son," he said. "There's not a woman in the world who won't buy a lie she wants to believe."

Jon jerked his eyes open. He was losing it. Weeks of endless toil on the Cliffhanger project and a lousy Friday and Saturday night, topped off by this Sunday, bloody Sunday had given him the willies. He looked at his watch: 10:31. If he could just get out of the beanbag chair, he could get in at least a solid hour of work before meeting Tracie and reviewing what a lousy weekend they'd both had. Jon might have a surfeit of mothers to entertain, but on this weekend, he was careful to be extra attentive to Tracie. Without a mother, the day hit her hard. Not to mention her holiday article. God! He'd forgotten the article! She had E-mailed the draft to him and it was really good, but you never knew what it would look like when it was published in the *Times*. He'd been so busy today, he hadn't had a chance to get the paper or even to look at a copy. He'd better do it on his way over to Java, The Hut.

Actually, work was the only part of his life he had under control. Unlike Tracie, he had a successful career, liked and respected his boss, a wild woman who'd been in on the start-up of UniKorn. Bella was great, his staff was great, his job was great, and the money was great. Now he'd been given control of the Parsifal project, and if he made it happen, well, the sky was the limit. And he *could* make it happen. Parsifal was the code name for the project Jon had fought for since he'd joined Micro/Con almost six years ago. He was trying to bring together convergent wireless technology for a laptop/TV/phone product so advanced, he wasn't allowed to let his right department know what his left department was doing. It would make him or break him, and it was certainly taking up every minute of his time. But if Parsifal worked, no one would ever buy a TV or phone from Panasonic again.

It was just that in the last three or four years, there'd been no time for a social life, and when there was . . . well, it was safe to say it was very definitely less than great. He thought again of his bad Friday night, followed by a worse Saturday evening, and winced. Maybe his reasoning was faulty. He rationalized his lousy social life because of his demanding career. But perhaps one of the reasons he worked all the time was because it was easier than going out. When he tried, as he had this weekend, look what happened.

Jon groaned aloud and sank deeper into the chair—such as it was. The beanbag cupped him at just the right tilt. He didn't feel like thinking anymore, nor did he want to sign on and see how many urgent E-mails he'd gotten in the last twenty-four hours while he bombed out with women and took care of his mothers—both step and natural. There would be mounds of work. Jon took a deep sigh. Every one of his employees thought that their problems were the most difficult and impossible for them to solve without either his help or his praise. He sighed again. He loved his work and he'd do the E-mail now, for half an hour. One less thing to do tomorrow morning. But he'd be sure to leave by eleven-thirty. Seeing Tracie was the high point of his whole week.

Chapter 6

Java, The Hut was just one of the 647 coffee shops in Seattle, but to Jon it seemed different from all the others. It was suffused with memories of the hundreds of Sunday-night "breakfasts" that he and Tracie had shared, fifty-one weeks a year for seven years. From the time they met in French class and crammed together until today, the two of them had bitched, studied, laughed, chewed each other out, and even cried (he briefly only once, she at great length more than a dozen times) over mochaccino at Java, The Hut. Jon sat there now, finished with all work and all mothers for the time being. He waited for Tracie to show up.

He had the *Seattle Times* spread in front of him and was shaking his head as he read the hatchet job that Marcus had made of Tracie's article. "You look like my Lab when 'e's got water in 'is ears," Molly, their usual waitress, said to Jon. Molly was a tall, slender blonde in her early thirties. A transplanted East Ender from London, she'd worked at the café since Jon and Tracie had begun coming there. Word was that she had been a rock bitch, one of those "successful groupies" who actually toured and slept with two important rock idols. Molly never spoke about it but Jon had heard she'd been with someone from INXS. Tracie claimed that after it Molly had made someone from Limp Bizkit hard. Whoever it was, it appeared that Molly had been dumped or had landed in Seattle and liked the town.

Rumors had run rampant that there might be a room or even a whole wing dedicated to Molly in the Experience Music Project, and that her first diaphragm was among the museum's eighty thousand rock artifacts. Jon had never believed any of it, and the opening of the museum last June had proved the rumors false, but even if they had been true, it wouldn't have changed Jon's feelings for Molly. She was acerbic, witty, and warm—at least to him. If she wasn't exactly a friend, she was a long-standing acquaintance and every time he rode by the blowsy, shimmering EMP, twenty-one thousand metallic shingles and the flapping, bright colors made him think of Molly.

"On your own, then, luv?" she asked now, though she knew the answer. Jonathan still shook his head as she indicated the empty seat with a jerk of her head. "The usual, then? Adam and Eve on a raft? Or are you going to wait for Little-Miss-Sorry-I'm-Late?" Molly asked sarcastically.

"I'll wait," Jonathan replied.

"Loyal, just like my Lab." Molly left the table briefly, then returned with his favorite drink. "One mochaccino light while she takes you for granted."

Jon looked up at her. "You really don't like Tracie, do you?

"Bingo! What insight. That must be why Micro/Con pays you the big bucks."

"But why?" Jon asked innocently. "She's so nice."

"She's so stupid. Thick as two short planks," Molly said matter-of-factly as she placed his coffee in front of him, then straightened the place mat and silverware opposite.

"Hey! She is not," Jonathan answered defensively. "In college, she had a four point oh in everything—except maybe calculus. She graduated with honors."

"Oh. Summa cum stupid," Molly said as she turned around, only to see Tracie looking in through the window advertising the Mother's Day special. "I'll leave you to it."

A glowing Tracie entered and hurried toward Jonathan. Of course all the other guys' eyes followed her, but she acted oblivious to that. Jon sometimes wondered whether or not she knew the effect she had on men. He quickly crumpled the newspaper and tried to hide it, pulling out the latest *Little Nickel*. He smiled when she sat opposite him in the booth.

"Sorry I'm late," she said. "Nice try, but I already saw the butcher job. Marcus always cuts my best parts. Could my editor be Edward Scissorhands' evil twin brother?" Tracie shrugged out of her coat, then picked up the menu. He knew her well enough to know she was upset, but also not to push it now. "I'm starving," she said, then looked at him as if for the first time. "God, you look beat!"

Jon smiled and shrugged. "Today was my annual Mother's Day Olympics."

Tracie moved the menu away from her face. "Oh God! I was so wrapped up in my article and . . . everything. I completely forgot! Did you see all the steps? And how did you squeeze in your actual mom?"

"I saw mine for lunch."

"Did she like the earrings?" Tracie's face lit up with hope.

"She loved them!" Jon assured her. "And I took all the credit. But she sends her love. I saw stepmoms one through five before or after."

"You actually visited the toad who wouldn't let your dad come to your high school graduation?"

"Oh, Janet's not so bad."

Tracie snorted. "You have way too much compassion and too many mothers. I've got neither."

Jon had to smile. "That's probably why we're such good friends—opposites attract. Did you miss your real mom this Mother's Day?" Jon asked gently.

"You can't really miss what you don't remember." Tracie repositioned the menu to avoid looking at him. In all the years they'd been friends, she'd never spoken of her mother's death. Jon felt awkward, and there was a momentary silence between them. "Anyway," Tracie said, "Laura's at my house baking enough empty carbohydrates to stock a kindergarten bake sale."

Just then Molly rejoined him. "So, luv. Poached eggs on toast?" she asked Jon.

"Yeah. Gotta have 'em."

"And for you?" Molly asked Tracie, arching her brows with what seemed to Jon a bit too much attitude.

Tracie looked searchingly at the menu. "I'll have . . . the waffles, with a side of bacon." Molly didn't write it down. Instead, she just stood there. Tracie closed the menu decisively. Molly still didn't move. Tracie looked pointedly over at Jonathan. Molly remained standing there.

"You shouldn't eat pigs," Jon told Tracie. "You know, they're more intelligent than dogs."

"Don't start," Tracie warned. "Next, you'll begin imitating the singing mice in *Babe*. So, you had the whole Mother's Day trial while I had the Mother's Day article fiasco. But that wasn't all. Get ready to end your winning streak, because I had the worst weekend of my entire life." She looked up at Molly, who was still standing there, looking as permanent as the red London phone booths. Tracie waited her out. "I'll have my coffee now, if you don't mind."

Molly finally started to walk away, but Tracie reached out and took hold of Molly's arm, as she always did. Jon restrained a laugh. "Wait. I think I'll have the pancakes. The pancakes and a side order of ham." She stared at Jon. "The hell with the pigs." She turned back to Molly. "I mean it this time."

Molly heaved a big sigh, obviously bored, and pulled up a chair and sat down.

"Excuse me?" Tracie said rudely. "I don't remember asking you to join us. And I think I placed my order."

"Admit it to yourself," Molly said. "You want scrambled eggs and you want them dry."

"I told you pancakes. . . ." But Tracie wavered and then gave in to herself. "Yeah. Okay. I'll have the eggs."

"No chips, slices of tomato on the side." Triumphantly, Molly showed Tracie the order was already written down, then sashayed off to the kitchen.

Tracie waited a minute to regain her dignity. Jon just looked at her. For years now, they'd been meeting every Sunday to discuss their romantic lives, such as they were. And Molly's eavesdropping meant she probably knew the facts as well as they did. "So, my weekend has to make me the winner," Tracie told him. "It was a social nightmare."

"Let me guess: On Friday, Swollen Glands never got to play and Phil was pissed off and got drunk. On Saturday, the Glands did get to play, but they didn't invite Phil, so he was pissed off and got drunk. Then he flirted with some girl, you walked out of the club and hoped he'd follow. He didn't, so you went home. But he came back very late to your place, where he passed out in the foyer."

"You think you know everything, don't you?" Tracie asked, sounding half-amused and half-annoyed. "You aren't always right." She paused, but Jon waited her out. "Well, he didn't pass out in *my* foyer," she protested at last. "But you got the rest right."

Jon sighed and shook his head. "Trace, why don't you give this guy the keys to the street?"

Just then, Molly returned and placed Jon's plate carefully on the table in front of him. She slung Tracie's across the table.

Tracie looked down at the scrambled eggs quivering on her plate. "I know it's stupid . . . but I really love him."

"It's not love; it's obsession," Molly told her as she refilled Tracie's coffee mug. "It's not even an interesting obsession."

Tracie tilted her head toward Molly but looked at Jon. "She doesn't like me," Tracie announced.

"That's not true," Jon said in what he hoped was a consoling voice.

"Yes it is, rather. I've been listening to your 'istory of bad boyfriends for dog's years. You 'ave one of these wankers after another. Frankly, you bore me." She walked to the next booth.

Jonathan called after her, "Molly! Don't be mean."

And then came the moment he was dreading. "So how was *your* weekend?" Tracie asked.

Chapter 7

Jon had a problem. He told Tracie everything, or almost everything, which was good. But looking like an idiot and a goofball and a pathetic excuse for a man was not so good. He needed her empathy and advice, but he was afraid of her pity. So, usually, he made a joke of his pain. Now Jon raised his hands and clasped them over his head. "The undefeated world champion with the worst social life in America . . ."

"Well, with Mother's Day, it would be—"

"No. It was the disasters *previous* to Mother's Day that hurt."

Tracie raised her eyebrows and scrunched up her eyes in an exaggerated move of remembrance. She was really cute when she did it. "Oh God! I'm so sorry! I forgot! The look-see didn't work out?" Tracie sighed. "What about the big date?"

Molly returned with coffee and poured it out for Tracie, then shook her head and left. Tracie leaned across the booth and lowered her voice. "What happened? What went wrong with the look-see?" Her face assumed a look of horror. "You didn't wear that plaid jacket, did you?"

"No," he assured her. "I wore my blue blazer."

Tracie, her mouth by now full of coffee, almost did a spit take. "You wore a *blazer* for a look-see?"

"Yeah, I—"

"*Never* get dressed up for a look-see. The whole *point* is to appear casual." Tracie sighed with frustration at him, not for the first time. "So . . . what happened?"

"Well, I walked into the bar; she waved. She was attractive in a skinny, redheaded way. So I went over to her and gave her the flowers. . . ."

"You brought flowers?" Tracie cried, her hands flapping in exasperation. "God, that stinks of desperation."

"Maybe that's why it lasted eleven minutes. We'd hardly begun to talk when she said she'd left clothes in the dryer and didn't want them to wrinkle."

"That's a new wrinkle in lame excuses," Tracie told him. They both let the horror of it sink in for a few moments. Then, as always, Tracie brightened. Jon was certain her optimism was genetic. "Oh, forget about it. I'm sure she wasn't a natural redhead anyway. The drapes never match the rug." Jon managed a grin and Tracie grinned back. "So what about Saturday night? You know, the date with that woman you work with? The one you yearn for with the lust of a thousand pubescent boys. What's-her-name?"

"Sam. Samantha," Jon reminded her. For a moment, he wondered why he always knew every friend and boyfriend of hers by given, middle, and nicknames but she . . . He sighed. "Actually, it was worse," he admitted.

"How could it possibly be worse than an eleven-minute look-see?"

"Well, for one thing, I was meeting her outside. For another, it was raining. And for a third, she never showed."

Tracie's lower lip dropped in real surprise. Then she exaggerated it, just to cover. "She *totally* stood you up? She wasn't just late? I mean, you waited long enough?"

"Two hours."

"Oh, Jon! You stood in the rain for two hours?"

"Yeah. I didn't mind that as much as the fact that I have to see her tomorrow at work."

"Ouch!" Tracie winced, his upcoming humiliation on her face, then tried to recover. "At least tell me she called and left a message with a plausible lie," she begged.

"Neither. No message at home, work, not even an E-mail. And I'd left messages for her on all three."

Tracie grimaced. Jon flushed, embarrassed again. "I wish you hadn't done that," she said.

Jon got defensive. "Well, what should I have done?"

Tracie narrowed her eyes. "It reminds me of the Dorothy Parker line: ' "Shut up," he explained.' "

"But how else could she know I was waiting?"

"Like she needed to? You weren't humiliated enough already?"

Now she was irritated with him. Jon saw something in her face that looked too much like pity. "Well. What else could I do?"

Before Tracie could answer, Molly returned to their table, obviously drawn by bits of the conversation she'd overheard. "Find girls who want to date you? An older woman, perhaps," Molly suggested as she batted her eyes at him. Tracie didn't even look up but Jon managed a wan smile. "Oh, I guess that's a dumb idea. But then I didn't go to college." She whisked their empty plates away and sashayed back to the kitchen.

Tracie sighed. "Okay, Jon, you win. Your weekend was worse. I think that's eighty-three consecutive weeks. A new world record." She scribbled on a Post-it pad she pulled from her purse and stuck it on Jon's shirt. It had a blue ribbon drawn on it.

"Great. Winner of the Losers."

Tracie stopped to consider him for a moment. "You know, it's not *all* your fault. Women tend to gravitate to . . . trouble. Men who are . . . challenges. You know, on Friday, my friend Laura arrived . . ."

"Laura? She finally came? Will I at last get to meet Laura?" Jon had been hearing about Laura for years.

"Sure, but the point is, she's come to stay with me since she broke up with Peter. She's nuts about him, but Laura calls him an IPPy—"

"And that would be?"

"An Intimacy-Phobic Prick. So I think maybe women prefer pricks until they give up on them."

"It's not fair; I try so hard."

"To be a prick?"

"No. Not to—"

"I know. That was a joke. But see, maybe that's the point: You try too hard and you're . . . too nice."

"How can you be *too* nice?"

"Jon, *you're* already too nice. *You're* too considerate. I mean, look at the data. Today, you visited your mom *and* all wicked stepmothers. You're too nice."

"That's ridiculous," Jon told her.

"I know it doesn't make sense to you," Tracie agreed. "It doesn't even make sense to us. And I don't think we like to suffer. But I know we hate to be bored. Take Phil, for example: He fascinates me. He keeps my life so interesting."

"He's a bass player, for God's sake," Jon said, totally exasperated. "Dumber than dirt. *And* self-involved. *And* selfish. You call *that* interesting?" he asked, then realized he'd probably gone too far and maybe hurt her feelings.

Tracie only smiled. "You have something against guys who play four-stringed instruments or something?"

Jon calmed himself. "Not all. Just him. He's not worthy."

"But he's so cute. And the sex!" She blushed.

Jon looked away. That was his punishment for going too far. There were some things he didn't need to know. He sighed. "I'd give anything to be able to land chicks the way guys like Phil do. If I could just learn to get dumb. Or pretend to be selfish . . ." He paused. "Hey, Tracie, I'm getting an idea."

"You *always* have ideas," she said, getting up. "That's why you're the Intergalactic Alchemist of Cosmology Development and Systems Conception Worldwide, or whatever it is you are over there in Micro Land."

"No. Not an idea like that," Jon said, getting up to join her. She couldn't leave yet. "I mean an idea about my *life*."

"Great. Can we discuss this next week? I need to go to the supermarket."

"For what? Panty hose?" Tracie hadn't been inside a supermarket in years.

"No. For baking soda. And flour."

"Are you doing a science project? Or is it something for your hair?"

"It's to bake," Tracie said, attempting a dignity she couldn't quite achieve with him.

"Since when do you bake? And why do you need to at midnight?" Jon knew Tracie well enough to know that she thought the black thing in her kitchen with the door in the front was where you stored extra shoes. And he hoped to God she didn't have buns in her oven. "Is this some trick to try to get Phil to turn over and play dead? Because your baking will kill him . . . not that that's a bad thing."

"I'm not going to dignify any of that with a response," Tracie said, rising.

Jon got up, too. He didn't want to show how desperate for company he was. And also he was interested in the mystery of Tracie's new domesticity. Then it came to him. "It's your friend, your friend Laura from San Antonio. Isn't Laura a chef?"

"So what?" Tracie said as she shrugged into her jacket. "It doesn't mean that I don't know how to do things, too."

"You know how to do a lot of things," Jon agreed. "You're a really good writer, a good friend, and you know how to dress. You're great at picking out gifts for mothers. But baking . . ."

Tracie gave him a look. "She's from Sacramento," she corrected him, which was her way of acknowledging he was right.

Jon smiled. "I'll help you grocery shop," he offered.

"What? Don't you have to work, or sleep? You always need to do one or the other. Anyway, it's the most boring thing in the world."

"Not to a man who offered to fold laundry and was turned down," Jon pointed out. "I can push the cart for you."

"If that's what you want." Tracie shrugged and started to walk away from the booth as Jon went through his pockets and hurriedly threw a twenty onto the table. Without turning around, Tracie spoke: "You're overtipping again. See, your problem *is* that you're just too nice." Tracie shook her head as she wound her way through the deserted tables. "Women don't want nice guys."

Jon's excitement was mounting. Exactly. Why hadn't he thought of this before? It was perfect, a conception that came to him complete from beginning to end, as the Parsifal project had. He had to get Tracie to understand, to agree, and to make his vision a reality. But he was good at that. "See you next week," Jon shouted to Molly, then caught up with Tracie as she walked through the door.

"So what's your idea?" Tracie asked as she pulled a shopping cart from the corral. "If you're planning another fake, on-line Girls of the Silicon Forest calendar, I'm out."

"Come on, Tracie. I'm serious. I gotta make a change before I need Viagra."

"Oh, don't be so overly dramatic," Tracie told him as they walked up the paper-goods and health-care products aisle. She looked him over with her peripheral vision as they panned the dairy counter. "Your sell-by date hasn't expired. You're good for another two or three years yet."

"I'm not being dramatic. I'm being realistic." He took a deep breath. He had to get her cooperation. "I want you to teach me to be a bad boy," he said.

Tracie was about to pass the hair-care products when she stopped and turned around to look directly at Jon. "Huh?"

He felt his heart actually thumping against his ribs. He gulped down a breath. "I want you to train me to be the kind of guy that girls always go for. You know, the kind of guy you're always going with. Phil. Before him, Jimmy. And you remember Roger? The skin-popper. He was *really* bad. And you were nuts about Roger."

"*You're* nuts," Tracie said, and pushed the cart forward, leaving him behind her. She grabbed a bottle of Pert—a shampoo she'd never select if she wasn't flustered—and Jon quickly caught up to her in the almost-deserted baking-supplies aisle.

"Please, Tracie. I really mean it." He had to both calm her and create a wave of enthusiasm. He reminded himself that he knew how to build project teams.

"Don't be ridiculous. Why would you want to be a bum? Anyway, it's impossible. You could never act—"

"Yes, I could. I could if you would teach me." Overcome objections, he told himself. Then enlist her talent. "Remember what a good student I was in school? Come on, Tracie. Look at it as a challenge, a way to use all the research you've gathered from those tattooed boyfriends of yours." He observed her interest. Now, create desirable opposition. "Otherwise," he said, as casually as he could, "Molly is right."

At the mention of the waitress's name, Tracie stopped again and turned to face him. "Right about what?" she asked, brusquely. Then she turned away to examine the flour.

"Repetition compulsion," he explained, his heart beating hard. He'd hooked her. "You've just been repeating yourself for no reason for the last seven years. Wasting time. But if you could become an alchemist . . ."

She crouched down, reading the label on one of the lower flour sacks. "Who would have thought there were so many different kinds of flour?" she asked, a mere distraction technique he'd simply wait out. "Do you think she wants sifted bleached or sifted unbleached or unsifted unbleached or unsifted bleached?"

Jon remembered Barbara's biscuits of fifteen hours earlier and grabbed the presifted bleached. "This kind," he said, handing her the package. She stood up and accepted the bag. "So how 'bout it? Will you teach me?"

She shrugged, placed the flour in the cart, and began to move down the aisle. "Okay," she admitted. "Maybe I can write a pretty good feature and blow-dry my hair on a rainy day in Seattle without getting frizz. But I can't bake, and no one could teach *you* to be bad. You can't be bad, so this can't be serious." She turned away.

Jon suddenly felt desperate. He imagined seeing Samantha at work the next morning and could hardly bear it. Plus, Tracie was right: It was much worse that he had called. What made him so unutterably stupid at times?

But despite her disclaimer, Tracie could help him, if only she would. She held the key, but she wouldn't give it up. What kind of friend was that? He told himself he had to go for a strong close. He'd succeeded in getting million-dollar project allocations. He could do this. He grabbed her by the arm and spun her around, looking directly in her eyes. "I've never been more serious in my life. And you're the only one who can help. You know all my dirty little habits *and* you've got your Ph.BB. You majored in Bad Boys all through college and you're doing your graduate work at the *Seattle Times*."

"Well, it would be a challenge, that's for sure," Tracie said, smiling at him. With affection. Yes! he cried to himself, though he didn't let his victory show. Tracie raised her eyebrows and with them her last objection. "But why would any alchemist want to turn gold into lead?" she asked, and took his hand warmly.

"Because the gold really wanted to change," Jon told her. "What if the gold *begged* the alchemist?" He knew, right away, he'd gone too far.

She let go of his hand. "I don't think so, Jon. I love you just the way you are," Tracie said, sounding just like his mother.

"Yeah, but no one else does," he reminded her, but it was too late. She shrugged and again moved down the aisle.

"I couldn't do it. Hey, did I say baking soda or baking powder?" she asked, looking at dozens of each stacked neatly on the shelf.

"You said soda," he told her. "And you could make me over if you wanted to."

Tracie paused. He hoped she was considering the project, but after another minute she shook her head. "I think I have to get baking soda. But maybe it was baking powder."

Jon sighed. "What's the difference?" he asked, dispirited.

"You use them for different things."

"Duh. And what would those things be?" he asked. He was angry with her and he wasn't going to let her get away with anything. "And how are they different?"

"Baking powder makes cakes rise."

"I can read cans, too, Tracie," he told her. "So what about baking soda?"

"Well, you can brush your teeth with it and you put it in your refrigerator to deodorize it."

"And your friend from Santa Barbara forgot her Crest or was knocked over by the odor of your Frigidaire?"

Tracie gave him a look, then shrugged and threw both products into the cart. She turned toward the front of the store and marched away. Jon followed her. He wouldn't give up on this brainstorm. He hadn't gotten where he was at Micro/Con without persistence. Maybe humor would work. He crouched down, holding on to the cart handle, and began begging, the way kids beg their mothers for stuff in all stores. "Please? Please will you? Please? Come on. I'll do anything. I promise."

Tracie glanced around, clearly embarrassed. "Get up!" she hissed. He knew she hated public scenes and was counting on it. "Jon, you have a great apartment, a terrific job, and you're going to be rich—as soon as you cash in your Micro stock options." She tried to ignore the old woman with a basket over her arm and the tall young man with a cart full of beer. "Get up," she repeated. "There have been plenty of girls who liked you."

He didn't get up. "But not *that* way," he whined. "It's never *that* way. Women want me as a friend, or a mentor, or a brother." He tried to keep the bitterness out of his voice. Bitterness didn't sell projects. Anyway, Tracie was one of those girls, foremost among them, but he didn't need to say so.

"Come on. Stand up," she begged again. "People are looking." Actually, the two had wandered off and now there was only a clerk, who wasn't looking, because he was too busy affixing price labels directly onto grapefruits. Tracie left him. Fine. He'd use her embarrassment against her. He could make it work for him. Tracie pushed the cart to the checkout line at the front of the store. Good—there were lots of people around. Jon helped Tracie put the groceries on the conveyor belt. Still on his knees, he whined loudly, "I want interesting girls. The hot girls. But they all want bad boys."

"Get up," she hissed. "You're exaggerating." Unfortunately, it was too late for a crowd to gather. He'd have to use his trump card: her innate honesty.

"Come on, Tracie. You know it's true."

"Well . . ."

The cashier finally stared at the two of them. Then she shrugged and totaled the purchases. Tracie fished in her bag for the money. Jon sighed, stood up, and looked blankly at the rack of tabloids and women's magazines. His knees were hurting. Begging was hard work. Then he noticed a *GQ* magazine. Some young movie star was on the cover, one who had recently dumped his girlfriend, publicly, on TV, right before the Oscars. Jon looked back at Tracie and pointed at the magazine cover. "I want to look like one of *those* kind of guys," he said.

"It's not just about looks," Tracie told him, picking up her bag. "You're good-looking . . . in a nice-guy kinda way."

He took the bag from her and the two of them began to walk out. "Right. And that guy doesn't look nice. He looks hot. *He* didn't take his stepmoms out on Mother's Day." He turned back around and pointed to the guy on the cover. "What *did* he just do? You know."

Tracie glanced at the magazine and shrugged. "He just told his new girlfriend that he'd like to see other people," she told him, and walked out the exit.

Jon followed her. "I could do that! If I had a girlfriend. And if you'd help me," he pleaded. "Look at it as your dissertation." He ran back, grabbed the magazine as a reference point, threw a five-dollar bill on the counter, and raced after Tracie. "You're an expert," he told her. "Only you could distill all the rotten behavior that you found so adorable and inject me with it."

Tracie was at the door of her car, fumbling with the keys. She took the bag from him, opened her door, and got in. "Forget this, would you?" she requested. "You're just having a larger dose of your weekly Sunday self-hate than usual. You'll be fine tomorrow."

"Yeah. When I see Samantha," he agreed glumly. "That will make me feel real fine."

"Oh, Jon, just get on your bicycle and go home," Tracie told him, so he did.

Chapter 8

Tracie's one-bedroom apartment was sunny, long, and narrow. It wasn't exactly small, but the kitchen consisted only of a sink, a half-size refrigerator, and an old black gas oven—which she did keep her extra shoes in. Now, for privacy, a temporary screen concealed one end of the place, a "guest room," so that Laura could have some privacy. Other than the cot, screen, and sofa, the only other real piece of furniture Tracie had in the living room was a desk covered with notes and photos and Post-its for article ideas. In fact, the whole apartment was covered with Post-it notes stuck on various surfaces.

Now at almost 2:00 A.M., after her day of sex with Phil and weird late-night breakfast with Jon, she was exhausted. She entered the place as quietly as she could. But Laura was up, busy with mixing bowls and cookie sheets. And—to Tracie's complete surprise—Phil was there, too, lying on the sofa and strumming his bass guitar. He looked over at Tracie. "What took you so long? I blew off a rehearsal to be here. Plus, Bobby would have bought me free drinks because he just got his tax refund."

Before she could answer, Laura responded, protective as usual. "It sucks to be you," she told Phil cheerfully.

Tracie tried to ignore Phil. Phil was odd, and in some ways adorable. He showed his affection like this, by turning up because he missed her but not being able to admit it. Every time it happened Tracie got a kick out of it. He looked sexy, stretched out there, but he knew it, so she'd act cool. "What are you doing?" she asked Laura, who was cracking two eggs at a time into a bowl.

"Welding a crankshaft."

"You're cooking something, aren't you?" Phil said, as if he'd just discovered DNA.

"Not cooking. I'm *baking*," Laura told him. She smiled at Tracie. "Did you get the baking soda?" Tracie nodded. Back in Encino, a weekend had never gone by without both brownies and sugar cookies. Laura baked from scratch, even back then. Tracie's only contribution had been licking the bowl.

"My mother used to bake," Phil offered. "Chickens, hams."

Laura rolled her eyes, then took a tray of cookies out of the oven. She lifted up one and gestured toward Phil. "Stupid want a cookie?" she asked with a cheery smile.

Tracie couldn't believe it. She waited for Phil's scowl, but instead he merely held out his hand. Tracie watched, amazed. Maybe the way to a man's heart *was* through his stomach.

"Wow!" Phil said as he sucked down the sugar cookie. "These are *amazing*!"

"Yeah. Fat and sugar can be a really powerful mood elevator," Laura said. "I'm hooked." She patted her hip.

Tracie hated the way she put herself down. "Laura, what's the difference between baking soda and baking powder?" Tracie asked.

"I know that," Phil offered. "One's a liquid and one's not. Easy."

Laura snorted. "Oddly enough, baking soda is not fizzy and you do not drink it through a straw," Laura told him. She turned back to Tracie. "You know, baking soda is like cream of tartar. You don't have to use them often, but when you need them nothing else will do. Boy, at Easter, I could have sold my supply of cream of tartar for more than you'd get for crack cocaine. The housewives of Sacramento were frantic."

Tracie smiled. She'd forgotten how odd, how unique Laura's humor was. Who else but Laura would be able to create a sentence combining crack and cream of tartar together.

"Cleanup time!" Laura announced, but Phil just picked up another cookie. Tracie shrugged. Phil didn't clean up his own place. Laura began to wash dishes, so Tracie covered and finished putting away the last of the ingredients.

"What took you so long?" Phil asked her, wiping crumbs from his mouth.

Tracie moved Laura over by hitting her gently with her hip and washed her hands. "It was the weirdest night. Jon asked if I could do a makeover on him."

Phil laughed. "A makeover on Techno-Nerd? What did he want to be made into?"

"Somebody more like you," Tracie said as she sat down on the sofa and slipped out of her shoes.

"Mr. Micro T. Stock Option? Now, *that* is impossible," Phil said. "The guy was born to wear glasses and work a day job. Day jobs were invented for people like him." Tracie was about to jump to Jon's defense, but then she noticed that Laura had left a bowl at the side of the tiny kitchen counter. She was about to bring it to be washed when she realized what it was. Gratefully, she picked it up and began to wipe the glass with her finger, then inserted the finger in her mouth.

"Just how many shares does he have, anyway?" Phil asked.

"Somewhere around thirty thousand, I think," she said, shrugging as the sweetness hit her tongue.

"Wow! So he's really rich. You'd think he'd never be lonely," Laura said. "When do I meet him?"

"Forget it," Phil told her. "You're better off with Jeff, and his IQ is in the double digits. But at least he has rhythm. He's still talking about you."

"Jon just doesn't get opportunities with the kind of women he likes," Tracie said.

"Too much money and you can't get a honey," Phil said. "And the guy wanted to be like me?" He laughed.

"Maybe I'm his type," Laura observed.

Tracie ignored her. "And what makes you think you're so impossible to imitate?" she asked Phil.

"Nothing. But he's so fuckin' lame. Totally void."

"Yeah," Laura agreed. "Never like a guy under thirty with a day job and a fortune in stock. That's my motto."

Phil missed her sarcasm and nodded. "Well, anyway, it's hopeless. You couldn't do it," he told Tracie.

"*He* thinks I could do it," Tracie retorted. Why was Phil so cruel when he spoke of Jon?

"Oh, Techno-Nerd thinks you can do anything."

"She could do it if she wanted to," Laura snapped at Phil as she rinsed off the last cookie sheet and retrieved the now-clean bowl from Tracie.

"Yeah. He has more faith in me than you do," Tracie told him. "What if I did change him, make him a hottie?"

"You should, and maybe write a feature on it," Laura said. "You know, a kind of day-by-day diary. People love makeovers."

It was a good idea. Plus it would really antagonize Phil, and she was in the mood to do that now. "Yeah!" Tracie agreed.

"Yeah? What, are you crazy?" Phil asked. "Why would you want to waste time writing about crap as ridiculous as that?"

"Oh, I don't know," Tracie said. "Everyone is interested in transformations. It's archetypal. You know, like Jung." Phil worshipped Jung. "The old Cinderella story."

"But I thought you weren't interested in *old* stories," he said. "You're interested in *new* stories."

"Yeah," Laura said. "Phil showed me one of his new stories." She caught Tracie's eye. Her mouth curled into the W it made when she didn't want to laugh.

"Really?" Tracie asked. Despite Laura's contempt, she was hurt. Phil had rarely shown her any of his work. "What did you think?"

"I think it could have been improved by characters and a plot," Laura opined. "Otherwise, it was great."

"Thanks," Phil said, as if he hadn't just been insulted. "It's a collective unconscious kind of thing." Well, Tracie thought, he probably didn't care about what Laura felt about writing. But why had he even shown her anything? "Anyway, even if you wanted to write crap like that, you couldn't make it happen," Phil added. "Making him cool would be like trying to refrigerate the Amazon. Too big a job. Impossible."

"Wanna bet I could?" Tracie asked.

"Bet what?" He reached out a finger to wipe the edge of her mouth, but Tracie dodged away. None of that stuff now, and certainly not in front of lonely Laura.

But there was a wager here. A legitimate way to address her gripes, teach Phil a lesson, and maybe move their relationship forward—or end it. "Bet you household money," Tracie said, inspired.

"Whoa. I don't pay household money." He almost dropped the latest cookie he was conveying to his mouth.

"Exactly my point, Phil. You eat here and sleep here most of the time, but you don't pay rent, or even chip in on the groceries."

"You know I can't, baby." He looked over at Laura then put his arm around Tracie and walked her over to the screen. He lowered his voice. "I'm still paying off the amplifier, and right now I'm even behind on my share of the apartment rent," he told her, gently pushing her toward Laura's bed.

"Not here!" she said sharply. What was he thinking of? "Anyway, if you gave up your place . . ."

"I think this is the point in the conversation where I diplomatically withdraw to provide you with the privacy you so obviously require," Laura said as she wiped her hands on the pathetic excuse for a dishcloth that Tracie had dug up somewhere. "I need a good, long, loud shower," she told them, and disappeared into the bathroom.

Phil took Tracie by the arm, went into the bedroom, pulled off his boots, and pulled her onto the bed. "Come over here," he said, and reached out to her.

"Phil. Stop. Seriously! Listen to me for a minute," Tracie insisted as he took her by the shoulders and pulled her to him. "If you moved in . . ."

Phil removed his arm from her shoulder and slid it under the pillow. All at once the emotional temperature dropped fifty degrees. "Hey, I have to have my own space," he told her, and turned to the wall, obviously wanting her to end the subject, or, better yet, fall asleep.

"But you were so sure about Jon. You afraid to bet?" Tracie egged him on. "If I can turn Jon into someone cool, would you give up your place and pay half the rent here?"

"It's not going to happen," he insisted.

"But if it did?"

He turned around, looked at her, and then grinned wolfishly. "I'd do whatever you wanted. But what if you can't?"

Tracie thought about it some more. "Then you can use this place as a free hotel where you drop your laundry and eat your meals but never have to make the bed." She paused again. "Oh, wait. You're already doing that."

Phil sat up. "Look, I told you, relationships are tough for a musician. You knew that going in. Right?" She nodded. "Relationships are like baths: At first they're okay, but after a while they're not so hot."

"Is that what you think about us? That we're not so hot?" she asked, getting off the bed. She didn't want him if that's what he thought.

"No, baby," he said soothingly. "How can you ask that after this afternoon?" His voice got husky. He pulled her back to him, though she kept her body stiff and resistant. "Hey, I was just raggin' on you. Look. I brought you something." Phil held out his hand and opened his fist. In his palm was a black velvet ring box. Her heart jumped and she threw her arms around his neck. "Oh, Phil!" she breathed.

* * *

Tracie was in front of the mirror in the ladies' room of the *Seattle Times*. She was applying Great Lash mascara while Beth looked on. She had dark circles under her eyes. She and Phil had been up till four, fighting, making love, and then fighting again. God, I need a haircut, she thought. She'd have to call and beg Stefan for an appointment.

"Then what?" Beth asked.

"So he's like, 'I need my own space.' "

Beth sighed. "My mother told me she would rent a warehouse for all the guys in Seattle I've dated who needed their own space."

The ladies' room door opened. Allison, the tall blonde who'd been at Cosmo and who could easily win a young Sharon Stone look-alike contest, entered the ladies' lounge. Beth and Tracie eyed her hostilely. She joined them at the mirror.

"Hi," Allison said as she needlessly fluffed her already-perfect hair.

"Hi," Tracie and Beth said simultaneously, and with precisely the same lack of enthusiasm.

There was a moment of silence. Allison kept playing with her hair. "So," Tracie continued, "Phil said he wanted to get married, but I'm like, 'I don't really know you well enough. I'm not even sure you're right for me.' But I took the ring anyway," Tracie told the reflection of herself and Beth.

Beth stopped putting on her lipstick and almost dropped the tube. "He asked you?" she asked. "I mean, he popped the big one?" Tracie covertly eyed Allison in the mirror. She finished her hair.

"Bye," Allison said.

"Bye," Beth and Tracie echoed at the same time as Allison exited the bathroom.

"Phil gave you a ring?" Beth asked after the door closed completely. "For real?"

"No, for Allison. Phil gave me a ring *box*. With a guitar pick inside."

"A *guitar* pick?"

Tracie imitated Phil's voice from the night before to make a joke out of her disappointment. " 'It's my first one. I didn't know I wasn't supposed to use one with a bass.' " She paused the way he had when he'd seen her lack of enthusiasm. " 'Hey. It means a lot to me.' " She went back to her normal tone of voice. "Well, it *does* mean a lot to him. You know, he lives for his music and his writing. He just doesn't think about material things like rings." Beth didn't say a word. "Well, he *doesn't*," Tracie insisted, then showed Beth the pick, which Phil had had a jeweler drill a hole through, now on a chain around her neck. "Doesn't Allison just get on your nerves?"

Beth became animated again. "You have no idea. Last week, she started dating this new guy. He was calling the office about six hundred times a day. By Thursday, he was waiting outside for her at lunch *and* after work. On Friday, she actually got a restraining order."

"No shit," Tracie said as she slipped the mascara wand back into its base.

"No shit! And he's not a mental patient. He's a big orthodontist in Tacoma," Beth added. "I swear she has the power to cloud men's minds. And I think she's after Marcus."

With a worse-than-usual display of neurosis and bad taste in men, not to mention career suicide, Beth had started up an office affair with Marcus. Now she tortured herself over it daily. Tracie thought Beth might be right about the Allison-Marcus thing, but there was no sense admitting it. "Well, you should give him to her on a silver platter."

"Noooo," Beth keened. "I mean, I admit he's troubled. But I love him." She blotted her lips and stood up to go. "Anyway, he's not mine to give."

"So let her have him. They deserve each other."

"But I . . ."

Tracie couldn't believe that Beth was still hung up on the jerk. "Oh, Beth, he dated and dumped you! You should have him up on harassment charges." Tracie began to throw her makeup in her purse. "Why are guys like that? My girlfriend Laura with Peter? Me with

Phil? And you with that bastard Marcus? How come they're so immature and selfish?"

"They're a challenge." Beth sniffed as they walked down the hall. "I mean, if Phil and Marcus did what we wanted all the time, it would get boring."

Beth was, of course, insane, but Tracie had to admit she recognized what Beth meant.

"Let's face it. The difficult ones make us feel special. You know, with Marcus it was like if I got *him* to love me, I was really something."

Tracie thought of Phil and how difficult he was. Then she remembered Jon and his request. Maybe he was right. Could she do it? Would it work? She sighed. "Sometimes I think we're just masochists. But Marcus is definitely a sadist."

"Never mind Marcus," Beth told her. "Look at Phil! He's not good enough for you, Tracie. I admit he's cute, but he's no good. And he'll never make a commitment." She grabbed the pick swinging around Tracie's neck. "That is just pathetic," she added.

"I don't know," Tracie said, feeling the glimmer of an idea. "I may have a way to force him to. *And* simultaneously get a good feature out of it." They got to the corner where they had to part.

"Don't bet on it," Beth said.

Tracie smiled. "I just might," she told her friend.

Chapter 9

Just outside of Jon's office, there were dozens of carpeted cubicles filling a space almost the size of an airplane hangar. The noise of beeping phones, copiers, printers, and fingers tapping keyboards made a low but constant thrum. Jon was tired from having to deal with his mothers, working on Parsifal, being out late last night with Tracie while she shopped. But now, sitting here, he had to muster up enough strength to pay attention. After all, this was his department, his kingdom. A bunch of Micro/Con guys were deep in tech development talk while he, the enlightened despot, listened, trying to keep his eyes open.

Jon looked up from the discussion group he was in and saw Samantha walking toward his office. His kingdom crashed around him faster than the "I love you" virus crashed the Filipino E-mail system. He remembered he was the Winner of the Losers. Humiliation was walking right up to him. There was something about Sam that Jon, or any other guy, for that matter, couldn't resist. She was one of those tiny freckled redheads, tough in her job, but she had a sweetness—no, an innocence—that was a total magnet. He wanted to catalogue every one of her freckles as if they were constellations in the night sky. And that wasn't taking her legs into consideration—so long, so lean, so perfectly proportioned.

Sam was in marketing at Micro/Con. Most marketing folk were empty suits, but she was a smart woman with a sense of humor, a lot like Tracie. He had first met her at last year's sales conference, when the Crypton-2 had been completed and was ready for public release. The auditorium was filled with three hundred people—most of whom were uptight salesmen—but Jon couldn't get over Sam as she stepped up to the podium and began her pitch with an insanely off-color joke about a midget and a washing machine. Not only had she made the guys roar, but she'd managed to be very ladylike at the same time. Even now, Jon chuckled at the memory. She had gusto. She had a certain aura about her that was magical. She was incredible. No one that Jon knew—not even Tracie—would be able to pull something like that off and get away with it. For months, he'd had her on his radar, always aware of where she was. At last, he'd gotten up the courage to sit next to her at a couple of meetings. He'd passed her funny notes; she'd laughed. He sat next to her in the cafeteria one day, and then he'd asked her out. She'd agreed, then stood him up.

Now, seeing her in the hallway, he wished he could get away with not having to speak to her. She was involved in a discussion of her own with some marketing gunslinger. They were all so damn slick. All style, no substance. Jon froze, then became visibly uncomfortable. He hoped the guys around him didn't notice. She couldn't pretend not to see him. He wished he could disappear or just push his head through the 100 percent natural fiber industrial carpeting beneath his feet and pull an ostrich, but there was no chance.

"Oh. Hi, Jon," Samantha said calmly. She continued down the hall without missing a beat, her long legs a receding dream.

"Hi, Sam," Jon responded in a voice about an octave too high. God, her casualness was worse than being ignored! Now he could tell he'd been totally forgotten.

Then Samantha stopped. "Oh, hey. Sorry about Saturday," she

said over her shoulder, as if she'd just remembered it. Well, maybe she just had.

"Saturday?" Jon asked, his voice under control. Hey, he could get amnesia, too.

"I wasn't sure if it was on or not, and then I got tied up and I was—"

"No problem," Jon said cutting her off. Then he separated from the group and entered his office. He could hear the staff murmuring outside his door. Dennis said, "Man, what did she do with Jon that made *her* sorry?" Someone else made another wisecrack, one he couldn't hear, and everyone laughed. He jumped when the phone began to ring. For a moment, he was tempted to ignore it, but he couldn't. It might be Bella, his boss, with new info on the Parsifal funding. He picked up the receiver.

"Do you like surprises?" Tracie's voice asked.

"Hit me with one." He sighed. Anything would be a good distraction from his current modality.

"What if I said this isn't Tracie? That it's Merlin and I've considered your proposal?"

Marlon? Brando or Perkins? He was so tired, he felt fuzzy-headed. What was she talking about? Had he been so desperate Sunday night that he'd gotten drunk and asked her to marry him? He was confused. Then it hit him. The tutoring. Jon flung the papers he was holding onto a chair and sat down. "Tracie, I'll do anything. *Anything.*"

"First of all, we'd have to buy you some decent clothes," she said.

Jon couldn't help thinking of Emerson—"Never trust an endeavor that requires new clothes." "My credit card is yours," is what he said to Tracie.

"You'll have to change your hair."

Hey, I'd like to change my whole head, he thought. But he just said, "Transplants, or just the color? I'll do either," he assured her.

Tracie giggled. She had a really cute giggle. "A good cut will do for starters. And you need to start working out."

"No problem. I can work out or in. All I do is work."

"You know I mean at a gym!" Tracie remonstrated. "Partly to be buff, partly to meet people. Okay. So . . . for a start, you'll have to get rid of your home answering machine. A*nd* your E-mail."

She'd gone crazy. He was director of an entire R & D division, working on a cutting-edge project. "What? . . . How would I get my—"

"That's the point. Rule Number One: Unavailability."

"To women maybe. But I do have business to transact."

"You've been doing nothing but work for the last six years. You're going to have to change some of your ways to get cuties."

He thought of Sam. "Okay. Okay," he said. "Just give me the rules."

"Rule Number Two: Unpredictability. Lose the watch."

He began to unfasten the band from his wrist. "It's not hip, right? I should wear a different one? A Swatch?"

She groaned. "God no. Bad boys just don't *need* watches. You're either fashionably late or inconveniently early, but *never* on time."

"Plus, no logos. No little alligators, no boomerangs. If people want to read, let them buy the *Times*, not stare at your chest. And forget your Micro/Connection wardrobe."

"I don't *always* wear Micro/Con stuff," he said defensively. He looked down at his chest. It said FROM FLOPPY DISK TO HARD DRIVE IN SIXTY SECONDS. Perhaps his argument was weak. Actually, he hardly ever noticed what he wore.

"Not if you sleep in the nude. But whenever *I've* seen you, you've been branded. And it is so *lame*."

Maybe she was right. "I'll put on a real shirt," he promised.

"So, your homework assignment: Tomorrow, you go to work without a watch and no Micro/Con. Then we'll meet at your place tomorrow at seven."

Jon was a good student. He'd always gotten the extra-credit points and the trick questions right in school. It was only in his personal life that he screwed up. "Is this a test? Am I supposed to be late? Or early?"

"On time," she told him in a stern voice. "Don't play those games with your alchemist."

Jon hung up, smiled, and swirled around in his desk chair. Yes! Soon he'd have the Samanthas of the world and all their freckles at his feet.

Chapter 10

Tracie walked into her apartment and nearly fainted from the scent of rosemary and thyme in the air. She began salivating immediately. She never had any food in the place, because she'd eat it if she did. This was . . . overwhelming.

"Hi, honey. You're home," Laura sang out. The table was set with Tracie's nice china, salads were already put out, and Laura opened the door enough for Tracie to see something really good seemed to be roasting in the oven. "I didn't know how you felt about duck, so I made chicken à l'orange," said Laura. Tracie frowned. She thought that took hours—though she'd never even read a recipe. And she was starved, but she was also getting concerned. As far as she knew, Laura hadn't been out of the apartment in the last three days. Plus, neither of them needed this many calories.

"Honey, you can't go on like this," Tracie said as she sat down at the table. Laura pulled a small dish from the oven. On it was a tiny bit of bread smeared with something and decorated artfully with a few leaves.

"Have a cheese savory," said Laura cheerfully, ignoring Tracie completely. She was already drinking a glass of red wine and poured some out for Tracie. Tracie couldn't resist, but she knew she'd hate herself in the morning. It was funny—after only a few days, the two of them were acting like a long-married couple.

"Laura, this is impossible," she said as she popped the savory into her mouth. Then she couldn't do anything except make animal noises because it was so delicious. All thoughts of dieting left her head. "Can't we have these for dinner?" she asked. Laura laughed. "Don't worry. Everything is that good."

Laura was telling the truth. Tracie only came back to her senses after the flan that her guest had made for dessert. Only then—replete with food and guilt—did she begin to shake her head. "We're getting fat. I can't take this rich food every night."

"Don't be silly," Laura said in her best Julia Child imitation. "What's rich about a little sour cream and truffles and foie gras and cheese?" She winked. "It's not like I'm baking farm cakes." But she might as well be. Laura's cooking was rich.

With some difficulty, Tracie got up from the table and dragged herself over to the sofa. She was stuffed. "Okay," she said. "That was it. I'm locking up the pans and from now on we're spending our lunchtimes at the gym."

"I am not friendly enough with gymnasiums to call them by their first names," Laura sniffed. "I don't *do* gymnasiums."

"You didn't do them in Sacramento. You *do* do them here," Tracie told her. "And you are way too talented not to be cooking. You've got to go out and find some catering jobs. Better yet, get a job as a chef. You always wanted to do that."

"Hey, babe, you're not doing your transformation on *me*," Laura said. "You're doing one on Jon, and even that's not a good idea. It'll end in tears, as my mother used to say."

"Your mother used to tell you sex felt bad," Tracie said as she attempted to find the place where her waistline had been only a few days before. Now it wasn't just the top button but the entire zipper of her slacks that had to be loosened. "Jon *asked* me to do this."

"Yeah? Well don't you see that every single thing you're going to do will be a criticism of him? At some point, he's really going to resent it. Maybe my mother lied, but there's an old Chinese saying: Why does he hate me so? I never did anything for him. That's based on truth."

"Don't be silly," Tracie said. "Jon will be grateful for anything I do to help him."

"Mmm? Remember when you used to try to do diet consulting for me?"

"You didn't ask me to! And I stopped!"

"Look," Laura explained, "if Jon doesn't resent it, *Phil* is going to start to. Too much attention paid to someone else."

"Are you kidding me?" Tracie asked, then wondered if Phil would drop by that night, as he said he might. "Phil doesn't notice anything I do. I'd *like* it if he was jealous."

"We shall see," Laura told her, and blinked like an owl. Tracie hated it when she acted wise.

"We shall see. And maybe we won't. But we will be at the gym," Tracie told her. "Beth and some of the girls from work go there three days a week. So are we." She got up and put her arm on Laura's much higher shoulder. "You're gonna look great on the StairMaster," Tracie predicted.

Seventies music blared in the background of Simon's Gym. A roomful of women were working the circuit. "Susan went out with a guy, and when they started making out, she found out he was wearing a toupee," Sara, one of the junior reporters at the *Times*, said.

"That's a pucker," Beth answered.

"What's a pucker?" Tracie asked, sitting at the rowing machine, her head bent between her knees. She was so tired, she thought she might puke.

"It's the female equivalent of a wilt," Sara explained. She held her finger up and indicated the loss of an erection. "So accountants are a pucker."

"What else?" Tracie asked, still breathing heavily.

"Shoe salesmen," Laura offered from the StairMaster, raising her left knee to her waist. The seventies album continued, "Let's all celebrate and have a good time."

"Brokers—stock or real estate. And security guards," Sara chimed in while doing a warm-up side stretch to the left.

"Did you ever date a security guard?" Laura asked Sara.

"As if," Sara said as she side-stretched to the right.

"Oh, computer guys," Beth added as she changed the weights on the new device she was about to mount. It looked frightening and maybe sexual. "Seattle is full of them. They're a bore. For some reason, they think you really care about their serial ports." The music stopped for a minute and so did all the women. Then Kool & the Gang started in.

Sara grabbed a sweat towel and wiped off her brow. "Yeah," she agreed. "Mothers always try to set you up with guys in the computer industry. But they're like lepers. I think they all ought to be forced to wear bells around their necks and yell 'Unclean, unclean' when they come at you."

"Mothers?" Tracie asked, remembering her article and wincing.

"No. Geeks," Sara explained. "Unless, of course, they're vested." Sara never quite got another person's joke, but she was sweet. Laura, who only liked sweet pastries, rolled her eyes. "I'm not into marrying for money, but I heard Allison talking, and she knows exactly how much every stock is worth. She said she's looking for some guy who's floated his own IPO, whatever that is."

"Allison," Tracie said dismissively. "As if a rich man would look at her."

"You don't think Allison's beautiful?" Sara asked.

"Nah," Tracie said. "She looks too much like Sharon Stone, but with a better ass."

"Hey, girls, speaking of asses," called Beth. "It's bicycle time."

"No, let's do the treadmill first."

"Let's eat lunch first," Sara suggested. "I'm starved."

"How about naptime first?" Laura asked, wiping the sweat off her upper lip.

They moved past the line of stationary bikes. The four of them each stepped onto a treadmill, punched in numbers, and started to walk. "So we know what we don't like, but what is it about challenging boys we do like? Why are we addicted to difficult men?" Tracie asked.

"They're such a big challenge," Sara said. "There're loads of them at the *Times*."

They were stepping in sync and their arms swung. "Yeah. It isn't easy to get a bad boy to love you, but you feel like if they did, it would really be an accomplishment," Beth added.

"I think they appeal to our maternal instinct," Laura responded.

"Get outta town!" Sara and Beth answered at the same time.

Tracie wished she had her Post-its.

"No. Listen," Laura continued. "It's like we get to practice on them. You know, they need attention like an infant."

"I think it's because they're easy," Beth said.

"Boy, are they *not* easy," Sara added.

"But they are in a way," Beth asserted. "You never get really close to them, so you never have to test your own ability to love."

All of them stopped, silent. For a moment, none of them wanted to meet one another's eyes. Even Tracie, the reporter, felt uncomfortable.

They all dismounted the treadmills and proceeded to the bicycles.

They were late getting back to the office from the gym. Beth was gathering her papers in a frenzy while also trying to brush her hair. Tracie entered her cubicle area. "Come on, you'll be late. Your hair looks fine. And Marcus will ignore you anyway."

"I just hate these meetings."

"Everyone does. But today I'm going to beard the lion in his den. I've got a really great feature idea."

Beth looked at her doubtfully as she exited her office and Tracie followed her down the hall. "You're crazy. Why discuss it in front of everyone and let him humiliate you?"

"Because I think I can get support from everyone. This is a really good idea. Funny. Cute."

"And we all know how Marçus loves funny and cute."

As the door to the conference room opened, Tracie could see that the meeting had been in progress for a while. She turned and shot Beth a look to tell her they were screwed. As she took her seat, she tried not to make eye contact with Marcus. He sat at the head of the table, an unlit cigarette jiggling in the corner of his mouth as he talked. "Nice of you to join us, ladies. Beth, did you get your piece on the new mayor finished?"

"Not quite, but I can get it in tomorrow."

"It better be good." He turned his attention to Tracie. "As for you, I want a feature on Memorial Day." Tracie tried not to show her excitement. It was the only holiday she cared about. She'd been hoping for this, and she had even planned to do some interviews with World War II veterans. She tried, though, not to show any enthusiasm. Marcus kept going around the table. "As for you, Tim, I'd like the indoor picnic story by Friday. And Sara, you get the author interview. I think this week Susann Baker Edmonds is in town," Marcus added, yawning.

Sara huffed as Allison tried getting Marcus's attention by flinging back her perfect blond mane. "Uh, Marcus? I thought I could cover the Radiohead concert."

"Forget it. You just want to sleep with them," Marcus said nonchalantly. "Well, if there aren't any more ideas or pitches, class is dismissed." He stood up.

"Actually, I have an—"

"Ah, the lovely Miss Higgins. Last Moment Higgins?" Marcus asked, and walked up behind Tracie.

"I'm sorry," Tracie said.

"I'm Sorry Higgins. I. S. Higgins. Don't Edit Me Higgins. Yes?" He put his hands on her shoulders.

She hated it when he did that. Though she really didn't like making eye contact with him, either. "I have this idea for a . . . well, for a makeover piece."

"What? Like those women's magazines do? The beauteous Allison tried to thrust one of those at me, and even *she* couldn't get me to bite. . . ." He must have smiled at Allison, because she had a look on her face that was like a child being noticed by her daddy. "Although I was very tempted. But not by the story. But as for you, Miss Higgins, the answer is no."

"Wait," Tracie snapped back, then twisted around in her chair to look at him. "I thought we could do it a little differently. I thought, well, there are so many computer nerds with money here that we could do a man—I mean watch a man get made over from a nerd to, you know, someone like you."

"Miserable and alcoholic," Tim murmured under his breath.

Marcus shot him a harsh glance. "I heard that." He looked down at Tracie. "What do you really mean, Tracie?"

She swallowed hard. "You know, sort of a spoof on those girlie makeovers. But also a real service article. Where a doofus could get a cool haircut, hip clothes. The dorky restaurants to avoid and the cool ones to go to. We could take a person and do a real *Pilgrim's Progress*."

"Could be cute. But how would you find someone who would agree to do it?"

"It would make the guy look like a real meat loaf," Tim said, sharing his opinion with the group.

"That makes you a candidate," Marcus shot back at him as he went to the door to leave. He paused and turned back to the table. "But that reminds me of something. It's time we did a survey piece about the best meat loaf in Seattle. Tracie, you take it." Marcus looked at Tracie. "I want a big piece with a lot of local places described in a positive way."

Tracie couldn't believe it. "And do they all win for best meat loaf?" she asked. "We wouldn't want to make any of our advertisers mad."

Marcus didn't even blink. "Only one winner, but a lot of four-star meat loaves. And Allison, could I see you in my office?" He pulled the door handle and slid out of the room.

Chapter 11

Jon was straightening up, getting rid of the take-out containers, pizza boxes, and back issues of computer magazines he had piled up. In his vast living room, there was a dusty but complete home gym, a fabulous entertainment system, half a dozen computers, and a small sofa. Once he got his new laptop, he'd finally unhook all of these. The doorbell rang and he looked down at his wrist, then realized there was no watch. Was it seven already? He looked up at one of the computer consoles. It was 7:20. He chucked the boxes in his arms into the hall closet and went to the sofa and picked up the rest of the magazines, threw them in the closet, too, and then turned to the full-length mirror on the back of the door. He slid the door open.

Tracie walked in, looked around, and hit her head with her hand. "Do you live here, or is this where you perform surgery? And the least you could do is listen to music instead of the business station KIRO. Did your stock fall or something?"

"I didn't even hear that it was on," Jon said. "What's the matter?" he asked, unsuccessfully trying to keep the plaintive note out of his voice.

"I don't have time to begin the list," Tracie said. "It doesn't matter, though. Rule Number Three: Never show them where you live."

Jon pulled out a Wizard 2000 and started to enter Tracie's wisdom into it. He'd already memoed himself on her other commandments. He was almost ready to keyboard it, when—

"Put that down!" Tracie told him.

"I'm just using it for notes," he protested. Tracie took it from his hand and put it firmly on the aluminum coffee table.

"Not anymore." She took off her jacket and handed it to him. He was about to hang it in the closet, but then he remembered the pizza boxes and thought better of it, smoothing the suede, folding it, and putting it over the back of the sofa. Tracie put down her bag, walked to the window, and turned around to face him. "So, back to Rule Number Three: Never show them where you live. No girl is going to come over here. It would ruin everything."

"They don't come over here now," Jon admitted. And it was too bad. The view was spectacular. "Not even my mother." Not that he spent much time here. He was always working.

"Then again, you don't get to go to *their* places now, either. Follow my rules and you will. You know, you're really kind, and so good at what you do. You deserve to have a wonderful woman in your life."

"Well, I do, but I don't sleep with you."

"Right. But now you can have both." She paused. "It's funny. You manage to do so well in work, but you can't pull your private life together. I can't manage to break through with work."

"And your personal life is okay? Excuse me, but your career *and* your boyfriend need a shot in the arm."

Tracie gave him a murderous look. Jon shrugged and moved to the refrigerator. "You want a drink or something? I've got cranberry juice and cranapple. Good for your urinary tract, you know. I think I also have—"

"Stop!" She got up off the sofa and went toward him. "Rule Number Four: Never offer them *anything*. You make *them* offer. That's the key to the whole thing. And never use either 'urinary' or 'tract' unless you're a vet, a gynecologist, or a religious fanatic." She took him by the lapels of his jacket. For a moment—a very brief moment—Jon thought she was going to kiss him. That or head-butt. "They're going to be asking *you* to go to bed with *them*."

"Them? More than one?" he asked, and realized his voice had risen an octave.

Tracie just ignored him, pulled on his lapels, spun him around, and twisted his jacket right off him. "Well, not at first," she said. "That's the advanced class." With a flourish, she threw his jacket in the wastebasket.

"Hey!" he began to protest, then remembered her stricture.

"No sports jacket. Ever. And no checks or plaids. Solid colors only. And dark ones. In fact, to begin with, we're going with the Henry Ford approach: any color you want, as long as it's black."

"Black? But I don't— Every—" he stopped himself. "Fine," he said.

Tracie walked around him slowly, like an officer inspecting the troops. "Where did you get that haircut?" she asked.

"Logan's."

"Never go there again except to clobber him. Stefan will try to fix it. If I beg him." She looked down at his legs. "Forget khakis. And you don't wear anything from the Gap, Banana Republic, J. Crew, or L. L. Bean." Jon was desperately trying to remember what she was saying, wishing for his Palm Pilot, and attempting not to take offense, all at the same time. "Look, if you wear this stuff, you'll just create a pucker in women."

"What's a pucker?"

Tracie made her big eyes bigger. "It's the female equivalent of a wilt in a man. There are some looks that are so bad, they make us pucker up to be sure we would never carry any of that genetic material."

"More information than I require." He tried to think of what, if anything, in his wardrobe was left. "So where do I get my—" he began.

"You wear either cool stuff from thrift stores or really, really expensive Italian clothes," Tracie said. "And you mix them. Let's go through your closet." She stalked across the room and pulled open the door to Jon's walk-in. He followed her. The clothes were meticulously arranged by pattern. Checks on one side, plaids on the other, descending down the color scale from light to dark. Tracie moved down the middle of the aisle like a machine gun mowing down soldiers. She pulled the first sports jacket off a hanger and dumped it on the floor. "No." She pulled the next and dumped it, too. "No and no and—ecch! No!"

"What's wrong with madras?"

Tracie ignored him, except to give him a withering what's-right-with-it? look. She opened his bureau drawers one after the other and scrabbled through his stuff. Jon panicked for a moment and wondered if there was anything that he . . . Well, he had no time to think, because Tracie threw him a black crewneck sweater, jeans, and—in desperation—pulled off her own belt. Jon cringed.

"No! Not the strap! Are bad clothes a whipping offense?"

"No, but spending real money on this crap probably is. We definitely have to go shopping. I'm not sure I can pull more than one cool outfit out of this. Okay? So here's the point. You *are* going to change: what you wear, what you say, where you go, what you eat."

"What I eat? Maybe we're talking too much change," Jon said.

"Hey, you asked for this. You get it." Tracie raised her brows. Silently, she gave him the belt and pointed back to the closet. He headed over to strip off his clothes behind the door.

"Change now?" She gave him a look. "That was just a question," he said as he slipped into the straight-legged jeans.

"No questioning the alchemist," Tracie called from somewhere near the door. "Otherwise, the magic doesn't work."

Tracie was going through his coats and jackets again. She began to bundle all the rejected clothes together and stuff them into a plastic bag.

Jon stepped out from the closet. Now he felt meek and small, like the real Oz. Tracie dropped the bag and looked him over. "Well, that's better. Except the shoes. No more sneakers."

"No more sneakers? But . . ." Tracie raised her brow and spun on her heel. "That wasn't a *but,*" Jon hastened to tell her. "It wasn't even a question. It was . . . a clarification. So what do I wear instead of Nikes? Sandals?"

Tracie turned back to face him. "Only if you think Jesus had a hot social life. Look, footwear is very important. Nice guys wear Nikes, or Top-Siders, Keds, or Converse. Boring! Sexy guys wear Doc Martens or boots." She squinted and looked him over again. It made Jon feel . . . peculiar. Surely she was taking this too far. "Look," she said with a sigh. "I have to tell you about the pants thing."

"What pants thing?"

Tracie seemed not to hear him. "I'm really trusting you by telling you this, but I feel you have to know. Most women have a pants thing."

"What?" Jon asked. He was afraid she was going to tell him that he had to stuff socks in his crotch and that women picked out their lovers and husbands based on bulge factor. He just didn't think he could bear it, but before he could tell her to stop, she began with a completely irrelevant question.

"Did you see *Out of Africa*?" she asked.

"The movie?" he replied.

"Yeah. With Robert Redford and Meryl Streep."

"No," he said.

"How about *Legends of the Fall*?"

"I don't know anyone over fourteen who saw that one."

"Well, there were some of us," Tracie informed him. "And it was all about the pants thing. A lot of women have the pants thing."

"What the hell is 'the pants thing'?" he asked.

She sighed. "It would be easier if you'd seen the movies. But it's all about a certain kind of pants. Not tight, tight ones . . ."

Relief flooded Jon like water on a service station's bathroom floor.

He wouldn't have to stuff his pants, though he wasn't sure what kind of pants he wouldn't have to stuff.

"But not those pleated pants, either. God, not those pleated khaki Docker things that make men look like throw pillows when they sit down. You want pants that are flat in the front. I mean, Robert Redford was already a middle-aged wrinkle bunny when he made *Out of Africa*, but he looked so damn good in those pants. My friend Sara says it's the swoopy hair thing, but most women I know admit it's the pants thing."

"Where do you get those pants?" Jon asked, mesmerized.

"I'll have to go with you. Because it's not just that they're flat in the front; it's also the way they hug your . . . back."

"How high do they come up?" Jon asked, imagining some kind of one-piece overall. "They cover my back?"

Tracie shook her head in despair. "I mean your butt. Sometimes, I admit, women look at men's butts."

"Not our crotches?" Jon asked.

"Don't be disgusting," she said dismissively. "Why do . . ." Then she looked up and was silent for a moment.

He couldn't imagine what she was seeing on the ceiling, but it was clear that she liked it. Maybe it was Robert Redford's butt. "It's a funny thing," she said. "It also has to do with the textiles. Nothing shiny. No. A man in shiny pants is . . ." She shook her head to get rid of the thought. "It has to be a smooth, firm fabric. See, it's about butts, but it's also not about butts. If you know what I mean."

Jon hadn't a clue. But he didn't want her to stop now. He felt as if he might be about to witness a biblical revelation.

"It's like most naked butts are not that cute, but one that's in a nice pair of pants, that's just sitting there kind of cupped by them, not too big, not too flat, just kind of narrow yet full . . ."

Forget this! "You are an embarrassment to yourself and others," Jon said. "Tracie, are you telling me responsible adult women make choices based on trousers and footwear? Details like that?"

Tracie opened her big eyes even bigger. "Jesus, Jon. In all these years, I never knew you were so ignorant. You know what they say: God is in the details. We—women—talk about details for hours. You guys are the big picture; we *are* details."

"But *I* am details. I was a computer analyst for four years. Nothing but details."

Tracie nodded, but not in a positive way. "Exactly. Wasn't that just the time your celibacy kicked in?" Jon tried to think back, afraid that Tracie might be right. "Look. Trust me on this one. It's not that there's anything wrong with your job. It just isn't sexy. Don't tell *anyone*."

Slightly hurt, Jon shrugged. "But what if they ask what I do?"

"And they will. Women want to know everything. You just be vague. Vague drives women out of their minds."

"In a good way or a bad way?"

"Both." She laughed. "It took me three months to find out if Phil was an only child. But the point is, they'll come back for more. Just clear your throat and tell them you're . . . in sales. Let *them* try and figure out if it's drugs or rebuilt engines."

"So let me get this contradiction straight: Women are driven crazy by vague and they go over details like monkeys on fur."

"Right. Beth from work spent an hour and thirty minutes today discussing the cable-knit fisherman's sweater that this guy she went out with wore on their first date and if it meant he was gay."

"Did it?" he asked. She picked up a black jacket and threw it at him. Jon struggled into it.

"Yeah, unless he's a fisherman," Tracie said, smiling at him. At seeing Tracie's pleased face, Jon struck a series of supermodel poses. "*Okay.* Now you're put together."

Jon went to the mirror and checked himself out. He had to admit he looked different—and improved. The crewneck sweater, one he only wore over a polo shirt, kind of hung off his shoulders in a sexy way. And the pants, though a little uncomfortable, were tight enough along the legs to make him look a little taller.

"Look at your buns!" Tracie said. "Wow! You've had hidden talent all this time."

He blushed, but it didn't stop him from half-turning to look over his shoulder. "Have I got the pants thing?" he asked, hoping it might be true.

"Well, the pants aren't perfect, but it's easier to fix that than the butt. Okay, this is what you're wearing from now on."

"You mean every day? How do I keep it clean?"

"The French only have one outfit and they wear it over and over."

"But they're used to body odor in France," he protested.

"Look, wash it out every night until we go shopping. It's worth the trouble."

"Can't we do it on-line?" he asked. "That's how I buy most of my stuff."

"Oh, that's why it looks that way. Do on-line shopping if you want to have on-line sex. If you want it up close and personal, we're going to have to feel the goods, babe." She looked him over. "You actually look really presentable."

He eyed himself in the mirror. He had to admit he looked a lot more like a man and less like a Salvation Army hanger. "I think this is a good look for me," he said.

"Meet me tomorrow night and we'll go shopping," Tracie told him. "It's something I'm very, very good at. And bring your cards."

Chapter 12

The first place Tracie dragged Jon to shop at was Secondhand Rose's, a hip vintage-clothing emporium north of the city. Jon looked around at the odd clerks and the rails stuffed with even odder clothes. "Tracie, this is used stuff," he said.

She didn't have time to explain. "No it's not. It's vintage," she told him, and started tearing through the first rack. She could get him shirts, sweaters, or even jeans that were new, but to replace that impossible Micro jacket, she'd need something that didn't look as if it came right out of the Gap. In her opinion, the key to really interesting dressing for a man was not to be *too* different from anyone else, except in a single particular: a fabulous jacket or a great pair of boots. And it had to be something that couldn't be ordered from a catalog or bought at a boutique—that showed no originality or interest. A Prada jacket cost big bucks, but any asshole with a platinum card could buy one. Tracie was looking for something unique, something that would fascinate.

Maybe that was why it was so hard to find something worn, unique, and appropriate. In a way, this would still be like being a billboard, but instead of advertising Bill Gates or Ben & Jerry's or Micro/

Con, you were advertising yourself—your inner self: "This is the kind of guy I am. One who bought this black lambskin jacket twenty years ago and wore it until it was the texture and thinness of baby's skin. And I love it." She looked at Jon appraisingly, her eyes partially closed.

Then she went back to the rack. Now, what jacket will tell people who Jon is—or, more to the point, who he wants to be? Tracie kept making the hangers squeal as she shoved them along the rack, past bowling jackets, polyester sports coats, and the tops of leisure suits. Nothing. Nothing. Then she stopped. A possibility. A long black frock coat with narrow lapels. She told him to hold it. Then she noticed the expression of horror on his face.

"This?" he asked, his voice almost matching the pitch of the hangers. "You want me to try it?"

"It's a start," she told him grimly, and began again to tear through the rack. A guy up ahead was also working it, and it looked as if he knew what he was doing. He was dressed well, cool, and was probably rich. He'd get all the good stuff.

Her nervousness made her hurry, and she almost missed a gem: a tight little black leather shirt hanging inside out. She looked at it and then eyed Jon, who was standing beside her, useless. He was watching her as if she had suddenly sprung a leak or something.

She searched and searched. At last, despite the guy ahead of them and the lack of decent material on the rails, she had accumulated a small pile of possibilities, which Jon was holding as if he was afraid of infestation. She'd even found a cool pair of trousers from a morning suit that might work. She took Jon to the corner where the dressing rooms were clustered and pointed to one. "Go ahead," she said. "Try these on." He stood there motionless.

"Did these come off dead people?" he asked.

"Who knows?" she asked. "Just put them on. The pants and long jackets first."

"Did you know the bubonic plaque was caused by fleas in people's clothes?" Jon asked her.

She ignored him and pushed him into a cubicle. "Put them on," she insisted. She waited. And waited. "What's taking so long?" Tracie called in to him.

The dressing room door opened very slowly. Jon stepped out wearing an outfit that looked a lot like the one Lincoln might have been shot in. The black frock coat was to his knees, and the long striped pants—well, he'd never be a Goth. Tracie snapped a photo, then gave him a thumbs-down. "Thank God," Jon muttered, obviously relieved, and disappeared back into the dressing room.

In a few minutes, the door opened again. This time, Jon was in an Austin Powers jumpsuit with a puff-sleeved shirt. Had she picked *that* out? Tracie was horrified. He looked like a gay space clown.

"That isn't for you," she said. "Where did you find it?"

"It was here on the rack," Jon said, shrugging.

She looked into the dressing room. There was also an orange overall and an aqua calf-length skirt. "Were you going to try *that* on?" she asked, hearing the same voice her stepmother had used when she inquired if Tracie would jump off the roof if her Encino friends did. God, there was something about shopping that brought out the bully in her.

She took the extra stuff out of the room and pointed to the garments she'd selected. "Only those," she told him. "This other junk must have been left behind by some circus carnies." Couldn't he tell the difference? If he couldn't, then he really *was* hopeless.

He tried on two more garments and she gave him another couple of thumbs-down. Jon shrugged each time and, in return, gave Tracie a grateful look. At least he went back into the dressing room. It was starting to look like a waste of time, until the door opened and Jon walked out in a pair of torn blue jeans and the supple black leather shirt. Now Tracie paid attention.

It wasn't perfect, but it was moving in the right direction. She walked around Jon appraisingly. She added the loden coat. Yes! He actually looked interesting. Maybe even good. She gave a high school cheer but then stopped in midjump. Now one of those sports jackets, the one near the end of the rack. She ran off and returned with a battered but stylish tweed sports jacket that she made him exchange the loden coat for. She regarded her living science project. Unbelievable. Now he actually looked hot.

Now that they were at the shoe store, Jon could at last sit down. He flopped back into the chair as if he'd been pushed. He'd never been so tired. Who knew shopping could be as exhausting as the Olympic decathlon? No wonder young women were so buff. Even Tracie—who once had held the Ms. Young Encino Shopper title—was tired from their bout with the stores. Jon, with none of her battle experience, must be absolutely dead, she thought. But there was one item still not crossed out on her Post-it list, and she was nothing if not thorough.

And who would have suspected that Tracie was such a shopping maniac? She was relentless. Some primal passion glinted in her eyes as she pounced on what looked to Jon like more useless and boring textiles. They'd been at it for hours, it seemed, and he'd spent more on clothes today than he had in the last two decades.

Now Tracie was holding up shoes for Jon's approval. These were suede, and awful. He contorted his face in an expression of distaste. Tracie pointed to another pair. Well, they weren't bad, if you liked pimp shoes. Jon sat up, trying to show some interest. Tracie handed him the left shoe. He picked it up gingerly.

"Not bad," he admitted, trying to muster some enthusiasm. Then he turned it over and looked at the price on the bottom of the shoe. He nearly fainted. You could support a Moldavian family for a decade on that amount.

"That's what good shoes cost," Tracie told him as if she could read his mind. He knew he better keep still if he wanted her help. He did as he was told, trying them on. Tracie flashed his credit card and forced Jon to buy them. At the counter, the owner smiled. Behind the head of the owner, written in Roman-style type, was a sign that proclaimed THE SOLES ARE THE SOUL OF THE BODY. Tracie pointed to it, nodded at Jon, and nudged him, as if to say, You see? Jon hunched his shoulders in defeat and put his feet into "de shoes."

Tracie stood beside Jon outside the shoe store. He was wearing the cool shoes, as well as the great jacket she'd found, but he'd begun to show his fatigue. Poor guy. Just another couple of stops.

"You're doing great," she said, and took his hand, leading him across the street toward a toiletries store. As they passed a young woman in the crosswalk, she turned to look back at Jon. Yes! Although Tracie noticed, Jon didn't even realize the girl was interested. What's wrong with his radar? Maybe he hasn't used it in so long, it's permanently broken, she thought.

She nudged him. "You're being checked out," she whispered.

Like a dork, he began to crane his head in every direction. Finally, he saw the girl. He returned her glance and then, to Tracie's horror, spun in a slow circle to show himself off.

"Are you nuts?" Tracie hissed, grabbing his arm and pulling him into the store. "Don't you know how to behave?" she asked him, as stern as a mom reprimanding a nine-year-old. "Never let them know you're looking back."

"But then how will they know I'm interested?"

"You're not supposed to be interested in them. They're supposed to be interested in *you*."

"But then how will we get together?" Jon asked. It was a reasonable-enough question, but somehow Tracie hadn't actually imagined that part. She'd thought of renovating him and about the before and after, but not about seeing him walk off with the girl in the crosswalk. But, of course, that was the whole point.

"We get to that later," she said, and took him to the men's cologne and aftershave counter. A group of bored saleswomen at the counter tried to glom on to them, but Tracie dismissed all but one—the oldest, most motherly one. The sales clerk proceeded to spray thirty different scents on various areas of Jon's body: his wrist, lower arm, upper arm, elbow, and neck. Tracie watched Jon twist with each spray and thought that ever since she'd met him back in college, he'd been dorky but kinda cute. Now, she noticed. Maybe he'd grown out of his dorky stage. When had that happened? Was it only now, with some cool clothes on, or was it earlier and she'd never seen it? "What do you think?" the saleswoman kept asking, and it wasn't in a motherly way at all.

In fact, a small crowd of saleswomen were gathering. Tracie looked at Jon. Once she had stripped off the ugly veneer of lameness, he was kind of cute, and there was something so sweet about the way he took the saleswoman and her advice seriously that it attracted the others. He was too inexperienced to know that fragrances were about hype more than anything else and that saleswomen would tell a size-fourteen customer in a size-ten skirt that she "really looks great." As her mean but shrewd stepmother used to say, "They lie like they breathe." Now the coterie consisted of two younger women, one blonde and one a horrible fake red, who began to flirt and bat their lashes at Jon.

"I think he's an Aramis man," the blonde who repped that line said.

"What's an Aramis man like?" Jon asked.

"Handsome. Important. And single." The blonde looked at Tracie. "Is she your sister?"

"No. I'm his mother," Tracie snapped, then looked at Jon, who appeared to be blushing. "We're looking for something a lot more subtle than you have to offer," she declared, and turned back to the older woman.

Meanwhile, the redhead had picked up Jon's left arm and was nibbling on it the way you might pick at corn on the cob. Jon smiled at the redhead with a kind of goofy look. Tracie yanked his arm away.

But by this time, the saleswoman had run out of available skin on Jon's wrists and arms. She picked up a crystal vial and smiled at him. "You might like this," she said. "It's very expensive, but I think it would suit you." She sprayed it on his neck and turned to the blonde. "What do you think, Margie?"

Margie immediately moved close to Jon and put her face up against his chest, nuzzling his neck. Tracie couldn't believe it! These women were without shame.

"It's got patchouli in it," Tracie said. "Nobody has worn that since 1974."

"It's coming back," Margie said, and then she looked at Jon. "I hope you do, too." Jon blushed again.

Tracie felt as if she was losing control of the situation, and she didn't like it. When the older saleswoman picked up another bottle and started to open Jon's shirt to spray some cologne onto his chest, Tracie slapped her hand away. "We've already got plenty to choose from," she told the woman. Jon kept sniffing like a beagle, while all three of the women gave him the eye but kept their hands off. Jon seemed to be enjoying the attention, until all at once he began to sneeze.

And it wasn't just one sneeze. It became three and then a dozen. In no time, he was spraying them all with bodily fluids. Even the blonde backed off. Tracie handed him a tissue. Freed of the fan club, she finally selected Lagerfeld. The saleswomen cheered and, despite his sneezing, Jon held the purchase over his head like a trophy. He grinned and, without being told, reached for his credit card.

Out on the street, Jon struggled with most of the bags. "I'm exhausted," he said.

"Yeah, shopping can wear a person out," Tracie agreed, but she was exhilarated. And when they passed a car stopped at the light, an older blond woman lifted her sunglasses to give Jon a better once-over. "You're ready," Tracie said.

"Ready for what? A couple of anti-inflammatories and a day of bed rest?"

In the safety of Java, The Hut, Jon, in some of his new regalia, and Tracie were seated at their regular table, packages piled around them. Molly approached, but Jon was too tired to raise his head to say hello. He pulled his feet out of his new boots. They already hurt.

"What are you doing 'ere? And where's Jon?" Molly asked Tracie. For a moment, Jon thought he might have disappeared from fatigue. But Tracie smiled, as if she knew what was happening.

"That's for me to know and you to find out," she told Molly, doing another Encino imitation.

Molly handed a menu to Tracie and then handed one to Jon. When Jon reached up to take the menu, she stopped, squinted at him, and did a double take. "Bugger all! That is you, isn't it?" She looked at Tracie with renewed respect. "You go, girl! Brilliant!" Then she turned to Jon. "Stand up, Cinderella." Molly took his hand, pulled him into the aisle, and then walked around him slowly. "My God! You look bloody marvelous. And you 'ave trouble written all over you."

"I do?"

"Big-time! Where did you get that fab jacket? And the excellent jumper?" Molly asked.

Since he had no idea what a jumper was, he only shrugged. "Tracie helped me," he said.

"Bloody marvelous! I love everything but the glasses. You going to get 'im some Elvis Costello ones?" she asked Tracie and gave her a look of something close to respect. "I take it all back. You're not useless," she told Tracie. She looked back at Jon with concern. " 'e looks tired."

Tracie shook her head. "No. His eyes are too good. He's going to get contacts."

Jon felt as if he had really disappeared from the table. Is this what women meant when they said men "objectified" them? Jon wasn't sure if he disliked it, but it felt odd.

"Tracie, I can't wear those things." Jon took off his glasses and rubbed the bridge of his nose.

"Wow!" Both Molly and Tracie exclaimed simultaneously.

"Is it because 'e can't focus 'is eyes?" Molly asked Tracie. "Or is it 'is eyes themselves that 'it you?"

"I don't know, but it works for me," Tracie cooed. "You've got to give them up," she told him.

"I'll be hitting walls and doors if I can't wear my glasses," Jon whined.

"Great! Scars are a real turn-on," Tracie said as she stood up, stepped back, and looked at him from a different angle.

"Why not? Did you ever try?"

"Call me crazy, but I can't stand the idea of pushing tiny bits of glass into my eyes."

"Well, it's either contacts or flying blind, because you can't wear these," Tracie said, twirling the glasses in her fingers. "You look like a newborn puppy, blinking like that."

"On 'im, it looks good."

Embarrassed, Jon felt himself blush, and he took his glasses back. Then Molly noticed the motorcycle helmet on the table. Oh, don't go there, Molly, he thought.

"Did you get a motorbike, too, luv?" she asked, as breathless as an original Beatles fan at Shea Stadium.

"No. Tracie said I just have to carry the helmet as if I have a bike."

"It was my one cost concession," Tracie told Molly, unusually chatty with the waitress for a change. "Plus, he'd probably kill himself on it and ruin all my work."

"Thank you for that compassionate expression of concern for my welfare."

"Is 'e tattooed? Or pierced?" Molly inquired.

Tracie took a disappointed breath and sighed. Jon knew that sigh. She'd be trying to talk him into a Suzuki GS 1100 before the end of the week. "He drew the line." She looked at Jon. "You know, I never noticed how heavy your beard is."

"Probably because I usually shave twice a day."

"For real?" Molly asked, raising her brows. "That's a lot of testosterone, darling."

Tracie stared at him, thinking. "From now on, you also can't shave—except once every three days," she pronounced.

"Oh. The old George Michael thing," Molly said, nodding in approval. "It would work."

"But I wouldn't," Jon told them. "I can't show up at work like that—looking hungover."

"Why not? It would make women wonder about your private life," Molly said, leering.

"Yeah. And then you might get one," Tracie added.

Molly crossed her arms then and looked down at both of them. "So, what are you two fashion victims 'aving? I've never served you dinner, so I'm curious."

"I'll just have a beer," Tracie told her.

"I'll have a mochaccino."

Tracie made a face.

Molly went off to fetch the drinks. Tracie leaned across the table. "You do look really good, Jon. And you were so patient. You didn't yell once. As a reward"—she paused for effect—"I'll buy you the mochaccino. It may be your last."

"Promises, promises." Jon sighed. Now that it was over, it seemed as if the episode had had a certain kind of charm. He imagined Tracie and himself years into the future, talking it over: Remember that time we shopped till you dropped? Back in the days when people didn't do all their shopping on-line?

Tracie got up from the table. "More lessons as soon as I come back from the ladies' room. . . ." She was off, and Jon sighed in relief.

Molly returned with their drinks. She slipped into the empty seat opposite Jon and looked him over again. "Bloody amazing," she said. Then she took his hand. "But Jon, don't you think this might be going a little too far? It might be fun to play fancy dress just once, if you got invited to the Oscars or something. But changing your whole persona . . . well, on some level, it must be scary."

"Especially when I look in the mirror, or at next month's MasterCard bill," Jon agreed. "But I've seen five or six women look at me tonight. That's never happened before."

"I've never 'ad cirrhosis of the liver before, but that wouldn't mean 'aving it now would be a good thing, would it now, luv?" Molly responded. "I mean, so what if a girl looks at you now? It's not the real you, is it?" She paused. "On some level, this is a betrayal of yourself." She waited for another moment, silent, letting that sink in. Jon was too tired for this. He just sat there, rubbing one foot with the other under the table. She looked around the restaurant, as if that would explain what she wanted to say. "I don't want to throw a spanner in the works, but 'ave you been to Freeway Park?" she asked.

Freeway Park was built on the roof of a highway. It was beautiful, with waterfalls and big lawns and terraces. "Sure," he said. "I watched them build it."

"Well, I can never rest there," Molly said. "No matter 'ow lovely and serene the fountains and the grass look, underneath it, there's insane traffic going in both directions. What I'm trying to say is, it doesn't matter if you pave over yourself with good sod." She plucked at his arm. "You're still you underneath these clothes. Think about what you Americans call your 'inner child.' Isn't 'e weeping?"

"I don't have an inner child, Molly. I have an inner dweeb, and he's doing the mambo because he thinks he just learned the magic words: 'Open sesame.' "

Molly shook her head. "I predict that at some point your inner dweeb is going to start fighting with this outer wild one," Molly warned. "Mark my words."

"What a world! A girl goes to the bathroom for two minutes and her so-called waitress becomes a psychiatric aide," Tracie cried. She stepped up to the booth and used her hip to evacuate Molly. "Traitor! I thought you were being too nice! Jon doesn't need any bad pop psychology advice from you."

"You're right. 'e's getting more than necessary from you."

Tracie ignored Molly. "You know, I was thinking. You need a new name. Jon is weak and Jonathan is lame."

"Oh. Perfect! Now it's not just 'is wardrobe and personality. Even 'is name needs changing," Molly said.

Tracie continued to ignore her. "Have you ever had a nickname?"

"My dad used to call me Jason sometimes, but I think that was because he forgot what my name really was," Jon admitted. "And my second stepmom called me 'the pest.' "

"It doesn't quite convey the sense of danger and sexual urgency I had in mind," Tracie told him. "How about Eric? I always thought that was a sexy name."

"Look, get real. I can't just have a totally new name," Jon protested.

Molly began to laugh. " 'ow about Big Swinging Dick?"

"I like it," Jon chimed in with excitement. "Or Big Swinging Richard, if I go formal."

"As long as it's not Little Richard, luv." Molly added. "Although I always 'eard 'e was *very* well equipped." Whether it was from fatigue or nerves or humor, Jon joined in Molly's laughter.

Tracie ignored the two of them. "There's got to be something . . ."

"Tracie, I'm not changing my name," Jon insisted.

"How about Jonny?" she asked. "Guys named Jonny are cool. Johnny Depp, Johnny Dangerously, Johnny Cash. They wear black and they're intense. They're heartbreakers."

"Yeah, like Johnny Carson," Molly agreed. "Or Johnny 'oliday, the French wanker."

He calmed down. "Well, I always wanted to be called 'Bud.' "

"Bud?" Molly asked. "Like on a tree? You can't be serious."

"No, like on a TV show. *Father Knows Best*. An old sixties thing," Tracie told Molly. "I wanted to be 'Princess.' "

"Now, that's perfect for you," Molly said sarcastically.

"Enough of that," Tracie said to Molly. "So, it's Jonny. And now that you're cutened up enough, I want you to go out on your own and start trolling for skank."

Chapter 13

A warren of a thousand tiny shops stacked on a Seattle hillside, the main fresh-food market of Seattle was a hive of produce sellers and their customers. But the market had become a lot more than that. Well-dressed Yuppies walked through, selecting endive or frisée for their dinner salads as they sipped their lattes from paper cups marked Counter Intelligence. It was incredible how espresso had become the craze of Seattle. Espresso drinkers had a language all their own—Milky Way, grande, skinny, extra foamy, half-caf. Jon always asked for a McD's spill, which meant the temperature should be as close to boiling as possible. Though he had been born and raised in Seattle, he still didn't know the names of most of the special coffee drinks.

Like most natives of any city, Jon didn't take advantage of what Seattle had to offer. He had never taken the Bremerton ferry, just across from Pike Place, still hadn't gotten to the EMP, never hung out in Gas Works Park, and he'd avoided the market, partly because when he was younger it was tougher and navy guys often hung there—a draw for hookers. What with work and the few dates he had, he hadn't been to Pike Place in years. When he wasn't working, Jon hung out at the Metropolitan Grill, which was the favored place for all Micro/Con employees. Here, though, there were Asian women dressed in Gucci, naval officers, a few hippie chicks wearing clothes they might have gotten from their mother's closets, an African-American who was wearing a turban and had a parrot walking across his shoulders, as well as the usual tourists. Jon's head was spinning.

But he was here to "troll for skank," as per Tracie's order. He stood in front of a baked-goods stand. Well, no time like the present. A blond woman, short and thin and dressed all in gray, stood outside. She looked like a nice person, so he tried to catch her eye. She avoided his glances, though, so he gave up. Blondes were cold, anyway, Jon decided.

Looking across the way, he spotted a tallish brunette in jeans and a green sweater. She also looked like good company—until she smiled. Jon wondered, for a moment, how much lipstick the average woman ate in a year. A tubeful? Two? What was in that stuff, anyway? Red dye number two? Did he eat it when he kissed a girl? (Not that he was in any danger of being poisoned lately.) Lipstick on the teeth, he decided, was a definite turnoff, but she did smile at him. He pushed himself forward and approached her. Now what? For a moment, he panicked. Why hadn't he prepared a line, a hello, a speech. God, he was standing there with his mouth open like a guppy. *Think, Jon, think.* "Do you know what time it is?" he finally managed to ask.

The brunette's smile faded. She looked him up and down. "No," she said, turned around, and walked away.

Embarrassed, Jon cowered next to the candle shop entrance behind him. God, I'm such a loser! Then he wandered over to a third woman, this one a little older and maybe a little less attractive. "Do you have the time?"

"For what?" the woman asked, then winked and waggled her eyebrows in the same bad Groucho Marx imitation that Tracie did. Jon froze for a moment, not expecting the response. Then, when he was idiotically silent, she shrugged and walked away.

On the other side of the marketplace, Tracie, Laura, and Phil wandered into the crowd around the seafood section. "This place is a caterer's dream!" Laura exclaimed.

"Yeah, but it's a tired musician's nightmare. It's a tourist trap. If you know any schmuck with a straight job, you'll meet him here on a weekend morning," Phil said.

"Pay no attention to him," Tracie told Laura. "Just look at this food. Maybe you'll set up business in Seattle instead of going back." She giggled. "Wait till you see the fish."

"Oh God. Not the fish," Phil moaned. "Next it'll be the fountain."

"What fountain?" Laura asked.

"The one at the Seattle Center. The water is choreographed to music," Tracie explained. Just to punish Phil, she added, "We'll go there after the Underground Tour but before the Experience Music Project."

"Oh, goody, goody, Mom," Laura said. "But what's so great about the fish? Good selection?"

"It's all in the delivery," Tracie told her, taking Laura by the arm and moving her toward the center of the seafood stands.

Laura looked up at a sign that read WATCH OUT FOR LOW-FLYING FISH. "They're kidding, right?" Laura asked. Just then, a screaming vendor whipped a flounder across to the cashier at the center of the stall. It almost whapped Laura in the head. "Oh my God!" she cried out.

"Okay, she's seen the fish. Can we go home now?" Phil asked. "Let's go back to bed." He yawned.

Tracie could see that Laura was embarrassed. Tracie could have kicked Phil.

"Hey, listen," Laura said. "I don't want to be in the way. I can just wander around by myself and you two can have the apartment to yourselves for the afternoon."

"Don't be silly. I love doing this. If I need privacy, I can go to Phil's."

"No you can't." Phil yawned again. "Bobby brought a band over. They've crashed at my place."

"That's not the point," Tracie said. "The point is, we're showing you Pike Market and we're thrilled to have you here." Tracie emphasized the plural and shot Phil a warning look.

"Oh, yeah," Laura said. "A thrill for Phil. Look, I'm going to take a look at that candle shop again. Some dork tried to pick me up there. Maybe I'll get lucky twice."

"Fine. We'll see you in a minute," Tracie replied as Phil pulled her in the opposite direction.

"That was really rude," Tracie told him angrily.

"What?" Phil asked. "Yawning?"

"Saying you wanted to go home." How could she explain that acting romantic in front of Laura was unkind? God, it might make Laura miss Peter.

"Hey, I worked late last night," he reminded her, as if she didn't know it.

"Yeah, but she's my friend. And it's my apartment."

He put his arm around her and lowered his voice. "And it's your bed, but let's both get into it." She felt a shiver down her back. Then, as if he felt her weakening, he leaned in and nuzzled her ear.

"Phil, I have to work this afternoon. I really have to come up with a couple of original ideas."

Phil put his hands on either side of her face. She loved it when he did that. "I have some original ideas."

"Not ones I can write about for the *Seattle Times*," she said, and laughed. She couldn't help it.

Leading her by her shoulders, he maneuvered her into a doorway next to a lobster tank. Just then, Tracie looked up and, through the lobsters, spotted a Micro/Con jacket. She peered through the glass. Jon. She'd forgotten that she'd told him to "troll" for a date. He looked lonely and glum. She pulled out of the doorway. Jon saw her and brightened, coming up beside her and Phil. "Hey, guys!"

"Hi there!" Tracie exclaimed.

"Hi!" Jon repeated. Phil didn't bother with a greeting.

"Didn't I tell you to forget this Micro/Con stuff?"

"The jacket, too?" Jon asked. "But I love my Micro jacket!"

"Jon, honey, you got to make them believe that *nothing* about you is Micro," Tracie said in her Mae West voice. "Anyway, what are you? A man or a billboard?" she asked.

"What difference does it make?" he asked her in return. "The new clothes are too confusing. I'm still not sure what goes with what. And I saw Samantha at work yesterday, but in spite of my new outfit, she blew me off."

"Don't worry," Tracie said in a voice she probably meant to reassure him with. "In two weeks, she'll be begging to be seen with you. You'll have to . . ." There was a pause, as if even she—his fan and guru—actually couldn't imagine the scenario herself. But she was a true friend. "You'll have to get a restraining order to keep her away," Tracie predicted.

"Yeah. Just call me Tommy Lee Delano," Jon joked.

Phil laughed. "As if you could land a babe like Pamela Anderson. Look, I'm gonna bum a cigarette." Without waiting for a response, Phil wandered down the aisle. Tracie allowed herself a tiny withheld sigh as she watched Phil's receding back. So, she noticed, did another woman.

"He's a pain in the ass, but doesn't he have a cute butt?" she asked Jon.

"I'm not an expert, but that redhead seems to think so."

Tracie glared at Jon, shrugged as if she didn't care, and stopped at the produce in front of her and, with exaggerated concern, began to select tomatoes carefully.

Jon watched Phil, who'd begun effortlessly talking to the redhead who'd been eyeing him. Jon wondered whether Phil's butt looked a lot better than his own or if it was something else that attracted women's attention.

"How do people do it? It's hard for me, but for some people it's so easy," he said, still watching Phil.

"I wonder the same thing. But Laura's been cooking since she was a kid." Jon realized he'd been talking about Phil but that she was talking about Laura. Love was blind. "It isn't just an instinct; it's a learned skill. Her dad taught her. And she's willing to teach me. You want a ripe tomato but a firm one." Jon watched as the redhead took a cigarette out of her mouth and handed it to Phil. He took it and put it to his own lips. The redhead looked like a ripe tomato all right. "It's got to be really red, too. Because you want it sweet."

Jon came back from his reverie. "I didn't know there was so much to a tomato. What are you making?" he asked, not that he was interested in that.

"Spaghetti sauce. Phil doesn't like to eat anything canned."

Oh God. Couldn't she get it? "Phil! Forget Phil. Tracie, you're such an idiot. You deserve someone . . . well, someone so much better." Jon raised his voice and called out to Phil, who was just leaving the redhead, apparently to come back to Tracie. "Do you know what the bass player got on his IQ test?" he asked.

"Uh-uh," Phil grunted.

"Drool," Jon replied, and looked at Tracie for a reaction. She giggled but then covered it by putting the bag of tomatoes in the basket. "What do you call a bass player with half a brain?"

"Gifted," Phil snapped. "I've already heard all of these from the band."

"You haven't heard this one. I just made it up. What's the difference between a bass player and a pig?" Tracie gave Jon a raised eyebrow, but he wouldn't stop. He turned to Phil. "A pig won't stay up all night trying to fuck a bass player." Then he glanced at Tracie. "Present company excluded," he said, as if that would make everything all right.

Phil flipped Jon the bird. "I'm getting those smokes," he said, and walked away.

"Okay," Tracie said, and watched him stride down the aisle. Then she turned to Jon. "Please. Don't antagonize him," she begged. She paused for a moment. "You know, I've been wanting to talk to you about an idea that Marcus shot down. But I'm actually thinking of writing it freelance and sending it around."

"That's great," he said. "Anything I can do to help? I'll proofread it, edit it, or—"

"That's not exactly what I was thinking about," Tracie said. "It's more like I wanted to put you in it."

"What? Another one of those profiles? I'm not interesting enough . . . unless the Parsifal project comes together. Then I'll be on the front page of every tech section in the country. Don't worry, I'll give the exclusive to you."

His morning wasn't going well. Jon believed in facing reality, no matter how unpleasant. So first he'd gotten blown off by three women, his jacket had been dissed, he'd had to watch a jerk succeed where he'd failed, and now he'd pissed his best friend off. As if that wasn't enough, there was a new embarrassment in the making.

Jon looked down the produce aisle in horror. There, coming at them with a full basket, was the brunette from the candle store, the one who had leered at him. Now she smiled with such a friendly smile that for a moment she was very pretty. Then he realized she wasn't focusing on him. She was smiling at *Tracie*. God! She was a lesbian! That would explain—

"Hey, congratulations. You traded Phil in for a new model?" she asked Tracie.

Jon looked from her to Tracie. Tracie was looking back at the brunette attentively, but she certainly didn't act surprised. They must know each other, he thought. The brunette gave him the once-over. "He looks familiar," she said. "I think you once tried to play Twenty Questions with me." She smiled at Jon. "Well, I guess Tracie gave you the right answers. Congratulations. She's a great girl. Did you have to kill Phil to get her? Or just give him a buck?"

"What are you talking about?" Tracie asked, but Jon had a nauseated feeling that he knew. "Do you think he's a—"

"I don't think anything," the brunette said smoothly. "I hardly think at all. You just look cute together. But are you mute?"

Jon was worse than mute. He was speechless, frozen in the kind of embarrassment he'd only experienced in that dream when you're naked on-stage and you've forgotten your lines. Because, with growing horror, Jon realized he'd tried to pick up Tracie's best friend.

"Laura, Jon. Jon, Laura," Tracie said over the grocery carts.

"The famous Jon," Laura cooed, almost laughing.

Tracie could swear that Jon blushed. God, he was impossible! He couldn't even meet a friend of hers without acting as if it was a big deal. Tracie tried to remember if Jon had been so retarded back in college. "The infamous Laura. You're the Sacramento cook, right?" Jon murmured, his face still red.

"Caterer," Tracie corrected. She didn't need these two not getting along.

"I seem to have interrupted something again," Laura said in the silence.

"We were just talking about Tracie's writing. How great it could be."

"Ha! *Could* is the operative word," Tracie said, sighing.

"You can't help it if your stories are cut till they bleed to death," Jon said defensively.

"Well, I could quit."

Tracie began to push her cart to the next aisle. Laura shot a grin at Phil as he rejoined them, with yet another bummed cigarette in his mouth. "You'd be a great columnist. Better than Anna Quindlen," Jon said.

"Who's Anna Quindlen? Do I know her?" Phil asked.

"Just a Pulitzer Prize–winning journalist," Laura said. "Now she's moved on to novels."

Phil shrugged. "I don't read commercial stuff," he said.

"Tracie, you really should write something independently, something you could be proud of," Jon continued, as if the Phil/Laura interruption had never happened. "Your dad would write you fan letters and all the kids from journalism school would send you résumés."

Tracie stared at him. No matter what, Jon always spoke up for her.

"Give it a rest!" Phil exclaimed. Tracie was dumbfounded by Phil's anger, but she didn't want to push his button. She knew that he was depressed over a rejection he had just gotten from some literary magazine. Of course, his work was so different from hers. It was dense and indirect. But it was best not to talk too much about her writing. It just antagonized him. He couldn't take it seriously, and she couldn't, either, because it was just commercial nonsense, after all.

"Laura, do you use white or Bermuda onions in your tomato sauce?" Tracie asked to change the subject.

"I prefer red."

Phil wandered off again. Tracie couldn't help but sigh out loud. She moved to the onions. Jon and Laura followed her in silence. Tracie tossed the onions into her basket and, with Laura, headed down another aisle. "Look, I've got to get a few things. I'll see you later," Jon said.

Tracie was surprised, because he usually stuck to her side like glue. Sometimes she actually had to whisper to him that he should go home so she could spend some time alone with Phil.

"Well, see you," Jon said. "Nice to meet you, Laura."

"Same here," Laura called back over her shoulder. "Let me know what time it is sometime."

"If you see Phil, tell him I'm ready to go," Tracie called out to Jon's back. She watched him walk away, and Laura watched, as well.

"So that's Jon," she said. "I think he's kinda cute, in an R2D2 kind of way."

"Jon? Cute? Yeah, I guess he is," Tracie agreed. "But is he cute enough to get himself a date?"

"Well, he acts like a dork. How much work have you already done on him?"

"I've just made a start," Tracie admitted.

"Why doesn't he have more confidence?" Laura asked. "He's smart and he's got nice shoulders."

"He's too smart," Tracie said. "You know, in that too-smart-to-be-good-for-you kind of way. He didn't have a father," Tracie said. "I think that really screws guys up, being raised by their moms."

Laura looked over at her and raised her eyebrows. "As much as being raised by their dads screws up girls?" she asked Tracie.

Tracie waggled her head the way they used to do back in high school. "Okay. Point taken," she said. "I shouldn't generalize, but you get the drift."

"Oh yeah, I get the drift. But do you?"

Tracie shrugged. "What?" she asked.

Laura laughed, then shook her head. "You are a mystery unto yourself," she told her best friend.

Chapter 14

Tracie sat across the table from Jon, observing him the way an artist might stare at a blank canvas. Well, she thought, it would actually be easier if he were a blank canvas. His clothes were a lot better—a black Armani T-shirt, the vintage leather jacket, and a pair of Levis 501s—but it wasn't coming together. His dorky haircut, his glasses, even his posture still spelled doofus. She knew what he would order, the way he'd eat it. It definitely wasn't sexy. Maybe Phil is right, she thought. I'll never win the bet, let alone get a feature out of this project.

Well, she'd never been afraid of a challenge. It hadn't been easy to get into the master's program or to talk her way into a job at the *Seattle Times*. It wasn't going to be easy to do this, either. Tracie sighed. "Okay," she told Jon. "People dating go out to restaurants a lot, so you have to be prepared."

"How?" he asked. "I've got my AmEx Card."

"No, no. I mean prepared to be . . . appropriate. Women notice everything. You've got to be careful of what you eat." She wrote a note to that effect on a Post-it pad.

"What I eat?" Jon echoed. "What do you mean?"

Tracie sighed once more, then began in earnest. "You're never ordering poached eggs or a Cobb salad again. Poached eggs are *not* sexy."

"Look, the truth is I don't even *like* poached eggs," Jon admitted. "I just love it when Molly yells, 'Adam and Eve on a raft.' It sounds so romantic."

"Only to you," Tracie told him. "Poached eggs are for invalids or babies, not for men."

Jon stared up at the ceiling, as if someone would have written permission for poaching across it. Exasperated, he asked, "Well, what's wrong with Cobb salad? I don't even eat the chicken. And I *like* Cobb salad."

"But you'd like getting a second date better," Tracie murmured, leaning across the table.

He had to agree. "No argument there."

Tracie smiled. The guy was highly motivated, as well as respectful. Maybe with a strong dose of both the stick of her disapproval and the carrot of sex, she'd stop him from being such a donkey. "Okay, here's what you have to understand: What women *see* you eat is important, especially when they're first sizing you up." She leaned back against the banquette. "Eating is like sex: You want to give the impression of both strength and restraint. Spontaneity, but with some health awareness." Jon was staring at her; that all sounded good, but confusing. Tracie paused. She was as impressed with herself as Jon was. She jotted most of it down on another Post-it. Then she remembered who she was dealing with and looked up, a horrified look on her face. "And for God's sake, don't tell them you're a vegan."

"I'm *not* a vegan," Jon whined. "I've told you. Vegans don't eat dairy or eggs. I'm a *vegetarian*."

Tracie rolled her eyes. "Whatever. Just don't tell them." Then, knowing him as well as she did, she continued. "And don't point out the difference. Remember, you're not an educator; you're a sex machine." She nodded to herself and wrote, "Educator—No. Sex machine—Yes" on yet another Post-it.

"So what exactly does a sex machine order to eat?" Jon asked. "Raw meat?"

From the corner of her eye, Molly, who up until then had been sitting over at her own dinner at a table in the back, stood up, noticed them, and came their way. Tracie braced herself for the usual hostility. "Bloody 'ell," Molly said, raising her brows almost to her hairline. "You rock my world." Then, and Tracie knew she did it just to annoy her, Molly bent over and gave Jon a kiss on the lips. He smiled up at her. When he smiled, Tracie had to admit he was kind of cute, even with the dumb glasses.

Well, it was easier to join her than to lick her. "Molly, could you help out here?" Tracie asked. "Pretend you're a waitress."

"Sure, luv. If you'll stop pretending to tip." Molly stood up even taller, straightened her shoulders, and pushed out her sizable chest. In a tiny voice, she said, "My name is Molly. I'll be your waitperson this evening. Our specials are vegetable lasagna and veal Parmesan and our water is tap. Can I get you a beverage to start?"

Jon laughed. That irritated Tracie. After all, she was taking this on as a serious project. And why did Molly always flirt with Jon? And why did he seem to enjoy it so much? She was way too old and—men! Tracie just dismissed the whole unworthy thing. "I'll have a mochaccino, please," Jon said.

Tracie gave him a thumbs-down. "No. From now on, you drink only beer, bourbon, or coffee—black."

Molly's brows went up again.

"I hate black coffee!" Jon protested.

"Not as much as you hate being dateless," Tracie reminded him.

"Check and mate," Jon agreed, and he turned to look up at Molly, shrugged, and made a face. "I'll have a beer."

"Can we see your ID?" Molly asked, to Tracie's horror. Jon actually began to reach for his wallet when Molly added, "Just joking!"

Tracie felt ready to cry. Or laugh. Jon getting carded on a date, oh God! She looked at him. You know, it's possible. She sighed. "I'll have one, too. Need *my* ID?" she asked Molly.

"Dream on, darling. So would these be pretend beers or real ones?"

"I'll spring for real," Jon told her.

"As you like it," Molly said, and moved off toward the bar, to Tracie's relief. But she kept eyeing the menu.

"Now, on to menu etiquette," Tracie began. "You're at the table, looking over the menu." She demonstrated. "*She* orders veal Parmesan. What do *you* do?"

"Tell her how they actually raise veal?"

"No! None of your political rants," Tracie warned.

"Okay. Okay. That was a pop quiz, right? I failed," Jon admitted. "Let me try again." He paused, thought it over, and started by lowering his voice to a basso profundo. "I say, 'Sounds good. I'll have that, too.' "

Tracie looked at him, clearly frustrated. She shook her head. "No, you don't. You look at her hard, raise your eyebrows, and say, 'Geez, are you really going to get *that*? Isn't that a little . . . rich for you?' "

Jon stared at her blankly for a moment, as if waiting for a bell to ring. "Why would I say that?" he asked.

"To set the tone. To put her at the disadvantage. To tell her you've already thought of her thighs. To make her begin to think her thighs might not be good enough for you."

"All that happens when I say veal is 'rich'?" Jon asked, his voice almost a squeak.

"Sure," Tracie told him. "Women—all women in *this* country anyway—think they're too fat. Every mouthful they take is accompanied by guilt. Use it."

Molly arrived with two beers and two empty plates. "I've been listening to you two. Let me try to get this straight. Right now, I'm a real waitress bringing real beers, but I'm also pretending to be a waitress and I'm bringing pretend food, but not veal Parmesan." Molly put two empty plates in front of them. She looked at Tracie. "Kafka didn't 'ave a patch on you."

"Ignore her," Tracie commanded. "Now, what do you say to the waitress?"

Jon hesitated. "Nothing. You just told me to ignore her."

"I meant ignore *Molly*," Tracie said, totally frustrated. She wished Molly would stop with those flying eyebrows and go away. "This is what you do with the pretend waitress: You say, 'Wait a minute. Stand right there.' Then you say to your date, 'Doesn't she have the most beautiful eyes you've ever seen?' "

"It's 'igh time you noticed them," Molly agreed.

Jon stared at Tracie as if she'd just told him to go down on a duck or something. "Wait a minute. You're telling me to compliment my date's eyes to the waitress?"

Impatiently, Tracie shook her head. "No. No! I'm telling you to compliment the *waitress's* eyes to your *date*. This will either really irritate the shit out of her or fascinate her. Or both." She paused in her tutelage and thought about it for a moment. "Anyway, women often can't tell the difference between the two."

"I can," Molly volunteered.

Tracie slapped her forehead. "Okay. Molly can. But you're not dating Molly." Tracie wished Molly would go away once and for all. She wasn't as self-conscious about her advice when she was alone with Jon. But in front of Molly, it seemed absurd. "So," she continued, "I'm talking about normal women. Now we're going to cover the fine art of complimenting." Tracie stopped for a moment to jot "Compliments" on her Post-it.

"Why can't *I* take notes on this?" Jon whined.

"Because only hosers take notes," Tracie snapped. She ought to tell him about her idea for a feature, but . . . well, maybe later.

"But you're—"

"Look, just concentrate."

"But there's so much."

Tracie had to agree with that. Oh, I'll never win this bet, she thought. "Okay, to begin, it's actually easier for us to cover what you *don't* say. So, for a starter, never tell a girl *she* has pretty eyes."

"Why?" Molly asked, and, to Tracie's dismay, she sat down in a booth behind them, preparing to stay.

"*Everyone* tells girls they have pretty eyes," Tracie told Jon. "Who doesn't have pretty eyes? Calves have pretty eyes."

"Yeah, well you don't think about that when you eat veal, do you?" Jon demanded.

"Would you give the veal a rest?" Tracie fumed. "The point is, pick out something small, a tiny detail. *That's* what gets them."

Jon thought for a moment or two. She watched him, holding her breath, hoping for a good one. But his face remained confused. "Like what?" he finally asked.

Tracie exhaled with exasperation. "Be creative. You do it all day at work. It's what you're good at."

"Yeah," Molly interjected. "And didn't you take Creative Complimenting at university?"

Thank goodness Jon ignored Molly and focused on Tracie. She stared right back into his eyes, which were actually a really pretty light brown—and his lashes were *so* long. Tracie wondered, not for the first time, why long lashes were so often wasted on men. Her boyfriend in high school had had lashes just like Jon's. The first time they necked, he had given her butterfly kisses all over her face with them. Funny. She hadn't thought of Gregg or that in years. He'd been so sweet, not at all like Phil.

"Just help me with this a little. Nudge me in a direction," Jon was saying. "Like, should I say, 'Mighty nice pair of incisors you've got there'?"

"And they'll bite the 'and that feeds them, luv," Molly warned.

"That's the general idea, but . . . I don't know." She sighed. "Look, you have to develop a feeling for it. Pick out a single feature. Her eyebrows, her cuticles."

"Cuticles? What's up with that?" he asked.

He watched as Tracie got a kind of dreamy look on her face. "This guy back in high school—my boyfriend Gregg—once told me I had beautiful cuticles. I had no idea what he was talking about. But that he noticed was so . . . so *attentive*." She sort of shook her head, then looked at Jon. "It was hot."

Molly extended her own hands, examined them, and then looked at Tracie's. "You know, I 'ate to admit it," Molly said, "but you *do* 'ave beautiful cuticles." She looked at Jon. "She's good," she admitted. "Sick as a parrot, but good."

Tracie smiled. "That's it. It's time for video."

"At this hour? Tracie, I can't watch movies. I've got a world of work to do."

"It's part of your training," Tracie told him. And she was up and out, leaving him to pay the bill and to follow once again.

Chapter 15

After midnight, the Seattle night was soft. The air felt heavy with moisture, as it so often did, but the mild temperature left it Skin-So-Soft. It was the time of night where you either gave in to fatigue or got a second wind and went out to party. But work loomed. "Come on," she said, and quickened her pace.

"Come on, you," Jon said. In the light that spilled out from the big windows of Java, The Hut, he already looked much improved. She couldn't help but be proud of her handiwork. If you believed the Bible literally, it had taken God six days to make the world. He must have been a man, because look at what a single woman could remake in just a few evening hours: Jon stood, his feet widely spread on the damp pavement, his arms thrust down and out from his body. He might still have the posture of a dork, but not the look of one. Tracie knew Jon was five eleven—and probably the only man in America who was five eleven and didn't cheat and say six feet—but now he looked tall. Her decision on the clothes had made him all vertical lines. His jeans, his chest-hugging T-shirt, the length of his jacket—all moved your eye up as if he were a long dark column. The only horizontal was the line of his shoulders. Thank God he had shoulders. And the jacket's subtle padding gave him a little more shoulder than what he had.

Too bad about the head. Not that he was ugly, but the haircut, the glasses, even the way he sort of hunched his head forward, as if he wanted his face to get somewhere before the rest of his body, spoiled her work. He needed swoopy hair as well as the pants thing. Well, Rome wasn't built in a day, she told herself, giving God a little more credit and herself a little more time. Jon, of course, didn't have a clue that she was admiring him. She'd have to change that about him, too. The man seemed to have no radar receptors at all. What did he think she was doing while she stood on the damp sidewalk staring at him? Meditating? Mentally reviewing a recipe for quiche?

"Come on, you," he repeated. "I'm going home."

"No, no," Tracie said, slightly raising her voice. "Just one more thing."

Jon shook his head. "Tracie, I appreciate all your efforts and I'm really grateful, but I just don't think I can take one more bit of criticism tonight," he told her.

She had to laugh. "Don't worry. We're just going to take a walk, and I'm going to give you your homework assignment."

"More homework?" Jon asked, his voice almost breaking. "Tracie, I left work before seven. I don't think I've done that since I joined Micro/Con. That's considered a half day there. Plus, I usually work for a couple of hours at home. Which I obviously haven't done, but it's waiting for me. A few days ago, in the kindest possible way, you and every salesgirl in the greater Seattle area laughed at my shoes, my hair, my eyeglasses, and my underwear. I spent more money in three hours than I've spent in the last three years, and that *includes* when I bought my condo. And now . . ." There was a quiver in his voice that Tracie couldn't quite figure. Either it was real fatigue, real pique, or a really good put-on. "And now you tell me there's going to be homework?"

Instead of answering him, Tracie began walking down the sidewalk. She figured that before she got to the corner, he'd join up with her, and, sure as death and taxes, he was there—unlike Phil, who was always looking for any opportunity to cut and run, and who probably wouldn't even be home when she called him. In fact, she reflected as Jon somewhat sulkily matched her stride, Phil could absolutely be counted on not to be counted on.

All at once, she was flooded with affection for Jon and his dependability, his doglike devotion. She took his leather-clad arm, squeezed it, and they walked in silence for a few moments. "Are you taking me to be pierced?" he asked in a very small voice. "Please say no."

Tracie laughed and turned them toward the doorway of Downtown Video. "Here we are," she said. "This won't hurt a bit."

"Yeah. When I was a kid, that's what my dentist used to say just before he hit the soft, pulpy nerve. Speaking of which, why are we going in here? Did you just realize Phil can't live without yet another viewing of *Pulp Fiction*?"

"Yeah. I want to freeze-frame poor Marvin's brain splat, like before The Bonnie Situation, the way your nerdy pals do." She disdainfully walked past the usual browsers gathered around the new releases.

Jon, newly energized, caught up with her in front of the suspense section. "Hey, that's not fair. *My* nerds have just gotten into *My Dinner with Andre*. Victor is trying to create a *My Dinner with Andre* video game."

Tracie laughed again and headed to the classics. Downtown Video was no Blockbuster: Here, the classics did not include *Rocky* or even the original *Die Hard*. The collection was as quirky as Mr. Bill, the legend who owned the place. Occasionally, he refused to rent videos to the undeserving. He also prescribed them like medicine, or—in extreme cases—performed interventions. "These are good movies but bad life lessons," he'd said once. "In the book, Holly ends up in the middle of Africa. And the George Peppard character is gay." He'd made her read the novel, and told her she could take out the video only once a year. He also cut her off from her favorite—*Love with the*

Proper Stranger. "She should have had the abortion," he'd said. "Anyway, the Steve McQueen character will abandon her in about eight months and she'll have to raise the kid alone." "How do you know?" she'd asked, angry. "Because I was the Steve McQueen character," Mr. Bill had said more angrily than Tracie was ready for. "Look at me now. A lonely fuck without a family, a son I never met, and a video store." She'd never rented the movie again.

"Tracie, if you rent *GQ's Guide to Debonair Sophisticates*, I'm going to shoot myself right here," Jon said.

"You'd need a gun to do that," she reminded him, then swiftly selected three videos and marched over to the counter. Jon followed her. She reached for his video card. This might be a *long* rental. He handed it to her as meekly as he had handed over his other charges and she passed it on to the clerk.

Mr. Bill, busy with restocking, looked up. "Oh. Someone is having a James Dean retrospective," he said. He looked over at Tracie and Jon. "And it looks like Natalie and James themselves." Tracie smiled. It wasn't a bad thing to be compared to Natalie Wood. Mr. Bill then opened the boxes suspiciously.

"Don't worry," she told him. "*Love with the Proper Stranger* is still on the shelf."

"You're not doing *Out of Africa* again, are you?" Mr. Bill asked sternly. He shook his head and looked over at Jon. "Looks like you found Mr. Trouble anyway," he said disapprovingly.

Tracie looked over at Jon and then couldn't restrain the widest of smiles. What success! Mr. Bill—aging bad boy, font of all wisdom, the purveyor of movies, truths, and practical cosmologies—actually thought that Jon was a troublemaker! "Don't worry about a thing," she said to Mr. Bill as she picked up the bag and led Jon out by the arm.

She was really pleased with her work so far. As they walked back toward Tracie's car and Jon's bicycle, she swung the bag full of the videos. "What was all that about?" Jon asked her.

"Not important," she said, suddenly stopping to survey him. "Okay, stand against that light pole and lean on the bench. Let me take a picture." She pulled out her little camera and peered through the lens. Wow! This would be great in the paper. Was she crazy to think of it as a book cover? "You look pretty good," she told him.

"I do?"

Tracie didn't respond. All of this would be great material for the article. She'd have to remember to jot it all down. "Okay," she said. "Look like you have attitude."

"Any specific attitude?" he asked. "Or is arrogant condescension the entire library?"

"Give it your best shot," she said. Jon posed, his foot up on the bench. Tracie snapped a picture. Just to be safe, she took another. Seen through the viewfinder, he looked even better. You couldn't observe the uncertainty in his eyes, or the irony he wore the clothes with. But, she reminded herself, this project wasn't all for her. He had to figure out how to get himself a girl. All he needed was a little confidence. She threw the camera into her purse and moved closer to him. "Now we're going to practice the look." Tracie indicated the seat. Jon took it and she sat beside him. She stared into his face. "Now, *you* have nice eyes."

"Really? You never told me that."

"Well, you do," she assured him. "But you've got to use them." She waited for a minute, trying to think how to tell him in a way that wouldn't embarrass her but would be effective. "You have to learn how to make them smolder. Remember Al Pacino?"

"I always confuse him and De Niro," Jon admitted. "Look, growing up, my mom and I would watch stuff like *Steel Magnolias*. I missed a lot of the mob films." He paused. "Was Pacino Sonny or the young Don?"

"He was Michael, who had to kill Fredo. God! You are weird. *All* guys know that!" She sighed. "Roger used to watch *The Godfather* every night before he went to sleep. It's kind of a guy's bedtime story." She thought of those nights with Roger while she lay beside him, lonely because he was more involved with the Corleones than he would ever be with her. "Anyway, remember how Pacino used to stare at the Sicilian girl?" Jon probably didn't, but she figured he was afraid to admit it. "You have to look at me, or *any* woman you want, with a single stare that conveys your entire proposal."

"Didn't we already practice that?"

"Yeah, this may be the most important thing you'll learn. So . . ."

"What do you mean? Right here? Right now?"

"Right here, right now. On a greater Seattle transit bench. Just focus and look at me."

Jon stared up at the streetlight. She followed his glance and watched the mist that wavered across its luminous surface, creating a watermark in the very air. I might get old here, she reflected, but I'll never wrinkle. Jon continued staring at the misty light. "I'm asking you to direct this staring at me," she finally reminded him.

"I can't," he told her.

Tracie sighed and handed him the bag. "That's why we rented these James Dean tapes. *Giant*, *East of Eden*, *Rebel Without a Cause*. Watch the Ferris wheel scene in *Eden* carefully. Watch his hands. And the way he looks at Natalie Wood in *Rebel*."

"Tracie, these movies are forty years old!" Jon opened the bag and examined the tapes as if there might be mold on them.

"Yeah, but sex never goes out of style. He was the first great bad boy," she explained. "Meanwhile, just try to hit me with your best shot."

Jon sighed deeply, turned his upper body toward her, and put his brows together. He looked a lot like Superman trying to melt rock with his X-ray vision. She laughed and, immediately offended, he got up. "Come on, Tracie. I can't look at *you* like that."

"I'm sorry. I'm sorry," she apologized. "But I want you to be able to look at hairy bus drivers like that."

Jon tried again and failed again, though this time, they both laughed. "Well, that looked like it might lead to a bodily function," she said. "Though not one I'd want to witness," she added.

"You're disgusting," he said. Then he set his shoulders and tried again. This time, his eyes cleared and the uncertainty was gone. They were dark pools, and the color deepened to the shade of melted chocolate.

"Not bad. But more focus. Project that heat. Look at me as if you've *really* wanted me for years."

Jon figured that wouldn't be hard. He shot her a look that could melt steel from twenty yards. Tracie opened her own eyes wide and felt suddenly uncomfortable. "Uh," she said. "Uh-huh. That's . . . that's pretty good. Uh, maybe that's enough for one night."

Slightly dazed, Tracie stood up. Jon mussed her hair. "Come on, Professor. I'll walk you to your car. But what's my next step?"

"It's time to test the waters," she said. "You couldn't do it at Pike Place Market, so I'll have to find you a date."

Chapter 16

Jon hit the eject button on the VCR and the cassette jumped out of its slot like a Pop-Tart from the toaster. He'd watched *East of Eden* four times. The images of the sensitive, lonely Cal—played by James Dean—didn't strike him as sexy. The guy seemed like a typical bruised loser, not the kind of man women went for. The girl, Aber, going with Cal's brother, played by Julie Harris, didn't seem to go for Cal, either. Why should she? He was neurotic and moody. It seemed to Jon that it was pity that kept drawing her to him. The way he kept going to his father for approval—that whole frozen lettuce episode. Yikes. Why couldn't he accept that his dad was a useless, demented waste? No biggie. Jon's own father was a waste in most ways. And he wasn't even Raymond Massey.

Jon pulled the sweater over his head, shrugged himself into the weird used jacket Tracie had made him buy, and then stood in front of the mirror. It was easy to see himself, because all the clothes that used to hang in the closet, obscuring the mirror, were just about gone.

He had to admit it was a very different Jon who looked out at him. Maybe that's why he was no good at hunting down women. It was hard for him to think about them as scores or one-night stands. Yet, inevitably, some of them would be if he didn't like them enough to be with them permanently. That's where it all got so confusing. He hated rejection. But he'd hate rejecting a woman more. He thought of his mother, and all the women Chuck had rejected. God knew how many, since all Jon knew were the ones he'd actually married.

But Tracie was going to change all that. He was going to out Phil the Phils and finally use his head to figure out a way to do it. He had followed Tracie's directions—the really tough ones. He hadn't shaved, and his feet, slipped into boots, were killing him now. He was sure he would get blisters the size of kiwis, and probably just as green. Actually, he'd once read about a guy who died from infected blisters. If it happened to him, he hoped it would be after he got to make love with a woman or at least sleep with her. Tracie would feel very, very bad at his funeral. He had to admit that he looked good, but he sure didn't look like himself. He looked like some guy sneering at him. He sneered back, but that just made his reflection worse. Jesus, what am I doing? Next I'll pull a Travis Bickle and ask if I'm talking to myself, he thought.

Jon shook his head. He definitely didn't look like a chocolate Lab anymore. Maybe a weasel or some kind of dark fox. Well, he guessed that was the point. He took out his Samsonite with the broken handle and the wheelies. He was about to open it, when Tracie's tutelage paid off. He could see her perfectly adorable, slightly crooked nose crinkling in disdain. He could almost hear her say, "Wheelies are *definitely* a pucker."

For a moment, Jon wondered what kind of suitcase James Dean would have. But he couldn't remember the guy carrying anything but Sal Mineo in any of the movies. Maybe cool guys didn't take luggage. They traveled light. He sighed. All of this was so complicated.

But now, for his plan to work, he had to have some luggage. After scouring his place for a quarter of an hour, he settled for an old black duffel bag he'd used for laundry back in college. He threw a few pairs of running shoes into it for heft, filling out most of the rest with crumpled *Seattle Times* sheets—being careful to save all the pages with Tracie's features. As he zipped the bag, he hoped this was worth all the trouble. Not that he had much hope.

But despite his usual pessimism, Jon had to acknowledge *something* was undeniably happening. Maybe it was the new clothes. Maybe it was something in his attitude that Tracie's not-so-tender ministrations had changed. Whatever, it was clear that women were definitely behaving differently around him. At work, secretaries, analysts, and even a few of the female executives had started to greet him whenever he walked past them. Even Samantha had volunteered a hello. He was sure that never used to happen, except for a few he was actually friends with. And it wasn't just that. There was something about the way they said hello—something in their voices. It wasn't a come-on, exactly. But Jon was amazed that two simple letters combined, like *h* and *i*, were so musical.

The weirdest thing wasn't that women were noticing him. He guessed that was the point of this whole exercise. The weirdest thing was how he felt about it. Like in the grieving process, there seemed to be multiple phases, three of which he'd already gone through: denial, delight, and pain. Because while at first it had just surprised him, then tickled him, it now hurt his feelings. It had taken him a little while to figure that out. Of course, he knew he should be grateful for even the slightest notice. And he had been. But then some kind of shift had taken place and he had moved from delight at the attention to hurt feelings when even Cindy Biraling, the adorable blond secretary to the CFO, began to greet him (she was notorious for ignoring people, even when they stood with the front of their thighs touching her desk). Over the years, whenever he'd had to drop by or call Cindy, she'd asked not only for his extension but how to spell his name—a sure indication that she hadn't had a clue to what it was. Now she sang out, "Hi, Jonathan." It had started to make him mad. Why hadn't she said hello before? And how come she knew his name now?

But whatever new magic—and the mood that accompanied it—existed, it didn't extend far enough to grant him a date with Cindy—or anyone else at work. He still seemed to be as tongue-tied and moronic as ever with all of the women. Tracie had said that he needed to try himself out in another environment, where no one knew him, but he just couldn't face going into a bar. He'd tried for two nights and couldn't get himself to walk through the doors. All the humiliations of past look-sees and sitting on bar stools, all the past women's put-downs seemed to stand like the angel at the entrance to Eden, barring the way.

And it wasn't just walking into the bar. Somehow, the new attention from women at work had made him feel all his past social-life traumas more acutely. Facing a strange woman that, in Molly's terminology, he was going to try to "chat up" stopped him cold. It wasn't just that the prospect was daunting. He could have done it if it weren't for the Phils, always sitting easily at the bars, seeming to watch his fumbling technique, disdaining his pathetic openers and his feeble attempts at humor. It was as if the Phils of the world could see past his new black sweater and the 501s and the boots he was wearing.

And so he was left with figurative and literal cold feet. Jon had decided that he was going to have to find somewhere to meet women where he wasn't known and he wasn't up against the competition of a bunch of Phils.

Hence the duffel bag.

Jon picked it up. The newspapers partially filled it out, but it was still so light, he'd look strong being able to lift it effortlessly. He shrugged, wished himself good luck, and put on the Tracie-selected lambskin leather jacket. He sighed and tried not to feel guilty. The lambs had already been led off to their slaughter, and now he would probably follow them to his own. It's what he deserved for letting Tracie talk him into the jacket in the first place. His feet were freezing! And it would be drafty at the airport. He wished he could put on a pair of thick gray wool socks, but if God was in the details, his toes would have to freeze.

The buzzer sounded, indicating the taxi was waiting. He grabbed a Huey, Louie, and Dewey Pez dispenser for good luck, picked up the duffel bag, locked the apartment behind him, and rapped down the stairs to the dark street below.

The airport wasn't too crowded, which Jon figured was a good thing. And no one accosted him; plus, today there were no chanting Krishnas. He took those as good signs and immediately rode the escalator down to the baggage claim. He checked out the arriving flights, though he'd already targeted his. Of course, instead of the gambit, he could get an actual ticket and just choose to stand in line behind a pretty woman and chat her up. But he figured people were often nervous before flights. He really would be better off trying to get someone who was getting off a flight. But this was not without risks.

To be less conspicuous, he'd asked the driver to drop him off at the arrivals area, but the driver had said, "No can do. You got to check in and go through security upstairs." Jon considered explaining his mission, then changed his mind. From what he could see from the back of the haircut and the part of the driver's face reflected in the rearview mirror, the guy wasn't quite a Phil, but he could have been a Phil at an earlier time, before he lost a few of those teeth. Jon wasn't telling him anything.

So, walking across the wide baggage claim area, he surreptitiously eyed the group of passengers who'd just arrived on Flight 611 from Tacoma. Tacoma was nice. His uncle and aunt lived there. If a woman had been to Tacoma for business or even to visit her family, he figured she might be very pleasant. Of course, if she lived in Tacoma with her husband and was here to visit her mother, this was not a good thing. He began to scan the crowd. How could you tell? The DC10 held about 280 people. He told himself that at least one had to be female, attractive, and single. But how to tell she was available was another problem. He noticed a blonde, but she was a little too thin, too tall, and too pretty. There was something about the way she swung her head that made her hair move like ten thousand silky strings, and it gave him the feeling she was doing it to be looked at. She was probably considering a move to L.A. Way upmarket for him.

Next, he spotted a redhead with curly hair that seemed so alive, it looked professionally snarled. For all he knew, maybe it was. People probably paid to have that done. Anyway, the woman was cute, and that was enough. Okay. Here I go, he told himself. Instead of throwing his hat into the ring, he threw his bag on the carousel, walked around it as casually as he could, and tried to think of something to say to a total stranger.

It was only when he got right up to her side and saw her in three-quarter view that he realized she was very, very pregnant. Clearly, someone else had thought she was adorable, too. Well, there goes that plan.

With the blonde as too much of a stretch and the redhead about to drop a baby . . . Well, there wasn't a lot left. He eyed the crowd. The usual grandmothers with a toy under their arms didn't excite him, and the harried mothers with children in tow—children wild from the confines of the flight—were also a real stretch. It looked like everyone else was male, except for the person who was far taller than he, wearing silk pajama trousers and a Brooks Brothers–type oxford cloth shirt. It might have been a man or it might have been a woman. Or perhaps someone in the process of changing from one to the other. But since Jon had never had the faintest desire to reenact the famous *Crying Game* scene, he figured he had enough issues of his own to deal with and began to despair.

It was then, as his eyes moved away from the baggage carousel, that he began to fold, the state that for him preceded a complete rout. Then he noticed the young woman standing at the next carousel. He caught his breath. Maybe he wouldn't leave in defeat. A shaft of sunlight—rare in gray Seattle—illuminated her as if she were part of a medieval manuscript. She was perfect. In fact, she reminded him of someone. It wasn't the fine light brown hair cut just below the ears or her profile, which he could see was deserving of the very best cameo maker. It was something in the set of her shoulders and the way she stood that immediately attracted him. Tracie would stand just like that if she was waiting for her luggage. His heart leapt but then fell.

Because the woman—she might have been a year or two older than he, but not more than that—was obviously arriving on the flight from San Francisco. That was a whole different kettle of passenger. If she was *from* San Francisco and just here for a visit, she was probably going to be way too cool for him. If, on the other hand, she was from Seattle and had only *visited* San Francisco for a vacation, there might be a chance. However, if she lived in Seattle now but had originally been raised in San Francisco and had been visiting her family, she would . . .

Jon forced himself to stop the madness. It only proved there was bound to be some way or other that he could think himself out of doing what he feared most. He looked at the woman again. She was lovely. A Lovely Girl. "This is it," he murmured aloud. "Go for it."

He tried to slouch the way James Dean might and, unemcumbered by any packages and without a fanny pack, he stealthily moved toward The Lovely Girl. Completely unaware of him, she was standing with her weight all on her left hip. With her right foot, she was tapping a small tattoo. It wasn't an impatient tap exactly. It was more of a stretching exercise that she was executing with her adorable foot. In fact, as he looked more closely, he realized that all of her was adorable, from the peripatetic toes to the top of her head. Jon simultaneously felt a lustful pull in his loins and a lurch of fear in his stomach. This is dangerous physical work, he told himself, and, before he broke a sweat and ruined the Armani T-shirt Tracie had made him buy, he placed himself directly behind The Lovely Girl. Using all his willpower, he forced himself not to look at her but to stare blankly at the empty conveyor belt, just the way everyone else was.

He tried to count slowly to one hundred, but he only got to sixty-seven. After all, what if her bag came now? He cleared his throat. "Is it just my misperception, or does it take longer to get your luggage than to fly from San Francisco to Seattle?" he asked aloud. Okay, it wasn't a great opening, but at least he hadn't asked for the time. The Lovely Girl turned her head and he had a look at her profile. Her nose was long and slightly irregular, which, in his opinion, made her cuter. Her skin was luminously pale. This close, Jon could see very fine freckles strewn just across her cheekbones and over the bridge of her aquiline nose. There was something very tender about the tiny constellation. Meanwhile, she looked in his direction for a moment. Then she smiled.

"It does seem to take a long time," she said.

Her voice was water splashing over stones, champagne flutes clinking. Jon allowed himself another brief look at her and then tore his eyes away, remembering not to smile. He shifted his body, pulling in his stomach, thrusting out his pelvis, and crossing his arms over his chest. But then he didn't have a clue what to do or say next. The James Dean pose was a start, but The Lovely Girl had looked at him, was looking at him, with an expectant—or perhaps tolerant—half smile and was clearly becoming restive with the wait.

What came next? He could offer her a ride into town. If only he had a motorcycle. He sighed. Tracie had been right, as always. Oh well. He racked his brain. What could he say?

Just then, a bell rang, and in another moment, the conveyor belt began to move. A young boy, three or four, by the looks of him, began to move, too. He'd been crawling about on the dirty floor and then he'd crawled onto the carousel. For a moment after it began and the horns went off, the little kid was transported—not in a literal sense—but then as the belt lurched him forward and away from his mother, his mood quickly changed. He opened his mouth and a roar of anguish, much louder than a mouth that small seemed to be able to utter, streamed out. Poor kid.

"That's the one from the plane," The Lovely Girl said. Just before the toddler rolled by, Jon swung into action. He bent over and picked the little boy up, swinging him back to his mom's feet. Unfortunately, getting off the wagon train didn't stop the scout from screaming. The little kid's yell got even louder and his face was turning red. The Lovely Girl, as well as Jon's other neighbors, actually backed off. Jon didn't know what to do. He supposed picking the tyke up again was a good idea, but the boy was filthy, and— "Cut the crap, Josh," the boy's mother said, and took the poor kid by the left hand, gave him a yank, and—without thanks to Jon—led the boy away.

The Lovely Girl and the other passengers returned like the tide and she looked up at him. She had gray eyes, Jon's favorite color, and although they were a tiny bit more deep-set than might be considered absolutely perfect, they were more than good enough. But Tracie had told him not to compliment eyes, so he was out of luck there.

"She didn't even thank you," The Lovely Girl said. Surprise more than outrage was outlined on her pretty face.

"No, but later she's going to nominate me for a MacArthur grant," Jon quipped, hoping that those gray eyes wouldn't give him the blank look he usually got back from people when he made those kinds of jokes. Instead, she laughed. She actually laughed! Maybe this was all easier than he'd thought. Maybe it was only a question of showing up at the right place wearing the right kind of used jacket.

Now bags of every description began to slide down the chute and come around the carousel. It was only then that the implications of the fact that his luggage was on the wrong conveyor dawned on Jon. Well, he'd just pretend he'd lost his luggage. That happened all the time. It might make The Lovely Girl sympathetic, although it also might make him look like a schmuck.

Quickly, he thought about what James Dean might do if his luggage was lost, but none of the films gave him a clue whether that would happen or what James would do if it did. For a moment, Jon felt deep bitterness. What good was tutelage if you knew how to react when your lettuces rotted but not when the airline lost your luggage?

Desperate, he tried to think of something else to say to The

Lovely Girl. It was certainly too soon to ask for her name. The luggage coming out of the hatch seemed to be the only thing of interest to anyone. It came in two types—black and indistinguishable from every other piece or one of a motley collection of every kind of bag imaginable, all of which displayed neon yarn, glow-in-the-dark stick-ons, or duct tape so that the owners could distinguish the piece from the myriad others. As if that would be necessary.

So, what to do? Help her with her bag! He looked at The Lovely Girl out of the corner of his eye and tried to imagine her luggage. She would never have a tatty hard-sided avocado green suitcase with pink pearlized nail polish X's along the side. He shook his head as that bag rolled past, and then a miracle happened: *She* spoke. "Isn't it hideous?" she asked. "What people use as luggage, I mean."

In his amazement, he forgot to answer her. He was too busy thinking that she might actually—as Molly might say—"fancy" him. She'd spoken. And she'd spoken a thought he'd had. Maybe there was real possibility here. Well, no sense sending out the wedding invitations if he didn't respond.

"Their bags are as ugly as their travel togs," he said. God! Togs? Who used the word *togs*? Men in smoking jackets. Guys who wore ascots and used cigarette holders. He'd better explain that. . . .

"Oh, I know. My mother said air travel used to be glamorous. That people dressed up for it. Can you imagine? Did you see that getup the mother with the spit-up baby was in?" she asked, then paused. "Oh, probably not. You were in first or business, weren't you?"

It was unbelievable! Here she was, telling him he looked like quality and actually leading him on. Had it always been this easy, even though he hadn't known it and didn't have the tools? Could a leather jacket and the heel blisters make all the difference? Blisters were worth it.

Newly confident, Jon changed his position to what he considered a cooler stance. "I didn't see it, but I smelled something sour," he told her. He reached into his pocket and pulled out Huey, Louie, and Dewey. "Care for a Pez?" he asked.

She chuckled but shook her head. "You're funny. Do you live here, or are you in town on business?"

It was his dream come true, but just how should he answer the question? He'd expected her to ask that. Should he lie and make her believe he was a traveler? Tell her the truth and let her know he was a local? And what should he do about his bag on the other carousel? "I'm here scouting for talent," he said, then thought, What a lame thing to say.

But she didn't seem to think it was odd, or a lie. "You're kidding? I'm just here for a magazine shoot for Micro/Con," she told him. "They want to make their new motherboards look like a mother lode, if you get my meaning."

Holy mackerel! "Do you have any photos you can show me? Maybe I could help you out," he said.

"Let me have your number so that once I unpack I can get you a portfolio."

"Sure." Jon couldn't believe how easy this was. She wanted his number! Okay, so it was under false pretenses, but what the heck. "Do you have a pen and paper?"

The Lovely Girl rummaged through her bag but could only find a pen. "Here," she said, and thrust her hand, palm up, at him. "Write it here."

Wow! What could be better than this? Jon reached out and took her hand. A shiver went through him at the touch of her flesh. Calm down, he told himself. He jotted down the number and folded her fingers up into her palm. "Don't lose it now," he joked as he slowly released his grip on her hand.

"It's about time," she said, and Jon wondered if she meant that he'd been moving too slowly. Then she stepped toward him. Boy, she's aggressive, he thought, but she went right by him and was reaching out her hand when Jon realized she was after her bag.

"Let me get that for you," he said, pouncing on the opportunity. Great. She'd get her bag, leave with his number, and never notice that his bag was on the wrong carousel. He grabbed the bag by the handle, glanced at the name tag, and started to lift it off the rubber mat, then realized he was going completely against the rules. What had Tracie told him? To take, not give. This was old Jon behavior. He quickly let go of the bag as if the strap were burning-hot. The Lovely Girl, Carole Revere if her luggage tag was accurate, looked at him in mild surprise. "Sorry, Carole, I got a cramp in my fingers," he told her lamely. The suitcase was half on and half off the conveyor. It kept moving down the belt. The Lovely Girl gave him a funny look as she went to retrieve the bag herself.

Then she just stood there, holding her bag. What was she waiting for? He had apologized for dropping it. What else was he supposed to do? He must have had a strange look on his face, because The Lovely Girl started talking again. "I have two bags."

"Uh-oh," Jon said, and smiled at her. "I'm beginning to think my bag isn't coming." She'd notice he didn't have a bag. What could he say? The crowd from the Tacoma flight was thinning out. He forced himself to chuckle. "Wouldn't it be a strange coincidence if our bags were lost together?" he asked. "Being together would be our destiny." Oops, Jon thought, I might have gone too far, been too friendly with that comment. Hadn't Tracie told him that he was supposed to make them want him, not show he wanted them? But, based on The Lovely Girl's expression, he figured he was still doing okay. Just don't screw this up, he told himself. But that made him even more nervous. Keep calm, he instructed himself sternly. He looked at her again. She *really* was lovely.

"Maybe our bags have been confiscated. Maybe they'll check them for weapons," he said. God, that sounded crazy. What did she think he was talking about? He was only trying to be funny. "You know, like Ted Kaczynski or something." But she didn't smile. Maybe she didn't know who that was. "You know, the Unabomber." She nodded. He laughed with relief.

"Why would they search our luggage?" she asked, her voice totally reasonable.

Yeah. Why would they? What a stupid comment. He was insane

and he was blowing this. He had to reassure her. He was panicking. "Who knows what they do. Right? But I can guarantee that They definitely won't find a typewriter if They search my luggage. The Unabomber wouldn't travel without that piece of equipment." He tried to laugh. "My bag's guaranteed to be typewriter-free. In fact, it's so light, it could be stuffed with newspaper."

Oh no. Worse and worse. Jon was ready to weep, but he tried to keep his face completely neutral. From the corner of his eyes he again saw his bag, black and ominous, abandoned on the next carousel. The cheese stands alone. He felt sweat breaking out under his arms and on the top of his lip. Great. Now he'd look like Albert Brooks in *Broadcast News*. Flop sweat. He was a flop all right.

Jon glanced back at The Lovely Girl, whose face had sort of come together in the middle, her brows, her nose, her eyes, and her mouth all gathering at the center of her face as if for safety. "Not that my bag is stuffed with newspaper," Jon assured her. "It's the normal weight. I mean, it's even heavier than normal. And it's not like I could be the Unabomber. I mean, they caught *him*. My bag just isn't heavy because I don't have weapons or stuff." He laughed again, because he was dying. Maybe a joke would save him. "This trip, I decided to leave the weapons at home. Just this once."

The Lovely Girl turned her head toward her carousel. She moved away from Jon, and he knew he'd gone way too far with her. Then he saw her reach for her other bag. Miracle of miracles! Once she had it, she came back toward him. Relief flooded him.

But The Lovely Girl's face had changed once again. Now it was closed and aloof, again the face of a stranger. But her eyes darted back and forth, the eyes of a nervous stranger. Yes. He had ruined everything.

"I've got to go," she said coolly. "I'll give you a call when I get settled. And I hope you find your luggage."

Chapter 17

Tears rolled down Tracie's face, but she didn't wipe them off. She just blinked her eyes to try to clear them, then felt one tear glide to the crease beside her nose, tickling her. She reached her tongue up and delicately licked it from the top of her lip. It was just the slightest bit salty.

"How much salt?" she called out to Laura, whose backside was up, while her head had disappeared deep in an under-the-counter cabinet, looking for something. "Do I put in salt?"

Laura grunted and pulled her head out of the cupboard. "Nah. There's a lot of natural sodium in tomatoes. I think that the other seasonings and the natural salt of the tomatoes make additional salt unnecessary."

Tracie nodded, and a tear flew off her chin as she did so. It fell onto the chopping board and moistened an onion slice. She could have thrown the onions into the pot sooner to stop her eyes from smarting, since she had already cut them up as finely as she knew how, but she wanted Laura's approval first.

"You know," Laura said as she stood up, "if you put the onion in the freezer for a few minutes before you slice it, it doesn't make you cry."

"Well, if I had time and could remember things like that, I'd be the type of person who had my panty hose in the freezer, too, so they wouldn't run."

"Does that work?" Laura asked.

Tracie shrugged. "How would I know? I'm not that type of person."

"Thank God!" Phil called from the sofa. "Panty hose are enough of a turnoff. Icy ones would be beyond my tolerance."

Tracie picked up the chopping block and moved it to the skillet, where the butter was already melting. "So I just throw these in?" she asked. Then she saw red bloom against the cutting board and realized she had just cut not an onion but deep into the flesh of her thumb. "Ohmigod!" she said.

Laura was at her shoulder in a moment. Tracie held up her thumb, which was now leaking blood down her hand. A line from one of the Plath poems Laura and Tracie shared with each other came to mind. " 'Trepanned veteran,' " she said aloud.

"Hey, no quoting Sylvia when you're bleeding into the cassoulet," Laura said, and in a moment she had Tracie's thumb under the faucet, then dipped in peroxide, then swabbed with Neosporin and tightly bandaged. By then, Phil had gotten to the counter.

"Hey, girl. Cut yourself?" he asked. Then added, "Why don't you throw in the towel?" before he idly began plucking the strings of his bass. "You were meant for other things." He leered.

"Hey! Be nice. I'm making this for you," Tracie told him, and instead of the towel, she threw the onion into the sizzling butter. The room was immediately filled with a most delicious smell. Tracie felt like Martha Stewart. "Taa-dah!"

Laura nodded, then looked over the onions. "Stir them a couple of times. You want them brown, not burned." She then looked over to Phil and back to Tracie. "Pay some attention to him," she whispered. "He's begging for it."

"Whom am I making this for?" Tracie asked, her voice raised. "I'm working my fingers to the bone for him."

Phil just shrugged. Laura turned to him. "Remember the Partridge Family?" she asked.

"Sure," Phil said. "I hated Keith."

"That's just because you were jealous of him," Laura countered. Tracie almost laughed out loud. "Anyway, did you ever notice that when Danny played the bass, he *strummed* it? Like a lead guitar?" Laura said.

"Get outta town!" Phil replied.

Tracie wondered if he meant it literally. Between her time with Jon and the attention she paid to Laura, not to mention her time at the gym with Beth and the others, she wondered if Phil was getting a bit shortchanged. Well, Tracie decided, that wasn't necessarily a bad thing. Usually, he was the one shortchanging her, stretched between his rehearsals, his writing, and his other, less-defined activities. She looked at the pot of peeled and diced tomatoes already simmering on the other burner.

"You're really going to love this tomato sauce when it's finished," she said.

"Yeah," he agreed. "I'm really gonna love when it's finished."

Tracie turned to Laura. "When do I add the onions to the tomatoes?" she asked.

"When they're nice and brown." Laura paused. "You know, it's my duty to remind you that there are some schools that believe in simmering the tomatoes with the onions. I am of the school that believes that tomato sauce is a tomato sauce and everything is therefore added to *it*. And that browned onions are better."

The only time Laura was dead serious was when she talked about cooking or when she talked about Peter. Luckily, she'd done lots of the former and none of the latter in the last couple of days. "I am of your school," Tracie said, equally serious in tone. "I hope someday to be in your school yearbook and wear your school letter."

"What letter would that be?" Phil asked in his bored voice. "S for *slow*?"

"S for *sauce*," Tracie told him.

"S for *simmer*," Laura added. They both giggled.

"S for *stupid*," Phil responded. "Both of you. Or *b* for *boring*." He put down his bass. "God, this is dull."

"I know you are, but what am I?" Tracie dared to sing out. She and Laura used to shout that back at girls in Encino when they'd been called names. Fat and skinny, Jack Spratt, and even lesbos. She hadn't thought of it in years. She danced over to the sofa and put her arms around poor Phil. "Just think, homemade spaghetti sauce anytime you want it." She bent to kiss him, but he pulled away.

"Jesus," he said, "you reek." She put her hands up to her nose, and her eyes began to tear again.

"Phew." She ran over to the kitchen sink and began to wash her hands.

"That won't do any good," Laura told her, picking up a lemon, which she pounded with the handle of a knife and then deftly sliced in half with the business end of the same implement. "Here. Use this."

Tracie squeezed the lemon juice onto her hands and then quickly washed them again with dish detergent. After checking her simmering pot, she made her way back to the sofa and sat beside her simmering boyfriend.

"Come here, you," she said, and pulled him to her, letting his head rest against her chest. He began to pull away, but she captured the top of his head with her chin. "Forget that guitar for a minute and bring those talented fingers over here," she whispered. He turned to look at her and was about to say something, when the phone rang. She reached over. "Hold that thought," she told him, picking up the receiver.

Jon's voice exploded into her ear. "Okay, forget about it," he said. "It's a stupid plan and a stupid idea. Anyway, it's not going to work. I can't do it. . . ."

"Hello, Jon," she said calmly. Phil rolled his eyes and pulled his head away from her. Oh well. She'd just have to warm him up all over again. A woman's work was never done.

"It's not working," Jon said. "I'm not trainable."

"We haven't even started yet, and you're giving up?" Tracie admonished.

"*We're* the ones who never get started," Phil said, while Jon also spoke, but she missed his response. She patted Phil on the knee. There, there.

"What?" she asked Jon. He was babbling, something about the airport and then luggage and that she didn't know he was traveling, and then something about someone pregnant and . . . Phil was getting up to put his jacket on, so she had to grab his hand and pull him back on the sofa to kiss him before he actually left. When she got back to the phone, she heard Jon wrapping it up.

"A madman," he was saying. "She thought I was some kind of terrorist."

"It's a start," she said. It was clear that he'd tried to pick someone up. "Better a terrorist than a dweeb. Much sexier."

"No. It's better to be what I was than a failed Ted Kaczynski."

"I thought Ted Kaczynski was a failure," Tracie said, stroking Phil's arm. "I mean, he got caught, right?" Phil began to pay attention to the conversation.

"The sauce needs stirring," Laura called. "Am I making it or are you?" Tracie knew how seriously Laura took her cooking and she gestured to her that she'd only be a moment.

"Don't joke about this!" Jon was saying. "I mean, you weren't there. You can't imagine the look she gave me."

"Did you ever notice how Ted is a loser name?" Phil inquired aloud. "You know—Ted Kennedy, Ted Kaczynski, Ted Bundy."

"I have a policy not to date any Teds," Laura agreed. "With Eds, I decide on a case-by-case basis."

Jon was still talking, but Tracie hadn't been able to hear much.

She made "hmms" and "mms" to try to comfort Jon. When he paused, she waited a moment and then, to be optimistic, said, "Well, you may get a call from her."

"Get a call from her?" Jon echoed. "I'm lucky if I don't get a call from the police. You don't understand." Even from across town, Tracie could hear his sigh. "You had to be there," he repeated. "I'm hopeless at this. I acted like a madman."

"Girls could like a madman," Tracie said as reassuringly as she could manage. Phil began nibbling her ear and Laura put her hands on her hips to indicate sauce consternation.

"Not ones like this," Jon told her grimly.

"Well, you get an A for effort," she said. "You set your sights too high. It's just too hard to pick someone up cold without some common interest." She pushed Phil off her and got up.

"The sauce needs stirring," Laura repeated. Tracie got over to the stove, and in doing so, she missed something else that Jon had said. "Slow down. Slow down," she told him. Her comfort hadn't helped. From the pitch of his voice, she realized she'd have to take this more seriously. It was obvious he was deeply upset.

". . . because I'd worked it all out. I thought I had it perfect. But you can't work it out. You can't control it. 'Cause when I got to the airport and there was nobody good on that flight—I mean, there was somebody good, but she was too good, and, like I said, the other one was pregnant."

"What other one?" Tracie asked as she took the spoon and stirred the sauce. She felt pulled in too many directions at once. How did women raise two or three children?

"Did Danny really strum his bass?" Phil was asking Laura.

"Absolutely," Laura said. "And did you know Laurie was anorexic?"

"Get out! I had a huge boner for Laurie."

Tracie tried to silence them with her hand motions. Jon was still talking. "So I moved to the next carousel and started talking to Carole, and then my bag was on the wrong carousel, and I guess I panicked and said something stupid, and then she started to act as if I was—"

"Who is Carole?" Tracie asked as Laura handed her some big leaves, which Tracie had no idea what to do with.

"This girl I picked up at the airport," Jon said, his voice showing his exasperation. "Carole."

"I'm listening. I just missed her name." What else did I miss? Tracie wondered. "Where were you going?" she asked.

"Going? I wasn't going anywhere."

"Well, where did you meet this Carole?"

"Tonight. At the airport."

"So why were you at the airport if you weren't going anywhere? Were you meeting Carole?" Tracie didn't remember that there was any Carole in Jon's life. Meanwhile, Laura pulled out a leaf from Tracie's hand and threw it into the sauce.

Next, Phil made a gesture with his finger across his throat to say cut it short, but she couldn't. Laura took back the spoon. Tracie shrugged an apology. "I don't understand," she told Jon. "What were you doing at the airport?"

So, while she stirred the pot with one hand and held the phone to her ear with the other, he told her a long, crazy story that only Jon could tell. She laughed a couple of times, until she realized that that might hurt his feelings. Then she managed to keep a straight face during all the rest of the crazy recitation. Jon was one of a kind.

"So anyway, I wrote my name and number on her hand. Can you imagine how embarrassing?"

"Well, you'll never see her again."

"I might. I know she's got a gig with Micro/Con." Then he really lost touch with reality. "Do you think if I track her down, find her number, and wait a day or two until I call, she might go out with me?" he asked.

"I think she'd have you arrested," Tracie told him. "Look, you tried. Forget it. There will be dozens more. Don't sweat it. And you get an A for originality, as well as extra points for neatness. But it wasn't such a good idea."

"Why not?" he asked. "Just because I panicked? Maybe I could try it again?"

"No. Not that." She sighed and looked down at the sauce, which was thickening nicely. "I mean that the two of you had nothing in common except that you were both at the airport. You weren't even on the same flight. Usually, there has to be some kind of shared *something* to get things started," she explained. "So you were working against yourself there."

Actually, as she thought about it, his idea was pretty neat. Crazy, but so Jon. That he was capable of thinking it up made her smile. The fact that he wasn't capable of carrying it off was because he was Jon. He was nuts, but in a kind of adorable way. He'd eventually make some woman a really great husband. But first, she had to get him a date. She lowered the flame under her sauce. Laura nodded approval.

She tried to think of a place where people gathered—not at a bar or club, because she knew Jon would never be comfortable there, but— It came to her like an avalanche and she smiled at her own analogy. Perfect! Much better than an airport. "Look," she said. "I've got an idea. How about if I take you somewhere where you'll have something to talk about to women?"

"Are you talking to me?" Phil asked, raising his eyebrows. "Because I'm interested." Tracie frowned at him.

"Where?" Jon asked at the same time, his voice suspicious.

"That's for me to know and for you to find out," Tracie announced, again reverting to Encino talk.

"It's time to get serious here," Laura said, interrupting. "We've got some major seasoning that's got to go in." Tracie nodded to her and gave her the "just one minute" sign.

"Trust me on this," she told Jon, and she wondered if she could write about his airport fiasco in her article. It would be really hysterical, but that would be what he might not like. Guiltily, she thought she really ought to tell him about her article idea, but she certainly couldn't do it now, not after his humiliation, and not with Laura and Phil breathing down her neck. "Look, don't lose heart," she told him. "It was great that you took the initiative. Rome wasn't built in a day. The longest journey starts with a single step. . . ."

"Not enough cooks spoil the sauce," Laura said pointedly.

"A stitch in time saves time," Phil added.

"That's not right," Laura said to him.

"I get the idea," Jon told Tracie.

"It's nine," Laura was saying. "Nine."

"It's past ten-thirty," Phil responded.

"The saying is, A stitch in time saves nine," Laura was explaining.

"Nine what?" Phil asked.

Laura ignored him.

"Okay," Tracie told Jon. "So I have a plan. You in?"

"I don't know."

"You promised me I'd pass calculus. I promise you you'll get a date," Tracie assured him.

"Okay," he agreed, but he still sounded pretty demoralized.

"Nine stitches!" Laura shouted.

"I have to go. We'll talk tomorrow," Tracie told Jon.

"Okay." He paused. "Hey, Tracie, thanks."

"*De nada*," she replied.

With relief, Tracie hit the off button and laid the phone on the edge of the stove. "You have to put in the oregano and the rest of the herbs now," Laura instructed. "But I want you to add some more garlic first."

"I have to chop garlic again?" Tracie asked, dismayed. She had started with that even before the onions. She was never going to smell sexy again, unless Neapolitan kitchens were a turn-on for Phil. Remorselessly, Laura handed her the cloves and the chopping board. Tracie shrugged her shoulders and did as she was directed for a few minutes, until the phone rang again. She shrugged at Laura as if to say, Not my fault, and then picked it up. It was Beth.

"I'm going to call him. I'm sitting here alone and he's sitting there alone and there's no reason for me not to call him," Beth said.

"You're *not* going to call him," Tracie told her. "First of all, he's probably not alone. Second, he's made it clear he doesn't want a relationship with you. And, in case you've forgotten, he is your boss. You'll wind up not only losing his respect but your job, too."

"I don't want my job," Beth wailed. "It's torture seeing him every day but not being able to have him."

Tracie shook her head. Her hair fell into her eyes. She *had* to remember to book an appointment with Stefan. Beth groaned. How Beth could manage to get so emotional about a middle-aged, slightly balding, mean guy was beyond her. What Beth needed was a distraction. "You've got more important things to do," Tracie told her. "I want you to go through your closet and figure out what you'd wear on a Friday date."

"Why bother?" asked Beth. "I haven't had a date in months."

"You have one for next Friday," Tracie informed her. "I fixed you up." Laura was tapping her finger against the side of her forehead with the gesture that said, You're crazy. Then she pointed to the sauce.

"With who?" Beth asked, and Tracie could hear the curiosity and interest in her voice, though she was trying to sound disinterested. "Not one of those loser musicians of yours," Beth added. "I don't want to be stuck paying for their beer all night like the last time."

"No, no," Tracie assured her. "This guy's really cool and he's not a musician." Better leave a little mystery. She lied: "I'm not sure exactly what he does, but he's really cute."

"What's his name?" Beth asked.

"Jonny," she lied.

Laura now had both hands on her hips again—not a good sign—and Phil was seriously sulking. "I gotta go," she told Beth. "We'll talk tomorrow at work." At least that will give her something to think about, she figured as she hung up the phone and turned back to Laura.

"You're getting him a date?" Laura asked.

"Well, first I thought I'd take him to a place where he could pick up a girl for himself. But you know, in case it doesn't work out, he needs a date."

"I'll go out with him," Laura said. "I mean, just as a practice."

"Oh, that's all right," Tracie said as offhandedly as possible. "I don't think we should try that. Not after you dissed him at the market." She thought for a moment. "It'll be good for Beth. She's trying to get over Marcus."

"Beth from the gym?" Laura asked. "She's an idiot."

"Well, yes. But she's a cute idiot, and it's just a date."

Laura turned to the sofa as if to ask Phil . . . but Phil wasn't there. "Where did he go?" she asked Tracie.

Tracie shrugged. He must be in the bedroom, sulking. She covered the pot with the only lid in the house, one she had improvised with a plate and aluminum foil. "Can I leave this now?" she asked, feeling as if she were stretched in a half dozen directions. She had to go to Phil and make everything okay with him. And she had to do some work on her article, at least to bring her notes up-to-date.

"Sure," Laura said acidly. "How important is tomato sauce compared to true love?"

Tracie's hands really stank now from the garlic. "Give me a break, will ya?" Tracie asked her. "Also, while you're at it, give me another lemon."

"Sorry. No more lemons," Laura said brightly. "Except for the guy in there." She indicated the bedroom with a tilt of her head.

"Thank you," Tracie told her. "Pete's a great guy, too."

"But Pete is not in my bedroom," Laura pointed out. "I don't have to go in there and give lemon aid."

Phil was lying on her rumpled bed with his guitar next to him. He was breathing deeply, his face stuffed into one of her pillows. But somehow Tracie could tell he was faking. She used to do it herself when she was a kid and her father would check on her. She sat down at the foot of the bed and put a hand gently on his ankle. "Are you sleeping?" she asked.

He immediately picked his head up in an exaggerated start. "No," he said after a moment, rubbing one eye with the back of his hand. "I was just going to try out a few new licks."

There was something very intimate about knowing he was faking his composure, as if she had caught a child in a game of pretend. He was like a child in many ways. Tracie became almost shy. "Look, I'm behind on my meat loaf sampling and I also have to cover the opening act at the EMP for the *Times*. Remember? I thought you might want to go."

"To EMP? Jesus, that place is so lame." Again, Tracie could see that he was covering his disappointment. Bob had talked of the Glands playing at the Experience Music Project through some friend of a friend. But the gig—if it had ever existed at all—had never materialized or fallen through. Since then Phil had had nothing but criticism of the museum that had made news all across the country. Sometimes Tracie thought highly of Phil's iconoclasm and fierce independence but at other times—like this one—she began to believe that he simply rejected things defensively before they rejected him.

"Frank Gehry is going to be there," Tracie coaxed. Gehry was the genius who had created the Experience.

"So what," Phil said. "They spent two hundred and fifty million dollars on something that looks like the wreck of the Partridge Family bus."

"I'm going to try to get an interview with him," Tracie said. "My father knows him from L.A."

"Fine," Phil told her. "Use insider contacts that others don't have. I don't care if that's the only way you can make it, but don't expect me to watch or help."

Tracie shook her head. Why did he have to be so nasty? Sometimes she believed that each time they got close to one another Phil was obliged to spoil it by being what Laura would call an IPP. She shrugged. She wouldn't press him or chase him and after this behavior she certainly didn't feel like bringing him as a companion. Then she remembered that she had yet another agenda. She decided to try one more time.

"Are you sure?" she asked. "We could have fun. We could dance like we used to." When they'd first met, they danced all the time. She'd been impressed with his weird dance moves. They were . . . unique. He didn't dance like a white boy, but he wasn't doing some pathetic imitation of a rapper, either. He moved like a robot ballet dancer. It seemed to Tracie that they hadn't danced together in a long, long time. "Oh, come on," she begged.

Phil fell back onto the mattress. "Nah. I'm really into my playing."

That's such bullshit! Tracie thought. Annoyed and hurt, she tried to cover it. "Okay. I just thought you might want to meet Bob Quinto, the manager. And you know, he's looking for help booking. . . ."

"Are you trying to talk me into taking some kind of straight gig again?" Phil asked, sitting up now.

Uh-oh. Not this argument tonight. "No. I just think . . ."

"I just think you don't have much confidence in me. I don't appreciate that." Phil threw his long legs over the side of the bed and began to push one foot into his boot.

"Look, I'm sorry. I just thought he'd be a good connection for you. Then, afterward, I thought maybe you'd come back here and . . ."

"Forget it, Tracie. I've got a late rehearsal." He put his other boot on.

"Fine," she told him. "I want to work on my article about the makeover anyway."

"Fine," Phil repeated. "Then we're both busy. Too bad I didn't know that before I wasted all this time waiting for you." He stood up and put his guitar in its case. "Good luck with your sow's ear."

"That's not nice," she snapped.

"Oh, I think it's nice," he said. "Nice for you. Nice for your ego." He paused, then cocked his head and raised his voice. "You could be the next Emma Quindlen," Phil said, imitating Jon almost perfectly.

"Anna, not Emma," Tracie snarled at his back as he left.

Chapter 18

Tracie was driving over to Mom's, a diner on the other side of Seattle, where they served things like baked macaroni and home-style chicken potpie. She'd been turned down on the makeover article, but the idea of the best meat loaf in town was worthy. She sighed. After thinking for a while, she'd come up with an angle she liked: Guys in films noir always seem to have a cup of joe and some meat loaf, so she was getting Mr. Bill from the video store to find a few of the restaurant scenes from the thirties and she was going to sample all the meat loaf in town, as Jimmy Cagney or Humphrey Bogart might. Needless to say, Jon had insisted that she include Java, The Hut's, although Tracie didn't feel it was necessary to do any favors for the place. It wasn't as if they gave her good service.

After Mom's, Tracie was going to meet Jon at Java, and over another meat loaf sampling, she'd fit in another lesson. Despite his mission impossible at the airport—she giggled when she thought of it—she could see he was getting close to scoring, or whatever it was that guys called it. The fact that he'd even try on his own was incredible, given what a mess he'd been. But now that he was close, she also knew that Jon needed preparation in one more area. Tracie had thought long and—excusing the pun—hard about discussing sexual etiquette with Jon. She shrank from it, though.

The two of them were really best of friends, but while they talked about virtually everything else, she had never talked to him about sex. Somehow, while she could describe to Laura—or even Beth—the exact dimensions of a man's private parts and any peculiarity thereof, the idea of doing that with Jon gave her the willies. Of course, she didn't *have* to talk to him about willies. He had one and, one presumed, he knew how to use it. But what she knew from sad experience, as well as from the experiences of her friends, was that most men had not read the operating instructions for women's parts. If her work on Jon made him look good and sound good, it still wouldn't be enough, as far as she was concerned, if he couldn't also put them over the top sexually. She told herself she shouldn't expect too much from Jon—after all, she knew he hadn't had that much experience.

Freud had pondered on what women wanted, but he must not have asked his wife, or any of his female patients. Because, based on her own sex life and what she'd heard from her friends, what women wanted was oral sex, and plenty of it. Not that they necessarily liked giving blow jobs, though Tracie herself enjoyed it. The problem was that no matter how good you became at playing the skin flute, men usually left you with a lick and a promise. That is, if they went south of the border at all. Tracie was always deeply offended by men who had an aversion to going down on her but who expected her to look at their own private parts as if they were ice-cream cones with sprinkles. One of the things she loved about Phil was how much he seemed to like all of her body, and her secret place the best. It was also so much easier to have an orgasm if a man knew what he was doing. God, when she thought about the oafs she'd occasionally been with in college who'd thought that pumping away until a girl came passed for good sex! She had to tell Jon about delicacy and teasing, about developing a pattern and then, just when the next touch or stroke or flick was expected, to withhold it and go on to something new until a woman was almost out of her mind.

She crossed her legs, then realized she needed her brake foot. She was so deep in thought that as she was about to pull into the right lane for her exit, she didn't see the blue Maxima to her side. She swerved, got back into the exit lane, and reminded herself to keep her eyes on the road, even if her thoughts were "in the gutter," as her stepmom used to say. As she stopped at the off-ramp light, she thought again of Jon and winced at the idea of leaving him completely unprepared. It wasn't fair to him, or to women. And then there was the question of the real sexual politics: where you slept, whether you slept over, condoms and creams and all the rest. God, she hoped he didn't need help with that, too! She could just imagine having to take him into a pharmacy and asking for ribbed Trojans for him.

As she turned onto the main road, she smiled. She remembered the days back in Encino when she herself was so embarrassed that she couldn't buy tampons if there was a guy anywhere near the pharmacy counter. Instead, she'd have to go into a supermarket and buy Clorox, Ritz crackers, some Oreos, a carton of 2 percent milk, Rice Krispies, a few Lean Cuisines, Wonder bread, and *then* a box of tampons, which would, oh-so-casually, be sandwiched between the sandwich cookies and sandwich bread.

Those days were long gone. She could walk up to any clerk at any convenience store and ask for a dozen lubricated, spermicidal Ramses with reinforced tips. If the guy even raised his eyebrows, she was capable of smiling sweetly and telling him, "Make it two dozen. I'm having a gang bang." As she pulled into the parking lot of Mom's, she smiled at the thought.

A very full belly later, Tracie looked down at the second plate of meat loaf she had to face that day and then glanced up at Jon. "It's not as good as Mom's," she said, gesturing with her fork at the pallid slice.

"It's better," he told her.

What a lie! "Have you ever had Mom's?" she asked, whispering so Molly couldn't hear.

"No," he admitted. "But it couldn't be better than this."

"Oh, how would you know anyway?" she asked. "You're a vegan."

"No I'm not," he said. "You remember? Vegans eat—"

"Caught you!" she said, jumping at the chance. "You're *not* supposed to be talking about your dietary laws to any woman."

"I didn't know this counted," he said, defending himself.

"*Everything* counts. That's the whole point of what I'm trying to teach you." She steeled herself for another bite of meat loaf and an opening for her little planned discussion about the birds and the bees. She needed an opening, but she couldn't really think of one. "Look, we have to talk about . . . seduction," she said, and swallowed hard.

Just then, Molly came over to the table. "Is everything okay 'ere?" she asked, perhaps too sweetly.

Tracie actually had to look up from her plate just to be sure it was really Molly. "Everything's fine. Why do you ask?"

"Just doing my job," Molly said, and refilled their water glasses. Tracie looked at Jon to see if he was curious about this new behavior. But nothing registered on his face. God, now she'd probably hang around, and Tracie could *not* talk about sex with Molly listening. "If you need anything, don't 'esitate to ask," Molly said, and left them their table.

That didn't add up. "You told her didn't you?" Tracie said accusingly.

"Told her what?" Jon asked.

"About my meat loaf assignment! She's never filled our water glasses in all the time we've been coming here. I don't even think she's served us water until today. You rat!"

Jon, his mug at his lips, choked a little bit of coffee back into it. "What do you mean?"

"Well, there are . . . rules. I'm supposed to be treated like an average customer." She felt herself flushing.

"So what if I tipped her off? She's always treated you worse than average. Look at it this way: Molly's finally being nice to you."

"Jon, you aren't allowed to—"

"Hey, it's not a Micro/Con tech breakthrough. It's just meat loaf. Anyway, get back to the seduction. What do you mean by that?"

"Just that there are certain ways you should . . . do things. And certain things you should . . . avoid."

"What do you mean, *things*?"

God, he wasn't making this easy. " 'What do you mean, *things*?' " she imitated. "What I mean is that you need to have a way to get women hot for you." She thought of her afternoon's sexual review, the one that almost made her run off the road. "And the best way is to . . ." She just couldn't get right to the nitty-gritty. She would have to segue into it. "Look, sex is like a dance," she told him. "You know those Fred Astaire movies?"

"Is he another bad boy? Tracie, I don't think I have time for any more videos. I'm getting way behind at work as it is."

"You don't have to watch him. It's just that he was that skinny bald dancer, but he had some kind of sex appeal, because in every movie he'd do this dance with Ginger Rogers or some other woman, but it was always best with Ginger. She'd be angry with him, but when they started to dance, she'd pull away and he would pull her back. Then the moment he let her go, she'd pull away again." Tracie, still sitting, gestered with her arms and shoulders to demonstrate. "But then he'd grasp her hand or her wrist and pull her to him again. And in the end, his persistence and his grace would win her over. And then you'd feel her give in, when her body would melt into his. It was a conquest, sexier than sex."

Tracie felt herself heating up again. She paused, recovering herself. "Anyway, the whole thing about a seduction is that you have to be strong enough, magnetic enough to pull the woman toward you. But then you have to abandon her so that you can replay the seduction. It's that conquest thing that makes women *crazy for you*."

"They want me to conquer them?" he asked. "Didn't that go out with Tarzan? Anyway, that's not what James Dean does."

"Right. James Dean's characters were oblique. They never admitted that they wanted someone, though they yearned. You have to be like that, too. Act like you don't care, but let women *imagine* the yearning. If you actually yearn and they see it, it's kind of a pucker."

"Tracie, I think this is too complicated for me," Jon said, putting down his fork and wiping off his mouth with the napkin.

"Oh, come on. You are the guy who is figuring out Parsifal. You can do anything." She took a deep breath. "Look, it's best if they see you as a tragic figure. And if they feel that they can help you and heal you, that's cool."

"But my life isn't a tragedy," Jon protested.

"No, it's a travesty. That's the problem." She paused. How could she get him to understand? "You have to try and find some secret to tell them and be sure that you tell them you never told anyone. Make them feel as if they're the only ones that could ever understand you. Because you're so complex and they are so sensitive. That will make them feel special and important."

"What kind of secret? I never told anyone that I wet my bed until I was about twelve, but I don't think that's what you have in mind."

"Good thinking, Sherlock." Tracie didn't even want to know if what he'd admitted was true or not. As she leaned back to think for a moment, Molly swooped down on them again and silently collected Jon's plate, wiped up the crumbs off the table, and brought him a fresh napkin and the dessert list.

"Are you still working on yours?" she asked kindly. Tracie couldn't take this sort of treatment. Now she'd be forced to say something good about Molly's meat loaf. She wished she could have her plate taken away. She couldn't eat another bite. Not that it wasn't good, but she was sick to death of meat loaf.

"I'm still working on it," she told the lying limey waitress. As soon as the hypocrite left with the dirty tray, Tracie was ready to continue. "Jon, just make something up. Tell them that you saw your father shoot your mother. Or that you saw your mother shoot your father. Or they both shot each other and you've inherited millions but that you'd never touch the blood money."

"They'd like that?" he asked.

"Only if they believed you. And if you said you never trusted anyone else enough to share that. Then they'll trust you enough to sleep with you." Jon just shook his head.

"Now listen." Tracie continued. "When you *do* sleep with them, it's important that you don't sleep over. No matter how tired you are, or how late it is, you have to get out of bed and go home. Rule Number Five, and the most important: Don't sleep over."

"Never? But Phil sleeps over all the time," he protested.

"Well, he never did at first," Tracie admitted. "The point is, it leaves her wanting more. It's best if you can sneak out while she's sleeping."

"Without even saying good-bye?"

"Leave an elliptical note."

"Like what?"

"Like . . . like . . . 'You made me go.' And don't sign it 'love.' And *don't* leave your phone number." Jon's mouth was hanging open in disbelief.

"They make me come and then I write a note to tell them they made me go? Come on! Am I supposed to seduce masochists exclusively?"

"Look, this is just about hooking 'em. After you're together, you can do whatever you like. But in the beginning, they need to feel that you are special, that they are special, and that they have to be very special to get you. That's why you're not going to call them back."

Jon's eyes almost popped out of his head. "After I finally get someone to sleep with me? What are you talking about? If I don't call them back, how will I get to sleep with them again?"

"You don't need to sleep with them again. Sleep with someone else. Right now, for you, it's about wide experience."

"So I'm supposed to behave like a bastard?" he asked. "That's what women want? Bastards with the right pants?"

"No. Do you think we're stupid? We're complex. What we want is someone who behaves like a bastard but we can tame, or at least we think we can tame. We want someone who's tough—but who has a deeply tender heart we can conquer. A panther who obeys our commands. It's sort of the female equivalent of that old-fashioned guy thing."

"What? Mental illness?"

"No. You know, the thing where men didn't want girls who are easy, 'cause then anyone had them." She paused. "I once liked this guy Earl—"

"You'd like Earl Grey tea?" Molly asked sweetly, coming up behind Tracie. "I'll brew some up fresh." What was with this woman? Tracie actually preferred her as a bitch.

"No, I don't want any tea," Tracie said, and gripped the edge of the table to restrain herself from slapping Molly. "I'll let you know if I want something else." Molly nodded and left them again. Tracie shot Jon a look.

"Oh, let her be," he said. "She just wants you to say something good about this place. Now, who's Earl? I don't remember him."

"That's because it was before I met you. And because he didn't last very long," Tracie said. "Earl was smart, and nice-looking. But he kept telling me how beautiful I was. That I was as beautiful as his ex-fiancée. The fascinating woman who broke his heart."

"Yeah, so?"

"So, after hearing about her and being really jealous, I'm over at his place, and on a bookshelf, lying facedown, is this picture of a fat, ugly girl. I ask him if it's his sister or cousin or something, and he tells me it's Jennifer, his ex-fiancée. If he thought *she* was beautiful, then whatever he thought about me wasn't valid. I broke up with him."

"Tracie, you are crazy. I always suspected it, but now I'm sure."

"Jon, I am imparting secrets to you that men would pay hundreds of thousands of dollars to know. These are the things women discuss in ladies' rooms when they go off together. These are the things that will help you to seduce and abandon beautiful girls all over the country. Maybe all over the world," Tracie told him.

"So you're asking me to hurt women on purpose."

"Oh, Jon, it's just part of the bigger picture," she explained. "It's what they're looking for. Then someday a woman grows up and realizes she wants a man who knows how to treat her well."

Tracie wondered when that time would come for her. Then she thought again about her planned discussion of oral sex and other sensitive things, but she just couldn't go there. This had been enough for her. Who knows? Maybe Jon could be okay in bed. At least he was a sensitive guy. The problem was that he probably hadn't lost his virginity until a few years ago. Maybe she should just ask about that. She took the last forkful of meat loaf. "Umm"—she paused, chewed, and swallowed a final time—"let me ask you something," she said. "Who was your first girlfriend?"

"You mean a real lover or the first girl I liked?"

"A real lover," she explained.

"Myra Fisher."

Now she echoed him. "Myra Fisher? I don't remember any Myra Fisher."

"Well, you didn't know me then. Myra was back in eighth grade."

Her mouth dropped open. "Eighth grade!" He must have misunderstood. "No, I mean the first girl you actually slept with."

"Well, I didn't get to sleep with Myra until the ninth-grade class trip. But we were having sex at her house all through eighth grade. And in the summer between eighth and ninth."

"You never told me about that!"

"Well, I don't think it's appropriate to talk about what *you* might call 'my conquests,' " he said. "It's very personal. I just don't really talk about it."

"Not with anyone?" she asked.

"Not really. I mean, you don't, do you?"

"Uh, not really." She hoped her nose wasn't growing. She looked at Jon and began to wonder about him in a whole new way. "Wait a minute," she said. "That really tall girl back in college, the one with the really long hair . . ."

"Hazel," he said. "Hazel Flagler."

"Yeah. Did you and she . . ."

"Of course," he said.

"You never told me!" Now Tracie was truly shocked.

"Well, what do you think I was doing with her? She wasn't a chess player!" Jon said.

"You never told me," she repeated. Tracie wondered what other relationships he'd had that he'd never spoken to her about.

"Tracie, I grew up listening to women complaining about how badly men behave. I watched my father do it. Do you think after all that I was going to kiss and tell?"

"Kiss and tell? Jon, this isn't some Victorian novel. This is the twenty-first century. Don't you watch *Friends*? Or reruns of *Seinfeld*? People on *Jerry Springer* talk about sleeping with their brothers!"

"I have never been on *Jerry Springer*," Jon said with dignity. And for the first time, Tracie looked at him and imagined that there might be a lot of water running deep under the stillness of his dark brown eyes.

Chapter 19

The next week, Wednesday, Jon met Tracie for the much-discussed haircut. They swung open the salon door, the music blasted from inside, and instinctively Jon stepped back. "Come on," Tracie told him. "Avant-garde hair care is not for the fainthearted." She took his hand and pulled him through the portal. "Don't worry," she said blithely. "Stefan will take care of you."

For the first time in his life, Jon really doubted her. He didn't think so, unless she was implying the mafioso meaning of "taking care of." Well, what the hell. He felt half-dead already.

Was all of this really necessary to get a girl? It took so much time, thought, and energy. Wasn't the relationship supposed to require maintenance, not his wardrobe and hairline? As he was dragged through the reception area—a room filled with bright lights, incredibly loud technorock, and something that seemed like the decor from a very bad game-show set—he felt himself flinch. There was a point at which a man had to put his foot down, and he figured this was it . . . until the woman with endless legs and silvery gold hair down to her waist walked by. She nodded to Tracie and smiled—actually smiled—at him. She was the most beautiful woman he had ever seen. "Hi, Ellen," Tracie said casually, as if the goddess of love had not just walked among them.

"Who is that?" he whispered.

"What?" Tracie asked at higher than full volume, continuing to pull him along.

"Who is that?" he asked, this time shouting. He had fallen deeply in love. She was a dream. She was paradise. If not for the hellish music, he could imagine paradise with her. "Who?" he shouted.

"Ellen? That's Ellen," Tracie repeated, as if that clarified anything.

They'd crossed the reception area, walked through a bustling room of chairs and mirrors, and now Tracie led him down a much emptier hallway, though the music continued full blast. All the walking was taking him farther away from his goddess. Two other women walked by. Neither one was quite up to Ellen's standard, but both were truly, deeply beautiful. Wow! They nodded at either Tracie or him, and on the blind chance that he had been included, he nodded back. Neither one giggled or pointed. It seemed he was expected to nod back, just as they were expected to nod at him. Maybe, he thought, maybe Tracie *did* know something about all this after all. But he would not let Ellen drop. "Who is Ellen?" he repeated once the other two nymphs were safely gone.

"She's Stefan's wife," Tracie shouted casually, as if that didn't mean his entire world had just crumbled. They passed a dozen doors, until Tracie opened yet another one—into what had to be the Holy of Holies in this temple of beauty.

"Isn't Stefan gay?" Jon shouted, still reacting to the technorock. But as the door swung closed behind them, the noise ended abruptly. He was standing in a small, square, perfectly silent white room furnished with only a Star Wars–type barber's chair in the center of it. A tall man stood beside the chair, looking at him.

The guy was tall, six foot five or six, and fair, with very short hair and a scar across one blond eyebrow. Tough-looking. Jon broke the silence. "Hi," he said, his voice almost squeaking. "You must be Stefan."

* * *

"You don't realize the sacrifice I'm making here for you," Tracie said as she sat Jon down in a chair. "Just look at me. I'm the one that really needs a haircut, but just remember, you owe me big for this." She stepped back and leaned against the counter. Then Jon was approached by Stefan, who was like Edward Scissorhands crossed with Riverdance. He kept snipping and stamping his feet and jumping. Jon wondered if it was safe for Stefan to move that way with the scissors so close to his eyes, but he guessed Stefan knew what he was doing. After all, Tracie just sat there calmly through all the snips and jumps and didn't seem to notice that there was no mirror, no noise, and no people. Just Stefan and his heavy breathing and his crazy jumping around. It was the strangest haircut Jon had ever experienced.

Jon sat for nearly an hour with a man he had just insulted. Meanwhile, Tracie, who apparently didn't realize the terrible danger he was in, sat on a tiny stool near his feet, chattering away. Jon only wanted to dart out of the seat, out of the room, past the fatal Ellen, wife of this Balkan madman, and perhaps leave Seattle forever. But he was afraid to move because of the very sharp scissors that kept flicking around his head.

". . . and the bicycle," he heard Tracie saying. What was she going on about?

He was afraid to turn his head to Tracie, so he merely twitched his eyes toward her. It hurt to put his eyeballs so far into the corner of his eyes for very long. "What about my bicycle?" he asked. He would have liked to put his hand up to his head, but he was sure that Stefan would snip off a finger. Bits of his hair had been flying around the room for a long time.

"I said we still have to do something about your backpack and the bicycle," Tracie repeated calmly.

"What about my backpack?" he asked. "And nothing's wrong with my bicycle. What do you mean we have to 'do something' about my bicycle?"

"It's just that a bicycle is so uncool," Tracie told him. "I mean, how are you going to take a girl back to your place? Put her on the handlebars?"

"I thought I wasn't supposed to take them back to my place," he said, reminding her of her tutelage.

"Okay. Okay. So how are you going to take them back to *their* place?"

They were going to get into this now, and do it in front of Stefan?

"In their car?" he asked hopefully.

"And how do you get home from there?" She shook her head. "You know, if you didn't have a Schwinn, you'd own a Pacer." Jon didn't know for sure what a Pacer was, but he could tell it wasn't good, because Stefan laughed. "It's hard to date without a car."

"We can go in hers," he said. Jon had to admit he was beginning to see the difficulty, but he pushed on. "Or call a cab?" he asked weakly, knowing it wasn't a good gambit. He heard a little derisive snort behind him and wished that for just one moment he could have those scissors in his own hands. "Look. You know how I feel. A bicycle is safe, convenient, and has very low ecological impact. If I power a bicycle, I don't need to use any nonrenewable fossil fuel to get where I'm going."

"But you're not getting anyvhere. Not vith vomen," Stefan said, speaking for the first time.

Jon tried not to grit his teeth. When he watched *Rebel Without a Cause* and *East of Eden*, he could always see James Dean's jawline stiffen when he got mad. Now he didn't want the Demon Barber of Fleet Street to do him in. Stefan wouldn't hesitate to cut his carotid artery. Jon decided to ignore him. "Are you telling me I have to buy a car to get dates?" he asked, outraged. Tracie knew how opposed to automobiles he was. They were ruining the Pacific Northwest and tearing the hell out of the environment. How could she even propose the idea?

"Then how about reconsidering a motorcycle?" Tracie asked brightly.

"A motorcycle? I already told you that I'd be a danger to myself and others."

"But they're so cool," Tracie said, almost bouncing off the stool in her enthusiasm. "And girls really like guys who ride motorcycles."

"How do they feel about guys who've had an entire side of their face abraded by pavement?" he snapped.

"Temper, temper!" Stefan cautioned.

"We'll talk about this later," Tracie told him.

"No, we won't," Jon answered her sourly, and then he was spun around to face Stefan. Light glinted off the hairdresser's straight razor. For a moment, Jon thought Stefan was going to wield it, Sweeney Todd–like, but this nut was only holding up a mirror.

Jon looked into it. Oh God! He'd become Sonic the Hedgehog. His hair stood in spikes. The Demon Barber should have just killed me, he thought, and he put his hands over his skull protectively. Stefan, the albino Edward Scissorhands, took the last couple of snippets from Jon's new, totally renovated head.

"Unbelievable," Tracie said.

"Transformation," Stefan replied in a self-satisfied tone. But it was Jon who was transformed—but into what?

He continued to stare. Looking behind him, in the mirror's reflection, Jon saw Tracie hug Stefan. Then she danced wildly, full of approval, around Jon's chair. Well, she was his friend. He guessed she liked Sonic the Hedgehog. "Fantastic," she yodeled, and pulled him up from the chair. Maybe it wasn't as bad as he thought. Then Tracie plucked Jon's wallet from his back pocket as she whizzed by and handed Stefan his charge card.

"It's going to be the best two hundred dollars you ever spent!" she told him.

"Two hundred dollars!" Jon gasped. Then he looked at Stefan and the razor and swallowed. He figured it was better than getting mugged, though just as expensive.

Chapter 20

Tracie and Jon pulled up to the entrance of the REI parking lot. He'd been grilling her the whole way, but she'd refused to answer a single question.

Ignoring Jon, Tracie pulled a right, forgot to put on her indicator, and almost got backed into by a passing Saab. Other than that, they had no mishaps. "Let's go." Jon got out of the car, then tripped on the curb as he looked up to read the sign on the door.

"Oh my God! Not here!" Jon protested.

REI was a famous landmark on the outskirts of Seattle, near Interstate 5. It was probably the largest outdoor sports–supply store in the world. It was a gathering place for sports-minded ecoshoppers. Its distinctive architecture and the huge window drew the eye. From the door, he could see aisle upon aisle of mountain gear shining as hundreds of attractive young men and women shopped for equipment.

"Try to pick out a normal girl," Tracie reminded him. "One of these." She pointed at a whole gaggle of them, all willowy, all perfect, with teeth and hair and skin that shone. Jon felt himself growing smaller and darker, a blot on the landscape. Tracie gave him a little shove. "Place yourself near them, but don't come on to them. You have to play hard to get. You have to make *them* want *you*," Tracie told him. She gestured. They had come to an end of an aisle and before them was an enormous rock wall—at least six stories high—enclosed by glass. People were climbing its almost vertical face, visible to everyone in the store, as well as to passing highway traffic.

"Holy shit!" Jon gasped. He hated heights. He'd once told her that he was afraid to look out high windows because it made him feel like jumping.

"Class is in session. You look fierce now, but you have to *act* fierce."

"How? By hanging off a rock? Forget it!"

She'd known he'd balk, but she was prepared. "Come on, Jon. Climbing is the bomb. A real loner's sport. Women love loners. Think James Dean. Think *The Loneliness of the Long Distance Runner*."

"Hey, that guy only broke into a store and stole money. Then he went to London with a girl. I can do *that*. It's heights I don't like."

"Jon, there are a million girls here looking to meet rock climbers."

"I thought they wanted rock singers!" he whined. "You got a rock player. Don't make me."

Tracie decided to ignore him; she took a coil of rope from a shelf on the right and handed it to him, along with a carabiner.

"Try these on. At least *look* like a rock climber," she demanded.

Jon pointed to the space below the indoor rock. "Or like a Rorschach on that floor. Tracie, I watched all those movies. James Dean mostly moped and hung out against a corner of a wall. I can mope. I can rub against corners. James Dean never climbed rocks."

"Don't be so literal. Or so negative. Move with the times," Tracie told him. "I didn't tell you to climb rocks; I only want you to talk about it." She nudged him. A very pretty blonde walked by, and Tracie thought the girl gave Jon the once-over. Good sign. "Anyway, you don't ever have to climb. Just hang out with a piton and talk to a girl."

Jon rolled his eyes. "Talk about what?" He looked up the wall. "I know nothing about this."

"Think positive. They probably don't, either. If they ask you anything, tell them you like Black Diamond stuff. It's the best."

"How would you know?"

"I did an article." It was a lie, but there was no need to tell him about Dan. Tracie drew a black diamond on her yellow Post-it pad, pulled it off, and stuck it on his chin. Even with the Post-it goatee, he looked cute. Absently, he reached up and unpeeled the Post-it. Meanwhile, he kept looking up at the towering faux rock that half a dozen people were climbing. He kept staring as he crumpled the Post-it. It was as good a moment as any to let her little duckling sink or swim, so, quietly, Tracie moved off.

"Why am I thinking Wile E. Coyote? You know the cartoon where he orders the Acme rocket and . . ."

Jon turned back to Tracie, but she'd disappeared. Instead, a long-legged brunette was listening to him.

"A rock etand?" she said. Her voice was as smooth as the rock surface glinting in front of them. "I've never used one. Is it some new piece of equipment?" she asked.

Jon tried to regain his composure. The crumpled yellow note in his hand reminded him of Tracie's advice. And the girl was certainly pretty. "Yeah. Black Diamond. But I stick with the classics, don't you?"

"Absolutely," she agreed. "You climb much?"

"Oh, yeah. Been climbing since I was a kid." God! What men would do to get a girl! His father had once made him limp for a whole afternoon with some woman he was trying to get into the sack. His dad had been real nice to him, and at the end of the day, when the two adults dropped him off, the woman said, "You're a very brave boy." Afterward, Jon asked Chuck why she'd said that, and his father laughed and explained, "I told her you had lost your leg to cancer." And then there was that guy Tracie dated in her first year of graduate school who . . . He pulled himself back to the present and the opportunity that was walking past him on two very nice legs. He turned to look at this woman, who actually seemed interested in him. Her hair was long, and she had it pulled back in some kind of loose braid that started as part of her head on top and became a pigtail that followed her. Behind her, Tracie gave him the "okay" sign. Did that mean it was okay to lie, or that the girl looked okay, or that . . .

"I only got started last year, but climbing is . . . like a way of life," the brunette said, interrupting his moral dilemma.

"Yeah," he agreed, slick as his dad on his best day. "I need it like . . . oxygen. I need to be alone and depend on no one. I need to be a figure, black against a slab of schist." At the corner of the aisle, he pulled a James Dean pose. He hoped she noticed but that she hadn't, by some odd coincidence, been watching *East of Eden* the night before.

Apparently, she hadn't. "I know what you mean," she said with growing enthusiasm. Then, as if reconsidering, she blinked and turned away. Jon immediately felt a knot develop in his stomach. What had he said wrong? Was he going to blow this like he had blown it with The Lovely Girl at the airport? But she turned back to him. "I mean, I don't totally know what you mean because I haven't really climbed alone, but I want to. Do you do aid climbing?"

He didn't even know what it was. "All the time." What the hell, he figured.

She stopped at a section filled with pitons. "It's all so gear-intensive, you know. And everything costs so much. I need a fifi hook and some copperheads. Do you use any?"

"Oh, sure. I never climb without them," he said smoothly. This was scary. The more he lied, the easier it seemed to be. Was this what it had been like for his dad?

The thing was, he wasn't like his dad. He looked at the girl and he liked her. Okay, maybe he couldn't really climb, but he loved the outdoors; he bicycled everywhere. He bet she was as ecologically aware as he was. Maybe she wasn't a vegetarian—it probably took a lot of animal protein to scale a mountain—but as he covertly looked her over, it seemed liked she was the kind of girl he'd want to get to know, that he'd want to do things with.

"What brand do you like?" she asked.

"Black Diamond," he told her, and put his arm against the shelf behind him, trying to look casual. Instead, he almost fell, but luckily, she hadn't seen him falter, because she was lifting some kind of gear off a lower shelf. Jon didn't have a clue. It looked like something a Jew wouldn't welcome seeing coming his way during the Inquisition.

"What about Pika toucans?" she asked. He remembered Tracie's directive, and anyway, he wanted to touch this girl. Her skin was an even color all over—a kind of creamy white, with just the faintest suggestion of pink underneath. Her lips were pink. . . . Then he realized she was waiting for an answer.

"They're okay. I mean, they're not Black Diamond, but . . ."

It's now or never, he told himself. You have to touch her. Jon took her hand as if to look at the gear. "Wow. You've got beautiful cuticles." He could tell the brunette was charmed. She looked down at her own hands, held in his, and he thought she actually blushed.

"I do? Thanks. My name is Ruth, by the way."

"Bytheway. Interesting surname. Are you English?"

Ruth led him toward a line of people and joined them. Jon fell in behind her to keep the conversation going.

"You know, I only have an Edelrid fifi hook," she was saying. For a moment, Jon thought the whole thing was a joke or an elaborate put-on that Tracie had arranged. Toucans, fifis, copperheads. Was this a sport or a circus? But though he'd lost sight of Tracie, he hadn't lost his mind. This girl was enthusiastic and pretty cute and he was going to try to stick it out. "I hope it's okay," she was saying, "because I don't want to have to buy another one."

Jon eyed the checkout line. He guessed he'd have to buy the rope and the belt. He'd consider it just another wardrobe expense. But after another minute, he noticed there was no register ahead. What was this? Then, to his growing horror, he saw a guy at the front of the line throw up a rope and begin to ascend the rock while several other people rappelled down its huge height.

"Is this the checkout line?"

"No. It's a testing line. I always test gear first. Don't you?" Ruth asked.

"Every time I've bought anything here," Jon agreed, truthful for the first time. His mother had always told him not to lie. How in the world has this happened to me? he wondered as he looked with horror at the people at the front of the line. One after the other, they kept swinging themselves cheerfully onto the rock face as if it wasn't a suicidal act. He turned back to Ruth, who seemed to be moving her lips.

"Excuse me?" he asked.

Two more people threw ropes up. He could hear his heart beating against his chest wall. He looked around for Tracie. This has to be a joke, he thought as he and Ruth moved toward the desk. Jon began to panic. He was so very afraid of heights. "I don't have to test this line," he said as casually as he could muster.

"No, but I'm sure you want to try out the carabiner."

An REI expert came up to Jon. "Are you experienced?"

Before he could beg off, Ruth piped up. "He does aid climbing," she assured the guy.

"Then you can tie your own knot," the guy told Jon.

Yeah, around my neck, Jon thought. Or around Tracie's. Jon glanced from left to right, looking for a quick escape. The crowd hanging around to watch all looked like relatives of Madame Defarge at the guillotine. To his increasing nausea, he saw Tracie among them. Jon shot her a desperate look. She shrugged. He looked at Ruth, thought of her creamy skin, then took a deep breath and threw his line up the rock.

"Are you sure you want such a difficult route?" Ruth asked. Jon shook his head, grabbed the rope, and began to climb. Everyone else moved up the face like spider monkeys, but Jon inched along like something melting upward. "Don't worry. I've got you," Ruth called to him. Jon suddenly hated her with his whole heart. He hadn't realized she was a demented sadist bent on his extinction.

"Oh, I'm not worried," he called back, talking to force himself to move up two or three ledges of rock. He was now almost six feet from the ground. He looked over his shoulder and became so terrified that his hands shook and he almost fell. To prevent that, he began to move wildly, pushing himself into the stone while he scrambled up the rope. There was no place to perch, no surface that was anything but vertical. At last, he reached a ledge about twenty feet above the crowd below and grabbed it desperately. He hugged the rock like lichen.

The REI expert pulled out a bullhorn and called up to him. "Are you all right?" Everyone in the huge store stopped to stare. The crowd grew. So this was what people looked like from the ceiling of the Museum of Flight. He watched as Tracie scrambled to the front of the assembly below. Jon could see her, but instead of yelling encouragement, she began to flash pictures of him! No matter how long you know someone, you can't guess their reaction to things, he thought in a detached way. It wasn't a helpful response to his situation, but Jon didn't really mind, since he was going to die right here. "Please answer me," the guy with the bullhorn was calling. "Are you all right?"

Jon knew it was impossible to nod his head or even to move his lips.

"A clinger! We've got a clinger! Would all climbers please get down," the guy with the bullhorn bellowed.

A safety siren went off. People from all over rushed to look. Tracie backed off from the crowd. Meanwhile, Jon tried to make himself one with the rock.

After the humiliation of the paramedics' arrival, Tracie and a pale, disheveled Jon crossed the parking lot to get back to her car. Other people in the lot stared and pointed at Jon.

He's absolutely hopeless, Tracie thought as she pulled the car door open. She'd lose her bet with Phil, but worse, there was no article here. She couldn't make Jon over. He was a lost cause. Worst of all was Jon's future: He'd always be a geek and he'd wind up a bachelor "uncle" to her future children. God, she thought, he'll teach them bad habits.

After a silence that got them onto the highway and halfway back to Jon's house, he spoke. "So, did you see where Ruth went? I risked my life for her. Then she disappears." Tracie said nothing so that she wouldn't explode. "I gave her my number. You think she'll call?"

Is he for real? Tracie thought. "Not after they brought the oxygen for you," she told him.

"That was all totally unnecessary," he said. "I was just hyperventilating. I only needed a paper bag."

"Yeah. To put over your head." She sighed. He was no Sir Edmund Hillary, but, on the other hand, he'd never take advantage of some poor Sherpa. The worst part was his lack of perception. Didn't he know how bad this had been? It was more embarrassing than the airport fiasco. She told herself she shouldn't give up, but she'd definitely have to give him a tutorial before his date with Beth. "We've got to do a little brushup."

"Oh God," Jon groaned. "Not another lesson."

Tracie took her eyes off the road to give him a pointed stare. "You better not complain, mister," she said. "Not after this fiasco."

Jon shrank toward his door handle; then he began to protest. "Look, I can do it. I know I can," he said. "It wasn't like the airport. She was talking to me. She was liking me." He looked at her. She tried not to smile. "Don't give up on me, Tracie," he begged. "I know you're thinking of giving up, but don't."

She couldn't help it—she took her eyes off the road again to smile at him. "I'd never give up on you," she said. "In fact, I've got exciting news."

"I don't think I need any more excitement today," Jon admitted.

"Well, it's not for today. You have an official date. For Friday night."

Jon sat up straighter. When was the last time he'd had a real date? Was it during the present administration? "You're kidding. With who?" he asked.

"Whom," Tracie corrected, though she often made the same mistake. "A girl from my office. Really cute. Beth."

Uh-oh. One of Tracie's losers. Tracie was always reporting on them, but he couldn't keep their names straight. "Wasn't she the one in love with that stock car racer?" he asked suspiciously.

"That was last year," Tracie admitted, as if last year were a century ago. "There's been a club bouncer since then. And a newspaper guy."

Oh God. A Seattle-scene chickie. "She'll never like me."

"She will," Tracie insisted. "We just have a lot of brushup work to do before Friday. Can you meet me tomorrow?"

"I have a planning meeting tomorrow." Jon had been really lax at work. Instead of his usual twelve-hour days, he'd been cutting back, and back. At Micro/Con, a twenty-hour day wasn't enough. This new focus on his social life was going to catch up with him if he didn't put in some time at the office.

"Hey! What's more important—your career or your love life?" Tracie asked. She had a disconcerting way of responding to things he had only thought and not said. Usually, he enjoyed it: It made him feel understood. Now, however, he felt exposed. "No one ever died wishing they'd spent more time in the office," she reminded him.

Yeah, he thought. And no one got to be vice president of development if they had a social life. He sighed. "Okay. Okay. So where do I meet her?"

"Across from the *Seattle Times*. In front of Starbucks. Or inside if it's raining."

"And where do I take her?" he asked. He actually felt himself getting nervous already.

"Take her to a nice restaurant. But not too nice. Now, you remember the rules about ordering."

"Yeah, yeah," he said glumly. "No Cobb salads."

Chapter 21

Tracie walked up the dirty stairs to Phil's apartment on the second floor. The door was open. He always left the door open, which made Tracie nervous. Tracie knew she was a conservative, keep-it-zippered, lock-it-up kind of girl, but this was dangerous. Phil's neighborhood—near Occidental Park—wasn't the best one in Seattle. She didn't even like parking here. Once, her left fender had been scratched badly, and another time, her antenna had been broken off. She actually liked Phil to go to her place, but she refused to have him do it all the time. He almost lived there already. Hence the bet. So here she was, parked in a dangerous spot, climbing the dirty stairs, prepared for dirtier sheets, just to be with him and make her point and keep some kind of balance. She shook her head. Men were so difficult. She knew he'd rather be with her than live like this, but he wouldn't admit it. Tracie figured she'd better win the bet.

She walked in, and the big room—Phil called it that because he thought *living room* was a middle-class term—was in the usual shambles. She stepped delicately around the *objects*. From the doorway of his room, she heard a clicking noise and knew Phil must be writing.

That was so great—he wrote without a deadline, without the

knowledge he'd be published. She could never do that. She hated to interrupt him anytime he was writing, but to do it now and ask for a favor might be really difficult. She tried to figure out how to present what she needed from Phil to make her project happen. What she'd figured, after Jon's failure alone at the airport and the documented failure at REI, was that to get an article out of it, she had to have some success with Jon. She really needed to see him on a date. Maybe she should go with him and coach him. And it wouldn't hurt if she got some success pictures. She jotted a note on a Post-it to remind herself to take her camera along. But Phil wasn't usually interested in going out—unless there was a movie he wanted to see or a gig he was playing—much less in playing duenna to help her. Tracie sighed. She was making progress with Jon. Ruth, or whatever her name was, had really liked him until he had to go freeze on the mountain.

But Phil wouldn't care about that, and he wouldn't care about her article. He'd tell her she shouldn't be writing such middle-class trash anyway. And she guessed he was right, but somehow it didn't seem fair. She paid for the groceries that he ate with the middle-class money she earned. Don't be bitter, she told herself. You respect him because he's an artist, a free spirit. And there was something about him . . . his freedom and his anarchy that made him tremendously alluring. It was too easy to find a dog and domesticate it, especially if the dog was already hungry and weak. When you found a bobcat or a mountain lion and could domesticate it, that was an achievement. Jon was a little Dalmatian or Lab puppy, just looking for a home. But Phil was a wolf, and to get him to eat out of her hand without biting her was an endlessly fascinating task.

For another moment, she thought about the bet she'd made with him. If she won, he'd move in with her. She wondered if that was what she really wanted. Sleeping with him was wonderful, but living with him might present more problems. She loved his longing to be free, but sometimes she wondered why he couldn't mature a little, get a job, and act a little bit more . . . well, middle-class. Tracie wasn't looking for a diamond solitaire and she didn't want to wind up a rich wife in Encino, but everything middle-class wasn't hideous. Marriage and family and a nice place to live and good food—those were all what Martha Stewart would call "good things." Not only were they good, but Phil liked them, too. That's why he spent so much time at her place.

She moved closer to his door and stepped on the lid of a pizza box.

"That you, Tracie?" Phil asked without looking up.

"Yeah," she said, trying to imitate him. "I got home late from rehearsal."

Phil turned from the computer screen and rubbed his eyes as if he'd been typing a long time. "Hey, you don't have rehearsals."

"You win the prize," she said, and went up behind him to put her hands on his shoulders. They were so wide. "Hey, I need help."

"Got an itch that needs to be scratched?" he asked, stretching.

"Not now. I'm talking about my project with Jonny."

"Jonny? You mean Jon? The so called sexless savant?"

He'd been reading her notes for the article! Tracie blushed and crossed to the bed, away from him. She was careful to respect *his* privacy. He'd obviously been looking at her notes and Post-its. Well, she admitted to herself, she did stick them all over. But it still annoyed her that he was snooping. He'd be sorry. She moved a half-filled bottle of Evian. "That's just it. He doesn't look like a Techno-Nerd anymore. He's really coming along. Want to check him out?"

Phil turned back to the screen. "No."

She'd known that one wouldn't work. "I've got a date set up for him on Friday," she told Phil.

"Is Chelsea Clinton that desperate?" Phil asked. "And how will Mr. Techno-Nerd cope with all the Secret Service agents watching his every move? Not that he has any," Phil added.

"He's got moves. I taught him moves," Tracie said in Jon's defense. She hoped that despite her chickening out on her sex lecture, he did have a couple of his own. She paused. She'd have to try now to slip this in gently. "Look, I fixed him up with Beth from work." Maybe if she just made it sound casual and fun. "For Friday." She paused again. "So won't it be a hoot? We need to go out with them. Like a double date."

" 'Like a double date'? Now I know I'm dreaming. Or is this a nightmare?" Phil asked, his voice heavy with sarcasm. "Tracie, I don't date. I certainly don't double-date. And, if I did, it wouldn't be with that Techno-Nerd. Or your little friend Beth."

Well, there was nothing left but begging. "Come on, Phil. We don't have to be with them. I just have to watch him. Like a coach. I have to be able to help him if things go wrong. It's the first time." She paused. "And for reportage, I have to observe."

"That doesn't mean that I have to be subjected to it."

Sometimes he was so selfish and predictable that she wanted to kill him. "Phil, I swear to God. If you don't do this for me . . ."

"I don't want you helping him anymore," Phil said suddenly. He took her hand, put down the water, and pulled her to him. He cradled her between his legs. "This is taking up too much of your time," he said, nuzzling her neck. "You were gone almost all night. Plus, if you win, then . . ."

His moves gave her a shiver of pleasure down her back. "Then we're sharing laundry duties," she said, finishing the sentence for him. "You'd look so good over a box of Tide."

He pushed her away and stood up abruptly. "See," he said. "See! I told you! This is not what I wanted. And you want me the way I am. That's why you picked me. You don't want me in an apron, dusting the living room. Domesticating the outlaw is a lose-lose." He threw himself onto the bed. "I wish you'd just drop this stupid project of yours."

Tracie sat at the edge of his bed and put her arms around him. "Maybe my dad wants you as an in-law," she said, fibbing, "but that's not on *my* mind. Besides, Phil, I really want to write this piece." If child psychology didn't work, maybe teen psychology would. "You're just afraid I'm going to win the bet, right? And that you were wrong about Jonny."

"What's with this Jonny stuff?" he asked. "Anyway, I wasn't wrong. You can't turn that guy cool."

"Then come see," she said as he rolled her on her back and kissed her deeply. "Will you come?" she whispered, and he nodded his head in a silent promise.

Friday morning at work, Tracie was frantically typing at her PC when the phone rang. Without a missed keystroke, she reached over and pushed the headset button.

"Tracie Higgins here."

"I know that. I called you," Laura said.

"Are you going out to look for a job today?" Tracie asked her. She loved having Laura there, and she certainly didn't want Laura to go back to Peter, but she couldn't stay cooped up in Tracie's apartment.

"I have an interview at three o'clock," Laura said proudly. "And I thought I'd stop by afterward so we could have a drink."

"Great," Tracie told her. "That's great, Laura." Then she remembered that tonight Beth was going out with Jon and that she was coaching. "I can have a quick drink," she said, because she didn't want to let Laura down after her interview.

"Fine," Laura said.

"But it'll have to be quick, because I have to go out." There was a pause.

"Do I have to baby-sit Phil again?" Laura asked.

"Nope. He's going out with me."

"Wow! Congratulations," Laura said. "What's the event?"

"Jon's coming-out party."

"Why? Is he gay? It didn't seem as if he was gay."

"Don't be ridiculous," Tracie snapped. "He's going out with Beth."

"Oh, so tonight's the night. Circuithead meets Airhead."

Tracie was about to protest to defend both of her friends, but then her phone flashed. "I've got to go. I'll see you around five," she said. Then there was a call interrupt.

"Tracie Higgins," she announced.

"Are we still on for tonight?" she heard Jon ask.

She rolled her eyes. "Yes, you're still on. Why wouldn't you be on?"

"You know," he said, "I've had a lot of last-minute cancellations in my career. Plus, I really ought to work. I mean, I've slacked off lately and I'm so far behind. . . ."

He was impossible. He'd worked twenty-four/seven for years. He was using work as an excuse, when, in fact, he had no self-confidence. Beth hadn't even met him yet, and he still figured he was striking out. "Forget about the past," she told him. "You're a new man. You look bad, you act bad, and you are bad. You are a bad boy, a chick magnet. Think of Beth as nothing more than an iron filing."

"Hey, did you have those little games when you were a kid?" he asked. "The ones that had the face of a bald-headed guy and a bunch of iron filings in a plastic bubble? You could make them into hair or a beard by using the magnet?"

Tracie drew her eyes away from her screen and stared into the phone. "Jonny, don't ask any questions like that tonight, okay?" she suggested. "No Mr. Potato Heads, none of your imitations of Cartman from *South Park*. And don't sing the entire *Gilligan's Island* theme song. When in doubt, be silent."

"Silent. Right," he agreed from his end of the phone. "But do you have to call me Jonny? It's so . . . weird."

She thought his voice sounded a little hurt, but she told herself it was for his own good. "Yes. Get used to it." She tried to think of what he could do to guarantee Beth's interest. She paused. The best trick would be to be unavailable. But how? She remembered a fight with Phil and smiled. Yes! " Jonny, there's something I want you to be sure to do," she told him. "Some time after you flirt with the waitress, I want you to excuse yourself and go over to the bar and talk to a woman."

"A different woman? But I . . ."

The light for line two on Tracie's phone went on. " Jonny, hold on a second, will you?" She was liking his new name, she realized as she pressed down the button for line two. "Hello, this is Tracie Higgins. May I help you?"

"What I want from you is a little more than help," Phil said.

"Hold that thought, and hold for a second." Tracie pushed line one and continued with Jon—uh, Jonny. "Where were we? Oh, yeah. You're at the bar talking to a woman. . . ."

"Trace. For tonight, I already have a date. I couldn't get one girl. I can't simultaneously pick *two* women up."

"That's not the point," she said. "Think of it as a magic trick. It's illusion." She remembered Phil on the other line. "Hold a minute," she said, then punched her other button. "Phil, I'll be right with you." She punched line one again. "So, Jonny, just ask her what time it is. Or the best road to take to Olympia. Anyway, then I want you to write a phone number in pen on your hand."

"Whose phone number?" Jon asked.

"Just *any* phone number," she told him, exasperated. "Then go back to the table and don't say anything about it. Just make sure Beth sees your hand."

"Let her see it?" he whined. "Tracie, you're getting me nuts. This is cruel and unusual punishment. Maybe we should cancel this. I'm so behind on my work. And I'm not feeling well all of a sudden."

"Don't even think about getting sick," she warned him, "or it's back to airports for you. Anyway, she'll love you over this. It will make you seem like a conqueror. You can have anyone, but you picked her."

"But I might also be picking up someone else," he whined. He still didn't get it.

Tracie rolled her eyes. " Jonny, this is what dating in the new millennium is all about: cruel and unusual punishment. Now do you get it?"

"I got it. So I'm going to meet her in front of your building at five-thirty."

"But be sure not to come until about quarter to six," she said.

"But . . . ah. Okay," he agreed.

"See ya. Wouldn't wanna be ya!" Tracie sang out, using Encino-speak again. Only after she had hung up and gone back to work did she notice that the light for line two had gone out. Phil! She shrugged. She didn't know where to reach him, but Phil would call back.

Beth was primping while Tracie, Laura, and Sara watched the operation. "You ought to brush out your hair," Sara suggested. Tracie handed her a blusher and straightened up her collar.

"I already have, Sara. Thanks. God, I'll probably sweat like a nervous pig," Beth said. "I wish I'd brought my perfume."

"You want to borrow some of my Giorgio?" Laura asked, rummaging through her bag.

"Thanks, but no," Beth said. "I already put on White Shoulders this morning. Together, they might curdle. Is he really cute, Trace?"

"Yeah. He's cute . . . in a kind of James Dean way." Tracie figured she could plant that in Beth's mind.

But Beth asked, "Who's James Dean?"

"Some dead guy. An actor, right, who made sausages?" Sara said.

"You're so lucky, Beth. I haven't been on a date in four months. Tracie, why don't you ever fix me up with somebody? Doesn't Jonny have friends?" Sara asked.

"Tracie never used to know anybody good," Beth said. "Laura, where did she find this guy? I'd never heard of him," Beth pointed out as she applied some mascara.

"She's manufactured him," Laura told the girls, then grinned over their heads at Tracie. Tracie gave Laura a warning look, then looked at her watch. "You're going to be late," she told Beth. "And Laura and I are going out for a drink."

Beth panicked. "You're kidding! I still have to tweeze my left eyebrow. Who has a pair of tweezers?" she asked. "I look like Gorilla Girl." Laura handed her the tweezers while Tracie sneaked a peek out the window. Whatever time Beth got there, Jon had to be a little later. God, she hoped Beth wouldn't be too disappointed or diss him too badly.

"It's already twenty to six," Tracie announced. "You were supposed to be there ten minutes ago."

"Make him wait. They're always late for us," Sara said.

Beth plucked two invisible hairs from her eyebrows, returned the tweezers, picked up her bag, and was ready to run. "Hey, if we go to the elevator bank, we can see them meet across the street," Sara said.

"Let's go," Laura agreed.

So Laura, Tracie, Beth, and Sara wove around the homeward-bound stragglers in the hall. They got to the elevator and Beth pushed the button. "Wish me luck!" she cried.

Before they could answer, the doors opened and she got in the elevator. Just then, the disgustingly beautiful Allison dashed into the hallway. "Hold the elevator!" she called. "I'm late."

"As if I give a shit," Sara murmured, but of course one of the men in the car hit the open button, hoping that for just a few moments he could stand beside Allison and drink in her aura. Beth was standing beside Allison, and her glow faded, but Tracie refused to acknowledge that.

"Have fun," Tracie said. "He's a dreamboat."

The three remaining women watched the door close on her hopeful face. First Sara, then Laura, and finally Tracie drifted over to the window. They waited a few minutes, looking out onto the street. Soon enough, Beth was below them. They watched as she crossed the street and stood alone in the twilight.

"If that son of a bitch doesn't show . . ." Sara said under her breath. "You know, Beth's had it so rough."

"He'll show," Tracie said grimly, hoping she was right.

"She looks really great," Laura said a little wistfully, her nose almost pressed to the window. "So thin."

"Ha! I hope he comes at her from the front and doesn't see her ass first," Sara said.

"Sara!" both Laura and Tracie cried.

"Just joking," Sara said.

Below them, Beth stood there, shifting from one leg to another, trying to lean against a light pole nonchalantly. The girls all watched in silence for a few more minutes. Despite her nerves, or because of them, her face had that first-date brightness that turns into a glow when women fall in love.

"If he doesn't show, I'll kill you, Tracie," Laura said.

"If he does and he's good-looking, I'll kill you for setting up Beth before you thought of me," Sara grumbled.

"Hey, hey!" Tracie soothed. "Don't get so excited. You probably won't even like his looks."

Just then, Tracie saw him chaining his bike to a railing just around the corner. God! She hoped they hadn't noticed him yet. Like an idiot, he had the motorcycle helmet lashed to the handlebars. She had to tell him everything, including not to take the Schwinn to the date. It was amazing that he didn't get arrested for public lameness. Tracie watched as he grabbed the helmet, ran down the street, and then slowed at the corner. She saw him check his reflection in the drugstore window. Luckily, Sara and Laura still hadn't spotted him. So that when he made the turn and swaggered across the street, there was nothing to link him to the Schwinn.

"There he is," Laura said. Down below, Jonny crossed the street and approached Beth. Clearly, they'd made contact and were introducing themselves. Tracie stepped back from the two girls and surveyed their reaction.

"Oh God. He looks great!" Sara was saying. She put her face up closer to the window and cupped her hands around the side of her head to cut down the reflection and get a better view.

"Nice sweater," Laura commented.

"Nice jacket. I saw one like that last year in Ralph Lauren," Sara continued. "Looks like the guy's got some bucks. Not to mention a nice set of pecs."

"He's got a helmet! Does he have a motorcycle?" Laura asked. Tracie remembered that Peter had a motorcycle.

"Where's his bike?" Sara asked.

"He probably parked it around the block," Tracie said truthfully; then, to distract them, she added, "You know, he just broke up with someone."

From the window, they watched Jonny and Beth talking. Jon put his hand in his pocket and pulled something out, putting it right in front of Beth's face.

"Is that a lighter?" Sara asked. "But Beth doesn't smoke."

Tracie rolled her eyes as Jon put the Pez dispenser back in his pocket. She'd have to kill him later. Then he reached out and touched the end of Beth's hair. The two of them laughed over something. And, in the silence by the elevator bay, loneliness began to envelop the three women. Tracie couldn't help but remember how excited she used to get when she'd first met Phil—how she'd spend an hour trying on every possible outfit. She remembered how happy she'd get just seeing him. That reminded her. "Laura, come on. We've got to go," Tracie said. "I've got only twenty minutes for a drink and then I've got to meet Phil."

"Yeah, and I've got a story due." Sara sighed.

"I guess I'll get to work on my résumé tonight," Laura said. "That, and read the want ads."

The three women all sighed as one and then each turned her back on the window and walked away.

Chapter 22

A waitress stood at the table and looked expectantly at Jon and Beth. She looked at least a hundred and ten years old, one of those women who would work until the day she died.

They were at the Merchants Café, the oldest restaurant in Seattle, and their waitress was probably even older. Jon was nervous, but so far, he hadn't blown it. Before he'd left work, he had called and had another quick review session with Tracie. She was going to show up and observe from a distance, to help him through. He was determined to do this perfectly: remember the lines he was supposed to say, compliment the appropriate odd thing, and avoid any mention of his dietary habits. He would carry no luggage, and he wouldn't hang off any rock walls.

But somehow, as he looked across at Beth's pretty face, all the tutoring became a mishmash in his head. For a moment, he felt sad and wondered why all the charade was necessary. It just increased the gulf between them. But he had to admit that Beth was really cute and she was looking at him with more interest than he'd gotten from a woman in a long, long time. He told himself he was going to have to tough it out. He was absolutely committed to making all the right plays.

By now, the waitress was tapping her foot, impatient for their order. Jon remembered that there was something he was supposed to do when Beth selected her meal. He tried to think quickly, reviewing what it was. Something about veal? No. For a moment, he panicked. Then he remembered. He'd have to wait until she selected her choice.

"I'll have the Dover sole," Beth said to the waitress.

"Are you sure you want to order that?" Jon asked, proud that he'd remembered in time.

"Why? Isn't it fresh here?" Beth asked him.

Wait. That wasn't part of his tutorial. He realized, too late, that in Tracie's scenario, his date ordered something very fattening.

"All of our fish is fresh daily," the waitress said hostilely, as if any discussion of the fish reflected on her honor.

"I'm sorry. I'm sure it is," Jon said apologetically. He hadn't meant to insult the Merchants Café. How could he explain? Thinking quickly, he said, "Uh, I'll have the sole, too." He didn't particularly like sole, but it was a good peacemaking gesture. At least he hoped so.

"It comes with salad. You want potatoes or rice?" The waitress took the rest of their order without comment and then left, shaking her head. Meanwhile, Beth was staring at him, a half smile on her face.

"You're weird. You warn me not to have the fish and then you order it, too?"

Jon shrugged. Okay. He'd screwed that up, but he wouldn't screw up anything else. He tried to think of what James Dean might do. He probably wouldn't have ordered the sole. What had Tracie taught him? He looked across at Beth. She did have pretty eyes, dark, with a fringe of darker lashes, but he knew he wasn't supposed to say that. So when the waitress returned to the table and put two salads down, Jon took the old woman's hand to stop her. He looked at Beth.

"Doesn't she have the most beautiful eyes you've ever seen?" he asked his date.

But, even as the words were out of his mouth, he realized with a sinking feeling that it was very clear that the waitress's eyes were not beautiful. In fact, they were hardly visible, buried as they were in the folds of her wrinkled face.

"Oh, yeah. She absolutely does," Beth agreed, probably to make the woman feel good. Or because she thought Jon was trying to be sweet.

"Thank you," the waitress responded. Well, he hadn't made Beth jealous, but at least he'd made up for his fish insult. What next? This was so difficult. He sighed. Once the waitress left, he began to fiddle with his salad, afraid to speak and afraid of the silence.

"That was considerate," Beth said, using the voice that he'd heard all his life. "You're a sweet guy."

"No I'm not," Jon said with more force than he meant to use. Beth blinked the eyes he was not supposed to comment on. Great. Next he'd start babbling about his luggage and the Unabomber. She'd run screaming from the restaurant. Get a grip, he told himself. Beth was saying something about the place and he had to get out of his head and respond. "Are you from Seattle?" he managed to ask. God, that was lame, but at least it got her going. She began talking about each of the places she'd lived. But he got distracted. Because out of the corner of his eye, he saw Tracie enter the place with Phil and take a table on the other side of the restaurant. Oh, no. She had told him she would be there for him, but somehow he hadn't imagined Phil along with her.

Of course, she wouldn't be coming alone and he supposed that Phil—odious as he was—was better than Laura. In case he blew this, he didn't want the woman he'd accidentally tried to pick up to watch him go down in flames.

Tracie surveyed the room, caught his eye, and then waved to him discreetly. She slipped into a chair with her back to Beth and Jon. Then Jon realized that Beth was asking him a question.

"Huh?" he asked like a lunkhead.

"What kind of bike do you ride?" she repeated.

"A Schwinn . . . uh . . . Could you excuse me a minute?" he asked as she laughed.

"Yeah, sure, Jonny," she told him. He gritted his teeth. He hated that stupid name. He got up and started to walk toward Tracie's table, but Beth interrupted him. "I think the men's room is that way," she said.

"Oh, thanks. Yeah, right." He walked off in the direction that Beth pointed in, then managed to hide himself for a moment in the hallway and doubled back. He crouched, then ran to Tracie's table. He stuck his head up between Tracie and Phil. He'd just blank Phil out. Phil, and all the smooth Phils of the world. Jon focused on Tracie.

But he couldn't blank Phil out, because when he raised his head to Phil's eye level, Phil did a complete double take. If he'd had something in his mouth, it would have been a spit take. Though he was in no mood for jokes, Jon readied himself for the insult.

"Whoa, little dude! Is that Jonny?" Jon didn't bother to respond, but Phil continued. "Tracie, he looks good. I mean for him, he looks really good!"

Jon just decided to ignore him. "It's going all wrong," he told Tracie.

"Oh, really?" she said sarcastically. "Could it have been when you flicked your Bic at her?"

"It wasn't a Bic it was a Pez."

"Well, that makes all the difference," Tracie told him, but the sarcasm was lost on him.

"Okay, okay. I screwed up but how do I fix it?"

"How do you know you have to?"

"She's already told me she thought I was a nice guy."

Phil laughed. "Uh-oh," he said. "You can take the dweeb out of Nerdland, but you can't take the nerd out of the dweeb."

"Thanks, Yoda," Jon snapped.

"What were her words exactly?" Tracie asked.

"She said I was 'a sweet guy.' "

Phil laughed. "Shit!" Tracie said. She rarely used expletives, so Jon knew it was as bad as he thought it was. He'd tried to do his part. He'd tried to do everything she told him to. He'd tried to follow directions, he really had. The hair, the clothes, the restaurant, the things he was supposed to say, and not supposed to say, but it still wasn't working. Maybe he should consider a career in a monastery.

Despite his nervousness, he realized he was babbling, but he couldn't stop. "And she didn't order veal Parmesan, the waitress is older than my grannie, and when I pulled the beautiful eyes bit, she thought I was being sweet." He banged the table with his fist. "Why do they always think I'm sweet?"

Tracie tried to reassure him. "Calm down. Don't worry. They'll feel you're heartless enough eventually. This is only your first try. Just think of this as a practice. Did you do the phone number trick?"

"What trick?" he asked.

Tracie glanced over at Phil, then glanced back at Jon. "The one I told you about," she said. She took his hand and wrote on it with her finger.

"Oh, yeah," Jon said. "Yeah, I mean, no, but I will." Despite himself, he turned his head toward Phil, who, if he had to witness this humiliation, could at least be useful. "By the way, Phil, do you ride a Yamaha?"

Phil looked at him with disgust. "No, I play a Yamaha. I ride a Suzuki."

Jon had to get back and had no time to be as snotty as he would have liked. "Great. Thanks," was all he had time to say before he scurried back to the hallway. There he stood up, looking around for a woman to talk to before he wrote on his hand. But there wasn't a woman around, and even if there had been, Beth couldn't see him. He had to do *something*, so he just took out a pen and scribbled a phone number on his hand. Walking the way James Dean did in *Giant*, he swaggered back to the table, where their fish had already been served.

"I started without you," Beth told him. "I hope you don't think that's rude."

"No. Not at all." He put his hand out to reach for the tartar sauce and almost knocked it over. Beth caught it and held his hand for a minute. "Oh. Thanks," he said.

Beth colored and looked down. She noticed his hand. "Isn't that Tracie's phone number?" she asked him.

Goddamn it! "Uuh . . . yeah. Sometimes I forget it," he said as smoothly as he could. He figured he'd better change the subject. "So, to answer your question, I ride a Suzuki."

"A 750?" she asked as she put a piece of endive in her mouth.

Her mouth was very sexy. It was pouty, or whatever word women's magazines used when talking about fluffy lips. She had a very red lipstick on, and for some reason, it gave Jon a real tug in his lap. "Uh, yeah."

"I didn't know Suzuki made a 750. My brother rode a Harley." She finished her fish. "He said Japanese bikes were all crap."

"Well, that seems kind of ethnocentric."

He looked down at his own fish. It was cold, and he'd never wanted it in the first place.

"Don't you like your fish, Jonny?"

God! Every time she called him that, he thought she was talking to someone else. "Uh, yeah. Well, no. Not really," he admitted. "I just ordered it because you ordered it. But I'm not a vegetarian or anything," he assured her. There was a silence for a moment. He had to say *something*. "You have very nice earlobes," he said at last. "Very shapely."

Beth laughed. "You are too weird." She laughed again. They talked for a while. "I like your jacket. Where did you get it?" she asked.

"My girlfriend—I mean a girl who's a friend of mine—I mean a friend of mine who's a girl—she thought it would—"

She interrupted him. "Are you seeing somebody? I mean in a serious way?"

Had Tracie told him what to answer to that? If she had, he couldn't remember. "No. No. I—"

"You're not living with her, are you?" Beth asked.

He remembered his line for that. "No. I live alone. But you can't come over."

"Well then, let's go to my place," Beth said.

Jon put down his fork. Had he heard right? He almost asked Beth to repeat it but, with his heart and other parts of him leaping, he figured he shouldn't press his luck. He gestured for the check and left cash on the table as soon as it was handed to him. (Tracie had told him not to use a charge card, and anyway, he wanted to be quick just in case Beth changed her mind.) Now he just had to get her out the door before she noticed Tracie and Phil at the other side of the restaurant.

Out of anxiety, he took her by the shoulder and gently but firmly pushed her toward the door, turning her body so that she'd be angled toward the bar and not the other dining room.

She turned her head over her shoulder. "That's sexy," she said.

Jon couldn't believe it. As he was opening the door and about to disappear through it, he only had time to give Tracie a fleeting glance. She had her neck craned and, though he couldn't be sure, the expression on her face looked a little bewildered.

Chapter 23

Tracie lay in the dark, staring up at the ceiling, with both her dinner and Phil's leg pressing heavily on her. He was sprawled across more than his share of the bed, making the little groaning sound he made at irregular intervals just before he fell asleep. She tried to extricate her leg from under his without disturbing him, but it wasn't possible.

After Jon and Beth's quick departure from the Merchants Café, she and Phil had finished their dinner. Phil had also finished the entire bread basket, most of the second one—except for the piece she couldn't resist—along with a large salad with blue cheese dressing, and then a very rich dessert. She thought of one of the Encino sayings she and Laura had used when they were learning the times tables: "I ate and ate and got sick on the floor. So eight times eight is sixty-four." He had finished up with brandy and two double espressos. Just to keep him company, she'd had one. It must be the espresso, mixed with my natural anxiety for Jon, that's keeping me awake now, she told herself.

They had come in more than forty-five minutes ago and collapsed on the bed. Since then, Tracie had had trouble sleeping. She wasn't used to such a rich meal at that time of night, and she never ate bread and desserts. But she'd been so nervous, expecting an emergency call on her cell phone to explain what had gone wrong at the restaurant.

It hadn't been going well. She could tell that from Jon's feverish questions and his report on Beth's comments. Beth, of all her friends, wasn't going to like a nice boy. What went wrong? she wondered. She supposed it wasn't possible to change Jon, and his true-blue color had shown, despite the camouflage they had tried. Well, Beth's loss. She just hoped that Jon wasn't too decimated. She had done this to build his self-confidence, but it seemed it was working the opposite way.

She shifted her weight. Phil's long leg still hung over hers. Her right foot was going to sleep. She would have to nudge him to get out from under. He was such a bed hog, she wondered why she even wanted to win her bet. He'd been awful at the restaurant, imitating Jon and making fun of both of them. He ate like a pig, he never had any money, and though he was undeniably good-looking, he looked at other girls. Sex was great, but sleeping with him certainly wasn't easy.

But that didn't cause her insomnia. What she couldn't understand was why they'd left the restaurant so soon, why Jon hadn't called her, and why he didn't answer when she rang his phone. Of course, she'd told him that he'd have to work at being unavailable, but she hadn't meant unavailable to her. Knowing Jon, he just didn't want to bother her with yet more bad news. Still, she'd called four times already and let it ring, hoping he hadn't turned the phone off and that he would pick up so she could comfort him.

She decided to try one more time. As gently as she could, she pushed Phil's hip with her hand while she tried to wriggle her leg free. She had extricated her knee when he lifted his head. "What time is it?" he asked.

"Sleepy-sleep time," she told him. "Roll over." He did, and Tracie got up and looked over his shoulder at the clock. She picked up the phone, dialed Jon's number, and, when there was still no answer, decided to dial Beth. What the hell. Beth might ream her for setting her up, or for waking her up, but she could always pretend she was upset over Phil. She'd gotten enough calls from Beth over Marcus to make that all right.

But there was no answer at Beth's, either. "It's almost two A.M. Where are they?" she murmured to herself. Phil grunted. Worry now mixed with her curiosity. Maybe . . .

"Downloading recipes, for all I know," Phil said. He sounded incredibly cranky. He always did if he was awakened. "Come on, go to sleep. You're nobody's mother," he reminded her. "What's it to you?"

"Well . . . I just hope they're all right," Tracie told him, then sat back down on her side of the bed. She imagined Jon finally giving up and hanging himself in his new, pared-down closet. Or snapping, and attacking Beth like a sex-crazed weasel.

Phil turned over, but Tracie continued to stare into the darkness. In a moment, she heard his snores.

She was sitting on the sofa in the dark, trying to think of what she'd do next, when Laura got up from her futon and stealthily walked to the side table and lifted up the phone. "What are you doing?" Tracie asked.

Laura jumped in surprise and strangled a scream. "Oh my God! Tracie! I didn't know you were there."

"Obviously not," Tracie said. "Who were you about to call? No one in Encino," she said accusingly.

"I wasn't going to call anyone," Laura said.

"No," Tracie agreed, her voice mockingly sarcastic. "You just woke up in the middle of the night with a phenomenal need to dust the phone." Tracie narrowed her eyes, although in the dark she could barely see Laura's white shape. Has she been doing this all along, while I thought she was getting over it? Tracie wondered. "Since no 900 numbers have shown up on my bill, I have to think that you've been calling Peter," she said bitterly.

"No, Tracie. I swear I haven't been. This was the first time. It was just that I . . ." Laura sat down beside Tracie. She picked up one of the throw pillows and pulled it to her chest. There, together in their nightgowns in the darkness, Tracie was suddenly flooded with tremendous affection for her friend. It wasn't easy being Laura. Who could understand a big, funny, smart, wisecracking girl with a passion for cooking? Who would want to be with her, to love her as much as she deserved to be? Well, Tracie would, and any man who wouldn't was losing out. And not just on great dinners.

"I don't know. I watched Beth get ready for her date, and then you had to rush off to Phil, and it seemed like everyone had someone but me. And I thought of Peter. I know I shouldn't even think about him," Laura admitted, her voice full of pain. "I know that. But . . ."

"I know," Tracie echoed, putting her arm across Laura's shoulder. "It's hard to be alone in a world of couples. I hope that Phil and I don't make you feel left out. I'd hate that."

"No. No. You never make me feel like the third wheel. It's so nice that you'd even have me here." She paused. "It got really bad in Sacramento." Laura made a little choking noise. "You know, I don't want Peter back. It was just hearing Phil's snore that somehow made me so lonely." She paused, and Tracie could see a single tear roll down Laura's cheek. "I wanted to be next to my own snorer," Laura said, then sniffed. "So sue me."

"I won't sue you this time," Tracie told her, "but I am going to tell you that you have to give up the reruns of *Quincy*. Jack's a bad influence on you. You know, Mr. Bill at my video store won't let me watch *Love with the Proper Stranger* anymore."

"He won't?"

"Nope. And that's a good thing. You have to get out there again. Oddly enough, you're not likely to meet anybody in front of my TV or in my kitchen."

"You may have a point there," Laura admitted.

Tracie moved her hand to Laura's two and rubbed them. They were big and warm and capable, just like Laura. "Come on," Tracie said. "Don't you think it's time you decided to stay up here? Look for a job?"

"Well, I already went to one interview," Laura said hopefully.

"It's a start," Tracie told her. "And let me make you an appointment with Stefan to add some streaks to your hair. It'll be fun."

"Hey, what do you say if just this once we make farm cakes? I know how you love them." She took one look at Tracie's expression and backed off. "Okay. Okay. Just a pan of brownies from a box."

"I ate and ate and got sick on the floor. So eight times eight is sixty-four," Tracie sang as she got up to go to the kitchen. "And then we sit here on the sofa together and watch *Barnaby Jones* or whatever else is on."

"Really?" Laura asked, her voice full of enthusiasm again.

"Sure. Maybe you could wean yourself off Klugman with Buddy Ebsen," Tracie told her. "Think of Buddy as the patch. Did I tell you Jon wanted his nickname to be Bud?" Tracie asked, then wondered again for a minute what Jon was doing at that moment.

"Bud? You're dreaming, right?" Laura asked, and they both giggled in the darkness.

Chapter 24

Jon sat in one of his beanbag chairs, his helmet in his lap and with what he knew was a dopey look on his face. He couldn't get the half smile off his face, despite the fact there was a big Parsifal project meeting that afternoon—unprecedented for a Saturday—and he wasn't prepared to lead it. Instead of focusing on the next steps he and his staff had to take on Parsifal, he was replaying moments from the night before over and over.

Beth had been an enthusiastic partner, but a little too athletic and fast-tempoed. Jon had put his hands on her and slowed her down the way you would with a nervous dog. Every time she wanted to jump to some new position, he'd reminded her with his hands and his tongue—and sometimes by pressing his chest against her—to take it slower. He wanted her to savor each stroke, each caress, each flick of the tongue.

And, once she relaxed, she seemed to enjoy herself. He could tell that she'd had plenty of experience, but he thought she was probably more practiced at pleasing men than at taking her own pleasure. The first time they'd made love, he'd come far too quickly. But that had given him the advantage when they made love the second time, and using his hand as well as long, slow strokes, he'd been able to make her come.

At least he thought so. Jon sighed. The night with Beth had given him a new attitude. He was surprised that it didn't really bother him that he didn't know her very well and didn't think that he'd like her too much when he did. What they had done had just been healthy and fun, but the only thing he didn't like about sex with an almost stranger was that you could never be sure if your partner had come or not. With his last girlfriend, they had had an agreement that she wouldn't fake it. He hoped Beth hadn't, but he couldn't know for sure. Jon looked around the table in his office, imagining the faces of his department staff, who in the next half hour would all be sitting there looking at him. Not one of them, he guessed, would feel as good, as relaxed, as he did at that moment. Or as unmotivated. Or as unprepared. He hoped that they had not been goofing off as much as he had.

As the meeting time approached, he couldn't keep his mind on the matters at hand. Visions from the previous night kept coming back to him: his hand moving down Beth's back into the hollow right above the swell of her hips; the way her eyelids flickered when he moved his hand slowly from her neck to her breast. He moved his tongue against his top lip and then thought about her nipples and how they'd felt against his lips. He felt a stirring in his trousers and realized he better focus on Parsifal, since he'd have to stand up for a good part of the meeting.

Beth was nice enough, but kind of silly. If he wasn't playing the game by Tracie's rules, he didn't know what they would talk about. Yet he felt a tug toward the phone. He wanted to call her. No, he didn't want to talk to her; he just wanted to meet her somewhere for an instant replay.

More and more, he was coming to understand that all was fair in love and war. It wasn't that his father or Phil didn't like the women they hooked up with. They just didn't like them enough. Sex with a stranger—and Jon knew that Beth was a virtual stranger—could be a lot of fun, but afterward there wouldn't be much to say.

His phone rang again, but, as Tracie had warned him, he didn't answer it. That was really putting a crimp in his professional life, but, remembering the previous night, he knew it was worth it. Jon grinned. The thought that he could do it again gave him a little thrill. He thought of the women that were coming to the meeting today: Elizabeth, Cindy, and Susan. He certainly wouldn't mess with anyone who worked for him, but Samantha—she was a different story. Jon wondered if his new look might work on Samantha. His phone rang again, but again he ignored it. His assistant was calling everyone to remind them about the meeting. Again the phone rang. Annoyed, he got up to check the caller ID and realized it was Tracie.

He reached out to pick up the receiver and then stopped. He was embarrassed. He knew Tracie. She wasn't a reporter for nothing. She'd question him on every detail, and somehow it would feel bad to tell Tracie how much he'd enjoyed her friend Beth. It would, however, be equally wrong to pretend that he hadn't enjoyed being with her. He sat back down on the beanbag, and as it gave a sigh of escaping air, so did he. In a way, he owed last night to Tracie and many nights to come. Somehow, though, he really didn't want to talk about it with her.

He'd left Beth's apartment, just as he'd been instructed to do, but shouldn't he eventually call her? Tracie was going too far with that. Still, what she had prescribed had worked. And if he was honest with himself, he knew he didn't actually want a relationship with Beth. So what was he going to do? Tell Beth he'd like to see her again just for sex? Lie to Tracie and pretend the sex hadn't happened? Betray Beth and tell her it did?

Lauren, his assistant, stuck her head into the office. "George says he doesn't have the time line ready," she told him. Jon was out of the chair in a minute. "Goddamn it! How can we schedule each work step without the time line?" he asked. "We're counting on it."

Lauren shrugged. "He says he tried to call you but that he didn't get you."

"Well, he didn't leave a message," Jon said. What he didn't say was that he had rigged his voice mail so that it would always say his message box was full. Lauren shrugged again and disappeared. Shit, Jon thought. While he was getting laid, Parsifal was getting screwed.

He had to review his E-mail, get a copy of the database report, and check his new voice mail messages. Even though Tracie had told him to get rid of voice mail, he couldn't do it at work. Since he was used to getting half a dozen phone calls at home from Micro/Con people, just aborting his home system was traumatic. And using the filled-mailbox ploy was dangerous. Look at what had happened with George and the time line. He got on the phone and began to listen, a pen ready. "You have twenty-seven new messages." Jon groaned. It would take him until the meeting just to clear the messages.

The first message was from Tracie. "I called you at home, but you didn't pick up. Are you depressed? How did it go? Call me."

The second one was also from Tracie. "I've tried you about four times at home again. I'm dying to know how it went. Look, she's not worth getting upset over. There will be others."

Jon had to smile at that, though he felt a little guilty for not having called her. The third call was from his mother. "Hi, Jonathan. I know you must be working very hard, but I wanted to talk to you. It's not very important, but if you have a spare moment, give me a call."

Oooh. He hadn't seen or talked to his mom since Mother's Day. Of course, she thought he was busy with work, as he usually was. He told himself he'd call her back that evening.

The fourth call was also from Tracie, but it was from that morning. "Where are you?" she said. "Come on. Call me. I'm at work. I haven't heard from Beth yet. I hope you didn't murder her." The next call was really breathy, and for a moment he thought it was Tracie again, fooling around. Then he realized it was Beth.

"Hi," she whispered. "Last night was . . . well, you know what last night was. Where did you go? Thanks for leaving your number. Call me." Jon hunched his shoulders guiltily. Tracie had been very clear that he shouldn't reveal where he worked or give out his number, but when he'd snuck out of Beth's bedroom, he'd felt so guilty that he had left his Micro/Con number and he'd rigged the phone so that anyone calling in wouldn't necessarily know that it was Micro/Con. He sighed. This was all so much more complicated than he had imagined.

Jon repressed a grin and listened to the rest of his messages. There were four more from Tracie, each one making him feel more guilty, and two more from Beth. He wasn't the only one who called over and over again. Obviously, women did it, too; it was just that they had never done it to him until now.

His other messages were from George and some of his own staff members. All the news was bad. Jon was almost finished with the lot when there was a new woman's voice on the phone. "Hi, this is Ruth. We met at REI. Remember?"

Jon's eyes widened as he stared at the machine. How could I forget? he thought. "I hope you're okay," she was saying. "You know, I panicked on a climb myself. Anyway, if you'd like to get together and have a cup of coffee or something, I'd like to see you. I hope you don't mind if I don't leave my number. I'll just call you back later."

Holy shit! Jon was too shocked to listen to the rest of his messages. He couldn't believe it. Tracie wasn't just smart; she was the Goddess of Love. He would have to call her, despite his embarrassment, and he'd have to ask her what to do about Beth and Ruth. Maybe he didn't have to see Beth again. He could just move on to Ruth. After all, she'd called him. That might make it even easier. Of course, he didn't want to hurt Beth, but he figured he didn't have much in common with a Seattle club girl. Not that there was going to be much in common between him and an REI mountain climber girl. But who knew?

Jon dialed Tracie, but her line was busy and he didn't want to leave a message. What would he say? Mission accomplished? Lafayette, I was there? Best to see her in person, but when the beep sounded, he panicked and started rambling. "Tracie, I need to cancel our Sunday brunch. I'm swamped at work but I do have a progress report to turn in. Can you see me Monday night after work?"

He hung up the phone and went over to his terminal, trying to pull the Parsifal project together. He was whipping up E-mails in a frenzy when Samantha appeared in the doorway behind him. He saw her reflection in the terminal.

"Jon, do you have a minute?"

Jon allowed himself to look up at her, but only for a moment. "Actually, not right now," he said. "I'm kind of busy." He bowed his head, trying to hide a little smile. Did a man's luck just change completely with the roll of dice or a roll in the hay? It couldn't be, could it?

"I . . . I just wanted to apologize again for that mix-up."

"What mix-up would that be?" he asked. The phone rang. Yes! "Excuse me for a second, Sam." He picked up the phone. When he heard the voice again, he felt it was too good to be true. "Oh, hi, Ruth. Sure. I remember you." Unbelievable! How could he be so lucky? He could talk to Ruth while Sam watched. There *was* a God. "Well, actually, I haven't been climbing since," he told Ruth while he watched Sam's reflection. "No. I'd like to. With you. That'd be great. See you then, Ruth." He hung up the phone.

"Sorry," he said, turning to Sam, but then remembered he wasn't supposed to apologize for anything.

"That's okay," she said, and took a tentative step into his office. "Anyway, you know that Saturday we were supposed to get together?"

"When was that?" he asked, vividly remembering the night he'd stood in the rain.

"Oh, it's not important." He thought she blushed. Was it possible? Had *he* made the beautiful Samantha, homecoming queen of the marketing group, blush? "Well, what I mean," she continued, "is maybe we could get together tonight."

Jon looked up cheerfully, then gave her a slight frown. "Hey, I'd really like to. Maybe some other time. I've just made a climbing date." He paused. He was loving this. "You're not a rock climber, are you?"

"No. Not really." Now Sam paused. "But I'd like to try it."

"Well, maybe sometime," he said vaguely.

"Great, Jon. Are you going to have lunch in the cafeteria?"

"I think so," he told her. Then he said nothing. Absolutely nothing. He watched as she tried to leave. Just as she began to move, he spoke again. "Oh, and Samantha . . . my friends call me Jonny."

"Great, Jonny," she said. "Uh, do you still have my number?"

He nodded, but just barely. Then Jon watched Samantha walk out the door and down the hall. He got up, calmly closed his office door, and then did a huge freakin' victory dance around his desk.

It wasn't until late afternoon—after the Parsifal meeting and long overdue phone calls—that Jon got a chance to gobble a quick sandwich, leave his mother a message, and get to the toilet. He was in a stall, just finishing, when he heard Ron and Donald.

"I don't know," Ron was saying. "I mean, it seemed like he was totally in the dark."

"In the dark? It was Helen Keller night in the black hole of Calcutta," Donald answered.

Ron and Donald were probably two of his smartest staff members, but Ron had a head of unfortunate red hair—the kind that looked pink and thinned early—while Donald might have been five foot two if he stood up straight. Both of them were brilliant, but neither one was what Miss Manners might call "a social success." They constantly hung together, and everyone at Micro/Con called them "RonDon." Now Jon had a sinking feeling in his stomach that they were talking about him.

"Hey, George," Donald said. Someone else had joined them. "What was with Jon in the meeting today?"

"I don't know, but I don't think he had all his burners going. He didn't know anything about the database project," George said. "And it wasn't my fault about the time line."

Jon gulped. It was true. He'd missed all of George's calls.

There was flushing, and Jon almost thought they had left, then realized their conversation was continuing. "Something about Jon has definitely changed," Ron—or Don—said.

"You mean like he's not as supportive of off-loading to the database as he used to be?" George inquired.

"No. Not about work," Don—or Ron—said. "I noticed it, too. He looks different."

"Yeah. And . . . and I think the pets are noticing him," Ron—or Don—said. "Jennifer smiled when she gave him that FedEx this morning."

"Jenny Pet smiled at a lowly mortal?" George asked. "Inconceivable!"

Jennifer was undeniably cute, but probably only eighteen. She worked in the mail room, and when she made her rounds, all business activity stopped.

"You know, I think you're right. When he left the meeting to get the marketing data, the women followed him with their eyes," Don—or Ron—said.

"You mean like in those holograms of Jesus?" Ron asked, his voice cracking.

"Kind of like that, but with sex," Don said. There was a pause, and for a moment Jon again thought they might have left. Then Don continued. He'd obviously been reflecting, because when he spoke, it was slowly, with great deliberation. "I think Jon is . . . hot."

"Homo! Homo!" the other two chanted.

In his stall, Jon shook his head. They were worse than Potsie and Ralph. He couldn't believe they made six figures a year.

"Shut up, shut up," Don yelled at them. "Don't you see the important implications here?"

"What implications?" George asked.

"Jon's done something to change himself. Something that works with the pets."

"Yeah?" George said. "So?"

"Well, if Jon can do it, we can do it," Don declared triumphantly. Then someone entered the stall next to Jon, water ran at one of the sinks, and Jon figured it was time to sneak out.

Chapter 25

When Tracie finally fell asleep, she had troubling dreams. At twenty-two after six, one of them made her wake up in an anxiety sweat. She was with her old dog Tippy and she was surprised and happy to realize he was alive again. Then for some dream reason, she started painting him blue. The little cocker spaniel stood there patiently as she rolled paint on with a fluffy roller, blue, all blue, until only his eyes remained, looking up at her in a sad but unsure way. At last, she finished, and taking the last bit of paint from the can, she upturned it on his head, covering his eyes as well. Tippy began to run in circles, yapping the way he did, and then he began to attack her ankles. He was biting her over and over again, and her red blood was mixing with the blue paint when she screamed and awoke. It was a horrible dream and she didn't want to go back to sleep after it. Maybe it was anxiety from not seeing Jon Sunday night. God, the waiting around for his so-called progress report was driving her crazy. So, she took a long shower and extra time to blow-dry her hair—it was too long and she needed a cut. On her way out the door, she snagged two more of the brownies she and Laura had baked on the weekend, ate one, and put the other in her bag for later. After all, it was a Monday.

Mondays were always a bitch because Marcus met with the brass in the morning. Then he passed the joy along at the afternoon editorial meeting. But this Monday, Tracie didn't have the regular knot in her belly. She was eager to get the scoop from Beth. Jon's social life was going to be good for her career in several ways, she realized as Marcus walked by her cubicle and raised his brows in surprise when he saw her. She smiled at him as obnoxiously as she knew how and sang out, "Good morning."

After he was safely gone, she took out the brownie and coffee that she had brought and put it down on her desk. At least it wasn't a farm cake. Between Laura's cooking and Jon's love life, she was eating a lot more than usual. The sessions at the gym weren't going to be enough to keep up with these calories. But she was ravenous.

She was also more concerned and curious than she could bear. Where was Beth? She jumped up on her chair and scanned the floor to see if Beth was around. She wasn't, so Tracie jumped down just in time to miss Marcus as he doubled back for something or other. This time, she ducked so that he wouldn't pick on her too much later. No sense making it worse at the editorial meeting than it had to be.

Without Beth to debrief, she dialed Jon's work number. She didn't get him, so she tried Beth's extension. No answer. She drank her coffee, nibbling guiltily at the brownie until the coffee got too cold to drink and there was nothing left but crumbs. It was only then that she saw Beth's curls bobbing two aisles away.

Tracie was out of her chair in a minute and at Beth's cubicle before Beth even sat down. When Beth made the turn, she smiled at Tracie. Tracie followed Beth into her work space. "Well? Aren't you going to say anything?" she asked. She couldn't tell if Beth was angry at her for the fix-up or if she had to be angry at Beth for blowing Jon off.

"Oh, I knew you were going to do this," Beth said. "I thought about it this morning, showering. Okay, okay," she agreed, then sat down and ran a brush through her hair.

"Okay, what?" Tracie asked.

"Okay, okay, you were right. About everything."

Tracie paused, really confused now. "Which everything would that be?" she asked.

"Everything about Marcus," Beth said. "He's boring and fat and way too old. Plus, he's selfish in bed. You've been right all along."

"You spent the night with Marcus?" Tracie asked, her heart sinking. "I can't believe it."

"Not with *Marcus*. With *Jonny*," Beth said. She took out a compact and looked into the mirror.

"With Jonny?" Tracie echoed. "You slept with Jon—Jonny?"

"Ohmigod," Beth said. "He is *so* good. And he's so great-looking. I mean, I didn't really like him, not like him like him, but then I just figured it would be a good thing to do to get over Marcus. Jon was sweet, you know. But then he kissed me, and it became a lot more than distraction sex. I mean, the way he touched me. He's got the most incredible hands."

"You're talking about Jonny?" Tracie asked. She was stunned. "Jon Delano? You slept with him?" Tracie felt dizzy. Somehow, the idea of Beth and Jon . . . This was more information than she required. She realized then that she'd never thought about Jon as a sexual partner. She'd even failed to talk to him about it. Tracie, Beth, Sara, and Laura talked about sex frequently. Laura once described how Peter's peter took a decided turn toward the left and the benefits and problems that presented. When Sara slept with the guy who wasn't circumcised, she had rushed in the next morning to describe the whole thing—as it were—in complete detail. She called it a shar-pei. But this was different. This was far too personal.

Beth was hanging up her coat. "You know, I guess I was getting used to Marcus. He's smart and everything. I mean, you can't deny that, but he's kinda"—she paused and Tracie realized she had no idea what was coming next—"kinda tired, I guess. Or maybe just so experienced that he's not so into it, you know what I mean?"

"Maybe *selfish* is the word you're looking for," Tracie suggested. And for a fraction of a moment, she thought of Phil.

"Yeah," Beth agreed. "Selfish."

Tracie didn't need to be told that Jon was anything but. For some reason, she had never really considered how that aspect of his personality would manifest itself in his sexuality. Silly of her. Of course he was generous and considerate in bed, as in all things. He had a great relationship with a warm and considerate mother.

"I had a hard time figuring out what type of guy he is," Beth said. "I mean, at first he looked like a tough guy—you know, a kind of Matt Damon in *Good Will Hunting*. But then he was more like an eccentric, kinda like Johnny Depp in *What's Eating Gilbert Grape*. Once we got talking, I saw he had this really sensitive, sweet side, like Leonardo DiCaprio in *Titanic*. . . ."

"Is there any movie star he doesn't resemble?" Tracie burst out.

"He's not like Ben Stiller," Beth said, missing the sarcasm, as usual. "I slept with Jonny not because he seemed like trouble but because he was different. He really likes women." Then she put her purse away, opened a drawer, and took out a flacon of perfume. "Thank you so much for setting us up. I like him. I mean I *really* like him," she said. "And the sex was just so—"

"Please, please," Tracie said, putting her hands up in surrender. "I don't need to hear this."

Beth looked up from the mirror at her friend. "You're acting like you're mad at me for having sex with him or something," Beth said. "How come? We're both adults. We took precautions." She paused. "Did you ever sleep with him?" Beth asked. Tracie shook her head no. "He was just so unbelievable."

It had been a hellish editorial meeting. But she couldn't get over the bombshell that Beth had dropped. And after she'd reached Jon, the bombshell had been followed by a barrage. "It was great," Jon had babbled. "So much fun. Beth's a real good kid. Your advice worked liked a charm. God, it was great to have sex again. Tracie, I'll always be grateful to you. It's like giving me the words *open sesame*."

"Fine, Aladdin," she had snapped. "Just don't expect a thousand and one nights."

"Why not?" he had asked. "I think I'm on a roll. You know what happened?" She'd shaken her head, wordless at this turn of events. "Ruth from REI called this weekend. She called again this morning, and we're going to see each other. I'll tell you more when I see you."

Tracie had been speechless. She'd gone to the editorial meeting in a state of suspended animation. All during the meeting, she couldn't help but look at Beth and imagine her and Jon in bed. She didn't know if she was disgusted with Beth, angry at Jon, or just mad at herself. She'd barely flinched when Marcus abused Tim and mocked Sara. She didn't remember to shrink down in her chair. She didn't need to look at either of them and wonder why they hadn't quit. If they were self-respecting, they would have, but she supposed if that was the case, she wouldn't be here, either. Allison was the only one who had escaped unscathed, and Tracie would almost swear that that meant Marcus was sleeping with her now. But that wasn't certain reasoning, because when he had been sleeping with Beth, he had felt free to make mincemeat of her whenever it suited his fancy.

Mincemeat brought her back to what she had just finished: the article on the best meat loaf in Seattle. Stupid. She shook her head. "Now," Marcus had said. "I have been truly pleased by the work done for this fine establishment by the late—no, make that the lately early—Tracie Higgins. Putting on a little weight lately, Miss Higgins? Perhaps it was in the line of duty. Fine coverage of the meat loaf crisis." He showed his teeth to the table. "So, onward and upward. I understand there is a new trend toward designer cupcakes. Little tiny things with really good frostings and new kinds of toppings. The days of the multicolored jimmies are dead and we at the *Times* will cover it." He looked directly at Tracie. "A cupcake story, my little cupcake. And get in all the bakeries that advertise."

"You are kidding," she'd said.

"Afraid not. We'll put it in a Wednesday food section." Then he'd turned to Beth, who had done, Tracie had to note, an excellent job of getting through the meeting. "Are you listening?" Marcus asked her.

"No," she said. "Is it my turn?" Tim laughed into his hand and disguised it as a cough. Allison tossed her perfect hair. Tracie decided once and for all that she would write her article for some other publication and do her best to get the hell out of Dodge.

Photos and Post-its were taped all over the inside of her desk. All of her ideas about nerds, cool guys, and the differences between the two were jotted on charts and graphs. Jon before and Jonny after were immortalized in photos. Each step of his progress was minutely detailed. But somehow, the date with Beth changed things.

She had called around to all of her journalistic contacts, verbally pitched the story to a couple of them, typed several query letters, and faxed them in a flurry of activity that made her look as if she was truly dedicated to the *Seattle Times* and Marcus. Too bad for the *Times* that all of it was motivated by her need to get away from him. It was too soon to tell, of course, but it seemed as if *Seattle Magazine* or a laptop publication in Olympia might bite.

But what was she going to do next? Add another Post-it that said "Jon fucks Beth"? Would Marcus like to have the article now? In fact, her wall looked like it was yellow, with a bad case of peeling. You could hardly see the green wall under all the Post-its. She sighed. Lots of notes, but no writing.

When the phone rang, Tracie was glad for the distraction. But before she could answer it, Beth scurried across to the phone. As Tracie reached for it, Beth put her hand on the receiver.

"Can I answer that for you?" Beth asked.

"No," Tracie told her. "Not since you didn't answer all weekend. Anyway, since when do you want to answer *my* phone? Just since your date with Jonny."

"Yeah? So?" Beth sat down. "Did you talk to him? What did he say about me? Does he like me?"

"If you let me answer it, I might find out." Tracie finally picked up the receiver. "Hello," she snapped into the mouthpiece. Beth watched her as if she were performing surgery instead of talking on the phone. "No, I can't. I have a deadline for this stupid cupcake article. No, the food, not the musician. Well, maybe what I do is as important to me as what you do is to you. No. Maybe tomorrow night." Tracie placed the receiver in the cradle.

"That wasn't Jonny," Beth said, and Tracie figured she should get the Nobel Prize for that one. Beth's eyes were open wide. "You just blew off Phil?"

"Yeah." Tracie had the strongest impulse to smack Beth, though she didn't know why. It was just her face. She had never really noticed just how annoying it was. "He's so self-centered. He wanted to have dinner."

"When you see Jonny again, can I come, too?" Beth begged.

"No!" Tracie told her, then realized she was almost shouting. She calmed down. "Look," she said slowly, as if she were talking to a child, "Jonny knows your name and number. You know his. As you said, you're both adults." Tracie felt exhausted, as if she'd run a marathon or climbed the rock face at REI a dozen times. She wanted to go home, crawl under the blankets, and have Laura serve her anything but meat loaf instead of sitting here, looking at a glowing Beth and writing about cupcakes. "You two work it out from here on in," Tracie said. "Call him if you want to see him so much."

"I already called him three times," Beth admitted. Again Tracie really felt like slapping her, and she put one hand over the other, just in case. "You know," Beth continued, "he doesn't have an answering machine or voice mail at home. Isn't that weird?" Tracie just shrugged. "He's not married, right?"

"Would I set you up with someone who was married?" Tracie asked, and shook her head. What had Laura called Beth? An airhead?

"Well, do you think he has a steady girlfriend?" Beth the Relentless asked. "Do you think he lives with her?"

"I *know* he doesn't." If Tracie told Beth the truth about the lack of other options Jon—or Jonny—had, Beth would probably drop him like a hot potato. "At least he didn't," she admitted.

"I'll just try him again," Beth said.

"Don't you think it's a good idea to just give it a rest?" she asked. She realized, with an unpleasant start of surprise, that she didn't like Beth or Jon very much at all.

Chapter 26

Phil and Laura sat at Tracie's dining table playing cards. They were playing for peanuts: not low stakes, but actual peanuts, because, to Phil's disgust, Tracie had no chips. Tracie was looking over her notes and photos, but the laughter from the other room kept distracting her. Perhaps it was something else: She still hadn't really talked to Jon. It was odd: The article sucked, but the makeover seemed to be progressing nicely. Despite not knowing Jon's take on his date, Tracie was determined not to obsess over it. After all, this turn of events gave her an ending for her article. In fact, it justified the piece. She knew she should be grateful and just get on with writing it.

But the truth was, she couldn't get very far with it. Without a deadline, she was having trouble focusing. Right now, she wanted to eat something, or to call Jon, or to put on the TV, or to lie down just for a minute and close her eyes. To be honest, she wanted to join in the card game. It sounded like fun.

Tracie heard Laura slap her hand down on the table. "Gin!" Laura exclaimed. On her bed, Tracie shook her head in pity for Phil. All their girlhood card playing in Encino had taught her that no one could beat Laura at gin. She'd once stripped their entire Girl Scout troop of money, jewelry, and Barbie dolls.

Tracie smiled at the memory, then forced herself to look back down at the makeover piece. She sighed and decided she couldn't concentrate on the article until she talked with Jon and found out what was really going on with Beth.

Had Jon become so unavailable? Was he avoiding her? Stranger things had happened. Maybe Jon really liked Beth. Tracie knew that would be delicate to talk about, because she truly didn't think that Beth was nearly good enough for him, certainly not smart enough. But since Jon hadn't had anyone for so long, he might confuse sex with love. Tracie decided she'd have to try gently to guide him out of that idea, but she'd have to be sure that he didn't hurt or insult Beth in any way when he did it.

But who knew? Maybe it would work and she should just keep her nose out of it. After all, there were a lot of friendships that broke up when people fell in love and got married. She thought it had happened with the Beatles, but she wasn't sure which ones. Maybe when Paul married Linda.

Marriage! The idea of Jon marrying Beth was so ridiculous that Tracie didn't know whether to laugh or to shudder. God, what am I doing, sitting here wasting my time over the idea? she thought. She told herself again that the incident was probably just a momentary attraction and would burn itself out in a few weeks.

Tracie looked at her Post-it notes stuck on the door frame, the window, and flapping off of pages of printout notes. She sighed at the thought of gathering them up and putting them away. Nah. She'd leave them where they were.

Meanwhile, she could hear Laura rattling the peanuts as she pulled them to her side of the table while Phil was shuffling the cards. "Have you lost weight?" she heard Phil ask Laura. Surprisingly, the two of them seemed to be getting along lately, but that was sweet of Phil anyhow. Tracie smiled—he could be thoughtful if he tried.

"Maybe a little," Laura told him, obviously concentrating on her game. There was a very brief silence. Tracie sniggered. If Phil was trying to distract her from her game, his attempt would be useless. Laura was the only girl Tracie knew who didn't care about her weight. "Gin," Laura said.

"Shit!" Phil exclaimed. "You can't have gin. We only drew one card."

"Gin," Laura repeated, implacable.

"Misdeal!" Phil cried.

Ha! Tracie snickered. She knew that route was futile.

"You dealt," Laura told him.

Tracie could hear Phil complaining and gathering up the cards. The two of them argued for a while as Tracie tried to tune them out, knowing the irrevocable outcome. How long until Jon arrives? she wondered. What will he say? What's going on with him? She stretched out on her bed and might have dozed off for a few minutes. Then she heard her name drift into the bedroom. "So you know, I'm trying to follow some of your advice, but I don't think Tracie is noticing."

"Oh, I'm sure she is," Laura said in the distracted voice she used when she was counting cards.

Tracie immediately wondered what the advice was, why Laura hadn't mentioned it to her, and whether Phil had asked for it or if Laura had volunteered it. Phil was speaking again. She moved to the end of the bed.

"I think you're right. I think I used to . . . take her for granted or something," he was saying, "but you know, now I think she might be doing the same to me." Laura murmured something Tracie couldn't hear. Then Phil must have gotten up from the table, because she heard the refrigerator door opening. She snuck to the bedroom door and peeked out. Phil had pulled open the vegetable drawer and was removing a head of iceberg lettuce. How had that gotten in there? Tracie hadn't been grocery shopping, and Laura despised iceberg lettuce.

Phil proceeded to cut the greens in half, then into quarters, and put the pieces on three plates. He took them to the table. "You wanna eat?" he asked Laura. Phil put out three place mats and three folded paper napkins. Then he lighted a candle, but once he'd done that, he obviously didn't know where to put it. He looked around for a candlestick, then, not seeing one, he stuffed the lit taper into the top of an empty beer bottle, Chianti-style. What in the world was he up to?

"You know, women want different things at different times of their life," Laura was now telling him as she put away the cards, gathered up her peanut winnings, and turned to Phil. "I was going out with that nitwit in Sacramento because he was exciting. But when you get old—I mean, I'll be thirty in just two years—you want something more stable. Someone with a job. Someone who can give back."

Phil nodded as if he'd take this as gospel. Tracie felt her jaw hang open. She could hardly believe it, or what he did next, which was lifting an already-opened can of Chef Boyardee ravioli and dumping the contents into a waiting pot. She couldn't believe it. He was trying to make dinner!

Of course, his attempt was laughable, but he was trying. It was so cute, like Peter Pan trying to stick back his shadow with soap. He was about to turn up the flame, when Tracie left her room. She couldn't stand it any longer. Laura was still sitting at the coffee table, eating her winnings. Phil now had his back to her and was stirring the ravioli with a fork. Just then, the intercom rang. Jon had arrived at last. Tracie ran to press the intercom to buzz Jon in.

"Are we expecting someone?" Phil asked.

"Jon's just dropping by for a minute," Tracie told him.

"From what I hear, Beth says nothing Jon does takes a minute," Laura said, wagging her eyebrows.

"When did you talk to Beth?" Tracie asked Laura. It seemed as if Little Miss Busybody was talking to everyone behind her back.

"Most of this afternoon," Laura admitted, sweeping peanut shells into a wastebasket. "She kept waiting for Jon to call her back, which he hadn't, and she had to talk to someone about him in the meantime." Laura shrugged. "I was an obsession recipient."

Tracie shook her head. "Don't mention her," she warned Laura.

"Hey, I don't have dinner for four here," Phil announced as Tracie crossed the room to open the door.

"Oh, don't worry," Laura told both of them. "I don't have to join you."

"Don't be silly," Tracie told her. "This'll just take a couple of minutes. We're going for a walk; then just the three of us will have dinner."

Tracie opened the door, and as usual, they hugged. She was interested to see what Phil's reaction to the new Jon would be. So when Jon entered the living room, Tracie was behind him. Looking over Jon's shoulder, Tracie watched as Phil eyed him from the top of his black-and-blue spiked-up hair down to the soles of his new boots. The expression on Phil's face was one of surprise, quickly followed by dismay, and then replaced by false nonchalance. Watching the changes was like watching the three seasons bloom and fade in time-lapse photography, like they always did on the Disney Channel.

But when Tracie turned again to Laura, her friend's reaction—though a little more subtle—was more interesting and more of a tribute. Laura gazed unblinking at Jon and, for just a moment, her eyes had that longing, the expression that men got when they admired sports cars too fast or too expensive for them.

"Hi, Jon," Laura said in the voice that she used only when she was trying to be cute.

"I don't believe it," Phil blurted as Tracie and Jon walked into the room. Suddenly, she realized there was no way they could talk about what had happened in front of Phil and Laura.

Phil stood up, put down the empty Chef Boyardee can, and walked halfway around Jon. "You didn't buy this stuff," Phil said. "Tracie bought this stuff." He turned to Tracie. "Where'd you get that jacket?" he asked. "It's just like the one I used to have. I want a jacket like that."

"We got it at—" Jon started to say, but Tracie interrupted him.

"Never reveal your sources," she told him, touching his shoulder. "We're going for a walk," she told Phil and Laura, then grabbed her coat.

"What did you do to your hair?" Phil asked Jon as Tracie began to push him from behind. She had her hand in the spot between his shoulder blades, and before he could talk to Phil, she'd pushed him out the door.

"Be back in a half an hour," she called over her shoulder.

They walked down the stairs and out to the street before she let herself say another word. "You know, I just don't get you," she said once they were on the wet sidewalk.

"What?" he asked, but she could tell he was uncomfortable. He matched his stride to hers.

"I work with you day and night for weeks. I set you up with a date. I even coach you while you're on it. Then you don't even call me to tell me how it went. And I have to find out from my girlfriend that you slept with her!"

Jon looked down at the pavement and winced. "Was that information you required?" he asked. "I mean, I guess it was the point. Anyway, now you know. So, in a way, I guess I can say the experiment is over. It worked."

"That's *not* the point!" Tracie exclaimed. "I mean, why did you sleep with Beth?"

"Isn't that what you expected me to do?" Jon asked. "Wasn't that the whole point? Date 'em, do 'em, and drop 'em. *I* certainly didn't make that up."

"I don't think I ever put it that way," Tracie said.

"Well, it may not have been how you put it, but as I recall, we were working at ending my celibacy."

Tracie narrowed her eyes. "But not with my friend," she told him. "And don't feel so good about it. Beth is so desperate."

"And you don't think I was desperate after a yearlong dry spell?" He was whining like a Borscht Belt comic.

Tracie shook her head. She felt like slapping him. "Do you know how thoughtless this was?" she asked. "Not just doing it but doing it with Beth? We talk about our personal lives, and now I'm going to have to hear more than I would ever want to know about your sex life."

"Excuse me?" Jon said. "You two talk about your sex lives? I'm not making you talk about it. And anyway, if you didn't want me to sleep with her, why did you set me up with her? You made the date for me."

He was being utterly exasperating. "I didn't mean for you to sleep with her," Tracie explained. "It was just a practice date."

"You mean I was supposed to strike out?" Jon asked. "You were setting me up for failure? Another no-hitter for the guy who was batting zero?"

"You're not a batter and Beth isn't a ball," Tracie snapped. "She's been terribly hurt by Marcus, and I didn't mean—"

"Marcus, your boss?" Jon asked. "She was going out with Marcus?" He rolled his eyes and leaned against a mailbox until he realized how wet it was.

"I'm the one who has to hear about Marcus a hundred times a day. I know how disgusting he is."

"Beth was going out with your boss and you set me up with her? That's the kind of taste she has and yet you thought she'd be right for me?"

"I thought she'd be *wrong* for you," Tracie said. "Remember? You were supposed to be bad."

"Then you did mean for me to date her, do her, and drop her," Jon cried, triumphant.

"Don't tell me what I meant!" Tracie snapped.

They walked along the sidewalk in silence for almost an entire block. Then Jon stopped, took her by the shoulders, and turned her to him. For a moment, Tracie thought that he might be about to kiss her. "Tracie, you're my best friend. Why are we fighting? You told me what to do, and then who to do it with. And I did it. So why are you mad? If you don't want me to see Beth, I won't see her again. Just please don't be angry at me."

Tracie looked at him. Despite all the changes she had wrought, he was still Jon. His eyes were warm and pleading. She loved Jon. "I guess I was just hurt," she admitted. "I expected you'd call me right away."

"I was embarrassed," he said. "Plus, it was very late." He stopped. "I . . . I don't think guys talk about sex the same way women do."

"Okay." She sighed deeply. "The whole thing was ridiculous," she said. "I don't even know what I was aggravated about. It's just that Beth talked about nothing but you all day, and it drove me absolutely bonkers."

"She did?" he asked.

Just how sexually confident is he? she wondered. And how justified is his confidence? Looking at him now in his new clothes, at his new hair and his unshaven jaw, she realized for the first time that he might be very, very good indeed. She turned away so he wouldn't see her blush. It was weird to think about him in a sexual way—a little like thinking of your brother in that way. When he took her arm, she actually jumped.

"You're not still mad?" he asked.

"No, I'm not mad," she said. Once again, she thought this would be a good time to tell him about her idea for the article. Maybe if she told him, she wouldn't have so much trouble writing it.

When she got back to the apartment, all she wanted was a beer and a hug, but when she opened the door and looked in the refrigerator, then back at Phil's pouty face, she realized she probably wasn't going to get either one.

"Did you get any beers?" she asked him.

"No. If it's not here, I won't drink it," Phil said. "I'm trying to cut back."

Typical. He always thought of himself. "Speaking of cut, I have to get a haircut. You want a cut, Laura?"

"Yeah. But what I really need are streaks."

"Stefan is great with streaks. Jon goes to him."

"You know, that guy ought to be paying you tuition," Phil told her.

"And you oughta be paying me rent!" Tracie said, slamming the refrigerator door. Phil, oblivious, stirred the ravioli, picked up a bottle of Kraft French dressing, crossed to the table, and poured it on the lettuce halves with a flourish. "Dinner is served."

"You made dinner, Phil?" She looked at the pot. "Gee. I'm sorry. I'm just not hungry."

"But . . . I did it for you."

"Why don't you eat with Laura while I take a bath?" she suggested. "All I want to do is crawl into bed." Tracie went into the bathroom. Phil followed her.

"Tracie, this is important," he said. "I wanted to talk to you over dinner. I thought I might . . . There was this job—" He stopped talking. She was looking under the sink for her Vitabath.

"You mean with another band? Leave the Glands?" Tracie asked, shaking her head.

"No. I mean a real job," Phil said. "Well, it's like a trainee job. Can you imagine me in semiconductors?"

Tracie stopped rummaging under the bathroom sink and stared at him. "Did I just hear you say something about getting a job as a train conductor?" she asked him.

"That is *not* what I said. Jesus, if you paid half the attention to me that you're giving to the nerd and that article, you'd know what I'm talking about." He turned and walked out the door.

Fine. He could go home. All she wanted was a hot soak in her tub.

Chapter 27

Low conversation filled the Malaysian restaurant. Waiters and waitresses glided back and forth between the kitchen and the dining room with huge serving trays. Jon sat at a table in the corner with Samantha. He was in his James Dean/*Rebel Without a Cause* pose, just ending an intense story.

"I've never told anyone before," Jon said, then paused. Jon was nervously playing with the Goofy Pez dispenser. The ears were flipping around in circles. What now? he thought. For brevity's sake, he'd decided to combine two of Tracie's directives: He'd made up a tragedy and simultaneously told it as a secret imparted only to Samantha.

Samantha's sympathy, an altogether appropriate reaction to his story, filled him with contempt. He supposed it was because he'd made a sucker out of her with the lie. But if he told a stranger he was Mormon, or an orphan, or that his birthday was on Independence Day—it was actually on December 3—there would be no reason for them not to believe him. Lying to Samantha was no big trick. So why did it make him feel superior?

Something else troubled him: The more he lied, the easier it became. And the more it made him wonder if anything anyone said was the truth. How about his father? Had he also lied to Jon all those years like he lied to his mother? He paused and stared down at the table.

"I just can't get over how I misjudged you," Samantha was saying. "I mean, I'd noticed you, but somehow I thought you were . . ." She paused, and Jon wondered what version of the word *nerd* she was thinking of using. "Well, I just imagined you as very different," she said.

He nodded, then executed a perfect James Dean shrug. "Yeah. A lot of people don't see the real me." He sighed and looked down at the Pez dispenser. "My brother really loved Pez." He'd already figured out it was best if he didn't talk too much. If he did, he'd only screw things up or have to lie and remember what he'd said. Maybe that was why men like his father moved on: The lies got too complicated and the truth was unacceptable, so you just started over.

Samantha heard the sigh and reacted with greater attention. "What are you thinking?" she asked. "You can tell me." Her eyes were pleading. Lie to me, they said. Tell me something dramatic, something that makes me privy to the drama. "What happened then?" Sam asked, leaning toward him.

"He was on the back of my motorcycle . . . and I wiped out. There wasn't a scratch on me, but he"—Jon paused for effect—"he died." He let silence reign again for a few moments while he looked out toward the kitchen and worked his jaw muscle as visibly as he could. God, I'll wind up with a jaw like Jay Leno's by the time I'm done. He figured he'd better finish the story. "I've always felt responsible, but since then, I just don't get frightened."

Sam nodded her head. "I think I understand," she said, which was a good thing, because Jon certainly didn't. What bullshit! Women actually liked this crap.

The cute young Asian waitress came over to their table. Jon looked up from Sam and, in apparent surprise, took the waitress's arm. "Doesn't she have the most beautiful eyes?" he asked Sam as he smiled up at the girl. When he saw the reaction on Samantha's face, he knew he was golden.

The next morning, Jon was walking down the hallway at Micro/Con, feeling pretty cocky. He had his radar on for Samantha, when he spotted a familiar-looking woman in the distance. He'd all but slept over at Sam's the night before, and although they hadn't gone the entire distance, Jon felt that an excellent blow job was nothing to sneeze at. And somehow he knew that oral sex was Samantha's prelude to the real thing. It was her way of showing him she wasn't the kind of girl who went all the way on the first date.

Sam had been very sweet and giving—surprising in a woman who was so successful and assertive in the office—but perhaps he shouldn't be surprised. He was finding out that a woman's sexual personality wasn't necessarily obvious from her public personality. While he pondered this, he kept his eye on the woman he'd clocked in the distance. Until he realized who it was. "Carole!" he yelled. It was The Lovely Girl from the airport! Hadn't she said something about having Micro/Con as a client?

She turned around and, once she did, Jon did everything he could to recover his cool. He certainly shouldn't have yelled her name. Now he wouldn't run to catch up to her or anything. If she waited for him, maybe he'd just pretend to walk by her. No begging girls to turn around and look at him. It was a bad slip.

Sometimes he thought he'd never learn. But The Lovely Girl, Carole, once she saw him, approached slowly and, as she did, he watched recognition dawn across her face. He had assumed another one of his James Dean poses; this time it was the defiant one from *Rebel Without a Cause*. He hated the idea that she would remember him as a geek, that he had called out to her, and that she must realize he worked here, but he wanted to conquer. Maybe he could make his early gaffe of seeming as close to a serial killer as possible without DNA evidence work for him. Being dangerous yet respectable enough to work here actually might make him a more acceptable candidate. Maybe it was all for the best.

Carole eyed him up and down. "The plane, right?" she asked. He kept his face blank. Could it be that easy? No. Because then, her eyes flickered and she said, "Oh, the luggage."

Well, a good offense was the best defense. He managed a laugh. "Yeah. I lost my luggage and you misplaced your sense of humor." He paused. "Man, you completely missed my madman riff," he said, making a gesture with his hand over his head to indicate the joke had gone over hers.

To his surprise, she blushed. "Sorry. I was probably a little tense. I don't like lying. But . . . you look . . . different."

He shrugged. "Maybe it's the boots," he said, and she looked down at his feet.

"You work here?" Carole asked. "I didn't realize you worked here. Did you tell me that?"

He could see her relax. She smiled. Clearly, she was deciding he wasn't a maniac living in the woods, waiting for his next victim. Or if he was, he was a maniac who at least had excellent health coverage. "Sometimes I'm here," Jon said truthfully. For once, having been exposed as a guy with a day job would work for him. He smiled. He had to admit he was starting to get it. All you had to do was try to anticipate a woman's thoughts. "What is it that *you* do here?" he asked.

Carole smiled. "I can't tell you that," she said.

He shrugged. By asking, he'd lost a few points, but he didn't really care. After all, he had a date with Ruth tomorrow, one on the weekend with Samantha, and Beth kept calling. If she didn't stop soon, he guessed he'd have to sleep with her again just to keep his phone line open. He almost smiled to himself at the thought, but instead he looked at Carole. She wasn't just pretty; she was smart. And she was working at Micro/Con. They would probably have a lot in common. Jon wondered what it would be like to be with a woman who understood his work and the implications of it. Even Tracie didn't get it.

He smiled more broadly at Carole. "Can you tell me if you eat?" he asked.

"Eat?" she said. "Of course I eat."

"Can you tell me if you'll eat with me?"

She smiled back at him. "Of course I'll eat with you."

And afterward, you'll kiss me and then probably sleep with me, too, he thought hopefully. Jon grinned. This was a lot more interesting than Parsifal.

"Where?" she asked.

"I can't tell you that," he said, and she laughed. "If I told you that, they'd find me and they'd kill me."

"Don't you hate that when it happens?" she asked, and he realized she was flirting with him. Ah, flirting. He looked Carole over. She was funnier than Sam, and probably funnier than Ruth would be. And she was very, very lovely. But not quite as lovely as he'd remembered.

Jon was at a corner table at Vito's on Ninth and Madison with Ruth, the mountain climber. The room was dimly lighted and candles burned in tiny glass lamps at each table. He had just led her up to his obligatory drama/secret/I've-told-only-you story. "What happened?" Ruth asked breathlessly.

"I was a twin," he said. "But my brother killed himself. I was better at school, better at sports, better with girls. To me, it was never a contest, but I guess he just couldn't . . . compete. I always felt responsible." He paused for a moment, surprised to actually feel a bit of the pain of his lost imaginary twin. He shrugged. "Well, since then, I just don't get frightened."

"Really?" Ruth said, and he could see the sympathy blossom across her face.

When their chubby blond waitress approached the table, Jon stopped her from taking away his plate by putting his hand on her elbow. "Doesn't she have the most beautiful eyes?" he asked Ruth.

* * *

Jon leaned back against the banquette. He had gotten a corner booth at Java, The Hut, but he wasn't alone, waiting for Tracie. He was with Doris, the Asian-American waitress he'd met while out with Samantha. "What happened?" the girl asked him, as if her total existence depended on his next words.

"We were fooling around at target practice," he told her. "I'm a great shot, and he dared me to shoot a cigarette out of his mouth. You know, even though I was only fourteen and he was my dad, I said no. He got belligerent, but even so, I said no." He took out a Casper-the-Friendly-Ghost Pez, and offered it to her as if it was the Legion of Honor. Jon continued, "Then he bragged to all the guys, his pals, about my aim and bet them I could do it. It was a big pot. After he shot his mouth off like that . . . well, I had to try . . . and I shot his mouth off. Literally. It was an accident, of course." He sighed deeply. "But I always felt responsible. Since then, I just don't get frightened." He heaved another deep sigh, then turned his head toward the window, as if his dad was out there in the dark parking lot.

Molly came up to the table to give them their dinners. After she slid the hot plate across the table and handed each of them a plate, Jon grabbed her hand. He looked up into Molly's face. "Doesn't she have the most beautiful eyes?" he asked his date.

Chapter 28

Tracie sat at her desk, grumpy and resentful. She should be working, but since the morning editorial meeting, she'd lost all motivation. Instead of beginning a new draft, she picked up the phone and dialed Jon. She hadn't heard from him in days. Not only was she curious as to what was going on with him, but she needed to vent.

Nobody was as good to complain to as Jon. Laura only made jokes and tried to cheer her up. Phil tried to distract her. But Jon knew how to empathize.

Even before Tom Brokaw had written *The Greatest Generation*, Tracie had been deeply fascinated by Pearl Harbor and World War II. Her mother's father had died in the Pacific, and her paternal grandfather had served there. One of the few things she'd enjoyed in Encino were visits from Papa, and each time she'd ask him for stories from the long-ago war. So it came as a deeply unpleasant shock when, at that morning's meeting, Marcus had assigned a follow-up piece about local World War II vets to Allison.

"Marcus, I'm prepared to cover that. I have some material I didn't use in my Memorial Day story," Tracie had said.

"Thank you for that spirit of volunteerism and cooperation,"

Marcus had told her, "but I feel certain Allison will be able to meet the challenge."

It was so unfair. Tracie had been stuck with a lot of stupid topics for almost a year, and now a story that held real interest had been wrested from her. Her disappointment was so sharp that she couldn't even look at Allison without imagining what Marcus had made her do to get the assignment. In the meeting, Allison had glanced over at her, shrugged her shoulders, and given her a sorry-what-can-I-do? smile. Tracie would have enjoyed wiping the smile off her face with steel wool and a little muriatic acid. To add insult to injury, Marcus had assigned her a Father's Day feature. As if she didn't have a serious father issue, along with most of America. "Can I do deadbeat dads?" she'd asked, but Marcus had merely laughed dismissively.

She lifted the phone and punched in the Micro/Con number again. Not only was Jon still not available, but his voice mail was full and Tracie couldn't even leave a message.

"Have you heard from Jonny?" Beth asked from the doorway.

Startled, Tracie looked up. "No," she snapped. "And even if I had, I wouldn't tell you."

"Oooh," Beth cooed as she stepped away. "I guess it's best not to speak to you until the end of the day."

Tracie could hardly believe that Beth seemed to shrug off Tracie's mood as she went back to her cubicle. Usually, she was good for at least half an hour of obsessive pestering. Tracie was getting so tired of Beth's inquiries about Jon that she wished she'd never set them up together. How was I to know that it would go this far? Tracie asked herself. But with any luck, the whole situation would go away soon.

At least she'd made progress with the makeover article. It needed a good rewrite and an ending, but she thought it was funny and pithy, and even the photos looked good. She wondered if she had the courage to send the draft to *Seattle Magazine*. Then she thought big. They had seemed interested. Why not try *Esquire*? She had never been published in a national magazine. She knew she ought to look at some magazines and see who was on their masthead and what they were publishing.

Which reminded her: She'd finally gotten another appointment with Stefan, and if she didn't leave soon, she wouldn't be there in time for the haircut she so desperately needed.

Screw Marcus, Allison, and the *Times*. She'd be taking a long lunch today.

Music blared in the shop as Laura, with her hair in a hundred strips of aluminum foil, waited for her process to work. Meanwhile, Tracie was finally getting her hair cut by Stefan. "Not too short," Tracie instructed him. Stefan had granted a special dispensation and was allowing Laura to watch him while her hair was being processed.

"I know," Stefan said. "Never too short." He sighed heavily, as if he was tired of every hair on every head in Seattle. Tracie hoped he wasn't in a bad mood. Stefan in a bad mood was not a good thing. "How is your little experiment vorking?" Stefan asked, and for a moment, she didn't have a clue as to what he was talking about. Then Stefan continued: "He's some cute cookie boy." Tracie knew he was talking about Jon. "He vas in two days ago. I liked the blue. It vorked on him," Stefan said.

"Jon was in?" Tracie asked. "Jon came in here by himself?"

"Yes, two days ago," Stefan told her.

Tracie could hardly believe it. First of all, Jon had gotten a haircut just recently, and second . . . "How did he get an appointment before me?" she asked.

Stefan smiled, not at her, but to himself. He shrugged. Tracie just managed to catch the movement from the corner of her eye. "He is most persuasive, your cookie boy."

Laura giggled. "Cookie Boy?" she asked. "That's worse than Kissy Face. Do you really call him that?"

"No," Tracie snapped. "The only thing I've called him lately is ungrateful."

Tracie couldn't believe he'd made an appointment. Nor could she believe he had time for things like that but had no time to call her. Just then, the door opened and Beth, her hair plastered to her head in some kind of mud pack of color, stuck her head into the all-white sanctum, then walked in.

"No interruptions," Stefan said, holding up his scissors hand.

"Not too short," Tracie reminded him. "Beth, what are you doing here?" How many people could ditch work without the *Times* shutting down, and could they all be here? Was Allison getting a facial while Sara had a pedicure and Marcus got a perm?

Beth ignored Stefan and walked over. "Obviously, I'm not having root canal." She smiled. It was a big cheery smile. Tracie braced herself for the next question, sure to be about Jon, but Beth merely took a seat on the floor.

"No spectators, please," Stefan said, brandishing his scissors and then taking another snip off the top. Tracie looked nervously from Laura to Beth. If he was taking off too much, they would tell her. At least she hoped they would. Calm yourself, she thought. Stefan is the only man in Seattle you can truly trust. That's why you come here, put up with his idiosyncrasies, and pay his outrageous price. But she wished she had a mirror.

"Beth, you better go," she told her friend nervously.

"That's okay," Beth said. "Stefan doesn't really mind."

"So, how is job on Cookie going now?" Stefan asked.

"Just great. Almost too great," Tracie told him. "My friend Jon needed a lot of help, but he's looking good."

"Way too good," Beth agreed.

"You can be too rich or too thin, but you can't look too good," Stefan intoned.

"He's right." Beth groaned.

"I thought you hated him," Tracie told her. "Isn't he the guy who never calls you back?"

"He called me back just after I talked to you," Beth said with a triumphant but guilty little smile. "That's why I'm here. It's an emergency."

"I hope you told him to stick it," Tracie said, but she felt her heart dropping in her chest, because if Jon had called, and if he'd asked her out, Beth was going to go.

"I told him I'd love to see him tonight," Beth gushed.

"Tonight? He didn't call you for days and then he asks you out for tonight and you say yes? You are hopeless," Tracie told her.

"I figured it out," she said. "Jonny's a very sensitive guy. I just think he's afraid he felt too much for me. It scared him."

Tracie and Laura exchanged a look. Behind Beth's back, Laura rolled her eyes.

"He was afraid of his feelings. It happens with guys."

"Beth, sweetie," Tracie said in a kind voice, "you didn't scare him."

"Please vould the psychology convention convene at the university? Or in the insane asylum? Just not here. No speaking here," Stefan said firmly.

Beth paid no attention. "You know, he's just traumatized because of his brother's death," Beth told Tracie.

"What brother? Jon—Jonny's an only child," Tracie said.

"No," Beth said, shaking her head. "He doesn't like to talk about it. Except to me."

"Oh God!" Tracie groaned.

Laura rolled her eyes again and snorted. Tracie couldn't believe it. She'd taught him that trick—to come up with something dramatic—but that he'd actually done it, and succeeded! Even with Beth—not exactly a polygraph.

"What?" Beth asked, staring at Tracie. "Oh, don't be hurt. A lot of guys will confide things in me that they don't tell anyone else." She waved. "I gotta go. I don't want to be late for him."

"Get out of here," Stefan said, and Tracie didn't know if this was in response to Beth's comment or if he was trying to maintain creative control.

She ran out of the room, and Stefan, with a noise somewhere between a sigh and a moan, took two more snips at Tracie's hair.

Laura squinted her eyes and shrugged, then pointed wordlessly to Tracie's head. Tracie felt a tug of terror. "Remember, not too short, okay?" Tracie told Stefan again. "Isn't that unbelievable about Beth?" she said to Laura.

"Oh, yeah, that'll keep her going for another three months of obsessing," Laura said. "But I have to say, I think I'm over Peter."

"Great!" Tracie exclaimed.

"And I think I want to stay here in Seattle." She paused. "I'm looking for an apartment."

"Terrific!" Tracie told her, and she meant it.

"Yeah. I figured that would be good news," Laura said. "I've been a pain in the ass with my moping. Plus, I know it's been a strain to have me at your place. I know I'm kinda getting in the way of your thing with Phil," she added.

Tracie shook her head to say no, then heard Stefan's quick intake of breath and realized she had moved at a critical moment. "Sorry," she said to Stefan. "No problem," she told Laura, but Tracie felt guilty, since she'd so recently thought the same thing.

"I know you didn't mean to have me move in permanently. . . ."

"You're always welcome," Tracie said.

"In my country, ve say guests, like fish, stink in three days," Stefan said, and took another slice at her hair.

"So anyway, I can't afford a place without a job, and I can't set up as a caterer without capital, but they need a cook at a brunch place and—"

"You got a job?" Tracie asked, surprised and delighted.

"Yeah. I talked to the owner. It's a done deal."

"Do I get a discount if I go there?" Tracie asked.

"No, but as an incentive, I promise I won't spit in your food," Laura assured her.

"Great!" Tracie said. She tried to put her hand up to her ears to see if they were still covered, but Stefan hissed and pushed her hands away.

"Well, congratulations." For a while, they sat in silence except for the ominous sound of Stefan's scissors. "I really can't believe Beth," Tracie said after a moment or two to break the silence. "How could she have said yes to Jon after he'd dissed her so badly?"

"How could she say no when she likes him so much?" Laura responded, shrugging.

"You know, he told me he'd made a date with Ruth, that girl from REI. He's probably seeing other women, too. And he hasn't told me anything," Tracie complained.

"What does it matter to you what he does? I think you are obsessed with him."

"I'm not obsessed with him," Tracie protested. "I just need to keep my information straight for my article." She heard Stefan sniff. He was taking a very long time. He never took this long.

"That is so ridiculous. You can't get me with that crap, Higgins," Laura told her. "I think you're in love with Jon."

"Laura!" Tracie jerked her head to turn toward Laura and Stefan's scissors narrowly missed her ear.

"Stop it! Stop it! Stop it!" he cried. "This is about my head, not your heart."

"*My* head," Tracie corrected him. "And my heart has nothing to do with it. I love Phil. Jon is just my friend. He's always been my friend." Laura began to hum, as if listening to Tracie was a waste of time. "Come on. You know that, Laura," Tracie protested. "I'm just trying to do a job, that's all. I'm not obsessed with him."

"That's what you think," Laura said. "We always deny we're obsessed in the beginning."

Stefan made a frightening noise somewhere between the hiss of a radiator and the rattle of a snake. He stomped over to Laura, and for a moment, Tracie thought he was going to hit her. Instead, he unfolded a piece of foil. "Ya. That is true," he said. "You are finished." Tracie wasn't sure if he meant Laura was done with her streaking or that Tracie was in emotional trouble. Whatever, he returned and snipped again, this time at her bangs.

"Not too short," she repeated. "And I'm *not* obsessed," she told Laura.

"Yeah. And Marcus is a nice guy. Look, I live and breathe on Obsession Street. I own a place there. You just rent. And I got to tell you, Tracie, you *are* obsessed."

"No. I'm . . . annoyed. I'm . . . regretful," she protested. "The piece is really coming along, but Jon's . . . changed. He's not behaving like a good friend. He's hurt Beth and he's probably hurting other women. I just hate that."

"Maybe he needs someone to give him his comeuppance," Laura said.

"Can you believe it?" Tracie asked Laura.

Laura shrugged. "You have tampered with the rules of the universe. Now prepare to meet the consequences of your karma," she said in her most annoying Buddha tone.

Tracie moaned. "Oh God! I *have* to destroy this man's confidence."

"Yes," Laura agreed. "Return balance to the universe."

"Leave him alone. He is like cook in a candy store," Stefan said.

"A cook?" Laura asked, but Tracie raised her brows in warning. Never correct a hairdresser with scissors in his hand was the basic belief in her universe.

"I have to have him taken down by a real man-killer," Tracie said. "Have the hunter become the prey."

"Too bad you don't know a man-killer," Laura said. "Except for me, of course, but now I have a job. Maybe Sharon Stone is available."

"Laura, you're a genius!" Tracie exclaimed.

"I know, but do you think these streaks are going to suit me?" Laura asked.

Stefan took one last snip at Tracie's hair and spun the chair around. "Finished!" he said, pulling out a mirror.

"Oh my God!" Tracie moaned as she looked at her reflection. Her hair was *way* too short.

* * *

Tracie lay on the sofa, her shorn head wrapped in a towel turban, while Phil and Laura, who were cleaning up the lunch dishes, bickered, as usual.

"Oh, come on," Phil was saying. "Next you'll be telling me there's a special order for washing dishes."

"There is," Laura told him. "Don't you know that?"

"I know when you're pulling my chain," Phil responded.

"I wouldn't touch your chain with a dish brush," Laura said, brandishing the dish brush and tossing her beautifully highlighted mane of hair. "But I can't believe you don't know the order in which you're supposed to wash dishes."

"Bullshit. There's no order. You wash them when you run out of clean dishes, right, Baldy?"

Tracie murmured something from her fog of short-hair blues. But they didn't need a response.

"It's *not* arbitrary," Laura was saying. "It's based on what goes in your mouth first."

"What are you talking about? Is this some kind of dirty joke?" Phil asked.

"Get your mind into the detergent, where it belongs," Laura said with a scowl. "Mrs. Ogg always taught us that we have to begin with silverware, because we put silverware into our mouths. You wash them first, when the water is cleanest. Right, Tracie?" Tracie murmured again. "See. Then you put them aside and wash glasses, because you put glasses up to your lips."

"You're not fuckin' with me!" Phil said, and his face had a look of amazement, as if she was revealing the secrets of getting published or how he could actually play his bass guitar. "I'm going to write a poem about this," he announced. "Wouldn't that be a great piece, 'Chrome Dome'? Come play in the water with me," Phil said.

Tracie rolled over and groaned. Laura just shook her head. "Just let her be, would you? Look, pay attention. Next come the plates, because they don't get touched by your mouth."

"Well, my plate does when you do the cooking, because I usually lick it."

"Well, isn't that cute?" Laura said in her toughest voice. "Like that's going to get me to cook more often for you." But she blushed a little. "Anyway, the last thing you wash are the pots and pans, which even you don't lick." She handed him the pad of steel wool.

Tracie wished they'd just disappear. She wanted Phil to go home and leave her to dwell in her own misery. At least Laura was trying to help out by keeping him busy. Tracie had been on the sofa for a few days. She'd even called in sick at work. She tried to work on her next article for Marcus, but all she could think about was getting Allison to take Jon down a peg. But just how could she get Allison to agree to a blind date?

"I might not lick pans, but my roommates do," he said, and began scrubbing the pot without any protest.

"Aren't you too old for roommates?" Laura asked.

"Look who's talking," he taunted. "Hey, Tracie, come out from under those blankets." Tracie moaned as a response.

"Hey, I'm looking for a place," Laura said.

"You are?" he asked. "You going back to that dipshit in Sacramento?"

"No," she said as she peeled off her rubber gloves. She began to rub some cream over her hands, concentrating on the knuckles and cuticles.

"Why do you do that?" Phil asked.

"To keep my hands soft."

He reached out and took her right hand. "Yeah," he said. "They are soft." He paused for a moment. Then he looked back at the pot and began to scrub harder, looking away from Laura. "So, you really trying to move out? You found a place and everything?"

"You know," Laura told him, "I think Tracie might pay a little more attention to you if she could take you a bit more seriously. If you had your own place, and a real job and some kind of game plan."

"I have a game plan," Phil said, and scowled into the Farberware.

"And that would be living off the six dollars a year you make from your writing?" Laura asked. "Or would it be living off the free beers you make at your gigs?"

"It would be none of your business," Phil told her.

Laura shrugged. "Suit yourself," she said. "But you know nobody's adolescence lasts forever. Except Warren Beatty's."

"Who's that?" Phil asked.

"It's irrelevant. His job's taken," Laura told him. "Anyway, Seattle is full of jobs. All kinds of them. There's no reason why you couldn't find something you'd like to do that actually pays. It's not like you do anything during the day except sleep and mooch."

Phil put down the pot. "Well, fuck you, too," he said. "And fuck the horse you rode in on."

"Oh, leave Trigger out of this," Laura said in a good-natured voice.

"I need the free time to create," Phil said, sounding like a petulant child. "I need empty days to write."

"Oh, come on. You might be able to get Tracie to buy that crap, but not me, buddy. My dad was a writer. You know what he did?"

Phil shook his head.

"He wrote. That's what writers do." She stopped a moment and then patted his arm in a sisterly way. "Look, I didn't mean to hurt your feelings. It's just that I think you're not really happy."

"Who said you're supposed to be happy?" Phil asked as he slipped into his jacket. "Who said life is about being happy?"

"Nobody in Encino," Laura agreed. "But that's why I got the hell out. And I don't think it's about being happy, but I don't think it's about being stuck, either. I think you—I mean everyone—just moves toward what they enjoy and away from what they don't enjoy. That's all that you can do. And I don't think you enjoy sitting around all day and being fairly useless. Not to mention getting humiliated by rejections from pretentious magazines and imbeciles like Bob." She shrugged her big shoulders. "I just think the scene's gotten old for you. But hey, call me an optimist."

For a heart-stopping moment, the room was very still. Tracie winced, expecting Phil's screams to begin at any second. She heard him clear his throat. Then there was silence again. Maybe he'd hit Laura, or break something before he stormed out of the apartment. Instead, he cleared his throat again. "You know," he said in a very gentle voice, "I've been starting to think the same thing."

Chapter 29

Tracie sat in their usual spot at Java, The Hut, waiting impatiently for Jon. She fiddled with the tiny ends of her hair. She'd never had a cut this short. She *really* hated it, and hated Stefan, who'd cut it; Phil, who made fun of it; and Laura, who had just told her not to worry about it, that hair grew back. At least she could count on Jon for support. She looked at her wristwatch. She'd been here almost twenty minutes late, but he still hadn't shown up. It was unlike him.

Molly strolled over, and Tracie winced in advance. This wouldn't be pretty. "Bloody 'ell! You've joined a nunnery? I didn't even know you were Catholic. Plus, you're 'ere on time and 'e's late. It's the end of the world."

"I'm not *always* late."

Molly leaned against the chair. "Not if fifty-one weeks a year three years running doesn't mean 'always.' " Molly took out her order pad. "Shall we go through the usual pantheon until you settle for your scrambled eggs?" she asked. "Or are you just going to sit there pulling on the ends of your 'air as if that will 'elp them grow?"

Tracie dropped her hands to her lap. "Molly, underneath that nasty English exterior, you really don't like me, do you?" Tracie asked.

"No, actually, I don't," Molly agreed cheerfully.

Tracie was taken aback. She hadn't actually expected to hear that Molly hated her. For a minute, she didn't know what to say. "But why? I've never hurt you."

"I guess I just don't like fools," Molly said. "I'm the daughter of one and an ex-wife of another. Call me oversensitive, but it's given me an aversion to them." She shrugged.

"I'm not a fool," Tracie protested.

"Yeah, and I'm not a waitress." Molly pointed to the plastic name tag pinned on her chest. "Read the card." Then she pointed at Tracie. "Yours says 'Tracie 'iggins—part-time journalist, full-time fool'!"

"What did I do?" Tracie asked, and, for some reason, she thought of the dream she'd had where she was painting her cocker spaniel blue.

"What 'aven't you done?" Molly asked angrily. "You date jerks. One useless git after another, and you don't know enough to get over it." Molly slid into the seat across from Tracie. "And, since you asked, mind you, if that isn't enough, you're turning the only nice guy in the great Northwest into a jerk."

"Jon! He's not a jerk. He's just . . . a little more stylish," Tracie said. "And he feels better about himself," she added.

"At the expense of others?" Molly asked. "I know what's going on. 'e brings them 'ere for coffee before going 'ome. It's like my Moggy bringing 'is mousies to me before 'e finishes them off. Three different women last week! And 'e bragged to me 'e 'ad *two* dates on Saturday." Molly leaned closer to Tracie. "You took a warm, sensitive guy, a guy who knows 'ow to listen to a woman, a guy who knows 'ow to please—who actually *wants* to please—and gave 'im all the tricks of the trade that the cold bastards use on us. 'e's a full member of the Guild of Guys now. Do you know what you've done?"

Tracie stopped protesting, sat there a moment, and thought about it. "Something very, very, bad?" she asked tentatively. Molly stared at her, and everything the waitress had said came together in Tracie's mind with her dream, Phil's jealousy, and Laura's warning. She'd need a little help and a little luck, but she thought she could undo the damage she'd done. "Molly, you're right," she said. The waitress nodded. Tracie swallowed her pride. "Will you help me stop him being a jerk?"

" 'ow?" Molly demanded.

"Get me two tickets to Radiohead. You've got the connections." Though Molly had stopped traveling with the rock-and-roll bands, they still called and visited when they were playing Seattle. She knew—and had probably slept with—every roadie, not to mention most rhythm guitarists in the business.

Molly made a face that showed she doubted Tracie's motives. "What do I get out of it?"

"You get your nicest guy in the Northwest back."

"I'll think on it," Molly said, but Tracie could see by her expression she was sold.

"Thank you, Molly."

"Mind you, I'm not sure I can do it. And don't take 'im back all the way to where 'e was. I liked what you did when you just made 'im look better—let's face it, 'e needed a visit from the fashion police." It was the first time Tracie could remember Molly approving of anything she'd done. "But don't you see that changing 'ow 'e *acts* is altogether different from changing 'ow 'e *looks*?"

"I guess it is."

"You've betrayed women everywhere," Molly hissed. " 'e used to be gifted, now 'e thinks 'e's God's gift. There's a big difference." She gestured with her chin over her shoulder. "Take a look."

Tracie turned. Jon was entering the coffee shop. He had a new swagger, a new persona. "I really did wrong," Tracie agreed. Then Molly nodded her head and disappeared into the kitchen.

"Here I am! Your star pupil," Jon said as he slid into the booth, taking Molly's place. Tracie looked him over. She could see he not only looked good but felt good, too. She wondered how good Beth felt right now. "Hey, what's with your hair?" Jon asked.

"What about it?" Tracie asked, forcibly restraining her own hands from covering it. She couldn't believe that Jon was being critical of her.

"I don't know," he said, and shrugged. "Who did it? You probably shouldn't try anyone new. *I* just went back to Stefan."

"Well, good for you," Tracie said. "It was Stefan who gave me this cut."

"Oh, well. It's nice." He almost closed his eyes in a kind of wince. "Yeah," he said. "It suits you."

"And how does your life suit you?" Tracie asked coldly. "Is it time for a few more lessons?" She was about to tell him he needed lessons in courtesy and thoughtfulness and remembering old friends. But before she had a chance to begin, he agreed with her.

"Absolutely," he said. "But I guess it's the advanced class now."

She couldn't get over him, and he obviously couldn't get over himself. "Oh, really?" she asked, trying not to show her pique. "And what would that consist of? Orgies? Menages à trois?"

He laughed, as if all of this was a big joke. She wondered for a moment if Molly was right about *everything*. She didn't think so, but it looked as if she was right about Jon.

Then Jon's face got serious. Maybe there was a chance he, too, wanted to change back. "Well, to tell you the truth, I really do need help." He looked at her with his old expression, a kind of tell-me-how-please look. "Uh, Tracie, I don't quite know if I should ask this, but . . . how do I get rid of them?"

"Rid of whom?"

"Well, say"—he paused, as if trying to pull up an example—"Beth. She calls at least four times a day. I finally saw her just to get rid of her, but you can't get rid of her. No matter what you say, she doesn't give up. I mean, I know she's your friend, and I don't mean to be disrespectful, but I think she needs to work on her self-esteem. Meanwhile, I don't know what to do."

Tracie took a deep breath. This was the Jon she knew. Maybe he wasn't an insensitive prick bastard. Maybe he was merely inexperienced, a little stupid. And, apparently, very, very good in bed. She blushed.

"Oh, don't be mad," he said, mistaking her reddening face for anger. "She's nice and all, but she's . . ."

Tracie told herself she had never expected Jon and Beth to be a permanent thing. She'd expected Beth to be cruel or bored by Jon. She had miscalculated, and that was an error of judgment on her part, not his moral wrong. And she supposed that it was no worse for Beth to be obsessed with an disinterested Jonny than a disinterested Marcus. In fact, maybe it was better because Jon couldn't fire her. Tracie took a deep breath. "Look, if you have to blow someone off, always use the INYIM line."

"What's that?"

Tracie spelled the initials on the damp tabletop between them. "INYIM. 'It's not you, it's me.' You know . . ."

"I've heard that from women!" Jon exclaimed.

"Yeah," she agreed. "We use it all the time, too. But it's sexier, somehow, from men. You know, 'I can't settle down. I'm a rambling man.' " She paused. "When I was teenager, every time I heard that song 'The Wanderer,' I'd get furious."

"The guy that went from town to town?" Jon asked.

"Yeah. You know, the kind of guy who could never settle down. When you're that kind of guy—"

"You're like James Dean!" Jon said.

"Yeah. The type of guy who says, 'You're the kind of girl I could love but . . .' "

"I got it, I got it," Jon said, excited and enthusiastic again. Then he leaned forward, so close that she could count the tiny wires of beard on his cheek and chin. "Hey, listen to this: I bagged Samantha."

Tracie recoiled as if she'd been bitten. "Why don't you shut up?" She asked him, and rose. Without thinking, she swung her arm as if to hit him. Jon put both of his hands in the air to ward her off.

"Wow! What's that about?" he asked. "I thought you'd be pleased with my progress."

"Progress? You don't call me back. You date Carole and Ruth and don't call Beth, except to break up with her! Then, out of boredom, or weakness, you see her instead—and you sleep with her to keep her hooked?" She had to stop to catch her breath. "You tell me that you 'bagged' Sam. *Bagged?* You really liked Sam. That's the way you tell me you had sex with her?"

"Hey, don't be mad. It was safe sex," he protested.

This was too much. Tracie got out of the booth, grabbed her jacket, and started to walk to the door.

Jon caught up with her and grabbed her hand. "Isn't this what you trained me for?" he asked. "I figured you'd be impressed with all I've done. I swear, Beth and Sam and Ruth all liked it."

"Ruth! You slept with Ruth, too?"

"Ruth and I didn't do much sleeping." Jon grinned. Tracie couldn't get angry again—she couldn't get over it. Had he always been a weasel in sheep's clothing? He was looking at her dazed face. "Hey, we had fun," he told her. "It means you've taught me well, Yoda. Wasn't that the point? Do you realize I even got it on with Enid from my building? Enid, the personal trainer."

"Enid?" she asked, her voice raised. Most of the people in the restaurant looked up. "*Enid?* She . . . she . . ." Tracie knew she was sputtering, but there were times you got beyond words. "She's ten years older than you, and a drunk. And a slut!"

"I'm not going to marry her, Trace," Jon said, his voice lowered. "It was a casual thing."

"I can't believe you slept with her. She's nuts, and you should be ashamed."

Molly came over to them. "We don't do take-away," she said, and led them back to the table. Putting both her hands on their shoulders, she sat them down, pulled out a pad, and looked ready to take their orders. "You 'ave some talking to do. Meanwhile, the usual?"

"No," Jon said matter-of-factly. "New man. New menu. Waffles."

"You want 'am with that?" Molly asked.

Tracie couldn't believe it. As if she would eat with him, as if all of this was okay. "No," she said. "He doesn't eat pigs—he fucks them."

Molly smirked. That only made Tracie more furious. "You are disgusting," she said to Jon. "I don't want to eat with you, I don't want to sit with you, I don't even want to talk with you."

Tracie looked at Molly. "Forget brunch," she told the waitress. "He's too busy for brunch with me." She got up and stomped away.

Chapter 30

Tracie was a woman with a mission, a female on a quest. Unfortunately, as she passed people, they said, "Hi," usually followed by "Some haircut!" Or "Ears lowered, huh?" or just "Tracie?" This was not the look she'd choose for walking into the enemy camp, but she imagined herself as Saint Joan. Her voices were telling her, Jon must be taken down. The fact that she'd have to use another enemy of women to achieve her goal didn't bother her.

She paused at Allison's cubicle. There was no denying the girl was gorgeous. She was looking over some work and her hair fell straight as a plumb line from the crown of her head across her pale cheek to the surface of the desk. She was so involved in what she was looking at that she didn't notice Tracie, so, without invitation, Tracie moved toward her desk.

"Hey, Allison. I wonder if you could do me a favor?" Tracie asked.

Allison looked up with a not very favor-oriented expression. Her perfect cerulean blue eyes blinded. Tracie automatically touched her tiny twigs of hair. "I know. My hair's too short," she said, precluding a first strike by Allison.

"Oh. Have you changed your hair?" Allison asked, and Tracie felt more insulted even than when Tim told her it was a bad Sinéad O'Connor impersonation. But as she stood there and looked at Allison, she realized that Allison was the kind of girl who probably didn't notice anything different about another woman.

"Anyway, I got free tickets, including a backstage pass, to the Radiohead concert and I told a friend of mine he could go, but my boyfriend is really freaking. So I wondered if . . . well, would you mind going with my friend?"

It was the first time Tracie had ever seen Allison look anything but bored. "You're kidding, right?" she asked, and her eyes—if possible—got even bigger. "I tried to get press passes for two weeks. I mean, I did *everything*." Tracie thought of the way Allison played up to Marcus and wondered whether "*everything*" included sexual favors. But somehow, Tracie thought that Allison was the type of woman who liked to tempt but not deliver. With her, men lived on the promise of sex, not the reality. "I'm dying to go," Allison added.

"Great! So you'll go out with my friend Jonny."

Suddenly, Allison's flawless eyes narrowed into Siamese-cat slits. "Hey, wait a minute! I mean, this isn't some dorky cousin you're fixing me up with or something?" she asked.

Tracie had a feeling that Allison liked only men who were the possession of other women. "Ha." Tracie laughed. "No. No blood relation. If he was, our dates would be incest. Actually, this is the guy Beth dropped Marcus for."

"Really?" Allison asked. "I didn't know that Beth had dated Marcus. Anyway, I thought he dropped her," Allison said, exposing herself as both a liar and an idiot at the same time.

Tracie shrugged. "I don't really know the details," she said as casually as she could manage, although the impulse to pull out a Remington and shave Allison's perfect locks suddenly became incredibly strong. "All I know is that he briefly dated Beth and that all the girls in the newsroom want him. But I've started going out with him, although my boyfriend doesn't know. So just go to the concert, keep my seat warm, and he'll take you out to dinner first, if you want to."

She watched as a light as small as a struck match began to glow behind the turquoise pools of Allison's pupils. Actually, her whole face began to glow with the perfect light of a smooth glass lantern. If her forehead were transparent, Tracie was sure she could have seen little wheels and gears grinding away as Allison compared the thought of stealing a man from Tracie with the risk of being found out by Marcus. "Okay. Sure."

As if her own thought had conjured him up, Tracie heard a gurgling noise behind her. She turned and found Marcus standing in the doorway of the cubicle. How long has he been there? Tracie wondered. Maybe it was she and not Allison who was risking her job. "So, speaking of the man that half the girls in the newsroom want," Tracie said in a bantering tone. Marcus didn't smile. Tracie felt a flutter in her stomach, and both women looked at him silently.

"Tracie, can I talk to you a moment?" Marcus asked, then turned on his heel after he gestured for her to follow him. She walked behind him down the hall. Had he heard everything she'd said? Even the fiction about Beth dumping him? Tracie decided that if he fired her, she would sue. She didn't know for what, but the guy was a hound.

The walk across the newsroom seemed endless, and when she got to his office, she was almost shaking. A lot of heads followed her perambulation, but nobody said anything.

"I heard a rumor," he said as he sat down in his chair and threw his feet up on the desk. Tracie wasn't sure if she should sit down or not, but she decided to. God, was he going to talk to her about how she'd fixed up Beth with Jon? Or was he going to yell at her for her idea to use Allison as a tonic? Or had he overheard her complaining about losing the Memorial Day follow-up piece and her theory on how Allison had gotten it? She held one hand with the other in her lap and had to use all of her self-control not to let one of them rise and pull at the pathetic stubble of her hair. "I hear you're thinking of freelancing," he said.

"Freelancing?" she repeated like an idiot, but his comment had come out of left field, or someplace further away, if there was someplace further away than that. How could he know? Had someone from *Seattle Magazine* snitched on her? Did they all run in the same pack at Seattle's toniest parties?

"As a full-time employee here, you are strictly forbidden to offer work that has not been presented for publication here to other outlets."

Tracie couldn't believe it. He was bothering her about the piece he'd turned down? For the first time, instead of being frightened of Marcus, she noticed something—nervousness, or fear?—behind Marcus's bravado. But what could he be afraid of? And how did he know about her query letters?

"I'm not sure that I'm going to freelance anything," Tracie said as truthfully and calmly as she could. "But if I do freelance an article, I would always hope that it would be published here." She paused and tried a smile, although what she really felt like doing was taking a bite right through the end of his shoe and into his big toe. "Anyway, Marcus, the only thing I've been working on—aside from your assignments, of course—is the makeover piece you rejected."

"What makeover?" he asked, and stood up. He began to pace back and forth along the windowed wall behind his desk. She could see that in profile he was still quite handsome, although the beginnings of a double chin weakened his otherwise-strong face. He crossed his arms, then turned and caught her looking at him appraisingly. It was his turn to smile and, probably to make her more uncomfortable, he passed the desk and began pacing behind her.

"Oh," he said. "Are you talking about that technotransformation, 'Mild One into Wild One' by the inversion of a single letter?" Tracie craned her neck, but each time he came into view, he turned and walked in the other direction. She decided to ignore his pacing and stared out the window instead. She kept quiet. "Maybe I was a little bit premature," he said. "I'd like to take another look at it."

Tracie knew that she should say no, that what she needed was an article to run somewhere else and without his butchering, but she wasn't sure if she could stand up to him. "It's just in draft form," she informed him, listening to his restless footsteps.

"I don't mind," he said and, from behind her, he put his hands lightly on her shoulders. She jumped in her seat and he took them away.

"Okay," she said, sounding to herself like the old Mary Tyler Moore character when she was startled by Mr. Grant. "I'll give you a draft right away." Then she was up and out of his office in a heartbeat.

"Tracie, can I talk to you a moment?" Marcus asked her again late that afternoon. Do I have a choice? she wondered. He stepped into her cubicle. "I read the draft of the dweeb makeover. I'm deeply surprised. It's actually pretty good. You're wasted on these stupid holiday pieces. There are some other assignments I'd like to see you working on."

Is he serious? What's going on? she thought.

"Come on with me," he said. She thought that he'd leered, but with Marcus, almost every expression was that unpleasant.

"Really?" she asked, and then wanted to bite her tongue. She had to learn not to react to either his praise or his criticism. What am I? His puppy? She followed him down the long hall that ran in the back of the building. Her thoughts kept her from noticing that Marcus had stopped, and she almost bumped into his back. He turned to face her. The hall was momentarily deserted, and he leaned against the wall, crossing his arms in that gesture of self-sufficiency she had come to know and dislike.

"Do we have a release from this guy?" Marcus asked.

"Uh. Sort of."

"What does that mean?"

"It means not yet, but I can get one. He's a friend."

"Not after this piece comes out." He laughed, then looked around. Tracie couldn't help it—she, too, turned her head, as if the enemy were listening. That was why she was so surprised when she turned back and saw he was leaning in, inches from her. He pushed Tracie against the wall and stretched both arms to either side so that she was backed against the wall, penned in by his arms and only inches from his smirking face. She could feel his breath on her forehead. "How about we edit it tonight . . . together?"

She couldn't believe it. He was actually putting a move on *her*. She thought of bringing her knee up between his legs, but she needed the job. "Marcus . . ." she began. He leaned closer, his mouth almost on hers. She squirmed down the wall. "I don't think so."

"Come on. Don't play shy with me. I know how you look at me in those editorial meetings." He was about to try to kiss her, when Tracie gave him a really big push, big enough to throw him off balance. He stumbled, and she couldn't help it—she pushed him again. Then she saw Tim and Beth standing just behind him. How much had they witnessed? Marcus fell to the floor. Beth stopped and stared at him. Tim, reluctantly it seemed, bent to give him a hand up. Embarrassed, Marcus slapped it away and stood.

"By the way, I'll need that Father's Day piece by the end of the day."

"But you said—"

"Your mistake," Marcus told her, and turned and left her alone in the hall.

Later on in the afternoon, when Tracie was finishing the Father's Day piece, the Radiohead tickets arrived. Wow! Molly had come through for her. She'd have to leave bigger tips. She had to get this article turned in. She'd called Jon over and over. She had to reach him, or she'd be stuck giving these tickets to Allison for nothing. Just then, the phone rang. It rang a second time, then a third. She needed a distraction, so she took the call. "Hello, Tracie Higgins here," she whispered into the receiver.

"Hello there, alchemist. What's up?" Jon asked her.

"Hey, I'm glad you called. Boy, have I got a girl for you tonight!"

"I can't tonight. I'm going out with Ruth."

"Well, cancel Ruth, because this girl is *really* something."

"I guess it won't hurt Ruth to be on hold a little longer, right?" Jon asked. "She's a climber. She likes to hang around." He paused and then laughed. "If I blow her off for tonight, I'd be Ruthless."

"Right." Tracie half-chuckled at the lame joke just for him. He'd be punished for it all tonight. "Come by here at six-thirty. I've got tickets to the Radiohead concert. Come to my office and I'll brief you."

"Okay. See you later, then."

Chapter 31

Jon had felt so bad after Tracie walked out on him at Java, The Hut that he couldn't concentrate on anything and so he had gone to visit his mother. He told himself that he owed her a visit, but it was for him, not her, that he'd gone. She'd made him chicken and noodles, one of his favorite comfort dinners, without even being asked. "Honey," she'd said, running her hands through his new haircut, "you look so tired. Working hard?" He hadn't said "hardly working," though that was closer to the truth. He'd only nodded. "Jonathan dear, why don't you get yourself a dog?" she had asked. It was the kind of crazy question only mothers would ask. But there was something sweet and even right about the question. All at once, Jon felt a yearning for something true and loyal and warm. He almost told his mother about the fight with Tracie, but he was too ashamed of the rest of his behavior.

So, expecting not to hear from Tracie at all, he'd called her, needing to apologize. He'd been delighted that she seemed happy to hear from him, and even more delighted about the date she'd set him up with. He had thought Tracie was really mad at him, and he'd been ready to do whatever it took to make peace. Although he'd loved this whirl of sexual activity, and had no intention of giving it up, he knew that he needed Tracie as a friend. In fact, she was his only close friend. She was also the only one who knew who he really was right now. And this Chick of the Universe sounded too good to be true, but Jon wasn't even nervous. He had the concert tickets in his pocket, one of his new Armani shirts on, and the magic jacket, which seemed to do the trick. He hadn't shaved since Monday, and he knew he looked good, because, although he still didn't have the confidence to sit at the bar, he'd walked past it and several women had turned their heads to check him out.

Anyway, with Tracie back on board, he had his confidence back. She'd seemed so angry at Java, The Hut, but, though he still wasn't sure exactly why, seeing her at her office had reassured him. She hadn't apologized or anything, but maybe setting up this date was her way of making peace. Tracie wasn't good at being wrong. And he didn't need her to say "Sorry about that PMS episode" or "Too bad I took out my anger at Marcus on you" to make up. She'd acted normal—no, even nicer than normal—when he picked up the tickets. She'd even approved of his outfit and straightened his collar before she sent him on his way. So that was all right.

He didn't have much interest in Radiohead—in fact, aside from *Karma Police*, he couldn't remember ever listening to anything they'd recorded. But Tracie had briefed him on the Chick of the Universe's passion for Thom Yorke, and Jon's only regret was that he hadn't had a chance to watch MTV to get a few of Yorke's moves down. If he could copy James Dean, he could surely imitate Thom Yorke. This girl—for a frightening moment he couldn't remember if she was Alexandra or Allison, but then he figured he'd call her Ali and be safe—would just have to settle for James Dean, the way the other ones had. He smiled slyly and shook his head. In a way, it was lucky he hadn't known it was this easy; if he had, he probably would have flunked out of high school.

He sat at a bistro table, ordered a beer, and when it arrived, he began swigging it and waiting. He didn't have a watch to check, but he was sure he was late. How late was she going to be? He wondered for a moment if he had the wrong restaurant, or if he'd been given the wrong information by Tracie. But no, this was the place, and what the hell: If Ali didn't show up, he'd just call Ruth, or even Beth, and tell her he'd copped a couple of great tickets and ask her to go with him. And if he couldn't reach one of them, he might actually approach the bar. There might be other girls there in love with Thom Yorke.

Bored, he picked up the menu. It was the usual bistro fare: fancy burgers, *pommes frites*, chicken paillard. He was just putting the menu down when he saw her. She was standing across the room, looking around. She wasn't the Chick of the Universe. She was much more: She was an angel. Jon knew immediately that this was the woman Tracie had set him up with, and he blessed her in his heart. Every man and woman in the dining room paused to look at her. And then, as if in a dream, but also as inexorably as his own death, she moved slowly toward him. She was tall, and aside from her shoulders, she was very wispy. Her legs began at the floor and went on forever. Her hair was an indescribable silvery blond, and he would give his life to stroke it.

Be cool, he told himself. Neither Thom Yorke nor James Dean would even blink were she to join one of them. All of Tracie's training flashed through his mind. He tightened his hand around his glass and forced himself to take another slow sip to steady himself.

"You must be Ali," he said to her as she reached the table.

"Allison," she said. Her eyes flicked up and down over him and he could feel her sizing him up. "You must be Jonny."

He nodded, because it was best not to talk again until he had control of his vocal chords. She was breathtaking, and there was something about her skin that reminded him of the perfectly smooth sheen of the screen on his new laptop. What do you talk about to a goddess? He found himself as tongue-tied as he'd ever been in the Micro/Con hallway with Samantha. God, he couldn't afford a relapse now, not when the Chick of the Universe was sitting across from him. He was about to really fuck up and ask her how she liked working at the *Times*, or whether she'd majored in journalism, or what her horoscope sign was, when he remembered that he was not supposed to talk too much. He moved his jaw in the approved James Dean manner, picked up his beer, and sipped it again. He'd wait this one out.

And it was a good thing he did. Because although Allison must have been used to dozens—no, hundreds—of men trying to impress her and entertain her, she wasn't used to silences except for those that she maintained. He was white-knuckled by the time she spoke, but that gave him time to slow his breathing and get himself back with the program.

"What do you do?" she asked.

"About what?" he responded, and her eyes blinked. Then she almost smiled. Her lips, which had been perfect in repose, were even more desirable when they opened. And her teeth! Ten thousand orthodontists dreamed of making a cast of teeth like that to show future clients.

They talked a little bit, and she wanted to know about his job, his family, what kind of car he drove, and a bunch of other desultory stuff. But while they talked, he realized he'd learned to play the stupid game so that he could graduate permanently to a woman like Allison. Why would you need any other woman if she wanted to wrap her arms around you, to put those lips against yours, to let you touch a square inch of her perfection?

As Jon sat across from Allison in the dim light of the bistro, he fielded her questions successfully but couldn't get over how beautiful she was. This was the best score he'd had so far.

And then the waitress came over to get their dinner order. For a moment, Jon thought he'd just ignore the girl, who was only a dim shadow of Allison's beauty. But something inside him spoke. He hadn't planned it; it just happened. He was on automatic pilot! Jon found himself doing a double take and turning to Allison. "Doesn't she have the most beautiful eyes you've ever seen?" he asked.

Chapter 32

The next morning, Tracie found herself humming as she walked down the corridor at the *Times*. She was early again, still in her coat and holding a paper bag with a cup of coffee and a muffin. Beth was in her cubicle, and she looked up. "Hi, Tracie," she said as her friend breezed by, but Tracie knew she wouldn't get off that easily. She stopped humming, aware that she was being followed down to her desk by Beth. She sighed. Well, soon all this would be over. Beth could become obsessed with someone else; soon she'd have her friend back, and things with Phil would go back to normal.

"Have you heard from him? Did she shoot him down?" Beth asked.

Tracie shrugged, though she knew that wouldn't end the questioning.

"She shot him down, didn't she? She's such a fool!" Beth cried.

"Beth, I have more important things to do than track every blip in the love life of my friends," Tracie told her. She took off her coat, hung it up, and sat down. Sara entered the room.

"Did you hear?" she asked.

"Hear what?" Tracie wanted to know.

"It's about Allison. It's something about Allison," Beth said breathlessly.

And then Sara smiled with the superior look of a person who has heard office gossip a minute before anyone else. Tracie shook her head and turned away, opening up her breakfast bag.

"Well, guess who just called in sick?" Sara asked.

"Marcus?" Tracie inquired. "Gee, I hope it isn't hysticular cancer," she said.

"Allison! Allison called in sick? On an editorial meeting day?" Beth asked.

"Marcus will kill her," Sara said.

"She's fearless. She probably iced Jon," Tracie said confidently, then smiled. She opened the bag and took out the farm cake and her coffee. "Beth, I thought you were getting help to get over these obsessions. What does your therapist say?"

"He's just interested in prescribing new meds for me. We don't really talk. He's more of a mental bartender. Speaking of obsessions, I thought you were through with those chocolate cream cheese muffins. You know, they're addictive."

"I haven't had one in awhile. Just this once . . ." Tracie began.

"You're worried about something," Sara said.

"No I'm not!" Tracie answered a little too quickly.

"Okay. So tell us what Jonny said about Allison, then," Beth insisted.

Tracie turned away from them. "He didn't say anything. He didn't call," she admitted.

"He didn't call? Oh my God! He always calls. Oh my God! Tracie, she's got him. She's got him, just like she got the others. He's just a fish on her hook, another pike on her lure, a trout," Beth ranted.

"Would you please cut the fish talk? I can't take fish analogies on an empty stomach."

"Poor Jonny," Beth said, shaking her head. "He deserves better." Tracie knew that as far as Beth was concerned, Beth was the only thing better. Oh well, everyone had their blind spots. Then Tracie's phone rang. "It's him! I bet it's him. I'll get it," Beth exclaimed, going for the receiver.

"Excuse me! I think this is *my* phone and *my* office," Tracie reminded her.

"Well, it's definitely your *cubicle*," Sara quipped. The phone rang again.

"Please let me pick it up," Beth begged. "I'll give you fifty dollars next payday." The phone rang once more and Tracie tried to reach it, but Beth blocked her way. Tracie, too, was dying to hear what had happened, but she wouldn't reveal that for fifty dollars, a hundred, or even for a farm cake. How many rings before it kicked into voice mail? Usually three, but sometimes four. She tried to reach past her friend, but, like a goalie on speed, Beth blocked her again.

"Beth, stop it!" Tracie said. "Have some self-respect."

"God! This is better than *The Young and the Restless*," Sara joked.

Feinting to the right, Tracie grabbed the receiver from Beth's left side before Beth could pick it up. "Would you guys grow up?" she said as she placed the receiver to her ear. "Hello."

"Tracie? It's Allison." Ha. Tracie could torture Sara and Beth now, payback for their harassment. Plus, she'd get to hear how Allison had leveled Jon, and she'd savor every minute of the story. She didn't like to think of herself as a bitch, but he really deserved it, and he'd be glad of it in the end.

"Oh, hey, Allison," Tracie said smoothly. As she expected, her words galvanized Beth and Sara. Sara's eyes opened so wide, they might have popped, while Beth's curls actually looked as if they were standing on end. Sara jumped up from the desk and came to Tracie's side, motioning to get at the receiver, while Beth immediately did the same on the other side. Tracie tried to wave the two of them off while she listened to Allison.

"I've got this problem, Tracie. I can't get out of bed." Tracie thought that's what she heard, but Allison's voice was getting even lower. She sounded awful.

"Is it the flu?" Tracie asked.

"No. I just can't get out of bed." Beth gave Tracie a sharp elbow in the ribs, not because she'd heard what Allison said but because she couldn't. Tracie had the phone pressed tightly against her ear.

"Well, there's a lot of virus going around. And you have laryngitis for sure."

"No I don't. I'm not sick," she said in a whisper that sounded annoyed. There was a pause. "I can't get out of bed because I don't *want* to. I'm here with Jonny and . . ." Tracie fell into her chair, nearly knocking Sara over.

"Oh shit," Sara said. "This'll look great for Marcus."

Beth and Sara tried again to listen in, but then they noticed that Tracie's expression had changed from her superior smile to a grimace. She turned her back to the two girls, who were watching her intently. She felt as if her head was spinning. She'd missed something that Allison had said. ". . . I just can't get out of bed. I don't want to ever again. And I'm exhausted."

"But . . . but . . ." What could she say? He's not really that good in bed; he's just my friend? Don't believe what you see and feel; he's really a dweeb? Don't be nice to him; punish him because he deserves it? "But . . . the editorial meeting," she said lamely.

"The hell with Marcus and the meeting. This is just too good."

"It is?" Tracie asked before she could stop herself. After all, she was a girl who had blown off work for a bad haircut. "It is?" she asked again.

"The best!" Allison whispered in a knowing voice.

Well, if anyone knew, it would be Allison, Tracie thought bitterly. What was wrong with this picture? Beth was pushing her on one side and Sara on the other, but Allison was talking again.

"Tracie, I owe you an apology. I never thought you liked me very much, but I guess I was wrong."

No you weren't, Tracie thought. But you're wrong now.

"What?" Beth said. "What did she do to him?" Tracie elbowed Beth and covered the phone with her hand.

"I guess I just want to say thank you," Allison continued. "Jonny told me what close friends you are and . . . I'm just really grateful to you for the best night of my life." Allison's voice sounded teary and she stopped as if to catch her breath. "Thanks," she said.

"You're welcome," Tracie replied.

"Oh, he's waking up. I have to go," Allison informed her. "Thanks again, Tracie." And then the phone went dead.

Tracie put the receiver down and slowly turned back to her two friends. "She spent the night with Jonny."

Beth groaned. "I can't stand it. It's just not fair."

"She's in bed with him now," Tracie said, shocked to feel tears rising in her eyes. She suddenly felt incredibly lonely. "I don't get it. I mean, how good *is* he?"

"*Really* good," Beth told her, then got up slowly and turned to leave. "Maybe I should go back to Marcus," she said as she walked out of the cubicle.

Sara looked at Tracie. "What are you going to do?"

Tracie forced herself to sit upright in her chair, picked up her farm cake, and took a huge bite. "Wait till Sunday's brunch," she said with her mouth full. "I'll *kill* him."

Chapter 33

Jon lay against Allison, dozing, his legs against her silky backside. Her skin was one of the wonders of the world. He moved against her, freshly aroused, his cock bumping gently against the small of her back. For a moment, he thought of Parsifal. If there were a way to build *this* into a virtual reality game, he could buy Bill Gates out in a matter of months.

Jon smiled. Last night, like the previous two nights with Allison, had been incredible, but it topped a whole series of successful nights. If he wanted to think of his recent sexual successes as conquests, Allison was Waterloo and he was the Iron Duke.

His cock moved again. He supposed there would never be a more perfect moment in his life. Yet something was missing. He thought, for some reason, about the Bible: not because Allison was a blessing, though she was very angelic in appearance, but because of the way the Bible described sex. In the Bible, when men slept with women, they "knew them." In a way, he could understand that, because the act of mounting Allison, of seeing her beauty naked and open beneath him, was an act of knowledge. And when he entered her, there was a thrill of possession and of a deeper, more forbidden knowledge.

But he did not know Allison. Not in any real way. Perhaps someday he would, but he had no idea what he would find. All he knew right now was that she was exquisite and that moving on her and in her and over her had become a pas de deux, more erotic and beautiful than any ballet. But he also knew that he was lying next to a stranger. And he was worse than a stranger to her: He was an imposter.

Jon's eyelids fluttered. He sat up and stretched. Allison rolled onto her back, exposing not only her lovely face and the aureole of wheat-light hair on the pillow but also her absolutely perfect breasts. It was amazing, but he felt himself stand up for her again, as if three times hadn't been enough.

Actually, to be honest, the sex, though good, hadn't been terrific. Allison was used to being pleased, and she was nowhere near as good a lover as, say, Beth, but just looking at her had given him enough of a thrill to make up for the difference. So he was thinking about another attempt, when his phone rang.

He had taken her to his place—breaking the rules, which Tracie would not have approved of, and here was his punishment. He thought for a moment of just ignoring the phone, but he didn't want Allison to think she was that important to him, or he'd never get another shot at her. He hoped it wasn't Beth. So, on the second ring, he reached over and picked up the receiver.

"Hey, Jon. Do you know what day this is?" a male voice asked, and he nearly dropped the phone.

"Dad?" he said, but then he didn't know what else to say. He hadn't heard from his father for at least two years, except for one postcard he had gotten from Puerto Rico, and then a letter from San Francisco begging him to invest $100,000 in a new venture that his dad and two other losers were trying to start. He had barely been able to understand the prospectus, but he had sent his father a money order for a thousand dollars and a note that wished him luck. He hadn't heard from him since then.

"Dad . . ." he repeated. Beside him, Allison turned and lifted her head, leaning it against her arm so she could look at him. But he didn't want to be looked at right now. He sat up and threw his legs over the side of the bed, turning his back on her.

"It's my day, Jon. It's Father's Day. Remember? And I *am* your father."

There was a defensive yet pleading tone to his voice that made Jon very uncomfortable. Had he been drinking this early? Jon still didn't have a watch, but it was early—*very* early for drinking. Of course, he didn't know what time zone Chuck was in—or even what hemisphere. Maybe it was cocktail hour in Singapore.

"I wondered if you'd have the time to meet me?" his father was saying. "I came a long way, son, to see you."

Jon shrugged a little. If his father was calling him "son," it was definitely a sign that something was wrong. His father never liked to admit that he was older than thirty-five, which made it awkward to have a son Jon's age. As he aged, his women hadn't, though there'd been a frightening decline in quality. Jon sighed and hoped his father didn't hear it. "Sure," Jon said. "Sure I can meet you."

"Shit! Shit," Tracie said as she looked at the papers spread out on her living room floor.

"Come on, his eggs aren't that bad," Laura said. They were having a late breakfast, prepared—oddly enough—by Phil. He had insisted. Though the eggs were cooked until they were brown and the potatoes were uncooked, so that they were unpleasantly crunchy, Tracie had hardly noticed. Instead, she was mourning the abortion Marcus had made of her feature on Father's Day. It hadn't been easy to think of an original angle, but she'd been pleased with the piece, since what she'd managed to do was a piece about alternative fathers. A priest who had helped raise a dozen orphan boys, a Yuppie who was Big Brother to a wheelchair-bound fatherless nine-year-old, a guy who had run a summer camp and served in loco parentis for dozens of boys, as well as a couple of grandfathers who were raising their grandsons.

It had run four full columns in length, but it had been cut to less than a column, mentioning only the grandfathers in detail, with the others given barely a sentence. And someone else had supplied the usual crap about where "normal" kids were bringing "normal" dads to celebrate, along with a list of restaurants serving special brunches. Enraged, she glanced at the byline and found that while her name was on it at the bottom, it did add "With special reporting by Allison Atwood." "Goddamn it!" Tracie said, and threw the paper halfway across the living room.

Oblivious to her pain, Phil chose that moment to ask, "How do you like the eggs?"

She could hear Laura stifling a laugh behind her, but she managed to suppress her own rage at the paper long enough to turn to Phil with a tight smile. "Really good. Thanks." What she thought was that she'd cooked him probably a hundred breakfasts without any fuss, and, usually, without any thanks. But if a guy fried up one goddamn egg, he expected the Nobel Prize.

"Really? You like the eggs?" Phil asked, probably because they hadn't praised him enough, and Tracie wondered, not for the first time, if she could perhaps somehow manage to live without sex.

Tearing himself away from Allison had not been as painful as the apprehension of what little treat Chuck Delano had waiting for him.

Jon didn't hate his father. It would be easier if he did. Instead, what he felt was a kind of indignation cut with pity. It was the pity that had gotten him out of his bed, into his clothes, and into a taxi. He wondered again what was waiting for him.

When Jon was just a teen, his father had made him go with him on several of his little excursions. Chuck—he didn't want to be called Dad—would sit across from some young woman but direct conversation to Jon. "Now, son, I want you to meet my new girl. Isn't she a pip?"

There had been a lot of those, because, though Jon hated to acknowledge it, his father was a good-looking and sometimes charming guy. But when Jon was in his early teens, Chuck had been at the top of his game. As his career had ebbed, so had his looks, and he'd found more solace in Southern Comfort than the entire Confederacy had. And more and more frequently, Chuck had used him as a prop to help with the women. He hadn't had a choice—his father had visiting privileges—and a part of him had wanted to see his dad. What kid didn't? As Jon hit maturity, Chuck certainly still hadn't. Just before he'd left Seattle for parts largely unknown, he'd taken Jon out for the last time. Another one of his jobs had ended in disaster, and after a few drinks and a lot of self-pity, Chuck had become maudlin. "Gotta start again somewhere," he'd said. "Got it all planned out. And I want you to be a part of it. You're my flesh and blood." Jon had been working at Micro/Con for a few years, but his father told him to quit. "You'll never get rich working for someone else," he said. "Take it from me. I'm striking out on my own." Striking out was more like it.

Jon hadn't noticed a very young woman peering at them from the bar until his father pointed her out. She looked like a ninth grader. Jon had almost thought she was interested in him, but he'd been sure the proof she carried was fake. "I was thinking of asking her," Jon's father had said. "Asking her what? How she scored on her PSATs?" Jon had asked. "No. No. To marry me," his father had answered matter-of-factly.

Jon had the taxi drop him at the corner near where he was meeting his father. The neighborhood was getting seedy, not far from the bus station. What in the world could he get his dad? A pint of Southern Comfort? A one-way ticket to South America? He entered the drugstore in the middle of the block.

He settled on some aftershave, the classic, stupid Father's Day gift. While the clerk gift wrapped it, he remembered that Phil lived somewhere around here, and that Laura had considered a place in the neighborhood until Tracie warned her off. Despite the wind that was making his eyes tear, he smiled. He'd have an earful for Tracie tonight.

His father had given him an address just a few blocks north of where he was now, a restaurant called Howdies. In another block, Jon could see it, the kind of big, grim, noisy place that people who took long-distance buses stopped at to eat.

As he swung the door open, an automated voice shouted, "Howdy." But that was about it as far as the theme went. The place was a grim collection of Formica-topped tables and molded plastic chairs. It was cavernous, and along one long wall ran a food service where hot tables offered up yesterday's meat loaf, macaroni and cheese, mixed carrots and peas. Jon felt as forlorn as the bowls of browning iceberg lettuce that sat, unwanted, in a row across the top of the salad section. From the entrance, he saw the ghostly glimmer of a white face under a cap and an equally white hand beckoning. Jon walked down the long aisle toward his dad.

He tried not to make a noise or stare once he saw him clearly, but it would have been equally cruel to avert his eyes. Chuck seemed to have aged two decades in the two years or so since Jon had last seen him. His father began to struggle to his feet, but Jon waved him back and took the chair opposite. He didn't kiss or hug him, but he did hold out his hand. His father's was thin and his skin was amazingly papery. Jon was too shocked by his appearance to say anything. "Hello, Jon," Chuck said. "You're looking well." It wasn't the best opening, since Jon couldn't give the standard "Yes, so are you." He fumbled in his pocket and then silently handed Chuck his gift. Chuck took it and looked at it blankly, as if it were a meteorite or a ball of buffalo mozzarella. "What's this?" Chuck asked.

"It's . . . it's . . . it's a present. You know, Father's Day."

Chuck stared at it and but didn't move to open it. Then he shook his head a couple of times. "You're a really good boy, Jonathan. You take after your mother's side of the family." Involuntarily, Jon nodded. "You're looking good. Still crazy after all these years, huh?"

It was a song that his mom and Chuck used to sing together when they were in a good mood. Jon remembered driving to Vancouver, with them singing happily in the front seat while he chimed in from the back. "Still can't afford a car?" his father asked, and when Jon was about to protest, Chuck raised his bony white hand to stop him. "I'm only joking," he said. "I know how well you're doing."

"You do?" Jon asked.

"Your mother keeps me up-to-date. On the Internet. Thanks for coming to see me, son," Chuck said, and Jon felt his heart tighten in his chest. The "son" business was usually the beginning of the financial requests. But it didn't materialize this time. Chuck talked about his place in Nevada, gardening, and the Seahawks, Donald Trump, the upcoming election, and an episode of *Frasier* where Niles and his father both seemed to want to date Daphne. None of it added up to anything, and Jon kept waiting for the touch, the angle, until his father lifted up the brim of his cap and ran his hand over the stubble of his shiny head. "It itches like hell," Chuck said. "They told me that was normal after chemo." It was only then that all the pieces fell into place. Before Jon could say anything, Chuck leaned forward and looked him in the eyes for the first time. "I've got a good chance," he said. "It hasn't metastasized. I have some radiation treatments to go through and then, with luck, I'll be right as rain."

"Good," Jon managed to choke out; he didn't feel strong enough to ask a single question about what kind of tumor, whether it had been operable, what the percentage of success was. . . . It all flashed through his mind, but he looked across at the shriveled shell of his father and didn't ask a thing. "You look good, Chuck," he said, and for the first time, his father laughed.

"You're too fucking much," Chuck said, shaking his fragile-looking head. He'd always been so vain. Jon wondered if he cared anymore about his looks or was only focused on survival. Again, he thought it was too personal a question to ask.

In fact, he didn't have much to say. "Good luck," he murmured at last. "If there's anything I can—"

"Well, I did wonder if there was any chance I could be put on your medical plan?" Chuck said. "That would be a big help. I don't really have the kind of benefits that give you priority seating in the waiting room."

"Hey, don't worry about that," Jon said. "I can talk to my benefits coordinator tomorrow." He doubted he could get his father, a man with a preexisting condition, who he hadn't lived with for fifteen years, any coverage, but he could certainly pay for whatever treatment might cure or comfort Chuck.

"Or maybe your mother could get me reinstated," Chuck added. "I thought about going over to see her while I'm here. Is she hooked up with anyone now?"

"Yes." Jon lied as smoothly as if he'd been doing it all his life. The last thing his mom needed now was to nurse her dying ex-husband. "You'd like him. He's a professional wrestler."

"I never should have left your mother," Chuck admitted.

"You never should have cheated on her, either," Jon said, and then regretted letting that slip, but his father merely nodded his head.

"Don't make my mistakes, Jon," he said. "Find a good woman. Stick with her. You'll never regret it."

Chapter 34

Molly was talking to a customer and didn't notice when Tracie walked in, which was a relief to Tracie. Phil had been really talkative all evening and kept trying to keep her from leaving. But she was here on time, despite Phil, and proceeded to go to her usual spot to wait for Jon. Just as she was slipping out of her raincoat, Molly approached her with two steaming mugs of coffee. "You 'ave no one to blame but yourself for this little turn of events," Molly said as she placed the two cups on the table and slid opposite Tracie in the booth.

"Excuse me? I don't remember inviting you to join me."

"Well, if I don't, you're going to be 'ere alone this time," Molly said as she pushed the sugar holder toward Tracie's hand. "We're making some doughnuts in the kitchen. You'll be able to dunk them. In your tears," she added. "I take it the tickets didn't work. And I 'ad to fuck a roadie to get them. Waste of a good favor, I call it."

"I think you're being a little overdramatic," Tracie said with as much dignity as she could muster. "Anyway, I have nothing to cry about."

"Being stood up by your friend after all these years won't upset you then?"

"What are you talking about? I'm early and Jon's a little late. What's the big deal?"

"No, luv. 'e was late *last* week. And a *little* late the week before. My bet is that this is the week 'e doesn't show at all, Radiohead tickets or no."

"Don't be ridiculous. We meet for this late brunch every Sunday, no matter what. Except for the time he had his appendectomy," Tracie told Molly, as if she didn't know. "I'm his best friend."

"You're a lot more than that." Molly stood up and looked deep into Tracie's eyes. "Face it: You're a scrambled egg girl who thinks she should like something different. You don't even know what you feel about 'im, do you? 'e was at your beck and call and you were too stupid to appreciate it."

"I did that?"

"Yes, Dr. 'iggins." In disgust, Molly got up from her seat and walked toward the kitchen.

Tracie sat alone in the booth, staring out the window. Bored with the lack of activity outside, she started to fiddle with the packets of Sweet 'n Low. There were eleven—a very unsatisfactory number. She tried to arrange them in three rows of four, but the last, short row annoyed her. So she reorganized them into two rows, the top with five and the bottom with six, but that looked like a pyramid without a top. So she did one at the top, a row of two under that, a row of three beneath that, and a row of four underneath. But then she had one left. What the fuck? she thought, then tore it into a star shape and put it at the top of the triangle that now became a Christmas tree. She got the Sweet 'n Low all over everything. The powder that spilled all over could be snow. Too bad it's mid-June instead of Christmas, she thought sourly.

" 'aving fun?" Molly asked on her way by the table.

Tracie sighed. Maybe Molly was right about her. Maybe she was a scrambled eggs kind of girl, a person who liked to work under deadlines, have assignments, and didn't know when she loved somebody. After all, Laura had said the same thing a week ago. She glanced down at her watch—only another nine minutes had passed. *Where the hell is he?* she thought. She'd always taken his promptness for granted. But he'd come early because . . . he loved her best. She felt water rise up to the bottom of her lids. Somehow, she'd counted on that. Who did he prefer now? Who was he with? Ten minutes passed. Tracie couldn't take the waiting any longer. She got up and went to the phone booth at the back of the coffee shop. She punched in Jon's number, but there was no answer. "Damn it!" She hung up the receiver and dialed his work number—he might have fallen asleep over his terminal—but all she got was the same recording saying his mailbox was full. "Goddamn it!"

She marched back to the booth, passing Molly, who was taking another customer's order. Molly looked up and smiled at her with an unbearable I-told-you-so grin. Tracie gathered up her raincoat and bag, stalked across the floor, pushed the door open, and stormed out.

She put her bag over her head to shield her hair from the rain and walked quickly to her car, fumbled with the keys to unlock her door, and finally managed to get inside. *Why the fuck do I live in a city where it always rains? What's wrong with me?* She drove like Mario Andretti through the wet, deserted streets of downtown Seattle. The rain was coming down so hard, it was like a sheet sliding down the windshield. She glanced at the console clock, which told her Jon was now—wherever he was—forty-eight minutes late for his date with her.

Tracie squealed up to his downtown building, parked illegally in front of it, and left the emergency flashers blinking. She hustled out of the car and ran up the stairs to his loft. Ridiculous! His rent was exorbitant, but he had no elevator, no amenities. So like Jon!

Her hair—what there was left—was glued to her head from the rain. *What does it matter anyway?* she thought, and she took her right hand and slid it across the top of her head to try to get rid of the excess moisture. When she got to his door, she was panting, but it didn't stop her from banging loudly. If he was in bed, she'd pull him out and drag him into the rain and let him hang there by his collar like a wet puppy. But there was no response. Despite the clear reality that no one was going to answer, she kept hammering. Well, she had to do something. She rooted through her handbag, found a pen, but couldn't find any paper. She was reduced to using a pad of small Post-it notes. She began to write on the first one "I can't believe that" and she smashed it onto the door with her fist. The words were smeared from the dampness of the rain, but it was still legible. Then she wrote, "after all these years you'd" and, running out of room, she tore off the page and also stuck it onto the door. She continued to write another: "completely forget about our" and she squished the Post-it against the door beside the other two. There was plenty more to say. Luckily, she had two pads of Post-its. "Ungrateful." "Thoughtless." "Rude."

She wrote, tore off another, and wrote again. The only sounds she could hear were the rain hitting the hall window, her own heavy breathing, and the scratch of her felt-tip pen on the tiny yellow papers.

By the end, Tracie had twenty-three Post-it notes stuck all the way down Jon's door, telling him what a pig he was and how she would never see him again.

Then the wave of anger receded and left only sadness behind. She looked at his door. It was ridiculous, just as she was. No dignity at all, just like her. He'd probably see them and laugh. Maybe he'd see them with Allison beside him. For a moment, she was tempted to tear all of the smeared notes down off the door. She chucked the remains of the pad into her purse and left.

Tracie got back in her car and tried to drive herself home, though the tears were making her vision cloudy. By the time she got to North Street, she was sobbing so hard that she was gasping for air. She pulled the car over to the side of the road, yanked her sweater partway off so that her arms were free but her head was covered. She used her free hands to wipe her covered face.

When she took her hands away from her face, she caught a watery glimpse of a bicycle whizzing by her. What a city! Rain all the time and nuts out in it. Her tears kept falling, and she kept making moans and hiccups. But finally, unlike the rain, her tears stopped. She wiped her swollen face, put her car in gear, and accelerated to get back on the road. She drove past the bike that had just gone by her. "You idiot!" she said aloud. "Haven't you heard of mass transit?" she asked into her rearview mirror as she drove away from the bicyclist.

It was a short ride on empty streets, but it felt as if it took a week to get home. She was exhausted, as if she had run all the way. When she finally reached her house, she parked quickly and got out of the car, slammed the door, and ran through the rain to her building entrance.

Chapter 35

Jon had gotten back to his place after he left his father waiting for the bus. He had hardly been able to climb the stairs to his loft, his knees had been so weak. If he had never liked the image of his father as a carefree womanizer, the image of him as a pathetic, regretful, sick man was no better. Jon had managed to walk in the door without crying, only to find Allison still lying on his sofa in nothing but his one remaining Micro/Con T-shirt. She was watching TV. He had to cover his shock, because he had completely forgotten she'd still be at his place.

"Where have you been?" she asked unreproachfully. And he had to endure chitchat and a bunch of questions about his job, how long he'd been at Micro/Con, whether he had stock options, and what his relationship with the founders was. He wasn't even able to lie, based on Tracie's rules. He just tried his best to be civil until she moved toward the bedroom. Then, when she bent over to pick up a shoe, he felt himself rising to the occasion, and he went to her for the only comfort she knew how to offer.

"I thought you'd never ask," Allison said with a smirk.

Well, maybe once for the road, Jon thought, and looked at his wrist. He still didn't have a watch, so he glanced at the clock on the other side of the bed. Shamefully, the reality of his father was erased by the drug of Allison's body and he used it hard, losing himself in an exhausting encounter. It blanked out everything, and for that, he was grateful. Shakespeare had gotten it wrong: It wasn't music that had the charms to soothe the savage breast. It was the horizontal two-step. But once he awoke from the postcoital drowse, the image of his father lifting his hat to scratch his bristled scalp came right back. Some Father's Day. And then he remembered that it was Sunday night and tomorrow he had Parsifal and the progress meeting to—My God! Tracie! He sat up as if powered by a 1K-megahertz chip. He was almost forty minutes late already.

He jumped from the bed and began to dress in a frenzy.

"Where are you going?" Allison asked in a sleepy voice.

"I . . . uh . . . I just remembered," he began. What could he say? I just remembered I forgot my friend? I just remembered I have to meet another woman? I just remembered I don't want to make love to you? "I . . . uh . . . left my clothes in the dryer," he told her lamely as he slid his right foot into his shoe and grabbed his sweater. He ran for the door.

"Wait!" Allison called out. "When will . . ."

He was jiggling with the lock and the chain that was across the door, so he couldn't hear what she'd said. Tracie would be enraged! He couldn't believe it. In seven years, he hadn't missed one time . . . nor had she. Well, except for his emergency appendectomy. He threw the dead bolt, turned the knob the other way, and finally got the door open.

"When will I see you again?" Allison asked from the bedroom door. She had the sheet wrapped loosely around her, one pink nipple just peeking over the top, her hair a tumbled blond sheet over her shoulders. Allison stopped and put her hands on her waist. "You're such a dick," she said.

Jon blinked, once, twice, then three full times as he let the words sink in. "I am?" he asked, his voice delighted with enthusiasm. She looked like a goddess. A goddess he had worshiped with his body. Jon shook his head. Amazing! Amazing!

"I'll call you," he said. Tracie was waiting; he really had to go. He was out the door, down the stairs, and out in the wet in a moment.

He was lucky. Unbelievably, a cab was passing. He hailed it. He was already damp, but he settled into the backseat. "Java, The Hut, on Canal," he told the driver. "Hurry!"

There was a clock on the dashboard. It was even later than he thought. What would he do if Tracie had already left? Well, he had left his bike in the alley back at Java, The Hut. He'd take it, bike over to her apartment, or, failing that, bike up and down the streets until he found her and apologized.

Somehow, he thought that might not work. Not because he wouldn't be able to find her, but because she wouldn't accept the apology. She'd probably been subjected to forty-six solid minutes of taunting from Molly, the Manchester Menace. He cringed, thinking of what Molly might say to Tracie if she had the opportunity to get her alone.

He had a feeling she might be enraged, and he wouldn't have been surprised if she'd torched Java, The Hut as well as anything else that annoyed her right now. When the cab slowed down near the coffee shop, Jon didn't wait for the car to come to a complete stop. He threw money on the front seat and thanked the driver as he jumped from the moving vehicle. He ran around the back of the taxi and flung open the door. He looked toward the table that he and Tracie always sat at. As he glanced around the room, he saw Laura in the kitchen doorway and Molly sitting down at a booth.

What was Laura doing here? Was Tracie so angry at him that she'd refused to come? Maybe he wasn't late; maybe he was being stood up by Tracie. Or, a best-case scenario, she was in the bathroom or checking up on Phil on the phone. He approached Molly, who was picking at a plate of scrambled eggs. He grabbed her arm. She looked up at him, her face expressionless, but he knew immediately what had happened.

"She was here, right?" he asked Molly, his heart dropping.

"Right," Molly said, and went back to her plate of scrambled eggs.

He couldn't believe it. He'd broken years of tradition. He felt sick to his stomach and more than a little frantic. "Molly, I'm a jerk and I know it," he admitted. "You know it. But please, do you know if she went to my house or back to hers?"

Molly shrugged. "Actually, I don't know," she told him. "She doesn't really confide in me."

Laura had ambled over from the kitchen. He turned to her. "Please, Laura," was all he said.

"I didn't see her go, but I'd guess she headed toward your place," Laura offered. "And she borrowed a knife," she added.

Jon didn't know if she was joking or not, but he didn't care. "I'm getting my bike," he told Molly, and turned and ran through the restaurant, literally jumping over backs of empty booths. He ran through the kitchen, almost upsetting a tray of scones. Outside the back door, his bike was leaning against the railing, where he had locked it up. He dropped the key in his haste and then fumbled with the padlock. When he finally got it off, he turned the bike around and pedaled down the wet cobblestones of the alley and out into the street. The rain hit him full then and he hunched his head against it as he turned toward his building.

It was a long, cold ride, and without his poncho, he was drenched to the skin long before he got home. But he wasn't cold. He was actually sweating, both from fear and exertion. He *had* to catch her before she left. When he pulled up to the front of his building, he was short of breath, but he had to manage the fucking stairs. So he galloped up them two at a time to get to Tracie faster. He was gasping as he opened the fire door to his hallway and his heart was thumping hard against his chest wall. It felt as if it skipped a beat when he saw the hallway was empty. She was gone, and if he could find her, she'd be even more furious. As he approached his door, he realized she was furious already. He saw the Post-it spectacular and, without reading it, spun around and ran down the stairs.

At the foot of the staircase, he grabbed his bicycle, cursed himself for not having a car, and maneuvered it through the doorway and back out into the rain.

He began hating everything about himself and his life. Why did he have to be born in Seattle and still live there, a place where it always rained? And why was he so stubborn? How come he had never bought a car? Adults have cars. And how could he be so stupid as to have forgotten his appointment with Tracie?

He always felt as if Tracie were an orphan. He was her family. Her mother was dead and her father was as good as. She had been waiting for him while he had been lying beside a naked stranger. In all the years and with all the boyfriends that Tracie had had, she had never—not once—skipped their Sunday appointment. What would he do if she hadn't gone home? Would she have gone to Phil's? Did he know Phil's exact address? He couldn't remember it, if he had ever known it.

The rain was dripping down his face, falling off his chin and onto his chest. The downpour had gotten more intense, and the visibility had worsened. He was only a block from her house. He pedaled harder and then saw the brake lights of a car only a few feet in front of him. He swerved to avoid it, realizing that it had pulled over to the curb because of the downpour. That was close, he thought. I'd better be more careful. He couldn't afford not to make it to Tracie's.

Just as he came around the corner of Tracie's street, he saw her car pulling into the parking space and he watched her get out. He threw his bike down. It splashed into a puddle, but he didn't care. He began to run toward her. "Tracie! Tracie!" he shouted, but either she didn't hear or she was purposely ignoring him.

Chapter 36

Tracie had run into her building, but she'd still gotten drenched. Now she shivered as she stood in front of her door, fumbling with her keys. She had to hurry. She'd heard Jon call out to her and she'd seen him out of the corner of her eye as she'd run into the lobby, but she didn't want to see him like this—or maybe ever. She just wanted to get into her place, lock the door behind her, crawl into bed, and never get out. But her hands were shaking, and Jon stepped off the elevator and came up behind her before she could get in.

"Tracie . . ." he said, but she ignored him and continued to try to get the door unlocked. Jon moved closer to her. He was even wetter than she was, but she would not turn around, even when she felt his chest pushing against her back. He reached out for her hand, but she slapped him away. How dare he touch her?

She got the door open and tried to push herself in, leaving him out in the hall, but he was too fast for her and managed to get his shoulder into the doorway. "Go away," Tracie said, still keeping her puffy red face averted. "Get out!"

"Tracie, you have every right to be angry, but you have to—"

"I don't have to do anything," Tracie said.

"But I—"

She turned to face him. What did she care? Let him see how bad she looked. He meant nothing to her. "Did you have your appendix out again?" she asked him as viciously as she could. "That would be the only acceptable excuse."

"Don't you think that's a little harsh?" he asked.

"No," she said, and tried to close the door on his shoulder.

"Ouch!" He sucked air in through his teeth and pushed the door open.

"Don't come in here," she warned him. "You're not welcome." She looked around behind her. Where were Laura and Phil when she needed them? "You hurt me. Really hurt me," Tracie said.

"I'm sorry. I never meant to," Jon said, trying to console her.

"Who was with you?" she asked. "Beth? Was it another pity fuck? Or was it Ruth? If you were Ruthless, it must have been Carole in from San Francisco." She turned her back on him and walked toward the sink. She was still hiccuping. A woman had no dignity when she was hiccuping. "Oh, or maybe you were doing Enid. I'm sure it was very aerobic." She hiccuped again, filled a glass with water at the sink, and was about to gulp it down, when he answered her.

"It was Allison, actually," he said, "but I saw my—" Before she could even think about it, she had thrown the water across the kitchen and into his already-drenched face. Jon choked and put a hand up as if warding off a blow. They both stood there, frozen for a moment. "I deserve that," he said. "I know I've behaved badly. But don't act as if you have no part in it."

"Oh, go ahead and blame me," she said. "Next, you'll rape someone and tell them that they asked for it." He grabbed her by the shoulders. "Let go of me," she said as she tried to pull away.

"Not until you talk to me. Not until you calm down and listen and talk to me."

"Go talk to Allison," Tracie spat out at him. She tried to pull away, but his hands were too strong. She just couldn't bear it. She was so disappointed, and so angry, and so ashamed that she turned her head away, covered her face, and began to cry.

Then Jon softened his grip and cradled her in his arms and—at last—as if he had been waiting for years to do it, he kissed her gently and then wildly, passionately. At first, momentarily shocked, Tracie struggled, but then she kissed him back. It was heaven. It was . . . everything. She began to shiver. Jon left her mouth and kissed her face, then licked the tears that still clung to her lashes. His own lashes were wet with rain, and at last she felt them against her cheek and brushing her lips and her brow. Then he found her mouth again with his own.

Her shivering increased and she couldn't tell if it was from the cold or the heat. His wet clothes were pressed against hers, but she could feel the heat of his body through them. She couldn't think, only feel, and this felt so natural, and at the same time so extraordinary, so unexpected Then anything resembling thought was completely gone. "You're cold," he said, holding her face in both his hands. "Don't you know enough to come in out of the rain?"

"I don't know anything," she whispered, and nestled her head against his chest. She was surprised but grateful when he picked her up, carried her to the bedroom, and took off her wet jacket and shirt. Tenderly, he wrapped the coverlet around her shoulders, "You're shaking, too," she said.

"Not from the cold," he told her.

"Come here," she said, and he took off all of his wet clothes, right down to his shorts, and climbed into bed next to her. She wrapped her arms around him and for a moment they lay still under the blanket. She could feel his hipbone against her thigh. His breathing was shallow; then she realized it matched her own. As if on cue, as if the moment was preordained, they turned toward each other. She felt him hard against her and shivered again.

"Are you still cold?" he asked, and in answer, she kissed him.

* * *

Tracie awoke, the afterglow of wonderful sex still surrounding her like an aura. She turned her head on the pillow. Jon was awake beside her, looking at her face with love and wonder. "You are so beautiful," he told her.

"Oh, come on. I—"

He covered her mouth with his hand. "You are so beautiful. So beautiful," he repeated, and though she had thought she didn't have any tears left in her, they filled her eyes again. With wonder, he ran his hand from a rib to her waist and then around the swell of her hip. "You're so . . . beautiful," he said. "Your breasts are perfect, so soft, so vulnerable. They make me think of new puppies—blind, but so alive and responsive."

"Puppies!" She laughed. "Where did you get that idea?"

"I don't know. My mother said I should get a dog." They both laughed; then he kissed her again, long and hard. She pulled away.

"Jon, I've been really stupid."

"You're adorable." He said it in a way she had been hungry to hear all her life.

But she had to tell him. She had to apologize for how ridiculous she'd been. How blind and foolish "No. No. I didn't know what I wanted. Molly told me . . . scrambled eggs. . . ." Oh, how could she explain? "I just didn't see—"

Jon kissed her. It was another perfect kiss. Then he looked at her. "Did you major in cute at school? Or do you still take lessons?" he asked. "Did you know I love your earlobes? I've always loved them." He bit one gently and she shivered. "They're adorable."

He stretched out, luxuriating in the bed. "I feel like we're the only two people in the world. Like Adam and Eve on a raft." He paused and lifted himself up on one elbow. "Will you let me eat poached eggs now?"

"Right this minute?" Tracie asked. She thought she was pretty cute, but he was gorgeous.

"Well, not right this minute," Jon said. "There's something else I want to eat first."

"Again?" she asked, and hugged him. She was so happy, her chest hurt. The strangest thought flitted into her head. She wanted to die right then so that she would always be this happy. "You can eat anything you like," she told Jon. "Just promise you'll never leave me." She looked deep into his eyes.

Very seriously, Jon looked back at her. "I have to leave you," he said. "I have to pee."

She laughed, relieved. "Okay, but just this once. And hurry."

Jon got up and walked past her desk. He crossed to the bathroom, but on his way, he noticed all the Polaroids Tracie had tacked up. They were arranged in a before-and-after format. Tracie's eyes opened wide. She sat up. Oh my God! Did I ever begin to tell him . . . to ask him . . . Her mind raced to everything she had there, every stupid, shallow observation, every silly adjective, and, worst of all, the bet. She closed her eyes and made a futile prayer that he would just turn and keep heading to the bathroom, but he didn't. He read a few of the Post-its. Then he saw the printout of the article. Again, she breathed a silent prayer that he wouldn't pick it up, but he did. His face dropped.

Tracie couldn't believe that she could go from such total joy to such complete misery in less than a minute. She wanted to cry out, to tell Jon to drop the article, to ignore it. Oh, she knew she should have told him about it so long ago.

Jon's face had gone white and he put the draft back down on her desk. He walked over to the damp pile of clothes beside the bed and began to fumble with his shorts, then his jeans.

"Jon, don't," she said stupidly.

"I have to go," he told her, his voice dead. Then he looked up at her for the first time since he'd seen the snapshots. "I don't like to stay over," he said. "I like to sleep alone."

She recognized the words she had taught him. She jumped up, wrapped the sheet around herself, and stood up. "Are you using the bad-boy treatment on *me*?" she asked. Then it occurred to her that maybe all of this—standing her up, following her, seducing her—

could have just been an elaborate part of his new persona. God, was that it? Had all of this been just an act, a taste of her own medicine? She began to shiver again. "What am I? Just another notch on your floppy disc?" she asked him.

He was already pulling his shirt on. "And what am I? Your chance at being the next Anna Quindlen?" Jon snapped at her. He thrust his arms into his jacket, snatched up the article, and threw it in front of her. "You did this to me so you could get a big byline?" he asked.

"Of course not. I did it because you asked me." How could he think that? And even if part of it was true, hadn't what they just shared transcended all that went before? "I began the article because—"

Jon turned his back on Tracie and walked out of the bedroom. She ran behind him, clutching the sheet around her. "Jon! Wait."

He was at the door, but he turned to her. "I can't believe it. I'm a photo op. A story? 'A nerd.' That's how you saw me? 'A corporate weenie'? Very complimentary."

"Jon, once I began writing it, I knew I could never submit the thing."

"But this is the way you once saw me," Jon said, looking at one of the photos he still clutched in his hand. He shook his head, crushed the photo, and threw it onto the floor. "You know, I was a little afraid when we made love that you might be doing it for the wrong reason. But until now, I never thought I was just a career opportunity." He smiled, but it was a mean smile, one she had never seen. "What was this going to be? The climax of the piece?"

"Jon, I—"

He shook his head. "You say you love me, but you mocked me and used me in this stupid newspaper piece. You and Marcus must have had some good laughs over this. How about Beth—was she in on it? And Laura? Did she see it? Did you and Phil read it in bed together?"

"Jon, when I started, I thought it was a good idea. I put a lot of you and a lot of my love for you into it. And it's good. But I'll just tear it up. I always meant to ask your permission, and then, somehow, it all got too sensitive and—"

"Sensitive! Ha, that's a laugh," he said. "There will be a special on *Nightline* the day you become sensitive. You're the one who taught me to hurt people," he reminded her. "You're the one who taught me the fun of being Mr. If-I-Tell-You-a-Lie-I-Can-Fuck-You-and-Forget-You. Sensitive?"

"Forget the piece."

"Forget *you*!" He turned to go.

"Wait! Five minutes ago, you promised never to leave me. You've been my friend for seven years. I told you the article was a mistake. I was going to dump it. But you treat me like this now?"

Jon moved to the door. "Hey, it's how you like to be treated. Didn't you teach me that? All the tricks. Women seek pain, right? They want to be treated badly. I'm a good student, even if you didn't let *me* take notes."

"Please. Jon, I love you."

"What does love mean to you? Betrayal? Forget this. This is . . . nothing." He opened the door, then turned back to face her. "Are you going to tell Phil about this?"

"About what? Nothing happened, right?"

Jon turned and closed the door behind him. Tracie could only manage to wait until he'd safely gotten out of range before she burst into sobs.

Chapter 37

Tracie hadn't slept all night, but she looked as if she hadn't slept for a week. She'd been caught coming in late—real late—and she hadn't even been able to duck her head in the traditional gesture of apology. So, an hour or so later when Marcus called her into his office, she knew the news wouldn't be good. She'd also heard from Beth, who'd heard from Sara, who'd overheard Allison talking to Marcus, that he was furious because Allison had dropped him. That wouldn't sweeten his mood. He was such an ass.

But as ridiculous as Marcus and his romantic life was, hers was worse, and she knew she was in no position to judge. Molly had been right about everything: She was a fool, and it was depressing to think of how she'd hurt Jon, been hurt by him, ruined the most important friendship she had, as well as all chances for true love.

Because she did love Jon. And it wasn't because he looked good now, or that she'd finally discovered what a thoughtful and gifted lover he was. It was because she'd always loved him. She had simply been too stupid to know that she did. And for that, she'd be punished, probably for the rest of her life. She'd called Jon more than a dozen times, in an imitation of Beth. The irony wasn't lost on her.

Jon hadn't called her back and wouldn't take her calls at the office. She wasn't sure that she could get him to forgive her.

Now, however, she had to see Marcus and probably get another lousy assignment. Marcus sat at his desk with his sleeves rolled up. He looked like he was in the middle of some major editing job. His blue pencil had already slashed veins and arteries on whatever story corpse he was working on. He was slashing so energetically, he even had a streak of blue along the side of his mouth, as if he might have been editing what he said, though Tracie knew better than to believe that.

She looked at him and suddenly felt that she couldn't bear one more snotty remark, one more insult. She took a single step into the room. "Yes?" she asked.

"That Father's Day article was pretty good," Marcus admitted. "With Allison's help," he added. She just stood there. It's odd, Tracie thought; once the worst thing has happened, other things that frightened you before no longer have any power. She remembered feeling this way just once before, after her mother died. The two girls who used to tease her mercilessly, her teacher, who frightened her, and even the Rottweiler at the end of her block in Encino had no longer held any terror for her at all. Let them all do their worst; she didn't care. In a way, the desolation then had been peaceful, just as it was now. She looked at Marcus calmly. There wasn't anything he couldn't do to her.

"Yup. Couldn't have done it without her. But it's too bad it was cut down so much," she told him calmly. "Maybe on my next assignments, they can be longer. But just try not to make them holiday pieces."

"That's a deal," he said rather affably. He picked up the papers he was working on and tossed them onto the credenza. "Sit down," he said.

"No thanks," she told him, and leaned against the doorway. There was a time when she would have done that to be insolent, but now she just didn't care.

"Well, I'm going to run the nerd makeover. It's actually pretty funny," he said. "I thought we might also run a sidebar with Ted Waite; Steve Balmer, the new head of Microsoft; and maybe Marc Grayson—you know, the head of Netscape. And maybe Kevin Mitnick, the hacker that just got out of jail. I thought we'd show him in his orange jumpsuit as a before and then I'd have the photo department do a montage on all of them after. Mitnick has got to find some girl to support him, since they won't even let him work at a McDonald's. Poor bastard. Live by the computer, die by the computer."

At that moment, Tracie wished Marcus would die by his computer. Her equilibrium, her dead calmness, had disappeared as he spoke. Jon might never forgive her for what she had done, but he'd certainly kill her or himself if the article was published. "You can't run the article," she said.

"Look," he told her, "I know all about your little talks with *Seattle Magazine*. But you can't publish there if I put in a first claim. We have the option, and I'm sure you did this on company time."

"Marcus, you can't publish it," she repeated.

He picked up the pile of papers off the credenza and waved them at her. "After all the time you put into that? And the time *I* put into it? It's the only good thing you've done."

"Marcus, you can't run it. . . ." How could she explain? Why would she explain to an idiot like him? "It . . . it will hurt people," she said.

"Oh. Well," he intoned, deeply sarcastic. "Well, if it will hurt people . . ."

She looked at him and knew that she couldn't stand him for one more minute. He was an egotistical, self-important, bullying hack and she was sick and tired of it.

"Look, if you run it, I quit," she told him.

"Really?" Marcus said with that same sophomoric tone. "I have a better idea. You're fired."

"Great," she told him. Her calmness returned. Sometimes complete desolation, a totally empty landscape, was best. "I'll go clear out my desk," she said.

To any observer, it would have been clear from the detritus on the bed that Tracie had been lying there for several days. There were the remains of a take-out pizza, empty ice-cream containers, half-full cereal boxes, magazines, rumpled newspapers, and books. She couldn't read much. Mostly, she cried, slept, and watched *Ricki Lake*. Sometimes she watched *Jerry Springer*, but it made it her feel worse about herself. Today, Ricki had brothers and sisters who slept with each other and who wanted the world to recognize their love. Either the show or the mud-pie ice cream she had eaten along with some Ritz crackers was making her queasy. So she hit the remote, turned on her side, and pulled a blanket up over her head. The phone rang and she listened to see who was leaving a message, but it wasn't Jon, so she didn't take the call.

She must have dozed for a while, but she woke when she heard the rattle of her lock. By the time she came out from under the blankets, Laura had entered the bedroom and was looking around. "Wow. Worse than I thought. I bought everything you asked for but the cookie-dough ice cream. That was too decadent."

"Yours is not to reason why, yours is but to shop and die," Tracie said.

Laura sat down at the foot of the bed, got up to remove a plate with toast crusts, and then sat down again. "You're the one who looks like you're going to die. Look, I know you feel really bad. Maybe you even fucked things up permanently with Jon, though I think you two may work it out," she told Tracie. Tracie merely groaned. "Still, you have to get out of bed eventually," Laura said.

"No I don't," Tracie contradicted. "I have no job, so I'm not going to the office. And I'm not going to the gym ever again. It'll take at least two years before I need another haircut. This is it."

Laura looked into the bag of groceries, pulled out a package of

Goldfish, and opened them, popping a handful into her mouth and passing the rest to Tracie. "But what will happen to you?" she asked.

"As long as there's pizza delivery and cash to pay for it, I've hit the mattress and I'm staying right here," Tracie declared. "I've ruined my life. Molly was right. I'm such a fool."

Laura got up, went over to the dresser, and took bread, cream cheese, and a jar of Welch's grape jelly decorated with the Spirits of Mickey Mouse from the bag. Laura opened both spreads, laid out the bread, and, using her finger as a knife, began to make two sandwiches. "Molly's a wise woman. And a nice boss." She handed a sandwich to Tracie.

"Ummm." The soft white bread, the creamy cheese, and the sweetness of the jelly comforted her. Before she swallowed, she pulled herself up into a sitting position. She wanted to die, but not the way Mama Cass had.

Laura sat down beside her and took a bite of her own sandwich. "So what did Molly say?"

Tracie dripped a glob of jelly onto the blanket, smeared it up with her forefinger, then licked it. "She told me I was wasting my time with idiots, when Jon loved me. Jon was right there in front of me all the time. And I couldn't appreciate him." She took another bite of the sandwich. If she kept focused on her regret that soon it was going to be gone, she couldn't think about her regrets over Jon. "Why do women go for bad boys?" Tracie asked Laura. "Why do we make ourselves suffer when there are nice men around? Why don't we see them?"

Laura shrugged. "Because God is a sadist?" Laura asked, getting up to make another pair of sandwiches.

Tracie ignored her flippancy. "Why did you think you loved Peter and I thought I loved Phil and Beth thought Marcus was worth obsessing over?"

Laura handed her another sandwich, sat back on the bed, and crossed her legs. "I figure it's just one of nature's ugly little jokes on women. A phase we have to go through, like menopause or bloating."

She took a bite of her second sandwich. "The worst irony is that in about five years, we're going to start looking around for nice guys to marry. And all the ones we blew off in high school and college and in our early dating years will be taken—you know, the nerds like Bill Gates and Steven Spielberg and Woody Allen. The guys who couldn't get laid for two decades and now get to sleep with movie stars and models because they're so smart and powerful."

Tracie threw herself back down onto her rumpled pillows and let her cream cheese and jelly sandwich rest on her chest. "I've messed up my whole life. I'll die miserable and alone."

Laura shrugged. "What about Phil? You don't have to be alone. You could probably stay with Phil, even if he is unpublished, unemployed, and has an unrealistic sense of his self-worth."

Tracie listened to Phil's description. "Wait, I think I'm falling in love with him all over again." She paused for a moment and then shook her head. "Phil! He's bored me for a long time. I just didn't notice."

"Oh, I don't know," Laura said. "He's not so bad. I kinda—"

Tracie interrupted her by sitting up. The two sandwich halves flew down the length of the bed and hit Laura's arm, flopping onto the blanket again. "You know what really bothers me? I can't believe I didn't notice Jon until I dolled him up and got all the other girls interested." She shook her head. "I didn't see who he was until I ruined him."

Laura picked up the two sandwich halves and handed them to Tracie, who shook her head. If she ate anything else, she'd vomit, and since she wasn't going to get out of bed, she didn't like to think of the consequences. "I love him, but I deserve to be alone here the rest of my life." She flopped back down. "Believe me, it will be better for the world this way," she said, staring up at the ceiling.

"Well, look on the bright side," Laura said cheerfully. "You've finally realized you love him. I've known it for at least a year."

"Great, be like that. Be the smart one. If you had told me that then, I could have had him. Now I have to get in line behind Allison, Beth, Samantha, Enid, and Ruth."

"Wow!" said Laura. "They're all hooked, huh? It's a good thing he never slept with me." She paused for a moment, as if considering whether or not she should say what she had on her mind. As always, she decided against discretion. "Was he as good in bed as Beth said he was?"

"Better." Tracie groaned, began to cry, and pulled the blankets over her head. A few minutes later, she controlled herself and wiped her eyes and nose on the blanket, then looked out from under it. Laura still sat at the side of the bed.

"Tracie, I don't think this is healthy," she said in what had to have been a whopper of an understatement. "Are you sure it's over with Jon? You're never coming out of your apartment again?" she asked.

Tracie nodded. "This is not a negotiation, Laura. I've taken myself hostage and nobody gets out of this place alive."

Laura nodded and shrugged. "Then it won't bother you that something else really bad has happened. Something worse than your fight with Jon."

"What? What could possibly be worse than this?" Tracie asked.

"The article ran."

Tracie jumped up as if hit with an electrical current. "Get out! It didn't!" she said. "Marcus fired me, but he wouldn't—"

Laura took the newspaper out of the paper bag and threw it on the bed. "It did. And he would." She grabbed the paper and began riffling through it. "Page one of the Living section," Laura told her.

Tracie got to it, surveyed the damage, and moaned. The article took up the whole front page, and it continued on the third and fourth pages. It also carried the ridiculous makeovers of the hacker and the high-tech CEOs. Tracie moaned again. "Oh God. I'll never make up with Jon now. He'll never speak to me. Fuck Marcus! That lying scumball." She began to scan the piece. "Oh no. The best man on the planet, and I've made a laughingstock of him."

Just then, Tracie heard the door locks as they started to be released one by one. For a minute, she thought it was Jon, then realized who it had to be. "Oh God! Phil's here." Tracie heard the last lock release; then the door opened and Phil's footsteps crossed the living room.

He entered the bedroom. But he was a different Phil. He looked like the subject of some makeover from hell. He'd had his hair cut and his act was cleaned up significantly, but in all the wrong ways. He still wore jeans, but he had a lamé sports jacket on. He carried a briefcase, as well. He approached the bed, yet he didn't notice Tracie's condition or the junk all over. He just swept a spot clear and sat down next to her. Tracie was too exhausted to comment. Laura, however, did a double take. "Phil, is that you?" she asked.

"Hi, Laura," he said cheerfully. "Hey, Trace, notice anything different?"

"You got a haircut?" she asked. "Yours is too short, too."

He smiled. "You'll get used to it. And that's not the only change. I got a job."

Laura stood up. "Hey, guys. I'd better go. I've got the evening shift at Java, The Hut. Trace, call me later." She reached down and rubbed Tracie's foot, then left the room.

Alone in a dirty bed with Phil, Tracie felt unbelievably claustrophobic.

Phil smiled at her, as if she looked as pretty as a picture with her butchered, greasy hair, her oldest nightgown, and the dirty coverlet. "Tracie, you won the bet," he said. "I saw the article. And I'm ready to be committed."

"We look like we both are," was all Tracie could manage to say.

"Great. You got me. Fair and square. I got my stuff packed to come here."

Tracie groaned and rolled over in bed. "That's all right, Phil. The bet idea was stupid. You shouldn't play with people's lives to win a bet."

"Well, stupid or not, I'm ready to move in," Phil said.

Tracie didn't respond. Her life was a nightmare. She just lay under the covers, promising herself she would never move or speak again.

"Hey. You sick or something?" Phil asked. Tracie knew he was self-involved, but she'd never thought he was an imbecile until now. Phil pulled the blankets down from her head, and though she tried to catch at them, he was too fast for her. He reached into his briefcase and took out a paper bag and a black velvet jewelry box. He handed it to Tracie. "This will make you feel better."

Tracie rolled her eyes. "Phil, I gave up farm cakes and I don't need another guitar pick right now."

"It's not a guitar pick," he promised. "Open the box." Tracie did. There was a tiny diamond in a traditional engagement setting. She tried not to let her jaw drop. No wonder Phil had never been able to succeed as a bass player. He had the worst timing in the world.

"Marry me, Tracie," Phil said. "I love you."

Tracie looked at the ring, then back at Phil, and burst into tears. She was so frustrated with her own stupidity that if she could have, she would have torn her own head off.

Lovingly, Phil took Tracie in his arms. "Oh, baby. I know. I love you, too," he told her. "I'm sorry I put you through such hell. I guess I just had to grow up a little. You know, start thinking of other people." Tracie sobbed louder. He held her tighter. "It's okay," he said. But of course it wasn't. "Thanks for putting up with me and going the distance." He patted her back. Tracie hated to be patted.

"You know, Laura helped me think this through. I've set new priorities, Tracie, and you're my number one." She sobbed harder, but he didn't seem to notice.

"Your article was really good. You're better than Emma Quindlen."

"Anna," Tracie sobbed, dangerously out of control.

Phil looked at her with concern. "Honey, calm down. You got to try on the ring."

She couldn't. She'd rather cut off her hand. The man that she'd thought she desired for so long, the man that she'd tricked herself into thinking she cared about was not only ridiculous but also a stranger to her. "I . . . I . . ." She tried to stop crying, wiped her eyes and her nose with her fingers, and looked at him. "Phil, do you think my earlobes are adorable?"

He shrugged. "I don't know. I never noticed."

Tracie began to wail again. Phil stood up, reached over to her bureau, and handed her a Kleenex. Then he turned his back to the bed and took off his sports jacket. He laid it carefully on the chair beside the bed, then patted it as if it were a good dog. "I got to take care of this baby," he said. "I think it was the jacket that got me the job."

"What job?" Tracie managed to ask.

Phil turned back to her, and for the first time, she saw the T-shirt he'd been wearing under the jacket. It had a huge Micro/Con logo on it. Wordlessly, she pointed at it and began to scramble off the bed in horror. "What? How?" she managed to say. "Why . . . are you . . ."

Phil looked proudly down at his chest. "Oh, yeah," he told her. "They didn't just give me the job. They gave me the T-shirt and a thousand dollars' worth of stock. Isn't that neat?"

Chapter 38

Jon was sweating. He was moving as fast as he possibly could. The last time he'd felt this kind of panic was when he was being chased by the neighborhood dog, notorious for biting anyone that got within fifty yards of his owner's yard. But this time, Jon was trying to escape himself. He had managed to get into the Micro/Con building undetected early enough that morning and get himself set up on the treadmill in the workout room. Now, however, people were starting to come in, and he knew it wasn't his imagination—he was the focus of everyone in the room. Usually, people would stare blankly while they pedaled a bike, pulled on the weight bars of the bench press equipment, and walked on the treadmills. But this morning, it was the stare of wonderment, of recognition, of celebrity. That's what happens when your best friend splashes you all over a section of the local newspaper, he thought.

He couldn't believe that Tracie had been so spiteful as to publish the article because of their fight. But he guessed he'd just never really known her. He'd been so upset, he'd had to spend the night at his mother's, and that hadn't been easy, either. She hadn't approved of the article, but she'd kept urging Jon, "Call Tracie. I don't know why this all happened, but I do know that a friendship like yours and Tracie's shouldn't end like this. Call her." Then she'd talked a lot about forgiveness, and visiting his dad in the hospital. Jon had been upset enough to think—but not say—that it was a lot easier to forgive someone who had ruined her life than it was to forgive someone who had ruined his.

He still hadn't actually taken in his visit with his father. After he'd gotten over his pity, he thought he was angry at Chuck, too. What was this Mother's Day and Father's Day about anyway? Why wasn't there a children's day? Chuck had just used the holiday as a wedge, as a way to get Jon to see him without having to actually apologize directly for all of his childishness and thoughtlessness over the years. It was easy enough for his mother to preach forgiveness: Grandpa had been a really good father and a really nice guy. He'd filled in for Chuck more times than Jon liked to remember. Next Father's Day, Jon decided, he was going to go to his grandpa's grave and thank him. Maybe, that is, if he didn't die of embarrassment between now and then.

Jon tried to avert his eyes from the other employees who had come in to work out—or to gawk at him—but it wasn't an easy thing to do. What he wanted so desperately to do was to hit the stop button, jump off the rubber track, and tell them exactly what Tracie had done to him. How she had violated him. How she had exposed him as the town clown. How she had made him the Micro/Con mascot. But Jon opted for jogging on the treadmill. His head was pounding with every step he took. How could she do this to me? he thought. He couldn't remember having this feeling of pain in his chest since his father left him and his mother so long ago. Sure he had felt badly for all the other women his father had been with and dumped, but this hurt was something that Jon couldn't get past.

He wiped the beads of sweat from his forehead before they could roll into his eyes and sting. Though that wouldn't be so bad, he thought. Then my vision would be impaired and I couldn't see everyone looking at me. He wondered if the hurt he felt was what he had inflicted on all the women he had slept with since this whole transformation started. Especially Beth—she was the most persistent of all of them. Well, he was definitely his father's son, thanks to Miss Higgins.

Why had Tracie decided to sleep with him only after he had been with all the others? Was she jealous of them? Had she wanted him all this time? Or did she want to see if he was doing the sex thing right and take notes on that, too? Jon couldn't take the pressure of the room any longer, so he stepped off the treadmill and left the gym. He used his towel as a shield, pretending to wipe down his wet face and neck.

At least the changing room was empty and he was given a moment to gain his composure before having to step out into the hallway. He had managed to get halfway down the hall on his way to his office, when he was met by Samantha. Jon almost wished for the time when it was only a daydream to have her come up to him. But what she did to him was beyond even his own wildest dreams. "You rotten little bastard!" Sam spat in his face, and before Jon could respond, she had slapped him across the face.

Great, if all the other women at Micro/Con had this reaction, he would be black and blue by noon. He put his hand up to his face and continued down the hall. He couldn't help but look into the doorways of the offices along the way. Luckily, most were empty, so he was fortunate enough to get down to the main room, where all the cubicles were located in his department. All that came to his mind was the possibility of a reenactment of the scene in *Jerry Maguire* when Tom Cruise goes to leave his job and everyone stands up and watches him go to the elevator. If only he were leaving, Jon thought. He thought that he could stand up to them and say that the article Tracie had written for the paper was not his mission statement, that he'd had nothing to do with it. Then everyone would go back to what they were doing and never give any of it another thought. He stopped at the entrance to the big room. Everyone was working away and no one really looked up at him; they were doing what they usually did every morning when he came into his office. Could be worse, he thought as he entered his office.

He decided he'd shut the door on the rest of his staff today. That way, anyone wanting entry would have to be announced first. As he turned from the door to head to his desk, he was taken aback by Carole, who had perched herself on a beanbag chair.

"Good morning, Mr. Bad Boy," she said with a sheepish grin on her face. "You're the talk of the commissary today."

Jesus! He didn't need this, not after all he'd been through already. "Good morning," he said quietly, and went to sit in his chair. "Can I help you with something?"

"I'm going home today and I wanted to say it's been a pleasure having met the 'Sexless Savant' of Seattle." She grinned again.

"I didn't have—" he began, but she got up from the chair and put her finger up to her mouth to signal him to be quiet.

"You don't have to explain anything to me, Jonny," she said in a snotty voice. "A boy's gotta do what a boy's gotta do. You'll manage." Then she stepped closer to his desk and pointed to a memo. "Based on what this says, you should have spent a lot more time on Parsifal than on me and all the others."

Jon looked down at the paper. Shit! It was from Dave, his division supervisor. He scanned the words and the word *failed* was in bold capitals in the second paragraph. He pushed his chair back from the desk and Carole went to the door. "Good luck," she said. "Maybe we'll meet at Carousel B again sometime."

Finally, his day was over. Jon walked out of the office building and headed toward his bike. Tracie stood beside it, her hand on the seat. When he saw her, he stopped for a moment, then turned back toward the Micro/Con entrance and began to walk away. "Jon, please,"

Tracie called, and came up beside him. "Just let me explain and apologize."

He shook his head. "I didn't know you were a liar."

"Jon, I swear. I was going to ask your permission before I—"

"Permission to humiliate me?" he asked, interrupting her. "I don't think I would have granted that, even for you."

"Listen! Marcus had rejected the idea months ago. I was—"

"But when he changed his mind, you stepped up to the plate, huh?"

"Marcus promised he wouldn't run it. . . ."

"Who do you think you are?" he asked. "*Who?* What gives you the right to play God?" He couldn't believe how callous she had been, how she had used him as a pawn to get closer to Phil. For a moment, his anger rose so high, he could understand how men hit women. "Interfering with people's lives. Changing them altogether."

"But you asked me to," she reminded him.

That was true. What had he been thinking of? Jon thought of his father and all that he had put his mother and stepmothers through, as well as the pain he had caused. Jon shook his head to snap himself out of his reverie.

"You know," Jon said to Tracie, "maybe Molly is right. For a smart girl, you're really dumb. Maybe I was asking you something different. Maybe I was asking you a more important question than why I got blown off by Samantha."

"What? What were you asking me?" she demanded.

Jon turned his back on her and walked away. He wanted her to melt, to disappear. Instead, she followed him. Christ! He didn't need anyone watching more drama in his life. But Jon couldn't keep silent. "After being my best friend for more than seven years, maybe you should have known what I was asking. And why," he spat out at her.

"If you wanted me, why didn't you say so? Why didn't you tell me, or make a move on me?" she demanded. "I'm not a mind reader."

The unfairness of that stung him. "Why should I? So I could hear that you loved me but you just didn't love me in 'that way'?" He felt a pain and a rage he hadn't known was there. "Do you know how insulting that is? Do you think I needed to hear that said aloud by you?" he asked. "You were smart enough to pull off this charade so that women would fall for me. You were smart enough to turn me into a newer, better version of my dad. You were smart enough to write an article that makes me look like the jerk I am. But you're not smart enough to know about subtext? What kind of writer are you?"

Now tears were actually rolling down her cheeks, the cheeks he'd covered with kisses. "Jon, I love you. I made love to you. . . ."

"But not until you changed me. Not until half of the women in Seattle had slept with me first." He finally got his fucking bike chain. Tracie came up beside Jon and gently touched his arm. He pulled away from her so violently that she stepped back. "I wasn't good enough for you before. You didn't notice me, or you took me for granted or . . . something. Anyway, you didn't want to make love to me then."

Tracie put her head down and her hands up to her head. He wouldn't let himself care how pathetic she looked. He'd seen her look this sad over morons she'd dated once. When she did answer, it was a whisper. "I think I always did want to make love to you. You were the only one who really knew me, Jon. But I was stupid. And I think I was afraid. Jon, do you know how much our night together meant to me? Do you know how much I loved it, how much I love you?" she asked.

Jon turned to her. "And you weren't afraid of Phil?" he asked. Tracie raised her head and gave him a guilty look. And then his hope was smashed, because he knew her well enough to know she'd done something very wrong. Despite his accusation, she wasn't a liar. Maybe the article had been a mistake. So what was it that she had now disclosed with that look? What had she done in the last twenty-four hours that she shouldn't have? . . . "Who did you sleep with last night, Tracie?" he asked.

Tracie lowered her gaze, but not before he saw her blush. Now he knew he was right. "Phil, but I . . . but he had just . . . we didn't . . ." she stammered.

He didn't want to hear another word. He actually got sick to his stomach and thought he might throw up right there on the macadam. "I was alone, Tracie. And that's what I'd like to be now," Jon said abruptly, then mounted his bike and rode off.

Chapter 39

Jon's mother kept giving him two pieces of useless advice. "Call Tracie, Jonathan," she said. "And get yourself a dog. A nice golden retriever maybe."

"I don't want to call her. I want her to be struck by lightning," he muttered, his mouth full.

"Why, Jonathan Delano!" she exclaimed, but then she backed off.

The problem was that he couldn't find anything that assuaged the pain. He wasn't so humiliated anymore—people were such jerks that having his picture in the paper had made him a celebrity on campus and some geeks had taken it seriously enough to try to emulate his "style." He put an end to that by stopping at the Micro/Con shop on campus and going back to his usual T-shirts and khakis. The hell with the pants thing.

But he couldn't seem to snap out of the pain he was in. One night, in total desperation, he picked up the phone. But he didn't call Tracie. He called Allison.

She seemed delighted to hear from him when he called. He'd tried not to—for both of their sakes—but in the end, he couldn't face another long night alone. By the time he picked up the phone, it was too late even to pretend to meet for dinner, so Jon asked if she wanted to join him for a drink, which he guessed was Bad Boy Talk for wanting to fuck. Or maybe Bad Boy Talk for wanting to fuck was asking her if she wanted to fuck. He wasn't sure. But he knew he needed a drink or two, or six, and some company.

He met her at Rico's, and he had already had a couple of shots of Southern Comfort before she got there. First, he'd asked for Dewar's and it was harsh, but now he was drinking in memory of his father—even if his father wasn't dead yet. Jon couldn't understand how anyone could like the taste, but after three drinks, he had to admit there was a certain logic to his father's drug of choice. It tasted like paint remover, but it was effective. He wasn't drunk, though. Tracie's betrayal and the bet she'd made with Phil would take at least a bottle of Southern Comfort—or paint remover itself—to erase.

He stared into his glass and wondered if he'd ever known her. He couldn't believe the Tracie he knew would make love to him the way she had when all along she was angling to get Phil to move in with her.

Phil! Jon ordered another drink, and the bartender was only too happy to oblige. Jon wanted to put the cold glass up against his forehead, but he took a sip instead. Maybe if Tracie's choice hadn't been Phil, he could have lived with it. Maybe. But Phil was a true idiot, pretentious and self-involved and—Hey, let's face it, he thought—not too smart. Jon had already vowed that he'd never see Tracie again, but earlier that day, he could swear he'd seen Phil walking across the Micro/Con campus. It couldn't have been true, but if he did see him anytime soon, Jon promised himself he'd do everything he could to beat the living crap out of the stupid bastard.

Just when he felt drunk enough to want to get drunker, he looked up from the bottom of his Southern Comfort glass and saw Allison walking along the bar toward him. All of the men turned their heads to follow her progress. She was beautiful; he knew that. Prettier than

Tracie. Definitely prettier than Tracie, he repeated to himself. Taller, and her breasts were bigger.

Every man at the bar wanted a chance to touch those breasts, but he was the only one who would be able to tonight. That is, if he didn't drink too much more Southern Comfort.

"Hi," she said, draping one arm around his shoulder. Every other guy, all the Phils and all the losers, tasted disappointment along with their booze. He knew what that felt like. The problem was, he didn't care that he'd triumphed over all of them.

"What's your poison?" he asked her, just the way his dad did. She ordered an Absolut on the rocks, and Jon hoped she wouldn't drink too much, because she had to drive them both to his place, manage to get up the stairs with him, take off her clothes and then his. Sorry, boys, he almost said aloud. He'd take this one home. Fuck Tracie.

For a minute, he thought about fucking Tracie. He closed his eyes, not because he wanted to make the memory more vivid but because he wanted to push it away. He would sleep with Allison; he would rub his body against hers and it would feel good to both of them, and he hoped that on the other side of Seattle, where Phil and Tracie were rubbing their bodies together, she'd be thinking of him.

Allison moaned and Jon moved his hand to her shoulders, lifting himself up so that he could improve his thrust into her. "Oh, Jonny," she moaned again. He stopped, and then after a moment, when he didn't continue, she opened her eyes.

"Not Jonny," he said. "My name is Jon," but he'd already lost his erection and his desire to pump himself into her a second time. The first one had been enough, anyway: It had been an anger fuck, a fuck for the boys at the bar, all sound and fury, signifying nothing. In his bitterness and anger, it was pleasurable in a sickening way. The worst part was that she seemed to have liked it, too. He rolled off of her.

He was ashamed of himself. He was worse than his father—his father didn't, as far as he knew, sleep with women to punish them. He couldn't move from the bed, and it wasn't sexual exhaustion that kept him there.

Allison walked around his apartment as he lay there. Now he understood the wisdom of Tracie's rule to go to the woman's place. Could he ask her to leave? It seemed very harsh indeed. "So you've been with Micro/Con almost since the beginning," she was saying.

"Not really," he said. "I mean, I wasn't a founder or anything. I came in after the first IPO."

"But you must have a lot of stock by now," Allison said. "And a lot of options."

"Yeah," he answered, and wondered if he could tell her he was feeling sick. It wouldn't be a lie. But would it be enough to make her leave?

"You know, Marcus isn't even vested yet," Allison told him. "And he's not an officer of the company."

Was she talking about the slimeball at Tracie's office? "Really?" he asked, as if he cared. "The guy who harasses Tracie?"

Allison shot him a look. "Does he harass her, too?" she asked. "I swear, I'm ready to put in a grievance. But I figure now that Marcus knows Tracie's engaged, he'll probably lay off her. He doesn't seem to go for married women."

"Engaged?" Jon asked. He could swear he felt his heart stop. Maybe it was just his lungs. He couldn't breathe. "Tracie's engaged?"

"Oh, didn't you know?" Allison said casually. "I thought the two of you were such good friends."

Allison came back to the bed and put her hand gently over his crotch. Nothing happened. "I don't mind about that," she said gently. "You know, I don't think sex is the most important thing." She lay down next to him and put an arm across his chest. He could feel her perfect left breast against his shoulder, but it could just as well have been a throw cushion or a rubber duck. When she moved her hand between his legs again, he lay limp under her hand.

Tracie was engaged to Phil. The bass player wasn't just an idiot she'd outgrow. He was going to be, at the very least, her bad first marriage, and possibly the father of her children. With that thought, Jon could no longer control himself. He rolled away from Allison, out from under her hand, over to the side of his bed, and vomited onto the floor.

Chapter 40

Tracie stared out the window at the Seattle sky. As almost always, there was a gray cloud cover, but just now, as she looked, a hole had appeared and silvery light was shining through in that pattern that made the sky look magical. There must have been a lot of turbulence, because as she watched, the torn clouds began to come together again, first in shreds of mist and then, like a tissue over a healing wound, they covered the brightness and closed out the sun.

Tracie didn't allow herself to sigh—Laura noticed those and commented on every one she made—so she just took her eyes from the window, crouched down again, and dipped her roller in the pan of paint that she and Laura were slapping on the wall.

Laura's new apartment was going to be nice, but Tracie thought the mauve paint was hideous. She'd been too pleased at Laura's enthusiasm to comment on her paint selection—Laura had really gotten into DIY decorating. Home Depot was now her preferred singles' meet market. She'd already dated a cop she'd met there, as well as a sales rep and the supervisor of the paint department. She'd kissed him in the jacuzzi department. "You just love him for his discount," Tracie had joked, until Laura found out the guy wasn't divorced but only separated. She had dropped him like a hot portable grill. Tracie rolled the paint across the wall in the letter X that Laura had instructed her to do, then wrinkled her nose when she noticed the ten thousand tiny freckles of mauve paint that had sprung up on her arm.

"Too much paint on the roller," Laura told her as she rolled the adjoining wall. Laura looked at her and shook her head. "You'll never be a Kandinsky," Laura told her.

"So what?" Tracie responded. "I never wanted to play the violin." She rolled her eyes as well as more of the paint, and this time most of it stayed on the wall. The light that filtered in through the window reflected the mauve color on both of them and made Laura's complexion hideously sallow. This is not a color to paint a bedroom, Tracie thought, unless the next man Laura finds at Home Depot is not only legally single but also color-blind. It would make both of them look like hepatitis sufferers.

"You know, I've been thinking about it, and you're going to have to get a job," Laura said. She kept her back to Tracie and kept staring at the wall as she rolled up and down, up and down.

"I'm trying to write a novel," Tracie reminded her. "Believe me, it's work." Like a baby writer taking tiny steps, Tracie was learning a new schedule of writing in the morning, editing in the afternoon. She was writing about a girl growing up in a place like Encino, overcoming the death of her mother. It wasn't exactly autobiographical, but at least she could say the research came easily to her.

"I know. And I'm proud of you. It's not that I think you're lazy," her friend said. "It's because you have to get out."

"Next, you're going to tell me to run a personal ad," Tracie snapped, and when she put the roller back into the pan, she used a little too much energy and splashed the mauve paint onto the woodwork. "Oops," she said, and wiped up with one of the paper towels. Luckily, it was latex. It would take only an hour, instead of two days, to clean up.

Laura turned to her, ignoring the spilled paint. "Look, I've left you alone to mourn," she told Tracie. "Have I interfered? Have I told you you couldn't lie alone in your apartment every night like a dead salmon after the spawning season?"

Laura had been surprisingly good, or merely busy. Tracie had spent days, maybe even weeks, trying both to remember and forget every detail, every moment of the perfect time with Jon. When he'd told her he loved her, that he'd always loved her, it had been like a magical dance, the kind of thing that only happened in dreams—where you put on toe shoes and realize not only that you can effortlessly dance en pointe but that you also know every bit of choreography to the *Swan Lake* pas de deux. She and Jon had moved as one. Each touch had been so expected, yet so spontaneous, so new that Tracie had been able to hold the memory fresh for weeks.

Somewhere, she had read that women couldn't remember the pain of childbirth, because if they did, they would never go through it a second time. She didn't know if that was true, but she couldn't remember the joy, the perfection of her union with Jon because the pain of knowing that she would never have it again would be too much to bear. She had spent as much time as she needed berating herself, hating Marcus, blaming Phil, and every other wasteful, unfair emotion. But eventually, she had to give it up and more and more of her time became focused on the present, rather than the past. She didn't regret losing her job at the *Times*. She didn't regret her minuscule income. She didn't even regret going into the capital of the tiny trust fund her mother had left her. In fact, it was the first time she'd appreciated this money.

"I don't need a job, and I can't write if I take one," Tracie reminded Laura. "Anyway, if I budget my money, I can manage to take off the rest of the year, and I ought to have it written by then."

"Yeah, but if you have a job that doesn't require any mental energy, you'll be able to write better and you'll be able to hold out for *two* years," Laura pointed out. "Just in case it takes you a little longer than you thought to produce this." She grinned, picked up a brush, and began to cut a line along the ceiling. Tracie marveled at her steadiness. She was tall enough—or the ceilings were low enough—for her to do it without getting up on a ladder. "I think you better clean up now, anyway," Laura said.

"Why? My painting's not that bad," Tracie protested.

"Yeah, but Phil's coming over, and I don't think either of you wants to see the other one."

"Good point."

Laura had been seeing a lot of Phil. At least it seemed that way to Tracie, who never saw anyone except Laura. Of course, Laura didn't have too many other friends or even acquaintances in Seattle yet. But still, she seemed to be settling in. The apartment would be cute—aside from the mauve bedroom—and Laura seemed happy with her job at Java, The Hut. Tracie hadn't been there since her breakup with Jon, but Laura gave her detailed reports about the denizens regularly. Apparently, Jon had quit going there, too. That, or he had been edited out of Laura's running commentaries. Anyway, Tracie was glad about Phil, partly because she felt guilty about him and also because she was delighted to put down the mauve roller. "You know, if you want to date him, I don't have any objection. It's over."

"No, we're just bad friends," Laura wisecracked. "We meet once a week or so to bitch about our lives. It took him a little while, but he's starting to get good at it."

"You know, Jon and I started out as friends."

For a moment, Tracie allowed herself to think about the bitch sessions she used to have with Jon, but she pushed him from her mind, as she now forced herself to do several dozen times a day.

"Anyway," Laura said, "I really do think you should get a job as a waitress. They're looking for one at the restaurant. It's only part-time. It'll get you out. It gives you more material. And the tips aren't bad."

"Tips!" Tracie snorted. "What? Buy Micro/Con before it splits again? Plant my corn early? Come on, Laura, I'm not in college anymore. I'm not going to work for tips."

Laura pushed Tracie into the bathroom and handed her some soap. "Here's a tip," she said. "Wash those speckles off before they dry. And do everything else I tell you. I'm always right."

Tracie snorted again.

Tracie, upset and disheveled, was pushed into Java, The Hut by Laura. She forced her to approach Molly. Tracie was clearly reluctant. "Do you need another waitress?" Tracie asked.

"Yeah, like I need a wider arse," Molly told her. Then she looked Tracie up and down. "Why? You need work?"

"Well, I was sort of fired, but my boss says I quit, so I'm not sure if I'm getting unemployment. . . ."

Molly put up her right hand as if she didn't want to hear any more. With her left, she handed Tracie a Java, The Hut T-shirt. "At least you know the menu by 'eart," she said.

"See, I told you," Laura said to Tracie.

"See what?" Tracie asked.

"Will you hire Tracie?" Laura asked.

"I may do," Molly answered; then she sighed. "This probably will end my dream of becoming the next Starbucks, but what the 'ey."

Molly could hire her? "Don't I have to talk to the manager? Or someone?" Tracie asked. "I mean, I have no experience."

"Don't worry, you'll be punished for it, too, my lamb. I 'ope people tip you like you used to tip me," Molly said with a bit of sarcasm. "Isn't it obvious to you that this place 'as no manager?" she asked.

"So you own this place? I didn't know—"

" 'oney, there's a world of things you didn't know. But I think you're starting to learn." Molly paused. "It's over with Jon, then?"

Silently, Tracie nodded. "We kind of—"

"Say no more." Molly turned her attention to Laura. "You're late. The kitchen calls. And we're out of tomatoes."

"No problem." Laura flashed Molly a smile, then gave Tracie a thumbs-up sign.

Tracie looked toward the front window; the tree outside had gone from bud to full leaf and she had not even noticed. She was still working for Molly when the tree turned orange, dropped its leaves, and then spent close to a month covered with ice. It was the winter of her discontent.

Chapter 41

Jon walked with Lucky through the Pike Place Market. It was the first springlike day. People were out, and Lucky sniffed the air as if there was something new in it. Jon didn't even notice women who turned their heads to look at him. His last night with Allison had been his last night with anyone. He hadn't responded to Sam or Ruth. Even Beth had finally stopped calling. He had thrown himself into his work, but it was too late to save Parsifal. Alone, he weathered his first professional failure. He tied Lucky's leash to a railing beside some outdoor tables. Not that he had to: The dog would wait all day and night for him, leashed or not. He went into a shop to buy coffee.

Standing in line, he saw that the labels beneath the buns and cookies were Post-it notes. He stroked one with his finger, then shook his head. He didn't allow himself to think of Tracie at all. He had enough discipline now to enforce that rule. His loneliness at first had closed in on him as dense as a fog over Puget Sound. He didn't like to admit how many nights he had spent at his mother's trying to get himself through this little crisis. She hadn't said anything about it, always greeting him cheerfully, never asking questions. The only thing she did do was make one suggestion: "Why don't you go over to the pound?" He'd never thought of himself as a pet lover, but, at the same time, he felt like a dog at the pound: lonely, locked up—emotionally anyway—and seeking companionship. As he'd looked in the cages, there were all the canine losers in love's game: puppies too exuberant, dogs that had grown too big or not been cute enough or smart enough or lucky enough.

Jon got his coffee and a sticky bun he'd split with Lucky. The dog greeted him with exaggerated gestures of joy, waving her butt and tail. As he untied her leash and turned to go, he saw Beth sitting alone. He could duck her, but at that moment, despite Lucky, his loneliness was so great that he walked over to her. "May I?" Jon asked.

She looked up. "Oh, sure. How are you, Jonny?"

"Jon. Just Jon," he told her. "And this is Lucky."

"I didn't know you had a dog."

"Just got her awhile ago. As for me, I'm okay. How are you?"

"Oh, same old, same old," Beth said. She picked up her coffee and sipped it. She was also consuming a Milky Way. "It's not much fun at the paper. Marcus got sued for harassment by Allison, and without Tracie—"

"Tracie's not at the paper?" Jon asked. He'd forced himself not to read the features, to avoid looking for her name.

"Didn't you know she quit?" Beth asked.

"No." He tried really hard not to ask her anything more; he used all his willpower and yet failed. "When is she getting married?" he asked Beth, shamed and frightened by his lack of control. He couldn't allow himself to go back to the misery he had suffered these last months.

"Allison?"

"No, Tracie," he forced himself to say. He hadn't spoken her name since the last time he'd seen her, and he had promised himself he never would again. His mother had stopped asking how she was, though she hadn't ever asked what had happened between them. "I knew she and Phil were engaged."

"For about a minute," Beth said, making a face. "They broke up."

Jon tried hard not to show any reaction. But he felt dizzy. He didn't hear Beth's next words until she was up to ". . . and Tracie's working at Java, The Hut. At least she was the last time I saw her."

It was too much information to take in. He thought he must have heard wrong. "As what?" Jon asked. Perhaps this was some kind of bizarre joke.

"I'm not sure," Beth told him. "But I think you should check it out. I know how she feels about you."

"You do?"

"Come on. She's been in love with you for years. She just didn't know it," Beth told him. "You know, about some things, I'm not completely stupid."

"She loves me?" Jon asked.

"You don't hang out with a guy for seven years if you don't love him," Beth told him. "And you still love her. Don't you think it's time to end the fight and tie the knot?"

"Only to hang myself," he told her.

Chapter 42

Jon sat in a window booth, a menu covering his face. Outside Lucky lay under a bench to avoid the passersby. Jon couldn't help but notice that on the menu were half a dozen Post-it notes with specials listed on them. Beth must be right. The fluttering yellow tags on the menu were more beautiful to him than daffodils on a spring hillside. His heart was racing in his chest. He watched Tracie from a distance as she took an order, poured more coffee, then wiped up a table.

It was hard for him to watch her waitressing. In all the years he'd known Tracie, he'd never even seen her fold a napkin. Now, looking at her, he was experiencing something he thought therapists called "cognitive dissonance." But he'd had a lot of confusion over the last forty-eight hours about what he saw and what he thought he knew.

After he'd spoken to Beth, he had gone home and tried to work out what had really happened—not what he had thought had happened—between him and Tracie. As best as he could reconstruct it, Allison had lied to him about Tracie's engagement. And whether she had done it on purpose to alienate him from Tracie or for some other reason, he didn't know and probably never would. He'd searched out

Phil, and though it had caused him some loss of pride, he was sure it had caused Phil just as much.

Phil sat in the tiny cubicle in the department he'd been assigned to and probably felt humiliated while heads turned to see why such a junior employee was being visited by one of the honchos. Phil had bitterly confirmed Beth's story.

Tracie approached the table. "Can I take your order?" Jon lowered the menu and stared at her. Tracie started with surprise and could barely stand to look back at him. But bravely, she did. Their eyes locked and all that she felt for him was there in her facial expression. "What are you doing here?"

"What are *you* doing here?"

"I work here," she said. "Things at the paper didn't pan out."

"I heard you were engaged to Phil."

"That didn't pan out, either. I wouldn't marry a guy on the rebound." Then she bit her lower lip, as if she were punishing it for talking too much. She looked down at her order pad. He could see her try to pull herself together. "Can I have your order please?" she asked.

"Adam and Eve on a raft," he told her.

Tracie looked stricken. She teared up and had to turn her head away for a minute. Jon could hardly believe it. When she turned back, she was angry. "This isn't fair!" she said. "I know I hurt you, but I have to work here. Teasing me is—"

"I'm not teasing," Jon said, his voice as gentle as he could make it. "Who are you on the rebound from?"

"Who do you think?" she snapped and threw down the pad. She began to walk away. Jon leaped out of his seat at the booth and caught her hand. She tried to pull away. He turned her to him. Tracie hung her head to avoid eye contact. Tears fell. Jon looked over at Molly.

"Doesn't she have the most beautiful eyes you've ever seen?" he asked Molly.

"Oh! Don't tease me," Tracie cried, and tears formed in her beautiful eyes. She tried again to pull away.

"Play nice!" Molly warned him. "No rough stuff."

"So when are you getting married?" Jon asked. Molly gestured to Laura who came out of the kitchen to watch, her eyes opening wide, her mouth agape.

Tracie turned to him. "I told you: I'm not marrying Phil."

"Right," he agreed. "You're marrying me."

Then she stood still and Jon had a moment to think about how beautiful, how perfect every line of her was. If he had sculpted her himself he wouldn't alter a single line. "You're marrying me," he repeated, this time with all the love he felt for her.

"I am?" she asked, and he watched her expression begin to change, as if blood was flowing into marble and enlivening it.

" 'Course you are, stupid," Laura said from her doorway.

"You're all mad, the lot of you," Molly told them, pretending to scold. "Well, I suppose you two better get together. There's no one else in the greater Seattle metropolitan area who would 'ave either one of you." She shook her head in a mock reprimand.

"I'm marrying you?" Tracie asked him again. She blinked."Why?"

"Because you love me," he told her. "And you have for a long time. It's only now that you really know that," he said, explaining it to her and himself at the same time.

Tracie wiped her face, covered with tears, with the back of her hand.

Jon handed her a napkin and continued. "And because we'll have beautiful children. Because I'll be a great dad and you'll be a great mom. And because we both love Seattle and want to live here forever. And because you could use a part-time mother, and mine wants the job. Plus, she wants grandchildren."

Tracie swallowed, mopped off her face again, and threw her arms around him. "Those are enough reasons," Tracie said. She pushed herself against Jon's chest, and he breathed in the scent of her warm skin, her clean hair. She looked up at him, then sighed and nestled her head against his chest. It fit perfectly.

Jon put his arms around her. The fit was even better.

"I love you, Jonathan," Tracie said.

"I've always loved you," Jon told her. "And I always will."

And he was right.